THE DRAGON WAR

THE DRAGON WAR

THE COMPLETE TRILOGY

DANIEL ARENSON

Copyright © 2013 by Daniel Arenson

ISBN: 978-1-927601-12-9

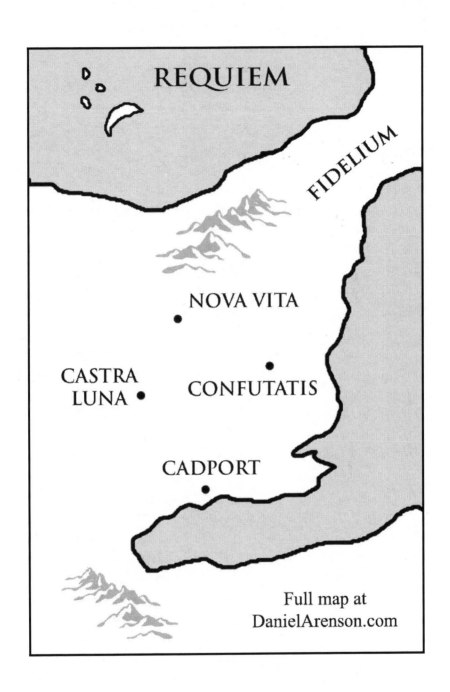

REQUIEM

FIDELIUM

NOVA VITA

CASTRA
LUNA

CONFUTATIS

CADPORT

Full map at
DanielArenson.com

BOOK ONE:
A LEGACY OF LIGHT

KAELYN

Kaelyn ran through the forest, clutching her bow, as above her the dragons shrieked and gave chase.

The night was dark; the treetops hid the moon and stars. Kaelyn could barely see. Her foot slammed into an oak's root and she tumbled, cursed, and leaped back up. She kept running. Her quiver of arrows bounced across her back. When she looked up, she saw them there, shades of black above the canopy.

Damn it.

Five or more flew above, and they had picked up her scent. Kaelyn snarled and ran on. Branches slapped her face. Her ankle twisted atop a rock, and she cursed and nearly fell again.

Just keep moving, Kaelyn, she told herself. *They can't see you through the trees. The cave is near. There is safety there. Just don't stop running.*

Dirt and fallen leaves flew from under her boots. Even in the cold night, sweat soaked her leggings and tunic, and her long golden hair clung damply to her neck and cheeks. A stream of fire blazed above. Kaelyn ducked and rolled. The flames roared, lighting the night, and for an instant Kaelyn saw a thousand black trees, mossy boulders, and a fleeing deer.

"I see the girl!" rose a shriek above. "Right below. I want her alive!"

Then the fire was gone. Wings thudded and air blasted Kaelyn. Claws longer than swords tore at the trees. Wood cracked and branches flew. Two red eyes blazed, their light shining on fangs and black scales.

Kaelyn leaped to her feet. She nocked an arrow. She fired.

The arrow whistled and slammed into the dragon. The beast reared and howled and clawed the sky. Kaelyn turned and ran.

The trees blurred at her sides. Fire blazed behind her. The dragons swooped and claws uprooted trees. A bole slammed down before Kaelyn, showering splinters and broken branches, and she yelped and fell back. A dragon landed upon the fallen oak. Its maw opened, a smelter of molten fire, and light bathed Kaelyn, and heat blasted her.

She fired another arrow, hitting the dragon's chest. The beast bucked and roared, spewing a fountain of fire. Kaelyn leaped, rolled down a rocky hill, and crashed into a tree. Pain exploded. She yelped, sprang back up, and fired a third arrow. She hit another dragon, then spun and kept running.

Damn it! she thought as she raced between the trees. Her heart thudded and her lungs ached. Her bruises blazed so badly that she ran with a limp.

They weren't supposed to be here.

But somehow these beasts knew about the boy in the city. Somehow they knew Kaelyn would try to reach him. She cursed as she sprang between more collapsing trees. If these dragons reached Cadport first, and if they found the boy before she did...

"Then we are lost," she whispered as she ran. "Then all hope is dead. Then the world will fall."

She snarled and ran up a hill thick with oaks and maples.

So I will have to kill these dragons. And I will have to reach the boy before he's found.

A howl tore the air above her.

"Kaelyn!" one dragon cried and laughed, a throaty sound like boulders tumbling. "Kaelyn, you little whore. Haven't you learned you can never hide from me?"

Ice encased Kaelyn's heart.

So the spies were right, she thought. Kaelyn had not wanted to believe, but now she saw the beast above her. *It's her. She knows. She's here.*

Flames roared. Blasting fire, a blue dragon swooped down before her, claws tearing trees and shattering boulders. Flames howled in an inferno. Red eyes burned. The beast's maw opened wide, and it shot a stream of flame across the forest. Kaelyn ducked and screamed, and the fire blazed over her head.

There was no doubt now. It was her.

My sister.

Kaelyn fired an arrow.

The shard whistled, slammed against the blue dragon, and snapped. The beast only laughed, nostrils flaring and leaking smoke.

Kaelyn had not wanted to use her magic. Not today. If she had learned anything during the long years of resistance, it was this: As a human girl, she was sneaky and silent and could hide in shadows. Dragons were burly, their scales clattered, and their maws leaked fire that could be seen for leagues. Humans survived in the wild; dragons were hunted and died.

And yet no arrows or shadows would help her now. This was no ordinary dragon facing her, a mindless soldier with weak scales. Here before her, atop a pile of charred trees, roared Shari Cadigus herself.

My older sister. Princess of the empire. The most dangerous woman I know.

Kaelyn tightened her lips, narrowed her eyes, and summoned her magic.

Wings burst out from her back with a thud. Green scales flowed across her, clanking like armor. Her body ballooned. Her fingernails grew into claws, fangs sprouted from her mouth, and a tail flailed behind her. As her sister howled, a blue beast roaring fire, Kaelyn flapped her wings and took flight as a green dragon.

She crashed through the treetops. She burst into a burning sky. Three other dragons circled under the clouds; they saw her, roared fire, and dived her way. Below, her sister Shari burst from the trees, smoke wreathing her blue scales.

Oh bloody stars, Kaelyn thought.

She spewed her flames, raining them down upon Shari. The blue dragon howled as the fire crashed into her. The beast kept rising through the inferno. With a curse, Kaelyn began to fly higher, shooting up in a straight line. Beneath her, her sister and the others blew fire and soared in pursuit.

Kaelyn shot into the clouds. For a moment she could see nothing but the gray mist; she was hidden here.

A pillar of flame rose before her, piercing the sky and nearly roasting her. Kaelyn cursed and spun the other way. Another flaming jet rose there. She ducked and nearly fell from the cloud cover.

"There!" Shari cried below. Her voice rang across the sky, high-pitched and demonic. "I want her alive—grab her."

Kaelyn flapped her wings. She rose a few feet, then leveled off and began flying south. At least, she thought she was heading south; she could barely tell within these clouds.

Stars save me, she thought. *None of this should have happened. Oh, stars, none of this should have happened at all. They'll be heading to Cadport now. They'll find the boy. They'll kill him. And it will be over.*

Dragons shrieked before her. Jets of flame pierced the clouds like spears. Kaelyn bit down on a yelp. She kept flying, daring not blow her own fire.

They can't see me, she thought. *I'll reach the boy before them. He's our only hope.*

She snarled and flew harder.

She had not thought more bad luck possible. As if the world itself conspired against her, the clouds began to thin.

Kaelyn dived and darted from wisp to wisp, trying to remain in cover. But it was no use. She was too close to the sea now. She could smell the salt on the wind. That salty air would lead her to Cadport and the boy who hid there.

It also dispersed the clouds, leaving her green scales to shimmer in the moonlight.

She looked over her shoulder.

She saw them there, the blue dragon and her three servants. A jet of fire blazed her way and Kaelyn ducked, barely dodging it. The heat blasted her. Claws reached out and grabbed her back leg, and Kaelyn yowled. She blew fire over her shoulder, hit the dragon who grabbed her, and tore herself free. She dived low. They followed.

A slim green dragon, she raced across wild grasslands, heading toward the sea. The grass bent under the flap of her wings, sending mice fleeing. The great blue dragon, a furnace of flame, and the three smaller black ones followed. Their fires blazed, and Kaelyn knew that she would die this night, and that with her the Resistance too would fall.

But no. Not yet. There! She saw it ahead—the hill and the cave. Hope bloomed inside Kaelyn like a flower from snow. She let out a cry, swooped, and flew toward the shelter.

Jets of fire blazed around her. Kaelyn darted like a bee, dodging them, until the cave loomed close. A blast of flame seared her tail, and she yowled but kept flying. With a roar, the green dragon shot toward the cave. It rose only as tall as a door, too small for a dragon to enter. Feet away from crashing against the hillside, Kaelyn released her magic.

Her wings and scales vanished. She shrank. She returned to human form. She rolled into the cave as a woman, sprang up, and ran into darkness.

A tunnel stretched before her.

Fire blasted behind.

Kaelyn raced around a bend in the tunnel and spun backward. The dragonfire crashed before her, hitting the stone walls and showering. Kaelyn took a few steps back. The heat bathed her, and she brushed sparks off her tunic and leggings. The flames kept roaring for a moment, then died.

Her sister's shriek rose outside like a storm.

"Get in there, maggots! Bring her out alive, or by the Abyss, I'll make a cloak from your skin. Go! Bring me the little trollop. I will break her."

Her clothes smoldered, and her leg throbbed with pain, but Kaelyn drew an arrow. Her fingers shook so badly she could barely nock it.

The fires died. Outside the cave, Kaelyn heard the clank of scales become the clatter of armor. The four dragons had released their magic.

"Now we will fight as humans," Kaelyn whispered. The tunnel walls closed in around her, too small for two to enter abreast. "One by one, I will slay you."

She stood, waiting around the bend, fingers shaking and lungs burning with smoke.

Boots thumped into the cave. Steel hissed—swords being drawn from sheaths. Kaelyn snarled and tugged her bowstring back.

The first man emerged around the bend—one of Shari's brutes. He towered above Kaelyn, a burly man clad in black steel. A red spiral blazed across his dark breastplate, and he clutched his dragonclaw sword. This one was a common soldier, no more than a thug.

Kaelyn's arrow slammed into his breastplate, drove through the steel, and crashed into his chest.

The man fell, and Kaelyn reached into her quiver for another arrow. Before she could draw it, a second man raced around the bend.

This one too wore black armor, and a helm of steel bars shadowed his face. His sword swung, and Kaelyn leaped back. The blade whistled before her, missing her belly by an inch. She nocked her arrow and fired. The arrow scraped the man's helmet, then slammed against the wall. The soldier cackled and swung his blade down.

Kaelyn scurried back and fell down hard. The man's blade hit the floor between her legs, raising sparks. With a snarl, she drew her own sword, a silvery blade named Lemuria after the drowned isle of ancient gods. She leaped up and thrust her steel.

Lemuria scraped against the man's breastplate, denting it. The brute grunted, spat, and swung his sword. He bore a longsword, thick and heavy, a blade for two hands; her sword was smaller and lighter, a single-handed weapon of thin steel. The blades clashed, spraying sparks, and Kaelyn growled.

No. I will not die here. The boy needs me. The Resistance needs me. She snarled. *I will live.*

She pulled her blade back, screamed, and fell to one knee. She drove Lemuria up. The blade crashed into the man's armpit where his armor's plates met.

Blood spurted. Snarling, Kaelyn drove her blade deeper, shoving it through the man's armpit and into his chest. Blood dripped down her arm. She pulled her blade free, and the man crashed down dead.

With a thin smile, her blade red, Kaelyn walked around the bend to see the third man there.

She charged toward him, their blades clanged, and Kaelyn swung Lemuria low. She swept the man's legs out from under him. He fell to his knees. With a shout, she drove her blade between the bars of his visor. Blood seeped out. The man gurgled, then fell silent.

Kaelyn stood panting. Her head spun and every breath sawed at her lungs.

Languid clapping sounded ahead. Kaelyn looked up.

At the cave's entrance, her sister stood in human form.

"Shari Cadigus," Kaelyn whispered. "Princess of the empire. The Blue Bitch." Her lips twisted. "My sister."

It had been years since Kaelyn had seen Shari, but the woman hadn't changed. Shari was twenty-eight years old, a full decade older than Kaelyn, and the two sisters looked nothing alike. While Kaelyn was short and slim, Shari was tall and muscular. While Kaelyn had golden hair and hazel eyes, Shari sported a mane of brown curls and dark, blazing eyes. While Kaelyn wore gray leggings and a green tunic, the garb of a woodswoman, Shari wore black armor, a crimson cape, and steel-tipped boots.

A rebel and a soldier, Kaelyn thought. *Sisters. Enemies to the death.*

Shari laughed, hands on her hips. "The Blue Bitch! So they still call me that, do they? A reference to my dragon scales, I imagine." She tapped her cheek. "You know, a man once called me that to my face. His skin still hangs somewhere in my closet."

Kaelyn raised her bloodied sword. "Shari, if you take a step closer, I will stick this in your neck."

A crooked smile twisted the older woman's lips. She raised an eyebrow and nodded. "So we will play. Like we did as children. I will enjoy that."

With a long, luxurious hiss, Shari drew her longsword. The blade was black and wisps of flame danced around it. The pommel was shaped as a dragonclaw, the crossguard like wings. Shari's leather glove creaked as she twisted her fingers around the hilt.

Kaelyn snarled and fear flooded her. She remembered the "games" Shari had enjoyed playing when they were young. Kaelyn still bore the scars across her body—the scars of Shari's blades, heated irons, and pincers, the toys of a sadistic youth who delighted in shedding her little sister's blood.

But tonight I will be the one spilling her blood, Kaelyn swore. She snarled and raised Lemuria before her. Her blade was smaller, her arms were shorter, and she wore no armor, but Kaelyn swore this to her stars. *Tonight I kill her.*

Screaming, she ran down the cave toward Shari.

Her sister smirked, swung her sword, and the two blades crashed.

"Yes, scream for me!" Shari said and laughed. She pulled her blade back and thrust, and Kaelyn barely parried. "You always did scream as a child when I cut you. You sounded like a sow in heat; it was the best part."

Kaelyn clenched her jaw and swung. Shari parried lazily, still smirking, her eyes mocking. Kaelyn tightened her lips.

Ignore her, she told herself. *Ignore her taunts. Focus! Be one with the blade. Kill her.*

She thrust her sword. Shari checked the blow.

"My my, you've grown feisty, little one." Shari barked a laugh. "Do you remember that time I caught you trying to eat dinner before me? Do you remember how you screamed when I drove my fork down into your hand? So many tears you shed!"

Kaelyn snarled. "My hand still bears that scar. That hand now holds the blade that will kill you."

With a grunt, she thrust Lemuria. Shari parried with a yawn.

"So far, not much luck there, beloved sister." Shari smirked. "Are you growing tired already, little one? You look a little winded."

Kaelyn swung her blade yet again, but Shari's defenses seemed impenetrable. *Damn it.* Kaelyn was a competent swordswoman, but Shari's skill with the blade dwarfed her own. Screaming now, Kaelyn swung again and again. The swords clanged, crashed against the cave walls, raised sparks, and kept flying. Shari wasn't even attacking, just checking every blow.

She's toying with me, Kaelyn realized.

Fear flooded her. Shari blocked the exit from the cave; fleeing was not an option here, yet how could she kill her sister? Shari hadn't even broken out in a sweat, and Kaelyn was so tired; her clothes clung to her, her throat burned, and she panted.

"My sweet little Kae," Shari said, and mock concern filled her eyes. "You look ready to collapse. Don't you realize, little sister? Did you never know? Of course your silly little... what do you call it? The Resistance? Of course this little *adventure* of yours was doomed to fail." She blocked another thrust and pouted. "Poor Kaelyn. Father will continue to reign. And I will follow him. And you, sweet sister, will wish that I'd killed you tonight. You will weep and beg for death many years from now, as you still hang in my dungeon, as my whips break your skin again and again."

Finally Shari attacked.

Her face changed, all the mockery vanishing, and rage flooded her eyes. With a snarl, she thrust her blade.

Kaelyn screamed as she parried. The blow was a terrible thing, a bolt of lightning, a striking asp. Kaelyn barely deflected it. The two blades crashed together, one long and black, the other slim and silvery.

Shari thrust again, and Kaelyn grunted and raised her sword. Her blade clashed against Shari's, but could not stop its onslaught. Kaelyn ducked and Shari's sword nicked her ear. Pain blazed and Shari laughed.

"Yes, bleed for me, harlot!" She swung her sword downward. "Bleed a little before I drag you home and make you beg."

Kaelyn leaped sideways and hit the cave wall. Shari's blade bit Kaelyn's hip, tearing her legging and drawing blood.

The memories pounded through Kaelyn: memories of a frightened, weeping child in a dark palace, memories of an older sister tying her, cutting her, and laughing as she wept. Tears stung her eyes.

No. Never again. You will never more torment me, Shari. You will never hurt me or anyone else.

The scar on her hand blazed, and Kaelyn screamed and drove Lemuria down in an arc.

Shari raised her sword. Kaelyn's blade slid down Shari's, raining sparks, and slammed into the older woman's pauldron.

Lemuria was perhaps slim and short, but it was northern steel forged in dragonfire, the blade of a princess. It cracked open Shari's armor and blood sprayed.

Shari screamed and fell back a step. Her eyes widened and she clutched her wound. Shock filled her eyes; she had obviously never imagined that Kaelyn could hurt her.

Kaelyn stood panting before her. She raised her blade, nodded, and smiled.

"Let us keep dancing," she said. "Or have you had enough?"

Now the duel truly began.

Now Shari fought with a snarl, all amusement gone from her brown eyes.

Now blades flew like striking lightning, and they danced, and the ringing of steel filled the cave, and Kaelyn snarled and drove her sword forward again and again, all the pain of childhood and war and wounds pulsing through her. In her rage, she struck down her sister's sword, screamed hoarsely, and slammed Lemuria so hard into Shari's breastplate the steel crumpled like tin.

Shari gasped. She stood frozen and her sword clattered to the ground. Her eyes widened and her mouth worked silently, but no breath found her.

Eyes narrowed, Kaelyn swung her blade, prepared to finish the job.

Still gasping, her breastplate caved in, Shari leaped back, and Kaelyn's blade sliced the air. Before Kaelyn could attack again, her sister turned, stumbled outside the cave, and shifted back into a blue dragon. She fled into the night.

For an instant, Kaelyn could not move. She wanted to chase. She wanted to run outside the cave, shift into a dragon too, and blow fire at her retreating sister. Yet for that instant, such pain and weariness filled her that Kaelyn could only stand panting. Her blade felt so heavy; she could barely hold it, and blood dripped down her thigh and cheek.

Be strong now. Pain can wait.

Kaelyn snarled, sucked in her breath, and raced outside the cave.

Shari was already distant, a squealing dragon coiling under the moon. Kaelyn did not know if she could even muster her magic now; she was too weak, too hurt. She ran, leaped into the air, and summoned the old magic with every last bit of will.

Pain exploded. Her magic coiled inside and she clung to it, refusing to release it. Scales flowed across her, and her wings beat, and Kaelyn flew into the night, a slim green dragon.

She could just make out Shari ahead under the stars; the blue dragon was flying north, no doubt to fetch reinforcement. When Kaelyn glanced over her shoulder, she saw the distant sea, the cliffs of Ralora, and the twinkling lights of Cadport, the city where the boy hid.

Stars damn it.

Kaelyn looked north and south, wings beating, breath rattling in her lungs.

Damn it, what do I do? Do I chase my sister? Do I slay the fabled Shari Cadigus, the cruel commander who killed so many of my men, who tortured me so many times? Or do I fly south to save the boy before the might of the Regime falls upon his city?

Kaelyn roared fire in frustration.

After all these years, she lusted to finally slay her sister. But her own vengeance would have to wait.

"Saving the boy is what matters now," she said into the darkness. "If the Regime approaches the city at night, or if they're already there... they will take him. And all hope will fall." Kaelyn snarled at the north where she could still see her sister fleeing. "This is not over, Shari. I will face you again. And next time, my blade will pierce your heart."

Kaelyn spun in the sky.

She flew south.

She flew to that distant port city. To the boy. To Rune Brewer and to hope.

RUNE

It was the last night Rune Brewer would see his best friend. He walked beside her along the beach, not sure how to say goodbye.

The moon glowed full overhead, haloed with winter mist. The light shone upon the sea, drawing a path into the black horizon. The waves whispered, their foam limned with moonlight. With every wave, strings of light glimmered, formed new shapes, and faded upon the sand.

"Do you know why I like the sea?" Tilla said softly, watching the waves.

Rune looked at her. The moonlight fell upon her pale face, illuminating high cheekbones, large dark eyes, and lips that rarely smiled. Her hair blew in the breeze, black and smooth and cut the length of her chin. She wore a white tunic, a silvery cloak, and a string of seashells around her neck. She was tall and thin—too thin, Rune thought. They were all too thin here.

"Because it's always different," Rune answered.

She turned to look at him. "Yes. Have I told you before?"

He smiled thinly. "Only a hundred times."

"Oh." She turned back toward the water. "Tonight the moonlight glows on the foam. Last night the sea was very dark; I couldn't even see it. Sometimes in the mornings there are many seashells, and the waves are shallow and warm and golden in the dawn. Sometimes the water is deep and the sand clear, and the waves near me are gray, and those far away are green. Sometimes there are crabs on the sand and fish in the water; other times life is hidden. Tomorrow there will be a new sea here."

Rune heard what she did not add. *But I will not see it. I will be far away.* He wanted to tell her that he would walk here tomorrow, that he would write to her about the water, that someday she might return and see the waves again. But the words would not come to his lips. Somehow speaking about tomorrow felt wrong, felt too sad, too dangerous.

So they only kept walking. Silent. The waves whispered. The remnants of old battles littered the beach: the rotted hull of a ship, wooden planks rising like whale ribs; a cracked cannon where crabs hid; an anchor overgrown with moss; and the shattered sabers of fallen sailors. Old wars. Old memories. Nothing but rot and rust in the sand.

Finally they saw the cliffs ahead, rising black in the night. As children, Rune and Tilla would often play under these cliffs, imagining the old battles fought here. They said that seven hundred years ago Elethor, the legendary king, had fought the tyrant Solina upon these cliffs. They said that the dead still whispered here, their bodies buried under the waves.

Rune and Tilla kept walking. Finally the cliffs loomed to their left. To their right, the waves whispered and raced across the sand. Here they stopped, turned toward the water, and stood still. A cold wind blew from the sea—it was the first moon of winter—and Rune hugged himself.

He smiled. "Tilla, do you remember how we used to play here as children? I always pretended to be King Elethor, and you were the wicked Queen Solina. Remember how we would fight with wooden swords?"

A thin smile touched her lips, but there was no joy to it. "Of course you always made me play the villain."

He raised his hands in indignation. "You wanted me to play the queen?"

Her smile widened and finally some warmth filled it. "Yes. I did. I think you would have looked nice in a dress."

He gave her a playful push. She fell back a step and sighed.

They sat in the sand. Rune opened his pack and pulled out a skin of ale—he had brewed it himself—and a wheel of cheese. Tilla's eyes widened to see it.

"Rune," she whispered. "Where did you get that?"

He shrugged and winked. "I have my ways."

Cheese was a luxury these days. Years ago, when Rune had been a child, he remembered eating cheese every day. But since the war had begun and trade died, cheese was rare as gold.

But this night was rare.

This was Tilla's last night home.

They shared the cheese silently, sitting side by side, watching the waves. They drank the ale. They had eaten here many times, the cliffs to their backs, the waves ahead. They could always talk here for hours, laugh, tell stories, play with the sand, and whisper of all their dreams.

Tonight they ate silently.

When their meal was done, they sat watching the water. Rune wanted to say so many things. He wanted to tell Tilla to be careful. He wanted to tell her that he'd see her again someday. He wanted to say *goodbye*. But his throat still felt so damn tight, and his lips so frozen, and his chest felt wrong, as if his ribs were suddenly too small.

Just say something, he told himself, staring at the waves. *Just... just make this a good memory for her, tell her stories, or laugh with her, or... stars, don't just be silent!*

He turned toward her, prepared to tell some old joke to break their silence, when he saw a tear on her cheek.

She was not weeping. Her lips did not tremble. Her eyes did not flinch. She only sat there, staring ahead, still and silent like a statue. Only a single tear glimmered on her cheek, not even flowing, just frozen there like part of the sculpture.

"Tilla," he said softly. "It... will be all right. It—"

She turned toward him, her face like marble in the moonlight.

"No, Rune," she said. "None of this is all right. None of this has been all right for years." She looked aside and her fists clenched in her lap. "This stupid, stupid war, and this stupid red spiral, and..." She looked back at him, reached out, and grasped his arm. "It wasn't always like this, Rune. I know. My father told me. Before the Cadigus family took over, there was trade here. Ships sailed this sea—tall ships from distant lands, ships with huge sails like dragon wings, and they brought cheese to Cadport, and fruits, and silks, and jewels, and my father had work then. He sold so many ropes to those ships. He showed me paintings of them, secret ones he keeps in the cellar. Stars, Rune! Those ships had so many ropes on them. It wasn't like today when we sell only a few ropes a year to farmers. And your father too, Rune—so many merchants visited his tavern, and they all wanted to taste his brew, and he was wealthy then. Both our families were wealthy; all of

Cadport was. Only it wasn't even called Cadport then. It was called Lynport, and—"

"Tilla!" he said. He placed a finger against her lips. "You know we can't say that word. We—"

She pulled his finger away. Her eyes flashed. "And why not? Why can't we speak the old name of our town? Why can't we look at paintings of ships, but have to hide them? Why can't we ever say, Rune, that things were better then, that maybe the Cadigus family didn't help us, that—"

Rune leaped to his feet. "Tilla! Please."

His heart pounded. Memories flashed through him. Somebody else in Cadport—and stars damn it, it was called Cadport now, like it or not—had once spoken like that. The fool had drunk a few too many ales at the Old Wheel Tavern, which Rune owned with his father. After his tenth drink, the red-faced loomer had begun to blabber about the old days, the one thing you were never to speak of.

"Back then, now, I could sell fabrics all over the world," he had bragged, teetering as he waved about his mug of ale. "Ships came, picked 'em up, and I got paid silver. That's called trade, it is. And no bloody fortress rose on the hill." He guffawed and spat. "No damn soldiers on every street in Lynport. Yeah, you heard me!" He waved his mug around, spraying ale. "Stand back, scoundrels, I won't be silent! *Lynport* our town was called then, named after Queen Lyana Aeternum, not after that bloody bastard Cadigus or whatever the Abyss his name is."

A crowd gathered around him. Wil Brewer, Rune's father, tried to pull the drunkard back into his seat. Rune himself begged him to be silent. All around, the other townsfolk hissed at the man to sit down.

But the soldiers who drank here did not hiss. They did not beg. They only stared, then rose, then grabbed the drunkard.

Rune never forgot that evening. He never forgot how the drunk loomer had screamed in the city square. He never forgot the *cracks* as the hammers descended. When his bones were broken, the soldiers slung the loomer's mangled limbs through the spokes of a wagon wheel. They hung that wheel from the courthouse and guarded it. The screams sounded all night, and all the next day, and it was night again before the loomer finally died.

That had been years ago, but tonight Rune still heard those screams. When he looked at Tilla, he could still hear those bones crack.

"Tilla, please," he whispered. "Please."

Her chest rose and fell. Her eyes still flashed. But when he held her hands, she let out a long sigh, and the flames in her eyes died, and she lowered her head.

"Rune," she whispered.

Her hands were warm in his, calloused from the ropes she wove. She had long, pale fingers that Rune could not imagine gripping a sword. How could this young woman, a mere ropemaker, his best friend, pick up weapons and go to war? They had played with wooden swords here many times, but this was real, and this stung his eyes and squeezed his chest.

"Rune," she whispered again. "Rune, I'm scared."

Tilla had been his friend all his life, and Rune had spent countless hours playing, laughing, and talking with her, yet he had never—not once—embraced her. Today he pulled her into his arms, and he held her, and she was warm against him, and he stroked her hair and marveled at its softness.

"I know, Tilla," he said. "I'm scared too. But it will be fine. I promise you, Tilla. Everything will be fine."

He was lying. She knew he was lying; he was sure of that. But it was what she needed to hear now, and so Rune repeated it, again and again, holding her close as the waves whispered.

"It can't happen twice to one family, right, Rune?" She looked at him with her large dark eyes, and suddenly she was no longer eighteen, a solemn young woman, but a child again. "It's impossible, right?"

He squeezed her hands. "You'll be safe, Tilla. The Resistance is small now; most of the resistors are dead. You won't have to fight. You'll train a lot, and you'll learn how to use a sword, but it will just be training. The war is dying down."

Rune still remembered the funeral. Five years ago, when the rebellion against the Cadigus family had flared, many of Cadport's people had been pulled out of workshops and farms, thrust into the army, and sent off to fight. Tilla's brother had been one of them. They had not heard from him for three years. Then one winter morning, soldiers from the north arrived in Cadport, carrying the young man in a coffin.

Hundreds had come to the funeral, Rune remembered. They had covered the cemetery, weeping and praying, and stars, how Tilla's parents cried. Even Rune cried that day. Only Tilla did not shed tears. She stood silent and still that day, staring at the coffin as they lowered it underground. Since then, she had rarely smiled and perhaps never laughed.

But it won't happen twice in one family, Rune told himself. *Tilla is eighteen now, and she will be a soldier, and she will train in some distant cold fort, but she will live. And someday, even if it's years from now, I will see her again.*

"Rune," she said, "do you think maybe... maybe in a few moons, when you're eighteen too, you might end up in the same fort?" She gave him a crooked smile. "Wouldn't that be something?"

He snorted a laugh. "There are only... what, about a hundred million forts in the empire?"

She shook her head and sighed. "Not that many, Rune. Not that many. Let's pretend, okay? Let's pretend. I would like that. I would like us to be in the same fort. Maybe if you ask them, Rune, maybe they'll let you." She grabbed his hands and squeezed them. "Will you promise me? Promise you'll ask them. They keep records of these things, Rune. They know where every soldier is stationed. Tell them you want to serve with Tilla Roper of Cadport. Tell them. Promise me."

Rune did not like thinking about his own enlistment. He was still a few moons shy of eighteen; tomorrow morning, when soldiers arrived from the capital to take Cadport's newest adults, he would still be too young. But in the summer, when they came again, he would be old enough. And he too would be given a sword. And he too would be sent off to some distant fort to train and to fight the Resistance.

No, Rune did not want to think about summer yet; summer still lay too far away, and this was bad enough, this was all the sadness and fear he could handle this night.

Tilla's eyes were large and damp as she stared at him. Her fingers clutched him desperately. Her breath shook. Tilla had always been somber, quiet, and reflective; she rarely spoke to the other girls in town but called them vapid and silly.

I've always been her only friend, Rune thought. *And she's always been mine.*

"I promise," he said. "I will ask to serve with Tilla Roper of Cadport. I will see you again, Till. I promise you."

She pulled him into an embrace.

The only two embraces of our lives, he thought, *both on one night.*

In the silence he could hear the waves again, and the wind billowed her hair so that it brushed his cheek, and when he tucked it back behind her ears, he found himself kissing her. She trembled against him, and her lips opened, and though they had never kissed before, this felt as familiar as her eyes or the memory of her smile. It was not a kiss of passion. It was not a kiss of fire or love or sex. It was sadness. It was salt and tears. It was goodbye.

"Rune," she whispered, "fly with me. One last flight. Like we used to."

He nodded and whispered, "One last flight."

It was years since the Cadigus family had outlawed the old magic. Only soldiers could shift now, and only when flying to battle. If others were caught using the old magic, they would not be left to die upon a wheel; they would be dragged into a dungeon and tortured for moons, maybe for years, before being allowed to die. But this night, in darkness between cliff and sea, all fear left Rune.

One last flight. Like we used to fly.

They stood up in the sand, walked several paces apart, and faced each other. The wind blew their hair and the waves sprayed them with mist.

Tilla shifted first. She closed her eyes and let the magic fill her. White scales like mother-of-pearl flowed across her, gleaming in the moonlight. Wings unfurled from her back, a tail sprouted behind her, and she grew until she towered above him. She stood in the sand, a pearl dragon with sad eyes.

It had been a long time since Rune had let the old magic fill him, the magic that flowed from the stars. Today he let the warmth fill him like mulled wine. He sucked in his breath, raised his head, and let the dark scales rise and clank across him. His fingernails grew into claws, and he felt his teeth lengthen and wings rise from his back. It felt as familiar and warm as her kiss, and he stood before her in the sand, a black dragon.

He lowered his head and nuzzled her, and she gave him a sad smile, and they took flight.

They were children of Requiem. They were Vir Requis, an ancient race blessed with starlight. For thousands of years, their people had flown as dragons, free and wild over forest and mountain. Today they flew in darkness, alone and afraid under the Draco constellation, stars of their fathers.

Their wings scattered the waves below. They rose higher until they glided over the sea, two dragons, black and white. They rose above the cliffs. Rune could see for miles along the shore and all the distant lights of Cadport.

Years ago, when they would first fly here, they would circle the moon and pretend that they could almost reach the stars. These days too many eyes could be watching the skies, and so they flew low over the water. They watched their shadows scuttle over the moonlight, and the cold salty night filled their lungs.

He looked at her. She looked back with a soft smile. They kept racing over the sea, flying south away from Cadport, away from what awaited her tomorrow, away from a place where no ships sailed, where not enough ropes could be sold, where drunk loomers screamed upon wheels and brothers returned in coffins. They flew over the water, and Rune wished they could keep flying forever, streaming forward until they reached whatever distant lands ships had once sailed from.

And why not? Rune thought. *Why can't we just keep flying? Why can't we see what lands we find?*

He looked ahead into the darkness, and a sigh clanked his scales.

No—those distant lands of ships and merchants had burned long ago. There was no more wonder in the world. Only this empire. Only the iron fist of the Cadigus family. There was no more light in the world, and no matter how far they flew, they could not escape the darkness.

But we can fly together one last night. Like we used to. Me and her.

They flew until the shore and the lights of Cadport disappeared behind them, then turned and flew back, landed upon the beach, and released their magic. They stood on the sand, a boy and girl again, and he held her hand.

"We will fly together again, Tilla Roper," he said.

She touched his cheek. "Remember this night, Rune. No matter what happens, remember how we kissed, and how we flew together, and even if we fight, and we bleed, and we're very alone and afraid, know that we have this memory. Know that we must stay alive so we can fly here again."

He wanted to say more, but could not speak; his eyes stung, and his throat tightened, so he only kissed her again and held her close as the waves lapped at their feet.

They walked back home in darkness, hand in hand.

Nobody knew whether Cadport, with its fifty thousand souls, was a city or a town. It was a common argument among its people; most elders longingly spoke of their rustic town, while youngsters boasted of their modern city. Whatever it was, tonight Cadport's brick walls, cobbled streets, and seaside boardwalks seemed dark and lonely to Rune. It was his hometown, but tomorrow it would feel empty.

When Tilla stepped back into her small home, Rune stood outside for long moments, then turned and walked alone down the silent streets. His throat still felt tight, and his lips were cold.

Instead of returning to his own home, he walked to the old port. He stood on the cobblestones and placed his hand upon an old iron cannon that pointed to the sea. Rune stared into those dark waters. He tried to imagine days long ago when ships sailed here, Tilla's father sold his ropes, his own father served ale to merchants, and life and laughter had filled this city, not soldiers and broken men on wheels and boys returning home in coffins. Rune's eyes stung and he could barely fathom that tomorrow night, he would walk on the beach alone, and Tilla would be gone—maybe for years, maybe forever.

"We were called Lynport then," he whispered. "And ships sailed here. And none of this would have happened."

But that had been long ago. It had been a different world. It was best to forget. Remembering brought pain, danger, and hammers that cracked bones.

Rune turned away from the water. He walked to the tavern that was his home. He stepped into the empty common room, walked upstairs to his chamber, and tried to sleep. But he could only lie awake, thinking of Tilla and her brother and what would happen in summer.

TILLA

She stood in the city square, hands clasped so tightly she thought her fingers would snap.

Be strong, Tilla, she told herself. *Do not show fear now. Even if your heart trembles, and even if your chest feels so tight you can hardly breathe, you must hide it. If you show weakness now, they will crush you.*

The others crowded around her—six hundred youths her age, all just turned eighteen this year. Their faces were pale. Their lips trembled. Tears flowed down one girl's face, and another girl was sobbing into her palms. A few boys huddled together, snickering and speaking of killing rebel men and bedding rebel women, but they too were scared; Tilla saw the sweat on their foreheads and the tremble to their fingers.

They laugh to hide their fear, she knew. *They will stop laughing soon.*

The Regime's soldiers surrounded the square, sealing in the youths of Cadport like wolves surrounding deer. They wore armor of black steel, the breastplates emblazoned with the red spiral, sigil of Emperor Frey Cadigus. Steel spikes tipped their boots, and steel claws grew from their vambraces. Crimson capes fluttered behind them. On their left hips, they bore swords with dragonclaw pommels. On their right hips, they bore their punishers, the tips crackling with lightning.

That last weapon scared Tilla more than the steel claws or blades. Each of these batons, their grips wrapped in leather, ended with a ball of spinning energy. Tilla had once seen soldiers torture a fisherman with their punishers. The man had writhed, wept, and screamed so loudly the whole city heard; his flesh still bore the scars.

They are demons, Tilla thought, looking upon these soldiers of the empire. *They were created to kill, to torture, to destroy.* She gripped her fingers so tightly she winced with pain. *And they will turn me into one of them.*

One soldier, a burly man who stood across the square, met her gaze.

Tilla froze.

The man's eyes were dead; his stare chilled her like a blast of winter through a door. He was easily the largest of the soldiers, probably the largest man Tilla had ever seen. He hunched over as if his arms were so beefy his back bent under their weight. Even so, he towered above the men around him; he must have stood almost seven feet tall. Lines creased his olive skin, and scars rifted his stubbly head. Dark sacks hung under his eyes, and his brow thrust out like a shelf. His armor was crude, all mismatched plates and chainmail cobbled together, and he bore no sword. Instead he carried an axe—not even an elegant battle-axe, but the heavy axe of a lumberjack, forged for felling trees.

This one must be Beras, Tilla thought with a shiver, unable to tear her eyes away. She had heard of him; everyone in this city had. Lowborn, once an outlaw, Beras was infamous for raping and strangling a girl two towns over. The Cadigus family had hunted him down... and employed him.

The brute kept staring at Tilla, his eyes blank, his expression dead. There was no humanity in Beras's eyes, no rage, no hatred, just cold ruthlessness. Tilla forced her eyes away and found that she had held her breath.

"Tilla!" whispered a girl beside her, a short and demure cobbler named Pery. "Tilla, what fort will they send us to?"

Tilla shook her head free of thoughts, blinked, and glanced at the girl. Pery was a pale, mousy thing, barely larger than a child. Her hair was so pale it was nearly white, and her eyes seemed too large above her gaunt cheeks. Her fingers were slim and quick, accustomed to helping her father make shoes. Could those small fingers ever wield a sword? Pery looked up, a foot shorter than Tilla and trembling like a rabbit cornered by a fox.

"I don't know, Pery," Tilla said softly. "They'll sort us when they're ready."

Pery's eyes swam with tears, and her fingers clutched at Tilla's tunic. "But... I can't go too far. I can't. My father needs my help at the shop. His joints hurt, and his fingers don't move quickly anymore, and..." She sniffed. "Tilla, do you think they'll station me at Castellum Acta here in Cadport—the little fort on the hill—so I can go home at nights to help him?"

"Maybe," Tilla said and patted the shorter girl's arm. "Maybe, Pery. Let's just wait and see."

Pery nodded, bit her lip, and lowered her head.

Dozens of other girls stood around them. Tilla stood tallest among them; she had always thought herself far too tall. Today she found her height useful. She looked over the heads of the others, scanning the crowds that stood behind the soldiers. Parents, siblings, or just curious townsfolk stood in the city streets, peering into the square. A few even stood upon roofs or gazed from tall windows. Many mothers were weeping and waving at their sons and daughters. Some fathers were beaming with pride and speaking about how their sons would slay resistors; most fathers looked as tearful and worried as their wives.

Tilla's own father did not stand here.

I saw my son recruited in this square five years ago, he had told Tilla last night. *He never returned.*

Tears had filled the old ropemaker's eyes, and Tilla had embraced him and whispered her goodbyes. He was not here today, but her father was in her heart; she would carry his love to wherever this war took her.

There was one more man in her life, and this winter morning, Tilla sought him, scanning the crowd of faces.

"Where are you?" she whispered.

Finally she saw him in the crowd, and her heart gave a twist.

Rune Brewer stood in an alley a few hundred feet away. Two soldiers stood before him, separating the new recruits from the crowd of onlookers; Tilla could only glimpse half of Rune's face. He leaned sideways, stood on his tiptoes, and gazed between the soldiers.

Tilla's eyes locked with his.

She wanted to wave to him. She wanted to mouth a goodbye. The youths around her were reaching out to friends and family, waving and weeping. But Tilla could only stand still.

Stars, she thought, fire blazing inside her. She wanted to do *something,* even shed a tear. And yet she could only stand frozen, staring at Rune over the hundreds of youths, and he only stared back, frozen too. Their stare seemed to last an era, and though still and solemn, his eyes cried out to her. They spoke of their lives: of wrestling together as children on the floor of the Old Wheel

Tavern; of forbidden flights over the sea at night; of Rune sneaking bread rolls and porridge over to Tilla's house when they could just not sell enough rope; and finally of what had happened last night, their first kiss, a memory Tilla knew would anchor her during the years ahead.

And then soldiers stepped in front of him, severing their gaze, and Tilla thought: *I won't see him again for years. Maybe never again.* Her eyes stung and she blinked. *My brother never came home. He left us from this very square, and we never saw him again. Will I ever return?*

Wings thudded above, interrupting her thoughts.

A roar sounded across the city.

Tilla looked up and clenched her jaw.

A blue dragon flew above, still distant but diving fast toward the square. The dragon was female; her horns were shorter than those of a male dragon, and her was body slimmer but no less powerful. A wake of smoke and flame trailed behind the beast.

Within an instant, the blue dragon was circling above the square. She howled a cry so loud, people across the city covered their ears and grimaced. The dragon's wings blasted Tilla's hair and filled her nostrils with the scents of ash, smoke, and oil. The dragon flew so low her claws nearly toppled the roofs of buildings. With another roar, she blew fire, forming a flaming ring around the square. The flames crackled, blasting Tilla with heat, then descended as a wreath of smoke.

Many youths cowered and whimpered. Since the Cadigus family had taken the throne, only soldiers were allowed shift into dragons; the magic was forbidden to everyone else, and many here had never seen a dragon display its might with flame and roar. At her side, Pery mewled and covered her head, but Tilla only stood tall and stared up at the blue beast.

This one is boastful, she thought and narrowed her eyes. *This one delights in fear. This one I will watch out for.*

Across the square rose Cadport's courthouse, a building of marble columns. Tilla's father would whisper that once, before the Regime, this had been a temple to the Draco constellation, the stars of Requiem. Today the banners of Cadigus hung from the building's balcony, black and long and emblazoned with the red spiral. With a final blast of fire, the blue dragon descended toward the courthouse, shifted into an armored woman, and landed upon the balcony.

The woman stood before the crowd, and Tilla sucked in her breath.

"Stars damn it," she whispered.

She knew this woman who stood on the balcony. She had seen this one in a dozen paintings; by imperial decree, they hung in Cadport's courthouse, guildhalls, and even Rune Brewer's tavern.

The Demon of Requiem. The Princess of Pain. The Blue Bitch.

"Shari Cadigus, the emperor's daughter," Tilla whispered.

Heir to the empire, Shari wore the garb of a soldier. She stood tall in leather boots and clad in black steel. Her breastplate sported the red spiral. Upon her hips hung her weapons: a black longsword and a punisher wrapped in red leather. A mane of brown curls cascaded down her shoulders, and her dark eyes stared upon the crowd in amusement; Tilla could see that amusement even standing a hundred yards away.

What was Shari Cadigus herself doing here? Every winter and summer, Tilla had come to this square to see youths drafted into the Legions. She had stood here seeing her cousins, her brother, and so many other townsfolk taken to distant forts to fight and die. Yet it was always some old, gruff soldier who arrived to lead the youths north. What was Requiem's princess herself doing here, so many leagues away from the glory of the capital?

Shari raised her right fist high, then slammed it against her breastplate.

"Hail the red spiral!" the princess shouted, voice ringing.

All across the square, hundreds of youths, eighteen years old and pale and shaky, repeated the salute. Hundreds of fists thumped simultaneously. Tilla hit her chest so hard, a gasp of pain fled her lips.

I will give the salute, she thought. *But my heart does not belong to the red spiral. It does not serve Emperor Frey or his daughter. My heart belongs to my father and his ropes, to Rune and his tavern, to secret flights above the water and a kiss I will not forget.*

Shari lowered her fist to her hip, nodded, and looked over the crowd. A thin smile played across her lips. Her head moved from side to side, scanning the youths. When her gaze fell upon Tilla, the princess nodded and pointed.

"There!" Shari barked at Beras, the burly soldier with the scarred, stubbly head; he stood below the balcony, axe in hand. "That one, Beras. Bring me that one."

Tilla stood frozen. Her heart thrashed. She could barely even breathe.

Beras's eyes remained dead and shadowed under his brow. With a grunt, he shifted into a dragon.

He was easily the largest dragon Tilla had ever seen, a beast of bronze scales, spikes, and black horns. The creature took flight, grunting and snorting smoke, and swooped toward the crowd.

When Beras flew directly above Tilla, he reached out claws like swords.

Tilla winced, ducked, and a yelp fled her lips.

Beside her, Pery screamed.

The claws closed, wings beat, and the bronze dragon soared. It took Tilla half a moment to realize she still stood in the square, hunched over and drenched in sweat.

Pery no longer stood beside her. Beras now flew with the cobbler's daughter in his claws.

Thank the stars.

Tilla couldn't help it. She breathed out a shaky breath of relief... and hated herself for it.

The bronze dragon howled and beat his wings, blasting the crowd with waves of stench. In his claws, Pery screamed and begged.

"Bring her to me!" Shari commanded, still standing on the balcony in human form. She laughed. "Place that mouse before me."

The youths in the square stood still, faces pale. The crowd behind them, separated from the youths by the soldiers, stirred and whispered. A graying woman reached out her hands—Pery's mother.

Beras flew to the balcony, hovered before it, and tossed Pery down. The girl thudded onto the balcony and mewled. With a grunt, the dragon flew down, landed outside the courthouse, and shifted back into human form. He stood still, clutching his axe.

"Stand up, darling!" Shari said to the fallen girl. "Stand up— you are a daughter of Requiem! Stand before me, child."

Pery rose to her feet and stood before the princess. She looked so small and frail, a good foot shorter than Shari, and wispy in her tunic next to Shari's armor and blades. The girl trembled and whimpered.

Be silent! Tilla thought, watching from the square. Her heart pounded. *Don't show her any weakness, Pery. You must be a soldier today.*

Tilla wanted to shout out to her friend. She wanted to shift into a dragon too, to fly to the balcony, to shake Pery and slap her until she stood strong and silent. And yet she dared not. Danger hung in the air. A wrong movement meant death now. All around the square, the people stood frozen; not a whisper rose.

Upon the balcony, Shari's face softened. Her lips pouted. The princess looked like a woman who saw a mewling, kicked puppy that begged to be hugged. She reached out and, with gloved fingers, caressed Pery's hair.

"Are you frightened, child?" Shari asked.

No! Tilla thought. *No, Pery, no. Tell her that you're brave, tell her you're strong.*

Pery looked around nervously. Her eyes scanned the crowd, and they fell upon Tilla, and the girl whispered something Tilla could not hear.

"My child!" Shari said. She touched Pery's chin and turned her face back toward her. "Don't seek answers there. Simply speak the truth. Are you frightened?"

Pery lowered her eyes, bit her lip, and nodded.

"I thought so," Shari said. She leaned over and kissed Pery's forehead.

A scream fled Pery's lips.

Shari stepped back with a smile.

No. Stars no, stars no. Standing below in the crowd, Tilla shook, and her heart thrashed, and tears filled her eyes. *Oh stars no.*

A dagger, its pommel shaped as a dragonclaw, thrust out of Pery's chest.

Tilla couldn't help it. She cried out.

"Pery!"

Everything seemed to happen at once.

Pery fell, blood gushing. Princess Shari stood above her and laughed. Pery's parents cried out below, reached toward her, and wailed, and soldiers dragged them into an alley. The crowd rustled

and whispered. A girl not far from Tilla fainted. One man shouted
and tried to run toward the courthouse, but soldiers held him back.

Tilla stood frozen, fingers trembling, and her eyes widened.
She had not thought things could get worse. She had not imagined
greater terror. She gasped and covered her mouth and her eyes
stung.

"No," she whispered. "Oh stars no."

Shari knelt above the body, snarling and laughing. She had
pulled the dagger free and thrust it into Pery's neck. More blood
gushed. Shari hissed as she sawed back and forth. Finally she lifted
Pery's severed head and held it above the crowd.

"See what happens to the weak!" Shari shouted and laughed.
Blood splashed her face, and the severed head dangled and dripped
in her hand. "See what happens to cowards!"

Some people wailed and tried to flee; soldiers grabbed them.
One man—Tilla recognized him as Pery's uncle—began driving
through the crowd. Soldiers twisted his arms, and one drove a
punisher into his back; the man collapsed and screamed, his flesh
smoking. Above the commotion, Shari laughed and tossed the
head off the balcony.

It arced through the air and slammed down by Tilla's feet,
splattering blood.

Tilla closed her eyes, clenched her fists, and swallowed a
lump in her throat. A tear streamed down her cheek.

I'm sorry, Pery. I'm sorry. May your soul find its way to our starlit
halls of afterlife.

"Beras, bring me another one!" Shari's voice rang above.
"That one—the one who cried out, the tall one beside the head.
Bring me her!"

Tilla's eyes snapped open.

The bronze dragon swooped toward her.

Tilla winced and sucked in her breath. Beras's claws closed
around her, and the beast lifted her.

They flew above the crowd. Strangely, no fear filled Tilla as
the dragon carried her toward the balcony. Perhaps after seeing
Pery's death, after flying in the night with Rune, and after losing her
brother to the war, no more fear could fill her. The crowd spread
below, a gray sea, and Tilla looked back, trying to find Rune.

Before she could locate him, the dragon reached the balcony and tossed her down.

Tilla tumbled and landed on the balcony, slamming her knees against the floor. She inhaled sharply, gritted her teeth, and made no sound.

Below the balcony, the crowd hushed. All the whimpers, whispers, and wails faded into tense silence. Jaw clenched with pain, Tilla raised her head to see Shari standing above her.

Kneeling so close, Tilla saw that Shari wore finer armor than a common soldier. Golden filigree covered her steel plates, shaped as dragons aflight. The red spiral upon her breastplate was not just red paint but formed of a hundred rubies. Small golden skulls grinned morbidly upon her boots like spurs. The princess was a soldier, but she was also vain.

"My princess," Tilla said, still kneeling before her. She slammed her fist against her chest. "Hail the red spiral!"

Standing above her, Shari nodded approvingly. "Hail the red spiral! Well spoken, child. Stand. Stand before me."

Barely daring to breathe, Tilla rose to her feet. She raised her chin, thrust out her chest, and squared her shoulders. She stood tense and proud, one fist still against her breast.

This is the stance of a soldier, she thought. She was just the daughter of a roper, of course, but the daughters of ropers and cobblers would die today. Soldiers would live.

I must live, she thought, her throat tight. *My father lost one child already. I must survive.*

Shari scrutinized her, her brown eyes narrowed. Tilla was among the tallest women in Cadport; she stood almost as tall as Rune, who was taller than most men. Her arms were strong from weaving ropes and carrying casks of Rune's ale. And yet she felt short and frail beside Shari; the princess stood several inches taller, and even her armor could not hide her powerful body.

Many call her the greatest warrior in Requiem, Tilla knew. She could see why.

"You stand well," Shari said and nodded. She placed a finger under Tilla's chin and raised her head higher, examining her jawline. "Show me your teeth, child. Open your mouth."

Rage flooded Tilla. Was she a recruit or a horse? She snarled and hissed. If Shari noticed her anger, however, she curtained windows. "You are either very brave or very cunning. Which one will remain to be seen." She tapped her dagger against her hip. "I will keep an eye on you, Tilla the ropemaker. I will watch you like a poor drunkard watches a tavern's last mug of ale. If you stray one inch... if you make one mistake..." Shari sliced the air with her dagger. "...your head will rot with the other one."

With that, Shari slammed her dagger back into its sheath, turned to the crowd, and shouted.

"All right, you miserable lot! Beras will lead you out. We're heading north to make you soldiers. You will crush the Resistance, or you will die in their fire!"

With that, Shari leaped off the balcony, shifted into a blue dragon, and flew so low over the square the youths had to duck. With a grunt like a beast in heat, the dragon disappeared over the city roofs.

Beras shifted too. The gruff, silent man became the bronze dragon, grabbed Tilla in his claws, and carried her back to the square. He tossed her down among her comrades. Tilla fell again, banging her hip so hard she gasped and saw stars. She forced herself to her feet among hundreds of other recruits.

Around the square, the soldiers drew their punishers; the tips crackled with lightning. They began herding the crowd forward, shouting and cursing.

"Move it, scum!" one soldier shouted. "Move!"

"Go on, maggot!" another said. "Damn you, move, or I'll make you move."

They thrust their punishers. Bolts crackled, youths yowled, and smoke rose from seared flesh. The soldiers laughed and kept goading the crowd forward, cruel dogs herding sheep. Soon all six hundred youths were moving across the square, then following Beras down Cadport's main street. The youths jostled against one another, looking over their shoulders with darting eyes.

Tilla moved among them, limping and wincing with the pain. Her hip and knees throbbed; bruises would cover them tomorrow. As the recruits flowed into the street, Tilla kept looking over her shoulder, trying to see Rune among the crowd of onlookers. She saw parents, grandparents, and siblings, but they were all strangers. Where was Rune? She wanted to give him one last look, to whisper to him, to call out one last goodbye, maybe even reach out and showed no sign of it. As Tilla snarled, she bared her teeth, and Shari got her look at them.

"Good," the princess said. "White, sharp, straight." She grabbed Tilla's arm and squeezed it. "Strong arms; slim but ropy. What is your profession, child?"

Tilla stared into her princess's eyes. "I was a ropemaker, Commander. I will be a soldier."

The princess barked a laugh. "This one will be a soldier!" she shouted to the crowd.

When she turned back toward Tilla, a dagger gleamed in her hand.

Tilla gasped. Fast as striking lightning, Shari placed the blade against Tilla's neck.

Tilla froze.

Her heart thrashed.

Shari snarled, holding the blade so close Tilla felt it nick her skin.

"You are confident," the princess hissed. She leaned so close to Tilla their faces almost touched. "You are a haughty one, aren't you? Nothing but a ropemaker. Nothing but a pathetic little worm. And you think you can be one of my soldiers."

Tilla froze, daring not speak; if her neck bobbed, the blade would slice it. She only stared back, not averting her eyes from Shari's fiery gaze.

There is madness in those brown eyes, Tilla thought. *There is cruel But there is cunning too; there is method to this madness. I must play her ge to live.*

She chanced a whisper, allowing the blade to scrape her s

"If you teach me, my princess, I will fight for you, and I kill for you, and I will grow stronger. I am not afraid. I am no weak like the other girls. I will fight for the red spiral until my drop of blood."

And I will live, she thought. *I will spit upon the red spiral in dreams every night, but in the days, I must survive. The weak will die. be strong, and I will live to return to Rune.*

Shari pulled back her dagger, and Tilla took a quick, h breath.

"You are an interesting little worm," Shari said. She narrowed her eyes and scrutinized Tilla, as if trying to peer touch his fingertips. But she could not see him, and the faces of the crowd swam around her.

With tears and whispers and the memory of blood, six hundred of Cadport's children, eighteen and old enough to die, swept out of their city walls... and into a wilderness of steel, snow, and fire.

RUNE

For a long time, Rune stood in the empty square, staring at the blood on the cobblestones.

The recruits were gone, Tilla among them, and Rune's heart ached at their loss. The crowd of families and onlookers dispersed slowly, many among them teary, leaving the city square empty. Yet Rune remained standing here, staring at the blood, unable to calm his thrashing heart.

They cut off her head, he thought. *Stars, they cut off her head right here, and we stood in the square and did nothing, and they almost killed Tilla too, and we only stared like sheep frozen before the wolves.*

He clenched his fists. The blood seeped between the cobblestones and ran toward his boots. A priest had lifted Pery's head, chanted a prayer, and placed it into a bag for burial. But Rune could still imagine it—its mouth open in a silent scream, its eyes still wide with fear, blood dripping from its neck.

"I'm sorry, Pery," he whispered. "We should have helped you. We should have done something."

Thousands of people had watched the execution, and each had magic to shift into a dragon, to thrust claws, to roar fire. Only a hundred guards had surrounded the square.

We should have shifted! Rune thought. *We could have saved her! We could have slain the soldiers, and...*

He sighed.

And thousands more soldiers would have streamed here from the capital, he thought. *They would have burned this city to the ground and slaughtered us all.*

He turned and began walking home.

He normally took the wide main road, but today, Rune walked on narrow side streets, seeking solitude. His boots thumped against the cobblestones. Houses and shops rose at his sides, built of wattle and daub; oaken beams formed rough frames, and white clay filled the space between the timbers. Rot darkened these wooden frameworks, and holes dotted many roofs; since the port had closed a few years ago, few could afford to maintain their homes. Only Cadport's largest buildings—like the courthouse, the fort on the hill, and the prison—were built of brick. The Cadigus family now ruled those.

It wasn't always like this, Rune thought. He watched a thin little girl sit outside her home, hugging an equally thin dog. *When I was a child, we'd run playing down these streets, laughing and banging wooden swords together.*

It had been years since he'd heard children laughing; children today did not play, but scavenged and begged for food.

Rune fished through his pocket, found a copper coin, and tossed it toward the skinny girl. Her eyes lit up. She caught the coin and ran off.

"Buy something to eat!" Rune called after her, but she vanished around a corner, and he did not know if she heard.

As he kept walking, again rage filled Rune. He remembered standing at the docks with Tilla years ago; they'd been younger than that thin girl. They'd watch the ships from foreign lands approach, bearing sacks of grain, exotic fruits, strong dry wine, and many other treasures. The ships would leave days later, laden with Requiem's crafts: ropes Tilla's father wove, shoes Pery's family cobbled, ale Rune's father brewed, and many other goods.

Nobody in Cadport was hungry then, Rune thought. It wasn't even called Cadport in those years, of course; it had been Lynport, the jewel of the south.

But then... then the war broke out, the Regime's great war to purify the world of "lesser nations". Then the Cadigus family burned those distant lands. Then those ships sank, and the port closed, and Cadport began to rot.

"And now this," Rune whispered. "Silence and hunger and blood upon stone."

And Tilla torn away from me.

He kept walking until he reached the boardwalk along the sea. He walked upon the cobblestones, watching the gray waves beat the sand below. A breakwater thrust into the water like a stone dragon, and upon it rose the old lighthouse; it hadn't shone in years. Docks still spread out into the water, but their wood was rotted, and many planks had fallen and floated away. Rune could barely remember the ships that would dock here; the only sign of life now was a stray, thin cat who wandered the beach, seeking dead fish.

Rune kept walking. To his other side, shops lined the boardwalk, but their wood too decayed. Most doors were boarded shut. Years ago, these shops had sold ale, wine, meat pies, and even women for lonely sailors. When the ships stopped sailing here, the shops fell to ruin; one now housed a scrawny orphan girl named Erry, a waif Rune sometimes brought food to, and the others housed rats.

Only the Old Wheel Tavern remained in business, Rune's home. When Rune reached it, he stood outside for a moment and stared. The cold wind whipped his cloak and ruffled his hair.

"Home," he whispered.

The tavern stood three stories tall, built of wattle and daub. Tiles were missing from its roof, and mold had invaded its timbers. Only one of the three chimneys pumped smoke.

By summer, I'll be eighteen too, Rune thought. *And I'll be carted off with hundreds of youths. Who will help Father then?*

He sighed. He knew the answer. Wil Brewer was growing older, and he depended on his son's help. Without Rune, the tavern would become another ghost hall like the dozens along this boardwalk.

A gull circled above, cawing a laugh as if the bird could read Rune's mind and was mocking him. Rune smoothed his cloak, opened the tavern's door, and stepped inside.

The shadowy common room greeted him. Scratches covered the hardwood floor like cobwebs. Odds and ends that Rune's father collected bedecked the walls: an old tapestry showing dragons aflight in a starry night, antlers on a plaque, a canvas map of the city, and two fake swords—forged from cheap tin—crossed upon a shield. At the back of the room stood the bar, its surface waxed a thousand times. Mugs hung above it from pegs, and behind the bar, casks of ale and wine stood upon shelves. Ten tables filled the room; all were empty today.

Hands in his pockets, Rune stared up at the ceiling. A wagon wheel hung there, topped with candles, forming a makeshift chandelier. It gave the Old Wheel its name. When Rune had been a babe, the tavern was called *Lyana's*, named after the legendary Queen of Requiem who had fought a battle at Ralora Cliffs outside the city. But of course, Lyana had been an Aeternum, a queen of the old dynasty. Today all memories of that dynasty were forbidden. And so the tavern's name had changed. And so everything had changed.

"Father!" Rune called out. "Father, are you home?"

A shadow scuttled. Paws scratched across the floor. A large black dog came lolloping from the kitchen, leaped onto Rune, and began to lick his face.

"Hello, Scraggles," Rune said and patted the mutt. "Are you alone here? Guarding the place?"

Scraggles panted, a wide smile across his face. Some folk, Rune knew, claimed that dogs couldn't smile, but they had never met Scraggles. He was an old hound now but still acted like a pup, happy and careless. His tail wagged furiously, dusting the floor, and Rune felt a little better.

"At least I still have you, Scrags," he said, but then a lump filled his throat. In summer, when Rune himself was drafted, he would be torn away from his dog too. Scraggles was getting on in years; when Rune returned from his service, the dog would be gone.

Rune blinked his stinging eyes. The tavern seemed too silent, too cold, even with Scraggles jumping against him. Tilla used to visit here most days. They would play dice or mancala, a southern board game a ship had once brought from the desert. They would sweep and polish the tavern while talking about their lives. Sometimes they would just sit by the fireplace, sip ale, and say nothing, but feel warm and safe and close.

Five years, Rune thought. *Five years in the Legions.*

She had been gone for a couple hours, and already Rune wanted to pound the walls, fly toward the capital, slay the emperor, and bring Tilla home.

"Father!" he called out again. He wanted to see the man, the only other soul he now had, aside from his dear dog. Where was the old brewer?

Leaving Scraggles in the common room, Rune trudged upstairs. The second floor of the Old Wheel held the guest rooms for merchants and travelers; those rooms were now empty. He kept climbing to the third floor where his own chambers lay.

He entered his room, and his breath died.

Upon his bed sat the most beautiful woman Rune had ever seen.

He froze and stared.

The beautiful woman stood up. Her clothes were torn and bloody, and she bore a bow and sword.

"Rune," she said, "we must run. They are going to kill you. They are coming."

Rune blinked, looked over his shoulder, then back at her.

"Excuse me," he said, "do I...?"

She stepped toward him, grabbed his arm, and narrowed her eyes.

"You don't know me, Rune Brewer," she said. "But I know you very well. And you must trust me today. We leave—now. Or we're both dead." She began tugging him toward the door. "Come."

He stood frozen, squinting at her. She was not from Cadport, that was certain; she spoke with the northern accent of the capital, a great metropolis many leagues away. And surely, Rune would have noticed a young Cadport woman so, well... so perfect.

Rune had seen beautiful women before. As a hot-blooded young man, seeking beautiful women was among his main pursuits. With her pale skin, noble features, and midnight hair, Tilla was beautiful; Rune had always thought so. And he had noticed Mae Baker too, a girl up the road with a strawberry braid, pink cheeks, and shy eyes. Even Erry the waif, who lived sandy and scrawny on the docks, had big brown eyes that Rune liked looking into.

But he had never seen anyone like *this* woman. She seemed to be about his age, maybe a year or two older. Her mane of hair cascaded down her back, a deep golden color like honey. Her eyes were hazel, her features feline; she reminded him of a lioness. Her body too was catlike, slim and lithe, a body made for leaping and running and climbing. She wore deerskin boots over tattered gray leggings, a blue cloak over a green tunic, and a belt with a golden buckle. A sword hung from that belt, and a bow hung across her shoulder. She had obviously seen battle recently; a bloody line ran across her hip.

He squinted, a dim memory pulsing inside him.

She looks familiar, he thought. Had he seen her before after all? He would have remembered a woman so beautiful, yet his memories only flickered, a soft glow he could barely see.

"Come on!" the woman said and tugged him. Her eyes flashed and she bared her teeth. "We're getting out of here."

Rune stood still, not allowing himself to be moved.

"I'm quite sorry," he said, "but if you're going to drag me out of my home, the least you could do is introduce yourself first."

She groaned, released him, and darted toward the window. She peered outside and cursed, then turned back to him.

"Kaelyn," she said and gave a mocking curtsy. "Good? Now *come on.* They're outside. They'll be here soon, and they'll be thirsty for beer."

She grabbed him again and tried to pull him outside, but he yanked himself free.

"Who is out there, Kaelyn?" he said. He walked to the window and peeked outside. "It's only a few northern soldiers. They drink here whenever they're in Cadport. We could use some business, and—"

"You woolhead!" Kaelyn said and pulled him away from the window. She yanked the curtains shut. "You idiotic boy! Stars know why they even *bother* trying to kill you." She grabbed his arm, twisted it, and began manhandling him toward the door. "Move it and be quiet!"

Then, finally, Rune understood.

He sighed.

The young woman was mad. No doubt, she was some wandering halfwit cast away from her northern town, sure that the world was out to kill her. Stars knew how she had ended up in his bed.

He planted both feet firmly on the ground, refusing to budge; he stood a foot taller than this woman, and he weighed a good deal more, and if he didn't want to move, she wouldn't move him.

"Look," he said, "Kaelyn or whatever you're called. Why don't I fetch you a pint of ale and a bowl of soup—on the house—and I'll even give you a bed for the night. In the morning, I can—"

Steel flashed.

She drew a dagger from her boot.

Before Rune could react, she placed the blade's tip against his back.

"That's right," she said. "Be silent. Good. Now move! Out the door and downstairs, or I'll stab you. You'll thank me for this later."

The knife pierced his tunic; he felt the cold tip between his shoulder blades, almost cutting him. He sucked in his breath and winced.

"Kaelyn, are you... kidnapping me?"

Rune had always imagined kidnappers as gruff, scruffy men covered in mud, their blades rusty and chipped, their odor less than pleasing. Kaelyn had the mud part right—her boots and leggings were coated with it—but she was definitely not scruffy, and Rune thought that she smelled rather nice.

But she only shoved him forward, keeping the dagger pressed against his back. "Out the door, boy. And keep your hood *low*. Hide your face or I stab you."

She grabbed his hood and, standing on tiptoes, tugged it low over his face. When he glanced over his shoulder, he saw her do the same with her hood. He noticed that, despite their ragged condition, her cloak and hood were woven of fine fabric. The cloth was a costly blue. Blue dye came from distant isles where mollusks leaked the color; Rune rarely saw blue fabric in Cadport. Kaelyn's cloak had been through rough times—tatters, mud, and burns marred it—but it had once belonged to a noblewoman.

So she's a thief, Rune thought. *She stole her cloak from a lady, then dragged it through the forest. She probably hopes to kidnap me for ransom.* He sighed. If only she knew his father had no ransom money to pay.

"Move!" she said and shoved him. "Go on, good boy— downstairs."

He grumbled under his breath, but he walked. The dagger poked his back; he thought it might have nicked his skin. Kaelyn kept pushing him forward. They left the room, crossed the hallway, and began walking downstairs.

"Kaelyn," he said, "will you please calm down and listen? If you're after money, we have none. If you want a good meal and a bed, I—"

"Keep walking!" she said and kept manhandling him downstairs. "And be silent. Bloody stars, they're almost here."

"Who's alm—"

"Hush!"

A thud filled the tavern—the front door slamming open. Boots thumped and the voices of soldiers cried out, demanding ale and food. Their armor clanked and their cries filled the tavern.

"Bloody stars," Kaelyn cursed. "Is there a backdoor to this place?"

Rune looked over his shoulder at her. Her face was pale. She was chewing her lip and whipping her head from side to side, seeking an exit, even though they still stood in the stairwell.

Rune thought of calling out. If he shouted, the guards would hear and rush onto the stairs.

And... Kaelyn might stab me before they arrive.

"Go on!" Kaelyn said. She pressed the dagger closer, close enough that now Rune was sure she nicked him. "There must be a backdoor for supplies; every tavern has one. Lead me there!" She snarled into his ear. "And if you lead us anywhere near the common room, this dagger goes right into your heart."

She gave his arm a twist, and he groaned.

"All right!" he said. "All right, I'll lead you there. Stop poking me."

He decided to humor her for a while. Sooner or later, she would tire of holding the dagger against his back. When that happened, he'd break free. The girl was just hungry, scared, and probably on the run from the Regime. Once she felt more comfortable and was far from these soldiers, she would let her guard down. He would flee her then. After all, she couldn't keep her dagger pressed against him forever.

"Come on," he said with a grunt. "In here. We'll sneak out through the kitchen."

They walked downstairs, moving close to the common room. Over the stairs' bannister, Rune saw the shadows of the soldiers as they bustled about. A few were banging the tabletops and calling out for ale.

"Rune!" Kaelyn warned. "If they see us..."

"Don't worry," he said. "And stars, loosen your grip. You're ripping my arm off."

The stairs led down to a hallway. To one side, casks of ale stood piled up; the shadows and sounds of the common room leaked from behind them. To the other side, the hallway curved toward the pantry and kitchen. Rune led them there, moving away from the common room and into a chamber stocked with sausages, flour, jars of preserves, bottles of spirits, and dried fruits.

"Where's the backdoor?" Kaelyn demanded.

"Be patient!"

They kept walking. Soon they entered the kitchen, where embers glowed in the hearth. Plates, mugs, and pots lay piled high on shelves. Beyond them a backdoor led into an alley.

Scraggles lay on the floor, gnawing a bone. The black mutt raised his head and stared at Rune, then at Kaelyn. With a growl, the dog leaped to his feet. His tail straightened like a blade, and he began to bark wildly at Kaelyn.

Behind in the common room, the soldiers fell silent and chairs creaked.

"Oh bloody stars!" Kaelyn said. She shoved Rune forward and grunted. "Go, go!"

She manhandled him around the dog, wrenched the door open, and shoved Rune into the alley. She hurried after him, dagger still pointed at his back, and slammed the door shut, sealing Scraggles indoors. She looked from side to side, cursed under her breath, and began pulling Rune down the alley.

"Come on!" she said. "Move quickly and silently. You try to escape me, or you make a sound, and you're dead. Trust me— that's a better fate than what these soldiers would offer you. They'd make you wish you were dead."

They hurried down the alley, cloaks fluttering around them. Cold wind moaned, and behind them Rune could still hear Scraggles barking. The alley walls closed in around them; it was just wide enough for him to walk comfortably. At least, he would be comfortable if Kaelyn weren't twisting his arm and goading him on.

"You do realize," Rune said as they walked, "that Cadport is swarming with hundreds of soldiers? They stand at every street corner—even on days without a recruitment. How are you going to avoid them? Or is your plan to just live in this alley for the rest of our lives?"

They reached the alley's end. Beyond two shops spread a wide road lined with homes.

Kaelyn tugged him back and positioned herself beside him, pressing her dagger against his waist. She gripped his arm and snarled at him.

"All right, listen to me, boy," she said. "You and I are nothing but a couple on a stroll, do you understand? I've hidden my dagger under my cloak's sleeve, but don't you doubt it—it's still pressing against you, and if you try to escape, I'll shove it into you." Her voice softened and she sighed. "I'm doing this to save your life, you know. Well, you don't know, but you will soon enough, Rune. Keep your hood low; these soldiers would kill you on sight."

Rune glared at her. "What's going on here, Kaelyn? Who are you? Why do you think these soldiers want to kill me? I've spent eighteen years around soldiers, and—"

"Not Princess Shari's soldiers. Do you really think Shari herself, the daughter of Emperor Cadigus, would visit this backwater town for a mere recruitment? The recruitment is a facade. She's here to find you, Rune, and to capture you. Her soldiers know your face. They know your name. They know to take you on sight. They weren't just in your tavern for ale; they were there for *you*." She looked at him strangely. "If they catch you, Rune, they will bring you to the capital. And they will torture you. They will break you upon the wheel, or disembowel you alive, or flay you, or quarter you. Do you know what quartering is? That's when they tie bulls to your four limbs, then send each bull running a different direction. And finally, when you've screamed long enough, they will cut off your head and stick it upon the city walls."

Rune felt himself blanch. "Stars," he whispered.

"Am I scaring you?" Kaelyn asked and narrowed her eyes, scrutinizing him. "Good. Because I'm scared too. And I want you to be scared; fear will keep you silent and moving. You might think my dagger cruel; it's nothing compared to what Shari would do to you. I'm taking you into the forest, and I'm going to bring you to the only man who can help you now."

He raised his eyebrows. "And who might that be?"

Behind them, a door slammed open.

The Old Wheel's backdoor.

Soldiers called for an innkeeper.

"Damn it!" Kaelyn said. She pulled Rune out of the alley and onto the wide, cobbled road.

A dozen of Cadport's people walked here. Their faces were pale; they were still shaken after the morning's beheading.

Two men stood outside a butcher shop, clad in black robes and hoods. Rune had never seen such men, and shivers ran down his back.

He could not see their faces; within the shadows of their hoods, they wore iron masks. Around their waists, they wore ropes heavy with knives, needles, and pincers—the tools of torturers. Strangest of all, neither man had a left hand. Their arms ended with axeheads strapped to stumps.

They serve the Axehand Order, Rune realized with a shudder.

He had heard of the Axehand, a religious order of fanatics who worshiped Frey Cadigus as their god. They were assassins, enforcers, and torturers—Frey's personal thugs. Every man of the Axehand Order, they said, completed his training by lifting an axe and severing his hand; the same axe was then strapped to the stub, a reminder of their loyalty to Cadigus. Rune had never seen their kind in Cadport before; many had whispered that the Axehand Order was only a myth.

"Keep walking calmly," Kaelyn whispered, and for the first time, softness filled her voice. "Come on, Rune. This way."

They walked down the road, heading away from the two axehands. Even after they'd left the robed priests behind, the chill lingered along Rune's spine.

Shops and houses rose at their sides, three stories tall, frowning down upon them. Whoever passed them by did not spare them a glance; the people stared at their shoes. As they moved down the street, Rune glanced over at Kaelyn. Her lips were pursed, her eyes darting, and her skin pale.

The whole thing is ridiculous, Rune thought. *If the soldiers were after me, why did they sit in the common room calling for ale? Why didn't they storm upstairs or burn the tavern down?*

He sighed. Kaelyn heard the sigh, glared at him, and pushed her dagger close.

"Keep walking," she whispered.

They moved through Cadport, street by street. They passed by the old amphitheater, a great ring of stone where singers and actors would once perform, and where the Cadigus family now executed the city's criminals. They walked around the granite statue of Emperor Cadigus, twenty feet tall, his fist upon his chest and his hard eyes watching the city. They walked down narrow streets filled with more townsfolk and soldiers, then across the square where Pery had been killed.

Finally they approached the city walls and the northern gates. Five guards stood here, each one bearing a sword, a shield, and a crackling punisher.

"This will be the tricky part," Kaelyn whispered as they walked. "Just act natural. If the guards ask, you and I are simply going into the forest to collect firewood. Do you understand?"

As Rune walked, he thought that he did understand... and it chilled him.

Stars, oh stars, he thought. *How didn't I see this? Kaelyn isn't just some common thief. She's... she's one of them. A member of the Resistance.* He swallowed. *Of course.*

The Resistance lived out in the forests, they said. They hid in trees and holes and secret tunnels, and they fought the Cadigus family, and they hated order and law and life. They stole from good folk to fill their coffers, and they weren't afraid to slaughter the innocent. Rune had heard all about their deeds.

He thought back to that day two years ago, the day they had buried Tilla's brother. Hundreds had come to the funeral. Soldiers whispered that Tilla's brother had fought nobly, slaying many resistors before they swarmed him. They said Valien Eleison himself, cruel leader of the Resistance, was the one who'd landed the killing blow. All joy had left Tilla that day; Rune had not heard her laugh since.

Every year, Cadport's soldiers—hard men trained in northern forts—caught a few resistors in the forest. They chained them outside the city courthouse, disemboweled them alive, and left them to die. If they caught Rune with a resistor now, he realized, they'd do the same to him.

His heart pounded and cold sweat trickled down his back, but he managed to nod.

"I understand," he whispered in reply.

"Good," Kaelyn said. "Beyond those gates is safety. Follow my lead, and we'll soon be in the forest. There is haven at my camp. Just be calm and silent."

As they walked toward the guarded gates, Rune's heart pounded.

Bloody stars, he thought. A forest camp? The woman *was* a resistor; now there could be no doubt. Rune held no love for the Cadigus family, but if Kaelyn thought she could involve him in her war, she was dead wrong. He was only a brewer. He wanted no trouble, and Kaelyn was made of the stuff.

They reached the gates, hoods pulled low. The guards stared at them from behind their visors, and their hands clutched their punishers. Their leather gloves creaked, and the rods' tips crackled with red lightning.

"Good morning, my dear men," Kaelyn said from the shadows of her hood. "My brother and I seek to collect firewood outside the city gates. Would you be so kind as to—"

Rune had heard enough. His heart thrashed against his ribs. His breath quickened. This was too big for him; outside in the forest, a thousand of these resistors could be lurking, and stars knew what they wanted with him. Rune would not wait to find out.

If I want to escape, now's my chance.

While Kaelyn was looking at the guards, Rune gave her a mighty shove.

She fell a few steps backward, gasping. Her dagger left his side and gleamed, suddenly exposed.

"She has a dagger!" Rune shouted to the guards. "I'm not her brother. She's a thief or a resistor. She—"

"Oh merciful stars!" Kaelyn shouted. She cursed, sucked in her breath, and shifted.

Wings burst out from her back. Green scales clanked across her. Rune gasped. He had never seen anyone but soldiers shift in Cadport; if carrying a dagger could land her in the dungeon, shifting was a capital offense. The green dragon soared and blew fire. Rune stumbled backward.

The guards at the gates cursed. They began to shift too, bodies ballooning and armor morphing into scales. Before they could complete their transformation, Kaelyn reached out her claws toward Rune. He leaped back, trying to dodge them, but she moved too quickly.

Kaelyn, an emerald dragon wreathed in flame, scooped him up like an eagle grabbing a mouse. She shot up so fast that Rune's head spun. He shouted, his legs kicked, and the wind whistled around him. The claws were so tight he could barely breathe.

"You bloody fool!" Kaelyn roared, wings beating. She rose so high the houses looked like toys below.

The guards began to fly too, metallic dragons roaring flame. Pillars of fire blazed up toward Kaelyn and Rune.

"Kaelyn, what the Abyss are you doing?" Rune shouted, kicking in her grip.

She banked sharply. Jets of flame blasted at their side, narrowly missing them. The heat baked Rune. The dragons below kept rising, and more fire blasted their way.

"It's the boy!" one of the dragons below shouted. "The brewer's boy Shari wants. Grab him and kill the girl!"

More jets of flame soared. Kaelyn banked again, and the fire screamed only feet away. The heat seared Rune and he shouted out.

What the Abyss was going on? Why did Shari want him? Could Kaelyn have been speaking truth all along?

Kaelyn rose so high the air thinned and Rune could barely breathe. Clouds streamed around them. With a howl, Kaelyn spun and began to swoop.

Wind screamed.

Blackness tugged at Rune and he gagged.

Five metallic dragons, guards of the city, came soaring toward them.

Kaelyn rained her fire.

Flames exploded across the world, and the dragons below howled. Kaelyn crashed between them, and her tail lashed, and her fangs bit, and blood showered. The metallic dragons bit and clawed all around, their fire blasted, and Rune screamed.

Kaelyn shot past the last dragon. She dived so close to the city that Rune—still held in her claws—nearly slammed against the rooftops. She began to rise again, the dragons in pursuit. More soldiers across the city saw the battle, shifted, and began taking flight.

Kaelyn cursed. "You bloody blockhead, Rune! You got us killed!"

She rose and flew above the city walls. The forest streamed below them. When Rune looked behind, he saw a hundred dragons, soldiers of Cadigus, shooting toward them.

He also saw something that chilled him far, far more than all the soldiers in the empire.

At the boardwalk, a building was burning.

The Old Wheel tavern.

Rune gasped and his eyes stung. Kaelyn kept streaming forward, cursing and beating her wings, and the dragons kept pursuing, but Rune could see nothing else.

The rest of the city still stood; only his home blazed.

They were looking for me, Rune realized. *Kaelyn was right.*

A blue dragon took flight from the blazing tavern. The beast screeched and clawed the sky, wings wide and tail flailing.

Shari Cadigus.

"Bring me the boy!" the blue dragon screeched. "Kill my whore of a sister, and bring me the brewer's boy! Bring me Rune Brewer!"

In her claws, Shari held a charred body. With a disgusted howl, she tossed the corpse down, and it crashed onto a nearby roof.

The body was badly burnt, but Rune saw that it wore a red and green cloak.

Rune knew that cloak. It was his father's favorite garment.

Tears filled his eyes, and Rune screamed out, and the world spun around him.

Then Kaelyn flew higher, crashing into the cover of clouds, and the city disappeared. The clouds streamed around them. Rune's eyes stung, his chest tightened, and he couldn't breathe.

The Old Wheel. My father. Stars, they're gone. Shari burned them.

"Father, no," he whispered, clutched in Kaelyn's claws. His voice rose to a howl. "What have you done, Kaelyn? What have you done? I'm a wanted man now, I—"

"You were wanted from the day you were born!" she snapped. "You just didn't know it until today. Thank me for pulling you out of your tavern moments before Shari burned it, or you'd be dead too."

"Kaelyn, what's going on?" he demanded, tears in his eyes. "Where are—"

Fire roared.

A hundred jets of flame pierced the clouds, shooting all around them. Hundreds of howls sounded behind, and Shari's voice pealed across the sky.

"Grab them!" the blue dragon screeched in the distance. "Burn them! Bring me my sister and the boy!"

Kaelyn howled, tightened her claws around Rune, and kept flying.

TILLA

The cart trundled down the road, jostling the recruits against one another. Tilla gasped for breath and clung to the girls around her. They had packed them like cattle, and even in the cold winter day, sweat drenched Tilla and she felt faint.

"Tilla!" whispered the girl beside her. "Tilla, can you see anything? You're tall!"

Tilla frowned down at the girl, the daughter of a baker, her blue eyes wide with fear, her cheeks pink, and her strawberry braid slung across her shoulder. Rune had been infatuated with the girl, Tilla remembered; her bakery stood only a few buildings away from the Old Wheel Tavern. Tilla herself had bought bread there, but could not remember the girl's name. She was a soft, doll-like thing, pretty but too fragile. Tilla could not imagine this one ever wielding a sword.

"What could I possibly see?" Tilla said and gestured around her.

The cart had no windows. It was wide enough to house a dragon... or about a hundred girls cramped so tightly together they couldn't even lift their arms. The shorter girls gasped for breath. At least Tilla was the tallest among them; her head rose above the mass, allowing her to breathe the hot, fetid air. The forest road was paved with rough cobblestones; the cart bumped and tilted with every turn of its wheels. The girls would have fallen were they not packed so close together.

"I don't know!" said the baker's daughter, and tears filled those large blue eyes. She clung to Tilla's hip. "Maybe you can see a crack, or a very small window, or..." The girl sniffed, then began to quietly weep. "I just miss Jem. I love him so much."

Tilla rolled her eyes. She remembered Jem Chandler, the girl's love. He was a useless dolt who spent more time drinking at the Old Wheel than crafting his candles.

They had not seen any of the boys all day, not since leaving Cadport. Outside the city walls, Beras and his soldiers had herded the female recruits into three cramped, rotted carts. The boys had been rustled into their own carts. Beras had driven his punisher into the backs of those too slow to climb in.

Dragons pulled these carts now, dragging them over bumps, ruts, and slopes that left the recruits bruised and whimpering. It had been a long day: a day of sweat, of gasps for breath, of recruits whispering and praying and—like the baker's daughter—weeping incessantly about loved ones.

"What's your name?" Tilla asked, not unkindly, and touched the girl's shoulder.

She sniffed and looked up at Tilla with damp, red-rimmed eyes.

"Mae," she said. "Don't you remember? You bought bread from me once. Mae Baker."

"Well, Mae, as I see it, you have a choice now," Tilla said. "You can cry and weep and mope for your boy. Or you can shut your wobbling lips, stop crying onto my shirt, and maybe act like a soldier. Okay?"

Mae's eyes widened, her jaw unhinged, and for a moment she just stared as if trying to understand if Tilla had truly said those words. Finally fresh tears filled her eyes.

"But I don't *want* to be a soldier!" Mae said. "All I want is my Jem, my sweet Jem who loves me."

Tilla glared at her. "Well, you *are* a soldier now. Or at least you will be when we reach whatever fort they're taking us to. I don't want to be a soldier either, but given that we don't have a choice in the matter, you can either cry yourself to death, or you can toughen up."

But the girl seemed not to hear her. She covered her eyes and began mumbling something about how her father was the richest baker in Cadport, and how he would save her from this place, and how handsome Jem Chandler was going to run away with her, and how Tilla would be so sorry she hadn't joined them.

Tilla heaved a sigh.

I'm not going to make any friends here like this, she thought. She had never been friends with any of these girls back in Cadport. She had always thought them moon-eyed, empty-headed peasants. It was no wonder she had never bothered learning their names. Standing here in a cart of them only confirmed her distaste.

It's little wonder Rune was my only friend in Cadport, she thought. She missed him. Perhaps not with tears and trembles the way Mae missed Jem, but she missed him nonetheless.

Where are you now, Rune? she wondered. *Are you brewing ale for the soldiers, or walking along the beach, or thinking about me?*

Her eyes began to sting and Tilla growled. She tightened her lips, narrowed her eyes, and clenched her fists. No, she could not think of Rune now. She could not cry, especially not after admonishing Mae.

I have three choices now, she thought. *I can try to escape this cart, run into the forest, and live on the run, and if the Legions ever catch me, I will die. Or I can stay here and weep and yearn like Mae and the others.* She raised her chin and grinded her teeth. *Or I can do this properly, and I can become a real soldier, and I can banish this pain from my chest and these tears from my eyes.*

She mulled over each option. Running seemed the worst of the bunch. Tilla had seen deserters caught before; the Cadigus family made sure every citizen in Cadport came to see them quartered by mules. Tilla rather liked having four limbs, so running was out of the question.

As for moping, she did not relish that option either. Thinking about Rune wouldn't get her back to him any sooner. Thinking about home would only weaken her. There was no point missing home now; or at least, she could try to suppress her homesickness. She could push those thoughts deep down where they couldn't hurt her. After all, how would weeping and yearning help her survive?

And so that left only one option.

I will play the game, she thought. *I will become the soldier they want me to be. For now, I will play by their rules. And maybe I can survive the next five years. Maybe I will learn enough to fight and live once they cart us off to fight the Resistance.*

Tilla nodded. Here in this cart, surrounded by the weeping and trembling girls, she vowed that she would *live.* If she had to fight a war, she would be strong and she would survive it, and in five years she could return home. In five years, maybe she could see her father and Rune again.

She looked at Mae, who still wept at her side, and iciness clutched Tilla, for she knew: Once their training was complete, and they were sent to fight, Mae would die.

She would die first.

Tilla closed her eyes and tried to forget Pery's head splattering down at her feet.

The cart kept trundling on and on. Finally whatever sunlight leaked through cracks in the walls faded. Darkness fell over the cart, and even the heat of a hundred bodies pressed together could not warm Tilla. She had not eaten, drunk, or sat down since that morning. Her back, feet, and stomach ached. Wolves howled outside, wind shrieked, and still the cart kept rolling.

"Tilla," Mae said, speaking for the first time in hours, "are we going to keep traveling all night?"

Tilla grumbled at the baker's daughter. "How should I know? Do I look like Beras?"

The girl whimpered and bit her lip. "Don't say his name," she pleaded. "Don't say the name of that man. They say he... he..." She sniffed. "It's horrible, but they said he r-r-... he did something horrible to a little girl. And then he strangled her to death." She shuddered. "Please don't say his name."

Tilla wondered if the stories were true. Had Beras the Brute truly raped a child, then strangled her and buried her body? Had the Cadigus family, impressed with his cruelty and reputation, hired him based on that merit? Tilla did not know, but after seeing Shari Cadigus behead Pery, she was inclined to believe it.

A woman like Shari would find a child-killer her perfect companion, she thought. Tilla looked at her boots and clenched her fists. Yet like it or not, Beras was the one leading this caravan. And Shari Cadigus, the emperor's daughter, was the one who had recruited them.

I might find them repulsive. But if I'm to survive, I must follow them. Tilla gritted her teeth so mightily it hurt. *I will live. I will return home. I will not be another Pery.*

After what seemed like hours of darkness, the cart finally slowed to a halt. It came with both a sigh of relief and a chill of fear.

The girls around Tilla looked at one another, mewling and whispering. Mae grabbed Tilla's arm, squeezing it so hard Tilla grunted and yanked herself free.

"What's happening?" Mae whispered.

"Hush!" Tilla said. "Be quiet, Mae, and be strong. No more tears, okay? If you want to live, you can't cry. Wipe your eyes."

Sniffling, Mae obeyed. After knuckling her eyes dry, she bit her wobbling lip so hard it turned white.

Boots thumped outside, and a voice cried out hoarsely across the convoy, the words muffled. The door of her cart jolted madly, keys rattled in the lock, and a low voice muttered curses.

Mae trembled. The hundred girls in the cart fell silent, and all eyes turned toward the door. Tilla squared her shoulders, straightened her back, and raised her chin. She could easily stare above the shorter girls, and she sucked in her breath and held it.

The door yanked open.

Beras the Brute stood outside in the night, holding keys in one hand, a torch in the other.

The girls inside the cart stared, frozen. Beras stared back, his beady eyes shadowed beneath his thrusting brow. Dark sacks hung under those eyes, tugging them down toward his cheeks. His face was ashen, and though close-shaven, his beard was so dark it left his cheeks in perpetual shadow. He wore no black, polished steel like the other soldiers, but crude plates of iron over patches of mail. Even this suit of metal could not hide his size; he easily weighed twice as much as Tilla, a blend of muscle and fat that pushed at his armor.

For a long moment, he merely glared at the girls. He grumbled, then hawked loudly and spat. A few girls started and Mae whimpered.

For the first time, Tilla heard Beras speak.

"All right, you miserable lot of whores," he rumbled. "If you ask me, you're good for nothing but spreading your legs in a brothel, the lot of you." He spat again. "But since Shari Cadigus thinks she can whip you into soldiers, you're mine for a few days until you reach your barracks." He clutched his groin and tugged it. "Any one of you harlots moves too slowly or disobeys my orders, you'll get a taste of this." His voice rose to a howl. "So move—now! Off the cart!"

For an instant, rage bloomed inside of Tilla. It coursed through her and spun her head. How dared this man threaten them? There were a hundred women in this cart, and each one could turn into a dragon. He was one man, one miserable murderer who—

She gritted her teeth.

He's one miserable murderer who's a darling of the empire, she reminded herself. *Unless you want to shift into a dragon and have that empire hunt you down, obey him.*

The girls began exiting the cart, silent, their eyes darting. Tilla moved among them. When she stepped outside, cold air stung her, so shocking after the stifling cart that she gasped. She found herself on a roadside in a forest clearing. All around the glade, dark trees rose naked to claw at a starless sky. Six carts camped here in a ring, and Cadport's youths were stepping out from each one, faces pale. At every cart, a soldier stood shouting, threatening to flay, whip, or behead anyone who moved too slowly. The shouts rose across the forest.

"Move it, maggots!" howled one soldier.

"Form ranks, worms!" cried another and raised his punisher, its tip crackling.

Tilla had seen soldiers in Castellum Acta, the small hilltop fortress in Cadport; she knew about forming ranks, but did the others? The six hundred recruits stumbled into the center of the clearing. Around them spread the carts and twenty soldiers or more, each holding a crackling punisher.

"Form ranks—move it!" one soldier howled, a gaunt man with one eye. "Or I swear, blood will spill tonight."

The other soldiers all shouted and thrust their punishers, goading the recruits closer together. All around the clearing, the trees creaked and distant wolves howled.

"Come on!" Tilla hissed and grabbed a girl beside her. She pulled her forward and stood her in place. "Stand here. You— Mae. Stand behind her, like this. Go. And stand tall and still, don't slouch!"

The girls glanced around nervously, but they stood where Tilla directed them. She grabbed their shoulders, pulled them straight, and shoved their chins up. Around them, the other recruits saw and followed suit.

"Form lines!" Tilla whispered, moving between the others. "Three soldiers deep; that's the standard form. Go! And stand straight."

Finally the recruits began to form ranks. They stood in three lines, every recruit a foot apart from the others. Tilla took her spot at the front line; Mae stood to her left, trembling and standing so straight her heels did not touch the ground.

Tilla stood frozen, barely daring to breathe. She stretched her own back straight, kept her arms firm at her sides, and raised her chin. She had seen this formation in Cadport before—it seemed the most common one—but she knew there were other formations too. Which one did these soldiers demand? If they formed these ranks wrong, and she was responsible, would they behead her too?

When the ranks were complete, and the recruits stood at attention, Beras began trundling down the lines. He lolloped like a bear, armor clanking and axe clattering against his back. His torch crackled and he grunted as he walked.

"He walks like he got a thorny stick up his arse," whispered a girl beside Tilla, a scrawny little thing with short brown hair, an upturned nose, and fiery eyes. "You reckon he likes to shove sticks up there, Tilla? I knew me a man once who—"

"Shh!" Tilla hushed her.

She remembered this skinny girl—an orphan named Erry Docker, a dockside urchin who slept on the beach and ate whatever she stole. Some whispered that Erry was the daughter of a long-dead prostitute. Others whispered that Erry herself had taken up the profession and already bedded a thousand men.

"I was only—" Erry began, eyes flashing.

"Hush!" Tilla said.

Beras kept lumbering around, indeed moving much like Erry had described. The recruits stood silently.

"I could have bedded two whores by the time you formed ranks!" Beras shouted. "If you cannot form ranks here, in a guarded camp, how will you survive at war? When we send you miserable worms to fight the Resistance, do you think the enemy will wait for you to form the lines?" He spat and shouted hoarsely. "They will butcher you, and skin you alive, and they will rape your flayed bodies as you thrash and beg to die."

Tilla's throat tightened. She had heard many stories of the Resistance. They whispered that these rebels, wild men and women who lurked in the forests, were even crueler than the Cadigus family. They were bloodthirsty.

They killed my brother.

Cold sweat trickled down Tilla's back. Could the Resistance be hiding in *this* forest, waiting to charge with steel and fire?

Beras kept moving down the lines, inspecting each recruit in turn.

"In a few days," he called out, "you will reach your barracks, and they will try to train you, to turn you whelps into soldiers. If you ask me, they'll be wasting their time. I don't see soldiers. I see cannon fodder." He stopped before one boy, leaned close, and sneered. "You're a skinny one; I bet you weigh less than my axe."

The thin, pale youth kept standing still. "Yes, my lord," he whispered.

Beras grunted and walked on. He paused before another girl, licked his lips, and ogled her.

"And you," he said, "you are soft and rounded. You're made for a brothel, not a barracks." He spat at her feet. "I bet two coppers you end up in one. I'll be there to break you in."

He kept moving and stopped before a tall, broad youth with black hair. Tilla recognized him as Jem Chandler, the lazy lout who spent days drunk at the Old Wheel—the youth Mae pined for.

"You!" Beras barked. "You've got some meat on you. Big lad. You think you can be a soldier?"

Jem stood so stiffly it looked like his bones could shatter. He managed to nod.

"Yes, my lord."

Beras spat at his feet. "I'm not a lord, boy. And you're not a soldier and never will be. What did you do back at that cesspool you call a city?"

Jem held his head high, the veins straining in his neck. "I'm a chandler."

"Chandler!" Beras rumbled. "What the Abyss is that—you rolled over in a whorehouse for sailors?"

"I... I made candles, my—" Jem bit his lip. "I just made candles. But I can be a soldier. I can fight. I'm strong."

Beras snorted. "Are you now? We will see. Fight me." He tossed his torch down; it crackled upon the earth. "Come on. Show me how you fight, boy."

Jem looked aside nervously and licked his lips.

"I—"

Beras drove his fist into Jem's belly.

Tilla winced, clenched her jaw, and held her breath.

Jem doubled over, gasping for breath. Standing before the youth, Beras changed—his eyes burned with wildfire, his lips pulled back from his yellow teeth, and drool ran down his chin. He was like a rabid beast. He swung, and his fist *cracked* against Jem's head.

At Tilla's side, Mae whimpered.

"Hush!" Tilla whispered to the girl. Her fists trembled. "Don't make a sound!"

Jem lay on the ground, hacking and coughing blood. Beras laughed and kicked him, again and again, as the youth mewled.

"See the mighty candlemaker!" Beras announced, arms raised and fists bloodied. "See the boy who thought himself a soldier!"

With a laugh, Beras kicked hard. The steel-tipped boot drove into Jem's head. The youth's neck snapped, and Tilla closed her eyes and struggled not to gag, not to faint.

Stars, oh stars. Her eyes stung and the world spun around her. *Another death.*

"You lot are nothing but maggots!" Beras shouted. "You think you can be soldiers? You can be dead! You will be fed to the cannons, and your flesh will rot in the fields. You are nothing! You will be nothing. You are worms and if any of you doubts it, I will crush you."

Tilla opened her eyes and looked at Mae. The girl was trembling. She bit her lip so hard blood trickled down her chin. Tears streamed down her cheeks and she whimpered.

"Hush!" Tilla warned. "Mae, you—"

"What's this?" Beras demanded. His boots thumped. Tilla turned to see him marching toward her, fists at his sides. Blood splashed his boots.

Tilla fell silent and straightened, standing as stiff as she could.

The stench of sweat and blood flared as Beras came to stand before her. Tilla was the tallest girl here, and taller than half the boys, but Beras towered above her; he made her feel small as a child. He thrust his head close, scrutinizing her, and his lips peeled back. His teeth were rotten, and his breath assailed her, scented of corpses.

"Well, well," the brute said. "Look at what we've got here. My, you're a tall one." He reached out. With rough fingers, he grabbed her throat and squeezed. Pain shot through her; it took all her will to suppress a gasp. "I like tall women."

Tilla dared not look into his eyes, but she stared at his forehead with all the strength she had in her. His fingers squeezed her tighter. She could barely wheeze. She managed to whisper through the pain.

"Shari Cadigus liked me too." Her breath rasped, but she kept staring at the spot between his eyes. "You remember. You were there."

Beras kept his hand around her throat, crushing her, and glared. He hissed and his breath blasted her face, and she nearly gagged at its rot. His beady eyes burned.

"Yes," he hissed. "I remember. You're that whore I grabbed in my claws. The Abyss knows what Shari saw in you. You look like nothing but a cheap harlot to me." He spat onto her boot. "Shari isn't here. You remember that. You remember that well. Over here, on this road, you are mine. What's your name?"

"Tilla Roper," she whispered, voice raspy.

He leaned closer. He whispered into her ear. "I'll be watching you, Roper. You are trouble. You make one wrong move, and you will envy that boy whose misery I ended. You I would not kill so quickly."

He released her, turned around, and kept trundling down the lines. Tilla allowed herself to gasp with pain. She sucked in air. Her throat ached and her head spun, and she could still smell his rot.

"Now get to bed!" Beras shouted. "We keep moving at dawn. Get some sleep, and if I see any worms crawl, I crush them."

With that, the brute stepped into a cart and slammed the door shut. One soldier began dragging Jem's body into the woods; the others entered the other carts, leaving the recruits outside in the clearing.

Nobody dared speak. Nobody even dared whimper or cry. Six hundred recruits lay down, glanced around, and huddled together.

Tilla lay on the hard, cold earth. The wind moaned and chilled her, and rain began to fall. She shivered and her belly ached; she had not eaten all day, and she didn't know when she'd eat next. The forest creaked around them, and the wolves kept howling.

Another death, Tilla thought, the blood dancing before her eyes. *Another memory that will haunt me. Oh Rune. If you knew how bad it was, you'd have hid me under your tavern's floor with your old books.*

Mae curled up at her side, and tears streamed down her cheeks. Though she had vowed to be strong, Tilla felt her own eyes dampen. Perhaps it was the death she had seen. Perhaps it was the cold, the hunger, or pain. Perhaps she simply missed home. But her own tears fell, and her own lips trembled. Here, in the dark night, she did not feel like a soldier, only like a young and frightened girl.

"Jem," Mae whispered at her side and shook, sobbing quietly.

Tilla wriggled closer to the girl. The rain fell upon them. Lying in the mud, Tilla embraced the baker's daughter. Mae wept against her shoulder, and Tilla shed her own silent tears. They held each other as rain fell, wolves howled, and the night wrapped around them like claws.

RUNE

They ran through the forest as the sky burned.

Smoke blazed in Rune's lungs. His chest ached from where Kaelyn's claws had clutched him. Branches slapped him and roots snagged at his feet. A green dragon, Kaelyn had crashed through the treetops a mile back; they had been running in human forms since, side by side.

A hundred dragons screamed above, soaring and swooping and tearing at trees. Their flames blazed across the sky in crisscrossing lines. Rain fell and smoke blew above the forest.

"Find them!" rose a shriek above. The blue dragon soared— Shari Cadigus blowing fire. "Bring them to me alive, or bring me their charred corpses, but find them!"

Rune snarled and kept running. His lungs blazed, his knees throbbed, and his chest felt ready to collapse. He looked at Kaelyn, who ran at his side. Sweat dampened her mane of golden hair, and mud covered her clothes. She ran with bared teeth, her eyes narrowed. Her sword clanked at her side, and her bow bounced across her back.

Rune looked up. The forest canopy was thick; he could barely glimpse the dragons between the branches. For now they were hidden, but how long would that last?

"Kaelyn, they will burn down the forest," he said. "You can't possibly outrun a hundred dragons, they—"

She glared at him. "They will not burn their empire. This is Shari Cadigus, and these are her lands; she still loves Requiem in her twisted way." She panted and wiped sweat off her brow, but kept running. "Keep your voice low."

She scuttled over a boulder, climbing as deftly as a squirrel. Rune cursed and scrambled after her; she had to grab his wrist and pull him over. They ran down a hillside bumpy with roots. Vines tangled around Rune's feet, and a dragon swooped so low that he cursed and fell into the mud.

The dragon shrieked and roared fire skyward. Claws uprooted a tree. Rune cursed and ran aside, scurrying under the cover of an oak. Kaelyn ran at his side, and they raced between more trees. Fallen leaves and moss flew from under their boots.

"Tear down the trees!" Shari screamed above. Rune could not see her, but he heard her wings thud, and the trees bent as in a storm. "I can smell them. They cower below."

Rune cursed and panted. Sweat drenched him. He had been running for so long. He could run no longer. Perhaps he should surrender, should explain to Princess Shari that this was all a mistake; surely she was mistaking him for somebody else. He had nothing to do with Kaelyn or the Resistance. He was just Rune Brewer, and Kaelyn had tried to kidnap him, and he just wanted to go home.

Only there is no home anymore, he remembered, and his eyes stung. *Shari burned it down. And she killed my father. And like it or not, I'm stuck with Kaelyn now.*

"Kaelyn," he whispered between pants. "Kaelyn, where are—"

Her eyes lit up and she flashed a grin. "Here!"

She darted toward a mossy, twisting oak. Rune paused from running, and as soon as his legs stilled, pain bolted up them. His head spun and his chest felt full of fire.

Had Kaelyn gone mad? Rune had expected a camp full of warriors, or a hidden castle, or... not just a tree.

"Kaelyn!" he said and glanced skyward. Dragons streamed above the branches, dipping down to uproot trees. One beast grabbed a pine so close, Rune cursed and ducked. The roots yanked up, raining dirt and moss, less than a hundred feet away.

He looked back at Kaelyn. The young woman was scrambling around the tree, muttering curses and kicking the earth. She got down on her knees and began rummaging through the leaves.

"Stars damn it!" she said. "Come on, where are you—"

A dragon swooped fifty yards away. Another tree was uprooted and howls rose. The blue dragon dived above, wings bending the trees, and blew fire across the sky.

"They're near!" Shari howled. "I smell them. They're close! Tear up every tree."

Rune ducked and grasped a rock, as if tossing it could defeat dragons. He snarled and prepared to die.

"There!" Kaelyn whispered in triumph. She straightened, holding a rope that rose from the fallen leaves.

"Kaelyn, we need an army, not a rope—"

Before Rune could finish his sentence, Kaelyn yanked the rope, and a trapdoor opened upon the forest floor. Leaves and grass covered its top; below, a stairway led into darkness.

"Well, go on!" Kaelyn said. "Close your mouth and get down there."

Rune dutifully closed his mouth. Just as another dragon dived, he rushed forward, passed under the trapdoor, and leaped onto the staircase. Kaelyn jumped down beside him and tugged the trapdoor shut.

Before Rune could examine his new surroundings or even take another breath, thuds sounded in the forest above. Even through the trapdoor, Rune knew that sound: dragon claws landing in the forest. Flames crackled outside, wings flapped, and dragons screeched.

"They were here." Shari's shrill voice rose above. "I smell them. I see their prints. They ran here moments ago."

Great nostrils sniffed above, loud as a bellows. Kaelyn cursed and gripped her sword. With her other hand, she drew her dagger from her boot. For an instant, Rune thought she'd threaten him with the blade again. Then he saw that she was holding its hilt outward, offering it to him. Rune took the dagger and gripped it.

Shari screamed above, a sound of fury like storms and mountains cracking.

"Uproot every tree!" she cried. "Spread across this forest and find them. If you cannot, I will decimate you. Spread out! Find the whore and the boy."

With that, wings beat, fire crackled, and Shari's shrieks faded into the distance. The other dragons seemed to follow her.

Rune let out a shaky breath. He lowered his head, breathed raggedly, and tried to calm his thrashing heart. His muscles cramped, his breath sawed at his throat, and his skull felt too tight.

At his side, Kaelyn too breathed in relief. She wiped her brow again, only smearing sweat and mud across it. She released her grip on her sword.

"Come, Rune," she said. "Down the stairs and into the darkness. We're safe—for now." She managed a weak glare. "No thanks to you; you almost got us killed. You're more trouble than you're worth, if you ask me. From now on, you listen to me, and you follow my every order—no questions. Is that clear?"

He grumbled under his breath. "You sure have a way with people. But I'll listen to you for now, at least until I can rest and eat. You do have some food and drink squirreled away down here, right?"

She gave him a withering stare, then turned and began walking downstairs. He followed. The steps were dug into soil and rock, reinforced with planks of wood. Roots thrust out from the walls, and a family of mice huddled in a hole. The air was colder down here, and the place smelled of moss and soil.

After descending twenty steps, Kaelyn reached into an alcove dug into a wall. She produced two candles and a tinderbox.

"Here," she said and passed him a candle. "Hold this and do try not to set yourself on fire."

She opened the tinderbox and rubbed flint against steel. Sparks flew and Kaelyn lit their candles. The orange light flickered, and they kept descending.

The stairway led into a narrow tunnel. A wooden framework held the walls and ceiling; the floor was mere soil. The tunnel was so narrow it pushed against Rune's elbows. Kaelyn walked ahead and he followed silently. He wanted to pester Kaelyn for answers, but her talk of fire reminded him of that morning. The Old Wheel burning. The charred corpse of his father. Rune lowered his head and walked silently, candle in hand.

The tunnel took them to a round chamber; it was roughly the size of Rune's bedroom back at the Old Wheel. Kaelyn moved about the room, lighting more candles in alcoves. The light fell upon casks of wine, shelves of preserves and sausages, a rack of swords and bows, and chests of tunics and cloaks.

"Do you live here?" Rune asked.

"I live nowhere," she replied, not turning to look at him. "This is what we call a gopher hole. Stop—don't go looking around for gophers, you won't find any. It's just what we call these hideouts. They're safe places we can use when traveling."

She rummaged through a chest and produced some bandages. She closed the lid, sat upon it, and peeled back the rents on her legging. Grimacing, she examined the cut along her hip.

Rune knelt before her and reached for the bandages.

"Let me take a look," he said. "I know a bit of healing; I stitched a wound on Scraggles once."

She gave him a sidelong glance. "Scraggles?"

"You met him." He gave her a wan smile. "He barked at you."

She yanked the bandages away from him. "I will tend to my own wound, thank you. You go... go look at the swords or something. I hope you know how to use one." She sighed and rolled her eyes. "Of course you don't know how to use one. You were an innkeeper. I suppose that if Emperor Cadigus ever attacks us with a mug, you'll know how to clean it."

She began to tend to her wound, wincing. Rune grumbled and paced the chamber, this "gopher hole". He felt less like a gopher here and more like a trapped dragon; fire fumed inside him. His boots thumped against the earthen floor.

"You're right," he said. "You're right, Kaelyn, I'm no warrior. I don't know how to use a sword. And I've cleaned a lot of mugs in my day. I *am* an innkeeper and a brewer; that's all I want to be. You're the one who dragged me here at dagger-point. You're the one who got me into this mess." He stomped toward her, grabbed her shoulders, and glared at her. "Why, Kaelyn? Whatever feud you have with the Cadigus family, why did you drag me into it?"

She looked up from her wound and laughed mirthlessly. "Feud with the Cadigus family? Boy, did you not hear Shari call me her sister? I *am* the Cadigus family."

He frowned. He gave her a piercing stare, taking in her golden mane of hair, her feline features, and her sharp hazel eyes. Then he barked a laugh.

"You?" he said. "You are nothing like Shari Cadigus. Shari is... well, first of all, she's much taller than you. And she has dark hair and dark eyes. And, well... she's more of a warrior. You're kind of small and sneaky. Aren't the Cadiguses supposed to be big and tough and scary?"

Kaelyn glared at him. "I didn't say she was my twin sister. I have one twin already, a madman of a brother, and pray you never meet him. And no, I'm not like Shari. I'm not big, or tough, or particularly cruel." She sighed. "Why do you think I ran away?"

Rune stared at her with narrowed eyes.

Stars, he thought, *she's serious.*

He clutched his head.

This is bad.

He had heard of Kaelyn Cadigus, of course—the princess who had escaped the palace and joined the Resistance. But Kaelyn was a popular name, and somehow—with all the fire, running, and blood—Rune had not pieced things together.

His head spun.

"This is bad," he muttered. "Oh stars, this is bad." He pointed at her. "*You* are Kaelyn Cadigus."

She raised her hands to the heavens. "Stars bless us, he can be taught! What gave it away?"

Rune resumed pacing the room, tugging at his hair. He remembered that winter two years ago, the winter Kaelyn Cadigus was said to have escaped the capital, flown into the forest, and joined the rebellion against her father. Soldiers had stormed through every city, town, and farm in Requiem that season, tearing through homes, burning farms, torturing and killing and seeking the girl in every last hovel. They had never found her, but some whispered that Kaelyn Cadigus had risen high in the Resistance, ranking second only to Valien Eleison himself, the uprising's leader.

"Oh bloody stars," Rune said. "I'm here with Kaelyn Cadigus. No wonder they were hunting me. They must have seen you sneak into my tavern. Stars, woman, you're the most wanted soul in Requiem, do you know that?"

She gave him a wry smile. "No, Rune, I'm not the most wanted soul in Requiem—maybe second or third. Most wanted? My dear boy, that honorable distinction goes to you."

It was his turn to raise his hands in frustration. "Me? Merciful stars, Kaelyn, your sister didn't even know I existed until you sneaked into my tavern. Why did you drag me into this?" He shook his head as he paced. "That's it. I have to turn you in. No other choice. I'll fly to Shari, and explain that this was all a mistake, and—"

"And she would break your every bone, and flay your skin, and disembowel you alive, and laugh as you scream and beg," Kaelyn said. "I've seen her do it to others. Rune, come here. Sit down beside me. I have some things to tell you. You'll want to sit down for them."

She wriggled sideways on the chest, making room for him. He glowered down at her, but she only looked up with large, sad eyes, all their mockery and anger gone. Suddenly Rune again realized how beautiful she was, and stars damn it, he was a young man, and a beautiful woman still muddled his mind and dissipated his anger. With a sigh, he sat down beside her.

"Well, it's about damn time you told me what's going on here," he said. "So talk. I'm listening."

She placed a hand on his knee and looked at him softly. Her fingers were slim and warm; her eyes were warmer.

"Rune," she said, "do you know how my father came into power?"

He nodded. "Of course I do. We had to sing his songs every harvest fair. Requiem was weak in the old days; the Aeternum Dynasty had weakened it. Griffins ravaged our kingdom. Phoenixes burned us. Desert warriors rode wyverns to shatter our halls. We were hunted, afraid, dying. And then... Frey Cadigus flew to the capital, a great general leading a host of loyal dragons. They took the throne. They cast aside the weakness of the old dynasty. They hunted and slaughtered the griffins, the phoenixes, and all those who had hurt us. They turned Requiem from a frightened, crumbling kingdom into an empire. Requiem is strong now; Frey Cadigus made her strong." Rune's lips twisted into a grimace. "At least, that's what they taught me as a boy. That's what they forced us to sing. If you ask me, your father is a right bastard."

"That," she said, "he most certainly is. And yes, I too heard the stories of how weak the Aeternum Dynasty was. I grew up hearing horrible stories, Rune. My father would relish in telling them. Stories about how the griffins tore apart our children, spilling entrails and blood; how phoenixes burned our people so that their skin peeled and they ran flaming; how wyverns invaded from the south, how their acid melted flesh and left us deformed and forever screaming." Kaelyn sighed. "Those stories might be true; they are written in books from before my father's rule. But those books grieved for our fallen, for all the wars we fought. My father did not grieve; he *raged*. He blamed the Aeternum Dynasty for weakening Requiem, for allowing our enemies to kill us. He would mock the old dynasty's *compassion* and *righteousness*, spitting out those words like insults. He told me that he delighted in killing them. He told me how he slaughtered the old Aeternum king, his wife, and his children. When telling these stories, his eyes would light up, and he would lick his lips, and he seemed almost in rapture."

Rune nodded. "Like I said—right bastard. But I know all this. Stars, Kaelyn, the whole empire knows that the Cadigus family hated the Aeternums, that they are... how does Frey put it?" Rune puffed out his chest and spoke in a deep, bombastic voice, imitating the speeches he had heard soldiers delivering at Cadport. "We are strong now. We will never fall. We are mighty and powerful and no enemies will threaten us again, and any weakness within us must be crushed." He rolled his eyes. "I've never met your father, but stars, every soldier of his I've seen repeats the same thing. An army of parrots, he has."

"Deadly parrots," Kaelyn said. "Big ones who can blow fire." She smiled and lowered her head. Her hand still held his knee. "Rune, you said I don't look like my sister; that is true. Did you ever wonder why you don't look like Wil Brewer, the man you called father?"

Rune had smiled at her jest about fire-breathing parrots; now his smile vanished, and pain twisted his chest. *My father.* Again Rune saw it: Shari rising from the burning Old Wheel, clutching the charred corpse in her claws. *She killed him. She killed my father.* He clenched his fists and tears burned in his eyes.

All his life—gone. His kindly father. His home. His books. All burnt and gone. He wondered if his dog, at least, had fled the flames; yet even if Scraggles had escaped, would Rune ever see his pet again?

Everything is burnt, he thought and a lump filled his throat. *Everything is lost.*

"Oh, Rune," Kaelyn said, voice soft. "I'm sorry. Truly I am. I didn't mean to... I..." She touched his hair. "I know this is painful. I know this is confusing. But hear me now. There will be time to mourn, but first you must hear everything I say."

He looked at her, silent. His eyes stung, and tears blurred his vision. He nodded, unable to talk.

"Rune," she continued, "this is going to be hard to accept. You might not believe me, but you must hear this. When my father took over the throne, he slaughtered the Aeternum family, every last one—the king, the queen, the princes, the lords and ladies... all but one Aeternum. All but the babe of the family. All but you."

Rune rubbed his eyes and sighed. "I had a feeling you were going to say that." He gave her a sidelong glance. "And damn it, you didn't disappoint. Yes, I've heard of this missing Aeternum babe. I realize he vanished around the time I myself was a baby. Stars, Kaelyn, every boy in Cadport my age was mocked for being the missing Aeternum."

Kaelyn's eyes narrowed and flashed. "Well, he really is you. Your true name is Relesar Aeternum, son of Ardin, heir of a dynasty four thousand years old. My father hates you—he hates you more than all the griffins and phoenixes that ever flew. He's been hunting you for seventeen years now, since I myself was only a babe. Why do you think Shari showed up in your city?"

"To enlist recruits? To behead a girl and terrify us into obedience? Because she likes the seaside air and the mild southern winters?"

"Because she was looking for you." Kaelyn jabbed him sharply in the arm. "You look like your father, the old king. Damn it, you're the spitting image. I've seen the man's paintings. People noticed. *Soldiers* noticed. You have the same dark hair, the same gray eyes, the same straight nose..."

"Kaelyn, that describes about a million people in Requiem!" He laughed. "So the old king Aeternun had brown hair and gray eyes—stars above, that proves it!"

Kaelyn looked at her feet; she twisted them uncomfortably. "Well, I... might have had something to do with Shari showing up. We've known about you all your life, Rune. Our leader, Valien, is the one who placed you at the Old Wheel Tavern; you were only a few moons old. Since then, the Resistance has been watching you. We'd visit the tavern. We'd drink your ale. We'd make sure you were safe, that the Cadigus family hadn't found you. And, well..."

Kaelyn bit her lip. "I'm sorry, but we grew careless. Shari's soldiers saw our movements. They knew we were visiting Cadport. They followed me one day to the Old Wheel, and they saw you there, and they put two and two together." She looked back at him, her eyes rimmed with red. "I had to look after you, Rune. I had to. You understand, right?"

For the first time, Rune realized where he had seen Kaelyn before. Of course!

The young, demure priestess had visited the Old Wheel the last two winters, claiming to be on a pilgrimage to Ralora Cliffs, the place where Requiem had fought a battle hundreds of years ago. The priestess would wear a headdress, heavy robes, and a hood, but Rune remembered her large, hazel eyes.

Kaelyn's eyes.

He rose to his feet so suddenly he nearly knocked the chest—and Kaelyn—over. He rushed toward a wall, grabbed a sword that hung there, and sliced the air. His jaw clenched and anger constricted his throat.

"Shari followed you!" he said, staring at Kaelyn with burning eyes. "I knew it. I knew it! And now my father is dead, and I'm stuck in this hole, and if they catch me, I'm dead too. And... stars, Kaelyn, how could you..."

He let his sword drop; it thumped against the ground. He fell to his knees beside it, covered his eyes, and felt Kaelyn's hands in his hair.

"I'm sorry," she whispered. She knelt before him and embraced him. "I'm so sorry—for everything. But you're safe now."

He lowered his hands and stared at her. Her face was inches from his, soft with concern.

"Am I, Kaelyn? Am I safe?"

"Safer than you were." She touched his cheek. "Believe that, at least. You are safer here."

He let out a long, shaky sigh. He felt too weak to stand up again, to ever leave this hole.

"What now?" he said and lowered his head.

"I will take you to see Valien, our leader. He has known you all your life; he smuggled you out of the palace when my father

killed your parents." She nodded. "He is wise, the wisest man I
know. He'll know what to do next."

"Valien Eleison," Rune whispered.

Like everyone in the empire, he had heard of Valien—the
disgraced knight turned resistor, the silver dragon with one horn.
Some called him a hero. Others called him a brute, a drunkard and
thief and murderer. And some, Rune knew, said that Valien
Eleison himself was the man who slew Tilla's brother.

And I will meet him, Rune thought and swallowed. *I will meet
the man who crushed my best friend's soul.*

Kaelyn nodded. "But for now, eat and drink something.
There is food and wine here. It will be a long journey, and you'll
need your strength." She looked at the fallen blade. "And you'll
need that sword."

"I thought you said I wouldn't know how to use one."

Though her eyes were still damp, Kaelyn managed to flash a
grin. "You wouldn't, but I'd like a spare, and I'm not carrying two."
She stood up, grabbed an apple from a shelf, and tossed it toward
him. "Eat this. And kick your boots off. We're staying the night.
You're stuck with me in this hole for a while longer."

On any other night, being stuck in a burrow with a beautiful
woman—overnight, too!—would have made Rune feel like the
luckiest man in Requiem. Today the apple tasted stale, and he
missed home, and he missed Tilla and his father.

When his apple was eaten, he lay down by a wall, and Kaelyn
lay beside him. She covered herself with her cloak and placed her
cheek upon her palm.

"Goodnight, Rune," she said.

"You're not going to stab me in the middle of the night, are
you?" He rubbed his side. "Your dagger nicked me back there."

She grinned again, a grin that showed all her teeth. "No, but
I do kick when I sleep." She gave him a mock kick. "You're safe
from Shari's fire, but no promises that I won't kick you to death."

"Fair enough." He closed his eyes. "Goodnight, Kaelyn."

Goodnight, Tilla, he added silently, wondering where she was
now, and whether she too had a dry, safe place to sleep.

Goodnight, Father, he thought. He wondered if the old man's
soul had risen to the starlit halls of afterlife... and how crazy Kaelyn
was for claiming Wil Brewer hadn't been his father at all.

SHARI

She flew back toward Cadport, shrieking and blowing fire. Her blood pounded in her ears. Her wings beat, bending trees below. Six of her warriors flew around her, metallic dragons blasting fire and howling.

The boy escaped.

Shari screeched and streamed above the city walls.

This backwater will pay.

"I seek Rune Brewer!" Shari screamed to city. She flew above the streets and homes, smoke streaming behind her. "You let the boy escape."

She swooped, reached out her claws, and slashed at a home. Its clay walls collapsed, and the family inside wailed. Shari rose higher, breathing fire.

"You will bring me the boy!" she cried. "You will bring him to me, or this city will burn."

She dived over a square and blew fire at another home. Its roof burst into flame. The family inside screamed and fled into the street.

Shari snarled, rage pounding through her. This foul southern city was conniving against her. This was a hive of resistors; she knew it. How else could Kaelyn have smuggled the boy out?

She turned to look at her warriors, six iron dragons who flew behind her.

"Each of you," she said, "grab two of this city's vermin. I don't care who. I don't care how young they are. Grab a dozen of these filthy maggots and break them upon a dozen wheels."

The six dragons blasted fire, grinned toothily, and swooped.

Claws slammed into homes. Walls collapsed and people ran through the streets, wailing.

Shari beat her wings, flew toward the hill above the boardwalk, and circled around Castellum Acta, citadel of this city. She screeched orders, voice pealing across the sky. A hundred soldiers streamed out of the craggy fortress, shifted into dragons, and streamed above the streets. The city shook and jets of fire crisscrossed the sky. Homes burned.

"Raise twelve wheels!" Shari howled, wings beating back flames across the city. Smoke filled her throat, and she roared hoarsely. "Raise them outside the courthouse!"

As thousands wailed and fled across the city, her soldiers dragged twelve wagon wheels into the city square, that same square where Shari had spoken to the recruits. Dragons dived and grabbed people from the streets—men, women, and children.

"Break their bodies!" Shari shouted, flying above.

Her six dragons returned and rallied around her. Each clutched two people, one in each claw. They dived, tossed the people onto the square, and pinned them down. Soldiers streamed from alleyways to form a ring around the plaza.

Shari landed upon the cobblestones and blasted fire skyward. She roared so the entire city could hear.

"Break them!" she cried. "Shatter their bones and hang them here. I want the city to hear them scream!"

The twelve, selected randomly from the thousands, squirmed and tried to flee, but they could not escape the claws that pinned them down. One of them, a young man with wide eyes, tried to shift into a dragon, to break the law of Cadigus. Scales began to appear across his body, but the dragon above him, one of Shari's soldiers, pressed his claws down. The young man below wailed and his magic left him.

"Break them! Bring hammers!"

Soldiers walked forward in human form, clad in black armor and bearing great hammers. The dozen townsfolk wailed, trapped under the claws.

"Please!" one begged, a young girl no older than ten. "Please..."

Another wailed, an old woman with white hair. "Please, my princess, have mercy—"

The hammers swung.

Bones snapped.

The dozen screamed.

Shari stood, snarling and snorting smoke, and laughed.

The hammers swung again. Again. Snapping limbs. Snapping spines. Shari laughed.

"Sling them onto the wheels!" she commanded.

The soldiers dragged the wailing, broken bodies onto the wagon wheels, slung limbs between spokes, and tied the dozen down.

"Hang them on the courthouse balcony!" she commanded, laughing and blasting smoke.

Her soldiers laughed too. Ropes were slung over the balcony, and Shari smiled; had she not met the ropemaker's daughter at this very place?

The wheels were raised to dangle off the balcony like bloodied wind chimes. Upon each one, a shattered body twitched and wept. Shari stood in the square, still in dragon form. She was tempted to blow her fire, to roast these wailing bodies and taste their flesh. But no, she thought. No. She would let them linger here. She would let them scream a while longer.

She flapped her wings and rose high above the square. The city rolled around her. From up here, she could see Castellum Acta upon the hill, the boardwalk lined with rotting shops, the docks that stretched into the sea, and the abandoned lighthouse upon the breakwater. In the north, beyond the city walls, stretched the forest where the boy had fled.

Shari roared her cry, making sure every soul in Cadport heard.

"I seek Rune Brewer!" she shouted. "You let him flee this city. This is your punishment. These bodies will hang until they rot!" She blew fire down at homes, torching roofs. "You will bring me information about the boy. You will tell me where he fled. Or next moon, I will break a hundred bodies, then a thousand, then ten thousand, until none are left alive." She screamed so loudly her eardrums thrummed. "You will bring me Rune Brewer or you will die!"

People streamed into the square below her, weeping and wailing and reaching out to those dying upon the wheels. They were the families of the broken, Shari realized, and her grin widened.

Good, she thought. *Let them see their beloveds suffer. This city sheltered an Aeternum.* She shrieked and blasted fire. *They will suffer greatly until he's mine.*

She spun and flew away. Once she had crossed the city walls and flew over the forest, a chill claimed her belly, overpowering the fire of her rage.

She had told her father she would return the boy.

She had vowed to drag Relesar Aeternum back to the capital, he a broken wretch and she a glorious ruler. She had promised her father this gift within the moon.

Frey Cadigus, she knew, was not one to take disappointment well.

She howled, thrashed her tail, and blasted fire.

"You will pay for this, Kaelyn!" she roared. "I will break you too, and I will break the boy, and I will break this city, and the world itself will weep until Relesar is mine."

With fire and roars, Shari flew north, heading to the capital, to her father... and to the rage of an empire.

Daniel Arenson

LERESY

He flew on the wind, a red dragon snorting fire, and licked his maw. He saw it below, rising glorious from the forest.

"My birthday present," he hissed, and smoke curled from between his teeth. "It's mine. My own."

He was eighteen today, a grown man, and his first fortress—the first of many he would command—shone below. Obsidian tiles covered its limestone foundations, reflecting the winter sun. Its four corner towers rose like skulls upon scraggly necks, their tops snowy. Their banners flapped in the wind, hiding and revealing the red spiral, sigil of his house. A fifth tower rose above the grand hall, twice as tall as the others. Upon it ticked a great clock, its four dials as large as dragons, the hands shaped as blades.

"Castra Luna," whispered the red dragon. "The oldest standing fortress in Requiem. My birthright."

As he flew over the forest toward the castle, Leresy Cadigus, prince of the empire, grinned and breathed his fire.

The forest streamed below him, pines and oaks bending under the flap of his wings. When Leresy drew closer to the fort, he saw hundreds of soldiers in the courtyard, mere scurrying ants from here. He narrowed his eyes and found himself salivating.

Yes, he thought. *Yes, lots of new recruits here—young, afraid, and female.* He licked drool off his maw. *So much flesh to claim. So much to taste, to savor, to conquer.*

Some in the capital had wondered, Leresy knew, why he had demanded Castra Luna for his birthday gift. His older sister Shari had scoffed.

"You could have any fort in Nova Vita!" she had said. "You could command knights, seasoned warriors, and garrisons of legend. And you choose... a training outpost halfway across the empire?"

She had laughed, and Leresy had only stood before her, silent, a small smile on his lips. So little she understood. So little

84

she knew of what lurked here in Castra Luna, this distant southern pile of stone.

Here lurked real power, more than Shari could imagine in her small, petty mind, the mind of a warrior.

"You think like a fighter," Leresy whispered into the wind. "Like a brute. Like the mindless killer that you are. But I want more than the glory of war, dearest sister. When I am done here, I will have such power that you will kneel before me."

Flames exploded within him. He clenched his jaw and blasted fire skyward. Shari thought herself so mighty, so proud, so powerful. As Leresy circled above the fortress, he roared his rage, a shriek that could tear through human eardrums.

You might be heir to the empire, Shari, but soon even you will quake before me.

He now flew directly over Castra Luna, the ancient fortress that had been guarding southern Requiem for seven hundred years. He dived toward the courtyard and flew so low the soldiers below—fresh meat just carted in from the backwaters—had to duck. With a grin and howl, Leresy blasted fire across the courtyard, then soared again. His wings stirred dust below, and he shrieked to the sun.

He rose high above the courtyard and blew fire. He had seen enough of the soldiers below to whet his appetite. Half were frightened, pale farm boys no older than himself—fools for him to crush under his heel. The rest were ripe females, and Leresy snorted and grinned and felt his pulse quicken.

I will savor them, he thought. *This fort is mine, and they are mine. I own these bricks, and I own this flesh.*

He flew toward the command tower, the tallest among them, a great spire of obsidian. It rose hundreds of feet tall, flaring into a capital like a flanged mace. Its clock ticked upon it, a masterwork of black and red gears that clanged the noon hour as Leresy approached.

He flew between towering black spikes, each taller than a dragon, and landed upon the tower roof. He snapped his teeth and grinned. Below him spread the fortress, barracks and armories and courtyards, and beyond them the snowy forests rolled into haze. He blasted fire upward, a beacon of his dominion, and shifted into human form.

Wind whipped him, trying to tear off his cloak. The rooftop spikes towered around him. When he peered off the roof, the height seemed dizzying. For an instant Leresy faltered, and his heart leaped, and he was sure he would fall to the courtyard below. He gritted his teeth, clutched his sword, and trudged across the roof.

A trapdoor lay below him, carved of bronze. Leresy grabbed the knob, pulled the door open, and found a ladder leading into a chamber. He entered, closed the trapdoor above him, and descended the rungs.

Once his feet touched the floor, he cursed.

The room was bare, cold, and utterly distasteful. Disgust washed Leresy, and for a moment, he wondered if he had made a mistake flying here. Only one wall held a tapestry, and even that tapestry was plain, black fabric emblazoned with the red spiral—cheap dye. The furniture was bare pine, and no gold or jewels adorned it. The bed's mattress was stuffed with straw, not feathers; Leresy could tell just by looking. The chamber did sport a stained-glass window, but even its design was simple—it showed a dragon atop a red spiral—compared to the majestic stained glass of northern palaces.

Leresy's lips twisted and he snarled.

"At least they have a proper mirror," he said and stepped toward it.

The mirror rose taller than a man, and Leresy admired his reflection. Whenever he felt sour, his reflection could lift his spirits.

He was remarkably good-looking, he thought. He placed his hands on his hips, raised his chin, and felt his mood improve. His hair was woven of purest gold, short enough to look like a soldier's hair, but long enough to shine. His eyes were blue as sapphires. His cheeks were smooth, his lips full and pouty.

Some said he looked like his twin, the filthy traitor Kaelyn, but of course, Kaelyn would be wearing rags now and crawling through the mud. Lersey's dress was immaculate. Not a scratch spoiled his armor of black steel and gold. Not a single errant thread marred his fine cloak of crimson wool and fur. An apple-sized ruby clasped that cloak, and ancient stones—each one taken from the grave of a great hero—embossed his scabbard.

But his greatest treasure, greater even than his jewels and
blades, was his punisher. Leresy's lips peeled back. Delicately, he
drew the rod from his belt and held it before him. The finest,
softest leather wrapped around its grip. Upon its rounded head,
red lightning crackled and flared. Leresy's breath quickened and his
eyes narrowed. He could already imagine the flesh he would burn
with his tool, the screams he would hear, and the trembling females
he would break and tame and invade.

"My birthday gift," he whispered, holding the punisher
before him; it throbbed in his hand. "My birthright. My—"

A creak sounded behind him—the trapdoor being opened.

Leresy spun to see a burly old man descending the ladder
into the chamber.

The man wore leather armor studded with iron bolts—the
crude armor of the outposts. White scruff covered his cheeks, and
snow and mud stained the hem of his cloak. A longsword hung at
the old man's side, but no jewels adorned it; it could have been
taken off a dead mercenary. Leresy's lips curled in disgust.

"Lord Raelor," he said, letting that disgust suffuse his voice.
"Look at your garb. I've seen farmers dressed finer. Look at your
beard. I've seen cleaner hair on seaside whores. And you call
yourself a lord?"

The burly old man sucked in his breath. His eyes widened
and he knelt.

"Prince Leresy," he said gruffly, head lowered. "You surprise
me with your visit, my lord."

Leresy snarled, stepped forward, and grabbed the man's
collar.

"And I suppose you don't like surprises, old man," he said
with a sneer. "If you knew I was coming, would you have
improved your appearance? Would you have shaved your scruff, or
washed that fleabag of a cloak, or prepared this room for a prince?"
He spat on the floor. "Castra Luna is the oldest standing fort in the
empire. Did you think you could allow it to rot, and the capital
would sit by idly? Stand up."

Raelor rose to his feet, his armor and joints creaking. His
eyes were small, blue, and cold, the eyes of a hardened warrior, but
Leresy saw fear in them too, and that pleased him.

"My prince Leresy," he said. "Aye, it is a gruff life here in the south, far from the northern comforts of the capital. If you are tired from your flight, however, we have strong wine in our cellars, and—"

"Do I look tired?" Leresy narrowed his eyes. "Are you saying I look tired, old man?"

Raelor stiffened. "My apologies, my prince, I merely—"

"But I *will* have some wine." Leresy turned away from the man and stomped toward a table; a jug of wine stood there by a pewter mug. "Have you no servants here to pour your drink? Truly, this is a cesspool of a fort. Things will change around here."

Lips curling, Leresy poured his own wine. It was the first time he'd had to pour his own drink. He sipped, swished the liquid in his mouth, then spat it onto the floor.

"Pig piss!" he said. He spun back toward Raelor and glared. "Do you drink pig piss here in the south, Raelor?"

The old man's eyes hardened; Leresy could see the hatred and fear locking horns behind those eyes.

"If the wine is distasteful to you, my prince, we can order other vintages shipped in. We receive shipments every moon, and—"

"You won't be around for that, Raelor," Leresy said. He pulled the scroll from his belt and tossed it forward. "A letter for you. Read it."

Raelor stared at Leresy for just an instant longer, just a heartbeat, but in that space of a breath, Leresy saw the man's well of hatred... and he grinned.

Good, he thought. *Good—hate me, old man. It will make this all the sweeter.*

The scroll bore the emperor's official seal, a red spiral surrounding the initials F.C. — Frey Cadigus. When Raelor looked at the seal, he sucked in his breath and blanched.

Leresy's grin widened. *A letter from the emperor is rarely good news,* he thought and licked his lips.

With stiff fingers, Raelor broke the seal, unrolled the parchment, and his eyes darted as he read. His skin grew paler, and a drop of sweat rolled down his temple. He rolled the scroll back up and looked at Leresy.

"My lord prince," he said. "If I have failed in my duties, allow me to mend them. My family has ruled Castra Luna for generations. We have served the empire loyally. We—"

"You," said Leresy, "are relieved of command, Lord Raelor. Oh, I'm sorry... but you are not a lord anymore at all, are you?" He *tsk*ed his tongue. "That makes you... nothing. Nothing but an intruder in my fortress."

More sweat rolled down Raelor's face. His fingers began to tremble. "Please, my prince. My family... allow me to..." His lips shook, his throat constricted, and he could speak no more.

Leresy allowed mock concern to soften his eyes. He stepped toward the larger man and placed his hand on his shoulder.

"Your family is safe in the capital!" Leresy said. "Do not worry, my good man. The empire remembers your loyal service. And your family will remain safe; we will not harm them. Not if you relieve yourself of duty honorably. The empire allows you this great, final honor."

Raelor's neck bobbed as he swallowed. He stared at the floor, and his teeth grinded, and his forehead glistened. When he looked back up at Leresy, red rimmed his eyes.

"Why?" he whispered. "Why, my prince? How have I failed?"

Leresy shrugged. "Because it's my birthday. And this is what I wanted." He gestured at the dagger on Raelor's belt. "Go on then. Do it. Just... not on the rug."

Raelor raised his chin. "And my family...?"

"We will make it painless," Leresy said. "Do this now, and they will not suffer. It will be in their sleep." He snorted. "I would have preferred to watch them broken and hear them scream—perhaps the rack or an old-fashioned quartering—but my father is more merciful than I am. Well, go on then! Don't test that mercy."

Tears dampened Raelor's eyes, but he managed to keep his chin raised. He gave a final salute, slamming his fist against his chest.

"Hail the red spiral!" he said, stepped back, and drew his dagger. With a gasp and blinking stare, he shoved his blade into his neck.

Leresy stood above the dying man, watching him writhe and bleed out onto the floor and rug.

Damn it, he thought. *I told him not to stain the rug.*

The blood seeped and ran between the tiles. Leresy sighed. This damn tower—the whole stinking fort—would need to be scrubbed and remodeled before it was fit for a prince.

A voice spoke behind him.

"Same old Leresy... still not killing his own enemies."

Leresy spun around and saw her there.

He grinned.

"Nairi," he said.

A backdoor stood open by the tapestry, revealing a staircase that plunged lower down the tower. Nairi stood in the doorway, hands on her hips. A crooked smile played across her lips.

Leresy felt his blood heat; stars, he had missed her. Her short blond hair had grown a little longer, just long enough to fall across her brow and ears, but her green eyes still shone with the same old mockery. When she walked toward him, the sway of her well-rounded hips still stirred his loins. She too was dressed crudely—she wore tan leggings, a steel breastplate, and muddy boots. She carried a rough sword across her back—it wasn't even jeweled—and a punisher hung at her waist. Only the black rose engraved upon her breastplate, sigil of her house, denoted her nobility.

When she reached him, she placed a finger under his chin and closed his mouth.

"Careful, my prince," she said. "There's blood on the floor, and your tongue nearly rolled that far."

With a snarl, he reached behind her, cupped a handful of her backside, and squeezed.

"Why kill my enemies myself?" he said to her. "My blade is far too fine to dirty with the blood of pigs. And you, Nairi, you too are a pig." He sniffed. "You stink of oil and dirt, and you're dressed like a peasant's daughter. Do you forget who you are? Did life here in this outpost turn you into a commoner?"

Nairi raised an eyebrow and gave him a mocking smile. "It's true. My clothes are dirty and foul; the clothes of a warrior. Why don't you remove them from me? I can see that's what you want." She patted his cheek. "Such a refined prince does not dirty his dagger..." She reached down to his breeches and grabbed him. "...or any of his blades."

He snarled and shoved her back. He walked toward the table, grabbed the wine, and drank deeply, pig piss or not. After slamming the mug down, he walked toward the bed, sat on the mattress, and stared at Nairi. She stood with one hand in her hair, smirking at him.

Stars, the woman drips sex, he thought.

"Well?" he said to her. "Go on. Get those clothes off."

"Somebody's impatient!" she said. She pouted and began unbuckling her breastplate.

Leresy leaned back and breathed deeply. *Perfection,* he thought as he watched her undress. *Exquisite perfection.* Piece by piece, she tossed aside her garments and armor, and Leresy's smile widened. The young woman was sex in boots, and her father...

Leresy licked his lips. *Her father is the most powerful, feared man outside my family.* He couldn't help but snort a laugh. *Once Nairi and I are wed, even my brutish sister will fear my might.*

Nairi pouted, naked before him, and crossed her arms across her breasts. "You laugh at my naked body?"

"No," Leresy said. He stood up, approached her, and grabbed her waist. He dug his fingers into her and snarled. "I claim it. Your body is mine. Today is my birthday, and I take this castle, and I take you."

He shoved her facedown onto the bed. When she tried to flip onto her back, he pressed her down.

"Ler—" she began.

"Lie still. Don't talk." He mounted her. "Scream if you like."

He reached under her torso, grabbed her, and took her roughly, and she screamed. Stars, he made her scream, and Leresy smiled and drooled above her.

"You are mine," he hissed into her ear. "Don't you forget that, Nairi. I am your prince, and you belong to me."

With a grunt, he rolled off her and lay at her side. The mattress creaked beneath him.

I was right, he thought as he stared at the ceiling. *The mattress is stuffed with straw. Raelor, you bloody peasant. I should torture your family after all. I'll start by making them sleep on this mattress.*

He turned to look at Nairi. For once, no mockery shone in her eyes or twisted her lips. She looked almost shy, almost demure.

He had hurt her. *Good.* He had made this feel like the first time, and in his bed, she now felt like a newly deflowered maiden.

And in this bed I will deflower many more, Leresy thought. *As soon as I replace the mattress, that is.*

"Soon we will be wed," he told her. "I haven't told my father yet. I will when the time is right; I'll fly to the capital and let him know in person. I will tell your father too."

Fire coiled through his chest, and his fingers trembled. Yes. Nairi's father. He was perhaps an ugly bastard, all bald and lumpy skin—not nearly as intoxicating as his fresh young daughter—but he was powerful, and if Leresy craved anything more than female flesh, it was power.

His lips curled.

Soon you will fear me, Shari, he thought. *When I'm married to Nairi, the son-in-law of the Axehand Order's commander, you will fear me. Once I'm wed into the Axehand, even you will be unable to hurt me. Even you will shiver when I approach, dearest sister. You've tried to kill me so many times. Don't think I don't know this, Shari. But soon, very soon, the tables will turn.*

"I would like that," Nairi said, her voice small. She propped herself up on one elbow. "Would we fly and tell them together? I haven't been to the capital in a year now. I would like to return."

He spun toward her and frowned, disgusted. "The capital?" He snorted. "What do you want to visit the capital for? Nova Vita is a cesspool, all politics and rules and..."

And Shari trying to kill me, he wanted to say, but bit down on the words. No. It was best Nairi did not know about that. In the capital, there was his father, his sister, and motley nobles with daggers forged for stabbing backs. But here... here in the south there were perhaps crude mattresses, bare chambers, and peasant armor, but there was also dominion. Here, Leresy was lord.

Once I'm wed to Nairi, I can return to the capital as a lord as well. Once Shari is killed, I will be heir.

"Never mind that," he finished. "The capital will be ours in time. Get up. Get dressed. Don't you have recruits to train?"

Some of the fire returned to her eyes. "Don't you have a floor to mop of blood?" She rose to her feet, lifted her clothes, and began to dress herself. "To answer your question, yes. There's a new shipment of fresh meat rolling in today—six hundred recruits from a southern backwoods called Cadport." She hopped on one leg, tugging up her leggings. "Cadport! What a ridiculous name. Why does your family insist on naming everything after itself?"

He scoffed. "I'll do the same to you, wench. Nairi Cadigus you'll be when I'm done with you."

And yet his belly tightened. Cadport, Cadport... where had he heard that name? He sucked in his breath, realization hitting him. *Bloody Abyss.* His sister had said something about flying down to Cadport; she had taken that brute Beras with her, a halfwit she had hired a few years back. Were these two events connected?

What are you up to, Shari? She had flown to the southern port, and now hundreds of its youths were arriving here, where Leresy was staking his claim. He grinded his teeth. Stars damn it, his sister was up to her own schemes; he felt it in his gut.

I'll have to marry Nairi soon. I'll have to grow close to her father. He clenched his fists. *And then my sister will die.*

Nairi fastened the last buckle on her breastplate, then slung her sword across her back. She nodded down at Leresy, who still lay abed.

"Come see them roll in, my prince," she said and grinned. "Lots of fresh meat for you to terrify. You should enjoy that."

Oh, but I will enjoy their fresh meat, he thought. *Though not the way you think.*

He had spent his love only moments ago, yet already Leresy felt his blood heat again. Yes, he would break in many of those recruits—with sword, with whip, and here in his bed. He wondered briefly whether Nairi would like to join him in his conquests, then decided against it. It was best not to share this with her; at least, not until after he wed her and killed Shari.

He left the bed and smoothed his robe.

"Are there any servants in this pile of bricks?" He nodded down at the corpse. "The thing stinks already."

She strapped her punisher to her hip; it was clad in the blood-red leather of a phalanx commander.

"Come, my prince," she said, "and don't worry; I'll send up a recruit or two to dispose of the corpse. We have no servants here, but we have thousands of youths to break, to train, and to command. They will do your dirty work. Come, let's go introduce them to the great Prince Leresy Cadigus."

She patted his cheek, winked, and turned to leave the room, hips swaying with reclaimed swagger. Leresy stood a moment, admiring the view, then followed.

They climbed back onto the tower's roof. They stood in the wind, looking down at the fortress. The smaller towers, the courtyard, the grand hall, the armory, the kitchens—they all looked like stone blocks from up here. Around them rolled the forests. A single, cobbled road snaked across the land, leading from the camp's gates down south. Leresy was a child of the north; to him, Castra Luna was as south as he could imagine. But the empire stretched even farther from this outpost, all the way to the Tiran Sea where Cadport lay, and beyond that sea to the endless deserts.

My birthright, he thought. *Once my father and sister are dead, all these lands will be mine.*

Movement caught his eye. A convoy was moving north along the road, heading toward the camp. Leresy counted six carts, each one wide enough to house a phalanx of recruits. A dragon tugged each cart down the road, and smoke plumed from their nostrils.

"Here they are!" Nairi said, standing beside him. The wind ruffled her short blond hair, and she smiled crookedly and clutched her punisher. "The fresh meat rolls in. Let us go greet them."

Her lips peeled back in a hungry grin, and she shifted. Gray wings burst out from her back. Her fangs shone. She took flight as an iron dragon, roared, and blew fire at the sky.

Leresy followed suit. He shifted into the red dragon, roared a spray of fire, and flew after her. They circled above the fort, howling their flames, and waited for the recruits to roll in.

As Leresy flew, he grinned and licked his chops. His chamber perhaps was bare, and the mattress rough, but Leresy thought he would enjoy his eighteenth birthday after all.

TILLA

The cart trundled forward, and they were close now. Dragons shrieked ahead, fire crackled, and Tilla could feel it. After ten days in the wilderness, they were nearing their destination.

What fort will it be? she wondered, standing in the dark cart as a hundred other girls pressed against her. She tried to remember all the forts she knew within ten days of Cadport, but there were too many. It would have to be one for training recruits—seasoned soldiers didn't share forts with recruits—but that only narrowed it down by a couple of forts.

She went over all the names she had heard soldiers speak of. This could be Castra Nova Murus, a great fortress in the east; that would be good fortune, Tilla thought, for soldiers said a benevolent lord commanded Murus. Or it could be Castra Alira, a dilapidated fortress in the west; Tilla remembered soldiers saying the rooms there were rough, but the training light.

Or it could be... Tilla swallowed and twisted her fingers. She did not want to be grim but had to consider the possibility. They could be rolling toward the infamous Castra Luna.

Tilla clenched her jaw, remembering the stories. They whispered that Luna was not only the cruelest fortress in the south, but in the entire empire. They said obsidian tiles covered the old bricks of Castra Luna, as black and cold as the heart of its commanders. They said recruits were broken there—physically and mentally. Tilla had once met a soldier who had, they said, trained in Castra Luna; the man had been a mute, grim killer, a demon in human flesh.

Her own brother had trained at Castra Luna. He had never come home.

Tilla sucked in her breath.

No, she thought, *the odds are against it. It won't be Luna. Please, stars of my fathers, don't let it be Luna.*

She moved through the crowd of girls, heading toward a cart wall. Two days back, the cart had overturned, and a crack now opened in the wall, too high for the other girls to peek through, but just the right height for Tilla. She jostled her way forward. The other girls moved aside, mumbling prayers. Tilla reached the crack, stood on her toes, and peered outside.

Her heart sank.

A snowy forest rolled around her, the trees bare and dark. Above the branches, still about a mile away, Tilla saw black, glimmering walls.

Obsidian. Castra Luna.

A hand tugged at her sleeve.

"Tilla, what do you see?"

Tilla turned to see Mae peering up at her. The baker's daughter bit her trembling lip. Other recruits gathered around and peered at Tilla, all whispering.

"What do you see?"

"I hear dragons flying, are we close?"

"Tilla, where are we?"

In darkness, Tilla thought. *At the gates of pain. In a world we might never escape.*

She raised her hand.

"We've reached a fort," she began.

"Which one?" demanded Erry Docker. The scrawny waif's short, brown hair lay in tangles, her knees were skinned, and her eyes flashed. "Tell us the bloody fort's name, Tilla."

"Are we at Castra Murus?" called another girl. "My brother trained there."

Mae Baker began to weep. "But I want to go home! I don't want to go to *any* fort. I want to go back to Cadport... Please... My father will be so angry, he's going to come save me..."

Tilla had to shout over them all. "Be quiet! Don't make noise or Beras will hear. You know he hates noise. We've reached the fort of Castra Luna." The girls began to whisper and weep, and Tilla raised her hands and spoke louder. "You will be safe here! I promise this to you. I know men who trained at this fortress, and I will protect you."

"How will *you* protect us?" Erry said and spat onto the floor. "You're just a pissant recruit like us. Bloody bollocks, I could take you in a fight, I reckon."

"No you couldn't, Erry!" said Mae, tears in her eyes. "Tilla is stronger than us, and she's about twice your height, so be quiet. And stop cussing; my mother said a girl should never cuss. Princess Shari liked Tilla too, you all saw it, and even Beras was a little afraid of her." She clung to Tilla and her lips wobbled. "Tilla is going to look after us here."

Erry rolled her eyes and groaned.

The shrieks of dragons grew louder, and Tilla peered out the crack again. She cursed under her breath. Two dragons were circling above the fortress, blowing pillars of fire. One was red, male, and long of fang. The other was female, and her scales were an iron gray. Both sported gilded horns; these ones were nobility.

And they are cruel, Tilla thought. *I can see it in their fire. They will try to break us.* She clenched her fists at her sides. *But I will not be broken. Whatever horror awaits here, I will survive it. I will see Cadport and Rune again.*

The cart kept trundling, and the black walls grew closer. Cannons lined their battlements, and soldiers in leather armor manned each gun. Tilla had seen cannons before, long and narrow things along Cadport's boardwalk; not far from the Old Wheel stood the oldest cannon in Requiem, a rusted sentinel watching the sea. But these cannons dwarfed Cadport's like greatswords beside daggers. Each gun was long as a dragon; she could have climbed into the barrels.

She swallowed. These cannons were not built to blast ships, she thought. They were built to slay dragons.

"Tilla, bloody dog dung, what do you s—" Erry began, but Tilla hushed her and kept staring outside.

The gates of Castra Luna rose ahead. From where she stood, Tilla could only see half of one door. That door loomed twenty feet tall, its oak engraved with carvings of the red spiral. The sigil also appeared upon black banners that draped the walls and fluttered from the tower tops.

But Castra Luna hadn't always been a Cadigus stronghold, Tilla knew. She thought back to the old, banned books Rune kept hidden under the Old Wheel's floor. Once this had been a castle of House Aeternum. The great Princess Mori Aeternum had raised this place from a small, southern outpost into a great castle, and many princes and princesses of Aeternum had ruled here, a beacon of southern light. In old drawings, Tilla had seen a castle of bright bricks, of green-and-silver banners sporting Aeternum's two-headed dragon, and of justice and light. Today... today she saw a prison of darkness.

The doors creaked open, revealing lines of soldiers. A chill ran through Tilla. Each soldier stood stiff as a statue, clad in leather armor studded with iron. Each bore a longsword. Helms hid their heads, bowls of black steel. They seemed to her not human, but automatons of metal, leather, and cruelty.

This will be me soon, Tilla thought. *I will no longer be Tilla Roper of Cadport. I will be one in a line, a soul broken and remolded into a killer, nothing but a machine—no more alive than the cannons upon the walls.*

Several carts rolled ahead of her own. They vanished under the archway, and Tilla's cart soon followed.

And so we enter the long, cold night, she thought and her throat tightened. She missed Rune so badly her belly clenched. Perhaps, she dared to hope, when he was drafted in summer, he would be sent to Castra Luna too. Would Tilla still be stationed here then? And if so, would Rune even recognize whatever demon they molded her into?

Six carts rolled into Castra Luna's courtyard. Through the crack, Tilla saw the brutish Beras lumbering about. He was howling, banging on cart walls, and unlocking the doors. Saliva sprayed from his mouth as he shouted.

"Out, vermin!" He growled and spat. "We've carried you maggots for long enough. Out, you miserable lot of bastards and whores!"

When the brute reached Tilla's cart and tugged the door open, the light nearly blinded the recruits inside. A few whimpered and covered their eyes. They had not seen daylight for ten days now, not since leaving Cadport, aside from what little light fell through the cracked wall.

Cadport's youths stumbled out into the courtyard like prisoners from dungeons, pale and blinking and frail in the sun. The sky was white, and the small winter sun reflected off the fort's obsidian walls. Tilla blinked and struggled to steady her limbs. Throughout the journey, they had been fed but scraps—old bread, burnt sausages, and some moldy cheese. Their training had not even begun, and already Tilla felt weaker than she'd ever been.

She looked around her, trying to focus her eyes. The recruits stood in the courtyard, still wearing the same tunics and leggings they had worn when leaving Cadport. A thousand other youths surrounded the square, but these ones were not weak. They did not tremble or blink or whimper. They stood in armor, silent, faces blank.

Tilla looked beyond them to see walls and barracks, all carved of the same obsidian, all bearing banners of the red spiral. A tower rose above them, the tallest she'd ever seen; it must have stood three hundred feet tall. It sported a great clock as large as a wagon; its hands were shaped as swords, ticking in an eternal battle. A hall stood below the tower, large enough to house a thousand men, and upon its walls perched two dragons, red and gray.

The red dragon stared directly at her, and Tilla felt as if an icy fist punched her.

Lust filled that red dragon's eyes—lust for her flesh, for her blood, and for her very soul. The beast stared into her, licked his chops, and snarled. Smoke rose between his teeth, and Tilla tore her eyes away. Her heart thrashed and her fingers trembled.

"Form ranks!" Beras bellowed, lolloping around the courtyard. "By the Abyss, if you embarrass me now, I'll flay your hides. Form ranks, sons of whores!"

Standing beside Tilla, Erry smirked. "He still walks like he got a stick up his arse. I bet he stick 'em there good himself."

Tilla glared at the skinny ragamuffin. "Don't you ever stop talking? Come on, form ranks; stand behind me."

Cadport's recruits shuffled together, forming ranks as Beras and his fellow soldiers barked orders. They had formed ranks every night for ten days, and they moved faster now. The girls stood in lines to one side, the boys to another. As always, Erry Docker stood to Tilla's right, smirking to herself, and Mae Baker stood to her left, biting her wobbling lip.

When they all stood in three lines, Beras stared at them in disgust.

"Miserable maggots," he said and spat again. "Bloody waste of time, you are. Good riddance to you. I deliver you now to your new masters. My only regret is I won't be here to see you broken."

He marched down the lines, huffing and thumping his boots. When he walked by Tilla, he paused and turned toward her. His beady eyes narrowed and he snarled. His breath wafted between his crooked teeth, scented of rotting meat.

Tilla stood stiff and frozen before him, chin raised. Her heart pounded, but she dared not say a thing, not even breathe.

"Oh, I'll miss you, child," Beras said, voice rough as his face. "I'll be seeing you again, don't you doubt it. You'll spread your legs for me yet." He spat onto her face. "You'll be mine, whore."

With that, he stepped back, shifted into a bronze dragon, and took flight. With a few flaps of his wings he was gone, leaving only a wake of smoke.

Tilla stood, knees weak and nausea rising in her. Belas's foul spit clung to her face, but she dared not wipe it off. The last recruit who'd moved in formation had been dragged off, hung from a tree, and beaten until his ribs snapped. And so she stood, breathing hard and struggling not to gag as the saliva dripped down her cheek.

"Recruits!" rose a female voice above. "Face north!"

Around the courtyard, a thousand soldiers spun upon their heels, slammed their boots down, and faced the grand hall. Fumbling and glancing around, Cadport's recruits followed, a breath late. Tilla and the others stood facing the hall. Upon its walls, the two dragons—red and gray—glared down at them, smoke pluming from their nostrils.

The gray dragon blasted fire skyward, then shifted. She stood upon the walls in human form, hands on her hips and a smirk on her face.

She was a young woman; she looked not much older than Tilla herself. Her yellow hair was just long enough to fall across her brow, and mockery filled her eyes; Tilla could see that even from here. She wore tan leggings, tall boots, and a breastplate engraved with a black rose. A sword hung across her back, and a she held a punisher in one gloved hand. Its tip crackled.

"Welcome to pain!" the young woman shouted. "Welcome to blood, to tears, and to death. Welcome to Castra Luna! I am Lanse Nairi, but to you, I am a goddess, I am a mother, I am a tyrant, and I am your savior." She smirked. "To me you are worms to crush."

Lanse. Tilla had heard that word before. It was a rank, she remembered. Tilla knew little of rank; she did not know how lofty a lanse was.

Lofty enough to command me, she thought. *But then again, that is probably everyone here other than my fellow recruits.*

"Today," Nairi continued, "we have a new lord in Castra Luna. Kneel, servants of the red spiral. Kneel before Prince Leresy Cadigus!"

Nairi gestured toward the red dragon, who snorted fire and shifted into human form.

The recruits below gasped, paled, and knelt.

The red dragon now stood as a young, golden-haired man. A smirk played across his lips. Unlike the others in this fort, Prince Leresy wore no crude leather. The finest steel plates formed his armor, each filigreed with golden dragons. A cloak hung across his shoulders, the crimson fabric lined with fur and probably worth more than all the coins in Cadport. A sword hung at his belt, its pommel shaped as a dragonclaw, its scabbard jeweled. A red spiral, shaped of rubies, shone upon his breastplate.

Shari's younger brother, Tilla thought, glancing up at him as she knelt. *Ten days, and I've met two of the emperor's children, and I don't know which one frightens me more.*

"He's looking right at you," Erry whispered from the corner of her mouth; the urchin knelt beside her. "The prince. Bet he wants to thrust right into you with his royal rod, and I don't mean his punisher. Not bad-looking, he is. Bloody bollocks, Tilla, but all the menfolk stare at you. I also need to grow a pair of big—"

"Shush!" Tilla whispered.

Terror froze her, but it seemed nobody had heard the exchange. She glanced back up at Prince Leresy. He stood on the wall, looking down upon the courtyard, and again he met her eyes.

She shivered. She had heard of Leresy's cruelty; everyone in Requiem had. They said that every week, Prince Leresy walked through the capital, seeking a woman he fancied. They said he favored mothers. When he found one, he would slaughter her family before her eyes, take her to his palace chambers, and force himself upon her. In the morning, they whispered, servants would collect the woman's battered corpse from the courtyard outside Leresy's window.

And now this prince—this monster—stared right at her across the crowd. His smirk grew, and he gave her a wink. He licked his lips—slowly, luxuriously, as if savoring the taste.

Tilla forced her gaze away. Her belly twisted and her heart pounded. She released her breath, only now realizing she had held it.

I must never stare at him again, she thought. *He is the most dangerous man in Requiem.*

"Children of Requiem!" the prince cried. He had the high voice of a youth, but carried it with the arrogance of a man. "I welcome you to my home. Rise."

The recruits rose to their feet, those newly arrived and those already armored.

"Hail the red spiral!" Prince Leresy shouted and slammed his fist against his chest.

"Hail the red spiral!" shouted thousands of recruits below, and thousands of fists thumped against chests.

To her left, Tilla heard Mae whimper. To her right, she heard Erry smirk and whisper something about sneaking into the prince's bed. But Tilla only stood still and silent, and though she had vowed to never look at the prince again, she could not help it. She found herself once more glancing his way.

He met her eyes and stared. The stare seemed to last forever, and in his eyes Tilla saw haughtiness, lust, and unending malice.

Without another word, the prince spun on his heel and stepped away from the battlements. He vanished, leaving Tilla feeling as empty and violated as a ransacked home.

"All right, you miserable lot of filthy maggots!" Nairi shouted above. She shifted back into a gray dragon and took flight. "It's time to sort your useless arses into phalanxes. A bloody waste of time, if you ask me." She blasted a pillar of fire. "Commanders, to the courtyard! Fresh meat!"

With roaring fire and thudding wings, five dragons appeared, rising from behind the grand hall. Fire and smoke filled the air. Scales clanked. Orders rang. Soldiers rushed about the courtyard, goading recruits with crackling punishers. Welts rose on flesh and recruits screamed.

Tilla moved with the crowd, her belly knotting.

Her life in Castra Luna began with fire, smoke, and pain.

RUNE

They climbed the hill, cloaks billowing in the wind, and beheld a landscape of ruin.

Rune stood for a moment, frozen, and softly exhaled. At his side, Kaelyn nodded and took his hand.

"My father's cruelty," she said. "Here it lies below us. Here we hide. Here we fight him."

They had been traveling through the wilderness for ten days now, keeping off the roads. At least, Rune thought it was ten days; it all blurred into one long, confused dream of hiding in holes, scurrying between trees, and living off dwindling supplies of dried meat, rough cheese, and stale bread. He had fled Cadport wearing everyday clothes—old boots, woolen pants and a tunic, and a warm cloak—and the journey had worn them into tatters. He was down one notch in his belt already, and he felt about a day away from losing another notch.

And here... here they reached the end of their journey, and Rune realized: He would miss the long days in the wilderness.

"Why this place?" he said, a chill tingling his spine. He turned to look at Kaelyn. "In the entire empire of Requiem, with all its forests and mountains and swamps and deserts, why hide here?"

She stood watching the ruins. The wind ruffled her golden, wavy hair and pinched her cheeks pink. She held her sword's hilt, and suddenly she seemed so sad to Rune, sadder than he'd ever seen her. Years ago, a wandering bard had traveled to Cadport, entered the Old Wheel, and played a song upon his harp. Men had wept to hear the music of old forests, ancient kings, and starlight upon marble columns. Rune had never forgotten that song, that sadness of longing and beauty; today he saw the same song in Kaelyn's eyes.

"It is safe," she said softly. "Imperial dragons fly here, but they don't land. No one but the Resistance walks among these ruins. We can hide here, survive, arm ourselves... and dream." She turned to look at him, and her eyes glistened with tears. "This place reminds us. Everywhere you look here, you will see my father's evil. It keeps us strong. And one day, his collapse will begin here—in this place that he crushed."

Rune looked back at the fallen city.

Confutatis, he thought. He knew of this place. He had seen its maps and cityscapes in the books hidden under the Old Wheel's floor. Only twenty years ago, this had been the capital of Osanna, a kingdom east of Requiem, a land whose people could not shift into dragons but rode horses, wove silk, studied the stars, and honored ancient alliances with the Vir Requis. In the old pictures, Rune had seen spires scraping the sky, temples with silver domes, thousands of homes and streets, and white walls topped with banners. It had been a place of life, science, and creation.

Today he saw a place of death, ash, and shattered stone.

The white walls lay fallen. The streets and homes lay shattered. The stems of towers rose like broken ribs, barely taller than men. The city spread for miles; a million souls must have lived here. Today Rune saw no life but for crows that circled above.

All who lived here—dead, he thought. *Cadigus killed them all.*

"Why?" he whispered. "Why would your father kill so many, crush an entire city?" He spun toward her, eyes stinging. "These people had no magic; they could not become dragons, could not defend themselves. Why, Kaelyn?"

"Because he is proud," she replied, looking upon the city. The wind billowed her blue cloak. "Because he is cruel. Because he is hurt." She sighed. "My father... when he was younger, he trained to be a priest, did you know?"

Rune frowned. "A priest? Your father? I've met priests; they tend to be meek, humble, and kind. I've seen statues of your father. He doesn't exactly seem the priestly type."

"He isn't," Kaelyn agreed. "But he was born into poverty, the son of a logger. His father beat him, and priesthood was an escape. A temple could give him food, shelter, and most importantly—books. My father had always craved knowledge."

"He doesn't seem the bookish type either," Rune said, remembering the man's statues. Even carved in stone, Frey Cadigus scared him. The emperor was a tall, powerful man—or at least sculpted that way—clad in armor and bearing weapons. Yet the statue's eyes would always frighten Rune the most. Those eyes stared, cold and always watching, from a hard, lined face. Those eyes seemed crueler than the man's sword.

"Books contain knowledge, and knowledge brings power." Kaelyn tightened her cloak around her. "He spent years in temple libraries, reading every book he could find. He especially craved histories of battle; even then he lusted for blood. He read how the people of this land, of Confutatis, enslaved the griffins, rode them to war, and toppled the halls of Requiem. That was a thousand years ago, but to a skinny boy in a dark temple..." She shook her head sadly. "I think those stories stabbed him like griffin talons. He left the priesthood. He became a soldier, an officer, and finally a general powerful enough to take Requiem's throne. And then... then he became a killer." She gestured at the city. "Then he took his vengeance. Deep inside, he was still that boy in candlelit libraries dreaming of slaying Requiem's enemies. But now this boy had an army of dragons. And still this death lies before us." Kaelyn snarled and gripped her sword. "And here, Rune, here his own death rallies." She began walking downhill. "Come. I will take you to Valien."

Ash swirled around their boots. Charred trees and skeletons, their flesh picked cleaned, littered the hillside. Kaelyn squeezed Rune's hand. Her grip was warm, and when he looked at her, she stared back with huge, somber eyes.

At the foothills, the ruins spread around their feet. The shells of houses stood blackened, roofs gone, walls chipped like teeth in smashed jaws. Bricks, shattered blades, and cloven helms littered the streets, so thick Rune had to wade through them. Inside the homes, skeletons still lingered—soldiers grasping rusted swords, children hiding in corners, and mothers huddling over babes. Dragonfire had burned them; the bones were charred.

Rune could barely breathe. His throat constricted. His fists trembled. He wanted to reel toward Kaelyn, to shake her, to yell at her.

Why didn't the Resistance bury them! he wanted to demand. *How could you just let your father's victims lie dead here?*

Yet when he looked at Kaelyn, prepared to shout, he saw tears on her cheeks. She did not tremble. She did not weep. She walked tall and proud, clutching her sword and bow, a warrior. Yet tears for the fallen, even these strangers of a different kingdom, shone in her eyes. Rune felt his rage ebb, and sadness replaced it.

Requiem was once a noble, peaceful kingdom, he thought, looking around at the destruction. *This is what the Cadigus family has made us. Killers. Monsters. Demons of fire.*

They stepped over a pile of bricks. A doll's hand peeked from between them. A crow sat upon a smashed keystone, pecking at a human jawbone. Half a tower rose to their right, ending with a shattered crown; inside, Rune saw skeletons in rusted armor. Looking upon this death, Rune remembered the Old Wheel burning and Shari clutching his father's body, and tears stung his eyes.

The Cadigus family had done the same to his home and family. The dead of Confutatis were his brothers now, bonded in grief. His eyes stung and his breath shook.

I don't want any of this, he thought. He climbed over half a child's skeleton; the legs were missing. *I never wanted this! All I wanted was to live quietly, to see Tilla again, to help Cadport cling to hope. Not this death. Not this war.*

He lowered his head. He missed home. He missed his father, his dog, his books, and everything else. The pain filled his belly like ice.

Kaelyn squeezed his hand. He looked up to see her gazing at him softly.

"I'm sorry, Rune," she whispered. "I'm sorry you have to see this." She touched his cheek. "But you need to. You need to see everything Frey Cadigus has done. And you will need to remember this." Her eyes hardened. "You will need these memories when you face him."

He laughed mirthlessly. "Face Frey Cadigus? After seeing these ruins, Frey is the last person I want to confront."

"I know," she said. "Yet you are the heir of Aeternum, and he seeks you. He will find you. He will want to slay you himself. And you will have to fight him. And when you do, remember this place." She looked around her. "Remember why you fight."

Rune sighed, shook his head, and kept walking. He could not get rid of that lump in his throat.

"You're mad, Kaelyn," he said. "Mad! I joined you only because Shari burned my home. But to fight your father? The emperor himself?" He barked another humorless laugh. "I'm only a brewer. Not a warrior."

"You *were* a brewer," she whispered. "A warrior you will become. Valien will teach you. We are near."

They kept walking through the ruins. They walked across a wide, cobbled square strewn with hundreds of skeletons still clad in sooty armor. They passed a shattered temple; its dome was cracked open like an egg, skeletons slung across its shattered rim. They were walking down a street littered with bricks, shattered shields, and bones when a shriek tore the air.

A dragon shriek.

Rune bent low and scurried for cover. Kaelyn leaped at his side. They landed in a ditch, scuttled under a fallen statue, and huddled deep in shadow.

They had run for cover so many times over the past ten days. Rune's knees and elbows were skinned from a hundred dives under logs, brambles, or tangled roots. Yet in the forest, the leafy canopy had offered extra concealment. Here in these ruins, the sky was clear; peering from under the fallen statue, Rune saw the dragon in all its wrath and flame.

The beast had copper scales, white horns, and great black wings like curtains of night. It shrieked to the sky, then swooped and blasted fire across the street. Walls of flame roared before Rune, heat blasted him, and he cursed and grabbed his sword.

"Bloody stars!" he hissed. "I thought you said this place was safe, Kaelyn."

She knelt beside him in the shadows. The fallen statue stretched above them, forming a roof. Kaelyn's face glistened with sweat. She clutched a dagger in her hand, bared her teeth, and breathed sharply.

"Hush!" she whispered. "Keep your voice down. This dragon hasn't seen us. If he had, we'd be dead. They patrol these ruins several times a day."

Rune rolled his eyes. "And you chose your hideout here? Where your father's dragons patrol daily?"

She tightened her cloak around her. "Forests can be uprooted. Towns can be toppled. Forts can be crushed. This place is already dead—lots of places to hide, nothing left to tear down."

Perhaps Kaelyn was right, Rune thought. The forests had seemed to offer no more safety, and as for Cadport, well... Rune's chest still ached to remember Cadport. Perhaps no place was safe anymore from Frey Cadigus. Once this had been a distant kingdom; now it lay ruined. Now there was just this, just the empire, as far as they could go.

And Kaelyn thinks we can topple it!

Rune wondered if he was crazy to even be here. He could grow a beard to disguise his face, he thought. He could take up a false identity, move to a new town, and find work. He didn't have to fight this war. He didn't have to walk through death.

He had thought this many times over the past few days. And yet he had kept following Kaelyn through forest, field, and ruin. Why? Was it Kaelyn's big eyes and her body pressed against his? Or had he simply gone mad?

I can't keep doing this, he thought. *I'll listen to what this Valien has to say. I'll tell him I'm not the man he's looking for. And then I'll leave this place and forget about the whole damn rebellion.*

Finally the dragon shrieks faded into the distance. Kaelyn released her dagger and began crawling back onto the street.

"Come on," she said and looked over her shoulder at him. "Follow me. Another dragon won't be back for hours."

Rune sighed. "So said half the skeletons on this street, I reckon."

Yet as she walked down this street of death, he followed. In the distance, he could see the dragon flying into the southern horizon, a mere speck blowing a thread of fire. Crows replaced it in the sky; a few dipped down to pick at old ribs.

They reached a wide, cobbled boulevard that looked wide enough for a hundred men to walk abreast. This must have been the main street of Confutatis. Along its sides, the iron frames of chariots rusted, and the skeletons of horses lay shattered. The stems of lost columns, the shells of burnt towers, and crumbling walls lined the roadsides in a palisade of destruction. Far ahead, past mist and shadow, the path led to a shattered palace, its pocked walls rising from ash and ending in ruin. Even the crows did not fly above this street, as if they feared it.

"What is this place?" Rune whispered.

"Welcome," she said, "to the Boulevard of Bones. It leads through death. It leads through old fire. It leads to hope."

They began to walk down the street. The skeletons at their sides seemed to stare at Rune. The skull of a horse grinned. Ash carpeted the cobblestones; it muffled their footfalls and stirred around their boots. Rune was looking at the burnt skeleton of a child, a sword piercing its ribcage, when movement caught his eye.

He spun sideways, clutched his sword, and drew a foot of steel.

"Kaelyn!" he hissed.

An archer stood in the broken tower, peering through a crack in the wall. The man wore a gray cloak smeared with ash, and gray paint covered his face; he blended into the tower's bricks. Rune snarled and prepared to dive for cover, but Kaelyn gripped his arm.

"It's fine, Rune!" she said. "He's one of ours."

She pushed Rune's sword back into its scabbard and nodded at the archer. She raised her left hand, holding her index and middle fingers pressed together. Inside the shattered tower, the archer returned the gesture and lowered his bow.

As they kept walking down the boulevard, more movement stirred. Rune looked from side to side and blew out his breath. Dozens of archers hid here, each one cloaked in gray, the color of the ruins. They peeked from broken towers, from behind shattered walls, and from under fallen statues. As Kaelyn walked by, they each raised their hands in salute, index and middle fingers pressed together.

"Welcome, Rune," Kaelyn said softly, "to a voice of hope, to a light in the dark, to courage in an empire of fear." She gave him a sad look that spoke of her childhood, of countless deaths, and of hope almost lost under pain. "Welcome to the Resistance."

They kept walking down the Boulevard of Bones. All around among the broken towers, walls, and halls they hid— warriors of the Resistance. As Rune walked, his head spun. Every year in Cadport, soldiers of the Regime would speak of the resistors' evil and might. Every year, they would draft all those turned eighteen, cart them off to forts, break and mold them into soldiers, then send them off to fight the Resistance. Rune had always imagined hosts of demonic beasts mustering with fire and steel. But this... this was just a rabble. Here were only a few men—Rune doubted he saw more than a hundred—clad in rags and dust, their blades chipped.

This isn't an army.

The Cadigus Regime had been lying to its people, Rune realized. With fiery speeches and military terror, they had turned a toothless pup into a rabid beast. The wars against the phoenixes, the griffins, and the wyverns had ended years ago. With Requiem's external foes defeated, Frey Cadigus needed a new enemy, Rune realized. He needed a new way to terrify his people, to rally them around a threat. How else would a soldier keep his power? How else could Cadigus maintain his iron grip, if not with fear of monsters?

This Resistance is nothing but a ghost of a threat, Rune thought. *They cannot win. Not with me here. Not with ten thousand more men. This is a hopeless war. They only serve to give Frey Cadigus the enemy he so desperately needs.*

They continued down the Boulevard of Bones, this vein of destruction Cadigus had carved. With every step, they drew nearer to the fallen palace of Confutatis. Soon its ruin rose before them.

In one of the books Rune had hidden under his floor planks, he had seen an illustration of this palace. Its dozen towers had risen into the clouds. Banners had streamed upon its walls. Soldiers bearing red, green, and yellow standards had ridden horses through its gates. All of that was gone now. The towers lay broken. A single archway rose in a crumbling wall; its doors had burned away. A few walls still stood, and a few archers still manned their arrowslits, but that was all. If this was the heart of the Resistance, Rune thought, it was barely beating.

"Is Valien in there?" he asked.

Kaelyn tightened her cloak around her; it was flapping in the wind. She nodded and clutched her bow tight to her chest.

"He is in there," she said. "Our leader. Our guiding star. Valien Eleison, leader of the Resistance."

Rune shook his head. *She treats me like a child,* he thought, *yet she speaks of this Valien as a god.* How mighty could this Valien be if he dwelled in ruin? Was this truly a man to speak of in awe? Judging by Valien's home, they were going to see not a great leader, but a ragged outlaw barely better than those who roamed the forests, seeking travelers to rob.

They walked toward the archway. Several haggard men stood alongside it, their cloaks the same gray as the bricks, their faces ashy. When they saw Kaelyn, they lowered their bows and heads.

"My lady Kaelyn," one said.

"Welcome home, my lady," said another.

She nodded at them, the wind in her hair. She stepped through the archway into shadow. With a last look at the skeletons that littered the boulevard, Rune followed into the darkness.

TILLA

Six soldiers surrounded the square, standing on pedestals and shouting names from scrolls.

"Yar Potter!" one soldier shouted, a portly man with a dark beard.

"Sana Tanner!" shouted another soldier, a muscular woman with a thin nose and cold, black eyes. "Sana Tanner!"

Tilla stood in the square with the other youths of Cadport. As every name was called, that recruit moved to join the summoning soldier. As Tilla stood, waiting to be summoned, she squinted at the six soldiers crying out the names. Each wore a black breastplate and pauldrons. Upon each shoulder, they sported a red spiral.

"Lanses," Tilla whispered. "That is their rank."

When speaking from the walls, Nairi—the soldier with the short yellow hair—had called herself a lanse. The young woman now stood upon one of the pedestals, also shouting names from a scroll.

The lanses seemed young—Tilla guessed them little older than herself—but lofty and well groomed. Each displayed a different sigil upon his or her breastplate. Nairi sported a black rose; other lanses displayed red skulls, dragon heads, towers rising from thorns, and other emblems. These were no brutes like Beras; Tilla guessed them the sons and daughters of noble houses, their blood too pure to serve among the unwashed commoners.

She thought back to Cadport. Soldiers there displayed their rank—one or more red stars—upon black armbands; their shoulders bore no red spirals, and their breastplates sported no emblems. Only the lord of Cadport, a gaunt and dower man, wore red spiral insignia and displayed a sigil—his was a boar—upon his armor.

The lanses are young officers, Tilla understood. *Noble born. They wear their house's sigils upon their breasts. The others are the common soldiers, like I will become once I'm sorted.*

Standing on a pedestal, scroll in hand, Nairi shouted. "Mae Baker!" The young lanse looked over the crowd with narrowed eyes. "Mae Baker!"

Tilla looked to her left. Mae stood there, eyes wide and damp, face chalk-white.

"I..." Mae's lips trembled. "I... I don't..."

Nairi shouted louder and reached for her punisher. "Mae Baker, damn it, report to me!"

Mae sniffed, feet frozen on the ground. Her body shook.

"Go to her, Mae," Tilla said. She gave the girl a gentle push. "Go to Lanse Nairi and stand before her. It's okay."

Sniffing and looking around, Mae took hesitant steps forward. She looked over her shoulder at Tilla, as if unsure whether to proceed. Tilla gestured her on.

But Nairi was less patient. The officer snarled and leaped off her pedestal. As she marched forward, she drew her punisher from her belt. The tip crackled with red lightning.

"Are you Mae Baker?" the lanse demanded, marching toward Mae. Her every footstep clanked across the square.

Mae stood frozen and nodded, tears in her eyes.

With a snarl, Nairi drove her punisher forward, bringing its tip hard into Mae's stomach.

Smoke rose.

Lightning crackled across Mae.

The girl screamed, doubled over, and begged. Nairi stood above her, growling and shoving her punisher against Mae's flesh.

No! Tilla wanted to shout. She took two steps forward. She froze. She winced. *Please stop!* She wanted to rush forward, to shove Nairi back, to save her friend... yet she only stood staring, eyes stinging and feet frozen.

Finally—after what seemed like ages—Nairi pulled her punisher back.

Mae collapsed against the cobblestones, legs twitching and the last wisps of lightning racing across her before vanishing in smoke. Tears streaked her cheeks and she whimpered.

"Mewling dog," Nairi said. She spat. "When I call you, you *race* to me like an obedient pup." She raised her voice to a shout. "Do you understand me, you flea-bitten mongrel? Stand up, damn it!"

Mae whimpered, still lying on the ground.

"You better stand up, dog," Nairi said, teeth bared, and raised her punisher. "Do you want some more?"

Finally Tilla could move. She leaped forward, knelt by Mae, and reached under her arms.

"Come on, Mae," she said softly. "Stand up. On your feet. I'll help you."

She pulled the trembling, weeping girl to her feet. Mae stood shaking so wildly Tilla had to hold her up. Burn marks spread across her tunic.

"Well, well," Nairi said. She laughed mirthlessly, tapping her fingers against her thigh. "Seems like you have a guardian, Mae Baker."

"Just a friend," Tilla said quietly.

She stared at the lanse; for the first time, she got a close look at Nairi. Most women were shorter than Tilla, and Nairi was no exception; the young woman had to raise her eyes to meet Tilla's gaze. But Nairi was strong, far stronger than Tilla; she could see that. This young woman had not shaped her muscles from weaving ropes, but from swinging swords. Her stance, her haughty green eyes, and her bared teeth all spoke of a huntress, a thirst for blood and battle. Her yellow hair was short like a boy's, but her lips were full and red and cruel, and they twisted in disdain.

"What is your name, dog?" Nairi hissed.

"Tilla Roper," she answered.

Nairi stared at her, eyes narrowed and burning with green fire. Then she spat again, looked down at her scroll, and smirked.

"Good," she said slowly, as if savoring the word. "Very good. Tilla Roper—you're one of mine." She looked back up at Tilla. "I will enjoy breaking you. Go join the others! Take your pup with you."

Tilla's heart sank.

Stars, oh stars, I've been sorted into Nairi's phalanx. She swallowed. *The one officer here to use her punisher—and she's now my commander, and already I've angered her.*

"Go on, move!" Nairi shouted and snarled. She thrust her punisher, forcing Tilla to leap back.

Clenching her jaw, Tilla began to walk toward the pedestal, helping Mae along; the young baker limped upon shaky legs, and her clothes still smoked. As Nairi kept shouting out names, the two girls reached the pedestal. Several other recruits already stood there. Looking around, Tilla saw Cadport's youths forming six groups.

They're called phalanxes, she thought; she vaguely recalled hearing the term. Looking around, it seemed that each phalanx held a hundred recruits. A lanse commanded each group.

Tilla squinted and tried to understand how each phalanx was formed. Who had written the names on the scrolls? Had they been sorted randomly, or was there some method here—farmers to one phalanx perhaps, tradesmen to another? All Tilla saw was that male lanses led three phalanxes; they took command of Cadport's boys. Women commanded the remaining three; the girls of Cadport were sorted into these.

The lanses continued shouting out names. More and more girls kept joining Nairi's phalanx and crowding around Tilla.

Finally Nairi shouted out the last name. "Erry Docker!"

The slim girl, her short brown hair mussed across her brow, raised her chin and marched to stand among them.

"Well, griffin guts," the waif said and flashed a grin. "Tilla-bloody-Roper. I thought I was rid of you, I did. Looks like I'm stuck with you." She shoved her way among the recruits, giving Mae Baker a particularly strong push. "Shove off! Make room."

Tilla was strangely relieved to see the fiery, foulmouthed girl among them. In Cadport, Erry was known as the city's chief troublemaker. An orphan, she claimed that her father had been a dockhand, and that she would beat bloody anyone who claimed otherwise. Behind her back, many did claim otherwise; they whispered that Erry was born of a dockside prostitute and a penniless, foreign sailor.

Whoever Erry's parents had been, they had died or left Cadport years ago. Until her enlistment, Erry had lived alone upon the docks, as feral as a stray cat. A *dock rat* they called her, an urchin with a filthy mouth, skinned knees, and gaunt belly. Cadport's girls whispered that Erry herself was a prostitute; half the boys bragged that they had bedded her.

Yet I too have always been an outcast, Tilla thought. At least Erry had some fire to her, which was more than Tilla could say about Mae and the others; they all stood here pale and sniffling.

The sorting was complete. From her height, Tilla could see Cadport's youths fully divided into six phalanxes—three for the boys, three for the girls.

"Move it, maggots!" Nairi shouted.

The lanse marched between them, shoving them aside, and leaped onto her pedestal. She raised her punisher high; it crackled above her head, incurring several whimpers from the girls.

"Listen up, you daughters of whores!" Nairi continued, holding the rod above her, a beacon of light and pain. "Form ranks—groups of threes! Triple up—now!—or I'm going to shove this punisher down your throats."

Around the courtyard, the other lanses were shouting similar orders and threats.

Tilla began to move. She grabbed Mae, who was still whimpering, and placed her upon a cobblestone.

"Stand still!" she said. "Form the middle line. Erry, you stand behind her—"

"You will form ranks silently," Nairi shouted, "or I'll cut your tongues from your mouths!"

Tilla bit down on her words. Lips tight, she pulled Erry to stand behind Mae, then moved to stand before the baker's daughter. At her sides, the other recruits scurried into their own ranks, forming three lines before Nairi.

The lanse stood, fists on her hips, and scrutinized the lines with narrowed eyes. Her lips curled in disgust.

"Hail the red spiral!" she shouted.

A hundred fists slammed against a hundred chests. Behind her, Tilla heard Mae sniff and Erry snicker.

Flexing her fingers around her punisher, Nairi marched up and down the front line, snarling and cursing. When she passed by Tilla, she paused, thrust her face forward, and glared.

"Roper," she said, voice dripping disgust. "You open your mouth again when I'm giving orders, and you will taste this punisher." She shouted. "Do you understand me, worm?"

Tilla raised her chin and swallowed her pride.

It's just a game, she told herself. *Just a game. Nairi is just like me, just a girl, just somebody sucked into this war. We must play this game for now.*

"Yes, Nai—"

The lanse drove her punisher forward, shoving its tip against Tilla's chest.

Pain exploded.

Fire raced across Tilla.

She clenched her jaw, but a scream still fled her lips. Sweat drenched her. The fire! The fire burned her, twisting in her teeth, in her fingers, burning her bones—

Nairi pulled the punisher back, leaving Tilla gasping. Tears filled her eyes, and it took every last bit of strength to stay standing.

"You will call me Lanse Nairi," the young woman said, "or you will call me Commander. If you ever call me anything else, I will press this punisher against you all night; by morning you will be begging to die. Do you understand me?"

Tilla could barely stay standing. She trembled. Pain throbbed across her chest.

"Yes, Commander!" she managed in a choked voice.

It's a game. Stars, let this just be a game. I will play by the rules, and I will survive this.

Nairi spat, left her, and kept marching down the lines. Across the courtyard, the other lanses were doing the same, and punishers crackled, and recruits screamed.

When Nairi reached the end of the line, she growled.

Tilla peeked from the corner of her eye.

The formation ended with a single recruit, a redheaded girl whose name Tilla could not remember. While all the others stood in threes, this recruit stood alone.

"You!" barked Nairi. "I said form into threes. Where are your other two?"

"I..." The girl faltered and sniffed. "There aren't enough others, Lanse Nairi. I... all the others formed into threes, but there are a hundred of us, and..."

Nairi snarled, grabbed the girl's throat with a gloved hand, and squeezed.

"Then you are useless," the lanse hissed.

With her other hand, she drew a dagger from her belt and drove it forward.

Tilla started, winced, and looked away. But she was too late. She had seen the blade enter flesh. She had seen the blood.

Behind her, Mae whimpered and even Erry gasped. The red-haired recruit screamed. She thumped to the floor. She wept and begged.

Tilla glanced over again, just long enough to see Nairi thrust the dagger again, this time into the girl's neck. The lanse smirked, pulled the blade back, and licked the blood from it. Her eyes burned with hunger, and she bared bloody teeth.

No, this is no game, Tilla realized. She trembled and her chest still ached. *Only the strongest will survive here. I must survive this place. I must. I will see Cadport and Rune again.*

"The rest of you miserable lot!" Nairi shouted. She cleaned her dagger on the dead girl's cloak before slamming it back into her belt. "Your groups of threes—these are your flight crews. These are your fellow warriors. From now on, you will remain in these same flights! The two worms with you—they will stick to you like boils to a leper throughout your training. Do you understand me, whores?"

"Yes, Commander!" they shouted together.

Nairi smirked. "Welcome! Welcome to my phalanx. You are now worms serving me. You are now miserable slaves. You now live for one purpose: to obey my commands." Nairi drew her dark longsword and raised it. "This is the Black Rose Phalanx. This is your new family. This is your new temple. This is your new life. You have no more parents, no more siblings, no more home. Your life is now the Black Rose! Your life is to obey me, your commander. Do you understand, worms?"

"Yes, Commander!" they shouted.

As much as her chest hurt, and as cold as her fear pounded, Tilla was glad to at least make some sense of things. Leaving Cadport, they had been nothing but a mass of frightened youths carted like cattle. But now Tilla had a phalanx and a commander. Now Tilla had a flight—a group of three. Now she finally had some grounding.

There are thirty-three flights in a phalanx, she thought, vowing to remember the numbers. *And a hundred troops: ninety-nine soldiers and one officer.* She swallowed. *The Black Rose Phalanx had one hundred soldiers. One too many.*

Tilla still had a thousand questions. Did she herself have a rank—the way Nairi was a lanse? Would her flight have a name too, or did just phalanxes get names? Would her flight have a commander, or was she equal to Mae and Erry? The questions kept bubbling inside her, but Tilla dared not ask. She had never had a chance to learn these things. Her brother had served, but he had died in the war. Those soldiers who did return to Cadport never spoke of their service, and Tilla could now understand why.

A lump filled her throat. *If I ever see Rune again, we won't talk about this either.* Her eyes stung. *We'll forget all about this nightmare. We'll walk along the beach, and he'll kiss me again, and we'll just walk there forever and look at the waves.*

"Now march!" Nairi shouted. She turned and began walking toward an archway in the courtyard's wall. "Follow me—three lines! Anyone who breaks formation tastes my blade."

Mae whimpered. Erry rolled her eyes and smirked. But they all followed. A hundred legionaries of the Black Rose Phalanx snaked out of the courtyard, under the archway... and into a nightmare of blood and pain.

SHARI

Shari flew upon the wind, blue scales clanking, and blasted fire. Across field and forest, she saw the distant lights of the capital, and she cursed.

On any other evening, flying toward Nova Vita, the great torch of Requiem, would fill her with pride. Ahead shone the lights of Requiem's center of power, the mighty city that ruled the world. Ahead shone her birthright, a metropolis of a million souls, the heartbeat of her lineage. Ahead shone might, pride, and strength.

Yet today Shari did not fly home as a heroine wreathed in glory. Today she flew in fear. Today she did not fly leading a battalion of dragons all roaring her name, announcing her return. Today she flew alone in the sky, a single blue dragon in the sunset.

I've failed my task, she thought, and fire flickered between her teeth. *Today I will face no glory but the wrath of my father.*

She streamed over the fields. The walls of Nova Vita rose before her.

These walls snaked for miles around the city, thick limestone bedecked with obsidian tiles and lit with torches. Upon the battlements stood hundreds of cannons, each one as long as a dragon, mounted on gears fast enough to spin, aim, and fire within an instant. At each cannon, three men in armor stood vigil. Between the guns perched dragons clad in armor, their great dragonhelms topped with spikes. Thousands of warriors guarded this city, the jewel of the empire.

During the reign of Aeternum, enemies had attacked and destroyed this place—griffins, phoenixes, and wyverns. But Frey Cadigus swore: Nova Vita would never fall again. All his wrath shone here, a glory of blade and gunpowder and fire.

And tonight, the wrath of this emperor will fall upon me, Shari thought as she flew.

The city sprawled below her, lit with countless lanterns. The streets were arranged like a great wagon wheel, its spokes leading toward the palace of Tarath Imperium, an obsidian edifice whose battlements clawed the sky. Fortresses, amphitheaters, aqueducts—thousands of great structures rose here, monuments to the empire's might, and Tarath Imperium dwarfed them all. The palace rose before Shari, clawing the sky, its windows burning with fire like the eyes of demons.

I should flee, Shari thought. *I should turn around and fly away and—*

She scoffed.

And what, live like my sister? Become a forest wildwoman like Kaelyn, fighting my father in a hopeless war?

She shook her head, scattering sparks and smoke. No. Shari was still a proud daughter of Cadigus, still heir to Requiem, the greatest empire the world had ever known. She would face her father. She would take his punishment. And it would make her stronger.

She flew over the great Cadigus Arena, the largest amphitheater in Requiem, and saw prisoners chained as dragons, their maws muzzled shut, forced to fight packs of tigers and wolves. Past the amphitheater, she flew over the Colossus, a gilded statue three hundred feet tall, depicting her father staring with cold eyes, his fist against his breastplate. She flew over the fortress of Castra Academia, its walls and towers bearing the red spiral upon black banners—the great academy that trained the Legions' officers.

Finally she neared the palace, and fear roiled through her belly like a horde of icy demons.

Four thousand years ago, the stories said, the first king of Requiem—King Aeternum himself—had raised a column here, a pillar of marble and starlight. Requiem became a kingdom that day, and that marble column still stood; ancient magic let no claw, fang, or tail shatter it. King's Column rose hidden now, a white spine enclosed in black flesh. Frey Cadigus had extended his palace, letting it spread like a growth. Today black walls, towers, spikes, and turrets covered the original marble the Aeternums had raised. Today this was no longer a place of beauty and peace, but an edifice of might—Tarath Imperium, terror of the empire. Dragons in armor perched upon its battlements. Men stood vigil, ready to fire cannons. Torches crackled and the dragons screeched and blew fire.

Black stone. Flame. Death. *My home.*

The guards upon the walls recognized her blue scales, gilded horns, and dragonhelm that bore the red spiral. They howled in salute. Those in dragon forms blew pillars of fire. Those who stood in human forms, manning the cannons, slammed fists against chests.

"Hail Shari Cadigus!" they chanted. "Hail the red spiral!"

Shari ignored them. The palace, its base wide with walls and barracks, tapered into a great steeple. This tower of obsidian rose a thousand feet tall, crowned with jagged spikes, a black arm clutching the sky in its claws.

Shari flew toward the tower top. Its spikes rose before her, taller than dragons, greater than most homes in this city. Shari flew between them, descended, and landed upon a stone roof. All around her rose the battlements of Tarath Imperium, a crown upon the empire.

The red and black clouds swirled above her, swarming with dragons. Shari shifted into human form. The wind whipped her, billowed her hair and cloak, and stung her cheeks. She snarled and marched across the platform, heading toward a staircase that led into the tower.

Twenty figures stood guarding the staircase, robed in black—men of the Axehand Order. Here were no simple guards; the axehands were elite killers, chosen for their cruelty and strength. Within the shadows of their hoods, they wore iron masks; they were forbidden to ever remove them, not even when they slept. At their waists, they sported the tools of their trade: pincers and blades for torturing their victims. Worst of all, they had no left hands; their arms ended with axeheads strapped to stumps.

They maimed themselves to prove their loyalty, Shari thought and shivered. *They lifted those axes, chopped off their own hands, and strapped the blades to the stubs. They are fanatics. They are ruthless. They are the only men I fear.*

The Legions fought Requiem's wars—a vast army hundreds of thousands strong. The Axehand Order was smaller, but far more dangerous. Its men were as much priests as warriors; they worshiped Frey as their god, and they spread fear of their lord across the empire.

Shari feared them too.

Seeing these men, shivers ran down her spine. She did not trust the Axehand Order; they were too fanatical. Soldiers in the Legions were broken, molded, and shaped into mindless warriors; all they knew was to serve. Shari had broken enough recruits herself to know that. But these axehands... they were too strong. Their order had gained too much power. Their commander, Lord Herin Blackrose, had grown too mighty.

Shari snarled as she walked past them, heading down into the tower. Someday, she thought, she might find an enemy not only in the Resistance, but here at her very doorstep.

As she descended dark stairs, heading deep into the tower, she left such thoughts behind her. Today she had greater concerns. Today she might find her greatest challenge not with the Resistance, not with the Axehand Order, but with her father.

She reached the end of the staircase, opened a door, and walked down a hallway lined with braziers. Her boots thumped. Shari snarled and clutched the hilt of her sword, as if that could save her now.

"You little whore, Kaelyn," she muttered. She drew her sword and swung it as she walked. "You and your boy will taste this blade."

Guards lined the walls, saluting their princess, fists slamming against breastplates.

"Hail the re—" one guard began.

With a snarl, Shari drove her sword into his neck. Blood flowed down the blade, and Shari growled as she twisted it. The guard gurgled, hanging upon the sword, blood in his mouth.

"This will happen to you, Kaelyn," Shari hissed. "This will happen to you, Relesar Aeternum."

She yanked her blade back with a gush of blood. The guard clattered to the floor. The other guards stood still and pale, fists still held to their breasts.

After several more halls and staircases, Shari reached tall iron doors. She paused outside them, for a moment frozen.

Father's chambers.

Frey Cadigus maintained a throne room in the base of the palace. It was a chamber an army could fill, a paradise of gold, torchlight, and treasures plundered from around the world. That grand hall mostly stood empty. For all his glory and might, Frey

Cadigus was at heart a soldier; he entertained guests in his throne room only several times a year.

Today, Shari knew, she would find him behind these doors in a humbler, darker place. These were the personal chambers of Frey Cadigus, far from his servants, his generals, and his gilt and glory.

Shari took a deep breath, steeled herself, and pushed open the doors.

She entered the wolf's den.

For a moment she blinked, eyes adjusting. Outside in the corridor, torches and braziers crackled, their light shining off the black tiles. In here, nothing but a few candles lit the darkness.

"Father?" Shari kept her sword drawn and bloody at her side. "Are you here, Father?"

She walked a few feet deeper and saw him.

Frey Cadigus, Emperor of Requiem, Slayer of Aeternum, stood with his back toward her. In statues and paintings, he wore fine black armor filigreed with gold. Here before her, he stood in a tan, bloodstained jerkin. His dark hair was thinning, but his shoulders were still wide and strong. Several meat hooks hung from the ceiling before the emperor. Upon one hung a wild boar, still alive and squirming.

Frey spoke without turning toward her; she could not see his face.

"You come to me, my daughter, with fear in your voice. You come to me alone. I smell fresh blood upon you, not the blood of a corpse."

Shari gripped her sword and bared her teeth. "I come alone."

The wild boar kicked and squealed, its cry echoing in the chamber. His back still facing Shari, Frey raised a dagger, grabbed the boar, and sliced its neck. The beast wailed and its blood gushed into a bucket.

"Fresh blood," Frey said and wiped the blade on his pants. "Ahh! Smell it, Shari. It is a wondrous smell, is it not? Tell me, my daughter. How did it smell when you shed the blood of the Aeternum boy?"

Shari lowered her head, jaw clenched. "Father, I..."

Slowly, bloody dagger in hand, Frey Cadigus turned toward her.

Today he perhaps wore no armor, no fine cloak, and no heraldry like in the paintings. In his bloodstained leather, however, he looked to Shari just as regal and cruel. His strength shone not from any armor or finery, but from the hard lines of his face, from the thinness of his lips, and from the cold, hard stare of his eyes, a stare as sharp and bloodthirsty as his blade.

"You let the boy slip away," he said.

Shari could not speak. Her throat constricted and fear pounded through her. There were none she feared more than her father—not the Axehand Order, not Valien the Resistor, and not an army of rebels. She lowered her head and nodded silently. Her blade dipped and its tip hit the floor.

Frey turned away. Muscles rippling, he thrust his dagger into the boar's stomach and pulled down, letting entrails and organs spill.

"I gave my useless son a useless fort," Frey said. He reached into the boar, bare-handed, and scooped out innards. "I gave him a pathetic pile of stones far south where he can't get into his usual trouble." He tossed organs into the bucket with a splash and looked over his shoulder, eyes hard chips. "I gave *you* a chance for eternal glory. And you let it slip between your fingers."

Shari glared and hissed. "I will find the boy, Father! I just need more time, and I need more men. He fled into the forests with Kaelyn. I need more dragons, and I can burn down every tree, and dig up every bolt-hole, and—"

"We used to be weak, you know," Frey said. He wiped his hand on his pants, turned back to the boar, and drove his knife along its flanks. "Not us, not the Cadigus family; we were always strong. But our kingdom. Requiem. We used to grovel before the world, and they would hunt us." He shoved his fingers into the boar and pulled down, peeling its skin; it came free with a tearing hiss. "Yes. They would relish our blood, and they reduced us to a quivering few. They butchered us like I butchered this boar. The Aeternum family did that to us; they had us kneeling in the mud before griffins, phoenixes, and men." He tossed the skin aside and stared at Shari. "I made Requiem strong. The boy, the Aeternum heir; he is a relic of that weakness. He is a drop of poison in the pure blood of dragons. If he meets that Valien, that rat and his rabble, the boy could become a figurehead. Valien will dream that he could place the boy on my throne." Frey snorted a laugh. "The man is a fool. He must be stamped out. Crushed. The boy must be taken from him."

"I will ta—"

"You will do nothing. You had your chance, Shari, and you failed." Frey snorted and began flaying more skin. "Maybe I should have sent your little brother on this task. Maybe—"

It was Shari's turn to interrupt.

"My brother is a fool!" she said and spat onto the floor. "Leresy is as great a fool as his twin sister. The two were always pathetic." She hissed. "But I am strong, Father. I am strong like you. I will make you proud and crush the Resistance, and I will bring you the boy so you can hang him here, gut him, and peel his skin."

Frey gave a choked laugh. "Will you now? You say your sister is weak. You say Kaelyn is a fool. Kaelyn is a traitor, that is true, but weak? Foolish? She found the boy before you did. You had one task—to beat Kaelyn to him. And you failed. So who is weak, Shari? Who is the fool?"

Flames seemed to burst through Shari, even in her human form. She snarled, screamed, and raised her sword as if she would strike her father down. He only stood still, staring at her with those hard eyes like granite.

Shari lowered her head.

Tears filled her eyes.

"I'm sorry, Father," she whispered. "I'm sorry. Please forgive me."

He stood staring, and no compassion or love filled his eyes. No, Shari knew; her father held no love for his children. He loved only Requiem, only the empire he had vowed to forever lead.

He gestured his head to the side. "The meat hook," he said. "That one there."

Shari hissed at him. Her legs trembled.

"I am no longer a child!"

"Today you are barely a worm," he replied. "Remove your armor. Remove this steel and hold that hook. If you let go, I will hang you there and gut you like this boar."

Shari wore steel plates; her father wore bloody leather. She held a longsword forged in dragonfire; her father held only a butcher's knife.

I can kill him now, she thought, snarling. *I can drive my sword into him and take his throne, and this empire will be mine. He will be the one to bleed, not me.*

Shari looked aside, eyes narrowed.

And Leresy would fly against me with his southern garrison. And that whore Nairi would summon her father, and the Axehand Order would descend upon me. The empire would collapse into war, and the Resistance would seize the chance; Valien would fly against me too, and his dragons would surround this palace.

Shari hissed. She hated her father but she knew: He held the empire together. He was the pillar of this realm, at least for now. If he died today, the world would burn. She would replace him someday, yes. But not with blood. Not with war. The time for her to pluck her fruit of power had not yet come.

So I will take his punishment, Shari thought. *I will take his wrath. Every lash will make me stronger. Every blow will stoke my flame.*

She removed her breastplate. She tossed it down with a clang. Eyes cold, Frey lifted his whip. Shari walked to the meat hook, held it, and closed her eyes.

Frey beat her. With every lash, Shari clutched the meat hook harder, grinded her teeth, hissed, but did not scream.

"You have failed me," Frey said and his lashes kept falling, tearing through her tunic, tearing into her skin and flesh. "Feel the pain of your failure."

Shari trembled and smelled more fresh blood, the third spill of the day; this time it was her own.

TILLA

"Move!" Nairi shouted, pointing her punisher at an archway. "Get inside, worms. Move your arses or I'll shove my punisher up them."

The Black Rose Phalanx marched along a portico of columns, moving toward the archway; it led into a shadowy barracks. As she marched among her fellow recruits, Tilla wondered what lay within those shadows. More pain? More officers who'd burn and cut them? What horrors lurked here?

"Move, damn it!" Nairi screamed, marching alongside them. "Into the darkness."

At her side, Mae was already weeping. Silent tears streamed down the young baker's cheeks. Even Erry seemed shaken; her face was pale, lacking its usual smirk, and red rimmed her eyes.

Tilla felt her own eyes sting. She had seen three of Cadport's youths killed already: young Pery back at home, Jem Chandler along the road, and now the red-haired girl—a girl who had only sinned by being one soul too many.

No. Tilla tightened her lips and kept marching. *If I am weak, I am dead. If I cry, I am dead. If I remember home, I am dead. I must be a soldier now, carved of stone, my heart of iron; thus will I survive this nightmare.*

"Move!" Nairi shouted and goaded a recruit with her punisher, making the girl scream and scurry forward.

The phalanx marched in three lines, entering the barracks one flight at a time. When it was Tilla's turn to enter, she clenched her fists and sucked in her breath, prepared for any horror that might lurk inside.

Stifling air, the smell of leather and oil, and shadows awaited her. She blinked and it was a moment before her eyes adjusted. When they did, she breathed a sigh of relief.

"It's an armory," she whispered.

The hall was wide, tiled, and topped with a vaulted ceiling. The recruits gathered here. Behind wooden counters, which reminded Tilla of the Old Wheel's bar, loomed alcoves. One alcove held shelves of helmets. Another held boots. A third brimmed with suits of leather armor studded with iron. The final alcove drew most of Tilla's attention; inside she saw hundreds of swords hanging upon racks.

Outside every alcove, a gruff soldier stood at the counter like a barman. As the recruits streamed into the main hall, these soldiers shouted out their supplies.

"Helms! Get helms here! Move it!"

"Leather armor—grab your armor!"

"Line up for swords, damn you—swords here!"

Tilla wasn't sure where to start. Despite the horrors of the day, she found a smile tingling her lips. It soon widened into a grin.

I'm going to get a sword! she thought. *And armor! What would Rune think of me now?*

Mae sniffed and clung to her arm. "But... Tilla," the baker's daughter said, and her lips trembled. "I don't *want* a sword."

Erry was staring around with wide eyes. "Well I do!" said the ragamuffin. "So watch out, Wobble Lips, because if you cry again, I'm gonna slay you right with it."

"Do you think..." Mae sniffed. "Do you think I can be a baker here too—like I was in Cadport? The Legions need bread too, right? There must be a bakery here somewhere, and maybe I can do that, not fight."

Erry rolled her eyes and snorted so forcefully she blew back locks of her hair. "Oh bloody donkey piss! Burn me, just grab a damn sword. Your days of baking are over."

Leaving the two to bicker, Tilla approached the alcove of armor. A grizzled old armorer stood there, cussing and spitting and shouting at the recruits.

"Here, runt," he said to one short, slim girl and tossed her a suit. "Smallest one I've got. Here, this is for you, pig." He tossed a larger suit at a larger girl. "Merciful stars, but you're going to need a leather sail. You! You—you with the big teats—bloody Abyss, how are you going to fit into a breastplate?"

A few of the girls smirked. Others retreated with their armor in tears. When it was Tilla's turn at the counter, the armorer gave her a shrewd look, scratched his chin, and nodded.

"Aye, you're a tall one," he said. "I like that. How about instead of suiting up, you suit down and slip with me into the shadows at the back?" He spat onto the floor. "I'll do my own slipping into a dark place."

Tilla rolled her eyes. "Well, haven't you just charmed me? Does that line ever work? Fetch me my armor, and maybe I'll forget to visit you again once I get my sword."

Behind her, she heard Erry snicker. Briefly, Tilla wondered if she had crossed a line; would she taste the punisher again for her words? And yet this gruff armorer wore no punisher or blade, and he bore but a single red star upon his armbands; Tilla guessed him too low ranking to threaten her.

All that matters in this place, she thought, *is your rank. Upon her shoulders, Nairi bears the red spirals of an officer; she is death in boots. This man wears the red stars of a lowborn soldier; he is what boots like Nairi's tread upon.*

Her suspicions were confirmed when the armorer grunted, scratched himself, and fetched her a suit of armor.

"Try this," he said. "Tall and slim; should be a bit tight on you, but that's how I like it." He licked his lips and hissed.

Tilla lifted the pack of leather and bolts—it was bundled together with straps—and retreated toward a bench where some recruits were already donning their own armor. After claiming a bit of bench, Tilla unwrapped the bundle.

She found a breastplate studded with iron rings, its boiled leather hard, brown, and tough as wood. This was no fine, steel breastplate like the one Lanse Nairi wore, or like the breastplates Tilla had seen soldiers in Cadport wear—but it was real armor, and it would protect her. Tilla rubbed her chest where Nairi had held a punisher against her, and she wondered if this leather breastplate would protect her from further abuse.

Along with the breastplate, she found tan leggings and a white undershirt, vambraces and greaves for her limbs, thick gloves, and even pauldrons of the same tough, brown leather. She was disappointed to see no armbands bearing insignia; even the armorer wore armbands.

I'll have to earn those ranks, she thought. She wondered how long it took to rise from recruit to soldier. She would not be a real soldier, she knew, until she had armbands with red stars.

"Suit up!" Nairi was shouting across the hall. "Damn it, cockroaches, suit up—fast!"

Tilla nodded, took a deep breath, and removed the woolen tunic and leggings she had worn all the way from Cadport. They were threadbare by now and smelled of mud and sweat and oil. The other recruits were undressing around her; after ten days in a cramped cart, all modesty had left them.

Tilla wriggled into her new leggings, then donned her leather breastplate. Unlike a corset, this breastplate had its straps in the front—three leather belts with iron buckles. When Tilla tightened her armor, she gasped for breath. The damn thing was too tight. Tilla considered returning for a larger suit, but Nairi was screaming that she would slay anyone too slow, and the armorer was shouting while he handed away the last breastplates.

Well, I'll have to lose some weight in this camp, Tilla thought, the armor squeezing her. *I have a feeling that it won't take long in this place. I'm already thinner than I've ever been.*

Mae and Erry approached her, each clad in their own leather armor.

"Merciful stars!" Erry said. She admired Tilla with wide eyes. "You look like a real warrior. That armor is skintight. Burn me, even I'd take you to bed in that suit."

"Don't be disgusting," Mae scolded her. New tears filled her eyes. "She looks *awful.* And I look awful in this suit. And... and... this whole place is awful."

With that, the baker covered her face with her palms and cried silently. Erry only rolled her eyes.

"Come on, girls," Tilla said. "Let's get some boots and helmets."

"And then swords," Erry said and grinned.

Tilla was immensely relieved to find boots her size. She thought that she could handle armor too small, but boots were one thing she needed to have fit well—and these fit beautifully. To be sure, the leather was as hard and unyielding as her armor, but Tilla thought that she could work it in. The boots rose tall above her leggings, ending just below her knees, and their toes were tipped with steel. As Tilla walked around in them, for the first time in her life, she felt powerful—a warrior.

I'm no longer helpless, she thought, and this was a new feeling for her. Back at Cadport, she had always felt lowly, outcast, hopelessly crushed under the weight of the Cadigus Regime. But here, wearing this armor and these boots, Tilla felt strong. She felt like a soldier.

And it feels good, she thought, and the thought surprised her.

At a third alcove, she found a round, steel helmet that fit nicely and left her face exposed; lined with wool, it strapped under her chin with a buckle.

"And now," she said to her flight crew, "we grab swords."

Erry grinned and whooped.

Mae, however, only sniffed. "Why do we even need swords?" she said and her lips trembled. "Aren't we supposed to fight as dragons? Why can't we just use our claws and fire?"

"Because," Erry said with an eye roll, "you're not always going to fight in the sky! Stars, Wobble Lips, but you are slow, aren't you? The Resistance hides in tunnels and caves and such. How are you going to fit in there as a dragon?" She grinned. "But we can get to them with swords. I'm going to stab them real good."

Nairi's shouts flowed over them.

"Back outside!" The lanse stood at the doors, shoving recruits outside, then glared at Tilla and her flight crew. "Grab your swords, you daughters of dogs, or by the red spiral, you'll taste *my* sword."

Tilla nodded, remembering the sight of Nairi's dagger thrusting into the red-haired girl. With her flight crew, she hurried toward the alcove of weapons. Most of the blades were already claimed. A soldier stood at the counter, balding and gaunt and blinking; he reminded Tilla of a giant ferret.

Erry banged her fist against the counter, as if ordering ale.

"Three swords please!" she said. "And make it snappy."

Tilla sighed. "When unarmed, Erry, never order around a man with swords."

The weaselly soldier grumbled under his breath, retreated to the back of the alcove, and returned carrying three blades. He delicately laid them on the counter.

"Take care of these," he said and gave them a longing pat. "Dragonforged, they are. Northern steel." He glared up at the recruits. "If you scratch em, I'll stick em into your guts."

"Well, why don't you just take them to bed with you?" Erry said with another roll of her eyes. When she lifted a sword, those eyes widened, and her lips peeled back into a grin. "Bloody stars, now this is a sword."

The scrawny, dockside orphan drew her blade and swung it, forcing Tilla and Mae to leap back.

"Be careful!" Mae said. She reached for her own sword hesitantly, as if reaching for a venomous snake, and her lips wobbled again.

Tilla lifted the third sword and hefted it. The blade was sheathed in a black, leather scabbard attached to a belt. She slung the belt around her waist, tightened it, and let the sword hang against her left hip. It felt light—lighter than she had expected—but just heavy enough for comfort. She closed her hand around the hilt, squeezing and releasing, but did not draw the blade.

My own sword, she thought.

Since leaving Cadport, Tilla had felt afraid, naked, and alone. But gripping this hilt comforted her. She had a weapon now. She was armed. She was a soldier. For the first time, Tilla felt that maybe the Legions were not a nightmare world. Surely, this was a violent place, and a dangerous one, but there were rules to it. If Tilla played by these rules, she could grow strong here.

Maybe someday I can be strong like Nairi, she thought, *and wear an officer's insignia upon my shoulders. I could command with justice, not cruelty, with pride rather than malice.*

Nairi was shouting again and herding recruits outside. Tilla hurried back out into the sunset. The rest of her phalanx crowded around her, all clad in leather armor and bearing swords.

"Form ranks!" Nairi shouted.

Perhaps it was the pride of armor and blade; this time, the recruits took formation faster than ever. Three lines formed. Boots slammed together.

"Hail the red spiral!" Nairi cried, and hundreds of fists slammed against hundreds of breastplates.

Tilla stood, chin held high. The sun was finally peeking through the clouds. She dared to feel a sliver of hope.

RUNE

They entered the wide, shadowy hall of Valien's crumbling palace.

Limestone pillars rose in palisades, supporting a vaulted ceiling. Dust, grooves, and holes covered the tiled floor and brick walls. Two lines of braziers crackled, forming a corridor of light. At the end of this corridor, a man sat in a chair, his head lowered and his face shadowed. A sword lay upon his lap; the man stared at it, not looking up.

A silent, dark majesty filled the hall, Rune thought. The kings of Osanna had once ruled from this place, presiding over courts of light and life. This man ahead, Rune thought, seemed a different sort of king—a king of death and darkness. He had no golden throne, only an old wooden chair. He wore no armor, only the garb of a forester. And yet Rune thought: He exudes his own regality, as strong as those true kings who had once sat here.

Rune looked at Kaelyn. She stood at his side, still and silent, but a light seemed to fill her eyes—a light of comfort and hope, hearth light shining at the windows for a weary traveler returning home.

She looked at Rune and a smile touched her lips. She held his hand and guided him forward. They walked across the hall, moving down the palisade of braziers and columns, and approached the shadowy man.

"Valien," Kaelyn said softly. "I've returned."

The man did not look up. He was polishing his sword, Rune saw, moving an oiled rag back and forth along the blade. Rune had a feeling that blade had been polished to perfection hours ago. His own father, when troubled, would polish the Old Wheel's bar over and over for hours, lost in thought. This man was polishing his blade with the same weariness.

Rune could still not see Valien's face, but what he saw of the man spoke of haunting memory, of pain, of a weight too great to bear. Valien's hair was long and untamed, hanging loose about his face; it must have once been a great black mane, but now white streaked it. The man's shoulders, though wide and strong, slumped as if bearing an invisible yoke. Valien's clothes had once been fine, Rune thought; they were made of thick wool and tanned leather. Yet years of age had worn them; the fabrics were now faded into mere memories of lost glory.

Seeing this man, Rune did not know how to feel. Many in Cadport, including his father, would whisper that Valien was a hero, the only man brave enough to stand up to the Cadigus family. Others said that Valien was a ruthless killer, that he had slain many soldiers from Cadport, including Tilla's brother. Standing here today, Rune did not know whether to feel awe, hatred, or fear.

"Lord Valien Eleison," he said softly. "The lost knight of Requiem."

Valien's hands stilled upon the blade. His body tensed. He still did not look up. After what seemed an eternity of silence, Valien snorted.

"Lord Valien Eleison?" he spoke in shadow, and Rune started, for that voice was rough and worn like beaten leather. "I haven't been a lord in many years, boy. And the House Eleison has fallen; I am its last survivor. You may call me Valien now; titles are nothing but a memory of light in darkness."

Rune wasn't sure how to respond to that. The Regime called this man a demon; others call him a hero. Standing here, Rune saw neither. He saw only a tired, broken man, the ghost of somebody who might once have been great.

"Valien," he said. "Just Valien then. And I'm just Rune."

For the first time, Valien looked up... and Rune nearly lost his breath.

He had seen hard faces before. Frey Cadigus, in paintings and statues, bore a face that Rune thought could wilt flowers. Tilla's face, when she was angry, was hard as granite. But this man...

Valien's face seemed carved of beaten leather stretched over iron. Grizzled stubble covered his cheeks. Grooves framed his mouth. But worst of all were his eyes. Those eyes were dark, deep, and haunted as windows in temples of ghosts. They sang of old pain and battles as clearly as tales in books or poems. He couldn't have been much older than forty, Rune thought, but his eyes seemed more ancient than those of old men.

"Just Rune," Valien rasped. "Is that so? Do you think you were brought before me because you are *just Rune*?"

Again, Rune was struck by that gruff voice. Valien spoke like a man being strangled. His voice was but a hiss, a scratch, a deathly gasp.

"Some might think me more than that," Rune said. "I've heard what Kaelyn believes. I come here to tell you: She is wrong." He shook his head. "I'm not the one you seek."

Valien snorted again. "Aren't you now?" He coughed and hissed like a man hanging from a noose. "I smuggled Relesar Aeternum out of the burning palace of his father, slaying Cadigus men as I held the babe. I brought the child, last heir of the dynasty, to an old tavern in an older port. I gave him a new name. I know you better than you know yourself, *Rune Brewer*. I've known you all your life, and so has Kaelyn."

The young woman, hearing her name, walked over to Valien and placed a hand on his shoulder. She leaned down, kissed his cheek, and whispered soft blessings.

When she straightened, she said, "Valien, I barely saved the boy in time. Shari arrived in Lynport the same day. I fought her. I wounded her. I smuggled Rune out moments before her men stormed the tavern." Kaelyn lowered her head. "She burned that tavern down, and she killed its keeper. I'm sorry, Valien; I did not mean for any blood to spill. I flew too slowly." She raised her head again, and her eyes shone with tears. "But he is here now. The heir to the throne. He will rally the people against Cadigus; he will bring us hope."

A lump filled Rune's throat. His eyes burned. Thinking about the Old Wheel still pained him so much he could barely breathe.

"Wait a moment!" he said, his voice too loud; it echoed in the chamber. "I will not be some figurehead for your Resistance. I hate Frey Cadigus too, but... I'm only a brewer. I'm not who you think I am. I—"

"You," Valien said, "were kept safe. We made damn sure of that. I've been protecting you all your life, Relesar, though you never knew it. I was in the Old Wheel many times, in shadow, watching you grow from a babe, to a boy, to a man. I made sure you never knew your true parentage; not until you were old enough.

You were safe in the Old Wheel." He sighed. "At least, safe until you went ahead and started looking like your father."

"Wil Brewer is my father—" Rune began.

"Your father was the last King Aeternum," Valien said. "I should know; I fought for him. And you, Rune, look exactly like him, damn you. The Regime noticed. And so... now you are here. You can no longer hide. The time has come, Rune, for you to accept your true heritage... and to take arms against the man who slew your family." Valien reached out and clutched Rune's arm, digging his fingers like an iron vise. "The throne of Requiem is yours. With your help, we will slay the tyrant and place you upon that throne."

Rune laughed.

He turned away.

He could not stop laughing. His laughter echoed through the hall, and tears stung his eyes, and he clutched his belly but could not stop. Valien and Kaelyn were looking at each other grimly, but that only made Rune laugh harder.

Tilla, his best friend, the woman who had kissed him—gone into the Legions. His father—dead. His tavern—burned. His life—torn apart. And now this! Now this ragged shell of man who ruled over ruins and bones—this disgraced knight—called him the heir of Aeternum. Rune paced the hall, tears streaming down his face as he laughed. As his world burned, as all hope for life faded, as everything he'd ever known crumbled around him, what else could he do but laugh?

"Rune," Kaelyn said slowly. "Rune, I know this is a lot to take in."

He tossed back his head, only laughing harder.

"Do you think so, Kaelyn?" he said. "I only just waded through skeletons to meet your grizzled old friend here—who looks barely better—and was told you want me to dethrone Frey Cadigus. Did I miss anything?"

Kaelyn stepped toward him and took his hands. "You don't have to dethrone him yourself, Rune. It needn't be your hand that slays him. But yes, you will sit upon his throne once we kill him."

He wiped tears from his eyes, chest still shaking with laughter. "Well, there's a relief. And tell me, even if I am this... heir of Aeternum... even if my true father was the king... who cares?

Kaelyn, you're Frey's daughter. Kill the bastard and you take the throne." He pointed a shaky finger at Valien. "Or you, old knight. You're supposedly a great warrior. If one soldier could start a new dynasty, why not another? Why not you—"

Valien rose to his feet and roared.

Rune's laughter and voice died.

He had not imagined this weathered man, a wreck who coughed and talked in a wheeze, could roar. And yet Valien now howled, and the cry—the cry of an enraged beast—filled the hall, echoed, and pounded in Rune's ears.

"Silence!"

Valien stomped forward so violently that Rune stepped back, but the man reached him and grabbed his collar. The fallen knight thrust his face close and snarled.

"I've not carried you through fire and blood to hear you mock me," Valien said, voice gruff as old leather cracking under stones. "You know so little. All your life has been sheltered. I made sure of that. You speak of things you do not understand."

Rune's laughter was gone now. Instead he found rage pounding through him, an inferno rising from his belly to sting his throat and eyes. He raged for Tilla leaving, for his father dying, for being taken to this place. He glared back at Valien with burning eyes.

"Is that my fault? You claim to have been watching me all my life. You kept me in the dark! And now you want to use me in your war as some... some figurehead? Look around you, Valien!" He swept his hands around the hall. "Look at this place. A shattered hall. Look at the city you dwell in! A ruin of skeletons. Look at your men! A few hungry souls with chipped swords and no armor. You speak of killing Frey Cadigus? Your war is hopeless."

"Then it is hopeless!" Valien howled. He shoved Rune back, and his eyes burned. "Then we will die! Then we will die like the rest of them—like your parents, like your siblings, like the knights of my order, like my—"

Valien froze.

His face paled.

His lip trembled.

The gruff man stepped back, whispering and staring at Rune.

Then, with a hiss, he spun around and marched into the shadows. He disappeared into the back of the hall, a door slammed shut, and Valien was gone.

Rune's heart pounded, his fingers shook, and his breath rattled his ribs. He turned toward Kaelyn. She stood by the empty chair, eyes sad like birds left to die in an abandoned cage.

"What was that all about?" Rune demanded. "Why did he just... leave like he saw a ghost?"

Kaelyn heaved a sigh. She looked over to the shadows where Valien had vanished.

"Because he did see a ghost," she whispered. "He saw *her* again."

Rune too looked toward those shadows, but Valien was gone and did not return. The room seemed to grow colder, and Rune hugged himself. He had just met the leader of the Resistance, the supposed hope of Requiem, the only man who had ever stood up to Frey Cadigus, raised his head, and said to him: This land is not yours.

And I saw only a broken, haunted wreck, Rune thought.

"Who was she?" he asked. "The woman he lost."

Kaelyn placed a hand on his shoulder. "Come, Rune. Evening falls. Let's go find a meal and a place to sleep. Valien needs to be alone this night."

She took Rune through a doorway, down a flight of stairs, and into a cellar filled with bookshelves, jugs of wine, and a bed. Several candles stood on a table, and Kaelyn lit them with her tinderbox. A painting hung on one wall, showing a woman with golden hair and sad eyes.

"Another gopher hole?" Rune asked.

Kaelyn smiled softly. "No. This one is a Kaelyn hole. My home—if any place can be called my home anymore. You can share it for now." She glared at him and jabbed a finger against his chest. "At least until we figure out what to do with you."

He frowned at the room and his stomach sank. "There's only one bed."

"Of course there's only one bed!" She bristled. "We're not running a tavern here, Rune Brewer. You will be quite comfortable sleeping on the floor. Well, I lied. You'll be cold and stiff, but you'll be *alive*, and that's all I care about."

With that, Kaelyn turned away. She hung her bow, quiver, and sword on pegs. When she doffed her cloak, remaining in only her leggings and tunic, Rune was struck by how fragile she looked. Armed and cloaked, Kaelyn had seemed a warrior. Now he saw only a slim girl, barely half his size. Her golden hair cascaded down her back, and her skin shone orange in the candlelight, and despite himself, and despite all this death and horror, Rune's blood heated.

She's beautiful, he thought. He found himself imagining what her body looked like under her clothes. With how snugly they fit, he didn't have to imagine much. His mouth dried.

She looked over her shoulder and glared.

"What are you looking at?" she said. "Stop standing there like a useless lump and get some food." She nodded at a shelf. "There, you'll find some bread and cheese. Slice us a meal."

Rune shook his head and blinked, banishing those warm, ticklish, disturbing thoughts. Kaelyn was a menace! She was bossy, she had dragged him from his home, and besides—he had Tilla. He had sworn to find her someday; he would stick to that vow.

They sat on her bed and ate a cold dinner. Rune wanted to demand more answers: about Valien, about this shattered palace, about what they planned next. But weariness tugged him so strongly he could barely chew his meal. When they were done eating, Kaelyn nudged him off the bed.

"Go on," she said. "There's a nice comfortable floor for you. I'm not sharing my bed with you yet."

"Yet?" he asked.

She gave him another one of her famous glares. "Not ever, but I thought that, for tonight, I'd give you just a bit of hope to help you sleep." A wan smile touched her lips, and she mussed his hair. "Get some sleep, Rune. Tomorrow we continue the fight."

When he lay on the floor, wrapped in his cloak, he looked up to see Kaelyn lying in the bed. She pulled a blanket over her and wriggled. A moment later, she kicked her leggings and tunic outside the bed, letting them drop to the floor.

Rune swallowed.

She's naked under that blanket, he thought, and again his blood began to boil. Stars, he could imagine her body there, warm and lithe and—

Stop it, he told himself. He turned away from the bed, so that he lay facing the wall. He closed his eyes and thought about Tilla instead. He remembered all those times they had walked along the beach, whispering or just walking silently. He remembered their kiss. He remembered her smooth, black hair that fell to her chin, and her dark eyes, and the rarity of her smile.

We will walk along that beach again, Tilla, he thought.

Sleep found him, and he dreamed of her at his side, sand under his feet, and waves under starlight.

TILLA

Tilla wasn't sure how she ended up being the standard-bearer.

Arriving in Castra Luna that morning—stars, it seemed like ages ago!—she had wanted to keep a low profile. This was hard enough to do with her height; she towered above the other girls. Now, marching ahead of the Black Rose Phalanx, bearing its standard while shouting out time, she stuck out like, well... like a tall, awkward girl in ill-fitting leather, shouting while waving around a huge banner.

It was night, but even that didn't help conceal her; braziers and torches crackled across the fortress grounds, their light falling upon her. Tilla sighed.

"Three, two, one!" she yelled, marching ahead of the other recruits. Their boots thudded behind hers in unison.

She hefted her standard; the damn thing was damn heavy. The pole rose ten feet tall. Upon its crest rose an iron rose inside a ring—sigil of the Black Rose Phalanx.

And of Nairi's house, Tilla thought sourly as she called cadence. Tilla herself was a commoner, her surname merely her trade, and she had no fine sigil of her own. Yet Nairi Blackrose was the daughter of nobles, and she bore the dark rose upon her breastplate, her sword, and now upon her phalanx.

Tilla looked over at Nairi. The young lanse alternated between marching ahead of the phalanx, leading its way around the fort, and falling back to inspect the marching troops. Her narrowed eyes stared at every thudding boot. Whenever a single soldier stepped out of time, Nairi swooped in, lashed her punisher, and a scream rose.

"You will learn to march as one!" Nairi shouted. "Or I will burn it into you."

Tilla kept calling time and marching. The standard was so heavy her arms ached, but she dared not lower it; the one time she had let it dip, Nairi's punisher had driven into her ribs.

I'm nothing but a tool to serve her, Tilla thought, watching the young noblewoman.

She wondered if commoners could ever rise in the Legions' ranks. Upon her shoulders, Nairi wore the red spirals of an officer, but she was nobleborn. Every lowborn soldier Tilla had known— back home and here in Castra Luna—only wore red stars on armbands; they fought and died, but did not command.

Could I become an officer too? Tilla wondered. *Could lowborn wear red spirals, or does my common blood doom me to a life of obeying orders and suffering the burns of punishers?*

She didn't know. Yet as she kept shouting—"Three, two, one!"—Tilla vowed that if commoners *could* rise somehow, she would find the way.

I will not serve as Nairi's standard-bearer forever.

As they marched, Tilla got to see more of Castra Luna. It was a sprawling complex, larger than she had first thought. They passed by the armory, a smithy where hammers rang, kitchens pumping smoke from a dozen chimneys, towering walls where dragons perched, and barracks of mossy bricks.

As they walked, Tilla wondered which building she would live in. They passed many structures, some squat and dank, others rising tall and topped with towers. Soldiers moved behind their windows. How many would share her room, and would her bed be clean, and would she have a little space to herself? Like it or not, this would be her home for several moons of training. Every building they passed, Tilla looked up nervously and wondered: *Will I be living in this one?*

Nairi led them toward a towering wall. Dragons stood upon its battlements between cannons. Oaken doors stood open in an archway, revealing a forest of barren trees and shadows. Patches of snow covered the forest floor, and a lone coyote fled, eyes golden in the night.

We're leaving the fort, Tilla realized and her stomach sank. As bad as Castra Luna was, she did not relish time in that dark forest. Beyond the gates, the trees creaked and swayed like lecherous old men, their branches hoary with snow. It was a place of shadows and whispers.

Nairi stepped through the gates, and Tilla reluctantly followed into the forest.

"Three, two, one!" she kept shouting, her voice hoarse, and heard her fellow troops marching behind her. She kept her standard raised high.

They left the fortress behind and walked down a gravelly road. Torches lined the roadsides, crackling as snow fell. The trees rose around them, reaching out branches to snag at Tilla's arms. Crows circled and cawed above. Cold wind blew, fluttering wisps of snow around her boots.

The road curved ahead. Nairi led them around the bend, and when Tilla followed, her stomach sank even further.

So here is my new home, she realized.

A great clearing lay ahead, nearly as large as the fortress grounds. Dozens of tents rose here, their cloth black and unadorned. A palisade of sharpened logs surrounded the camp, and troops patrolled it. Between the tents, more recruits marched and shouted in reply to barking officers.

It was harder than ever to hold up her standard. Tilla had not hoped for much—a roof over her head, walls around her, and a fireplace for the cold nights. Here, it seemed, she would have none of those.

Nairi led them through the camp, and Tilla looked around. Hundreds—maybe thousands—of recruits marched around her. Tilla recognized some faces from Cadport; other recruits were strangers, probably drafted from other towns. All these faces were pale, their lips blue and shivering, their breath frosting. Finally, after walking across half the camp, Nairi led her phalanx to a long black tent. It was barely larger than the cart that had brought them here.

"Halt!" Nairi barked.

Tilla slammed her standard down and her boots together. Behind her, her fellow recruits froze.

"Form ranks!" Nairi shouted. "Move it, maggots."

Tilla stepped back, still holding her standard. She formed ranks along with her fellow troops. Mae and Erry, her flight crew, fell in line behind her. Boots thumped down, and ninety-nine troops stood still and stiff.

Nairi nodded in satisfaction.

"This will be your home until spring," she said. "You will keep this tent clean. You will keep yourselves neat. You will all partake in guard duty, at least an hour a night—every one of you. Do you understand?"

"Yes, Commander!" they shouted together.

Nairi nodded. "You are my soldiers now. You will make me proud. You will keep your swords oiled. You will keep your boots polished. You will keep your armor neat, your fingernails clipped, your hair tied or braided, your bodies clean and groomed. I will inspect you every morning before dawn. If any of you break these rules..." She drew her punisher and raised its crackling head. "...you will taste this. Do you understand?"

They shouted their understanding.

"Good," Nairi said. She looked them over, one by one. "This is the Black Rose Phalanx. This is *my* phalanx. That means you will become the finest troops in this fortress—in the entire Legions. If any of you let me down, I will personally slice you open and drink your blood." She snarled. "You will find rations and supplies in your tent. I suggest you get some food and sleep. I will be back before dawn, and your training will begin."

With that, Nairi shifted into a dragon, took flight, and crashed past the forest canopy and into the sky. She disappeared into the night.

Everybody started talking at once.

"Pig's puke, what a royal pain in the arse that Nairi is!" Erry exclaimed and spat.

"Do you mean... we have to live here in the forest?" said Mae and whimpered. "I don't *want* to live here. I'm scared."

Other recruits were talking about seeing the prince, or how older relatives had served in Castra Luna too, or how Nairi was the daughter of Herin Blackrose himself, lord of the Axehand Order. A dozen other conversations rustled like leaves.

Tilla did not feel like talking. This had been the longest day of her life. Her muscles ached and her belly cramped with hunger; she could not remember the last time she'd eaten.

"Come on, girls," she said to Mae and Erry. "You're my flight crew; stay with me and let's find some food."

She stepped into the tent, and one by one, the other Black Rose recruits followed.

At first Tilla wondered if this was the wrong tent. There were no beds here, no chairs or tables, nothing but a great wooden chest and a few blankets on the ground. With a sigh, she realized she'd miss the wooden walls of the cart.

"Tilla," Mae said and sniffed back tears. "Tilla, where are the beds?"

"I don't think there are any," she replied, and surprising herself, she placed an arm around the baker's daughter. "Come on, let's see if there's food at least."

Erry beat them to it. She leaped toward the chest in the center, lifted its lid, and whooped.

"Battle rations!" she said with a grin. She pulled out bundles of leather and began tossing them toward the others.

Mae and Tilla grabbed a bundle each, unwrapped them, and found a wafer, a wheel of cheese, and a strip of dry meat. Tilla had not eaten all day, and this was not nearly enough; it was barely worthy of two bites.

"Not bad!" Erry said, slumped down to the ground, and began chewing on her meat, looking like some wild dog gnawing a bone. "Bit chewy. I've had worse."

Mae glared at the waif through her tears. "Of course you've had worse! You... you just used to live along the docks at Cadport. You probably lived off fishbones and garbage. But I was a baker." She sniffed at her wafer. "I can't eat this." She grimaced at her dried meat. "And I don't eat animals either."

"Well, starve then, Wobble Lips!" Erry said. "We'll be rid of your whining, at least." She stuffed the cheese into her mouth and chewed lustfully.

The rest of the phalanx, ninety-nine of Cadport's young women, sat on the ground and began to eat.

"Make some room," Tilla said to Erry, nudging the urchin aside with her boot.

When Erry had squirmed over, Tilla sat beside her and began to eat too. Even Mae, sniffing tears, finally sat down and nibbled a few bites. With everyone seated, they covered the tent floor; a mouse would've had no room to scurry between them.

"I miss home," Mae said. She leaned her head against Tilla's shoulder. "Tilla, do you remember home?"

Tilla laughed. "We haven't been gone a moon yet. Of course I remember home."

"Do you remember the smell of baking bread from my bakery?" Mae inhaled through her nostrils as if she could smell it. "I do. And I remember your shop too, Tilla. My father bought a rope there once. Oh—and do you remember the Old Wheel?" Light filled Mae's eyes. "I remember how we used to sing there sometimes—you know, the old songs of Requiem. Jem and I used to sing together, and..." Tears filled her eyes. "Oh Tilla... he just... he just died like that, in the forest, alone."

Tilla felt ice trickle down her spine, and guilt rose through her belly. She had been rolling her eyes at Mae all day, but of course the girl was teary; Beras had butchered her lover not days ago.

"Oh Mae," she whispered, pulled the baker's daughter into an embrace, and smoothed her hair. "Do you know what the old priests used to say?"

Mae sniffed and shook her head. "What did they say?"

Tilla held the girl close. "That when we Vir Requis die, our souls rise to the Draco constellation. A starlit palace rises there, the columns all white and glowing. The souls of our fallen drink, sing, and dine there forever." She kissed Mae's cheek. "Jem is there now, Mae, and he's at peace."

Mae looked up with teary eyes, holding Tilla and trembling. "Really?"

Tilla nodded. "Really. I promise."

"I like that." Mae closed her eyes, leaned against Tilla, and mumbled. "Thank you, Tilla. I'm sorry for crying so much. I'll be a good soldier. I promise. Just don't let me go yet."

Tilla nodded and kept stroking the girl's hair. When she looked to her other side, she saw Erry watching them. For once, the scrawny dock rat had no quip or smirk, and ghosts filled her eyes.

Erry chewed her lip for a moment, looked down, and suddenly blurted out, "My father wasn't really a dockhand."

Tilla turned toward her; the girl was furiously staring at her feet, her face was pale, and her fists were clenched.

"Erry," Tilla said softly, "you don't have t—"

"He was just a sailor!" Erry said, and now her eyes dampened, and she blinked them madly and punched her thighs. "He wasn't even *Vir Requis*. He was some... some soldier from

southern Tiranor—my mother didn't even know his name—and...
he paid for my mother at the docks. She was a prostitute, Tilla."
Erry looked up, tears in her eyes. "I just lied to people. I didn't
want them to know. I was ashamed of my mother and my mixed
blood. I'm nothing but... but a bastard, halfbreed, whore's
daughter!"

Mae gasped, eyes wide.

"Oh, Erry, that's all right..." Tilla said and tried to embrace
her, but Erry shoved her off.

"I don't need no hugs!" Erry knuckled her eyes. "And I
don't need no stinking pity. I'm strong. I've been strong and
fighting all my life on the docks. I'm just... a little less strong here.
But like it or not, we're stuck in this damn place now, and three of
us already died, and... I just need to be honest here. I need to tell
the truth, at least to you and Wobble Lips." A crooked grin
managed to creep through her tears. "But just to you two, so don't
go telling anyone else, or I'll shove my sword so far up your
bottoms, I'll use the blade to clean your teeth."

Mae scrunched up her face. "Oh, Erry, that mouth of yours.
It's horrible."

Erry opened that mouth wide and stuck out her tongue at
Mae. Then, with a mischievous gleam, she grabbed Tilla's arm.

"Now what about you, Roper?" Erry grinned at her. "While
we're all sharing secrets, what's yours?"

Tilla laughed. "My secrets? I have none."

"Everybody has secrets," Mae said. "I can't believe I'm doing
this, but I'm agreeing with Erry. Tell us, Tilla!" She tugged at
Tilla's other arm. "Tell us your big secret."

"Secret! Secret! Secret!" Erry chanted, bouncing up and
down on her bottom.

"All right, all right!" Tilla said, laughing. "Settle down first."
The two girls fell silent and stared with eager eyes like puppies
awaiting treats. Tilla continued. "Do you remember Rune
Brewer?"

Erry gasped. "You... you bedded Rune Brewer!" She began
to laugh hysterically. "Did the boy even know where to stick it?"

"Erry, your mouth!" Mae scolded, then turned back toward
Tilla. "Oh, Tilla, did you... really?"

"No, no!" Tilla held up her hands. "I just kissed him, that's all." She sighed. "It was the night before we were drafted. On the beach by Ralora Cliffs."

"So..." Erry said slowly, "he didn't know where to stick it."

Tilla roared and shoved her, and Mae squealed, and soon all three were shoving one another and laughing.

In the distance, the clock tower of Castra Luna chimed. Tilla fell silent, cocked her head, and listened. The tower was far, and soldiers still talked around her, but she managed to count twelve chimes.

"Midnight," she said and stretched. "This has, quite officially, been the longest day of my life. What say we get some sleep, girls? I have a feeling tomorrow will be just as long."

Tilla wriggled out of her new armor, breathing in relief as her body was freed from the tight, hard leather. She grabbed a blanket, wrapped it around her, and lay down. The blanket stank, and mold spread across it; at once Tilla's skin and throat began to itch. And yet she was so tired, sleep tugged at her at once. All around, the other soldiers were lying down to sleep too, pressed together like snakes in a pit.

"Goodnight, Erry," Tilla whispered. "Goodnight, Mae."

The two were already sleeping beside her, wrapped in their own moldy, tattered blankets. Ignoring her itching skin, Tilla closed her eyes and slept.

"Wake up, girls!" shouted a voice. "Damn it—guard duty! We ain't staying up all night waiting for you."

Tilla opened her eyes, blinked, and vaguely heard the distant clock tower chime again. Was it morning already? No, it was still dark. She counted only a single chime.

"It's one in the morning!" Erry mumbled beside her, wrapped in her blanket. "Frothy griffin snot, who's making that racket? By the emperor's hairy arse, I'm going to cut out their tongue."

Tilla rose, rubbed her eyes, and saw a young recruit—he wore no insignia upon his leather armor—standing at the tent entrance. She had seen his face in Cadport—he was a grocer's son—but she couldn't remember his name.

"Come on!" the young man called. "You girls going to get up, or do I have to walk around kicking?"

Tilla rose to her feet, realized she was wearing nothing but her underclothes, and wrapped her blanket around her.

"What are you on about?" she demanded. "Get lost before I do my own kicking."

He pointed at her. "Wear your damn armor, not a blanket. This is the Black Rose Phalanx, right? It's your guard-duty shift. You walk around the camp palisade three times, then wake up Red Blade Phalanx." He grumbled. "There are bloody siragis patrolling all over this place, so don't think of weaseling out. They got punishers. Now put on some damn armor!"

With that, the grocer's son turned and left the tent.

Bloody siragis. Tilla cursed. She had heard of these soldiers before; veterans back in Cadport would mutter about them. The sons of commoners, they wore three red stars upon their armbands, denoting several years of service. The siragis didn't have the noble blood for command; they were the officers' pet brutes. Tilla's body still ached from the wounds Nairi, a young woman like herself, had given her. She did not relish a confrontation with the siragis, hardened warriors.

"All right, you heard him!" Tilla said and clapped her hands. "Into your armor, grab your swords—quickly."

A moment later, the Black Roses emerged from their tent, tugging on boots and buckling swords to waists. When Tilla blinked in the night, she saw a men's phalanx outside their tent. Its soldiers were dropping bulging sacks; they thudded onto the ground.

"What the Abyss are those?" Tilla demanded.

The young grocer scowled. "Cannonballs," he said. "You carry them around the palisade."

"We what?"

"Three walkarounds!" he said, then showed her his arm; a welt rose across it. "If you drop your sack, the bloody siragis burn you. The bastards are patrolling all over the place."

His phalanx, ninety-nine young men of Cadport, turned and limped back to their tent, rubbing their shoulders and cursing. Ninety-nine sacks lay on the ground.

"Oh, piss and blood!" Erry said, trying to lift a sack. "Thing weighs more than I do."

Tilla peered into a sack. It held three cannonballs, each one nearly as large as her head. She lifted the sack with both hands. She grunted, slung it across her back, and nearly collapsed. The sack must have indeed weighed more than Erry. The other Black Roses were lifting their own sacks and cursing.

When Tilla stared ahead at the palisade, she saw the siragis standing there, watching. There were three of them, tall and burly men in black steel. Upon their arms, their three red stars gleamed in the torchlight. Their punishers crackled in their hands. Tilla shuddered. These men craved to burn flesh; she felt their bloodlust like heat waves.

"I can't... carry this!" Mae said, wobbling under her sack. Her sword swung between her legs like a tail.

"Oh, come on!" Tilla said and began walking, the sack across her back. "Three loops and we can get back to sleep. Black Rose! Follow me. Three, two, one!"

She began to march, gritting her teeth. Her back screamed under the weight. Her boots drove deep into mud. She reached the palisade that surrounded the camp, hefted the sack, and began her first loop. Her fellow Black Roses groaned and cursed and walked behind her.

"This isn't fair!" Mae said, jaw clenched as she trudged forward. "Why do we have to carry the same weight as the boys? They should make it lighter for the girls."

Erry spat and glared. "Dog dung. I can carry just as much as any boy."

Mae moaned. "Why do we need to carry cannons balls on patrol anyway? It's not like we even have cannons here! What, if an enemy attacks, are we to toss these balls at them?"

"You could just whine them to death," Erry said. The poor slight girl—the smallest one in the Black Rose—was wobbling and barely trudging forward. "Shag-a-dog, these things are heavy."

"Language!" Mae said, then squealed as she slipped.

Tilla could not guess the diameter of the palisade, nor how long it took to complete the first round. All she knew was: By the time they started their second round, her legs howled with agony, her toes felt ready to crack, and her spine creaked. She had to rest. She had to stop for just a moment—to catch her breath, to find some water, to let her heartbeat slow.

She paused for just a moment, let the sack fall, and wiped sweat off her brow.

Shadows leaped.

A siragi, burly and clanking in armor, lunged toward her. His punisher lashed out. Tilla cursed and leaped back, trying to dodge the weapon, but was too slow. The punisher drove into her side, and lightning shot across her. She screamed.

"Keep moving!" the soldier barked and pulled his punisher back, leaving Tilla's armor smoking. "Damn it, you stop again, I'll burn every last inch of skin off your flesh."

Tilla gasped and shook. "I—"

He raised his punisher again.

Heart thudding and fingers trembling, Tilla grabbed the sack of cannons balls, hefted it over her back, and began her second patrol.

Behind her, the other Black Roses trudged along, no longer speaking. Tilla heard only grunting, wheezing, and the odd whimper. She wanted to talk to her friends, but had no breath for words. She kept walking, step by step, inch by inch. All around in the camp, the other troops slept in their tents. Tilla envied them more than she had ever envied anyone else. Sleep—pure, beautiful sleep—was now her greatest lost love, greater than Rune, greater than her father, greater than home.

By the time she finished her second round, she was limping. Her back twisted, and her shoulders felt ready to dislocate. Sweat drenched her, and her throat blazed with thirst; she could not remember the last time she had drunk. It felt like every bone in her feet had cracked. When she looked over her shoulder, she saw the others looking the way she felt; their faces were pale, their hair damp with sweat, their lips tightened.

She wanted to rest, but the siragis raised their punishers. Tilla grunted and began her third round.

Pain.

Pain leaped through her bones and ground her spine.

Pain twisted her feet, clutched at her chest, and burned through her lungs.

Behind her, she heard a soldier fall, then smelled smoke as punishers burned flesh. Tilla turned to help the girl rise; punishers thrust her way too, and Tilla screamed. She kept walking, sack slung over her back. Step by step. Inch by inch.

Think only about every new step, she told herself, sweat blinding her eyes. *Don't think about anything else; just the next step, one after the other, and it'll be over.*

When finally the nightmare ended and the Black Rose completed its third round, Tilla's head spun. She dropped her sack to the ground, doubled over, and felt fire racing through her bones. The other Black Roses gathered around her, bedraggled and drenched in sweat.

"Come on, girls," Tilla said and wiped her brow. "Let's drag these sacks to the next phalanx and get some sleep."

Finally—it must have been close to two in the morning— Tilla lay back in her moldy blanket. She was too tired to even itch now. Everything hurt. Vaguely, she saw the other Black Roses collapse around her.

There are still a few hours until morning, she thought. *If I can only get a good, solid five or six hours of sleep, I...*

Her thoughts trailed off.

Sleep welcomed her into a deep, black embrace.

"On your feet!" The shout pierced the night. "Black Rose Phalanx—inspection! Form ranks!"

Tilla blinked. Her muscles cramped. Her bones ached. Somebody was shouting at the tent entrance. When Tilla rubbed her eyes, she thought that she saw Nairi there, a torch in her hand. Darkness still covered the world.

"Hairy horse dung," Erry cursed at her side, sitting up. The clock tower began to chime in the distance, and Erry counted on her fingers, then cursed. "It's only four in the morning!"

Nairi was still shouting. "Out, Black Roses—morning inspection! Move!"

The recruits stood up and shivered. Tilla's teeth chattered. It felt cold enough to freeze liquor.

"Armor!" Nairi screamed. "Swords! *Move!*"

The Black Roses moved in a daze, strapping on armor with numb fingers. Swords rattled and pale, numbed feet thrust into boots. They stumbled out into the darkness, ninety-nine souls half frozen, eyes blurred and breath fogging. Outside the tent, they formed ranks and stood shivering.

Nairi stared at them in disgust. Her torch crackled in her hand.

"Pathetic," she said and spat. "If we were under attack, you'd be dead by now." She began to pace along the lines, staring at each recruit as if staring at flies upon her dinner plate. "Buckles unstrapped. Boots covered in mud. Half of you are missing your helmets. Not a single sword is oiled." Her voice rose to a howl. "You are a disgrace!"

Standing behind Tilla, Erry muttered under her breath. "That woman needs a few cannonballs dropped onto her head."

Nairi did not hear, but kept pacing along the lines, cursing.

"Not one of you is properly armed and ready. I thought of letting you eat dinner today. I thought of letting you sleep a full five hours next night." She shouted so loudly her face turned red. "You will eat nothing, and I will let you sleep only three hours next night, and this will continue until you can pass morning inspection!"

Erry muttered again. "Next night? Morning? Tonight? I have no idea when's what and who's who. Is it morning or night now? Bloody stars."

"Shh!" Tilla said; Nairi was marching back toward them.

"Back into your tent!" the lanse shouted. "You have one minute. I want to see a proper inspection now—boots shining and swords oiled. Go, go!"

Nairi waved her torch, showering sparks and goading the recruits back into the tent. Outside, the lanse counted down the seconds. Inside, the recruits rummaged through the chest for oil. Finally—it must have been several minutes—they stumbled back outside.

"Second inspection!" Nairi shouted. "You are late. You have failed. You will not sleep for *two* more nights. Go, back inside! One minute. Again!"

Tilla sighed.

With pain and darkness and bitter cold, her second day at Castra Luna began.

KAELYN

She entered his chamber, her fingertips tingling and her throat tight. She took a deep breath, steeled herself, and spoke softly.

"Valien?" Her voice shook. "Valien, it's me."

He sat hunched before a hearth, his back to her. The firelight outlined his form but left him in shadow. He said nothing. He did not move. He could as well have been a statue.

Kaelyn sighed. Valien was in one of his moods again. Lately these dark spells had been coming more frequently. When they hit, Valien could brood here for hours, eating little, drinking much, and try as she might, Kaelyn could shine no light into his darkness.

It was a small room, hardly the chamber of a great warrior. In the stories Kaelyn's father told, the cruel Valien Eleison sat upon a throne of bones, commanded a hall of demons, and drank from goblets of children's blood. But this chamber was no larger than Kaelyn's own. Half the shelves bore books: ancient bestiaries, histories, and epic poems. The other shelves bore jugs of the spirits he drank, overpowering rye that made Kaelyn's eyes water and Valien's memories fade.

In Kaelyn's chamber, she kept a painting of her mother, the dearest woman she had known. Valien too had lost someone, yet no memories of that woman were allowed in this chamber. No paintings. No mementos. Just mentioning Marilion, his fallen wife, was enough to send Valien so deep into darkness he would not emerge for days.

"Valien," she tried again. "We must discuss the boy."

Still facing the fire, Valien grunted. "He is not who I thought he was."

Kaelyn gasped. "Valien! You said he's the spitting image of King Aeternum. You said—"

"I know what I said." His voice was raspier than ever, the death croak of a hanging man. He turned toward her, eyes red in the firelight. "He is the flesh and blood of Aeternum, that much is true. But he's not who I thought he was. He's not strong like his father. He's not brave. He's not wise." Valien grumbled. "The boy is a fool."

Kaelyn sighed. "He is young."

"So are you." Valien reached for a mug and took a swig of rye. "You're eighteen. You're his age, or only a year older." He snorted. "I was eighteen when I first joined the Legions, then the knighthood soon after. Yet this one..." He drank again. "Rune Brewer is nothing but a spoiled, soft city boy."

"He's not yet been hardened," Kaelyn agreed. "But I traveled with him for ten days. He knew where he was going. He stayed with me." She took a step forward and held Valien's shoulder. "That shows some strength. He will learn. Teach him."

Valien leaped to his feet so violently he knocked his chair back. It clanged to the ground, and Kaelyn started.

"The boy will not learn." Valien paced the chamber, teeth bared, face red in the firelight. "The boy brought us death and misery from the first day. I was wrong, Kaelyn. I was wrong to think he could bring the people hope."

He brought his mug to his lips and drank deeply. His cup held strong spirits—Kaelyn had tried a sip once and nearly choked—yet Valien drank down this liquid fire like water.

"Valien!" Kaelyn said. She stepped toward him, held his arm, and lowered the mug from his lips. "Valien, look at me. Please. Listen to me."

He looked at her. His eyes were wild and bloodshot. In them Kaelyn saw his pain, his memories, and his loss.

When he looks at me, she knew, *he sees her. She too was eighteen. She was my age when she died. When he looks at me, he sees his wife. When he looks at Rune, he sees the babe he saved while she died.*

He panted, breath raw, and Kaelyn embraced him.

He needs me now, she thought. *He needs me more than he needs Rune. He needs me more than his memories.*

"It's all right, Valien," she whispered into his ear as she held him. "Don't lose hope now. We have more hope than ever before." She touched his cheek. "And I'm with you, as I've been for two years now. I fly at your side—through fire, light, or blood, whichever will fall upon us."

You are weary, she added silently. *You are broken. And you are drunk. But you are our leader, and you are the greatest man I've known. And you will lead us home.*

He wrapped his arms around her, great arms that even now, even here, made Kaelyn feel safe and small; each of those arms was nearly as wide as her body. She laid her head against his chest and felt his heart beat against her cheek.

"I cannot guarantee that he will live," Valien said. "If once more we face the fire, and I must choose between him and another... I cannot guarantee his life."

Kaelyn looked up at him. Those old ghosts circled in his eyes like crows around a gallows tree.

"I know," she whispered. "He might die. So might the rest of us. For now, let him be a beacon of hope to the people. Let him be a torch in the shadow my father cast upon this land." She gave him a twisted smile. "Am I not the same? I'm the daughter of the emperor, a voice rising in defiance. Am I too not a symbol for your uprising?"

He grabbed her arms so roughly that she gasped.

"You are more than a symbol, Kaelyn." He snarled at her. "You are a bright blade. You are a lioness. You are—"

"—the daughter of Emperor Frey Cadigus," she said. "I am a statement and a banner of rebellion. Rune will be one too. You lead us, Valien Eleison, and you will lead us to victory. But the people... the people will rally around Rune." It was her turn to snarl. "I fly at your right-hand side. Let Rune fly at your left. Together—the last knight of Requiem, the daughter of Cadigus, and the son of Aeternum—we will topple this regime, kill my father, and place Rune on the throne."

Valien turned away from her. He walked to the hearth, placed his great hand—wide as a bear paw—against the mantel. He looked into the flames, head lowered.

"If I have to choose again, Kaelyn... if I..."

His voice died, and Kaelyn felt her eyes water. Valien rarely spoke about that night, but Kaelyn had heard the tales whispered in countless taverns and halls. Seventeen years ago, when Frey Cadigus had stormed the capital and slain the royal family, Valien had fought him; he still bore the scar of Frey's blade across his chest. That night, Kaelyn knew, Frey had given him a choice.

Valien had but moments to flee before more of Frey's troops swarmed the palace—just long enough to save the babe, the last heir of Aeternum... or to save Marilion, his young wife.

Valien fled the palace that night with a babe in his arms. His wife burned.

Tears stung Kaelyn's eyes, and she approached her leader, embraced him from behind, and laid her head against his back.

"You will not have to choose," she whispered.

He spun toward her, teeth bared, cheeks flushed red. He clenched his fists.

"When fire rises, we will all burn!" he said, eyes blazing like a rabid animal's. He clutched Kaelyn's arms, and his voice rose into a torn howl. "I will not lose you! I will not see you burn, Marilion, I—"

Kaelyn gasped and stared silently.

Valien's eyes widened. He shut his mouth. His face whitened. He looked aside and blinked and his fists trembled.

"I've had enough to drink this night," he rasped. "Leave me, Kaelyn. Leave me."

She touched his cheek with trembling fingers, and tears filled her eyes. "Valien—"

"Leave me!" he roared, waved his arms, and tossed his mug across the room. It smashed against a shelf, and more mugs fell and shattered, and Kaelyn turned away. She fled the room, eyes stinging and legs trembling.

RUNE

They flew in the night, a black and green dragon, two shadows under the clouds.

As Rune glided, the cold wind felt heavenly in his nostrils. Whenever he went only a few days without flying, the magic tingled inside him, and he lashed out, grumbled, and felt as if ants were crawling through his bones. He would fly with Tilla many nights above the water.

And now I fly with Kaelyn.

He looked at her. She flew to his right, the hint of fire in her nostrils like two embers. She gave him a sad smile and tapped him with her tail.

"What did you want to show me out here?" he asked.

"Be patient!" she said. "I'm taking you there. And be quiet; imperial dragons still patrol these skies."

They glided silently. Forests and plains streamed below and clouds hid the stars. Dragon eyes were sharp—sharper than his human eyes—but Rune could barely see more than smudges in this darkness. Some distant lights shone—fortified outposts of the Regime—but otherwise the land lay in shadow and mist. A drizzle began to fall, and Rune allowed just a little more fire to fill his belly, crackle in his mouth, and warm him.

He tried to imagine that these forests below, rolling shadows in the night, were the waves back at home, that those distant lights were Cadport waiting on the shore. He missed those waves. He missed the cobbled boardwalk with its shops, rusted cannon, and Tilla walking beside him. He missed the Old Wheel, he missed Scraggles, and he missed his father.

I miss home, he thought. But what was his home now? And who was his father? Rune did not know, and so many questions still burned inside him like the fire. As he glided through shadow and rain, ice filled his belly along with the flames. He looked at Kaelyn, and she met his gaze, and he saw the same sadness in her eyes.

"There," she said and gestured below. "There's an old ruined temple on the hill. Do you see it?"

Rune squinted. He could discern only vague shapes in this darkness. He thought he saw pale columns, some only broken stems, rising upon a hilltop.

"A temple," he said. "An old temple to Requiem's stars."

Kaelyn nodded and began diving toward it. "It *was* a temple. Priests used to worship the Draco constellation here. My father..." Kaleyn sighed. "He didn't like that."

Rune descended beside her. Wind and rain stung his face. A temple of marble columns had once stood in Cadport; Rune had heard the city elders whisper of it in awe. They said priests and healers would play harps there, sing to the Draco stars, and bless the city. Today that temple was a courthouse, its walls draped with banners of the red spiral, its marble columns stained with blood.

But there was no use for a courthouse here in the wilderness, and as Rune descended toward the ruins, he marveled at the columns. Their marble shone like moonlight. Some columns lay shattered upon the hillside, but others still stood, forming a rectangle. The roof they had once supported had fallen; its bricks lay strewn across the grass, pale lumps in the night.

The two dragons landed upon wet grass. Above them loomed the temple columns, two hundred feet tall at least. Rune tried to imagine this temple standing in its glory days—back when the Aeternum Dynasty had ruled. He could almost see priests' white robes fluttering between the columns, almost hear their harps.

When he looked above, Rune gasped to see the clouds part. The Draco constellation shone between them, the holy stars of Requiem.

"Our people used to worship these stars," he said softly. "My father would pray to them at night. He thought I couldn't hear. Many of Cadport's elders would still pray secretly, knowing that if any soldiers heard, they would be broken upon the wheel. Do you think those stars have any real power, Kaelyn?"

She stood at his side, a slim green dragon, and watched the constellation with him. The starlight glimmered on her wet scales.

"I've never doubted it," she said. "My father hates those stars. How he would rail against them! He would shout that these stars had never protected Requiem, that under their light, so many of our people died. He claimed that only he could defend this land, that only he was worthy of being called godly, not some lights in the heavens." Kaelyn blasted smoke from her nostrils. "Anything he hates so much must have power, Rune. And so I believe."

She shifted into human form. The rain dampened her hair, and her clothes clung to her. She smiled, spread out her arms, and twirled in a circle.

"Oh, you're one of those horrible people who loves dancing in the rain, aren't you?" Rune said.

He shifted into human form too, then hugged himself as the rain chilled him. Grinning, Kaelyn grabbed his hand.

"Dance with me," she said. "Join us horrible people for one night."

He tried to tug his hand free. "Bloody stars, Kaelyn, did we fly all the way here for this—to dance in the rain? I'm cold and wet."

"Poor baby." She pouted at him, then grinned again. "The stars shine between the clouds! The old priests would always dance when rain and stars met."

She began to skip around him, tugging his arm.

"You made that up," he said.

Yet she was tugging his hand too powerfully—damn it, the girl was strong for her size!—forcing him to spin around.

"Come on!" she said and danced around him, the rain drenching her. "It's fun."

He sighed and gave a quick, sarcastic jig. "Happy?"

"Not nearly enough." She placed both arms around him and pressed her body against his. "Just... do like this. Sway a bit. That will be an easier dance for your clumsy feet. Now go on! Put your hands on my waist—like this. Don't stand there like a block of wood!"

She grabbed his hands and placed them against her waist. Rune held her awkwardly. Even through her cold, wet tunic, he felt the heat of her body. She placed her arms around him, laid her head against his shoulder, and swayed gently. Her hair smelled of grass and flowers.

Rune rolled his eyes and allowed himself to sway with her.

"This is hardly the time to dance," he said. "Not here in the rain and darkness."

She looked up at him. "It's always time to dance, especially in the darkness."

Fast as a squirrel after a nut, she broke apart from him, grabbed his hand, and tugged him.

"Now come on!" she said. "I want to show you something. Follow me. Come *on*!"

She laughed and tugged him toward the temple columns. With a sigh, he allowed himself to be pulled. They leaped over a fallen column and raced between two standing ones, entering the ruins of the temple. Only the moon and stars, shining between gaps in the clouds, lit their way.

Bricks and shattered columns littered the grass here, lumps of white upon black. Kaelyn scurried around the ruins like a dog seeking a scent. Finally she approached the fallen capital of a column, its marble carved as leaping dragons, and tapped the ground with her boot.

"Here!" she said, leaned down, and pulled a rope from the grass. She tugged open a trapdoor.

"Another gopher hole," Rune said.

Kaelyn smiled. "My favorite one."

They walked down a rough, wooden staircase and into a chamber. Kaelyn scurried around the room, lighting candles that stood upon shelves. Orange light fell upon jars of preserves, jugs of wine, racks of swords and bows, and...

Rune gasped.

"It's... me?"

Upon one wall hung a painting, life-sized, of himself clad like a king. Rune rubbed his eyes and stared. His doppelganger wore a crown, a green cloak embroidered with silver birch leaves, and a golden broach shaped as a two-headed dragon—sigil of House Aeternum. The painted king held a wide longsword, its dragonclaw pommel clutching polished amber the size of a chicken egg.

It's Amerath, Rune realized. *The Amber Sword.* It had been the sword of the Aeternum kings for a hundred years.

Kaelyn came to stand beside him. She placed a hand on his shoulder.

"You look just like him," she said.

Rune tore his eyes away from the painting. He frowned at Kaelyn.

"What kind of joke is this?" he said.

She smiled sadly. "This used to hang in the royal palace. You gaze upon Ardin Aeternum, King of Requiem, the man my father slew." She looked at Rune. "Your father."

Rune could not believe it. Could not! Surely Kaelyn had found some painter to trick him, or used dark magic, or... Rune clutched his head. Wil Brewer was his father! The Old Wheel was his home! He was only a brewer, not a prince, not...

"Oh stars," he whispered.

Kaelyn approached a rack of weapons. A dozen swords hung there, the rough and simple blades of soldiers. Among them hung a bundle of green cloth embroidered with silver dragons. Kaelyn lifted the bundle, brought it toward Rune, and held it out.

"It's yours now," she said solemnly. "It's time you raised your father's sword."

Her eyes shone with tears. She pulled back the green fabric, unveiling Amerath, the Amber Sword of Aeternum.

It was the sword from the painting; every detail was the same. The candlelight danced along the black scabbard. The platinum pommel, shaped as a dragonclaw, clutched the amber stone. It was a large sword, at least four feet long, its hilt built for two hands. It looked heavy enough to chop down trees.

To Rune's surprise, Kaelyn knelt before him, holding the sword upon her upturned palms.

"My prince," she whispered.

Rune wanted to laugh. Her prince? Stars, she was an emperor's daughter! Yet he found no mirth upon his lips. Amerath beckoned to him, and Rune reached for the hilt and wrapped his fingers around it. The black leather was warm, soft, and worked in by many hands.

"The kings of Aeternum have wielded this sword for generations," he whispered.

"Draw the blade," Kaelyn said, still kneeling before him. Her tears shone in the candlelight. "Let its light shine in a temple of Requiem."

Rune took a step back. He drew Amerath, and its blade caught the firelight and shone, golden and red and white—a shard of memory and light. Despite its size, the sword was surprisingly light; it felt lighter than the Old Wheel's broom. Rune raised the blade and saw his reflection within. He held it side by side with the painting before him.

My father and me, he thought. *The same face. The same sword. The same blood.*

"It's true," he whispered. "Stars, it's all true, isn't it Kaelyn?"

She rose to her feet. "You loved Wil; I know it. He was a father to you too, more so than the king. This will not diminish your love for Wil Brewer or cheapen your memories of him. But now you have drawn Amerath, the Amber Sword of Requiem. Now the light of Requiem shines again in the darkness."

Rune sheathed the sword.

"Well," he said. "Lovely blade. Lovely painting. I do think I'll need a better cloak now, and maybe some fancy doublet and jewels, but overall, not bad." He looked around. "There's only one more thing missing."

"What's that?" Kaelyn asked

"A chair. I really need to sit down."

He stumbled to the corner, slumped down onto his backside, and leaned against the wall. His head spun, and he clutched it. Kaelyn sat beside him and patted his shoulder.

"No chairs here, but how about a strong drink?" she asked.

"I would *love* a strong drink."

She nodded, rushed to a shelf, and grabbed a bottle. She yanked the cork out with her teeth, sat back beside Rune, and passed him the drink.

"Here," she said. "It'll help."

Rune drank. It was strong rye—southern brew, he thought, possibly even from Cadport. The spirits burned down his throat and through his head. Stars, it felt good. He passed Kaelyn the bottle.

"I think you deserve a drink too."

She took a swig, then wrinkled her nose. "Horrible stuff. I don't know how Valien can drink it."

"It's *fantastic* stuff," Rune said. "And I reckon it's from my hometown or very near it. We would serve this in the Old Wheel." He sighed. "But the Old Wheel is gone now. And Wil is gone. And this sword is here."

Kaelyn leaned over and kissed his cheek. "And I'm here. I'm here to help you, Rune. You're not alone."

His cheek blazed; her kiss shot through him, stronger than the spirits. Rune drank again and Kaelyn leaned against him. He placed his arm around her and found himself stroking her hair— soft, golden hair like silk. Her breath fluttered warm against his neck, and she placed her hand on his thigh. They huddled in the dark and cold, passing the bottle back and forth.

"I don't like any of this," Rune said. "And I never wanted this war. I hold no love for your father, but I never wanted to pick up a sword and fight him. But yes, my home is gone now. My best friend is a soldier, and my family is dead. Like it or not, this is my life now."

"You have a new family," Kaelyn whispered. "You have me, and Valien, and the rest of us. You will never be alone. Will you fly with us?"

She was looking up at him, her eyes large and her lips parted.

"I will fly with you," he said. "I'm no warrior; I don't know how to wield this sword. But I can fly as a dragon and roar fire, and however I can help you, I will, Kaelyn. I will fly by your side."

She smiled tremulously and touched his cheek, and her tears fell.

Rune kissed her. He did not mean to. He did not want to. Yet he stroked her hair, and he kissed her, and her tears mingled in their kiss. It was warm and soft and wet, and it tasted of spirits, and Rune never wanted it to end. He held Kaelyn in his arms, and she was so small, a delicate doll held against him, and at that moment Rune loved her—loved this woman who had dragged him from his home into shadow and fire.

He pulled away from her, leaving her breathing heavily, her cheeks flushed.

I can't, he thought. *I have Tilla. I can't. This is wrong.*

Kaelyn leaned against him, wrapped in his arms, and smiled softly. She closed her eyes and slept in his embrace.

TILLA

Tilla stood in the square, arms pressed to her sides and chin raised. Her helmet topped her head. Her leather armor still squeezed her, so tight she could barely breathe. She kept her fist around the hilt of her sword.

Nairi stood before the phalanx, face twisted like a woman staring at dung upon her boot.

"Listen up, maggots!" the lanse shouted. "You are now divided into flights of three. These flights are your life! In tunnels and halls, you will swing swords in threes. In the skies, you will roar fire as three dragons. Every flight will have one leader—one attacker!—and two defenders. Do you understand?"

"Yes, Commander!" Tilla shouted along with the others.

It was the only acceptable answer, of course. One recruit, only an hour ago, had dared to ask a question. Nairi had driven her punisher into the girl for so long her flesh had cracked.

Flight commanders, Tilla thought and sucked in her breath. She knew that dragons flew in threes—two defending one attacker—but not how the attacker was determined.

I'm going to find out now.

"First flight!" Nairi shouted. "Forward."

Three recruits—those who formed the left flank of the formation—stepped forward. They glanced around nervously and clutched their swords. They were the daughters of farmers; Tilla vaguely remembered them selling eggs, fruits, and grains in harvest fairs. Today they wore armor and bore blades.

Nairi snarled at the farm girls.

"If you ask me, all three of you are worms. You should be squirming under my boots, not standing before me in armor." The lanse raised her voice. "The last one among you standing will eat and sleep tonight! The two who fall first—you will spend the night cleaning the outhouses. Do you understand?"

"Yes, Commander!" the three answered, faces pale.

"Your swords are blunt," Nairi said, "but they will still bruise flesh. Swing them! Last one standing will lead your flight."

The girls glanced at one another, hesitating.

Stars, oh stars, just swing your blades, Tilla thought.

Yet the girls did not move.

With a snarl, Nairi drew her punisher. She drove the crackling rod into one girl.

The recruit screamed. She fell into the dust. Her body convulsed, and Nairi knelt above her, growling and shoving her punisher against the girl's belly. The girl doubled up, weeping and begging and smoking.

Finally, after what seemed like ages, Nairi withdrew her punisher and rose to her feet. She spat onto the fallen girl.

"This one is out," she said. She looked up at the two recruits who still stood. "Go on—fight each other! Or I'll burn another one."

The two recruits swallowed, drew their blunt blades, and began to swing at one another. Steel clanged.

"Faster!" Nairi screamed. "Harder! Beat her bloody."

The steel kept clashing. Finally one girl disarmed the other, slamming blade onto wrist.

"Finish her!" Nairi ordered. "Beat her down."

The armed girl's eyes were damp, yet she obeyed. She swung her blunt sword against her friend's legs, sending her falling.

Nairi spat in disgust. "Useless cockroaches, you are." She snarled at the last girl standing. "You lead your miserable trio of worms. Drag the other two back to formation." She turned back to the ranks. "Next flight—you three, forward!"

The next flight stepped forward.

More blades swung.

As Tilla stood, watching each trio fight for leadership, she heard wings thudding overhead. She looked up to see a red dragon descend into the square, fire streaming between his teeth. Tilla sucked in her breath and her heart thrashed.

Prince Leresy.

The dragon landed before the phalanx, shook his head, and scattered curtains of smoke. He shifted into human form, placed his hands on his hips, and smiled. His plate armor shone in the dawn, black steel bedecked with gold. His golden hair shone just as bright.

Whispers and gasps flowed across the ranks, and Tilla's heart thudded. Smiling thinly, Prince Leresy stared directly at her—into her—and winked.

"Hail Prince Leresy!" Nairi shouted and slammed her fist against her chest. "Kneel before your prince."

Nairi knelt, fist clutched to heart. The rest of her phalanx, Tilla among them, repeated the salute and knelt too. Tilla kept her head lowered, daring not look up, but she could feel Leresy still staring at her.

Stars, why does he look at me among everyone? she thought. She only wanted to be a good soldier here, to fit in and fly low. And yet wherever she went, it seemed, she attracted trouble like flowers attracted bees.

"Back on your feet!" rose his voice; it was smooth and melodious and still carried the high pitch of youth. "Carry on, please. I've only come to watch my troops, not interfere."

Tilla made the mistake of glancing back at the prince—just a glance—and caught him staring at her. His lips peeled back and he licked his teeth. She looked back at Nairi... just in time to hear the lanse shout her name.

"Tilla Roper!" Nairi pointed her crackling punisher at her. "You and those two dogs of yours—forward! Let's see who among you will sleep tonight, and who will clean nightsoil from a ditch."

Heart pounding, Tilla stepped forward, leaving the formation of her phalanx. The square seemed to spin around her. She felt hundreds of eyes watching her—her fellow recruits, her commander, and her prince. She glanced over her shoulder to see Mae frozen, her face pale, and Erry trying to shove her forward.

"Roper, bring your two whores forward, or you'll taste my fire!" Nairi screamed.

It took some tugging from Tilla, and more pushing from Erry, to bring the trembling Mae out of formation and into the dust of the square. The three recruits stood together, trapped between the rest of their phalanx, Lanse Nairi, and Prince Leresy.

"Draw your swords," Nairi ordered.

Tilla drew her blade. She gave it a few quick swings. It whistled as it sliced the air.

Whenever Tilla had seen soldiers carrying swords—especially wide longswords like this one, their hilts large enough for two hands—she had thought them crude weapons for hacking and slashing. Yet this sword, even blunted, was light and agile. It felt no heavier than waving a sprig of holly. The blade was long and wide but flexible, and despite herself Tilla smiled. For the first time, she thought of soldiers not as brutes hacking with crude chunks of metal, but as artists mastering an ancient dance.

At her side, Erry was waving her sword around, slicing the air. The slim girl seemed just as impressed; her eyes shone, and her lips peeled back in a smile. Mae, however, wasn't even testing her blade; she merely held it before her, and it wobbled like her lip.

I think I'll only have one contender here, Tilla thought.

Nairi took a deep breath, opened her mouth, and seemed ready to order the duel start. Before the lanse could speak, however, the prince interrupted.

"A moment," he said, raising his hand.

Again he was looking straight at Tilla, and her heart thudded. He walked toward her, and Tilla stood frozen before him, sword in hand, not sure if to salute, kneel, or simply stand still.

When Prince Leresy reached her, his lips peeled back in a smile, but it looked hungry, the smile of a wolf. His eyes scanned her from top to bottom; they lingered against her breasts, which pressed against her leather armor. He reached out, fast as a viper, and clutched her wrist.

Tilla gasped.

He's going to kill me, she thought. *Stars, I did something wrong, and he's going to kill me now—just like his sister Shari killed the girl back at Cadport.*

But Leresy only turned her wrist, adjusting her grip on the sword.

"Here," he said. "Like this. Hold your right hand a little higher on the hilt. Now place your left hand beneath it near the pommel—like that. Give the blade a swing—from top to bottom." The prince stepped back, and Tilla dutifully swung her sword. Leresy's face split into a grin, and he clapped.

"Splendid!" he said. "Now here, move your left hand to the base of the blade—just above the hilt. Don't worry, it's not sharp. This is called half-swording—a different grip. Give it a try."

Leresy stepped back again, and Tilla gave the blade a few more swings. Holding the sword this way, her thrusts were shorter but more powerful.

"Good!" Leresy said. "You use this one for piercing armor. A strong soldier can break steel this way. Shorter range but tougher punch."

He stepped toward her again and reached between her legs. Tilla gasped, but Leresy only winked and moved her thighs apart.

"Don't get all flustered," he said. "I'm just fixing your stance. Here, like this—legs parted, right leg forward. Try again! This time strike my blade."

He drew his sword and Tilla's eyes widened. His was a beautiful blade. Its dark steel shone with ripples like midnight waves. Its golden, dragonclaw pommel clutched an egg-sized ruby. Tilla hated to attack such a beautiful weapon—what if she chipped it?—but Leresy beckoned her, and so Tilla swung her blade.

He parried. The two swords rang.

"Excellent!" Leresy said. He slammed his sword back into its scabbard. "What's your name, soldier?"

"Tilla," she said. "Tilla Roper."

Leresy nodded. "I'll remember you."

But there was no pride or kindness in his voice; there was only lust. Tilla had served tables at Rune's tavern when she could not sell enough ropes; she had seen such lust in the eyes of many drunkards.

He cares less for blades of steel, she thought, *and more for the blade between his legs—one he would thrust into me.*

Leresy clutched her shoulder and looked over at Nairi.

"This one is a warrior!" he announced.

Tilla glanced over at her commander... and what she saw chilled her more than Leresy's lust. Pure, blazing fire filled Nairi's eyes. Her cheeks flushed red. Her teeth grinded. She stared at Tilla with a look of such unadulterated hatred that Tilla felt herself blanch.

But... but it's not my fault! she wanted to shout out. *I didn't ask the prince to speak to me, I...*

For the first time, Nairi did not shout. She spoke in a low, venomous hiss, and it seemed to Tilla more cruel than all the screams in the Abyss.

"Let us see the great warrior in action," she said. "Fight!"

Immediately, Erry roared and launched into a wild attack.

Tilla gasped and raised her sword; Erry was charging like an enraged badger disturbed from its den. Yet Tilla parried only air. Erry wasn't attacking her; the diminutive urchin swung her blade against Mae Baker.

Mae squealed. She raised her sword in a useless attempt to parry. Erry's blunt blade slammed against Mae's chest, thudding against the leather armor.

Tears budded in Mae's eyes. She fell to her knees, and her sword thumped into the dust.

"I yield!" she cried and covered her head with her arms. "I yield!"

Roaring, her face red, Erry turned and came charging toward Tilla. Her sword swung in mad arcs.

"Bloody stars!" Tilla cursed and swung her blade.

She had never parried a sword before; she had to learn fast. Her blade checked Erry's onslaught. The short, brown-haired girl barely seemed fazed. She leaped back, then charged again, thrusting her sword. All around, the other troops gasped and a few cheered.

Tilla parried again. *Stars damn it!* Erry was no taller than her shoulders, yet the little beast seemed unstoppable. Her blows kept flying. It was like a rabid rodent attacking a wolf.

The blades clanged. Erry screamed. Her sword swung. The blade slammed down onto Tilla's shoulder.

Pain exploded. Erry's sword was blunt, and Tilla's leather pauldron stopped the blade, but the damn thing hurt. Agony shot down to her fingertips. Erry's blade swung again, and this time Tilla managed to parry, then attack.

Her blade swung. It slammed into Erry's hand.

The dock rat screamed, her fingers opened, and her sword fell.

Tilla kicked the fallen blade; it flew across the square. She breathed raggedly. She lowered her own sword, thinking the battle was over.

She was wrong.

Howling, Erry leaped onto Tilla and clung to her. The little demon bit Tilla's wrist.

"Erry, stars damn it!" Tilla shouted. Her own sword fell into the dust. "Get off."

Erry still clung to her, biting and clawing at her armor, trying to reach her face. Tilla fell to the ground. Erry fell upon her, scratching and screaming, her eyes wild.

"Fantastic!" Prince Leresy called somewhere in the distance.

"Abyss damn it!" Tilla said.

She lay on her back, Erry atop her. This dockside orphan was perhaps half her size, but fast and wild and strong. With a grunt, Tilla kicked and managed to flip herself over. Now Erry lay on her back, Tilla atop her.

"Damn it, Erry!" Tilla said.

The girl squirmed and screamed below her. Tilla cursed and finally managed to pin her down.

"Get off me!" Erry shouted, face red.

"Calm yourself," Tilla said. "Stars, Erry, I'm bigger than you and I have you pinned down. Do you yield?"

Erry stopped struggling. She lay still for a moment and scrunched her lips. She looked from side to side, as if deep in thought, and bit her lip. Finally she flashed a toothy grin.

"All right!" she said brightly. "I yield. Good fight. Now get off me, you lumbering mule, before I bite your face off. You're bloody heavy, you are."

Tilla grabbed her sword, rose to her feet, and helped Erry up. She then approached Mae, who still lay mewling in the dust, and helped her stand too. Tilla felt pride well up inside her. She raised her chin and thrust out her chest.

I won! she thought. *I'm flight commander! I've only been a soldier for a few days, and I can already command two others.*

She turned toward Nairi, expecting to see the officer give her a grudging nod. But Nairi was still glaring, hatred blazing in her eyes. That glare was so strong Tilla took a step back and swallowed.

She wanted me to lose, she realized.

"Splendid!" Prince Leresy said. He approached and clasped Tilla on the shoulder. "I must be a good teacher. I'll be keeping an eye out for you, Tilla Roper." He leaned down and whispered into her ear. "Perhaps someday you will visit my chamber, and I can give you some private lessons."

Tilla stood stiff and still. Her knees trembled only the slightest. She looked over at Nairi; rage still flamed in the officer's green eyes, but pain dwelled there too, and Tilla understood.

She loves the prince, Tilla thought. *Oh stars damn it, Nairi and the prince... and me in the middle.* She wanted to shout out. *This isn't my fault! I didn't ask for Leresy's affections!*

"Well!" the prince said. "I've seen enough for one day. Lanse Nairi, keep up the good work. You'll whip these girls into warriors yet."

With that, the prince shifted back into a red dragon, took flight with a cloud of smoke, and disappeared over the walls.

When the smoke and dust settled, Tilla turned back toward Nairi, hesitating. She gasped to see the lanse draw her punisher, snarl, and come marching toward her.

"Lanse Nairi," Tilla began, "I—"

Nairi drew her sword, slammed Tilla's blade aside, and drove her punisher forward.

Pain exploded across Tilla's chest.

She couldn't help it. She screamed and fell to her knees.

"You were to fight with swords," Nairi said through clenched teeth, shoving her punisher against Tilla. "I teach swordplay, not wrestling, you seaside scum."

Tilla gasped for breath. Lightning flowered across her. She screamed again. She tried to clutch at Nairi's wrists, to push the punisher back, but her arms felt rubbery like loose skin.

"Please!" she tried to say, but screams drowned her words.

Tilla fell onto her back and writhed in the dust.

"Please, no!" somebody called behind her.

"Lanse Nairi, please!" cried another soldier.

Tilla could barely hear them. Tears streamed down her cheeks. Nairi knelt above her, snarling, twisting her punisher as if trying to shove the rod through Tilla's chest. Smoke rose from her. Tilla's eyes rolled back. Darkness, pain, and fire flowed over her world.

RUNE

"Again!" Valien barked and thrust his wooden sword.

Cursing, Rune tried to block the attack. His own practice weapon blocked Valien's. A second thrust flew. Rune checked the blow; the two wooden blades clanked. The third thrust slammed into his chest, and Rune gasped and fell back two steps.

"Dead again," Valien said in disgust. "If I were Frey Cadigus, you wouldn't last five heartbeats."

Valien Eleison, leader of the Resistance, stood clad in a steel breastplate, tan breeches, and leather boots. Sweat matted his grizzled hair and clung to his stubble like dew to grass.

"If you were Frey Cadigus," Rune said, "I would shift into a dragon and burn your arse."

Rune wiped sweat off his brow. He wore a breastplate too, but Valien's thrusts—even with a wooden sword—left his chest aching. He imagined that bruises spread beneath the steel.

Valien spat into the dust. "Dragon? Frey Cadigus dwells deep in his fortress; its corridors are too small for dragons. You'd have to fight his guards foot by foot, man by man. I doubt you'd slay one before they captured you."

The ruins of Confutatis sprawled around them, a hodgepodge of fallen columns, the shells of towers, crumbled walls, and countless bricks strewn across dead grass. It was a tapestry all in whites, tans, yellows, and grays. Men and women of the Resistance, clad in robes the colors of these ruins, stood upon what remained of the walls and towers. They bore swords of real steel, and they clutched bows. They said nothing. They only watched.

Rune growled, raised his wooden sword, and swung it at Valien.

The older man scowled, knocked the blow aside, and slammed his wooden blade against Rune's shoulder.

"Stars damn it!" Rune cursed.

Valien snarled and whacked Rune's shoulder again. "Never curse by your stars. Your stars saved your life, boy. That's more than your skill with the sword would do, it seems."

Rune tossed that sword down, spat, and glared at Valien.

"It isn't fair!" he said. "You've been fighting all your life. You were a knight. I was a brewer until a moon ago."

"Pick up your sword," Valien said. His eyes blazed and his face reddened. "It isn't fair? Life's not fair, boy. Was it fair when Frey slew your parents? Was it fair when he toppled this city? Was it fair when my w—" The grizzled warrior stopped himself and gritted his teeth. "Life is cruel and death is crueler. You can cry about how things aren't fair, or you can stand tall and *make* things fair."

Rune stared at the man. Rage flared inside him like dragonfire. *You are why I'm here!* Rune wanted to shout. *You sent Kaelyn to drag me out of my home, to take me here, to...*

As fast as it had flared, his rage dissipated. He thought back to the night with Kaelyn in the rain. That sword—the Amber Sword of Aeternum—stood against a fallen statue only feet away.

Make things fair.

Rune grumbled, reached down to his fallen wooden sword, and lifted it.

"The wooden sword's too heavy," he said. "The Amber Sword is light and fast. I could parry assaults with that one."

Valien's face softened, and he sighed and nodded. "The wooden sword needs to be heavy," he said. "It will strengthen you. When you've trained with thick wood, thin steel will seem lighter than air. You are right, Relesar Aeternum. Until a moon ago, you were only Rune Brewer, not a warrior, and I've been swinging swords for longer than you've lived. But now you are a warrior. Now you too will fight. I will bruise you here, Rune, until your body aches so badly, you will even dream of pain. But it will make you strong." Valien smiled thinly. "When training is hard, the battle is easy."

"I don't want to fight any battle," Rune said.

Valien clasped his shoulder. "Nor do any good men. A brute craves battle. A coward flees from it. The wise man hates war, but will fight to defend what he loves."

"And what do we defend, Valien?" Rune asked. "What do we love?" He swept his arm around. "A pile of ruins? Bricks and broken statues?"

"An idea," Valien said. "A memory. A story as old as starlight. We defend the light of Requiem, even as darkness closes in around us. We defend the heart and soul of our people. And that, Rune, is one battle I am willing to fight."

Rune thought about this for a moment. Valien's words rang true to him. Rune too wanted to fight for light, for the soul of Requiem, and for justice. And yet... he wondered. Valien's men— some said Valien himself—had slain Tilla's brother. The Resistance had slain many legionaries. Those soldiers had not been bloodthirsty worshippers of the red spiral. They had been humble farmers and tradesmen—people like his friends from Cadport— torn from their homes, given swords, and sent to die. Frey was evil and deserved death, but could the same be said for his soldiers, the youths the Resistance killed?

Can light shine in a kingdom so shadowed in death? Rune wondered. *Can we ever light the beacons of justice after shedding so much blood?*

He did not know. But he nodded. Fighting was *something*, he thought—fighting was standing up, flying onward, and making a change. That, Rune thought, was still better than hiding in shadows.

Sweat dripped into his eyes, and he wiped it with his hand, then raised his wooden sword again.

"All right, old man," Rune said. "You're going to slow down soon, and when you do, I'll be the one making bruises."

With a grin that looked almost like a snarl, Valien nodded and lashed his sword, and the wooden blades clattered.

That evening, the Resistance gathered in the fallen hall of old kings, the place where Rune had first met Valien. Candles burned upon the craggy walls. Trestle tables stood topped with bread rolls, smoked meats, dried fruits, cheeses, and nuts. Men and women, their robes and faces dusty, raised mugs of ale and drank deeply. Steam, smoke, and the scents of the feast filled the air.

Hundreds of warriors filled this grand hall. Across the ruins of Confutatis, two thousand others gathered in burrows, abandoned homes, and old cellars. This city had become a place of bones and old blood, but today light and hope shone here again.

"It is the Night of Seven!" Valien announced, standing at the head table of his hall. He raised a goblet of ale. "Tonight is the holiest night of Requiem's stars. Tonight marks a thousand years since the heroes of Requiem, the seven who survived the Great Slaughter, stood and rekindled the light of Requiem." Valien raised the goblet higher, and hundreds of mugs rose across the hall, returning the salute. "We live in a time of darkness. Requiem lies cloaked in shadows—the shadows of the Cadigus Regime." The resistors hissed across the hall, and Valien spoke louder. "Tonight we say: Like the Living Seven, we will fight. We will keep our light blazing. Tonight let us drink for those old heroes, and let us vow to continue their fight."

Valien drank deeply from his goblet. Across the hall, hundreds of warriors drank from their mugs.

Rune drank too. The ale was bitter and dark, but it flowed well down his throat and warmed his belly. This feast, these candles, and these stories warmed him like the ale. Back in Cadport, soldiers never spoke of the Living Seven, the ancient heroes of Requiem. Soldiers never spoke of the stars. They only hailed the red spiral, worshipped Frey Cadigus, and mostly they hated—they hated the Resistance, they hated the old enemies of Requiem, and they hated the fallen Aeternum Dynasty for its weakness.

"Here there is no hate," Rune said softly into his mug. "Here there is memory and camaraderie and hope."

At his side, Kaelyn placed her mug down, wiped suds off her lips, and touched his hand. She smiled softly, and the candlelight glowed in her eyes. Their fingers twined together under the table.

"I'm glad you're here with us, Rune," she said and squeezed his hand.

Rune thought back to how he had kissed Kaelyn; this memory too warmed him. When he looked at her now, he could almost feel her lips again. Kaelyn's hazel eyes shone, her hair cascaded like waves of molten gold, and her smile warmed him more than hearth fire. His hand, which held hers, felt more alive than his entire body.

I want to fly with her again, he thought, *to dance in the night, to hold her body against me, to feel her lips against mine.* She drew him like heat draws a freezing man, so powerfully he could barely breathe.

With a bolt of pain, he tore his eyes away. He stared at the tabletop.

Tilla, he thought. *Tilla Roper. I walked with her on the beach. I kissed her too. I vowed to see her again.* His throat stung. *How will I find you now, Tilla? Do you too have food, friends, and a warm fire? Or are you cold and afraid, and do you need me?*

He felt a hand in his hair. Kaelyn was looking at him, eyes soft with concern.

"Rune," she said, "you look sad."

He forced a smile and drank some more. "Are you going to force me to dance again?"

She laughed. "Of course I am! Many more times. For the rest of your life. But not now—now we do not dance. Now we sing." She stepped onto her chair, raised her mug, and cried out to the hall. "Vir Requis, let us sing the song of our people. Will you rise and sing the Old Words with me?"

They rose across the hall, hundreds of men and women with gaunt faces but bright eyes, with calloused hands but raised heads. Kaelyn stood before them, and she sang, and their voices rang with hers. Rune realized that he knew these words—his grandfather used to sing them on quiet nights—and Rune joined his voice to theirs.

"As the leaves fall upon our marble tiles, as the breeze rustles the birches beyond our columns, as the sun gilds the mountains above our halls—know, young child of the woods, you are home, you are home. Requiem! May our wings forever find your sky."

They all drank again, and when Kaelyn turned toward Rune, her eyes were solemn, her smile gone.

"The song of Requiem," Rune said to her. "It is forbidden now."

She nodded. "My father forbade it, but it is old beyond reckoning; we have been singing this song for thousands of years. We will sing it again in the palace of Nova Vita, and starlight will fall upon us." She raised her mug again and cried to the crowd. "Blessed be Relesar Aeternum, rightful King of Requiem! Blessed be his name!"

The hall erupted with cries.

"Blessed be Aeternum!" they called. "Stars bless the rightful king!"

Their cries echoed all around. Men and women stood waving their mugs and chanting his name. Rune stood up too, uneasy. Maybe it was the ale, but the room spun around him, a sea of faces and voices and eyes.

"Blessed be Relesar Aeternum, the rightful king!" they cried.

Rune looked around, feeling his face flush and stomach clench. He wanted the ruins to collapse and bury him; never had so many eyes stared at him. He wanted to cry out: *But I'm not a king, only a brewer. Not Relesar, only Rune!* Yet he remained silent. He had accepted Amerath, the Amber Sword. He had drunk from these men's brew; if not as a king, then as a brewer, he knew the significance of that. And so he only stood silently. Perhaps it was the best thing he could do now.

They ate, drank, and sang long into the night—a night of light and heat and Kaelyn's hand holding his.

LERESY

He stood above the infirmary bed, looking down at the burnt, wretched girl. A sigh flowed through him.

"By the stars, Nairi," he said. "You didn't have to burn the damn girl half to death."

The young lanse leaned against a wall, arms crossed and face twisted into a scowl.

"Don't you bloody mention the stars," she spat at him. "Your father would beat *you* half to death if he heard you mention them."

Lersey rolled his eyes. "Oh yes—it's red spiral this and red spiral that now. Of course. Only you're forgetting something, my dearest Nairi." He pointed at her. "You are a lowly lanse, a junior officer not worthy to lick my boots, and I am your prince. Granted, a prince you're bedding, but your prince nonetheless. And if I want to mention the bloody old gods..." He raised his voice to a shout. "I will!"

Nairi only glowered at him; he could hear her teeth grind.

With another sigh, Leresy turned back to look at the bed. The soldier lay there, her eyes shut, her bandaged chest rising and falling as she slept. Burn marks stretched out from the bandage like cobwebs; they spread across her shoulders, neck, and arms.

A memory pounded through Leresy, making him wince. How many times had he seen Kaelyn lying wounded like this, all burnt and bloody? So often throughout their childhood, Leresy would stand weeping as Frey, or sometimes Shari, beat and whipped and burned his sister. So many times Leresy would kneel over his wounded twin, trying to comfort her, to heal her.

Just be strong, the boy would whisper to his twin. *Be strong and they won't hurt you.*

But Kaelyn had always been too weak. Leresy had grown strong and survived; Kaelyn had fled.

And now Tilla too lay wounded. Would she grow strong like he had, or would she shatter and flee like Kaelyn?

"Nairi has done a job on you, Tilla Roper," Leresy said with a sad shake of his head. "I'm quite afraid that when you do wake up, you'll be sore for a good moon or two."

Behind him, he heard leather creak and boots stomp toward him. He turned to see Nairi marching his way, her teeth bared. She drew her punisher and held its crackling tip between them.

"How about I finish the job now," she said. "I'll burn that whore into a scarred, twisted freak of melted flesh and sores. But I'll leave her eyes. Yes. I want to leave her eyes so she can see the monster she's become."

"Or," Leresy said, "you can calm yourself before I demote you from lanse to dung shoveler." He pulled her arm down. "For pity's sake, Nairi, put that thing away. You've had your fun. The girl fought well. Your job is to train warriors here, to cull the weak and foster the strong, not disfigure the best in your phalanx."

Nairi snorted a laugh. "So you think her the best in my phalanx? Have you seen them all fight? Or do you simply choose the tall ones with the nice t—"

"Nairi!" he roared. When she fell silent, his voice softened. "Nairi. Are you jealous? Yes, she is tall, and yes, she does have a rather splendid pair of breasts on her. I see them. I like them. I'm the prince of Requiem; I'll stare at as many splendid pairs of breasts as I like. But the only ones I'll touch, Nairi, are these."

He reached for her chest. She glared and slapped his hand away.

"Don't you touch me, Leresy Cadigus," she said. "Your father is far from this land. We are in the south here, and the Black Rose is my phalanx—mine to lead! You are a prince, yes, but you do not serve in the Legions. I do. Within the Black Rose, I am ruler, I am supreme." She hissed. "And if you ever interfere with my command again, and if you ever touch one of my soldiers again, my father will hear of it." She gave him a caustic grin. "You're not the only one with great parentage, Leresy Cadigus."

Leresy opened his mouth to retort, then closed it.

Abyss damn it, he thought. The woman was right. Leresy was perhaps the son of the emperor, but he wasn't heir to the throne—not until he figured out how to kill Shari, at least. But Nairi... Nairi was firstborn daughter of Herin Blackrose, lord of the Axehand

Order. If anyone in Requiem approached the emperor in might, it was Lord Herin.

And isn't that why you're here in the first place, Leresy Cadigus? he asked himself. *Do not forget your purpose. You're not here to bed young recruits with large dark eyes—at least, not only. You flew down to this wretched, southern cesspool to woo power. And power means Nairi.*

He had the grace to lower his head.

"Nairi, you are right. What can I say? I am a young, foolish man, and my blood is hot, and I think with my pants more than my head. What young man is different?" He placed an arm around the small of her back. "But the only woman I love is you, Lanse Nairi Blackrose. Not common girls. Not seaside soldiers. Just you, Nairi—my rose of Requiem."

He tried to pull her into an embrace, but she resisted and snapped her teeth at him.

"Do not try to woo me like I'm some common harlot," she said. "I've heard of your conquests in the capital; they say you bedded half the women in Nova Vita. Don't mistake me for another conquest. I am an officer in the Legions, not one of your courtesans."

Though she struggled against him, Leresy pulled her close, pressing her body against his. He hissed into her ear between clenched teeth.

"Oh, but I *will* conquer you." He slid a hand between her legs. "And you *are* but a whore. I know it. You know it. And I know that you love it. You are mine, Nairi Blackrose. I am your prince, and you are mine, and I will do with you as I like." He shoved her toward an infirmary bed, the one beside the cot Tilla lay on. "And I'm going to prove this to you right here."

She stood with her back to the bed, narrowed her eyes, and hissed at him like a cornered animal. He stepped toward her. Her grabbed her clothes, tore at them, and shoved her onto the mattress.

And he conquered her. And he showed her who she was.

"Who am I?" he hissed into her ear as he thrust into her.

"My... prince," she whispered.

"I own you, Nairi Blackrose. Don't you forget it. You do not command me. I am your lord, and I will be your husband."

As he claimed her and she moaned below him, Leresy looked over to the bed beside them where Tilla still slept.

You will be mine too, Tilla Roper, he thought as Nairi screamed and tugged at his hair.

Moments later, as Nairi was collecting her fallen clothes, Leresy approached a bronze mirror that stood behind the beds. He stared at his reflection and passed a hand through his golden hair, fixing an errant strand. He smoothed his doublet and nodded in satisfaction.

"I'm thinking of returning to the capital when the moon is full," he said, speaking to Nairi's reflection in the mirror. "I will announce our betrothal then. We've waited long enough, Nairi. I'm eighteen now. I'm of age. I'll not wait longer. Let us marry here, in my fort, this winter."

She looked up from tugging on her leggings. Her reflection met his eyes.

"You've only just claimed lordship over this fort," she said. "Already you rush to be wed?"

He turned from the mirror to face her. "I thought you would be glad," he said. "Were you not complaining of my wandering eye? Marriage sticks a dagger into that eye. Knowing you, you'd make sure of that." He stepped toward her and held her. "Nairi, I love you. I want to marry you this winter. Not in the spring. Not next year. Not in the capital. But here—in our fort, in our home, in our passion. I will fly to the capital, and I will ask your father for your hand."

She gave him a sidelong glance. "My father. That would be... my father the commander of the Axehand Order."

Leresy stiffened. "That is his position, yes. A useful servant to my family."

"A powerful servant," Nairi said. "Some would say not a servant at all, but... an ally, maybe even a danger. Sometimes I wonder, Leresy, whose backside you crave more—mine to bed or his to kiss."

"Can't I do both?"

It was a mistake, he knew; he regretted those words at once. And yet they tickled him, and he could not stop a grin from spreading across his lips. To his great, great relief, even Nairi's lips twisted into a small smile.

"My poor, lustful prince," she said and mussed his hair. "Lustful for flesh and for power; which will win?" She placed a hand behind his neck, craned her neck upward, and hissed into his ear. "I too play this game, dearest prince. I too crave power. And yes, you are powerful, Prince Leresy. You are powerful in my bed and in the courts of your father. Fly to the capital. Ask for my hand. We will wed this winter, here in Castra Luna, and someday I will be queen."

He raised an eyebrow. "You do know that Shari is heir to the throne."

She kissed his lips, smiled crookedly, and patted his cheek. "Not for long."

TILLA

She lay abed, wrapped in pain.

When she opened her eyes, firelight seared them. When she breathed, the air sawed at her throat. She tried to wriggle in bed and froze at once; the blankets rubbing against her skin cut her like blades.

What had happened? Tilla could barely remember. Her mind felt foggy. Thoughts floated like clouds, and she could not grasp them. She recalled only training with a sword, and Prince Leresy touching her legs, and...

Nairi.

The memory thudded back into her.

The pain! The pain had pounded through her for so long, so hot, all consuming; it had rattled her teeth, raised welts across her, and twisted her fingers and toes. Tilla had thought her bones would dislocate and her skin shatter.

It's not my fault! Tilla had wanted to cry, but she could only scream, beg, weep, and fall into endless agony and darkness.

"Tilla!" a voice said, muffled and distant and echoing, a voice from another world. "Tilla, can you hear me?"

Tilla blinked. Two shadows stood before her, dark blurs upon orange light. It seemed the shadows were speaking, but the voices sounded so distant Tilla could barely hear.

"Stars, Tilla, can't you hear me?" one shadow said, speaking louder.

"Oh, bloody puke soup, Nairi did a job on her," said the other shadow. "I swear, I'm going to grab that woman's punisher and shove it up her fat arse!"

"Language, Erry!" said the first shadow. "I told you to watch your language. You're not living on the docks anymore."

"As if this place is any damn better! How about you go eat hairy donkey bollocks, Wobble Lips. Get your mouth dirty for once."

The two shadows began to shove each other. Groaning in pain, Tilla forced herself onto her elbows and blinked vigorously. Slowly the shadows came into focus, becoming two young women. One was pale and doll-like, her golden hair braided—Mae! The other was scrawny, her short brown hair rising in tangles—Erry! Her two friends didn't even notice her sit up; they were busy hitting and scolding each other. Oil lanterns lined the wall behind them, lighting a stone chamber with several empty beds.

"Will you two stop it?" Tilla demanded, voice raspy.

"Now don't you butt in!" Erry said. "This is between me and Wobble Lips, and—" Erry froze and her eyes widened. "Tilla! Sweaty codpieces, you're awake and talking!"

Tilla fell back into bed and groaned. "Barely."

At once, the two girls leaped onto her bed and began to bounce and cheer.

"You're alive!" Mae said and hugged her. "Oh stars, Tilla, I was sure she *killed* you."

Erry was bouncing up and down. "I knew our flight commander would live! We're going to make you strong enough to *kill* that rat Nairi someday."

Every bounce of the bed sent pain thudding through Tilla, and she moaned.

"Ow, ow!" she said. "Stop it. Please."

The two soldiers froze.

"Sorry!" Mae said and gasped. "I... did I hurt you?"

Tilla waved weakly. "Never mind that. Just... sit still and speak quietly. Where am I? How long have been sleeping?"

"You're in the fortress infirmary," Erry said and gestured around at several empty beds. "You're the only one here now. Usually when somebody upsets the lanses that bad, they end up buried, not bedridden. You were damn lucky, Roper. You've been here for..." She counted on her fingers. "This is the second night."

"You need to count on your fingers for only two nights?" Mae said. "Stars, Erry, you are a dumb one."

"You're the one who thought the infirmary was the barracks for ground troops!" Erry retorted. "That's *infantry*. I told you that a million times, barnacle brain, Tilla was wounded, not drafted into the ground forces."

Mae sniffed and tears filled her eyes. "Well it's not my fault. I don't know all these soldier things. At least I can count properly!"

The two girls began to hit each other again, and the bouncing shot more pain through Tilla.

"Stop!" Tilla said. "Please." She rubbed her eyes. "How bad is it?"

The girls fell silent and Mae began to weep. Tilla dared to lift the blanket and look down at her body. She closed her eyes.

Stars.

Nairi had indeed done a job on her, as Erry had said. Below the blanket, bruises and welts covered Tilla's naked body. Her leather armor had perhaps protected her from dulled swords, but not from Nairi's punisher. She wondered if she'd forever carry these scars.

"It's... not that bad," Erry said. "Really, Till. Stars, I got beat up worse on the docks a few times, and I'm still standing." The waif snarled. "You're going to keep fighting, Roper, or I'm going to beat you up even worse."

Sniffing back tears, Mae reached into a pack she carried and pulled out a bundle of cloth. When she unwrapped the fabric, the scents of honey and bread filled Tilla's nostrils so powerfully her mouth watered, and she couldn't help but moan. Inside the bundle lay three plump pastries still steaming from the oven.

"Honey cakes!" Mae said. "With raisins in them. We, uhm... kind of... stole them."

Erry nodded. "It was a daring heist: sneaking out of our tent at night, breaking into the kitchens, grabbing honey cakes, and finally climbing the wall into this place. Forget being soldiers. We should become thieves."

"Oh, you were always a thief," Mae said to the girl. "She has a lock pick set, Tilla! Stars, a real one, with a bunch of little skeleton keys and wires and stuff. I bet she stole from at least half the houses in Cadport."

Erry raised her chin. "More than half! By the way, Mae, nice little doll collection you've got in your old bedroom. How old are you again—one?"

The two girls lifted their hands again, ready for more blows.

"Stop!" Tilla had to say. "Fight later. Now we eat."

"They're all for you," Mae said. "All three honey cakes. Erry and I already ate ours."

Tilla looked at the cakes. Each steaming pastry was larger than her hand. She did not imagine she could eat one, let alone all three. Yet when she bit into the first pastry, it melted in her mouth, rich with butter and raisins and honey. She closed her eyes and let out a sigh. She had not eaten a proper meal since leaving Cadport; she thought this was the best food she'd ever tasted.

"It's what the officers eat," Erry said. "Stars, Till, you should see their kitchen! Roast chicken, cakes, fresh fruits, wines..." Erry smacked her lips. "And all they give us is stale wafers, moldy cheese, and slop that's probably full of rat droppings. I need to be a lanse too someday."

Tilla finished the first honeycake. Her stomach still rumbled, and she was tempted to eat the remaining two. Instead, she wrapped them back into the cloth and placed them under the blankets. She didn't know how much longer she'd be here, or how scarce food would be.

"How are things back at the Black Rose?" Tilla asked, trying to keep her mind off her wounds.

"Awful!" Mae said. "We only got three hours of sleep last night too, and we failed the morning inspection. Erry's boots weren't polished."

"And your sword wasn't oiled!" Erry said, eyes flashing.

"Well, I don't know how to oil a sword!" Mae sighed. "Nairi said we can only sleep for three hours this night too, and we have to carry the cannonballs again soon. Erry, when did she say we have to—"

The clock tower chimed outside, cutting her off. Four chimes. Four in the morning.

"Wormy dragon vomit!" Erry said and leaped off the bed. "It's our night patrol time. If we're not there..." She made a beeline to the window, placed one foot upon the ledge, then looked back at Tilla. "Get better soon, Till. We need our flight leader back."

With a wink and a grin, Erry leaped outside into the darkness. Sniffing back tears, Mae followed; Tilla heard the baker's daughter thump against the ground outside and wail. Then their boots thudded and disappeared into the distance.

Weariness tugged on Tilla. She closed her eyes and slept.

It was another two days before the infirmary nurse, a severe woman with muscles like the ropes Tilla would weave, deemed Tilla healed. Tilla did not feel healed; bruises and welts still covered her, and when she tried to walk every step hurt.

"If you can walk, you can train," the nurse said, a scowl twisting her wrinkly face. "Now out! Return to your phalanx, soldier, and by the red spiral, stay out of trouble this time."

Tilla left the infirmary clad in her leather armor, which rubbed against her welts so powerfully every movement made her wince. Her sword hung upon her hip, her helmet topped her head, and fear gripped her heart.

What if Nairi hurts me again? she wondered as she stepped into the courtyard. Snow dusted the cobblestones and glided before her. *What if Leresy speaks to me, and Nairi gets jealous, and...*

Suddenly Tilla wanted to flee. She stood alone in this courtyard, the nurse still in the infirmary, her phalanx in the forest.

I can shift into a dragon, Tilla thought. *I can fly away from this place—back to Cadport, back to Rune.*

She stood alone in the snow and looked at the southern wall. No, she could not fly back home, she knew. If she fled the Legions, she would be an outlaw; the Cadigus Regime would hunt her down and slay her.

I can join the Resistance, she thought, *if I can find them.* Yet the stories she had heard returned to her: stories of the Resistance slaughtering babes, snatching children and forcing them to fight, burning farms and killing peasants simply to punish the emperor. As bad as Nairi was, surely the Resistance was worse. Even if Tilla could find the resistors, would she only stumble into a den of monsters? Would they kill her like they had killed her brother?

She sighed. No. There was nothing over those walls—Cadport was now banned to her, the Resistance frightened her, and Tilla did not fancy a life on the run, hiding in caves and forests.

All she could do now, she decided, was survive this training. Nairi would not command her forever. If Tilla completed her training, she would advance in the ranks. She would be assigned to a better fortress. She would become a warrior, a proud legionary of the empire, clad in steel and glory. Surely that was better than living as a filthy, frightened outlaw.

I'm going to show Nairi. She clenched her fists, and marched across the courtyard. *I'm going to be the best damn soldier in Castra Luna.*

She marched out the gates, took a deep breath, and headed back to her tent.

The clock chimed.

The snow fell.

Day and night molded into a blur of pain and weariness.

Every night, as the clock chimed one, the Black Roses emerged from their tent to carry their cannonballs around the camp. Every morning, as the clock chimed four, Nairi woke them with screams, threats, and thrusts of her punisher.

They fought with blunted swords, then sharpened ones.

They ran through the forest for hours, tasting the punisher when they fell.

They ate scraps. They slept shivering in moldy blankets. They drank melted snow when they could steal it. They were always hungry, always thirsty; they would fight for the last slice of stale bread.

Castra Luna brought them to the edge of humanity. The Black Roses did not bathe; they stole snow, melted it in their tent, and shivered as they rinsed their grime. They had no outhouses or chamber pots; when Nairi looked aside, they sneaked into the forest and dug holes, praying that Nairi would not shout and order them back into formation. Whenever the young lanse slept or ate, she left with them the hulking siragis, and they were worse; they thrust their punishers with glee, and once they whipped a recruit until she passed out.

More than the hunger and thirst, and more than the pain, Tilla longed for sleep.

I can live without food, she thought during the endless runs, marches, and swordplay. *I can live without water to drink or bathe in. But sleep... sleep I long for with every aching fiber in my body.*

And yet sleep, this most precious of lovers, was only allowed brief visits. An hour here, two hours there; that was all.

"Whenever they march us," Tilla whispered to her fellow soldiers, "I want to sit down. Whenever they sit us down, I want to stand and march."

Marching was agony—it was blisters upon her feet, cramping muscles, aching breath, and her spine twisting under the sacks of cannonballs. Whenever she marched, she prayed for it to end. She prayed only for rest—to sit, to rub her feet, to breathe again.

Yet whenever Nairi ordered them to sit—while they ate, while they listened to her speeches, while she demonstrated new sword thrusts—Tilla prayed to please, please stars, only to stand up, only to walk. Sitting down meant a visit from her greatest foe: weariness.

Whenever she sat, sleep leaped onto her at once, tugging more powerfully than all the ropes Tilla had ever woven. Blackness began to spread across her. Invisible demons tugged at her eyelids, forcing them down.

Sleep, Tilla, voices whispered. *Sleep, sleep...*

One time, sitting with her fellow Black Roses to hear Nairi praise the emperor, Tilla could not help it. Her eyes closed—just for an instant, barely more than a blink.

At once, Nairi pounced upon her. The punisher drove into her chest. Lightning crackled.

"You will not sleep as I speak, dog!" the lanse shouted and pulled her punisher back, leaving Tilla gasping. "Anyone who closes her eyes, I'll cut off her eyelids!"

And so whenever they sat—or even stood—Tilla bit her cheek, dug her fingernails into her palms, and used every bit of strength to stay awake, to keep her eyes opened.

Every time they sat or stood, a few eyes closed. A few recruits screamed under the punisher. Twice recruits fell asleep while marching, a feat Tilla had thought impossible; Nairi's punisher burned them.

How long had it been? A moon now? Two moons? Three?

Whenever we marched, we wanted to sit. Whenever we sat, we prayed to march.

That was how, Tilla knew, she would remember her training for the rest of her life—marching in pain and hunger, sitting through the agony of forbidden sleep, one or the other, again and again, day after day. A dreamscape. A blur. A nightmare of weariness, hunger, thirst, dirt, chiming hours, and endless pain.

During these moons, Tilla found comfort only one hour a day—her favorite hour of the day, the hour that kept her going, that made this agony bearable.

The morning hour right after dawn.

The hour they trained as dragons.

All her life in Cadport, shifting into dragons was forbidden. Dragons were not docile citizens. Dragons could blow fire, slash claws, and rise up against the Cadigus family. Dragons were outlawed.

It was one law that Tilla, all her life, could not obey. Since she was old enough to shift, she had craved Requiem's ancient magic, the magic that flowed from the Draco stars. And so she and Rune would walk upon the beach at night, shift into dragons in darkness, and fly over the water. She knew that many others in town shifted too; she had seen other youths above the waters at night, even some older souls.

But this—this was new. This was flying in daylight, in the open, not concealing her fire behind her teeth, but roaring it in great pillars of fury.

This was life in death, light in darkness, the beacon of her soul.

"Warriors of the Black Rose!" Nairi shouted, pacing along the courtyard before her troops. She drew her sword and raised it high. "Shift and fly!"

With that, Nairi shifted into a gray dragon, beat her wings, and took flight. Across the courtyard, her ninety-nine soldiers shifted and followed.

Tilla inhaled deeply and let the magic flow across her. For the first few days of training, her armor and sword would constrict her; she had ripped one breastplate trying to shift. Today her armor and blade were like parts of her, as familiar as her own skin. They shifted with her, melting into her body. Her wings sprouted from her back. Her white scales clanked across her. She soared and blew a pillar of fire.

All around her, the other dragons ascended too. Her flight crew flew around her, one defender at each side. Erry flew to her right, a slim copper dragon with blazing eyes. Mae flew to her left, a lavender dragon with white horns.

"Flight one!" Nairi shouted. "Flight two—charge!"

Three dragons swooped in from the east. Three more charged from the west. They crashed together with beating wings and blasts of smoke.

"Flight three, four—charge!"

When it was Tilla's turn to fly, she led her flight in assault. She screamed and blew streams of smoke, charging toward another flight of three dragons. Sparks and smoke flew. Their claws and horns, tipped with cork, slammed against scales.

In real battle, Tilla knew, she would breathe fire, not just smoke, and slash bare claws. Day by day, she practiced with cork and smoke, and she grew faster. Her defenders whisked around her, holding back the enemies, letting Tilla charge into battle.

Every day her flight won more rounds. Within a moon, Tilla's Three, as they called them, was ranked top flight in their phalanx.

Some days, Nairi cracked open cages of doves and sent hundreds of birds flying. The Black Rose dragons chased, blew jets of fire, and roasted the birds; for every dove that escaped, Nairi docked them a meal. Other days, they flew for hours over the forests, shifting from attack formation to defense and back again a hundred times—changing shape in the sky from arrows, to rings, to great V's like skeins of geese.

In the long days of impossible pain, it was freedom.

It was joy.

It was the song and light of dragons.

It's why I stayed, Tilla thought, flying over the forest with her phalanx, roaring fire and howling the might of the Legions. *It's why I never ran away when I had a hundred chances to. It was for this—wind in my wings, smoke in my nostrils, and fire in my heart.*

As the dragons of Requiem flew, Tilla thought: *I wish you were here with me, Rune. I wish we could fly together again—one more flight like those above the sea.*

That night, when she lay in her tent, Tilla thought of him. Her fellow soldiers slept around her, a great mass pressed together. Tilla closed her eyes and tried to remember Rune: his dark hair, his somber eyes, and his hand holding hers. Yet hard as she tried, every night his face seemed more blurred to her, and he seemed farther away.

"I miss you, Rune," she whispered.

But I also have a new home now. And I have new friends and a new purpose to my life. I have Erry and Mae and all the others—and an hour a day of wings and fire.

He faded into the shadows. She slept.

RUNE

"So I suppose you want to know about that night," Valien rasped, took a swing of spirits, and slammed down his mug. "The night I saved your life. Don't deny it, boy; you've been burning to ask. I've seen it in your eyes since Kaelyn dragged you into this place."

Rune stood at the entrance to Valien's dark, dusty chamber. Candles, bottles, and books covered the shelves. A spider wove a web in the corner. A log crackled in the hearth. Valien sat at an oaken table, his scruff thickening into a beard, and drank from his mug. His grizzled hair hung wild around his face—a face as rough and leathery as the ancient codices around them.

"Did you summon me here," Rune asked from the doorway, "to tell me the tale?"

Valien grumbled and snorted something that sounded like a laugh. He drank again, swishing the spirits before swallowing, then wiped his lips with the back of his hand.

"Ah!" he said. "Seemed as good a night as any to remember. I've had a bit... to drink. In with spirits, out with secrets, they say." He slapped his palm against the table. "If I didn't summon you, you'd be coming here soon enough to ask. I reckoned we'd talk when I'm nice and ready, with a hearth fire warming my bones and rye warming my belly. Come on. Step in. Sit down. Make yourself at home and all that, as you innkeepers say."

Rune hesitated. He had seen Valien gruff before. Stars, the man was always scowling and rasping and cursing. But this—this was worse. Valien's voice was slurred and scratchier than ever, and something about that invitation seemed less than welcoming.

"Come on, boy!" Valien said again. "Aye, I'm a bit drunk, but I won't hurt you. Sit down. I have some memories to spill, and well... you're the one to listen."

Rune did not want to enter this room. He wanted to return to the main hall, walk outside and look at the stars, or seek Kaelyn in her chambers; he had begun to teach her mancala, using a board he'd carved himself. At the same time... Valien was right. Rune had wanted to ask these questions, to learn more about that night. He knew the story, of course—everyone in Requiem did. He too had heard of Valien Eleison battling Frey Cadigus, snatching the last heir, and smuggling the babe out of the palace. Yet all those stories had been told in taverns, or at military rallies, or in dark caverns. Here before him stood the man himself, the great outlaw, the rebel leader; here was the story of Rune's life.

Rune entered the room, pulled back a chair, and sat at the table. Valien leaned forward and fixed him with a red-rimmed glare.

"They say you battled a hundred men with a broken sword," Rune said, "all the while holding the Aeternum babe—me—in one hand."

"Aye," Valien agreed. "They also say that Frey Cadigus stands eight feet tall and the sun waits for him to piss every morning before it rises. What do you believe, Rune?"

He thought about this for a moment. He answered carefully.

"I think," he said, "that I would very much like a bit of whatever you're drinking."

When Rune too held a mug and the warmth spread through him, he allowed himself to lean back. Valien seemed less frightening through the glaze of spirits, and after all, Rune had seen many drunken warriors at the Old Wheel.

"You're eighteen now, are you?" Valien asked after another gulp of the rye.

Rune nodded. "Almost—a moon away. If I were eighteen already, I'd have been drafted last recruitment with my friends."

He had almost said: *with Tilla.* He had stopped himself just in time. Valien did not need to know about Tilla Roper. Nobody did. That memory was pure, and Rune would not stain it with this war.

Valien sighed and leaned back. "Aye, still a youth. I was only a squire when I was your age. It was another few years before I was knighted—I was twenty-one and still too young for wisdom." The grizzled man's eyes seemed to be looking back upon better days. "Had my proper armor and all and a good sword; I still carry it. I served your father, and he was good man. And those were good days."

"Until Frey Cadigus flew with his troops into the capital," Rune said. "We've heard the story countless times in Cadport. They always tell us how Frey Cadigus, the hero, saved Requiem from its weakness, from the old corrupt blood."

Valien raised his eyebrows. "Cadport? No, we don't call it that here. Lynport is the name of your city. It was named after the great Queen Lyana Aeternum, an ancestor of yours. She fought a battle upon Ralora Cliffs outside the city. Cadport!" Valien snorted. "Frey Cadigus renamed half the cities in this kingdom after his miserable self. But it's still known as Lynport here, Rune, and you should call it that."

"My father did," Rune said. "My stepfather, that is, but I still think of him as Father. He would whisper 'Lynport' sometimes late at night after our tavern closed, but... it was a forbidden name. Once a man was caught saying 'Lynport' in our tavern. The soldiers dragged him outside, and..." Rune had to drink again. "Nobody's called it Lynport since, not even in a whisper."

"It's a good town," Valien said softly. He stared at the wall as if lost in memory. "A good town. Good, honest folk. It's why I took you there, Rune, why I placed you in the Old Wheel with your stepfather. And Wil Brewer kept you safe for seventeen years. Aye, a good town, and good folk."

"How did you know Wil?" Rune asked. "Why did he agree to raise me as his own, to place himself in danger, to protect me?"

Valien said nothing for a long moment, only stared at the wall. Finally he took a gulp of spirits, grimaced as he swallowed, and slammed the mug down.

"My wife, Rune," he said and clenched the mug so tightly, it trembled. "My wife. Frey Cadigus slew her the night I saved you. He stuck his blade into her as she screamed for me. I couldn't save her, but I could save you, Rune. So I took you to my wife's hometown. And I took you to her brother." He grumbled and sighed. "Yes, Rune. I took you to the only family I still had, to Wil Brewer. He lost his sister that night, but he gained a son."

Rune's head spun, and it wasn't from the drink.

"Stars," he whispered. "My father—I mean, Wil—spoke of losing a sister. I never imagined..."

"Of course you didn't." Valien scowled into his mug. "I told Wil not to speak of it. You were never to know who you were—

not until you were old enough, until you were ready to fight with us."

Rune lowered his head, and his belly felt cold. Guilt and sorrow swirled inside him. He tried to imagine losing the woman he loved, losing Tilla. Of course, Tilla wasn't his wife, and he had only kissed her once, but he loved her. She was his best friend, his companion all his life. If Frey killed her, Rune would become a ruin of a man.

I would become like Valien, he thought. *Hurting. Mourning. Seeking solace in my cups.*

"Valien," he said and looked up at the man. "I'm sorry for your loss. For Marilion dying. I know it must hurt, and—"

"Oh do you now?" Valien hissed and leaned forward, and suddenly fire filled his eyes, and rage twisted his face. "Do you know what it's like, boy? Are you sorry? What do you know of loss, of—"

Valien sucked in his breath, grimaced, and growled. He swallowed his words, then pushed himself back. He seemed to wilt. His shoulders slumped, and all the fire left his body.

Rune watched, heart thrashing.

"I..." he began.

Valien waved him silent. "It's not your fault, boy. I know you mean well. And... thank you." He heaved a rattling sigh and drank again. "I don't talk about her much, as you can imagine. She looked like Kaelyn, do you know?" He laughed bitterly. "Same age when she died. Same golden, wavy hair. Same eyes. When I look at Kaelyn sometimes, I... Well, never mind that."

"She was very pretty," Rune said softly.

Valien laughed. "Marilion was, and Kaelyn is."

"I'm sorry." Rune was surprised to find his eyes stinging, and his voice shook. He clenched his fists in his lap. "They say that you saved me while Frey killed her. If... if you weren't saving me, maybe you could have... you could stopped Frey from..."

"Maybe," Valien agreed. "But you were only a babe. What did you know? It was a bad night, Rune. It was a bad night for me, for you, for the land. Frey Cadigus and his battalions flew into the capital as heroes; we welcomed him, the great general returning home from the wars. He entered the palace unopposed. He was in the throne room before he drew his sword. I was there, and I fought him. I fought him well, and I suffered the wounds of his sword, and still I fought. But his men were too many; he slew your father, your mother, your older siblings. But you... you were a babe. You were in a nursery upstairs. I ran. I burst into your room. And I saw a soldier above your crib, a blade in his hand."

Rune leaned forward, clutching his mug like a sword. "And you killed him," he whispered.

"Well... I tried to," Valien said. "Thrust my sword at him, but he saw me in a mirror, and I was too weak, too wounded. He blocked my blade, and our swords shattered in a rain of steel. We fought with fists upon the floor. He grabbed my throat. He squeezed and squeezed and squeezed. I saw stars. I thought he would snap my neck. I kicked. I punched him. Still he squeezed. Finally—stars, I must have been seconds from death—I kicked down the mirror, shattering it. I grabbed a shard the size of my fist. I drove it so deep into his eye it scraped the back of his skull." He gave a gruff laugh. "He released me then. I wheezed and coughed on the floor like a wretch, every breath like a saw of fire working at my throat. He couldn't kill me, but he did ruin my voice; left it all gravelly and scratched, the bastard. Since that day, I've sounded like a man dying of consumption." He gave Rune a squinted, sidelong look and spat. "If you ask me, you weren't worth it, boy."

"Maybe I will prove you wrong someday," Rune said. "You kept me alive for a reason. You need me now. We're going to kill that bastard Frey Cadigus, and we're going to rename my city, and stars, Valien—we're going to get you a bath. You stink."

And I'm going to see Tilla again, he thought. *I'm going to save her from whatever fort they dragged her to. We're going to return to Cadport—to Lynport!—and rebuild the Old Wheel, and Tilla and I will live there together.*

"Aye!" Valien said, leaned back, and slammed his boots against the tabletop. "You know what they say. Good men stink of soil, oil, and other toil; villains smell of roses."

Rune was about to reply when the door slammed open behind them.

Kaelyn burst into the room. Her eyes were wide, her hair wild, and her fingers clutched her bow like a drowning woman. Her chest rose and fell as she panted.

Both Rune and Valien leaped to their feet and gripped their swords.

"What is it, Kaelyn?" Valien demanded.

"It's Beras," she said, panting. "He's back with news. He claims this one's worth gold. Oh bloody stars. He's waiting in the main hall."

They rushed down the corridor, boots thudding. As they moved, Rune frowned. *Beras.* Surely she didn't mean Beras the Brute, the infamous enforcer of the Cadigus Regime, the man Rune had seen deliver a trembling girl to her death in Lynport?

As they burst into the main hall, Rune's stomach sank.

It was him.

Rune cursed and drew a foot of steel.

The burly man stood in the crumbling hall, facing them. Circles hung under his eyes, black rings upon an ashen face. His armor was a tattered jumble of buckles, scraps of chainmail, rusted plates, and beaten leather. In his fists, he clutched his axe—not the axe of a soldier, but a great thing of wood and steel built for felling trees. Rune had seen this man in Lynport before, but only from a distance. Facing him in the hall, Rune felt a chill; Beras stood nearly seven feet tall, his shoulders wide as a wagon. Even before Frey Cadigus had taken power, Beras the Brute was feared across the kingdom, the most bloodthirsty outlaw in Requiem, a thief and murderer and rapist.

He raped a child once, Rune remembered and snarled. *He strangled her and buried her body in the woods.*

Frey Cadigus had been so impressed, the stories whispered, he had hired Beras at once, elevating him from outlaw to bodyguard.

"So this is the boy," Beras said, fixing Rune with a dead gaze. His lips peeled back, revealing rotted teeth. "So here is the so-called Whelp of Aeternum."

Rune growled and drew his sword. He doubted he could defeat Beras in battle—the man was twice his size, and his axe was larger than the Amber Sword—but rage pounded through Rune, drowning his discretion.

"You've stumbled into the wrong lair, Beras," he said. "I saw you in Lynport hiding behind the skirts of Shari, your mistress. You will find no such protection here."

Beras grinned—the grin of a feral beast. "The pup's got some spunk. You're a feisty one, aye. Normally I like me a nice girl to warm my bed, but you'd do fine. Come here, boy—let me take that sword from you."

Valien marched forward and stood between them.

"Enough!" the fallen knight said. "Rune, sheathe your sword. Beras, tell me your news."

Rune fumed. He wanted to leap toward Beras and stick his sword in the man's neck. Yet Kaelyn took his arm and pulled him back.

"Let them talk, Rune," she whispered. "Sheathe your sword. It's all right. Beras works for us."

Rune's head spun. He took a few steps back with Kaelyn until they stood in a shadowy corner.

"What?" he said and shook his head wildly. "Beras the Brute—the outlaw, Shari's henchman, the murderer and rapist— fights for the Resistance?"

Kaelyn sighed and kept her hand on his arm. "I wouldn't say he fights for us, no. And I wouldn't say he holds much love for us either, or for anyone. Beras is a mercenary, that is all. My father was a fool to hire him. Beras loves his wine, his women, and his blood, but one thing he loves more than all—his coin. Frey pays him to murder and torture. We pay him for information."

Rune growled, and it took Kaelyn's hand to guide his sword back into its sheathe.

"How could you employ scum like that?" he demanded. "Folk whisper about the Resistance being a rabble of outlaws and killers. When you pay Beras, you are only—"

"—gaining information we need," Kaelyn finished his sentence. "Rune. Listen to me. I have no love for Beras. I hate the man, and he knows it. But I hate my father more. What is Beras? Nothing but muscle. Frey Cadigus is the heart of the Regime; with Beras taking our coin, we can learn what we need to stab that heart. The wise work with small devils to slay the big ones."

"You cannot trust anything Beras says," he told her. "The man is a rabid beast. Anything he tells you will be tainted with lies."

Kaelyn raised an eyebrow. "Is that so? It was Beras who told us Shari was flying toward Lynport to kill you. His information saved your life that day. Beras is a rabid beast, it's true, but you owe him your life. And so do many others among the Resistance." She sighed. "War is rarely black and white, rarely goodness fighting evil; we are all different shades of gray. There are no pure means, only pure ends."

Rage still bloomed in Rune, and he wanted to retort, but more than that, he wanted to hear what Beras was saying. The brute was smirking and reaching out his hand to Valien.

"This one's a real gem," Beras said and spat. "Pay up! Gold this one's worth. No more of your silver. One gold coin now, another once I deliver your news. Go on! Still less than what you pay for your booze, I wager."

Rune's rage crackled with new vigor. He didn't know how Valien managed to stay calm. Yet the leader of the Resistance only nodded, fished through his pocket, and produced a golden coin. He slammed it into Beras's outreached, craggy palm.

"Talk to me, Beras," Valien said. "Share your tidings and I'll toss you another treat."

Beras chuckled, spat again, then bit the golden coin. "Aye, this is good gold, it is. All right. I'll share my tale." He leered at the shadows where Rune and Kaelyn stood. "You want your pups here while I speak?"

Valien nodded, and it seemed like all the drunkenness had drained from his eyes; those eyes now burned with an intensity Rune had never seen.

"I have no secrets from the emperor's daughter," Valien said, "nor from our king's son. Speak freely, Beras. Tell me all you know."

"A wedding," Beras said and barked a laugh. "The boy Leresy is making a grab for power—and for some young arse. Got his eye on Nairi Blackrose, daughter of Lord Herin, the bald bastard."

Valien nodded slowly. "It's a smart move for him. Leresy is second in line for the throne. Nairi's father could threaten Shari, if push comes to shove between the siblings. But this news is hardly worth gold, Beras. These rumors of Leresy courting Nairi have been flowing since the boy took command of Castra Luna."

Beras was chuckling—a horrible, bubbly sound like grime rising in a sewer. "Ahh, but you haven't heard the best part yet, my grizzled old friend. The wedding, you see! Ah, the wedding. The pup insisted on it."

"Insisted on what?" Valien demanded. His shoulders had lost their stoop, and he stood tall and proud as a knight. "Tell me your news, Beras, if you want your second coin."

"Oh, I'll have my second coin," said the brute. "Leresy Cadigus, that whore of a pup, demanded to have his wedding in his new home—Castra Luna itself. The whole clan will be attending—Frey Cadigus, Shari Cadigus, and Herin Blackrose. The whole bloody echelon of Requiem. They'll be there in ten days at noon—the first day of spring."

Valien stood silent for a long time. His face hardened into a blank mask. Finally he reached into his pocket, pulled out three more golden coins, and placed them into Beras's palm.

The brute grinned, barked a laugh, then turned to leave. He trundled out of the hall, gurgling his chuckle. The sounds of wings beat outside, and through the windows, Rune saw the bronze dragon take flight and vanish into the distance.

Rune stood still, fingers tingling around his sword's hilt.

Frey Cadigus. His children. Herin Blackrose. In one fort.

"Castra Luna is a training fort," Valien whispered. "It lies in the middle of nowhere, leagues away from any other fortress or town. The entire high command of Requiem... in an isolated fort full of young, green recruits."

Kaelyn shook her head mightily, her wavy hair swaying. "No. I know what you're thinking, and no. I know my father; he will suspect an attack. He will bring the Axehand Order with him, hundreds of his finest warriors, fanatical priests who worship him as a god. Valien!" She glared at the knight. "You can't seriously be considering this. We're *not ready*."

Valien stared at the wall as if he hadn't heard her. His leather glove creaked as he gripped his sword. His jaw too creaked, tightening under his salt-and-pepper beard.

"Valien!" Kaelyn said again. "We've talked of attacking in force. We agreed that we must first enlist more warriors. With Rune here, we can rally hearts. We can bring more men to our side. We can—"

Valien turned toward her, his eyes haunted.

"This is the best chance we've had in years," he rasped. "The echelon of Requiem—together, isolated. We've not seen such a thing since Frey Cadigus seized the throne seventeen years ago. We might never see it again."

Kaelyn's chest rose and fell as she panted. Her eyes flashed and she bared her teeth.

"Will you have us crash against the walls of Castra Luna now? Will you dash our hopes so soon after Rune joined us? Will you douse our flame just when it begins to burn? Valien." She held his hands. "Valien, listen to me, please. We need more time. We need to send men to every city, to spread the news of Relesar Aeternum fighting on our side. Many remember him. They will flock to his banner. They will fight with us. But we *need time*."

"Time is what we do not have." Valien grunted, gripped Kaelyn's shoulders, and stared into her eyes. "If we don't attack now, we might lose this chance forever. I've been fighting Frey Cadigus for seventeen years, and now is our chance to strike. To kill him. To reclaim our kingdom." He snarled and flames burned in his eyes; his face turned demonic. "Blood must now be shed. We will fly out in force. Kaelyn, you've been flying at my side for two years; fly with me now."

She pulled herself free and glared at him. "No, Valien! No, I will not. I will not let you just... just fly out and die. We had a plan. We've had a plan for years. Bring Rune here. Rally the people around him. Raise the kingdom in rebellion. Not this—not flying to face Frey in open battle." She looked away, eyes damp. "You don't know him. Not like I do. You haven't seen the Axehand Order, how they train... Oh stars. They murder babes for sport. I saw it. In their training, they... they snatch babes from mothers and use them for crossbow practice. They complete their training by severing their own hands; they do this with glee. We cannot face these men head on—not with the forces we have now, weary men of these ruins. My father would kill us, Valien. He would kill you."

Tears filled her eyes, and she embraced Valien and clung to him.

Rune watched from the side, feeling somewhat like a third wheel. He was not sure who he agreed with. He had seen the cruelty of the Cadigus Regime—Pery beheaded in Lynport Square, men broken upon the wheel simply for speaking the wrong word, and his friends carted out of the city like cattle. Rune did not relish flying to battle these people; the mere idea churned his belly with so much fear he almost gagged.

And yet... was Valien right? Was this a chance they had to seize?

If we kill Cadigus now, he thought, *I'll have my city back. I'll have Tilla back. The entire kingdom will be freed. No more breaking wheels, troops patrolling every street, or statues of Frey in every square. No more youths carted off and broken into killers.*

Valien turned to look at him, Kaelyn wrapped in his arms, a pale and fragile doll in his bear-like grip.

"It seems to me," the haggard knight said, "that it should be Relesar Aeternum, our future king, who decides."

Rune couldn't help it; he barked a laugh. The room swam around him.

"You want... *me* to decide?" he said, eyebrows firmly raised. "Only last moon you were calling me a green boy who knows nothing of the sword. Now you want me to choose whether we fly to battle?"

Valien raised his own eyebrows. "You are our king, or will be. And you know a bit of swordplay; I taught you. So what say you? Do we do as Kaelyn says—bide our time, rally the people around you, and eventually, years down the line, strike at the capital with greater forces? Or do we fly to uncertain battle now—seize this chance to end the war in ten days and crown you?"

Rune clutched his head and laughed again—a mirthless laugh that sounded almost like a sob. Valien's voice sounded far too casual to him.

"But..." he said, "but... stars, Valien! Don't ask me. You're the knight. You're the leader of this Resistance. And you, Kaelyn." He turned to look at her. "Kaelyn, you know your father better than anyone here. And you've been fighting this war for two years now. How can *I* decide this?"

He raised his hands to the ceiling, and his legs shook. Stars! Thousands of warriors hid in these ruins. Thousands of warriors would be waiting at Castra Luna, guarding the emperor. Millions of souls suffered throughout Requiem, and their only hope for salvation was the Resistance.

All these people, Rune thought, *all their lives... depending on my decision.*

"Oh stars," he whispered.

"It's true, Rune," Valien said. "I've been fighting this for a while now. So has Kaelyn. We're both experienced, seasoned warriors, and we both know exactly what to do. Only problem is... we want to do exact opposite things." He gave a rare smile. "It seems fair that you, who will be our king, give your first decree."

Kaelyn looked at Rune too, her eyes damp but solemn. She tightened her lips and nodded.

"Let us hear," she said, "what the heir of Aeternum decides." She stepped toward him, clutched his hand, and squeezed it. Her eyes softened. "Choose, Rune. I will respect your choice. Do we rally more men to our cause, or do we strike the snake as he leaves his lair?"

They were both looking at him, waiting.

How could he decide? How could he possibly know what to do? The fate of the empire—hinging on his word!

I am the child of great kings, he thought, but today he felt like only a boy, alone and afraid. Even Amerath, which hung at his waist, did not comfort him. It still felt like a foreign object, the weapon of greater men. He had accepted his dynasty but still felt like only a brewer, only Rune of Cadport, not King Relesar.

I miss you, Tilla, he thought. Whenever troubles had found him at home, he would talk to Tilla, and they would find a solution together. So many times they would walk along the beach, discussing their problems—a bad brew of ale, not enough customers buying ropes, or a hinge needing repairs.

But this... this was the world itself awaiting his word, and Tilla was far away.

What do I do, Tilla? What would you tell me?

He closed his eyes and tried to imagine her beside him. They were walking on the beach again in darkness. They flew over the water as two dragons, him black and she white. He held her hand, kissed her lips, and looked into her dark eyes. Tilla—pillar of his childhood, light of his life, the beat of his heart.

"You are in danger now, Tilla," he whispered in his dream. "You are in pain. You are a soldier of Frey Cadigus, the man I must kill. I have to save the world, but I also have to save you."

He stood in silence, eyes shut, and closed his fists at his sides. All his life, he had hidden in shadow. Walking in the night. Flying in the dark. Withering in his tavern as the Regime crushed his city under its heel. But now—now he stood among the Resistance. Now he had Valien, a great leader, and Kaelyn, a great light, to guide his way, to fight at his side.

"It is time," he said softly, "to rise from ruin. It is time to light the darkness with fire." He opened his eyes and stared at his companions. "It is time for war."

LERESY

He stood upon the northern wall, hand on the pommel of his sword, and watched his father's procession fly toward Castra Luna.

"Bastard always knew how to fly in style," Leresy muttered.

The dragons—five hundred or more—still flew a league away. Most were dragons of the Axehand Order; they wore black dragonhelms topped with blades, the steel engraved with the red spiral. They were missing their front left paws; great axeheads were strapped to the stumps, mimicking their human deformity. They flew in five phalanxes—four framed the procession, while the fifth brought up the rear.

Between these elite guards flew the emperor and his contingent. Frey Cadigus led the formation, a burly golden dragon, the largest among them. The emperor wore no royal raiment like the old kings of Aeternum, only the armor of a soldier; a steel helm topped his head, engraved with the red spiral, and a great breastplate—large as a boat—covered his belly where no scales grew. And yet none would mistake him for a mere soldier, for his horns were gilded, his eyes commanding, and his bearing noble. Every flap of his wings, creak of his scales, and snort of his flames spoke of his dominion.

At his right side flew his heir, the Princess Shari. Her scales were blue, her armor black, and she roared and blew flames.

The Blue Bitch, they call her, Leresy thought and snarled. *An apt title.*

He clenched his sword's hilt, hungering to spill his sister's blood. Shari would learn, he swore. After his wedding this night, she would learn that he, Leresy, was the strongest sibling, that he—the only son—would inherit the throne. When he was done with Shari, she would envy the miserable outcast Kaelyn.

He looked at the dragon who flew at his father's left side.

Here is my power.

Leresy's scowl twisted into a grin. Lord Herin Blackrose, lord of the Axehand Order, flew as proudly as an emperor. The old dragon had no scales, the result of some disease no priest or healer could name. The dragon's flesh rippled, naked and raw, covered in boils instead of scales, a pale yellow that reminded Leresy of pus. Lord Herin was a foul, twisted freak, a beast that belonged in a menagerie, not in command. But he was strong. Leresy would swallow his disgust for a taste of Herin's might.

"He will be my father-in-law tonight, Shari," Leresy whispered as he watched the dragons fly. "Are you afraid yet? You should be, Blue Bitch. You should be."

Wings flapped behind him. An iron dragon landed upon the wall at his side, smoke pluming between her teeth. The dragon shifted, then stood as a woman with short yellow hair, mocking green eyes, and black armor engraved with a rose.

"The guests arrive," Nairi said, placed her hands upon a merlon, and nodded. "Soon I will be a princess."

"And I the heir," he said. "With your father's help, Shari won't last long." He placed his arm around Nairi, pulled her toward him, and kissed her cheek. "You will be my queen someday, Nairi. Today we rule Castra Luna—tomorrow, the empire."

Leresy looked around him, giving his fortress a last inspection. He had made sure to whip this outpost into proper shape for his father. His recruits, all three thousand of them, stood upon the walls or in the courtyard. Leresy had dressed them in black, steel breastplates bearing the red spiral; he would not have them wearing sweaty leather for the emperor's visit. Each soldier stood stiff and still in perfect discipline; beneath their armor, their bodies bore the scars of punishers.

"You will make me proud today," Leresy hissed, inspecting their lines.

His eyes fell upon Tilla Roper and his pulse quickened. The young woman stood upon the eastern wall, a good head taller than the troops at her sides. Her face was pale, nearly pure white, but strong; her cheekbones were high, her nose straight, her eyes dark and proud. Leresy remembered reaching between her legs to correct her stance, and he sucked in air and hissed. He craved to reach there again, to touch her, own her, break her, to beat that pride out of her eyes. Tilla stood here a tall, proud soldier; Leresy ached to drag her into his bed, to make her scream, to shatter this shell of her strength and make her weep, to claim her.

Don't think you are safe, he thought, staring at her. *Don't think because I'm marrying Nairi that you won't be mine. I will break you, Tilla Roper. You think you are my soldier, but I will make you my whore.*

The imperial dragons roared their cry, and Leresy turned back toward them. Five hundred beasts of the Axehand Order howled together, announcing the emperor's arrival. It was the first day of spring, but the trees were still bare; they bent and creaked under the wind of a thousand wings. Blasts of fire rose to paint the sky red. The castle walls themselves shook. Only Frey Cadigus did not roar or blow fire; the great golden dragon merely flew with narrowed eyes, fangs bared.

"Welcome, you old bastard," Leresy said softly.

The old scars across his body flared, and Leresy clenched his fist around his sword, narrowed his eyes, and grinded his teeth. Frey had given him those scars, beating him throughout his childhood. Leresy knew every scar across him: those dealt by the rod, the whip, and the blade.

I will not have suffered for nothing, he thought. *Your cruelty made me strong, Father. I did not flee in weakness like Kaelyn. Your empire will be mine.*

He grabbed his banner, which stood in a ring upon the wall, and lifted it high. The banner unfurled, revealing the red spiral, sigil of his house.

"Welcome to Castra Luna!" he shouted to the approaching force. "I am Leresy Cadigus, Prince of Requiem! Welcome to my domain!"

The dragons approached, Frey at their lead, a great host of shimmering scales and fire. Leresy raised his banner as high as he could.

"Welcome, Father!" he shouted. "Welcome to Castra Luna!"

The emperor flew with narrowed eyes toward the wall... then overshot Leresy, not sparing him a glance. The rest of the procession did the same, the flapping of their wings nearly tearing the banner from Leresy's hands. His hair and cloak billowed madly. The dragons didn't even seem to see him, only flew above him, then began to descend toward the fortress courtyard.

Only Shari even spared him a glance, but her eyes were mocking, and she smirked and blasted smoke his way. Then she, too, overshot him and landed in the courtyard below.

211

Leresy spun around, fuming, to stare down at the courtyard. The five hundred dragons were landing and shifting into human forms. The axehands formed ranks, silent figures robed in black like ghosts. Their hoods and masks hid their faces. The sunlight gleamed on the axeheads strapped to the stubs of their left arms.

Between them, Frey Cadigus and Shari shifted into human forms too. They wore black steel, the plates filigreed with gold, and their cloaks were woven of rich crimson fabric. At once, they two began marching toward the fortress's main hall, not even turning back to glance at Leresy.

"Father!" Leresy cried from the wall.

Frey ignored him. The emperor snapped his fingers, and the gatekeepers—burly men in chainmail—pulled open the hall doors. Crimson capes billowing, Frey and Shari entered the hall and vanished into its shadows.

Leresy snarled.

Still a bastard.

He grabbed Nairi's arm.

"Come on," he said and began pulling Nairi down the stairs into the courtyard.

He entered the main hall of Castra Luna. The hall was wide, but its vaulted ceiling was low, and columns rose every few feet. This place, like every chamber in Castra Luna, was built with no space for dragons. Should the Resistance ever reach this hall, they'd have to fight here in human forms.

Frey Cadigus was already sitting at the high table, occupying Leresy's seat. Shari sat to his right, Lord Hiran Blackrose to his left. Several recruits, whom Leresy had stationed to guard the hall, were pouring wine as if they were servants.

"Make yourself at home, why don't you?" Leresy called out, marching toward his father. "Would you care for a seat? Perhaps some wine?"

Frey Cadigus finally acknowledged his son. He stared at Leresy, eyes narrowed and cold. The lines on his face deepened. He held his cup near his lips, but did not yet drink.

"Spare me your failed attempts at wit," the emperor said; his every word sounded like he was spitting. "And for pity's sake, what's that bauble on your head?"

Leresy touched the golden ringlet he wore in his hair. He had paid a small fortune for it; its golden wires twisted to form dragons aflight, their eyes made of diamonds, their scales rubies and sapphires.

"A symbol of my lordship," Leresy said, chin held high.

Frey grunted, rose to his feet, and marched forward. He grabbed the ringlet off Leresy's head, glowered, then snapped the priceless work of art in half. He tossed the pieces aside, and jewels spilled across the floor.

"I've seen finer trinkets on whores," Frey said, staring at Leresy. It was his old, withering stare, eyes hard and sharp as daggers. "You lead soldiers. Start behaving like one yourself."

Leresy squared his jaw. "I will—"

But Frey turned away, ignoring him. The emperor looked at Nairi, who stood at Leresy's side, and his eyes softened.

"Nairi Blackmore!" Frey reached out his arms. "Come to me, darling, and give an old man a kiss. You are looking more beautiful than ever. The south agrees with you, which is more than I can say for my son."

"My Commander," Nairi said, embraced the emperor, and kissed his cheek. "I am so pleased to see you, my lord. Welcome to our home."

Frey clasped her pauldron. "Ah! You wear good steel and speak well. Learn from her, Leresy! She is a real soldier; she cares for steel and fire, not tiaras. Come, Nairi! Sit with me at my table. Tell me all about these new troops you've been training for me."

With a wink at Leresy, she followed the emperor to the table, sat beside him, and began to share the bread and wine.

Leresy stood fuming. His fists trembled at his sides.

He's trying to enrage me, he thought, jaw clenched. *He wants me to scream. He wants me to embarrass myself before his men. I will not give him that satisfaction.*

He spoke loudly, letting his voice fill the hall.

"These recruits I've trained—yes, Father, *I* trained them— will receive their rank as the sun hits its zenith. Eat your bread and drink your wine! Soon the clock strikes noon, and you will see my gift to you. Three thousand soldiers will receive their rank, a new host for the Legions. They will watch me wed this night!"

Frey was chewing his bread and still speaking with Nairi. He looked back at his son and snorted.

"*You* trained them? Did you march with them in the mud, or blow your fire with theirs, or teach them the values of our empire—strength, honor, and eternal glory?" The emperor snorted again. "Or were you busy staring into a mirror, admiring your fine jewels, as Nairi broke in the troops? Yes, Leresy, I will most gladly watch three thousand recruits receive their rank. And I will gladly watch the woman who trained them—Nairi Blackrose—wed into our family. Now leave us! Go and cut your hair; it's longer than a woman's. Return to me looking like a soldier yourself before you present me with three thousand of them."

With that, Frey returned to his meal and conversation with Nairi.

As Leresy fumed, almost shaking with rage, he saw his sister looking at him from the table. Shari Cadigus, heir to the empire, was stabbing grapes with her dagger and eating them. She wore no helm; her curly dark hair cascaded across her armored shoulders. She swallowed a grape, winked at Leresy, and gave him a crooked smile. Then she slammed her dagger down, piercing another grape, and her grin widened—a wolf's grin.

Soon, Leresy, her eyes said. *Soon this dagger will thrust into your back.*

Leresy spun, fists clenched, and marched out of the hall. In the courtyard, he shifted into a dragon and took flight. He soared toward his tower, flames spilling from his maw.

You will die, Shari, he swore and blasted flame at the sky. *You will die, Father. Do not think you are safe. You mock me now, but you don't know my strength. I will crush you both in my jaws, and Requiem will be mine.*

He landed upon his tower, shifted into human form, and entered his chamber. He walked to his mirror and drew his dagger. With clenched teeth, he began shearing his hair, tearing nearly as much as he cut.

"I will play your game for now, Father," he said. "But when I'm done, this dagger will enter your heart."

His beautiful, golden hair fell around his boots, and his eyes stung.

TILLA

She stood in the courtyard, clad in steel, on the most frightening day of her life.

Today I will watch the prince wed, she thought. *Today I will receive my rank. Today I will become a soldier, ready for war.*

The tower rose above her, a shard of obsidian scratching the sky. Its great black-and-red clock chimed noon, and Tilla sucked in her breath, raised her chin, and struggled to calm her thrashing heart.

Her fellow recruits stood across the walls and courtyards, three thousand in all. Many were from Cadport, youths she had grown up with; the rest were from towns and villages across the south. They stood in their phalanxes, a hundred each. Tilla clutched the standard of her own phalanx, a black rose within an iron ring.

Nairi Blackrose herself, her commander and soon her princess, stood before her. She wore her finest armor this day, polished black plates engraved with roses. Her insignia—the single red spiral of a lanse—shone upon her shoulders.

Tilla herself wore metal for the first time. The prince had equipped all his recruits with real steel for this day. The armorer had forged Tilla's breastplate only days ago. It fit snugly, polished black and engraved with a red spiral upon the chest. Soon she would receive armbands, and each one would display a single red star.

I will be a periva, she thought. *A low rank, yes. But I will be a true warrior of the Legions, no longer merely a recruit.*

Her fingers tingled to think of it. After all this time—three moons of pain and dirt and sweat and blood—she would become a true soldier.

I made it, she thought. *I survived Castra Luna.*

Wings thudded, and Tilla looked up to see the emperor, the princess, and the prince—three dragons in armor—descend into the courtyard. Once they landed, they shifted into human forms.

Frey Cadigus stood in the center, the tallest among them. His dark, thinning hair was slicked back. His eyes, shards of stone, stared upon the troops that stood before him. His thin lips twisted, deepening the grooves around his mouth. His face was almost cadaverous, Tilla thought, but his armor shone, and his shoulders were wide and strong.

Frey raised his fist.

"Hail the red spiral!" he shouted, then pounded that fist against his breastplate.

Across the courtyard, the soldiers repeated the cry.

"Hail the red spiral!"

Fists rose, then pounded against chests. Tilla sucked in her breath, and her body tingled.

This is power, she thought. Thousands of warriors shouting together, united under one banner—this was glory.

She was no longer afraid, she realized. It was the first time in moons, maybe in years, that she felt no fear. She had come to Castra Luna a timid, terrified girl. Now she stood as a warrior, clad in steel, a sword at her side, shouting for the glory of her kingdom.

"Today you become soldiers!" Frey Cadigus cried to them. "You have trained for long moons. You have grown strong. You learned to fight with swords, to fly as dragons, to kill our enemies. But more importantly, you learned our moral code." He clenched his fist. "You learned of strength. You learned of honor. You learned that pity, compassion, and cowardice lead to decline and death. Requiem is strong! Requiem is a great blade and a pillar of flame. Requiem will never more fall. Hail the red spiral!"

"Hail the red spiral!" Tilla shouted with the others, fist raised.

The cry echoed across the fortress, across the forest, across the empire itself. Tilla held her head high, allowing the power to flow through her.

"Speak your vows," Frey called out, "and join the might of Requiem."

Across the courtyard, the ranks of troops held fists to chests and chanted together. Tilla spoke with a loud, clear voice.

"I hail the red spiral. I hail Emperor Cadigus. I vow to fight for Requiem. I will crush her enemies. With fire and steel, I will slay all who threaten her. I am strong. I am proud. I will allow no weakness, fear, or mercy in my heart. I am the fist, blade, and

flame of Requiem. The fatherland will never fall! Hail Requiem—
today I am her champion."

As Tilla chanted her vows with thousands of others, she felt
that strength rise through her. She had always been so afraid, so
weak; for the first time in her life, she felt pride.

Is this not better than fear? she thought. *Is this not better than the
woman I was—crushed under the emperor's boot, timid, alone? I was so afraid
then, but now I am strong.*

The lanses, commanders of the phalanxes, marched forward.
They carried boxes full of black leather armbands.

Nairi stood before her phalanx, hands on her hips, and
nodded.

"Today I am proud of you," she said. "I broke your bodies.
I broke your souls. I molded you into warriors. Today you are
soldiers of Requiem."

Tilla stared at the box. Each armband gleamed with a single
red star; it was the lowest rank in the Legions, but by the stars, it
meant she was a real legionary now. She felt her eyes dampen. All
her life, she had lived in hunger, poverty, and fear. Now she had
achieved something—a bit of honor. She would wear her insignia
proudly and know: *I survived and I have a purpose.*

Nairi began to call out names. Across the courtyard, other
lanses were doing the same.

"Erry Docker!" Nairi shouted, and the slim urchin stepped
forward.

"Yes, Commander!" Erry said, the shortest among them but
today standing tall.

"I promote you to Periva Erry Docker," Nairi said, reached
into the box, and produced two armbands. She buckled them
around Erry's thin arms; they gleamed with the new rank. "Hail the
red spiral!"

Erry saluted. "Hail the red spiral!"

The young orphan, now a warrior, returned to her formation.
Her face beamed.

"Mae Baker!" Nairi cried next, and soon Mae too wore
insignia upon her arms.

When it was Tilla's turn to walk forth, her knees shook, and
she clenched her fists to hide her trembling fingers.

"Yes, Commander," she said, standing before Nairi.

Nairi stared at her, eyes narrowed and shrewd. The lanse paused.

She's not going to promote me, Tilla suddenly thought, and fear washed her. *She still remembers how Leresy touched me. She's still jealous. She's going to pull out her punisher and hurt me—right here before the emperor. Oh stars...*

"Tilla Roper," Nairi said slowly, nodding.

Tilla's belly clenched with fear; Nairi was among the most powerful women in Requiem, and after tonight's wedding, she would only rise in status.

She could kill me here in this courtyard, Tilla knew, *and nobody would bat an eyelash.*

"Yes, Commander!" Tilla replied.

Nairi tilted her head, examining her quizzically. "You think you are a soldier, Roper?"

Tilla raised her chin high. "I will fight for the red spiral, Commander."

"Will you now?" Nairi leaned close and whispered. "Or will you just spread your legs for my husband?"

Tilla's heart thrashed. Sweat trickled down her back.

"I..." She stiffened and whispered back, "No, Commander! He is yours. You are a great leader, a woman of nobility and strength. I am but a lowly servant of the empire."

"You are *my* servant," Nairi said, teeth bared. "Do not think—not for an instant—that you are free of me today, Tilla Roper. You will remain in my phalanx. I commanded you in training; I will command you in battle. You will be mine for the rest of your service." She clutched her punisher and its tip flared. "If I see you near him, Roper, your last punishment will seem merciful. I will drive this punisher against you all night until you beg for death. Do you understand me?"

Tilla felt herself blanch. She took a shuddering breath.

"Yes, Commander," she whispered.

Nairi all but slammed the bands onto Tilla's arms, tightening them so hard it hurt.

"I promote you to Periva Tilla Roper!" she shouted, teeth still bared. "Hail the red spiral!"

"Hail the red spiral!" Tilla shouted in return, then stepped back into her formation.

Bloody stars, she thought. Her breath shuddered. She had thought that, after the wedding, she would be rid of Nairi. Wouldn't a princess of Requiem command entire battalions, not a humble phalanx of only a hundred troops? When Tilla had heard of the wedding, she had rejoiced, thinking that Nairi would leave her.

How will I fight under her heel? Tilla thought. *Is there any hope for me to ever leave the Black Rose?*

When all the troops had received their rank, Frey Cadigus raised his fist and shouted for the red spiral. The troops returned his call, three thousand new warriors of the empire.

Prince Leresy paced the courtyard and cried to the troops.

"Today you are warriors! I have trained you well. As my gift to you, you may stay to celebrate my wedding. You will feast with me! Today you will dine upon fresh meat and wine." Leresy raised his fist in salute. "Tomorrow you will fly to war, soldiers of Requiem. Hail the red spiral!"

LERESY

"Everything changes today," he whispered, perched upon the fortress walls in dragon form. "Today Leresy Cadigus rises."

He snorted fire from his nostrils. Below him in the courtyard, tables were set out in the open air. Winter was ending; the day was crisp but sunny. Smoke was pumping from the kitchen chimneys, and when Leresy sniffed, he could smell his wedding feast cooking. There would be roasted fowl, wild boar, lambs cooked in mint, and hundreds of pies and loaves.

It was a small feast, of course, compared to the splendor of the capital. Had he chosen to wed in Nova Vita, the Fire of the North, the entire city—a million souls—would feast with him. Banners of gold and crimson would flap from every roof. Ten thousand dragons would fly overhead, roaring for him. Troops would march down hundreds of streets, blowing horns and chanting his name.

Here in the south there would be none of that. Here in Castra Luna there would be some food, some drink, but mostly power. And power was what Leresy craved even more than splendor.

This is my domain, he thought and blasted smoke from his nostrils. *Here is my fortress, my rule, my home. Here I will form this great alliance, and from here my wrath will descend upon the capital.*

His troops stood upon the walls around him, all in human forms. Some faced the forests, keeping watch upon the horizons. Others faced the courtyard below; they would witness the glory of his wedding.

Again Leresy's eyes sought out Tilla. He saw her upon the eastern wall. She stood with her back to him, keeping vigil upon the woods. She held the banner of the Black Rose, a ring of iron upon a wooden pole—Nairi's sigil.

Strangely, seeing Tilla holding the sigil of his betrothed only made her more intoxicating. Tilla's hair blew in the wind, revealing her pale neck. She was a tall, noble warrior, yet so fragile, so afraid, so weak compared to his might. Leresy had always wanted to break her, to hurt her, to hear her scream, yet now he felt a strange need to comfort her.

What if he flew toward her, grabbed her, and carried her into the wilderness? What if they found some distant land to dwell in, just him and her? No more Shari plotting to kill him. No more Frey belittling him. No more Nairi craving his power and planning her ascent.

I could protect you from all that, Tilla, he thought. *I could shield you from all the pain in the world. I would hold you in the dark and we would feel warm.*

He looked away, grimacing.

No, he thought. He had worked too hard for this. He could not give up his ambitions, not so close to seizing his prize. He would have to play this game a little longer, to tolerate his family for a few more moons or years. But then... then he would strike. Then the throne would be his—and so would Tilla Roper.

Below in the courtyard, Frey Cadigus waited, clad in a burgundy robe and holding his scepter of power. Shari stood at his right side, Lord Herin Blackrose at his left. Before them, all across the cobblestones, five hundred axehands stood in formation—the men whom Leresy would soon rule.

"It's time," he whispered.

He took flight and dived toward the courtyard.

From the clock tower above, an iron dragon flew—Nairi Blackrose—and landed beside him. The two dragons, red and gray, stood in the courtyard before the emperor. Plumes of smoke rose between their teeth. They shifted together and stood in human forms, clad in black steel, awaiting their union.

Leresy looked at his father. He looked at the grooved face, the cold eyes, the thin lips. He looked upon this man and he hated him.

He looked aside at Lord Herin Blackrose, soon to be his father-in-law, and shivered.

Like all men of his order, Lord Herin wore black robes, and his left arm ended with an axehead instead of a hand. But unlike the others, Herin Blackrose—as their commander—wore no iron mask. Leresy thought it a pity; if anyone needed to hide his face, it was Herin. The man looked like a dying, furless cat. Herin was completely hairless; not merely bald, but lacking eyebrows and eyelashes too. He had no more teeth than hair; when his lips parted, they revealed bare gums. Wrinkles and boils covered his skin. Leresy could barely believe such a monster had fathered the beautiful Nairi. Lord Herin was a diseased freak, Leresy thought, but he was strong. His eyes blazed like steel in smelters. After the emperor, he was the strongest man in Requiem.

Finally Leresy looked at Shari, his older sister. She smirked at him, her eyes mocking, and gave him the slightest of winks. He knew what that wink meant. *I will kill you, Leresy,* she was saying, and he clenched his jaw.

Not if I kill you first, he thought.

He wondered where his twin lurked on this day. Was Kaelyn hiding in some tunnel, filthy and stinking? Did she run through some forest, dreaming of the day she could strike the capital? Was she bedding that vagabond Valien, the disgraced knight?

One day I will kill you too, Kaelyn, he swore. *One day I will kill you all—everyone in this damn, foul world.*

Emperor Frey raised his scepter, a rod of gold topped with a red spiral. He called out to the crowd.

"Today we join two great houses!" he said. "Today House Cadigus and House Blackrose become one. Today Requiem grows strong!"

The wedding began.

TILLA

She stood on the walls, her insignia upon her arms and her banner in hand—a soldier defending her emperor.

The forests rolled into the east, trees still bare, but spring began this day in Requiem, and spring had come to her life. She had arrived in Castra Luna in winter's cold, shivering and pale in a cart, no better than cattle. She had been frightened, weak, and lonely, yet now she stood in steel, armed with her sword.

I'm no longer that old Tilla, the one who was always so afraid, she thought. *I am a periva now. I am a soldier. And I am strong.*

Behind her in the courtyard the wedding began. Tilla could hear Emperor Cadigus speak of the union, joining two mighty houses. Tilla had been ordered to defend the walls and watch the eastern sky; she could not view the wedding, which pleased her. She had no wish to see Nairi's power grow. Watching the forest, defending these walls, was the task of a true soldier.

"Bloody Abyss," Erry muttered at her side. The girl clutched the hilt of her sword. "I was sure we were rid of that gutter stain Nairi. Is she really going to keep commanding us now in battle?"

Mae stood at Tilla's other side, her pale cheeks pinched pink in the cold. Her lips quivered, and she nervously tugged her golden braid.

"But I don't *want* to fight battles," she said. "Now that we're real soldiers, can't we just... guard walls? Standing here isn't so bad. I want to be a guard, not a fighter."

Erry snorted. "Wobble Lips, you want to spend your five years of service standing on a wall? Not me. I'm going to *fight*. I'm going straight to the front line to kill those bloody resistors." She snarled. "I'm going to burn them good."

"Hush!" Tilla whispered; the conversation was growing too loud, and she worried the sound would carry to the courtyard. If it did, they wouldn't have to worry about any battles; they'd be hanged after the wedding.

She returned her eyes to the east. The forests rolled into distant mist. Many called Castra Luna the most isolated fort in the empire, a single light shining in the wilderness. Tilla wondered where the next five years would take her, and whether she would see Cadport again before her service ended.

And will I see you again, Rune? And if I do see you, will you recognize the woman I've become?

Movement on the horizon caught her eyes.

Her thoughts died and Tilla squinted.

Thousands of shapes fluttered in the distant mist like a flock of birds.

"Nairi Blackrose!" the emperor's voice rose below. "Step forward and hail the red spiral."

Tilla squinted and leaned forward. Those were no birds. They were too large, too many. She could barely see them through the mist.

"Erry, you'd last maybe five minutes in battle!" Mae was saying, incurring curses from the shorter girl.

Tilla clutched her sword. Fear washed her belly. Whatever was flying ahead was moving fast. She thought she saw orange sparks rise among them. A few of the shapes glinted as if clad in armor.

"Leresy Cadigus!" The emperor's voice rose from the courtyard. "Step forward, hail the red spiral, and turn toward Nairi."

Tilla's fingers trembled around her hilt.

Stars no, stars, it can't be.

"Wobble Lips, maybe you'll die," Erry was saying, "but I'm a warrior. I'm going to *kill*."

We're all alone here, Tilla thought. *Alone in the wilderness. The emperor. The prince and princess. And us upon the wall.*

The horde flew from the east, and Tilla heard their distant cries.

"Dragons," she whispered, voice shaking. "Thousands of them. The Resistance."

"Exactly!" Erry said. "Tilla understands. I'm going to kill thousands of Resistance dragons, and—" The young woman gasped. "Stars, Tilla, what the Abyss is that in the east?"

"Your chance for battle," Tilla whispered.

The eastern dragons roared, and vaguely upon the wind, Tilla thought she could hear their words, just a hint of sound: *For Aeternum! Death to Cadigus!*

"Join hands!" Frey announced below. "Nairi Blackrose and Leresy Cadigus, I now—"

Tilla spun around toward the courtyard, raised her standard high, and shouted over the emperor's words.

"Dragons! Dragons fly from the east!" She waved her standard. "The Resistance attacks!"

LERESY

Leresy stood frozen, holding his new wife's hands.

"The Resistance!" Tilla was shouting from the walls, waving her arms. "We're under attack!"

Leresy blinked. He could not move.

He looked up. His father met his eyes, then shifted into a golden dragon and flew. Shari too took flight, a blue dragon blowing fire. The axehands shifted as well, and hundreds of dragons rose. Roars and thuds of wings filled the air.

Leresy could not move. He only stood, clutching Nairi's hands.

"Are we... married yet?" he said.

Nairi snarled and pulled her hands free.

"Damn it, Leresy!" she shouted, shifted into a dragon, and took flight.

"The Resistance attacks!" Lord Herin Blackrose was shrieking, circling above the courtyard, a wrinkled dragon with no scales. "Axehand—battle formations, surround the emperor!"

Leresy looked to his right. Nairi was flying above the walls, shouting for her phalanx.

"Black Rose—behind me! Assault formation, shift, fly!"

The hundred soldiers of her phalanx, Tilla among them, took flight as dragons. Thousands of the other legionaries were doing the same, grouping around their own commanders.

Leresy cursed, shifted too, and flew.

He had no phalanx of his own. He was not sure where to go. He soared higher than the others, so high that the thin air spun his head, and stared east. He saw the enemy there, and he snarled.

"The Resistance," he hissed.

Thousands of them flew from the east, roaring and blasting fire. They wore no dragonhelms or armor. They were feral beasts, unwashed and wild. They flew in no formations, but as a single rabble, howling and wreathed in flame.

Fear—stabbing, pulsing, all-consuming—washed over Leresy.

"Death to Cadigus!" the resistors were howling. "Slay the emperor and his children!"

They're coming to kill me, Leresy thought, staring at the horde. His wings shook. His smoke blasted uncontrollably. *Oh stars, they're coming to slay me upon the walls of my fort.*

Tears stung his eyes, and fire flared inside him, and Leresy soared higher.

"Into the barracks!" he howled at his troops. "Retreat! Retreat into the halls, lock the doors, man the walls! Defend this cast—"

His father roared, soared from below, and slammed into him.

The blow knocked the breath out of Leresy. He tumbled, and his father cudgeled him with his tail. Lersey spun in the air, fell a hundred feet, and barely righted himself.

"Assault formations!" Frey Cadigus shouted to the troops around him, his voice deep and steady. "Axehand—man the walls and await my orders. Dragon Legions—prepare for aerial battle. I will lead the charge."

The phalanxes began to take formation. These dragons had been soldiers for only several hours, but had trained well enough to form ranks quickly. Frey flew to their lead, then looked over his shoulder at Leresy. Disgust filled the emperor's eyes.

"Go defend your castle," he said, then turned and began flying east. "To war! To glory! Dragon Legions, fly!"

Thousands of dragons howled and flew behind the emperor. Shari flew at her father's side, roaring flames. Nairi flew ahead of her phalanx, shouting orders. They charged over the forests toward the Resistance.

Leresy hovered in midair, panting and trembling.

Before him in the east, the two armies crashed with exploding fire and blood.

Leresy stared, jaw open.

He had never seen so much blood.

One of the resistors, a burly beast of chipped scales, flamed a young periva. The dragon screamed and returned to human form, flesh peeling. Another resistor, a black demon with flaming eyes, lashed his claws at another dragon; this dragon too returned to human form, clutched spilling entrails, and tumbled to the forest below.

Do you fly here too, Kaelyn? Twin sister, do you howl with this mob? Leresy's eyes stung. *I always protected you, Kaelyn! When Father beat you, I always comforted you! Now you come to kill me?*

Leresy could not breathe. He could barely flap his wings. He let out a howl—he meant it to be a battle cry, but it sounded more like a wail.

"The prince!" roared a burly, silver dragon missing his left horn. "Leresy Cadigus, there! Slay the prince!"

Hundreds of resistors looked up, eyes blazing and fire burning, and began to fly his way.

Leresy screamed, spun around, and began to flee.

"Axehand!" he shouted as he flew. "Into the barracks! Into the hall! Defend the gates—defend your prince!"

The sky burned. Howls shook the walls. Leresy screamed and panted and landed in the courtyard. He shifted into human form and ran, arms pumping, into the grand hall of Castra Luna.

"Axehand! Into the hall—defend your prince!" His voice cracked. "That is an order!"

Outside the doors, fires blazed, and thousands of wings hid the sky.

Leresy panted, fell backward, and felt warm liquid trickle down his leg.

TILLA

Blood, smoke, and fire raged around her.

Thousands of dragons, soldiers and rebels of Requiem, covered the sky. Claws slashed. Fangs bit. Jets of fire howled. Dragons burned and bled all around. In death, their magic left them; they tumbled to the forest as humans, armor shattered, flesh charred, and limbs torn.

Terror. Terror clutched Tilla like claws. Her head spun. Ice filled her belly. Her wings could barely flap.

How could this be? I've only just received my rank! I can't—

"Assault formation, damn it!" Nairi howled, streaming before them, her gray scales caked with ash. The lanse roared fire, burning a resistor who swooped toward her. "Black Roses, form ranks— rally here! Charge!"

Tilla bared her fangs and growled.

No fear now. Just fire.

"Erry, to my right!" she cried. "Mae, my left! Soar!"

Roaring, Tilla beat her wings and flew after Nairi. She blew her flames. She howled her rage. Her flight crew flew at her sides, their horns at her shoulders in defensive positions. Around them, the other flights of the Black Rose flew, roaring and blowing flames. Above them, hundreds of resistors swooped, fire raining and claws stretched out.

"Hail the emperor!" Nairi shouted above... and the sky exploded.

Fire rained onto Tilla. She shut her eyes, screamed, and blew her own flames. A great weight slammed into her. She peeked to see scales and claws slashing. She howled. She thrust her horns. She bit into flesh and tasted blood.

"Soar!" Nairi shouted above. "Break through their lines— arrow formation, after me, fight!"

Tilla howled and rose through flame. Fire swirled around her. A dragon's head burst through the inferno, fangs biting, and Tilla slashed her claws. Blood rained and she kept soaring. Her flight crew screamed at her sides, blowing fire over her shoulders, clearing a path for her. A triangle of dragons, they rose after Nairi. Behind and around them, the rest of the Black Rose flew, a spearhead driving upward.

They burst through the rebel assault. Clear skies opened ahead. Tilla looked around, panting. The battle covered the sky. Bodies lay strewn over the trees. All around, dragons were battling. The Legions flew in phalanxes, lanses leading perivas. The Resistance flew as a mob, a wild mass of howling beasts; they seemed to have no ranks or formations, only their rage. Flames and blood showered. Tilla could barely even see the fortress, though it lay only a league away; smoke and blood curtained the sky.

"Swarm!" Nairi cried above. She flew toward the sun, turned, and dived. "Follow, Black Rose—rain fire!"

Tilla howled, spun, and swooped. Her phalanx followed. They crashed down, spewing fire. Dragons of the Resistance soared toward them.

The two forces slammed together.

The thud of crashing bodies shook the sky.

Flames burst and claws slashed at scales. Tilla screamed and lashed her tail, clubbing a dragon's head until its neck snapped; the resistor fell as a man, his skull caved in. Flames rose. A dragon at Tilla's side, once a seamstress from Cadport and now a soldier, screamed and burned. She lost her magic and tumbled, a human girl aflame.

In an instant of respite, Tilla looked around her. Her heart pounded and her chest heaved. The battle was moving closer to the fortress; the Resistance was still howling in berserk rage and pushing forward. The emperor was leading a charge against their northern flank, roaring flames.

Where is Valien Eleison? Tilla thought, tongue lolling as she panted. *Where is the leader of this rabble? I will slay him.*

She looked across the Resistance, seeking him. She had only seen him in paintings and drawings—a scarred, silver dragon, one of his horns chipped off. He was said to be the largest among them, a demon of bloodlust and fire. Where—

Tilla's breath died.

No.

Her head spun.

No, please, no, this can't be.

"Charge, break their lines!" Nairi was shouting hoarsely, her wings beating. A gash ran down her face, and blood splashed her scales. "Black Rose Phalanx, charge! Assault formation, go!"

The Black Roses began to charge. Tilla could barely move. She shook.

Oh, stars, it can't be him...

"Come on, Tilla!" Erry screamed at her side. The young copper dragon slapped Tilla with her tail. "Fly!"

Tilla looked over her shoulder to the east, and she saw him again. Tears filled her eyes.

A young black dragon.

"Rune," she whispered.

"Attack!" Nairi shouted.

Fire rained and dragons crashed against them.

Heart thrashing, Tilla joined the charge. She screamed. A claw slashed her shoulder, her blood spurted, and she blew her flames. She clawed a resistor and sent the beast tumbling.

"Break their lines!" Nairi was howling. "Hail the red spiral! Attack—for Requiem!"

Tilla looked over her shoulder again, seeking him. Yet the black dragon was gone.

No. No! It couldn't have been him. Tilla shook her head wildly. There were many black young dragons. How could this have been Rune?

And yet... the dragon had dived just like him. Tilla had flown alongside Rune so many nights. She would recognize his dragon form anywhere.

How could he—

"Death to Cadigus!"

The howl rose below.

Tilla whipped her head down, and she gasped.

A burly beast rose from flames. He was the largest dragon Tilla had ever seen, perhaps even larger than Emperor Frey. His left horn was missing; he had only a chipped stub. Scratches and dents covered his scales. And yet he ascended with the fury and might of a demon, blowing his flame and lashing his claws.

Valien Eleison, leader of the Resistance.

"Charge!" Nairi screamed and dived.

The Black Rose Phalanx roared and blew their flames.

KAELYN

She flew on the wind, roaring fire.

The battle raged around her, thousands of dragons crashing through flame and blood.

Her father's troops flew with horrible precision. Their phalanxes changed formation at a single order. They charged as arrowheads, breaking through the Resistance lines. They swooped in the shape of great claws, trapping resistors amongst them. They flew toward the sun, then dived, the light at their backs, blinding the Resistance before raining flame.

The Resistance fought like wildfire; the Legions were clockwork killers.

We can't beat them, Kaelyn thought, heart pounding against her ribs. She beat her wings mightily, rose higher, and blazed her fire. *They're too well trained. They wear armor. They fight like machines. We can't defeat them.*

"Kaelyn, you harlot!" rose a shriek ahead. "Come die in my flames!"

Kaelyn gasped.

She looked up.

"Nairi," she whispered. "Nairi Blackrose."

She had known the young woman all her life; they'd been born only days apart and raised together in the palace. Nairi's father was Lord Herin himself, the most powerful man in the empire aside from Frey. Nairi's house ruled the Axehand Order, enforcers and torturers.

Nairi herself tortured me in my childhood, Kaelyn remembered. The cruel young girl, with her mocking green eyes, would strut around the palace, spreading rumors about Kaelyn bedding common soldiers.

She always saw me as a rival, Kaelyn thought, teeth grinding. *She is the firstborn daughter of the Axehand; I'm the lastborn of the emperor. She is the prince's lover; I'm his twin. Two girls, of an age, equal in power: one cruel, the other hurt.*

"Kaelyn Cadigus!" Nairi was screaming, an iron dragon wreathed in fire; a hundred soldiers flew behind her. "The Whore of the Resistance! The traitor of the empire! Come to me, Kaelyn, and burn!"

Kaelyn snarled.

"Fly with me, Rune!" she said. "Keep to my right and blow your fire with mine."

The young black dragon flew beside her. Fear filled his eyes. Smoke burst from his nostrils, trembling with his breath. Flames charred his scales. And yet he reared, clawed the sky, and bared his fangs.

"We fly!" he howled.

"We charge!" Kaelyn shouted. "Resistance, fly! Slay the iron dragon."

Kaelyn roared and they shot forward. Around them, a hundred other resistors howled and blew flame.

The two forces streamed toward each other: a hundred dragons of the Legions, clad in black helms and breastplates, and a hundred dragons of the Resistance, howling wild and bare.

Streams of fire blazed and crashed together.

An instant later, the dragons shot through the flames and slammed together.

Kaelyn screamed. Flames showered her. Claws lashed her back, ripping off scales. Blood flowed.

"Scream for me, sow!" Nairi shouted somewhere above. "Scream like a pig as I gore you!"

Kaelyn roared flames and lashed claws. The Legions' dragons mobbed her. Blades topped their helms; one scratched along her leg, and more blood poured. Kaelyn howled and clawed the beast. It screamed, lost its magic, and fell as a young woman.

"Kaelyn!" Nairi cried above and laughed. "Come die, Kaelyn."

The iron dragon shot down, a shard of fangs and fire.

Kaelyn screamed, bucked, and raised her claws.

The two dragons, green and gray, thudded together. Flames engulfed them.

Nairi laughed and bit.

Fangs drove into Kaelyn's shoulder.

She screamed.

The gray dragon drove her fangs deeper, and her claws lashed, and Kaelyn writhed but could not tear her off. Pain exploded through her. She dipped in the sky. Nairi clung to her like a scaled leech, biting deeper, tasting her blood, *drinking* it.

"Rune!" Kaelyn cried, looking around for him, but could not see him. She could not see any of her dragons. The legionaries surrounded her, horns drove into her, and fire bathed her. Kaelyn screamed and the flames covered her. She bucked and clawed, but couldn't dislodge Nairi, and the beast's fangs drove deeper. Nairi's throat bobbed as she guzzled the blood.

Goodbye, Requiem, Kaelyn thought, eyes rolling back. *Goodbye, Rune.*

But no. No! She could not give up, not now, not so close to the end. Kaelyn growled. There was only one thing she could do now, one maneuver Valien had taught her. If she failed, she'd die at once. She would have to take that risk.

Screaming, Kaelyn released her magic.

She returned to human form.

She expected Nairi's fangs to tear through her. But Kaelyn wriggled, pushed back, and tumbled from the gray dragon's jaws.

She fell through fire and blood.

Above her, Nairi screamed and reared, then began to dive.

Kaelyn fell, cloak billowing, and drew an arrow from her quiver. She thudded against a dragon's back, tumbled over the beast, and kept falling.

Nairi swooped above, a dragon wreathed in flames.

Falling backward toward the forest, Kaelyn nocked her arrow and fired.

The arrow slammed into Nairi's eye.

The gray dragon screeched.

Kaelyn's back grazed the trees below. At once she shifted back into a dragon, soared, and roared fire.

Her flames crashed into Nairi. The iron beast screamed, blinded, an arrow in her eye and fire engulfing her.

"You will be the one to die!" Kaelyn screamed.

She flew higher, howling, and slammed her horns into Nairi's neck.

Pain exploded. Kaelyn's horns punched through scale and skin like blades through boiled leather. Blood showered Kaelyn.

She knew nothing but fire and blood.

Above her, Nairi returned to human form.

Kaelyn flew higher, the human Nairi skewered upon her horns. Dragons battled and screamed around her. Kaelyn shook her head wildly, tossing Nairi off.

The young lanse fell through the sky, pierced with holes, her eyes wide and mouth crying silently. She was still alive.

"Please," her lips seemed to whisper as she fell. "Please..."

Kaelyn snarled, dived, and blew a jet of fire.

The flames engulfed Nairi.

A burning corpse crashed through trees below, thudded into the snow, and lay crackling.

Kaelyn landed above the body, still in dragon form. Blood and ash stained her scales. She panted, and her tongue lolled, and her wounds bled. She snarled down at Nairi's body.

"You fell today, servant of evil," she hissed. "Your emperor dies today too. I killed you, Nairi Blackrose, and I will kill my father."

Kaelyn gritted her teeth, flapped her wings, and soared. She crashed back into a sea of dragons and death.

RUNE

"Tilla!" he cried. "Tilla!"

He had seen her! Stars, she flew here in the battle!

"Tilla!" he shouted again, seeking her. He had only glimpsed her white scales, and she was gone, drowned in this sea of fire and blood.

Was it even her? Did he truly fly in battle against Tilla, his best friend, the woman he loved?

"We have to turn back," he whispered. "Stars, we can't kill Tilla." He raised his voice to a howl. "We have to fly back!"

But it was too late. Nobody heard him. The battle raged. Dragons fell all around, returning in death to human form. Three legionaries charged and flamed a resistor; when the dragon became human again, the legionaries bit and tore the body apart. Two other dragons slammed into each other, and claws ripped down one's belly, spilling blood and organs. The trees below turned red. Smoke hid the sky.

This was slaughter. This was carnage. And Tilla was somewhere here in this sky... or lying upon the forest below.

"Tilla!" Rune shouted again and whisked between the battling dragons, seeking her.

"Rune, get back here!" Kaelyn shouted somewhere below. "Rune, fly among us..."

Her voice faded. Rune ignored her. He snarled and darted between the battling dragons, seeking Tilla. He crashed between legionaries, barely dodging their claws. He dived under a falling body; it thudded against his back, then rolled off and kept tumbling. Rune rose higher.

"Tilla!" he shouted.

Shadows hid the sun. Blue wings unfurled. A great dragon cackled above, spraying drool and blood from her jaws.

Shari Cadigus.

Two smaller, metallic dragons flew at her sides, wearing helms topped with blades.

"The pup!" Shari said and laughed. "The vermin child! Slay him."

The two metallic dragons bared fangs, plunged down, and spewed fire.

Rune snarled and soared toward them.

He swerved right, dodging one stream of fire. The other jet crashed against his shoulder. Rune screamed, his scales cracking in the heat.

Shari—the woman who'd murdered a girl in his hometown, who'd taken Tilla from him, who'd crushed the empire under her heel. Rage filled Rune.

I will kill you, Shari.

Screaming, he rose higher and slashed his claws. Blood showered from one metallic dragon's face. Rune howled and blew flames, bathing the other with fire. He drove forward, shouting, and clawed madly. Scales rained like coins from a cut purse. Rune blew his flames, lashed his tail, and the two metallic dragons screamed.

They lost their magic.

They tumbled, two men in cracked armor, and crashed into the forest below.

Rune looked up, panting.

Shari still flew there, a hundred yards above, her blue wings wider than his own. She laughed, mocking him. Her eyes burned. Bits of flesh dangled from her maw, the remnants of men she'd killed.

"Relesar!" she called down to him. "Tell me, has my sister spread her legs for you yet? How much did you pay her? Or was it the other way around?"

Rune snarled and soared, roaring fire.

Laughing, Shari swerved and dodged his flames. The blue dragon snapped her teeth at him, forcing him back.

"Who was the man who adopted you again?" Shari asked, eyes shining with amusement. "Wil Brewer, was it not? Was he close to you? I enjoyed burning his flesh."

Rune snarled. "Now *you* will burn, Shari."

He blew his flames.

Shari laughed, flapped her wings, and rose higher. She spewed her own fire.

The inferno crashed against Rune.

He screamed.

He fell.

His scales cracked in the heat, Shari laughed above, and Rune tumbled. He righted himself just in time to see Shari swoop. He raised his claws but was too slow. She crashed atop him, her fangs bit his neck, and his blood spilled.

"Yes, scream, whore!" Shari said and laughed. "Your father screamed the same way when we killed him."

He fell through the sky. More of her fire rained upon him.

I can't win this, he thought in a haze. *I was wrong, Kaelyn. I was wrong. I should have listened to you. I've led us to death.*

He blinked, gazed through the fire, and saw Shari charge toward him. No more amusement filled her eyes. She opened her maw wide, and her claws lashed.

"And now, Rune," she said, "it's time to die."

No, Rune thought. *No.* He could not die today. He could not let Kaelyn fall here, and Valien, and all the others. He had to save them, and he had to save Tilla.

Her flames crashed down.

Rune beat his wings, drove forward, and dodged the blaze. He soared. He flew past her. He spun and swooped, the sun at his back, and rained fire.

The blaze crashed against Shari and she screamed. Welts rose across her wings.

Rune slammed into her, lashed his claws, and tore through her wing. It ripped like leather under a blade. Air whistled through it.

Shari shrieked. She bucked. She lashed her tail, and its spikes drove into Rune, but he ignored the pain. He kept tearing at her wing, widening the rent.

"You will die!" Shari screamed and blew flame over her shoulder.

Rune shut his eyes. The flames roared across his back. The pain nearly broke him. He felt more scales crack across him. He clawed and bit madly. Blinded with smoke and fire, he felt the joint where her wing met her back.

He bit down hard.

He tore through cartilage.

He pulled back, ripping her wing off, and spat.

She tumbled below him, screaming, a dragon with one wing. The severed appendage caught the wind and flew away like a sail torn from a ship. Shari roared. She flapped her one wing uselessly.

Rune rained his fire. The flames crashed against her.

With a howl that sounded far too young and afraid—the cry of a hurting girl—the blue dragon returned to human form. Shari Cadigus fell screaming, a woman with blood on her shoulder, her armor shattered.

Rune dived after her.

"Shari!" he screamed.

Dragons flowed between them. Rune crashed into one, shoved the beast aside, and kept diving. Shari tumbled. Rune reached out his claws. He had to catch her, to kill her before she could escape. Another dragon shot between them. Rune cursed and slammed against scales. He leaped off, pulled his wings close, and roared fire. He kept swooping. He saw Shari below. He could almost catch her. He reached out his claws—

A white dragon streaked below.

Rune howled.

The white dragon caught the tumbling Shari, flapped wings, and flew westward over the forest.

Rune stared, heart freezing.

Stars no.

"Tilla," he whispered.

He hovered in the sky. His eyes burned. His wounds blazed. Then a dozen dragons charged toward him, roaring fire.

TILLA

She flew, the wounded princess of Requiem in her claws
Her eyes burned and her belly roiled.
I saved her. Oh stars, I saved her. I could have let her die. But I stopped Rune. I chose Shari over him. Oh stars.
She flew through smoke and fire, tears in her eyes. She looked down at Shari; the princess was writhing, and her eyes rolled back, and her lips mumbled. Blood poured from her shoulder blade. The forests streamed below them; half the trees were blazing and raising smoke that nearly blinded Tilla.
"I'm taking you to safety, Commander," Tilla said.
The fortress of Castra Luna rose ahead from the inferno. Cannons were firing from its walls. Smoke unfurled and the fortress shook. Dragons flew above it in defense; the Resistance had not yet broken through to the walls themselves. There would be safety inside those stone halls.
Why did I save her? Tilla thought as she flew over the walls. Stars, she could have let Shari fall! She could have tried to escape with Rune. She...
She was a soldier of Requiem.
Tilla nodded and blinked tears from her eyes.
She had sworn a vow when receiving her rank. She has sworn to fight for Requiem, to defend her lands, to protect her commanders.
I will keep an eye on you, Tilla the ropemaker, Shari had said that first day in Cadport. Tilla had sworn to prove her worth to the princess. She would prove it now.
She shot over the walls. The cannons fired beneath her, shaking the fort. Tilla dived toward the grand hall; its doors stood closed. Corpses of resistors, those brazen enough to have flown this far, lay strewn outside the gates.
Tilla hovered above the courtyard, her wings scattering dust, bits of armor, and a severed leg. She placed Shari down upon the cobblestones, then shifted into human form too.

"Princess Shari," Tilla whispered, kneeling above her. "You're safe."

Shari moaned and her eyes fluttered open. Blood filled her mouth.

"Tilla Roper," the princess whispered, voice hoarse, and spat out blood. "Tilla of Cadport."

She remembers me!

Despite the blood, terror, and pain, Tilla felt pride well up inside her. Hundreds of thousands served in the Legions—and Princess Shari remembered her.

If I save her life, Tilla thought, *she will reward me. I can rise above the Black Roses. She will promote me. She will grant me power.*

Tilla tightened her lips. She had sworn to survive in the Legions; this was the greatest thing she could do now.

"I'm going to save you, my princess," she said. "Can you stand? I'll get you inside. There is safety behind the walls. The enemy still fights above the forest."

She helped the princess to her feet. Shari slung her arms across Tilla's shoulders, and the two began to limp toward the doors. Tilla was the tallest woman in her phalanx, possibly the entire fort, yet Shari stood even taller, her body lithe but heavy with muscle and steel. Tilla struggled to support her; her knees ached and nearly buckled.

When she reached the doors, Tilla pounded against them.

"Shari Cadigus is here! Open the doors!"

Arrowslits lined the walls and turrets. Behind them, shadows stirred and men called out.

"Shari Cadigus!" The cry echoed behind the doors. "Open the gates!"

The doors creaked open, and Tilla entered, supporting Shari. The princess limped, most of her weight pressed against Tilla's shoulders. Once they were inside, the doors slammed shut again.

Axehands stood in the hall, arranged in battle formations, their namesake blades raised. The low, vaulted ceiling and crowded columns left no room for dragons; if the battle reached these halls, it would be a battle of blades.

Prince Leresy stood behind the Axehand formations. His eyes widened and he gasped.

"Shari!" he said. He ran between the axehands, shoving them aside. "Move. Move! Let me through." He reached Shari and stared at her, eyes narrowed. "You're wounded."

Still leaning on Tilla, the princess snarled. "Go back and hide behind your thugs, brother. The battle still rages."

Confirming her words, howls sounded outside. The archers at the walls cried out and began firing through the arrowslits. Thuds shook the doors, and fire burst around their frames.

"Break down the doors!" howled a voice outside. "Kill the prince and princess. Kill them all! Break inside!"

Tilla laid her princess on the floor, drew her sword, and stood above her.

She bared her teeth, sucked in her breath, and watched as the doors cracked.

VALIEN

The sky darkened into night, clouds brewed into a storm, and
Valien flew through dream and memory.

Rain fell in sheets, thunder boomed, and lightning flared.
Dragonfire reflected in every raindrop. Smoke rose like demons
and blood spilled. All around, through ash and rain, the shadows
of dragons spun, rose, fell, and crashed together with bursts of
light. Valien flew through a nightmare, a single dragon in a sea of
ghosts.

"Marilion," he whispered as he flew, still seeking her. "Do
you fly among these ghosts?"

Cannons boomed ahead. A cannonball cut through the
clouds and slammed into a dragon beside Valien. The dragon
collapsed into human form. The cannonball kept flying; the man
fell, limbs torn and tumbling.

Valien snarled.

I've come here to save the living, he thought. *And to avenge the dead.*

"Resistance!" he howled. "Follow my fire—to the fort! We
break through."

He blew a pillar of flame skyward, a beacon for his warriors.
Behind him, he heard them answer his call. Thousands of flaming
pillars pierced the clouds, spinning and roaring. The rain steamed.

"Claim this fort!" Valien roared and flew forward. "Death to
Cadigus!"

He beat his wings madly. He could still see little of the
battle; all around, the smoke, fire, and blood curtained the forest.
The battling dragons were nothing but shadows and firelight upon
scales. Yet Valien drove onward. He could hear the enemy ahead:
their cannons firing, their dragons calling, their emperor shouting
for the red spiral.

Yes, you await me here, old friend, Valien thought. *You who killed
my king, who killed my wife. I hear your call, Frey. I come to answer.*

He blew more fire, clawed an imperial dragon who charged his way, and kept flying. From smoke and fire, he saw them rising: the black walls of Castra Luna.

Years ago, Valien himself had served in this fort. Back then, the Aeternum dynasty had ruled here. Ivy had covered pale walls. The sons and daughters of Requiem had studied swordplay, dragonfire, and justice. Today no ivy covered the walls, only black tiles draped with banners of the red spiral. Today the youths studied no justice, only cruelty and murder.

Today, Valien vowed, *we cleanse this fortress.*

Cannons boomed.

Balls of iron flew through the smoke and clouds.

Valien howled, rose higher, and dodged a missile. Behind him, dragons screamed and blood sprayed him. Dark shadows leaped from the walls below, and pillars of fire blazed his way.

"Break down the walls!" Valien cried. "Resistance, follow— take this fortress!"

He swooped, claws outstretched. More dragons flew toward him, their bladed helms engraved with spirals. Valien bathed them with fire, then clawed their blazing bodies. He dived. A cannon fired toward him. He dodged the missile, landed on the gun, and roared his fire. Men burned and fell screaming from the walls. Casks of gunpowder blazed, and Valien soared, the flames licking his feet.

"Slay the enemy!" he howled. "Show Cadigus no mercy."

The Resistance descended from the sky, a rain of scales and claws. Hundreds of dragons landed upon the walls, towers, and courtyards, roaring their flames. Arrows shot from inside the halls and towers. Dragons clad in armor—frightened youths only moons into their service—fought and died.

Valien stood in the courtyard, tail lashing, breath blazing. Arrows clattered against his scales. A dragon shot toward him, and he flamed it; it crashed down in human form, a charred young man crying for his mother.

"Break down the doors!" Valien howled, pointing a claw at the main hall. "Slay all who lurk inside."

The main hall of Castra Luna rose from the fire, its columns wreathed in smoke; the Regime's echelon would be lurking inside.

Arrows flew from slits. One slammed into Valien's shoulder, and he roared.

We end this tonight, Valien swore and let flames fill his maw. He flapped his wings, prepared to charge at the doors and smash into the hall.

A cackle from above froze him.

Old pain flared in dark shadows.

Valien knew that cackle. He had heard that cackle the night his wife died. He heard that cackle every night since in his dreams. It was a rumble like thunder, like demons in the deep, like the death of all Valien had ever loved.

He looked up.

Through the rain and fire, he saw him there, a great golden dragon upon the clock tower—burly, demonic, wreathed in fire.

Frey Cadigus. Emperor of Requiem.

The man who killed you, Marilion.

"Valien!" the beast cried from above. "Valien, come to me! You have flown here slaying youths. Now face an emperor. Or will you run again, coward?"

Valien snarled, beat his wings, and took flight.

The clock tower rose before him, the tallest spire in Castra Luna—in all southern Requiem. As Valien flew past the great dials, the bells chimed midnight. Each chime clanged across the palace, as loud as the cannons. Valien kept ascending until he reached the tower's top. Black crenellations rose here like jagged claws reaching skyward.

Atop this dark steeple, the emperor waited.

"Valien!" shouted Frey Cadigus. "You've at last come to join your wife."

Frey's wings beat, churning cloud, smoke, and fire. Lightning blazed against the emperor's golden scales. His teeth shone. Flames crackled in his maw like a smelter. He seemed less a dragon than a primordial beast, a demon of the Abyss.

"*You* will die this night!" Valien called, hovering before the beast. "Your stronghold falls, Frey. Your reign ends here. Aeternum has returned; you cannot survive."

Frey cackled again, the sound of tar bubbling from the deep, and blasted his fire.

Valien howled and blew his own flames.

The two streams crashed together and exploded, showering sparks across the sky. Valien drove through the inferno, opened his maw, and slammed into the emperor.

The two dragons thudded together. They fell. They crashed against the tower, and its obsidian cracked. Lightning slammed into a jagged crenellation; its light revealed thousands of dragons still battling around the fort. Thunder pealed.

"You cannot defeat the power of the red spiral," Frey said. The gold dragon lashed his tail, shoving Valien aside. "The pup you brought here won't save you, Valien. Nothing can save you now."

Valien slid across the roof. The knob of a trapdoor drove into his flesh and snapped off, remaining inside him. Valien roared and Frey's fire blasted him.

Agony flared. Frey's tail cudgeled him again, and a spike pierced his scales. Valien howled, slid another few feet, and dangled over the tower's edge. Below him, hundreds of dragons battled across the walls and barracks.

"Now you can only die, Valien," said the emperor. The golden dragon loomed above him, a god of scale and flame. "Only die."

Frey's fire blasted down.

Howling, Valien leaped up.

The dragons crashed together in a shower of fire.

"You have already failed, Frey!" Valien howled, driving the golden dragon back. He clawed and bit at the beast. "Your daughter left you; she fights at my side. The heir of Aeternum flies with me too; the people rally around him. Your reign ends tonight. You—"

"Your wife, Valien!" Frey said, biting and clawing. "What was her name? Marilion, was it not?"

Rage flared in Valien, blinding him, spinning his head. He howled and blew flames.

"You will not speak her name here! You will—"

"I bedded her that night, Valien!" the emperor shouted, still laughing maniacally. "Did you not know? She spread her legs for me, and I thrust into her, and she loved it. She moaned with pleasure. I gave her a taste of a true man before I stuck my blade in her gut."

Claws lashed Valien. His scales fell like jewels. His blood poured. Frey roared his fire, and heat blasted Valien, and he howled. In the flames, he saw her again: His Marilion, his wife, his love. He saw her smile—that smile that always seemed so hesitant, trembling, a ray of joy breaking through her sadness. He saw her eyes again, kind eyes that carried so much old pain, yet which shone whenever he held her, whenever he kissed her cheek, whenever she sang to the birds they kept in a golden cage.

Marilion. Scarred and afraid, pure and loving, a moonbeam caught in a storm.

And he saw her dead. He saw the blood soaking her gown. He saw Frey's sword stuck inside her. The cage had fallen; the birds had fled. Her eyes had stared. Her smile had died.

Marilion. Timid and strong. Hurt and beautiful.

I will join you now, Marilion, Valien thought as the fire washed him, as the emperor's claws cut him, as his blood spilled. *I fly to you now, and we will meet in the starlit halls of the fallen. I will never let you go again, and your eyes will never know more pain.*

"Valien!" cried a distant voice, high and afraid. "Valien!"

Was it Marilion calling? Did his beloved shine down from the starlit halls?

"Father, no!" cried the voice.

Valien opened his eyes. Through the blood and fire, he thought he could see her—a green dragon in the storm.

Kaelyn.

Above him, the emperor chortled and turned his flames away.

"My daughter!" Frey called. "You've returned to me, traitor of Requiem! Come die too in my fire."

Welts and blood covered Valien. He wheezed and gagged for breath. He flapped his wings weakly and struggled to stand. Frey held his claws against his chest, pinning him down; Valien struggled and lashed his tail, but was too weak to rise.

"Kaelyn," he whispered.

The emperor was still laughing. "Fly to me, Kaelyn! You've betrayed your empire and your family. Come die in my fire."

Valien drew flame into his maw.

Kaelyn—a new light in his life. Kaelyn—daughter of his enemy, beacon of his soul. Kaelyn—the woman who looked so much like Marilion, the woman who stirred memories he feared, the woman Valien had vowed to defend.

I will not let you die too, Kaelyn.

She came flying toward them, a green dragon caught in the wind. Frey roared and blasted fire her way.

Valien howled, shoved himself up, and crashed against Frey.

The two dragons fell against the tower, cracking stones and shattering the trapdoor. Valien bit down hard. His fangs drove into Frey's shoulder, tore through scales, sank into flesh, and drew blood.

Frey screamed.

Valien lashed his claws. He pulled his head back, blasted Frey with fire, and thrust his horns. He pierced the emperor's chest, and blood spurted, and Valien kept clawing, kept biting, kept blasting his fire.

With crackling heat and shimmering scales, Kaelyn landed upon the tower and joined her flame to his.

Frey Cadigus burned.

His scales cracked.

His skin peeled.

And yet he laughed. He kept cackling. He spread his wings wide; they rose in flame like burning sails, spreading smoke. And still he laughed.

"Your fire makes me strong!" he called. "You are like me, Valien. You are like the thing you hate. You too are a killer. You too lead hordes to blood. You fight to slay a monster; you've become one yourself!"

With that, Frey Cadigus fell.

The golden dragon slammed against the tower top... and lost his magic.

Frey's smaller, human form—charred and clad in armor—crashed through the shattered trapdoor and vanished into shadows.

Valien leaped, shifted into human form, and jumped after him into the darkness.

He crashed down against a ladder, reached out, and grabbed a rung.

"Frey!" he shouted. "Face me, Frey! Does the great emperor run like a coward?"

He could not see the emperor; darkness cloaked the chamber. Lightning blazed outside the windows, illuminating tapestries stained with blood. Valien descended the ladder, placed his boots upon the floor, and drew his sword.

Located above the tower clocks, this was the chamber of Castra Luna's lord—once a benevolent princess of Aeternum, today the foul Leresy Cadigus. The prince was away now. A mirror stood against one wall, framed in gold, and firelight glowed behind a stained-glass window. A bed stood by a table topped with wine jugs. A trail of blood led across the floor toward a shadowy corner; groaning rose from those shadows.

Valien grunted, clutched his sword, and marched across the floor.

His torchlight fell upon a charred, bloody Frey Cadigus.

It ends now.

Valien raised his sword and kept marching, only feet away from the emperor.

A dagger gleamed.

Frey snarled and tossed the blade.

Pain burst across Valien. The dagger pierced his chest beneath the shoulder.

Valien's breath left him. Stars swam across his eyes. He howled and raised his sword again, prepared to land the killing blow, even if he died with it.

"Marilion lives, Valien!" Frey called and cackled, blood on his lips. "She lives in my dungeon, you fool!"

Valien faltered.

Horror thudded into him, sharper than the dagger.

Frey dragged himself up, ran toward the window, and crashed through the stained glass. Multicolored shards flew. Frey tumbled outside into the rain.

"Frey!" Valien howled, blood washing his eyes, blood soaking his shirt. He ran toward the window. He fell to his knees. "Frey!"

Outside in the storm, a golden dragon beat wings, spun toward the tower, and blasted fire.

"Valien!"

Hands grabbed his shoulders and pulled him back.

Kaelyn dragged him aside, and they pushed themselves against the wall, and flames bathed the room.

"Dragons of Requiem!" Frey shouted outside, voice ragged. "Fall back! Fall back to the capital."

Valien could hear no more. Was Frey dying? Did his injuries silence him? Had Valien himself died?

He held onto Kaelyn, and tears streamed down his cheeks.

"She lives," he whispered, trembling and clutching her. "She lives, stars, she lives."

The tower shook. Flames crackled outside. Thousands of dragons roared in a storm of sound and fury.

LERESY

Thuds shook the door. Chips of wood flew. Around the doorframes, dragonfire roared and blasted into the hall.

"Break down the doors!" cried voices outside, and again the doors shook. Splinters flew. "Slay everyone inside!"

Leresy stood trembling. His hand was so sweaty he could barely grip his sword. His head spun and his breath shook in his lungs.

"Do something!" he screamed. "Soldiers—slay them! Drive them back!"

He whipped his head from side to side madly. His trousers, soaked with his own urine, clung to him. The doors kept shaking—again and again. Every time the dragons outside slammed against them, more chips of wood flew, and more fire raced around the frames.

"Go on, kill them!" Leresy screamed, voice hoarse. His sword shook madly in his hand. "I order you! Are you disobeying your prince?"

And yet his soldiers—a mix of the Axehand and the Legions—only stood still, weapons raised, facing the door and waiting. Waiting! How could they just stand and wait like this?

"I order you to kill them!" Leresy cried, and his voice cracked. "You took vows. You swore to defend your price—now kill the enemy!"

He looked around madly, seeking an exit. There were no windows here, only arrowslits, and men stood there firing their bows. Who had designed this damn fortress? How could they not have built windows for escape? The enemy kept slamming at the doors, and outside the arrowslits, Leresy glimpsed thousands of the flying beasts.

Barbarians! A horde of unwashed outlaws! And his own men—soldiers trained for honor and strength—did nothing?

"Why don't you kill them?" he demanded, pacing among his troops. They only stood like damn statues, frozen and watching the

doors. He screamed so loudly, his voice became but a shrill rasp.
"I order you to get out there and kill them all!"

"They can't, you fool," Shari said. The princess sat slumped
in the corner, bandaged and bloody. Her face was ashen, but scorn
still filled her eyes. "They know war. *You* know how to fluff up
your hair, choose the finest embroidery, and kiss our father's arse.
Stand back and let them do their job, little brother."

Leresy spun toward her, baring his teeth. "Look at you!
Look at you, sister, the great warrior. You lie wounded and dying.
What do you know of war?"

Sitting in the shadows, she smirked. "Enough to fly out and
fight one, not cower in a hall."

"And yet now you too cower," he said. He raised his sword;
it wavered in his palm. "I should end your life now, Shari. I—"

A thud echoed across the room.

Leresy spun back toward the doors. A great crack had
appeared, showering splinters. Flames burst into the hall, forcing
his soldiers back.

Tilla stood among the troops, Leresy saw. Sweat drenched
her face, blood stained her armor, and yet she stood tall. She
clenched her jaw and held her sword before her, ready to fight.

"Do not let them break the doors!" Leresy shouted at the
soldiers. "If you let the enemy in, I will butcher you myself!"

He spun away, marched across the hall, and approached an
arrowslit. A soldier stood there, firing his bow. Leresy grabbed the
man and shoved him aside.

"Let me see!" Leresy said. "I must view the battle to lead
you."

He stared outside, and he felt the blood leave his face. Sweat
drenched him.

By the red spiral...

Their defenses had crumbled. Dragons of the Resistance
covered Castra Luna's walls. Their tails slammed at the cannons,
sending the great iron guns tumbling. Bodies of legionaries lay
across the courtyard, torn apart. Leresy saw strewn limbs and
severed heads and everywhere blood. The horde approached from
all sides; they covered the sky.

Leresy gasped for breath. His heart blazed with pain. This
hall, with its low ceiling and many columns, was too cramped for

dragons to enter, but the Resistance could still swarm in here as men, screaming and bloodthirsty and armed with steel.

I'm going to die, Leresy realized, and tears filled his eyes. Kaelyn was going to kill him. *Why, sister? I always comforted you. I was a good brother to you...*

"Fall back!" roared a voice outside, and great wings stirred the smoke. "Fall back to the capital! Dragons of Requiem—rally behind me. Follow!"

Leresy squinted through the arrowslit, peered up, and saw his father flying north. The golden dragon was badly wounded; his scales were cracked and charred, and gashes bled across his flesh. A few survivors rallied behind him and began fleeing north, breaking through the Resistance.

"He's leaving without me," Leresy whispered, and his fists trembled. His voice rose to a howl. "He's betrayed me! My father's betrayed me!"

He pulled back from the arrowslit, looked around wildly, and saw the doors shaking. More cracks raced across them. Fire blazed through.

I have to get out. I have to get out!

Leresy sucked in his breath. *Of course. The tower top!*

He began racing across the hall, shoving soldiers aside.

"Move. Move it! Out of my way!" He ran toward the staircase at the back. "Defend these doors. Defend these stairs!" Saliva flew from his mouth as he screamed. "Do not let the enemy in, or I'll hang you from Requiem's palace!"

He leaped onto the staircase, glanced back at the hall doors, and saw them shatter open.

A hundred dragons of the Resistance, beasts of fire and scale, shifted into human forms and raced into the hall.

Leresy ran.

He left the hall. He ran up the spiraling, stone staircase, heart thudding. Below, he heard the screams—so many screams. Steel clashed. Fire blazed. Shouts of "Requiem!" and "Death to Cadigus" rang across the fort.

Leresy shrieked, pumped his fists, and kept racing upstairs.

"Hold them back!" he shouted over his shoulder. "Soldiers of Requiem, I order you! Defend this fortress!"

He raced around and around. His breath rattled. He slipped, banged his hip, then leaped up and kept running. The fire blazed and the screams rose behind him. When he looked over his shoulder, he saw shadows racing upstairs; he didn't know if they were his troops fleeing too, or the enemy pursuing.

The stone staircase ended in a chamber of gears, springs, and bells. Upon the four walls, Leresy saw the inner faces of four clocks. A hundred gears, some taller than him, moved and clanged together. The clocks ticked. Ropes creaked and weights shifted. Instead of stone stairs, an iron stairwell coiled up toward a small door near the ceiling.

"Grab the prince!" rose shouts below. "Slay him!"

Leresy leaped onto the iron stairwell. He raced up, the gears and springs all creaking around him. He shoved the door open and burst into his chambers.

Blood soaked the room; men had fought here too. One window was smashed open, and outside, Leresy saw the battle raging. Thousands of dragons still flew, roaring fire; most were beasts of the Resistance, too barbaric to even wear armor. His father was leading legionaries through the encircling enemy, cleaving a way north.

"Leresy!" cried a voice below from the staircase. "Damn it, Leresy!"

It was Shari.

Leresy snarled.

"No, sister," he hissed. "You will not flee this place with me. This will be your tomb."

He spun toward the doorway and saw her limping up the iron staircase, pale and bleeding and screaming for him.

Leresy slammed the chamber door shut, grabbed the keys from his belt, and locked it.

Shari slammed against the door.

"Brother!" she screamed from behind. "Damn you, Leresy, open this door!"

He cackled. "No, Shari! You were too late to flee. Go fight with your troops, Shari! I thought you were a great warrior. So die like one!"

He ran toward his heavy bureau and shoved with all his strength. The bureau scratched across the floor, and Leresy pushed it against the door. Panting, he placed himself behind his bed next, gritted his teeth, and shoved. The bed slammed against the bureau. Nobody would be breaking through this door now.

"Leresy!" his sister screamed from the stairway. "Damn it, Leresy, open this door, or I'm going to butcher you like the pig you are!"

He laughed, spraying sweat and spittle. "Goodbye, sister! Enjoy your death!"

With that, Leresy ran toward the window, leaped outside into the night, and shifted.

Wind whipped him. Fire blazed below and smoke blinded him. Rain crashed down and lightning rent the sky, and everywhere the dragons flew. Below in the courtyard, Leresy saw more resistors pouring into the fort.

"Father!" Leresy cried; he spotted the emperor and his troops ahead, cleaving a way out. "Wait for me, Father!"

Dragons dived toward him, blowing fire. Leresy soared higher and rained flame upon them. He flew madly, tail lashing, and joined the retreat.

"Goodbye, Shari!" Leresy screamed over his shoulder, and delight filled him; he had perhaps lost this fort, but he had gained his inheritance. "Goodbye, you wretched pile of rocks!"

They broke through the ring of beasts. They streamed over the forests, bloody and charred and howling. A hundred dragons— the emperor, a cluster of survivors, and Leresy—howled and beat their wings and fled into the night.

TILLA

The hall had fallen.

Tilla screamed through flame, swung her sword, and cut a man. A column cracked beside her. A bearded warrior howled, charged her way, and their swords clanged. The walls shook. Fire burned.

The hall had fallen.

"Fall back!" somebody screamed behind her. "Up the stairs—into the tower!"

Tilla could not even turn around to seek the stairs. Warriors rushed all around her. Axehands fought at her sides, axes swinging and black robes fluttering. She had lost Erry and Mae; had they died? Bodies lay across the hall. Blood flowed around boots. Men screamed and blades swung.

I'm going to die here, Tilla thought. *The hall has fallen. I'm going to die.*

One soldier, a tanner from Cadport, tried to shift into a dragon. He ballooned in size, only crushing himself between the columns, floor, and low ceiling. Swords slammed into his flesh, and the dragon screamed, then returned to human form—a butchered boy, belly slashed open. The legionaries fell all around, their insignia only hours old on their armbands, and their blood washed the floor.

And I will fall with them.

The clock chimed above her five times. Dawn was near, a last light before the darkness.

We die at dawn, Tilla thought. She held her sword before her. *A new day rises; an empire falls.*

"Fall back!" the voice shouted behind. "Tilla, with me!"

Swords swung at Tilla. She parried blow after blow. She could not turn around, not without letting the enemy slay her. She walked backward, blocking attacks. Axehands screamed around her, clashing against the resistors, swinging the axes strapped to their stumps. Tilla kept retreating. Her boots slammed into a corpse; she stepped upon the dead man and kept moving.

"Tilla!"

Somebody grabbed Tilla's arm, and she spun around and raised her sword. Her heart thrashed and she screamed in rage, prepared to kill. But the hand grabbing her belonged to Erry.

"Erry!" she said. "Bloody stars, you're alive!"

The scrawny urchin looked half dead. Blood matted her short brown hair. Her face, normally tanned bronze, was ashen. Welts rose across her left temple.

"To the stairs!" Erry said. "Come with me, Tilla."

"Where's Mae?" Tilla shouted.

"I don't know! I think she fled with the others. The emperor is leading us north. Come on!"

Erry tugged and Tilla ran with her. Soldiers and resistors fought all around. The two Black Roses—if they still belonged to a phalanx at all now—leaped over bodies and onto the staircase. Blood stained the steps. The two young women ran, and behind them resistors screamed, and boots thudded.

"Take the stairs!" howled a voice below—the rough voice of the enemy. "Don't let them escape. Up the stairs! Death to Cadigus!"

"Dirty dog bottoms!" Erry cursed as she raced upstairs. "Stars, Tilla, did you think it would end like this?"

"We're not dead yet!" she shouted back. "Run!"

They raced up the spiraling steps. The battle cries echoed behind them. Swords clanged.

Pain flared on her calf. Tilla yelped and spun to see a resistor; his blade had nicked her. With a scream, Tilla swung her sword down, cleaving his hand. She kicked, and the resistor tumbled backward, crashing into men behind him.

"Tilla!" Erry cried.

"Keep running!"

They raced upstairs, breath ragged, boots slipping in the blood. Finally they emerged into the great clock room. Gears, larger than the greatest wagon wheels, turned and clanged all around. Ropes and weights rose and fell, and on each wall, a great dial ticked. An iron staircase coiled up between the gears like a giant spring, leading toward a door.

Tilla gasped.

Princess Shari stood at that door, ashen and bleeding. Blood filled her hair and stained her face. She was driving her shoulder into the door, again and again, but could not break it.

"He blocked the door!" the princess cried from above. "Leresy—he left us to die. Help me break it open."

Erry leaped onto the iron stairwell and raced up toward the princess. Tilla ran close behind. They reached the locked doorway near the ceiling. Below them, all across the chamber, the gears turned and ticked.

"Death to Cadigus!"

Resistors burst into the clock chamber from below, a dozen warriors in armor, their swords bloody. They ran between the gears, leaped onto the iron staircase, and began racing up.

"Erry!" Tilla shouted. "Help the princess break the door. I'll hold them back!"

Standing upon the staircase, Tilla swung her sword. It clanged against an enemy blade. She swung down, cleaving the man's helmet. He fell, blood gushing from his head, and crashed into the men behind him. Another resistor replaced him. His blade met Tilla's. She screamed and kicked, knocking the man over the staircase banister. He crashed into the gears below; they kept spinning, crushing the man between them.

"Break the door!" Tilla shouted. "Get out of here!"

She glanced behind her. Erry and Shari were both slamming against the door, cracking it. It opened an inch; something was blocking it.

Tilla spun back toward the enemy. She swung her sword again, parrying a blow. A red-haired woman was attacking her, screaming wildly. Tilla screamed too, blocked the mad attack, and thrust her sword. She pierced the woman's belly, sending her tumbling down; the gears crushed and swallowed her. Tilla glanced over her shoulder to see the door opened another inch.

"It's almost open!" Erry cried from above. "Hold them back just a little longer."

Another resistor charged toward Tilla. Another sword swung. Tilla parried and the blades clanged.

No.

Shock flooded her. Her eyes stung. Her heart froze, then leaped.

"Rune," she whispered.

The resistor below her, covered in sweat and blood, was him.

"Rune!" she cried.

"The door's almost open!" Erry screamed behind. "Almost there!"

He stared at her, face bloody and blade raised. He was thinner than Tilla had ever seen him. His eyes were colder than she'd ever known.

But it was him. It was her Rune.

"Tilla," he whispered.

His voice raised memories in her like waves over rocks. In the shadows of the chamber, she saw the sea again, the cliffs at night, the stars above. She felt the wind beneath her wings as they flew together. She felt his kiss again, lips warm against hers in the cold. She saw Cadport, two lost youths, and soft lights in the dark.

"Rune," she said, and tears stung her eyes. "You are here. How can this be?"

"Got it!" Erry cried above. "The door's open. Come on, Tilla!"

Yet Tilla only stood still, staring at Rune. He craned his neck up, peered over her shoulder, and snarled. Tilla had never seen him snarl.

"Tilla, I have to get through!" he said. "Shari Cadigus is escaping."

He took a step up. He made to run around her.

What do I do? Stars, what do I do?

She moved and blocked his climb.

"Tilla!" he shouted. "Tilla, she's getting away."

Tears streamed down Tilla's cheeks. She placed a hand against Rune's shoulder.

"I can't, Rune," she whispered. "I can't. I made a vow. I can't."

He shook his head in amazement. He tried to shove past her. She stopped him.

"Tilla, let me through!"

He grabbed her arms. She pushed him back.

"Rune!" Her tears fell. "Please, Rune, listen to me. I made a vow. I vowed to defend Requiem. You can't—"

"Shari is getting away!"

Rune grabbed her and tried to pull her back.

She wrenched herself free.

She raised her arms—only to block his climb—but he mistook her gesture for a sword's thrust. He raised his own sword. Their blades crashed together.

"Tilla," he whispered, and surprise and pain filled his eyes. "Tilla, how can you do this? How can you protect her? Stars! We can end this tonight. Fight with me—with us. Not with... not with these murderers!" His eyes burned red. "I don't know what they taught you. What did they do to you? Oh stars, Tilla—"

"I am Periva Tilla!" she shouted.

Her pain pounded through her. Her chest shook. Their swords swung and clanged again. All around them, the clock gears moved and clanged too, locked in their own duel.

"You are Tilla Roper!" Rune shouted back. "You are a ropemaker from Cadport, Tilla! Don't you remember? Can't you remember who you are?"

He tried to push by her. She blocked him again. Their swords rang.

"That girl is dead," she said, barely able to see through her tears. "I am a soldier now, Rune. I made a vow. I vowed to fight for my kingdom. I cannot let you pass. I cannot let the enemy through—"

"The enemy?" Rune said, voice torn. "Stars, Tilla, I'm not your enemy! The Cadigus Regime—the ones you protect—are the enemy. Tilla, can't you see?"

Her body shook. Her throat tightened.

"I see outlaws!" she shouted, weeping now. "I see a horde that burned my fort, that killed my friends, that slaughtered youths from Cadport. Stars, Rune! Six hundred youths from Cadport trained here! How many of your own townsfolk did you murder? How many of your own friends did you kill?" Her tears fell. "My brother served in this fort. He died serving two years ago—this Valien you follow murdered him! Now you murder too!"

Rune froze. He stared up at her, panting, his eyes wide with horror.

"I..." His sword trembled. "I didn't know. I didn't know the Cadport recruits were here. I—"

"You flew with monsters!" Tilla was panting now, barely able to breathe. "And now they're dead. Now hundreds of boys and girls—the people we grew up with—lie butchered across this fort. And you want me to let you through? I am Periva Tilla! I am a legionary of Requiem!" She slammed her fist against her chest. "I hail the red spiral!"

He stared up at her, frozen. A tear rolled down his cheek, trailing through blood.

"No," he whispered. "No, Tilla. You don't mean that. You can't—"

"Goodbye, Rune," she whispered, and a sob racked her body. "Goodbye."

She spun around.

She leaped through the broken door.

She raced across the prince's chamber, jumped out the window, and shifted.

Wind and lightning and dragons flurried around her. Thunder boomed. The fortress and forests burned below, and smoke shrouded the world.

"Tilla!" he cried behind her. "Tilla!"

She looked over her shoulder and saw Rune standing in the broken window of the tower, calling to her, a shadow in the night.

Goodbye Rune, she thought. *I love you. I love you always. But now you are my enemy.*

She turned her head north, roared a pillar of fire, and flew into the blazing horizon.

SHARI

She stood in her chambers, hand against the fireplace mantel, and stared down into the embers. The fire crackled and danced, a small battle whose light fell upon her. In the flames and shadows, she saw dragons aflight. She saw the Aeternum heir land upon her, claw at her flesh, and tear off her wing. She saw the deaths of thousands.

Shari Cadigus clenched her fists.

"You crippled me, Relesar," she whispered. "You stole my wing. You will suffer. You will scream like none have screamed before."

Her eyes burned. Her fists shook. The flames danced in the hearth, an endless war, their light red like blood, and in their crackle, she thought she heard screams again: the screams of men dying, of her own body tearing, the rip of leather, and—

A knock sounded on her door.

Shari turned from the flame.

She loosened her fists, took a shuddering breath, and raised her chin.

"I will not succumb to the night," she whispered. "I will not allow those flames to claim me."

She walked across her chamber, boots clacking against the tiled floor. Tapestries hung around her, depicting dragons aflight in war. Golden vases engraved with the red spiral stood upon her tables, and swords hung upon the walls. When Shari reached the door, she froze and took a deep breath.

Do not show her your pain, she thought. *No one must know. Here in the capital, weakness is death. Weakness is a stab in the back.*

She opened the door.

Guards lined the hall, faces hidden behind their visors. Tilla Roper stood between them, dressed in a steel breastplate, her new insignia upon her arms. Her sheathed sword hung at her belt. Her black, chin-length hair peeked from under her helmet.

"Commander," the girl said and saluted, slamming her gloved fist against her chest. "You summoned me."

Shari nodded. "Come inside, Roper," she said softly. "Close the door behind you."

She young periva entered. Shari led her across the chamber toward her table, poured two glasses of wine, and handed one to Tilla.

"Drink," Shari said. "Southern wine from your hometown."

Tilla opened her mouth as if about to speak, then closed it and nodded. She sipped.

"Thank you, Commander," she said.

Shari looked upon this young woman.

She's only eighteen, Shari thought. *A decade younger than I am, and frightened, and confused. But there is strength in this one. There is so much cruelty here for the red spiral.*

"I have a gift for you, Tilla Roper," she said.

She stepped into the corner and pulled back a silken veil, revealing a shield. Carved of oak and banded in iron, its surface was painted crimson. It sported a new sigil: a black cannon overlooking the sea.

"Is this... mine?" Tilla asked, narrowing her eyes.

Shari nodded. "Cadport has the oldest cannon in the empire, did you know? I visited it once; it stands upon the boardwalk, overlooking the sea. It no longer works. It rusted years ago. But it's a great symbol of Requiem." She looked at Tilla. "It will be a great symbol for you."

"For me?" Tilla asked and placed her glass down. "Commander, I'm but a commoner. I cannot have a coat of arms. I was not noble born."

"That is true," Shari said. "But neither was my father."

Tilla's eyes widened. "Frey Cadigus, the emperor... a commoner?"

Shari laughed. "The poor son of a logger. He excelled in the Legions. He began as a humble periva—like you. He rose to power." Shari lifted the shield and handed it to Tilla. "You will rise to power too. I vowed to you in Cadport, Tilla, that I will watch you closely. I have watched you, and I am pleased. Take this shield, Tilla of Cadport, and bear your sigil proudly. Hail the red spiral."

Tilla took the shield, lifted her chin, and blinked. She held the shield tight against her.

"Hail the red spiral," she whispered.

Shari smiled softly. She touched the young woman's cheek where a tear trailed.

"You are overcome with joy," she said. "That is good. You are a noble warrior and strong, but you must remember: Never shed tears. Never show weakness. If you shed a tear again, I cannot protect you."

Tilla nodded and blinked. "Yes, Commander. I vow to you: I will be strong. I will serve the Legions well."

Shari sipped her wine and looked back into the flames. They danced there, the old battle of light and darkness, of heat and endless winter.

"You will *command*," Shari said and looked back at the young soldier. "Tilla, you were meant for more than servitude. You are noble now. You were meant to lead dragons in battle, not *serve*. Would you like to train in Castra Academia here in the capital, to become an officer someday like Nairi was? The training is grueling. You will have to train there for long moons, and they will break you. But if you survive, Tilla—and I believe you will—you will wear red spirals upon your shoulders. You will become a lanse like Nairi, a young officer. You will lead your own phalanx in war."

Tilla's jaw shook, but she tightened it.

"Castra Academia," she whispered. "Commander! It is a fortress of legend. I would be honored. I vow to you: I will succeed. I will fight for Requiem."

They will break her there, Shari thought, looking upon this young girl. *She will miss the southern Castra Luna. In the academy, they train no cannon fodder like they do in the south. They train killers.*

"Good," Shari said and smiled. She lifted a scroll from her table and handed it to Tilla. "Only a Cadigus can appoint a cadet to Castra Academia. Take this scroll; it bears my seal. Fly there tonight. This scroll assigns you a chamber and commander. Your training begins tomorrow."

Tilla saluted, chin raised and lips tightened. She spun on her heels and marched away.

"Goodbye, Tilla Roper," Shari whispered, then winced.

Pain flared across her shoulder where Rune had torn off her wing. Even when she stood in human form, the wound ached, and Shari rubbed it.

"I will capture you, Rune," she whispered through the pain. "And you, Tilla, will kill him. I heard you speak with him. I will have the boy die at the sword of his beloved."

Shari snarled, gulped down her wine, then tossed the cup into the fireplace. It shattered, and the wine burned like dragons ablaze.

RUNE

Dawn rose over death.

A light snow fell upon Castra Luna, a lingering whisper of winter. A shroud of white clung to the bodies as if preparing them for burial. Hands rose frozen, fingers reaching toward the snowflakes. Dead eyes stared. Mouths screamed silently. Everywhere the ice and frost glittered in the morning, a blanket of stars.

Rune walked among the dead. The battle had ended.

"We claimed this fort," he whispered. "But we lost this battle."

He looked up at Kaelyn. She stood solemn at his side, snow in her long golden hair. The flakes covered her blue cloak and frost coated her armor, yet when she reached out and held Rune's hand, her grip was warm.

She whispered to him, "Battles are always lost. Where youths fall dead, the wise do not rejoice."

Rune lowered his head. "Castra Luna is ours. We claimed this fort. And yet... the emperor fled." His eyes stung. "I killed so many. For nothing."

He walked across the courtyard. Dragons of the Resistance stood upon the walls around him, watching silently. The bodies of legionaries lay upon the cobblestones, some torn apart, others still whole and peaceful like children playing in snow. Rune walked among them, holding Kaelyn's hand.

"I know so many of these faces, Kaelyn," he said. "This boy here—he was a weaver. I knew this girl—she used to sell eggs at the summer fairs."

"I'm sorry, Rune," she whispered.

He walked toward a fallen cannon and knelt by a body. It was a young woman, her strawberry hair braided. Her face was soft, doll-like, and her blue eyes stared.

"I know this one," Rune whispered. "Her name was Mae. She was the daughter of bakers. I used to buy bread from her."

His breath frosted and shook, and Rune lowered his head. His tears fell into the snow. "I'm sorry, Mae Baker. I'm sorry."

He closed Mae's blue eyes, the eyes of a friend.

"It wasn't your fault, Rune," Kaelyn said, kneeling beside him. "We couldn't have known."

He looked up at her. "I killed them, Kaelyn. I killed my friends. I killed... oh stars. Tilla was right."

Kaelyn's lips quivered, and she pulled Rune into an embrace so tight he could barely breathe.

"You didn't kill them," she whispered. "My father armed them. My father sent them to battle. We could not have known. Please, Rune. Please."

He held her for long moments, then rose to his feet. He looked around him at the dead, hundreds of them youths from his home.

"We will bury them," he said. "We will bury them with honor—every one."

He shifted into a dragon, filled his wings with air, and flew toward the clock tower.

Valien waited upon the roof, a silver dragon coated in snow, his left horn chipped away. The leader of the Resistance was staring north, his breath frosting. Rune landed beside him, and the two dragons—one burly and silver, the other slim and black— stared north together, silent.

Finally Valien spoke.

"Rune," he said in his deep, raspy voice. "Rune, listen to me."

Rune wanted to speak, but did not trust his voice to remain steady. He nodded silently.

"Rune," said Valien, "what we've begun cannot end here. We cannot let these deaths be in vain. You hurt. You rage. You know loss." He turned to stare at Rune, his eyes burning. "Do not let this be for nothing."

Fire filled Rune's mouth. He wanted to burn the old dragon, to rage, to break down the tower, to fly into the forests and hide forever in their depths.

"They're all dead," he said. "All the youths of my home. My best friend lived, but she serves the red spiral. What do I fight for now, Valien?"

The silver dragon snarled. Fire flared between his teeth.

"You fight for Requiem!" he hissed. "You fight for your father. You fight for your friends who lie dead below—yes, even if they fought for the enemy. We failed here in this fort, but we will fight on." That raspy voice shook now, and the dragon's claws gripped the tower so tightly they chipped the stone. "We will send word to every corner of the empire. We will drop scrolls upon every town and village. We will let them know: Relesar Aeternum has returned, and he rules the south, and he is king. Requiem will be freed."

Rune shook his head. "A king? Valien, my hands are stained in blood. How can I ever hope to rule Requiem?"

The silver dragon's rage seeped away. The smoke from his nostrils died. He sighed, scales clanking, and moved closer to Rune.

"Have you ever seen the capital?" he asked, voice soft.

Rune shook his head.

Valien took a deep breath that rippled his scales. He closed his eyes and a smile revealed his fangs.

"It's not much to look at now," the silver dragon said. "Now it's all banners of the red spiral, and marching soldiers, and towers of obsidian, and statues of Frey." Valien snorted. "Ha! But back then, Rune... back in the days of your father... you should have seen it! Whenever we'd fly toward the city, the guards would greet us from the walls, blowing silver trumpets. When we'd march through the streets, children would throw flowers at us, and people would smile. So many flowers, wine, pretty women..." Valien opened his eyes and winked. "You'd have liked that part, I think."

Rune lowered his head. "I've never seen a city like that."

"You will," Valien said. "You will, Rune. That is why we fight. Not for strength, glory, or any of that rubbish Frey spews. We fight for flowers, for wine, and for silver trumpets upon white walls."

"And for pretty women?" Rune asked.

Valien snorted a laugh; Rune did not think he'd ever heard him laugh before.

"Especially for pretty women," he answered. He nudged Rune with his wing. "Come on, Rune. Let's fly back to Kaelyn. The dead wait below, and we will bury them. And we won't forget

the living. You are king of the south now. You have returned."
Valien's eyes gleamed. "You will see the capital. I vow this to you.
We will fly toward the walls of Nova Vita. Silver trumpets will call
you home."

They took flight and Kaelyn joined them. They soared high
above the fortress, three dragons in the snow, and roared their
song.

Rune looked north. Beyond forest and mountain lay the
capital, too distant to see. The throne of Requiem awaited him
there; so did the emperor.

"And you wait there too, Tilla," he whispered.

The snow fell and Rune blew his fire. The flaming pillar
rose, a pyre for the dead, a beacon for the living... and a light for a
lost friend.

BOOK TWO:

A BIRTHRIGHT OF BLOOD

Daniel Arenson

KAELYN

They stood in the heart of evil, a woman and a man, two souls alone in a sea of steel, bloodlust, and fire.

All around them, line by line, stretched the ranks of a dark empire. Five hundred thousand strong they stood, the soldiers of the Legions, automatons of steel coated in plate and helm. Half a million demons. Half a million blades. Half a million souls screaming for blood and glory.

Youths broken and molded into beasts, Kaelyn thought, standing among them. Hidden within her helm, her eyes stung with tears. *The Legions crushed their hearts; only fire burns within these breasts.*

The soldiers covered the great Square of Cadigus, a cobbled expanse wider than entire towns. Not a boot strayed out of line. Fifty brigades mustered here, and within each, smaller units stood in perfect formation--milanxes divided into phalanxes divided into flights--paths running between them. Soldiers stood with drawn blades. Officers held the standards of Cadigus; each pole rose twice a man's height, topped with iron dragons perched upon red spirals. Flying above, a true dragon would see a great machine of metal, every soldier a single cog perfectly aligned, an imperial clockwork built to kill.

Kaelyn turned her head only slightly, for only a second, and glanced at the soldier who stood beside her. To the world, he was another legionary. Black steel coated him, the breastplate engraved with a spiral. His helm hid his face. He bore a dark shield and a longsword. He was one in myriads, a gear of metal and fire, identical to her and to half a million more.

He was, Kaelyn knew, the most important man in the world.

Be strong, Rune, she thought, wanting to whisper to him, hold his hand, and comfort him, but daring not. *We are in the lion's den. Be strong. I'm with you. Be strong and we will live.*

She looked back ahead. She vowed to not look aside again. One wrong glance, one tilt of the head, could mean bones broken upon the wheel.

Across the square, the palace loomed above the Legions. Obsidian tiles covered its bricks, the black stones so polished they shone white in the sun. Battlements lined the great hall, cannons peering between merlons like iron eyes. The banners of House Cadigus hung from the crenellations, each one sporting a red spiral against a black field.

Above this hall, stretching like a blade from a hilt, rose the tower of Tarath Imperium, the great steeple of the empire. A thousand feet it rose, piercing the clouds, the tallest structure the world had seen. Black were its bricks, and arrowslits squinted upon its walls. Its crest flared out into a crown of black spikes, watching Requiem in eternal vigil.

Before she had fled her father's rule, Kaelyn had once stood upon that black crown, a thousand feet above the empire. The city of Nova Vita, a million people strong, had rolled around her. Beyond the city walls, she had seen distant forests and mountains, Requiem sprawling into the horizons.

Today her father perched upon that crown. The Legions in the square below stood in human forms, soldiers clad in steel, but Emperor Frey Cadigus roared as a dragon. His golden wings spread wide. Fire shot from his jaws, a flaming pillar rising into the sky. His howl rang across the city; even standing below, Kaelyn winced at its depth and rage.

"Hail the red spiral!" cried the emperor.

Across the square, the Legions roared.

Half a million soldiers shouted together. Their fists rose, then slammed against chests. The sound exploded like thunder.

"Hail the red spiral!" the Legions shouted, and Kaelyn shouted among them.

The emperor's wings stretched like curtains of night, as if he could engulf the world. Smoke and flame rose from him. His eyes burned red. He perched upon the tower top like a gargoyle of molten fire, like a demon risen from the Abyss. He was scale, flame, and steel. He was the wrath and might of an empire.

He is my father, Kaelyn thought and her eyes burned. *He is the man I must someday slay.*

"An evil has risen in the south!" roared Emperor Cadigus. "A rot spreads. The Resistance raises its head in mockery."

The Legions howled, fists raised and voices torn in rage. The cries shook the square. The sound thudded in Kaelyn's chest and slammed against her ears. She shouted with them. She raised her fist and cried in fury. Yet she did not share the bloodlust of the thousands around her. She thought of how her father would beat her, how his hot irons would sear her flesh, and how his rod of lightning would thrust against her. The fires of old pain flared inside her, and Kaelyn screamed with the rest of them, letting her memories burn.

At her side, Rune shouted too, his voice hoarse, his fist raised. Kaelyn did not know where he found his rage, but she could guess. The Cadigus Regime had burned his home and slain his father. There would be rage enough in him to fuel a forge.

Emperor Frey blew fire, then shouted again.

"We have defeated the old enemies of Requiem!" His wings beat, churning flame around him. "We've slain the griffins, the salvanae of the west, and the weak men of the east. We've burned the desert barbarians south of our sea. The world is cleansed of their evil! Yet still darkness writhes among us."

The Legions roared in the square. They chanted for Requiem. They banged fists against breastplates. They were a smelter ready to spill over.

And they will cover the world, Kaelyn thought, standing among them in her disguise. *They will drown all lands in their shadow, unless our small light can hold back the tide.*

"We will slay the evil that has risen!" Frey howled upon the tower. "We will stamp out those who betray the empire. We will crush any weakness within us. Requiem must be united in its honor, pride, and strength." He roared fire. "We seek *purification!*"

The crowds below chanted, banging their fists.

"Purification! Purification!" Their cries rang across the city. "Hail the red spiral!"

Flames spewed from the emperor's maw and wrapped around him. He bellowed to the skies, wings roiling smoke and ash.

"All weakness must be eradicated!" he cried. "The sick must die. The old must perish. The traitors must be broken. Requiem will be pure in its strength and glory."

The crowds roared. "Purification! Purification!"

Kaelyn shouted among them. Rune did too. Her eyes burned.

So the stories are true, she thought. Whispers had reached their southern camp, speaking of the Axehand Order--the elite thugs of the emperor--slaying the sick and weak. Refugees spoke of axehands storming infirmaries and homes, snatching all those deemed impure. The ill, the handicapped, the wounded, the frail and old--all taken at night, never seen again.

"Purification!" chanted the crowds, banging fists against steel. "Purification!"

Above them all, the great golden dragon howled. "Requiem will be pure! Weakness will be crushed. The southern rebels will be broken. *Purification!* Axehands—reveal the prisoners!"

Men of the Axehand Order stood upon the great hall's battlements. Their black robes swayed. Their hoods hid their faces. Their left arms ended with axe blades strapped to stumps; with their right hands, they grabbed and twisted cranks. The banners of Cadigus, sweeping black fields emblazoned with red spirals, began to rise from the walls like curtains.

Kaelyn winced. Tears budded in her eyes. She couldn't help it; a wail fled her lips.

It was a mistake--wailing here could cost her life--but none heard her. All around, the other soldiers roared with renewed rage. Their shouts rang, battle cries of unending hatred, shrieks of primordial fire.

"Oh stars," Rune said beside her, voice shaking; Kaelyn doubted any of the screaming soldiers heard him either.

As the banners rose, Kaelyn stared at the unveiled, bloody walls of the palace. Tears streamed down her cheeks.

"I'm sorry," she whispered. "I'm so sorry."

Upon the castle walls they hung from chains, twenty wagon wheels. Each wheel held a broken man, woman, or child, their shattered limbs slung through the spokes. They were still alive. They twisted and bled, too weak to scream.

"Behold the rot among us!" Frey called from his tower, a beast of flame and tooth. "Behold the so-called resistors caught lurking in our pure city. See their might now! See their wives and children broken upon the wheels. See the impure and cowardly crushed!"

Kaelyn wanted to look away. She knew these men. She knew their wives. She had played with their children. Tears blurred her vision, her throat tightened, and her fists trembled, yet she could not look away. She stared at them, her brothers in arms, now shreds of humanity.

They were naked, their flesh whipped and burned. Their bones had been shattered with hammers. Their spines had been cracked. They coiled through the spokes like ropes of flesh, and they bled, and they whimpered. A few were children barely older than toddlers.

Kaelyn wanted to fly to them. She wanted to shift into a dragon, to burn them dead, to end their pain, then flee this city. Yet she could not. If she shifted now into a dragon, the Legions would swarm, and she too would be broken. She too would hang among her comrades.

She clenched her fists, trembled, and bit her lip so hard she tasted blood.

They served me. Her throat was so tight she could barely breathe, and she tasted tears on her lips. *They served my rebellion. I doomed them to this fate. I'm sorry, my friends.*

"So will happen to all who stain our purity!" Frey said from the tower top, voice ringing across the square. "Axehand Order— remove these wretches from the wheels. Send them to infirmaries. Heal their bones. Heal their spirits." His voice rose to a shriek, a sound like steam fleeing a kettle. "We will break them anew every year! They will hang here every summer, spines and limbs shattered, and we will heal them again, and break them again, and they will scream for decades, and we will never let them die. They will suffer! The enemies of Requiem will suffer! *Purification!*"

The Legions roared. "Purification!"

"Hail the red spiral!" cried the emperor.

"Hail the red spiral!" answered the crowds.

"Requiem is strong! Hail the red spiral!"

Kaelyn looked around her, feeling like a woman drowning in a sea of steel and hatred.

How? she wanted to shout. How could so many people worship blood? How could so many people cheer the torture of children? These were her people! They were fellow Vir Requis, children of starlight! They were born to an ancient race that, for thousands of years, had worshiped the stars and fought for justice. How could they now scream for blood?

Eyes burning, Kaelyn looked around at the howling soldiers. Though the slits of their visors, she saw young eyes. The eyes of boys. Of young women. Many were no older than her own nineteen years. And Kaelyn understood.

They were just babes when my father took the throne, she thought. *And he molded them. He forged their souls into his blades of darkness. He turned a generation into a machine of murder.*

Kaelyn looked up at her father. The golden dragon cackled atop his tower, wings drawing in smoke and flame, jaws spraying fire. Kaelyn snarled.

I will kill you, Father, she vowed silently. *You will fall. I will restore Requiem to starlight.*

The men upon the battlements twisted winches, and the wheels began to rise on their chains, leaving trails of blood along the walls.

Now Kaelyn could finally close her eyes. She wanted to reach out and clutch Rune's hand, but dared not. She prayed silently to the stars of Requiem, the old and forbidden gods.

Give them strength, stars of my fathers. Or show them mercy and let them die. Please, stars, let them die. Pity the children at least.

Yet could the stars even hear her? The ash and fire of Cadigus covered the sky. Darkness cloaked Requiem. The noble kingdom had fallen; the bloodstained empire rose.

The rally ended at sundown.

The troops marched back to their barracks. Their officers flew as dragons, blowing flames over the city roofs. The sun sank behind the walls and towers of Nova Vita, and Kaelyn's work began.

I will not fail, she swore in the shadows. *I will keep fighting. For the memory of those fallen. For the sacrifice of those suffering. I will do my task. The tyrant must die.*

In the night, she and Rune marched with the troops. Thousands of boots thudded along the cobbled streets. Thousands of faces stared forward through slits in dark visors. They moved through the city like a coiling snake of steel, each soldier a single scale. At their lead, their standard-bearers marched with their banners. At their sides, the city rose: rows of homes four stories tall, barracks of troops, smithies where hammers rang against anvils, the amphitheater where Frey executed his enemies, and everywhere statues of the emperor, fist to heart, eyes watching the city.

No civilians could be seen. The sun had fallen; the curfew reigned. Years ago, they said, light and laughter had filled these streets at night. Jugglers and singers would perform, merchants would hawk wine and pastries, and the people of Nova Vita would walk under ever-burning oil lamps. Since Cadigus had taken the throne, only steel filled these streets after dark. The singers, the jugglers, the merchants--they hid in their homes, languished in dungeons, or lay buried.

Kaelyn sneaked a look at Rune. He marched at her side, staring ahead, body stiff. He did not glance her way. He looked every inch a soldier, boots thudding and fist clutching his sword, but she saw the fear in him. She *felt* it.

Be strong, Rune, she thought, as if she could transfer those thoughts into him. *Be strong and we will survive.*

They marched with the Flaming Eye Brigade, a host of ten thousand warriors stationed here in the capital, tasked with defending Nova Vita. Rune and Kaelyn's armor, taken from the bodies of slain soldiers, fit snugly. Their armbands sported two stars each--the rank of *corelis*, low enough for officers to ignore, high enough to wield some respect among fellow soldiers.

Everything is perfect, Kaelyn told herself as she marched down the streets. *Our armor fits. Nobody can see our faces behind these helms. Nobody knows of the two legionaries we killed. We are nothing but two more cogs with perfect hatred.*

And yet fear pulsed through her, and every officer she passed sent her heart thrashing. What if something wasn't perfect? What if somebody found the corpses of the soldiers she and Rune were mimicking? What if they stood too tall or short? What if somebody saw their eyes through their visors and spotted the ruse?

What if we're caught?

Kaelyn swallowed a lump in her throat, knowing the answer.

If they catch us, they won't kill us. They will break us. They will hang us in the square every year, then heal us, then break us again, an endless cycle until our minds break too.

She tightened her lips and gripped her sword. She kept marching with the thousands, passing from street to street.

Then we must not be caught, she told herself. *We must not fail. We will do our task. We will live. And then we will flee far away from this place, back south to safety... and to Valien.*

They marched, passing from snaking streets to a wide boulevard. Ahead rose a fortress all in black, its walls tiled in obsidian, its battlements topped with cannons and armor-clad dragons. Torches blazed upon these walls, their shadows dancing like dead spirits rising from graves. Four towers rose here, capped with merlons like the teeth of stone giants. The banners of Cadigus thudded upon each tower, hiding and revealing red spirals.

"Castra Draco," Kaelyn whispered. "The heart of the Legions."

Its towers dwarfed the buildings around it. Its halls held three brigades, thirty thousand troops in all. The generals of the Legions ruled from this place. If Tarath Imperium was the heart of the empire, here was its iron fist.

Castra Draco. Center of Requiem's military might. She winced. *The place the two soldiers we mimic served.*

She glanced around. Thousands of troops marched, clockwork demons of fire and steel. Boots thudded in unison. Eyes stared ahead, never moving, never straying. The fortress loomed above, and Kaelyn swallowed. She could not enter those dark halls, the place where bones were broken, where souls were forged, where the wrath of Requiem simmered. In there she and Rune would have to remove their helms, unveiling their deception. If she entered that darkness, they would not emerge.

"Come on," she whispered under her breath. "Where are you, Lana?"

She looked up at the rooftops along the streets, seeking movement. She kept marching with the troops. The fortress grew closer, rising like a tombstone for a god. Soon they were only a hundred yards away. Kaelyn bit her lip and cursed under her breath. She sneaked another few glances to the roofs of surrounding homes and shops.

Hurry up, Lana, she thought, chewing her lip. At her side, she saw Rune too searching the rooftops, his fists clenching and unclenching at his sides.

What if soldiers had found the woman, friend to the Resistance? What if Lana now languished in a prison or lay dead?

Kaelyn stared ahead. The gates of Castra Draco rose only yards away.

We'll have to escape on our own, Kaelyn decided and sucked in her breath. Yet how could she? She marched among thousands. She and Rune moved in flawless formation, their boots thumping with the others in a perfect beat. If they fled now, they would be seen. They would be caught. They--

There!

A shadow appeared upon a roof.

Kaelyn sucked in her breath, and hope sprang in her chest.

The silhouette of a woman stood above, clad in leggings, tall boots, and a fluttering cloak. In one hand, she held a banner; her other hand rested on the pommel of a saber. The clouds parted, and moonlight caught her standard, illuminating a two-headed dragon, sigil of House Aeternum. The pale light shone upon the woman too, revealing mocking lips, a mask with only one eye-hole, and long black hair with a single white streak.

Lady Lana Cain, Kaelyn thought. *My dearest friend.*

"Soldiers of Cadigus!" the lady shouted from the roof and raised her banner high. "King Relesar Aeternum returns! See his banner. Hear his call. Requiem--may our wings forever find your sky!"

Chaos erupted.

The troops below spun toward the roof. Officers shouted orders. Soldiers shifted into dragons, armor morphing into scales, swords into claws.

"Death to the tyrant!" Lady Lana cried above, laughing and waving her flag. "Death to Cadigus!"

With that, the masked woman shifted and soared. A black dragon with a white stripe across her back, she vanished into shadows.

All around Kaelyn, officers shouted and pointed at the roofs. Dragons took flight. Fire spewed from maws, lighting the night. Cries and roars rang.

Rune stood staring, frozen in place. Kaelyn grabbed his arm and tugged him.

"Come on, you woolhead!" she said.

She pulled him away from the chaos and into shadows, praying no eyes were watching. But it seemed everyone was busy shouting, flying after Lana in dragon form, or watching the commotion--including Rune, who was still sneaking glances toward the rooftops.

"Come *on*!" Kaelyn said, tugging him.

They slunk into an alley, leaving the brigade and disappearing into shadows. Kaelyn began to scurry deeper into the darkness, her boots now silent upon the cobblestones. She pulled Rune with her. The sounds of the boulevard faded into a muffled storm.

A hundred yards into the alley, Kaelyn found a moldy barrel. She drew her dagger, loosened the barrel's lid with her blade, and pulled it free. She stood on tiptoes and gazed inside. Rotten turnips festered there, rustling with bugs.

"Bloody stars," Rune muttered and lifted his helm's visor. "Did she have to use rotten turnips? Why not a barrel of strong ale, or-- Ow!"

Kaelyn kicked his leg hard. "Quiet, Rune, and help me dig."

Standing on her toes, she reached into the barrel and rummaged through the rotten tubers. Bugs scurried around her fingers, and she thanked the stars that legionaries wore thick leather gloves. Rune rooted around beside her, grimacing.

"Disgusting," he said. "I think I felt a rat in there. Or maybe a turnip that's gone fuzzy."

"Quiet!" Kaelyn whispered and reached elbow deep. She rifled around, then smiled. "There! I feel it."

She gripped her catch and pulled, fishing out a bundle of leather. She brushed it clean, placed the bundle on the ground, and unwrapped it.

She revealed parchment placards, each about a foot long. Her eyes dampened.

Each poster displayed the sigil of House Aeternum--a two-headed dragon wreathed in leaves of birch, the holy tree of Requiem. Above the dragon's heads, inked in silver, appeared the constellation Draco--the stars of Requiem. Letters too were drawn upon each scroll:

"Relesar Aeternum, true king of Requiem, reigns in the south. Join the true king! Death to Cadigus!"

Beneath this, in smaller script, appeared the Old Words of Requiem, the forbidden prayer that priests had sung for thousands of years.

"Requiem! May our wings forever find your sky."

Rune stared at the posters and tapped his chin.

"Not bad," he said. "Lana did a decent job, though she could have added something about how I'm also breathtakingly handsome."

Kaelyn sighed. "We're here to spread the truth to the empire, Rune, not inundate the people with more lies." She grabbed a sheaf of posters. "Now lift half of them! It'll be a long night."

"I don't understand," Rune said as he stuffed placards into his pack. "Why wouldn't we just sneak into this city at night? Why bother seeing your father speak and marching down the streets? We could have just come to this alley in the first place." He shuddered. "Oh stars, Kaelyn, the rally... the men he breaks... And we just stood there and watched."

Kaelyn sighed, rolling up posters and shoving them into her own pack.

"We needed to be there," she said softly. "We need to see, hear, and shout his evil. We need to know the full rot of his soul." She lowered her head, still seeing those broken bodies upon the wall, and when she looked up at Rune, she saw them haunting his eyes too. "One must grasp the depth of evil before one can fight it."

When they'd packed all the posters, they crept back to the alley's mouth. Kaelyn heard nothing. The boulevard seemed barren. All the soldiers had either entered Castra Draco or flown in pursuit of Lana.

"Fly high, Lana," Kaelyn whispered and looked up at the sky, as if she could see her friend flying there. "Fly far. Thank you."

Her eyes stung. She knuckled them, tightened her lips, and stuck her head outside the alley. She peered from side to side. Seeing no one, she grabbed Rune and pulled him out into the street.

"Now come on," she whispered to him. "We're just two soldiers on patrol, part of the Flaming Eye Brigade. Curfew is on, the rally is over, so these streets should be quiet. If anyone stops us, we're just doing our rounds, and Castra Draco has our names to prove it."

They began to walk, moving away from the fortress. Kaelyn had grown up in this city; she'd spent sixteen years here before fleeing her father's rod and wrath. She knew these streets like the scars her father had given her. After walking several blocks, they reached a wide brick building. Smoke plumed from its four chimneys, and the scents of wine, ale, and roasted meats wafted. Behind the stained-glass windows, she saw the shadows of men moving, and she heard them singing hoarse drinking songs.

"The Green Duck," she said. "A favorite alehouse among the soldiers."

Rune raised an eyebrow. "The Green Duck? This is Nova Vita, heart of the Cadigus Regime. I figured alehouses here would have names like The Tavern of Steel, The Goblet of Glory, or Frey's Firkin. Something more... imperial."

Kaelyn allowed herself a wan smile. "This tavern predates my father's regime. He did rename Lynport after himself--and about half the other towns in the kingdom--but soldiers have been drinking in the Green Duck for two hundred years. If he changed *this* name, he'd truly have a rebellion on his hands." She patted Rune's cheek. "You owned a tavern; you know how soldiers are with their drink. Now quickly--help me with a poster!"

She looked around furtively. The street was empty. The soldiers inside the tavern were singing raucously. Kaelyn unrolled a poster, and Rune opened a bottle of glue. Within an instant, the poster bedecked the tavern's outer wall; it would greet anyone come to drink.

"Relesar Aeternum, true king of Requiem, reigns in the south. Death to Cadigus!"

Kaelyn grabbed Rune's arm and tugged him.

"Now come on! We have many more posters to hang, and the night won't last forever."

He walked after her, wincing. "Kaelyn, your fingers have bruised my arm by now--and that's with me wearing armor!"

She glared at him. "If we're caught, you'll have more than bruises. Hurry. And be quiet."

They walked down the silent street. Torches stood in palisades, lighting the night. Dragons flew in patrols above, blasting streams of fire that crisscrossed the night. Every few blocks, they encountered more soldiers. Most were other pairs on patrol, their rank low and their faces hidden behind helms; they did not spare Kaelyn and Rune a glance. On one street, they passed an officer; he bore two red spirals upon each shoulder, denoting him a *dialanse*, a young officer two or three years out of the academy.

"Hail the red spiral!" Kaelyn and Rune said, standing at attention and saluting.

The officer regarded them, gave a lazy salute, and kept walking down the street. His legs wobbled. This one was drunk.

If my father caught an officer wandering the streets in his cups, he'd have the man flayed, Kaelyn thought. But for now, she had more pressing concerns than the fate of a young commander. She kept marching down the streets until she and Rune neared the amphitheater.

It loomed before them, a great ring of stone, large enough to seat fifty thousand souls. Her father used to force Kaelyn to come here, sit in the upper tiers, and watch prisoners fed to lions and wolves. Frey rarely hanged or beheaded his enemies; to him, death was a show, a horror to celebrate. Frey was not a man for the noose or the axe, killings too quick for his liking. He lusted for disemboweling, for quartering, for flaying, for feeding flesh to wild beasts. And he delighted in sharing his love with his children.

Shari always loved the executions, Kaelyn remembered. Her sister herself had once broken a man upon the wheel, grinning as she swung the hammer.

Her knees began to shake, and sweat ran down Kaelyn's back. For a moment, the past pulsed too powerfully, memories of her family torturing its enemies... and torturing her. She too had felt their lust for blood. Her flesh still bore the scars of Shari's blades, of Frey's punisher, of the joy they took in beating her.

Only Leresy never hurt me, she remembered. *He always cried when Father and Shari beat me. He always comforted me afterward.*

But of course, her twin brother too enjoyed his bloodshed. Leresy would watch in fascination as beasts tore into flesh. He would stay up all night, reading books of old battles. He would collect torture instruments in his chambers like some men collected statues.

But he never hurt me, Kaelyn remembered. *I'm his twin. He sees me as part of himself. And he loves himself more than anything.*

"Kaelyn?" Rune whispered. "Are you all right?"

She looked at him. He was watching her in concern.

"No," she whispered. "None of this is all right. But we will make it right. Grab a poster."

Kaelyn kept guard, glancing around with her hand on her sword, while Rune glued a poster to the amphitheater's wall. They moved onward, two soldiers on patrol.

We don't have much time, Kaelyn thought. *When the first posters are seen, dragons will swarm. This city will burn.*

"Hurry," she said to Rune.

They kept moving. Kaelyn no longer sought buildings of importance; that was taking too long. Every shadowy wall she passed, she pasted another placard. They moved from street to street. Their bundles of posters dwindled. Soon they were down to twenty or fewer.

They left the wide, clean streets of northern Nova Vita behind, heading south into the slums. Here the houses rotted. Here beggars huddled in alleys, peering with frightened eyes, then scurrying into hiding as they saw Kaelyn and Rune. Stray cats stretched on roofs and rats scuttled in gutters.

"You want to raise this place in rebellion too?" Rune asked, looking around dubiously. "I thought you wanted to target lords and soldiers to rise up against Cadigus, not the poor."

Kaelyn smiled softly. "Great rebellions rarely begin with soldiers or lords; they rise from among the poor and hungry."

They walked between crowded, dilapidated buildings. Shop awnings touched above their heads, turning alleyways into corridors. The houses here had no glass windows like the abodes of the wealthy, only wooden shutters. Nightsoil flowed in gutters, and bugs scurried along the cobbled streets.

"Here," Kaelyn said and pointed at a wide, brick building. "This place. Let's hang one here."

It was the largest house in the neighborhood, but it nestled into shadows, hiding from the city. Laughter rose from within, and candlelight burned behind the curtains. A sign hung above the door; it read "The Bad Cats" and featured two cats licking their paws.

Rune squinted at the building. "What is this place?"

A door burst open, and a woman stumbled into the alleyway, squealing and laughing. She clutched scarves of silk to her naked body, and her hair hung wild across her shoulders.

"Come back here!" rose a man's voice from within, thick with ale and lust. "I paid good coin for you. Back in!"

The woman laughed, saw Rune and Kaelyn, and forced her mouth shut. She winked, held a finger to her lips, and rushed back inside.

"Oh," Rune said. "We had one of these places in Lynport."

He thought back to Lynport's brothel along the boardwalk. The Cadigus family had burned it down years ago, killing all those inside. Only one person had fled the inferno: a young girl with short brown hair and blazing eyes. Her name was Erry Docker; she had spent the following years living on the beach, eating crabs and whatever she could steal.

Kaelyn nodded. "My father does not approve of brothels; he calls the men who visit them weak. Yet he accepts some sins if they remain unseen. He allows this place to linger in the shadows to please his generals."

Rune raised an eyebrow. "You mean... the generals of the Legions visit a brothel in a slum?" He gestured around him at the rats and gutters. "They visit *this* place?"

Kaelyn smiled wanly. "As often as they can. I sometimes think this is the heart of the Legions, not Castra Draco. Here they are not generals; they are men thirsty for ale and hungry for women. Let these men see our posters. Let them know that you've returned. We'll hang one right on the door."

Kaelyn pulled a poster from her pack, walked into the alley, and faced the brothel's door. Candlelight glowed through the windows, and laughter and squeals rose. From the upper floor, she heard huffing and a cry of pleasure.

These patrons love freedom, laughter, and good cheer, she thought. *They might join our cause.*

She unrolled the poster, smeared glue across it, and raised it to the door.

Before she could hang the parchment, the door swung open. Kaelyn gasped.

The young man at the doorway rubbed his bleary eyes. His cheeks were flushed with wine, and he wore fine fabrics of crimson and gold. His fingers, heavy with rings, struggled to unlace his pants. Laughter rose behind him, and women called him to return to their bed.

"Hang on!" the young man called over his shoulder. "I got to piss, damn you. Don't put your clothes on, hang on!" He turned back toward the alleyway and took a step outside, nearly bumping into Kaelyn, then squinted at her. "Hello... do I know..."

He gasped and his hands fell to his sides.

"Leresy," Kaelyn whispered.

My twin brother. Prince of Requiem.

He stared at her, frozen.

"Kaelyn?" he asked, voice rising incredulously.

With a snarl, Kaelyn drew her dagger and thrust it forward.

Leresy screamed. He stumbled backward. Kaelyn was aiming for his neck, but sliced his cheek instead. His blood spilled and he squealed. He drew his sword and barreled forward.

"The Resistance!" he shouted. "Enemy in the alley! Men! Guards! Guards!"

Kaelyn cursed. She tried to stab him again, but he was waving his sword wildly. Soldiers came rushing to the door from within, drawing their own swords.

Rune grabbed her arm and tugged.

"Run, Kaelyn!" Rune shouted. "Fly!"

They turned. They ran. They shifted into dragons and flew.

They soared into the night, moving faster than falcons. The air roared around them, and the city dwindled below, its lights spinning and its streets spreading out like cobwebs. Kaelyn laughed and roared fire and her heart thudded.

"Death to Cadigus!" she shouted, letting her cry ring across the city. "Aeternum rises and Requiem will be freed. The tyrant must die!"

Her heart thrashed and her wings beat mightily. Rune soared at her side. Pillars of flame pierced the night, shooting between them, blazing and crackling and nearly burning her. When Kaelyn looked behind her, she saw a hundred dragons rising in pursuit.

Leresy flew among them, a red dragon shrieking and blowing fire.

"The Resistance attacks!" he screamed. "Awake, dragons of Requiem! Awake, Legions! Fly!"

Kaelyn turned and blasted fire his way.

Her jet blazed through the night and crashed into her brother.

"Kaelyn, fly!" Rune shouted and slapped her with his tail. "Don't fight them, just fly!"

She kept beating her wings. They streamed south. They soared into the clouds, and more flames filled the sky. Dragons swooped from above; Kaelyn and Rune darted between them, swiping their claws. More dragons rose from below. Thousands of flaming jets filled the air.

Kaelyn darted between the flames. Rune flew at her side. They rose higher and clouds enveloped them. Kaelyn could see nothing but Rune at her side, a black dragon nearly invisible in the night.

As they flew south, Kaelyn bared her fangs. She felt light fill her and the fire of battle burn her fear. Thousands of dragons chased them. An entire army roared behind, and fires lit the sky, yet Kaelyn grinned as she flew, and she had never felt more alive.

We struck in the heart of the capital. Now the empire knows Rune is our king.

The Legions roared behind, washing the world in fire, thousands of beasts with blazing eyes. Kaelyn and Rune flew through the night, leaving the city behind, until forests swayed below and the stars of Requiem shone above, the old gods guiding her home.

LERESY

He lay in the brothel bed, his face blazing and his head swimming.

"More wine!" he shouted and waved around his empty mug. "Damn it, more wine!"

Wine would dull his performance in this bed. He knew that. But he didn't care. He didn't have to prove anything to anyone anymore. Not to the whores of the Bad Cats, this rundown cesspool. Not to his men. Not to his father.

"Wine!"

What he did need was to forget. To forget the blazing wound on his face. To forget his lost fortress.

To forget Nairi.

"Bloody whore arses, I said wine!" he shouted, pushing himself up in bed. He blinked, shook his head, and tried to bring the room into focus.

The Bad Cats was a gaudy, stinking mess. Pastel curtains hid the windows, cheap wool woven to look like silk. Murals covered the walls and ceilings, depicting amorous acts and their cost. Each wall showed the woman and man in different positions, the price scribbled below the painted figures. Upon the ceiling, two women--painted in peachy pastels--were pleasing their client together. Leresy had chosen the ceiling's offering; it was the most expensive, but his pockets were deep, and his pain was deeper.

"My lord!" said Dawn, the golden-haired woman to his right. She kissed his ear. "Give your attention to me, not your cups."

At his left, Dusk--an olive-skinned beauty of the east--stroked his hair. "Give me your love, my lord, not her."

Leresy did not know their true names. He did not care. They were nothing but cheap flesh. They were nothing but filthy, base, false mockery. Yet he snarled, tossed his mug aside, and took them again. He closed his eyes while he used them. He did not want to see their flushed faces, their eyes fluttering with the mock pleasure he paid them to feign. He did not want to see these murals around him, their colors so bright they hurt his eyes. He moved in the bed,

and Dawn and Dusk moved with him, and behind his closed
eyelids, Leresy saw her again.

Nairi.

"She killed her," he whispered and his eyes stung. "My twin
did it. Kaelyn. She killed her. And now I'm dying too."

Dawn and Dusk were moaning so loudly--stars, they sounded
like hogs in heat!--they did not hear. Leresy let them keep doing
their work. He no longer knew where he lay. In the fog of wine,
he was back in Castra Luna. He flew upon the wind, a red dragon
roaring fire, and she flew at his side, an iron dragon with mocking
green eyes. Below them spread his dominion--his first fort, a
mighty outpost, a beacon of civilization in the wilderness.

"And they took it," he whispered and clenched his fists. His
eyes stung. "The boy Rune and my sister Kaelyn. They took
everything from me."

His fists trembled. He saw it again--the horde of the
Resistance howling his way, and the bodies of legionaries raining
around him, torn to pieces, entrails dangling and limbs severed.

Nairi was gone. His fort was gone. His hope for inheritance
was gone. All that remained was wine and cheap whores.

"Enough!" he shouted and opened his eyes.

He rose from the bed, shoving Dawn and Dusk off. They
fell to the floor, naked, and gazed up at him. Fear filled their eyes.

"My lord?" Dusk asked, her raven hair spilling across her
shoulders.

"I said wine, damn it!" he shouted, stepped toward her, and
slapped her. "I demanded wine, and you ignored me. Is there no
more wine in this whorehouse?"

Dusk recoiled, clutching her struck cheek. Dawn rushed to
her and embraced her.

Disgusting harlots, Leresy thought and spat. He grabbed his
clothes from the chair, dressed himself, and fished through his
pocket for coins. He tossed them a silver each.

"You're not even worth copper," he said and left the room,
slamming the door behind him.

Before him, the hallway swayed. Leresy had to hold the wall
to walk. Everything spun around him. Other patrons moved from
room to room, and women ran naked and giggling, but they were
only streaks of color to Leresy, only ghosts of sound. He had to

get out of here. This whole house was a nest of disease and filth. The walls were spinning and closing in around him; soon they would crush him.

I have to get out!

He staggered downstairs, falling the last three steps and banging his hip hard. A girl tried to help him up. He struck her, sending her sprawling, and pulled himself to his feet. Holding the wall, he made his way to the front doors and stumbled outside into the night.

The cold autumn air washed over him. His wound, an ugly stitched gash across his face, blazed with new agony. It was here, at this very doorstep, that his twin had slashed him. Whenever he stood here, the wound flared.

"I will cut you too, Kaelyn," he hissed into the shadows. "And I will cut you, Rune, and I will cut you, Shari, and I will cut this whole damn world until we all drown in blood."

Tears filled his eyes.

She scarred me and she killed you, Nairi, he thought, and a lump filled his throat. *She burned your corpse and buried you in a mass grave, and now you're gone. Now I'm nothing.*

He tried to remember every detail of Nairi--her short yellow hair that fell across her brow, her green eyes that were always so haughty and teasing, her pink lips and their crooked smile, her body clad in leather and steel, and mostly... mostly her power.

With his wife fallen, her father was beyond his reach. Lord Herin Blackrose, lord of the Axehand Order, would no longer serve him.

His love. His fort. His power. His face.

"You took them all from me, twin sister," he whispered and tasted his tears. "You will hurt so much when I find you. You will scream so loudly."

He stumbled through the city streets, holding alley walls for support. The smell of frying onions rose from one brick house, invading his nostrils like poison. Leresy fell to his knees, crawled toward a ditch, and retched. He had eaten only scraps all day; he now lost them.

He righted himself, wiped his lips on his sleeve, and kept walking. His father would be furious to see him, a prince of the realm, stumbling alone through the darkness. Princes should march ahead of brigades, soldiers and might surrounding them. Leresy smirked and tightened his cloak around him.

Anything that upsets you, old man, is good.

Finally he saw his new fortress in the distance, a shard of black rising from a dark square. A thousand legionaries served in Castellum Tal, a milanx of battle-hardened men. Leresy snorted.

Men! Who wanted to serve with a thousand sweaty, hairy, disgusting men? Back at Castra Luna in the south, Leresy had commanded thousands of youths, half of them soft females only eighteen years old and frightened. So many beauties had served him--Tilla Roper with her pale cheeks, that scrawny friend of hers with the short brown hair, and so many others to conquer.

Leresy stood in the night, staring up at his new home, at this pathetic little tower with its wretched milanx hidden inside. This was no place for him. This was no fortress for a prince. Yet his father, the bastard, had insisted.

"I demand another training fort!" Leresy had shouted at court, his eyes stinging. "I will break in recruits. I--"

The emperor had only snorted, glaring down from his throne.

"I'll not have my son whoring his way through the Legions," Frey Cadigus had said. "Do you want to train female youths or bed them?"

"Father!" Leresy had cried. "I will train them. I trained the last recruits and--"

"And we saw how that ended," Frey spat. "You commanded a fort for only three moons, and it crumbled. You had a chance to mold youths into soldiers, and you proved yourself weakest among them." He snorted. "My Legions are not your brothel, boy. You will no longer serve among women; they have softened you. You will serve among men now, hardened warriors who've slain enemies in battle. Maybe they'll teach you to be a man too."

Leresy walked across the courtyard, reeling from side to side. When he reached the tower, he banged upon the doors.

"Let me in, bastards!" he howled, pounding. "This is your prince. Let me in, sons of whores!"

The sound of laughter, howls, and song wafted from behind the doors. Leresy pounded with more vigor.

"Open these doors," he shouted, voice hoarse and slurred, "or I'll flay you all and make cloaks from your skin!"

Finally the guards pulled the doors open, and Leresy stumbled into his new tower.

The grand hall swam before him, a cavern of light and sound. Soldiers banged mugs upon tabletops, singing hoarsely. A few were so deep in their cups, they were dancing upon the tables, kicking off plates and mugs. Roasted boars and jugs of wine lay everywhere. Two stray dogs ran between legs, and three whores squealed, clutching silks to their naked bodies and fleeing pursuing men.

"Bring me wine!" Leresy demanded, marching deeper into the hall. His boots stumbled over discarded turkey bones, smashed mugs, and a drunken soldier who lay gurgling. "Wine, sons of dogs, and lots of it!"

When he had taken command of this fortress, it had been a dull, dreary place, its men automatons who knew only to march, drill, and shout "Yes, Commander!" like trained birds. Leresy would have gone mad.

A woman ran naked toward him, holding a jug of wine. He grabbed the jug, drank deeply, and slapped the woman's backside to send her scurrying off.

This, he thought, *is more like a fort for a prince.*

Soon he was lying across a tabletop, pouring wine from a jug, aiming for his mouth but mostly splattering his face. His scar blazed--it was only days old--but Leresy didn't care. Pain was good. Pain made him forget.

Wine poured. Men sang. Memory faded into numbness.

Leresy's eyelids fluttered and he smiled.

A shriek tore across the hall.

"What is the meaning of this!"

The singing died at once. Silence fell across the fort.

Lying upon the tabletop, Leresy pushed himself up onto his elbows. He squinted toward the hall doors. A figure stood there, blurred and shadowed. Leresy shook his head and blinked, struggling to bring it into focus.

"Shari?" he asked, squinting.

She came marching down the hall toward him, clutching her sword. Leresy rubbed his eyes, and finally she came into focus.

Shari was ten years older than him, and as a child, Leresy had always feared her. A sadistic youth, Shari had delighted in torturing him--cutting his flesh with her knives, burning his hands upon coals, and once even locking him in a coffin for a day. Today Leresy was a grown man, but Shari still frightened him. She was a tall woman, the tallest he'd ever known, and her body was as strong as any man's; Leresy could see that even through her black armor.

And today she was furious. Her dark, curly hair bounced, her eyes flashed, and her lips peeled back, revealing sharp teeth that had bitten him many times.

"Leresy!" she shouted. "What have you done to this place?"

Leresy shook his head to clear it. Still lying upon the tabletop, he managed a grin.

"Hello, sister!" he said and raised a random mug in salute. "Would you care for some wine, some food, or perhaps a lady of the night?"

She marched toward him. Her gloved hand reached out, grabbed his hair, and tugged. Leresy yowled. Snarling, Shari dragged him across the tabletop by the hair, then slammed him down onto the floor. His hip blazed with pain.

"Ow!" he said and struggled to rise. "Stars bloody dammit, Shari, you--"

She backhanded him. White light blazed. Pain flared across his cheek.

"You will not mention the old gods," Shari hissed and clutched his throat. "You are a son of Cadigus. You serve the red spiral. You--"

"Shari, why are you here?" He shook himself free. He leaned against the tabletop, feigning nonchalance; in truth he was hiding his wobbling knees. "Don't you have any prisoners to torture, puppies to eat, or Father's arse to kiss?"

She grabbed his collar, twisted it, and began dragging him across the hall.

"It's you who'll be begging to kiss it tonight," Shari said. "He demands to speak with you. I would be less comical, Leresy, and more afraid. Very afraid."

He stumbled behind her, his wobbly legs struggling to keep up. Mugs and bones clattered around his feet. She kept dragging him, marching toward the doors.

"Shari!" he said. "Let go, damn it."

He reached for his sword but found it missing. Stars damn it! He must have left it at the brothel again. He wanted to go back and fetch it. He wanted to lie in the bed upstairs again, to make love to Dawn and Dusk, to sleep, to drink, to forget. To do anything but see his sister and father.

I want to see you again, Nairi, he thought, and tears stung his eyes. *I want to die and fly with you through the halls of afterlife.*

But Shari would not release him. She dragged him outside into the night.

"Shari, let me go--"

"Be silent or I'll cut out your tongue, then feed it to you."

She tossed him back, growled, and shifted into a dragon.

Blue scales clattered across her. Her body ballooned, her claws scratched the cobblestones, and her tail flailed. Flames churned behind her fangs like a smelter, and her eyes blazed like molten steel. Her wings spread out in the night--one blue and veined, the other a contraption of leather stretched over wood.

"Twisted freak," Leresy said, staring at her.

The pup Relesar, a soft boy, had ripped off her left wing. Shari had built herself this prosthetic, this mockery of true dragon glory. The wood-and-leather apparatus creaked like a sail.

"You look like a fisherman's barge, Shari!" he screamed at her, voice hoarse, and laughed. "Look at you! A freak. A joke."

She flapped her wings and rose several feet in the air. Her claws reached out. Before Leresy could even stumble back, let alone become a dragon himself, she grabbed him like an owl grabs a mouse.

"Shari!" he screamed and struggled in her grip, but couldn't free himself. He tried to shift now, but her claws constricted him, keeping him in human form.

"Silence, brother," she said. "I'm taking you to him."

She flew. Her wings beat in unison, her true wing and her mechanical monstrosity. Leresy squirmed in her grip, screaming and cursing and spitting. The city rolled beneath him, a whirlpool of black buildings, streaming lights, and streets like veins in a rotted heart. Leresy gagged again, spewing wine into the sky. His head tilted back, he moaned, and he saw it there.

The ground lay above him, the sky below. The palace of Tarath Imperium hung like a stalactite, a thousand feet tall. It ended with a claw of black, jagged battlements. Torches flickered across it, and dragons circled the tower like flies around the hand of a corpse.

Tarath Imperium. The greatest tower in the empire. The home of his father.

It was the very last place Leresy wanted to go.

"We would have ruled this place together, Nairi," he whispered, head dangling. "It could have been ours. It should have been ours. But she betrayed us." He growled and wept. "Kaelyn betrayed us. We will kill her, Nairi! We will kill her."

His eyes fluttered shut. He barely noticed Shari shrieking, descending, and carrying him to the palace doors. Next thing he knew, he was stumbling on his feet again, wobbling so madly he almost fell. Only Shari, who marched while gripping his collar, held him up. He blinked, trying to bring the world into focus, and saw his sister dragging him into the palace throne room.

He blinked madly. Shari was in human form again; he hadn't even noticed her shifting back. He shoved her off.

"Let go!" he said. "Unhand me. I'm not one of your dogs."

He reached for his sword, then cursed when--yet again--he realized it was gone.

Shari laughed, released his collar, and shoved him so powerfully he stumbled several paces back. He hit a column, managed to remain standing, and glared.

The throne room of Requiem was, quite handily, the largest chamber Leresy had ever seen. Dragons could fly here and find it roomy. A hundred columns stood in two palisades, rising taller than the greatest pines. The vaulted ceiling sported paintings of dragons flying among clouds. More dragons, these ones battling phoenixes, coiled across the floor in a mosaic. That floor stretched between the columns, leading to the distant throne of the emperor.

Leresy hissed at that throne. His father sat there, the man Leresy hated most.

"Father!" he cried, voice echoing in the hall. "You wanted to see me, Father. I am here! Your son is here."

He lurched down the hall, swaying from column to column for support. He cackled as he walked, spraying saliva. Finally--it seemed like he walked for hours--he stood before Frey Cadigus, Emperor of Requiem.

The old bastard sat in that ivory throne of his, looking like some stuffed vulture. Leresy imagined him roosting on eggs and barked a laugh. Grooves framed the emperor's thin, frowning lips. His dark hair was slicked back. His shoulders were wider than Leresy's, and his pauldrons made them seem even wider. But his eyes, Leresy thought... his eyes were the hardest thing about him. Those eyes were black, narrow, and cruel. They could see better than eagles, he thought. They could see through him--through his stained tunic, through his skin, and into his very soul. Staring into them, Leresy found all his mirth dissipating. A chill ran through him, and he couldn't help but shiver.

"Father," he said, and suddenly his legs shook so badly that he fell to his knees. He knelt before the emperor, and tears burned in his eyes.

Frey stared down at him, looking like a man staring at a maggoty corpse. He placed a handkerchief to his nose.

"You stink of booze, vomit, and cheap whores," Frey said. "Stand up."

Leresy rose to his feet and swayed.

"You summoned me, Father," he said to the old vulture. Rage crackled inside him. Why was the old man just sitting there? "Why, Father? Tell me! Speak, damn it."

Frey rose to his feet and his face twisted, red with anger. His lips peeled back, revealing sharp teeth. When he stepped toward Leresy, fists clenched, he seemed more like a swooping vulture than ever. Leresy let out a yelp, stumbled a few paces backward, and fell down hard onto his backside.

"Father!" he cried, holding out his hands. "Father, please, don't strike me."

Shari laughed in the distance. Sweat drenched Leresy and fear churned his gut. Across his flesh, the old scars blazed--the scars Frey had given him throughout his childhood, beating him with belt, whip, and rod.

He's going to beat me again, Leresy realized and mewled. He scampered backward on his bottom.

"Please, Father!"

Frey leaned down, grabbed Leresy's collar, and yanked him to his feet.

"I said stand!" the emperor thundered. "Are you a prince or a dog to lick my heels? Stand!"

Leresy stood, trembling. Frey towered above him, so much taller, so much stronger.

"What do you want?" Leresy demanded, spraying spit. His voice cracked. "Why do you do this? Let me drink! Let me whore. Let me forget. Why do you bring me here? I don't want to be at court. I don't care about this place. Tell me what you want, and let me go sleep."

Frey's voice dripped disgust. "Oh, you can go sleep soon, Leresy. You won't be here long. You might not be here ever again. You are a disgrace of a son. I gave you a fort in the south, and you reduced it to rubble. I gave you a smaller fortress in the city, thinking Castra Luna was too big for you. You turned even this garrison into a hive of drink and debauchery." He snorted. "You don't care about this place, it is true. You don't care about anything, Leresy, that you can't bed or drink. But I wanted you here for this night. I wanted you to hear this in person. I want you to leave here tonight in shame, knowing what you've done."

Leresy barked a laugh. Tears streamed down his cheeks.

"I reduced Castra Luna to ruin?" he shouted and cackled. "It's your daughter Kaelyn who did that! She's the one who flew in with the Resistance. She's the one who slaughtered our men there, who toppled our walls. I defended that fort! I stood in its grand hall, a sword in my hand, and--"

"You cowered behind women, then fled through the window, leaving Shari to die," Frey said, voice twisted in disgust. "You fought? Did you even draw your sword that night? Have you ever slain an enemy, Leresy, or only run from one? You blame Kaelyn?" The emperor snorted again. "Kaelyn betrayed me, that is true, but she fought well that day. She did not flee from battle. She is a traitor, yes, but strong. She has more of my respect than you do, boy."

"Kaelyn is a whore!" Leresy screamed hoarsely, face burning. "She gave me this scar on my face! She is a dirty, cowardly dog, and I will kill her--"

"You will do nothing," Frey said. He reached out his arm, and Shari came to stand at his side, a smirk on her face. "My daughter Shari has proven herself my only worthy child."

Leresy guffawed. "Shari? She's a freak! She's a monster. Have you seen her wing, Father? I've seen better sails on slavers!"

"And I've seen slaves with more honor than you," Frey retorted. "You may blame Kaelyn, boy, but Castra Luna was your watch. And you let it fall. Shari, my daughter, will not disappoint me. The Resistance, cowards that they are, toppled the walls of Castra Luna and fled into the forests, knowing they could never defend the fort. I am giving Shari command of those ruins now. She will rebuild Castra Luna in my honor, and she will rule it well. It will never more fall under her command."

Leresy stared, his breath dying.

His lips shook.

No. Stars, no.

He let out a raw, anguished howl, reaching his hands to the ceiling.

"But Castra Luna is mine!" He shook his fists and stamped his feet. "You gave it to me, Father. To me! It was my birthday present!" He panted, frothing at the mouth, and screamed wordlessly. "You can't give it to Shari now. She's only... she's a monster! She--"

His voice morphed into nothing but a wordless, hoarse howl.

Frey watched him, eyes hard and cold. Shari stood at his side, her hands on her hips.

"Are you quite done whining, little brother?" she asked. She gave him a crooked smile and wink. "Don't feel bad. If you're a good little brother, perhaps I'll let you visit and muck out the outhouses." She smirked. "They can call you Leresy, Lord of Latrines!"

That was enough for Leresy. After all this night had brought him, that was enough. That made him snap.

He yowled. He reached for his sword a third time, again found it missing, and screamed. Then he remembered. His dagger! Of course! The dagger in his boot!

Cackling, tears and mucus and drool mingling on his face, he reached into his boot, drew the blade, and ran toward his sister. He screamed, dagger flashing in hand.

"Now you die, Shari!" he cried, laughing and crying. "Die, Blue Bitch! Die!"

He leaped and thrust his dagger.

She sidestepped, and the blade sliced the air.

He kept flying forward, tumbled, and crashed facedown onto the floor. His dagger clattered away across the mosaic.

Hands grabbed his collar. His tunic pulled back, choking him. The hands yanked him to his feet.

Frey Cadigus, Emperor of Requiem, began dragging his son toward the doors.

Leresy struggled. He mewled. He kicked. But he could not free himself. His father dragged him across the hall, between the columns and statues, over the mosaics, and under the painted ceiling. When they reached the doors, Frey tossed his son outside the palace like an innkeeper tossing out a rowdy barfly.

Leresy slammed against the stairs that led down into the night. He turned back toward his father, covered his face with his arms, and whimpered.

"Father!" he said.

Frey spat upon him, standing tall in the doorway, framed in the light of braziers. Shari stood behind him, her hands still on her hips, a sneer still on her lips.

"You have shamed me, Leresy," the emperor said. "You are henceforth banished from my court. You are henceforth banished from my city. You are no longer my son." He spat again. "Leave this city. You have one hour. If I see you again, Leresy, you will receive no such mercy. If I see you again, I will break you, hang your mangled body from this palace, and let the empire see your shame. Be gone!"

Leresy hissed and snapped his teeth.

"You will regret this, Father!" he screamed. He pointed a shaky finger. "You will regret this, Shari! I will slay you both. I will butcher you like the pigs that you are, and I will hang you here by your entrails."

With that, he stumbled down the stairs and nearly fell. He shifted into a dragon. He roared. He flew through the night. He sprayed his fire across the city; it fell in a rain of sparks.

"I am Leresy Cadigus!" he shouted as he flew, laughing and beating his wings. His fire rained and ignited roofs below. "I am Prince of Requiem. The throne will be mine--mine!"

Roaring, he dived toward his fortress, the slim tower of Castellum Tal. He slammed into the front doors in dragon form, shattering them, and rolled into the hall. He spread his wings wide and howled, and his dragon's roar echoed. All around, his drunken men fell, fled, or cheered.

"We fly out, men!" Leresy shouted. He whipped his tail, knocking over a table and shattering its mugs of ale. "We fly--now! Follow me and you will have all the ale, women, and gold in Requiem. We fly!"

His thousand men cheered in a drunken stupor, waving mugs, jugs, and swords.

Leresy spun around in the hall, his wings and tail knocking over more tables, and lumbered outside into the night.

"Follow!" he shouted over his shoulder. "Bring the wine with you, and bring the women. We fly!"

He soared. Behind him, his cheering men emerged from the hall, shifted into dragons, and flew after him. They rose in the night, a thousand drunken dragons blowing fire. Their flames lit the darkness.

Lord of Latrines? Leresy snorted a laugh. He would make her into a latrine! When he ruled the throne, he would chain Shari beneath the sewers and let the city piss on her. He laughed, imagining it.

Nova Vita sprawled below him. He flew, howling and laughing. He streamed over the walls, and his thousand dragons flew behind him, chanting his name.

They will be my army, Leresy vowed. *I will give them ale, women, and drunken songs. And they will give me a throne.*

They flew over the forests, leaving the capital behind. The night wrapped around them, cold and black like the memory of Nairi's death.

ERRY

A lone copper dragon, she flew over the forests toward her darkest nightmare.

"Oh, griffin puke," she cursed, wings flapping. Her heart thrashed against her ribs, and she blasted nervous fire. "Damn bloody piss soup. Damn the stars and damn the Abyss and damn Frey Cadigus's hairy arse!"

She snorted smoke from her nostrils. Her wings ached. Every fiber in her body screamed at her to turn tail, to fly back north, to flee the damn south and the memories that pulsed here.

"And damn you, Tilla Roper," Erry hissed. "Damn your long bones."

She flew on, grumbling and cursing and panting.

The forest rolled beneath her for leagues, its oaks, pines, and maples turning red and yellow with autumn. The colors reminded Erry of blood and fire. Last winter, it was blood and fire that painted these trees. Today autumn's beauty only chilled her.

The old pain dug through her. The wound on her temple had healed, and even the headaches had been receding, but now it blazed with new agony. A resistor had given her that blow, slamming his tail into her head. Worse than the physical pain were the memories.

As she flew, Erry saw the battle again before her. Cannonballs slammed into dragons, tearing their magic away, scattering their human forms in a shower of blood and limbs. Soldiers lay burning upon the trees, some dead, others still screaming in the inferno. And she saw Mae Baker--her dearest friend, her silly and terrified Wobble Lips--disappearing into a rain of fire.

"Wobble Lips!" Erry had screamed and tried to find her, streaming through smoke and flame. "Mae! Mae, where are you?"

She never saw the timid baker's daughter again. Erry had fled north with the emperor, the prince and princess, and Tilla. She had fled the fire, the blood, the swarm of the Resistance.

"I left you, Mae," Erry whispered as she flew back south, back toward that old nightmare. Tears stung her eyes. "I left you to die. I'm so sorry. But I will find you again. I will find you alive, or I will find your grave, but I will find you."

She flew on, a single copper dragon in an endless sky of memory.

Finally she saw it ahead, a stain upon the forest, a pile of stone and ash like a crater.

The ruins of Castra Luna.

"Maggoty fish guts," Erry whispered, and her throat constricted. She had promised herself she wouldn't cry--she had shed enough tears during the lonely nights these past few moons-- but her eyes stung anew.

Serving in a northern fortress, Erry had heard news of her old training outpost. They said that after conquering Luna, the Resistance had ravaged and abandoned the fort, knowing they could never defend it. Erry had imagined ruins like those from the Griffin War a thousand years ago--orphaned archways, crumbling towers, walls pocked with holes, a fortress that could be patched up with good masonry and elbow grease. Yet Castra Luna... for a moment, Erry wasn't sure she even flew to the right place. Nothing remained here. Not walls, not the shells of towers, nothing but bricks and ash strewn across a clearing.

"The Resistance took apart every damn brick," she said to herself. "Nothing is left. Nothing. Oh stars, Mae."

When she flew closer, she saw that hundreds of soldiers were bustling across the ruins like ants over a smashed hive. Dragons were tugging carts full of crumbled bricks, digging foundations, and clearing rubble. Men were building scaffolding of wood and rope. Outside the ruins, a thousand troops or more drilled in a forest clearing, marching between tents.

Erry swallowed a lump in her throat.

Castra Luna. The fort where she had trained for three moons. The fort where she had met her two best--her two *only* friends: Tilla Roper and Mae Baker.

"I miss you."

Growing up in Cadport, Erry had never had friends. How could she? She was the bastard of a foreign sailor from Tiranor and a Vir Requis prostitute. Her father had never returned to Requiem. Her mother had died many years ago.

The other children of Cadport had grown up in homes, sheltered, warm, and protected. Erry had survived alone on the docks. She lived with feral cats and stray dogs. She ate whatever washed up onto the shore and whatever she could steal. She shivered at night in abandoned hovels. She begged, she stole, and sometimes--she cursed to remember it--she bedded men for a warm meal or a roof on a stormy night. Her only friends were the animals she shared the docks with. She often went moons without talking, only growling and barking and hissing among the strays.

And then... then the blessed day came.

Then she turned eighteen, and she was drafted into the Legions.

They had given her boots--real boots of leather! After years of wandering the boardwalk barefoot, the boots felt like slippers for a princess. And they gave her food--real food! The other recruits would complain about the stale wafers and dried meat, but to Erry--whose meals had often been scavenged from trash--it tasted like a feast.

And best of all... I had friends.

Flying toward the ruins, Erry blinked tears from her eyes. For three moons, she had shared a tent with Tilla, Mae, and many other girls. For the first time, Erry had felt like she belonged. In the Legions, she was no half-breed dock rat. She was a soldier, same as the others. She did not sleep among stray cats and dogs on the beach, but beside friends. Beside Tilla and Mae.

"And now you're gone, Mae," she whispered. "But I will find you, Tilla. And I will serve with you again."

She looked down, blinking her damp eyes, and a gasp fled her maw. She squinted and flew lower.

Could it be...?

Yes. Erry felt her throat tighten. Just north of the ruins, a cemetery sprawled between the trees. At first she had thought that thousands of bricks lay strewn through the forest, cast from the ruined fort. Then she realized these were craggy tombstones.

Erry pulled her wings close and dived down.

She crashed through the treetops, landed on the forest floor, and shifted into human form.

"Oh bloody stars," she whispered.

The tombstones rolled around her, carved from the old bricks of Castra Luna. Thousands spread between the trees. Those trees creaked in the wind, and their leaves rustled, a whisper of ghosts. Erry shivered and hugged herself. Even in steel armor, a sword at her side, she felt as fragile and afraid as she had upon the docks.

She began walking between the graves, her boots crunching fallen leaves. Most tombstones bore no names; they were simply engraved with a single birch leaf, an ancient symbol of Requiem.

Erry tilted her head.

"The Regime engraves the spiral upon its graves," she whispered. "The birch leaf is an older symbol. The Resistance dug these graves."

She had not imagined the Resistance would bury the dead. She had always heard that they merely burned corpses, left them to rot, or even ate them. Yet somebody had dug these graves here, raised these tombstones, and engraved each one with a symbol of Old Requiem.

As she kept wandering through the forest, Erry saw that several scattered tombstones did bear names. She recognized some; here lay the fallen youths of Cadport.

Rune must have buried them, Erry realized. *He's from Cadport too. He'd know some of those he slew.*

She sighed and lowered her head. Back at Cadport, Rune Brewer had always been kind to her. He would bring her food to the beach sometimes. Once he even let her sleep in his tavern during a storm. Yet now the boy had become a resistor. Now he had slain hundreds; burying those he slew could not atone for that.

"In only a year, so much changed," Erry whispered. "Two kids from the boardwalk, one now a soldier, one a resistor. And so many dead."

She kept wandering, reading the names of the fallen, until she saw a tall tombstone upon a knoll.

Erry froze and stared.

A ray of light fell between the trees, lighting the tombstone. Ivy crawled over its craggy white surface, and cyclamens circled its base. The trees rustled, whispering to her. This grave seemed to beckon, and Erry approached it gingerly, holding her breath.

When she saw the name upon the tombstone, she lowered her head, and a tear flowed down her cheek.

"Mae Baker," she whispered.

She looked at her friend's grave and clenched her fists.

"Oh damn it, Wobble Lips!" she blurted out. "Why did you have to go and get killed, damn you? I *told* you to fly near me." Her fists shook, and she wanted to punch the tombstone. "I told you a million times--in assault formation, look *ahead* and blow fire, not at enemies beside you." She kicked the earth, sending leaves flying onto the grave. "Now look at you. Now look at you, Wobble Lips! At least I'm spared seeing your damn lips wobble so much. At least you won't bug me again with all your wailing and tears."

She closed her burning eyes and stood for long moments, fists clenched. Finally she sighed, opened her eyes, and touched the tombstone.

"Wherever you are now, Wobble Lips, just... don't get into any more trouble, all right? Not until I see you again. And for stars' sake, don't cry so much, okay? Be strong. We all have to be strong." Her knees trembled and she knuckled her eyes. "We're going to be so damn strong, Mae, you won't believe it." She patted the tombstone. "Goodbye, Wobble Lips. Goodbye."

She turned and left.

She walked through the forest, head low.

Soon she found a gravelly road. As she walked between the trees, heading toward the ruins of Castra Luna, she unrolled the scroll she had carried all the way from her northern fort. She clutched it like a treasure.

It had taken her moons to convince her officer to write this scroll, reassigning her here. At first, Erry had agreed to do anything for reassignment. And so she had spent a moon serving her officer as a slave--scrubbing his boots, sweeping his floor, oiling his sword, polishing his armor, and begging again and again for naught. She had then changed her approach. She spent the next moon wreaking havoc in her phalanx--knocking over pots, breaking three swords, crashing into other dragons in flight, and being the worst soldier she could be. She had suffered many punisher burns during that moon, but it was worth it. Finally, after Erry had lost yet another helmet, her commander agreed to send her south.

"Remember," Erry had said, rubbing the bruises of his punisher, "I want to serve in Castra Luna, and I want to serve under Lanse Tilla. Remember that--it has to be Lanse Tilla."

Her officer had scowled, cursed... and written the scroll.

"Soon I'll see you again, Tilla," Erry whispered as she walked down the gravel road.

All my life, she thought, *I've had only two real friends. One now lies buried. The other is an officer leading her own phalanx.* Erry took a deep breath. *I might still be a lowly periva and Tilla a lofty lanse. And I might have to serve under her command, rather than fight at her side. But I can be near her again. I can be with my friend.*

She knuckled her eyes, kept walking down the road, and soon reached the ruins of Castra Luna.

The Legions had built a palisade of sharpened logs around the debris, and Erry approached an opening where two guards stood. When she reached them, they frowned down at her, two beefy men in black steel. They moved to block the palisade gateway.

"Move it!" Erry said, craning her head up to glare at them. She stood five feet tall only on tiptoes, and these brutes towered above her, but she had fought men this size before on the docks. "I'm reassigned to this fort. Let me in, mules."

The guards wore a single red star upon their armbands. They were perivas, the same lowly rank as her. They snorted.

"You got to be eighteen to join the Legions, shrimp," one said and snorted. "You look about three years old. Get lost."

Erry rolled her eyes. "And you got to have a brain to join too, and I've seen logs with bigger brains than yours." She brandished her scroll at them. "Can you even read? This is my new fort. *Move!*"

With a great shove, she pushed between them and entered the camp.

Chaos awaited her.

Dragons trundled about, snorting smoke and dragging wagons of bricks and wood. Masons cursed and yelled at one another, jabbing fingers at building plans. Workers swung hammers, erecting scaffolding. Other dragons grunted as they dug ditches. Between these workers, hundreds of troops marched in clanking armor, trained with swords, and flew overhead as dragons.

A thousand legionaries must have bustled here, engineers and fighters alike.

"I'm looking for Lanse Tilla Siren," Erry said to one mason, speaking Tilla's new, noble surname. "She commands the Sea Cannons phalanx. Where do I go?"

The mason ignored her, rushed toward a worker, and began admonishing the man for using the wrong chisel.

Erry grumbled, spat, and moved on. She had to ask a dragon tugging a cart, three soldiers sorting through rubble, and another guard.

Finally the last man scratched his chin, sucked his cheek, and said, "Lanse Tilla Siren? Tall woman, sort of looks like a statue?"

Erry nodded. "That's her all right."

The legionary snorted. "You asked to serve under Lanse Siren? The Cadport Cannon?" He whistled. "You crazy or what?"

She growled at him. "You stupid or just an idiot?" She waved the scroll at him. "Yes, Tilla Bloody Siren, says so right here. Where is she?"

The soldier raised his hands in defense, and his eyebrows rose just as high.

"All right, little one, don't have a fit. It's just that, well..." He snickered. "Siren's got a bit of a reputation around here. Say she not only looks like a statue, but got a heart of stone too. Loves her punisher, that one does. But well... if you're a glutton for pain, you might like her." He gestured his chin to a gateway behind him. "Step out the palisade, down the road for two hundred yards, and look for a tent with a cannon banner. You'll find her there."

"Yeah, well, you're a glutton for... dumbness!" Erry said and marched away, fuming.

So what if people badmouthed Tilla? Erry had heard others say the same about her friend, even back in Cadport, calling her cold and haughty. But Erry had seen a different side to her. Erry had seen a kind, sensitive woman beneath the icy exterior. She had seen a friend.

I myself was always an outcast, Erry thought. *I myself was always called names. They called me a dock rat, a harlot, and a diseased stray.* She knuckled her eyes. *But I'm not. And Tilla isn't cruel. We're two outcasts, two lost souls from Cadport... and we'll get through these damn Legions together.*

She stepped through the palisade gates, walked down a dirt road, and saw a clearing between the trees. A hundred tents rose here, their black cloth emblazoned with red spirals. Troops marched between them, and several dragons flew above in patrol. If the ruins bustled with workers, here there were only fighters. These men did not wield hammers and chisels, but swords and shields.

Frey is mustering a new army here, Erry thought. *Green recruits used to train in this forest clearing. Now Castra Luna will house seasoned warriors to fight the Resistance.* She gripped her sword. *And I will fight with them.*

The tents displayed the banners of their phalanxes. Erry saw sigils of wolves, lions, dragons, swords, and many others. Each phalanx had two tents to its name: one large tent for the common soldiers, one smaller one for its commanding officer. After walking through the camp for several moments, Erry saw two tents bearing Tilla's banners--a cannon overlooking the sea.

When she walked closer, Erry saw the phalanx training in the dirt outside. A hundred perivas and corelis--younger soldiers sporting only one or two stars--stood in black steel, swinging swords. The clashing blades rang. A hulking siragi--an older, gruffer soldier with three stars upon his armbands--was moving between the lower ranks, barking at soldiers to correct their stances and thrusts.

Behind the troops, upon a boulder, stood Lanse Tilla Siren.

Erry's heart skipped a beat.

Stars, she thought and felt herself pale.

She hadn't seen Tilla in six moons, not since the battle here. But Tilla looked like she'd aged six years. Soldiers like Erry wore breastplates, vambraces, and greaves over tan leggings and tunics. Tilla now wore the full plate suit of an officer; the steel covered her from toes to shoulders, perfectly molded to her body. Her pauldrons displayed red spirals--the insignia of command. She did not bear the simple sword of a common soldier anymore, but a fine weapon with a dragonclaw pommel.

Upon her hip, she bore a punisher. Erry gulped. The wounds across her, those her former officer had given her, blazed anew. Did Tilla too punish soldiers with this weapon of lightning and pain? Erry remembered how Lanse Nairi had nearly killed Tilla with her punisher. Did Tilla herself now torture others?

But worse than the punisher was Tilla's face. Erry felt ice fill her belly. Tilla had always seemed pale and aloof, but this... this was different.

No color touched Tilla's face now; she could have been carved from marble. No emotion or life filled her eyes. As she stared upon her troops training, her eyes were dead. Cold. Hard as stone.

She looks like that statue of Frey that stands in Cadport, Erry thought and shivered. *She seems just as cold and cruel. Stars, what happened to her at Castra Academia? How, in only six moons, did they freeze her eyes?*

When Erry stepped closer to the phalanx, Tilla turned those cold eyes toward her, and their gazes locked.

Erry smiled and waved, expecting Tilla to smile too, to greet her, maybe even to rush forward and embrace her. But still no emotion filled those dark eyes. Erry didn't even see a flicker of recognition within them. Her heart sank.

Stars, doesn't she remember me?

Then Erry realized: Of course! Of course Tilla could not rush toward her, embrace her, or even acknowledge her. She was leading her own phalanx now! She had to act aloof. She had to be strong like Nairi had been. But it was all an act for her soldiers. It had to be.

Erry sucked in her breath, slammed her fist against her chest, and called out.

"Hail the red spiral! I am Periva Erry Docker. I report to duty." She raised her scroll. "I've come from Castra Lan. I'm to serve in the Sea Cannons."

Tilla's eyes narrowed the slightest bit, a movement so subtle Erry wasn't sure it even happened.

For the first time, Tilla spoke.

"Step forward, periva. Hand me that scroll."

Stars! Erry thought. Tilla's voice was even colder than her eyes. It didn't even sound human; it was the voice of a statue. Erry gulped, suddenly not sure this was an act at all. Briefly, she wondered if she had even found the right officer. Was this truly Tilla or simply somebody who looked like her?

Erry stepped forward and held out her scroll.

Everybody was watching them, she realized. The soldiers of the phalanx, a hundred men and women in steel, had stopped drilling and stared.

Tilla looked toward them, and her eyes narrowed further. "Keep drilling!" she shouted, and her voice rolled across the camp. "Do you think the Resistance is standing around gawking?"

The swords began to swing again. The men were hulking warriors, many of them standing well over six feet tall, their frames burly. Yet even they looked sheepish as Tilla commanded them.

Merciful stars, Erry thought. *She's even harder than Nairi.*

Tilla marched toward her, boots thudding, and snatched the scroll from Erry's hands. She scanned the writing quickly, then stared into Erry's eyes.

"Says here you're a troublemaker," Tilla said, scrutinizing Erry. "Says here you break swords, lose helmets, and earned the punisher every day. What makes you think you can serve here, soldier?"

Erry gasped. She wanted to shake Tilla madly, to scream at her. *Don't you remember me? You think I'm just some... some troublemaker soldier? I'm your friend! I'm Erry from Cadport!*

She glanced back at the drilling soldiers and forced herself to take a shaky breath.

It's just an act, she told herself. *It has to be. She's just acting this way for her troops.*

"Don't look at them, soldier!" Tilla barked. "I asked you a question. Look at me and answer."

Erry couldn't help it now. She gave a shaky laugh.

"Stars, Tilla," she whispered and shook her head. "Don't you remember me? It's Erry."

Tilla hissed. Her eyes blazed. She looked so much like a rabid wolf that Erry took a step back.

"Into my tent, soldier," Tilla hissed. "Go!"

With that, the young officer spun around and marched into her tent. Shakily, Erry followed her into the shadows, leaving the phalanx to drill outside.

Inside the tent, Erry saw a cot, a small table and chair, and a wooden chest. It was a small tent, maybe nine by nine feet, a retreat for an officer to find privacy from those she commanded.

Finally Tilla can drop her act, Erry thought.

"Well, this is nice, Tilla!" she said and allowed herself a hesitant smile. "Sure beats the old dirt we used to sleep on, right?" She reached for an apple on the table. "And they give you apples! Stars, I should become an officer too. I--"

"You will refer to me as *Commander*," Tilla said, eyes blazing. "Or you will refer to me as Lanse Tilla. Do you understand, soldier?"

Erry froze, the apple halfway to her mouth, and frowned.

"By the Abyss!" she said. "All right, *Commander.*" Erry laughed shakily. "You... you remember me, don't you? I--"

Tilla snarled. Erry could not believe it. The young woman-- her best friend!--snarled at her. Her lips peeled back, her teeth showed, and she growled like a wolf.

"Do not test my patience," she said. "I remember you, Docker. We trained together, yes. You know it. I know it. Those days are over." Tilla took a step forward, towering over the smaller Erry. "I am your commanding officer. That's all I am to you now. Do you understand?"

Erry stood frozen, almost too shocked to breathe.

Merciful stars, she thought. *What did they do to her at the academy?*

Her eyes burned, and Erry tossed down her apple in disgust. She spat on the floor.

"Well, dog dung, *Commander,*" she said, spitting out that last word like an insult. "You might remember me, but do you remember yourself? Do you remember who you are?"

Tilla clutched her punisher, and its tip crackled to life. "Be careful, periva. Be careful that--"

Erry snorted. "You think I'm scared of you, Tilla? You're just a common, seaside ropemaker's daughter from Cadport. Bloody stars, you and I pissed in the woods together. Now you act all high and mighty?" She laughed mirthlessly, and her eyes would not stop stinging. "Sweaty codpieces, Tilla! Don't you remember? I came here to serve with you again. Like in the old days. Like--"

Tilla drew her punisher. Lightning wreathed its tip.

"I will tell you this once more, periva," Tilla said. "Those days are over. You are no longer a recruit, but a soldier with insignia on your arms. I am no longer the woman you knew. I am your commander now and your officer. Salute me, hail the red spiral, and pray that I forget your words here today. Anyone else would hang for them. This is the one mercy I will show you."

Erry looked at the drawn punisher and barked a laugh.

"What are you going to do--burn me?" She snorted. "Go shove that thing up your fat arse, Roper."

Tilla moved so fast Erry barely saw it. The punisher drove forward. Lightning raced across Erry's breastplate, pain flared, and she screamed.

Her old officer had burned her before, short blasts that made her yelp and jump. Tilla was crueler. She kept her punisher against her, driving all its pain into Erry's armor, flesh, and bones. Tears ran down her cheeks. She fell to her knees. When Tilla finally pulled the punisher back, Erry doubled over, panting and spitting.

"If you will serve under my command, periva," Tilla spoke above, "you will show me respect, or you will burn."

Erry stared up, wincing. Stars floated across the tent. Tilla stood above her, her punisher still drawn, her eyes still dead.

Erry struggled to her feet.

She raised her chin, only as tall as Tilla's shoulders, but stretched to every inch of height she had. She slammed a trembling fist against her breastplate.

"I salute," she said through stiff lips. "I salute Cadport. I salute the friend I once had. And I salute the memory of Mae Baker, a memory you shame." She spat on Tilla's boots. "And you, *Commander*, can go lick horse dung."

With that, she fled the tent, shifted into a dragon, and took flight.

She soared above the clearing. She heard shouts, roars, and flapping wings behind her. Erry didn't bother looking back. She was among the slimmest, fastest dragons in the Legions. If she did not want to be caught, she wouldn't. She streamed over the forest and blazed fire skyward.

Damn you, Tilla, she thought. Her eyes dampened and she spewed her flame. *Damn you to the Abyss, and damn these Legions, and damn you, Mae, for dying, and damn you this stupid, stupid war.*

She didn't know where to go now. She didn't care. She'd had enough of forts. She'd had enough of damn commanders. She'd had enough of this whole damn world.

Erry Docker howled and flew into the horizon, tears in her eyes and fire in her throat.

RUNE

They climbed the hill, rose from the cover of trees, and beheld a canyon that halved the land.

"Cain's Canyon," Rune whispered, the wind billowing his cloak and hair. "Burn me, it's larger than I imagined. All of Lynport could fit in there."

At his side, Valien nodded and scratched his grizzled stubble. "Aye, and Lord Cain will brag to you about it, wait and see. 'All the people of Cadport could fit into my canyon!' he boasts to all who visit. The man's been hunkered down in there for years, and he never forgave Lynport for calling itself the Jewel of the South. He sees himself as a southern lord and Lynport as stealing his glory."

Rune sighed. "If he saw Lynport now, its homes rotten and its port dead, maybe he'd feel less jealous."

Valien raised an eyebrow. "Lord Devin Cain lives in a hole in the ground--literally. I think even a barren boardwalk is enough to stir his jealousy." Valien hefted his pack over his shoulders, rattling its pans and knives. "Come now, it's still a long walk there among the trees, and I dare not fly yet. The Legions patrol these skies too."

Rune stood for a moment upon the hilltop, staring down over the trees at the canyon. It stretched across the land as far as he could see. The forest plunged into it, trees tilting over its rim, roots sticking out like hair over a scar. Mist floated within its depths, and flocks of birds flew over the shadows, their cries echoing. Rune had seen wonders before: the towering Ralora Cliffs over the sea, the lost glory of Confutatis in the east, and the clock tower of Castra Luna. Yet he thought Cain's Canyon the greatest among them, certainly the largest; he could probably fit all those other wonders into its depths.

"Rune!" Valien's raspy voice rose from the trees coating the hillside below. "Come, follow. You're too visible up there."

Rune too hefted his pack, gripped the hilt of his Amber Sword, and began climbing downhill.

They walked between the trees in silence. They had been walking through this forest for three days now, leaving their camp far behind. Since abandoning Castra Luna, the Resistance had been hiding in the western forests of Old Salvandos, a lush wilderness of oaks, pines, and maples so thick no scouts could see through the treetops. Three thousand resistors still hid in their camp, living in holes, treetop nests, and hidden burrows.

Rune had found the camp a blessed change from the ruins of Confutatis, the fallen city where the Resistance had once hidden. The Legions had taken three resistors alive at Castra Luna and flown them north to the capital. That meant three bodies had been tortured, and three mouths had screamed of their old camp. And so, for several moons now, the Resistance had hidden in the wilderness. Their new forest home was humble, but green and safe. Walking here with Valien, Rune missed it. He missed his warm underground burrow with its soft bed of leaves. He missed drinking ale with his fellow resistors and whispering old stories of Requiem. And he missed Kaelyn.

You wait for me there, Kaelyn, Rune thought. *Watch over our people.* He squared his jaw. *I'll be back with aid. I promise you. I promise.*

"Rune!" rose the voice ahead, and Valien's leathery face peered from between the trees, framed with shaggy hair. "Move your arse. We have little time to spare."

Rune gave a mock salute. "I'm right on your heels, old man."

As they kept walking through the forest, Rune sighed. He had spent days now alone with Valien, whom he found far, far less pleasant company than Kaelyn. True, Valien was a great warrior, a strong leader, and a man Rune admired. But he was also gruff. He still cursed and drank too much. Whenever Rune slipped or fell behind, Valien had a sharp remark.

And the training. Stars, the training still left Rune bruised and cramped. Every evening, Valien insisted they practice their swordplay, and the man was ruthless, slamming his sword against Rune's armor again and again, denting it and bruising the flesh beneath.

"Tough in training, easy in battle," the former knight kept saying, but amusement always filled his dark eyes; Rune thought he rather enjoyed beating him black and blue.

The noon sun shone when they reached the canyon. A flock of cranes flew overhead, singing and beating their wings. The trees tilted over the crevice, clinging to the canyon's rim and nearly falling over. Rune approached gingerly, grabbed a pine, and leaned forward. The depth spun his head. The canyon plunged a mile deep, ending with a rocky floor. Mist floated in the depths like ghosts.

Valien came to stand at his side, wiped sweat off his brow, and stared down into the canyon. Burrs and mud stained his garb of leather and wool. He wheezed after the trek; the wound on his neck, suffered when saving Rune's life years ago, still pained the former knight.

"Remember," Valien said, voice a mere rasp, "Lord Cain rebelled against the Regime once. He was punished for it. His three sons were slain; Cain himself was spared, but forbidden to emerge from his canyon since. That was many years ago; you were just a babe. Cain now serves and fears the emperor. His daughter Lana is sympathetic toward the Resistance; you saw that in the capital. Lord Devin Cain himself might not hold much love for us." He stared at Rune. "We must be wary. We could find a great ally here, or we could find our deaths."

Rune squinted down into the canyon. "Where is he? You said he commands ten thousand men. I see birds and a few lizards, that's all."

Valien nodded. "I said he lives in a hole in the ground, didn't I? This is just a crack--far too exposed for the likes of Devin Cain." He squinted upward. "The sky is clear. We'll shift into dragons, fly down to the bottom, and walk from there in human forms. We're close."

With that, Valien leaped from among the trees and tumbled into the darkness of the canyon. Before he could hit the bottom, he shifted into a silver dragon, filled his wings with air, and slowed his fall.

Rune cracked his neck, hefted his pack across his shoulders, and leaped too. He dived into the canyon. The wind whipped his hair and cloak. The canyon walls rushed at his sides. With a deep breath, Rune shifted into a black dragon and stretched his wings wide. The wing caught them like sails. Rune slowed his fall and glided down.

318

The two dragons, silver and black, landed upon the canyon floor and shifted back into human forms.

A rain of cutlery clattered down around them. A fork nearly stabbed Rune in the shoulders.

"Stars damn it!" he said. "Damn pack never did close properly."

Valien grumbled. "Come on, we move. Quietly. This is not a safe place."

They began to walk along the canyon floor. Rune craned his neck back and gulped. The canyon walls rose a mile high; the sky was but a thin, blue strip above. Every footstep echoed.

As he looked at the craggy walls, Rune thought back to Ralora Cliffs at home. He remembered how Tilla and he used to walk there between the cliffs and sea. They would bang wooden swords, pretending to be old heroes. They would wrestle, whisper quietly, or just look out across the waves.

And one night we kissed, Rune thought. *And we said goodbye. And we vowed to see each other again.* A lump filled his throat. *And we did. We saw each other again... and we fought with swords of steel. And I lost her, maybe forever this time.*

He blinked furiously and banished those thoughts. Pining for Tilla would not help now. All he could do was keep fighting.

I can still save you, Tilla, he thought. *You are good at heart. I know it. I can still save you from the soldier they forced you to become.*

They walked for about a mile down the canyon, rounded a bend, and Rune's breath died.

"Oh merciful stars," he whispered.

Valien came to stand beside him and nodded. "Welcome to the Castle-in-the-Cliff, home of Lord Cain and his army."

Rune had seen castles before. He had seen the small Castellum Acta upon the hill in Lynport. And he had seen Castra Luna, a sprawling fort in the forest. But this was different. This castle was not built of bricks and walls. Lord Cain's home was carved into the cliff itself. The living stone had been chipped away, forming a portico of columns, turrets carved with dragon reliefs, and a balcony topped with statues of winged women. The facade rose as tall and lavish as a palace.

Or the world's largest mausoleum, Rune thought.

A wide stairway led from the canyon floor to the castle gates. No doors filled the archway; Rune saw only shadows within. Two statues surrounded the entrance, carved of the same limestone, a hundred feet tall each. Stone helmets hid their faces, and their fists--each one large as a mule--were held to their breasts.

"Are there no guards?" Rune said. "No doors? Do we simply walk in?"

Valien was holding the hilt of his sword. "Careful. We don't know if we meet friend or foe here." He lowered his voice to a growl. "And remember, Lord Cain has not left this hole in years, not since losing his rebellion--and his three sons. By now, he is not what you would call sane."

"Might take one madman to help us kill another," Rune said.

He marched across the canyon toward the towering facade. He craned his neck back, admiring it from up close. The columns, balconies, and dragon reliefs soared. The two stone guardians towered thrice the height of dragons. Rune shivered. Helmets hid the statues' faces, but Rune could swear they were watching him. He raised his chin, took a deep breath, and approached the stairs that led toward the palace gateway.

Dust rained.

Stone creaked.

"Rune!" rasped Valien.

Hands grabbed Rune's shoulders and tugged. He fell several paces backward. Stone slammed down ahead of him, showering dust, and the canyon shook.

"Bloody bollocks!" Rune cursed and scrambled several paces farther back.

Before him, a great stone fist--taller than he was--had slammed onto the ground. As Rune watched, coughing and rubbing his eyes, one of the stone statues straightened and returned its fist to its chest.

"Well," Valien said, still holding Rune's shoulders, "that explains why there are no guards."

Rune nodded, legs rubbery. Looking around, he saw that cracks covered the canyon floor around the entrance. Those stone statues had slammed their fists down many times before. He wondered how many people they had crushed.

A high voice rose ahead, echoing in the canyon.

"We meet again, Relesar Aeternum!"

Rune looked up.

"Lady Lana," he whispered.

She stood upon the palace balcony, a hundred feet above them. She held one hand to her hip, the other upon her sword's pommel. Most Vir Requis bore longswords, ancient weapons of wide, straight blades; Lady Lana, however, bore a thin, curved saber like southern sailors used to wield. Lana's hair billowed in the wind, a black mane sporting a single white streak. She leaped off the balcony and shifted into a dragon, her black scales bearing a similar streak across her spine ridge. She spread out her wings, landed before Rune, and shifted back into a woman.

"The Stone Guardians were built to slay any strangers who try to enter," she said, her accent highborn and meticulous. "Thousands dwell within this hall, and the Guardians know every one. In five hundred years, none have entered here without their blessing." She reached out her hand. "It's good to finally see you in daylight, Relesar Aeternum. The sun agrees with you. Or should I call you Rune?"

Rune clasped her hand and shook it.

Back in the capital, he had seen Lady Lana masked and cloaked in shadows. Today he saw a noble face with high cheekbones, arched eyebrows, and thin, pink lips. A patch covered her left eye; the right one was gray and bright and intelligent. She looked about thirty years old, but the white stripe through her hair gave her an older, wiser look. She wore a yellow belt over a gray tunic--the colors of House Cain--and tall boots over leggings. Her cloak was dyed blue, the color of nobility, and clasped with a pin bearing the sigil of Cain: two statues guarding an archway.

"Lady Lana," Valien said in his rasp of a whisper.

She turned toward him, and a smile touched her lips.

"My lord Valien." She reached out her arms, embraced him, and kissed his cheek. "Your stubble grows rougher and whiter every time we meet."

"And you grow more beautiful," he said and kissed her hand.

Rune raised an eyebrow. "Burn me, he's a romantic," he said. "Who knew?"

Valien growled at him. "A romantic who still kicks your backside in sword sparring." He turned back to Lana. "My lady, we are here to see your father. Will he speak with us? Will you take us to him?"

Her face darkened. "My father's mood has been dark and his mind addled. He has spent too many years in the shadows. You will not find him the man he was." She clutched the hilt of her sword. "His temper flares without reason. He sees demons in every shadow. He rails against the cruelty of Frey Cadigus one day, then blesses the man the next. He is feverish with stone and stale air. In years past, I could get him to fly within this canyon and see the sky above, even if he refused to fly into the forest. Now I cannot get him to even leave his hall." She sighed. "My father has been a broken man since Frey crushed his rebellion and killed my brothers. I do not know if you can enlist him, Valien. You have my sword, always, and I've tried to soften my father to your cause. I've praised the Resistance in his ears. Whether he listened, I cannot tell; he will not speak to me of this. Maybe he will speak to you. He once greatly admired you."

Valien nodded and sighed. "He was a good man, years ago. He was a friend. I pray that I find this same man today."

"You will not," Lana said, "but I will take you to him. Follow." She turned and began walking between the Stone Guardians. "Do not fear them! They will not harm my guests. Just walk close to me."

As they followed Lady Lana, Rune glanced up nervously at the stone statues, ready to leap back should they move again. Yet they remained frozen, stone heads raised, fists still clutched to their chests. Lana led them between the statues, up a wide staircase, and toward the gates of the Castle-in-the-Cliff.

Shadows loomed before them. The gateway rose taller than dragons, carved into the living rock of the cliff. More than a gateway, this was an ornate cave. Cold air blew from within, chilling Rune, and mist swirled. As he stepped through the archway, the sound of wind and distant birds faded. He entered a realm of shadows and fog.

When he blinked, he saw a great hall, larger than any he'd ever seen. Rows of columns stretched into the shadows. Upon each burned an oil lamp, the light barely piercing the darkness. A mosaic of dragons battling griffins covered the floor. Shadows hid the ceiling. Rune had walked a hundred yards before he even realized that guards stood between the columns, cloaked in gray and armed with sabers; the shadows nearly drowned them.

"Father!" Lana called out, and her voice echoed across the chamber. "Guests are here to see you. Will you speak with them, Father?"

As they walked deeper down the hall, Rune saw a throne ahead; it too seemed carved from the raw stone of the cliff. When they walked closer, Rune saw that a man sat there.

"Stars," he whispered.

Rune had always thought Valien--with his shaggy hair, leathery face, and grizzled stubble--looked rough and weathered. Yet the man upon this throne made Valien seem as well-groomed as a prince.

Lord Cain wore shaggy gray robes lined with fur. His walrus mustache bristled beneath a bulbous, veined nose. His face was as red and wrinkled as a dried apple. His hair was even redder, wild and tangled and streaked with white. Yet despite the snow invading his hair and the grooves lining his skin, he did not seem frail. His shoulders were still wide, his body stocky beneath his robes. His hands were large and strong, clutching the armrests of his throne. A curved blade hung at his side, its pommel shaped as a roaring dragon's head. When he looked up, his eyes blazed under bushy brows--black, deep, and shrewd.

"So, Lord Valien Eleison!" he called out, voice booming; it pealed across the hall. "You've come at last to grovel and beg for my aid."

The haggard lord rose from his throne. He was a large man, as tall and wide as Valien. He drew his sword and held it aloft. His forearms were wide and crisscrossed with scars. In his youth, he must have been a great warrior; he still stood with the pride of one.

Valien kept walking forward, not slowing down. Rune and Lana walked at his sides.

"I've not come here to grovel," he rasped. "Nor to beg. I come to see a man who was once great. I come to see if greatness can still be found within him, or whether he's become but a ghost, a withered puppet for a stronger lord."

Lord Cain cackled; it sounded less like a laugh and more like a man gagging. Spittle flew from beneath his bushy mustache.

"Aye, you've still got a way with words, you bastard!" Lord Cain said. He barked a laugh. "You always were the poetic one, weren't you? Reading your books like a woman." He snorted. "True men have no use for books, Valien, nor for your fancy words. We deal with blood, blades, and dragonfire."

"You will have the glory of all three," Valien said, "if you join our cause."

They reached the throne. Lana went to stand by her father's side. Rune and Valien remained standing before him. All around, the columns rose into shadows, and the guards stood still and dark between them. The lamps burned, casting flickering light.

Lord Cain turned to stare at Rune. Those dark, shrewd eyes narrowed, scrutinizing him.

"Is this your boy, Valien?" the entombed lord asked and grunted. "Is this pup the so-called heir you've been trumpeting around? He looks more like a girl to me. Ha! This one is prettier than my daughter. My arse is hairier than his cheeks." He thrust out his chin at Rune. "Do you talk, little girl? Or do you merely drag around behind your lord as a trophy?"

Rune felt his temper flare. He grabbed his sword.

"You know Shari Cadigus, daughter of the emperor?" he said to Cain. "You know of her missing wing? My teeth tore it off."

Cain snorted. "So you fought another woman, and you couldn't even kill her. And you think you can fight men in battle? You think you can slay Frey Cadigus?" He hacked a laugh. "And you want me to help you! I wager you need help to wipe your own backside."

Rune growled. "I flew to battle. I fought Frey's men. You haven't left this cavern in years! And you call me a--"

"Rune!" Valien said, voice rough, and his eyes blazed. "We've not come here to argue with Cain, but to seek an alliance."

Cain's laughter boomed and echoed across the palace. He clutched his belly. "Ha! This boy who would be king cannot even talk without his lord lecturing him. What sort of king allows a knight to interrupt his words?" He sat back upon his throne. "Be gone, boy, before I send word to the capital that you hide in my hall."

"Me, hide in your hall!" Rune said and snorted. "You've been rotting here for too long, old man. Will you not emerge to fight?

Will you leave your army here in the shadows to collect dust, or will you emerge into the sky as a dragon?"

All mirth left Cain's eyes. His face darkened, and his lips peeled back in a snarl.

"Emerge into the sky? A sky full of imperial dragons bearing Frey's sigil? Fly in a sky another man rules? No, boy. Am I not a man? Am I not a lord?" He spat on the floor. "I will not fly over another man's fields, forests, or forts. I am Lord Cain! I march and fly above earth that I own."

"You own nothing but a hole in a wall," Rune said, disgusted.

"Aye, little girl, and wouldn't you love to rule this hole in a wall? Wouldn't you love to command the army that dwells here? They are true warriors. They are true men, tested in battle, not babes fresh off the teat like you."

Rune took a step forward. "You want lands? You want skies to call your own? You want to see sunlight again, old man? I will give you land and sky if you join my cause. Fight with me, Cain, and I will give you what you desire."

Cain snorted. "Will you now, boy? You will give me lands, is that so? I will take what lands are mine, not have a whore's daughter give me a treat like a dog." He spat on Rune's boot. "If Frey should fall, I will command all the south of Requiem--from Castra Luna in the north, down to Ralora Cliffs in the south, and east across the plains of Osanna to the port of Altus Mare."

Rune's eyes widened and he guffawed. "But that's half the kingdom!"

"Aye," said Lord Cain and cackled. "Would you rather rule half a kingdom or all of nothing?"

Valien stepped forward, face red beneath his beard. "Enough, Cain! Enough of this bantering. Are you two leaders or fishwives?" He took another step forward and clutched Cain's shoulder. "Cain. We are old friends, you are I. We are both warriors. Now fight with us. Let us swing swords and blow fire together. Cadigus has you hiding in a hole like a rat. Join us, dethrone the man, and you will have the lands you crave."

Cain grumbled under his breath. He gave Valien a long look, then turned his eyes toward Rune; his tufted eyebrows turned with his stare like shutters.

"Does he know how to fight?" he said. "The boy is too soft and too young. Can he kill?"

Rune nodded, thinking back to Castra Luna, and ice filled his belly. "I've killed before. I fought at Castra Luna."

Cain barked a laugh. "Ha! Luna? You fought green recruits there, not hardened men. Can you fight a true warrior? When you fly to meet Frey and the Axehand Order, will you slay them, or will you fly away with your tail between your legs?"

Rune clutched his sword and drew a foot of steel. "I will fight. I will not run and hide."

Hide like you, he wanted to add, but bit down on the words.

"We shall see," said Cain. "Very well! I will fight with you. I will give you an army. But first, boy, you must prove your words. You must prove that you can indeed fight as you boast--fight a true warrior." He raised his voice to a shout. "Doog! Doog, here boy. Here!"

Footsteps thudded. Grunts rose from the shadows. Rune turned toward the sound and felt the blood leave his face.

Oh bloody Abyss, he thought.

A lumbering troll of a man came lolloping from the shadows. He towered seven feet tall, his shoulders wide as an ox, his belly flabby but his arms rippling with muscles. His feet were bare, the toenails yellow, and he wore only a tattered tunic. Iron rings circled his neck and ankles, as if he'd just been unchained from a dungeon. He grunted and chortled and drooled as he approached. But worst of all was not his size. The man had no face.

A great scar rifted his head from his right ear, across where his nose should be, and down to his left jowls. The wound drove into his head, two inches thick, leaving the man one eye and just the hint of a mouth.

"Here, Doog, here!" Lord Cain said.

The huge, scarred man trundled up to his master, then stood on wobbly legs. Saliva dripped from his wound down to his shirt.

"Merciful stars, Cain," Rune said.

Cain barked his laugh, fluttering his mustache. "Meet Doog. Do you like his face? Ha! I gave him that wound myself--slammed my axe so hard into his face he leaked half his brain. He kind of looks like the canyon we live in, doesn't he?" He turned to the poor soul. "Here, boy, I have a treat for you."

Cain fished through his pocket, produced a wafer, and held it out. Doog ate it from his hand like a trained hound.

"By the Abyss, Cain," Rune muttered. "He's a man, not a dog."

Cain spat. "Ah, he's got no sense left in him. Took it with his face, I did; he's more beast than man now. I trained him myself. Want to see him do tricks? Sit, Doog, sit!"

"We have no time for this," Valien interjected. "Cain, enough of your games. Rune will fight the poor soul. And he will defeat him."

Rune bit his lip, not so sure about that. Doog was perhaps a halfwit, but he was twice Rune's size. Each of his arms could have been a person on its own.

"Valien..." he began.

The gruff knight strode toward him, grabbed his shoulders, and leaned close.

"Is there a problem, Rune?" Valien said, and a hint of a smile touched his lips. "I've trained you well. You are young and strong. You can defeat him."

Rune looked over at Doog. The brute was chortling and drooling and begging for treats from his master. An ugly sound rose from his wound, halfway between a yowl and a mewl. Rune wasn't sure whether it sounded pathetic or terrifying.

He leaned closer to Valien and whispered. "Stars, Valien, he's bigger than Beras."

Valien shrugged. "Should make a bigger sound when he falls." His face grew somber. "Rune, understand--Cain is an old sort of fighter. You're used to fighting among resistors, men of honor and hope and light. Cain is a different kind of man. He will not follow starlight or dreams of Old Requiem. He will follow *strength*. He will follow a man he believes can be king. Show him your strength today, and he will lend us his army." Valien nodded. "When you joined our fight, I never promised you safety. You knew that battles lay ahead. You fought soldiers in a great battle. This man you must fight alone." He dug his fingers into Rune's arms. "And greater enemies await you; someday you will face Frey himself in battle. First you must pass this test."

Rune looked again at Doog. He was now howling and swinging his arms; Cain was goading him with a spearhead like a man riling up a war dog before a fight.

If Kaelyn were here, she would say this is madness, Rune thought. *She would urge for calm, for peace, for another way.* He tightened his lips. *Yet Kaelyn isn't here, and Lord Devin Cain is a different sort of man; Valien is right about that. I'll have to play by his rules today.*

He nodded. "I will fight him."

They left the hall--Rune, Valien, and a hundred dwellers of the castle. They stood within the canyon. Outside the palace facade stood Lord Cain, wrapped in his ratty cloak, his wild red-and-white hair fluttering in the wind. At his side stood his daughter, the Lady Lana, clutching the hilt of her saber; her hair too billowed, its single white strand like a banner. Around them stood a crowd of canyon soldiers.

These men were Cain's personal host; they had served his family for hundreds of years, and they did not wear the black steel of the Legions. Their armor was pale, their cloaks gray like the cliffs around them. They did not bear the longswords of the Legions, but curved sabers shaped like the canyon they dwelled in. They wore the red spiral upon their armbands, as decreed for all soldiers in the empire, yet not upon their breastplates; there they sported the sigil of House Cain, two stone statues guarding a gateway.

The actual Stone Guardians towered above the men. Rune glanced up at them, then back down at the cracks at their feet. He swallowed when he remembered how close their fists had come to crushing him.

"Remember, Rune," Valien said, leaning close to whisper in his ear. "You will fight as dragons here. Fly fast. Do not hesitate to blow your fire. We have flown many times in the night. Use the sun now; let it blind your enemy."

Rune nodded and looked over at that enemy. Doog stood in the canyon, his iron collar and anklets gleaming. The beast tossed back his head and howled, a roar so loud the canyon seemed to shake and birds fled. Spittle flew from the smaller canyon rifting his face.

"I'm afraid," Rune said. Ice seemed to encase his innards.

Valien nodded. "All wise men fear battle. Only fools rush fearless into a fight. The true warrior is not he who feels no fear, but he who conquers fear."

Rune nodded, forcing himself to swallow, and clenched his fists to stop them from trembling.

I will conquer my fear, he told himself. *I will fly fast. I will use the sun. I will win this. For Kaelyn. For Requiem. For Tilla.*

"Doog!" Cain shouted and raised his fists. "Crack his bones!"

Doog repeated the gesture, raising his fists to the sky, and his howl pealed across the canyon. The scarred, collared man shifted into a dragon. Scales of motley grays, blacks, and browns rose upon him, clattering like mismatched plates of armor. His claws drove into the canyon floor, and his tattered wings raised storms of dust. Long horns grew from his head, but like his human form, the dragon Doog had no face; the same scar drove into his dragon's head. A single fang thrust out from the crevice, and fire smoldered within. His head looked like a volcano ready to erupt.

"Rune, shift!" Valien shouted.

Rune summoned his magic. Black scales flowed across him, and he beat his wings and soared.

The scarred, metallic dragon howled and flew toward him, a beast of rattling scales and smoke and spurting flame.

Rune blew his fire.

The jet blazed across the canyon, roaring and spinning. Doog howled and his flames burst, not a neat jet, but a wild fountain like exploding barrels of gunpowder. Rune's stream crashed against the inferno, and fire filled the canyon.

Rune beat his wings and rose from flame. He flew higher. The canyon walls raced at his sides. Below he saw Doog thrash in the blaze, and then the beast soared too, howling and lashing his tail. Doog blew more fire. The beast had no jaws for blowing narrow, flaming streams like other dragons; instead he spewed burning showers thick with saliva.

Rune cursed. He had trained to dodge thin jets of fire; he knew how to bank around them, then blow his own flames. Toward him rose an inescapable inferno like an overflowing smelter. He kept soaring. The fire kept rising below; Doog was still ascending, spraying his heat. The canyon walls raced at his sides, trapping Rune. The fire was rising too quickly; he'd never reach the canyon top in time.

He cursed, shut his eyes, and swooped.

He screamed as he crashed through the flames. His scales blazed; he felt the flesh beneath raise welts. He burst from the blaze, stretched out his claws, and slashed at Doog.

Rune yowled. Sparks flew. Doog's scales were thick as steel plates. Rune's claws flared in agony, not even denting the beast's scales.

He kept diving toward the canyon floor, smoke rising across him. The men howled and shouted below. Valien was shouting commands, but Rune couldn't make out the words. Doog yowled above him, and when Rune glanced up, he saw fire crashing down.

Stars damn it!

Rune swooped toward the canyon floor, then leveled off and skimmed across the cracks and stones. When he glanced over his shoulder, he saw Doog crash down onto the canyon floor, cracking the stone before rising again with a howl.

They raced through the canyon. Rune flapped his wings with all his strength, streaming over the canyon floor. The wind roared. The canyon walls blurred. Birds fled overhead. Flames crackled behind him, and when Rune glanced behind him, he saw the beast following. Doog flew at a totter. A burly dragon, his belly slammed against boulders, his tail lashed at canyon walls, and his claws tore the ground. Dust and rocks rained around him, and he screeched from his wound of a mouth, spraying fire.

Rune cursed, looked back ahead, and flew faster. His lungs and wings blazed with pain. The Castle-in-the-Cliff vanished behind.

He wanted to attack. He had trained to fight dragons. Yet this felt more like fighting an erupting volcano.

Rune snarled.

I tore off the wing of Shari Cadigus herself. I fought an army of legionaries and axehands. I can defeat this beast too.

The flames licked his tail. Rune narrowed his eyes, lowered his flight to a mere foot above the ground, and raced toward a towering boulder that rose from the canyon floor like a lighthouse. Doog squealed behind him, flames showering across the canyon and singeing Rune.

With a howl, Rune reached the boulder, curved his flight, and spun around it. Flames crashed against the stone. Rune came shooting back toward Doog and blew his fire.

The jet blazed and roared. Doog screeched. Flames crashed against him and Rune rose higher. He overshot Doog and swiped his claws, driving them across the dragon's back.

Sparks showered. Rune screamed. One of his claws tore off and clattered down. His blood spilled.

Bloody stars! he thought. Did the dragon have scales of steel?

He kept racing along the canyon, now moving back toward the Castle-in-the-Cliff. When he glanced behind him, he saw Doog following. The flames had blackened his scales, but the dragon was still howling and sputtering his fire and drool.

Rune flew with all his might, but he was too slow. Doog's claws wrapped around his tail. Rune floundered, caught in the grip. He kicked, slamming his claws into Doog's ruined race. The beast bellowed. His mouth, a mere hole with one fang, opened inside his scar. He drove his head forward and bit.

Rune roared. The fang drove into his leg, and blood spilled, and fear flooded Rune.

I can't win this. I will die here.

He kicked and beat his wings madly, unable to free himself. Doog pulled him down, and Rune slammed against the canyon floor. Rock cracked beneath him. Claws lashed him.

"Rune!" shouted a distant voice; it seemed to be calling from another world. "Rune, on your feet--burn him!"

He looked up, blinking, but saw only flames. The heat blasted his back. His scales widened in the heat and cracked. Pain drove through him like daggers, and the howls of the beast tore through him. His blood splashed across the canyon floor.

"Rune!" shouted the distant voice. "Up, damn you! On your feet."

Valien.

It was Valien shouting in the distance. In the cloud of pain, memories of his training returned to him: long nights swinging swords, flying as dragons, blasting smoke, and lashing claws tipped with wood.

Valien. Leader of the Resistance. The wisest, strongest man
Rune had known. The man who raised the torch of Requiem, who
gave Rune hope.

I will not die today, Valien.

He snarled, shoved against the canyon floor, and flipped onto
his back.

Doog howled atop him, a demon of scale and flame, twice
his size and showering fire and blood and smoke.

*I maimed Shari Cadigus. I toppled the walls of Castra Luna. I can
defeat him.*

Doog's maw came lashing down, his fang thirsty for more
blood. Lying on his back, wings splayed out, Rune blew his fire.

The jet shrieked, crashed against Doog's face, and showered
back down onto Rune. He closed his eyes against the heat. The
weight lifted above him. Rune leaped up, beat his wings, and flew.

He raced back toward the Castle-in-the-Cliff. Behind him,
Doog howled and chased, claws banging against the floor, tail
chipping the canyon walls at their sides. They raced through fire
and dust and raining rocks.

I can't cut him, Rune thought. *I can't claw or bite him. I slammed
my fire into his head, and still he flies.*

Rune gritted his teeth.

He's too strong. He's too big. I cannot cut or burn him.

He roared, blood in his eyes.

I will crush him.

He saw the castle facade ahead. Cain and the others still
stood outside the palace, watching and howling and cheering. The
Stone Guardians framed the castle gates, a hundred feet tall.

Valien's words echoed in his mind. *The true warrior is not he
who feels no fear, but he who conquers fear.*

Rune roared and flew toward the palace gates. His wings
beat and raised storms of dust. In mid-flight, he released his magic.

He returned to human form.

He tumbled through the air, shouted, and landed at the feet
of a statue.

He looked up. He saw Doog flying toward him, belly
skimming the canyon floor, claws reaching out to tear him apart.

The statue creaked above.

Rune leaped back.

The burly, scarred dragon came flying beneath the statue. The statue's fist slammed down.

Stone drove against scales. The fist crushed Doog's head like a war hammer crushing a tin helmet. The dragon's skull caved in. Blood and gore gushed out. Doog's single fang tore free and clattered against the canyon floor. He gave a few last flaps of his wings, and his tail lashed... and he lay still.

Rune panted, still in human form, his clothes soaked with sweat and blood. Silence fell across the canyon. The hundreds of soldiers watched, not daring to breathe.

The stone statue raised its fist, straightened, and stared blankly ahead. Below, Doog's skull leaked. With a fluttering of dust, the dragon returned to human form. He lay dead, a burly man, his head caved in.

Rune stood, breath shaking, legs bleeding, and clothes smoking. He stared down at the corpse. He shook his head, clenched his fists, and looked up at Lord Cain with burning eyes.

"He was only a halfwit," Rune said, voice hoarse. "He was only a poor, scarred man with the mind of a child. And you made him fight." Rune spat. "I slew him, Cain. I slew him for you." He stepped up toward the lord, fists shaking, and hissed. "But know this--I will never more shed blood for your sport. I fly to kill Frey Cadigus next, and you will fight with me, or it will be your blood I shed once Frey's throne is mine."

Lord Cain stared back, eyes shrewd beneath his bushy brows. His lips twisted. His face was like beaten leather bristly with red and white stubble. His fists clenched too, veins rose in his neck, and Rune was sure the lord would strike him.

Then Cain snorted out a great laugh that ruffled his mustache.

"Aye, you scoundrel!" the lord boomed, grabbed Rune, and pulled him into a crushing embrace. He then shoved him back and punched Rune's shoulder. "Your cheeks might be as smooth as a virgin's teats, but you've got bollocks, boy."

He roared his laughter. It echoed across the canyon. Rune only stared, fists still tight. Sweat and blood dripped down his forehead, but he would not even blink. He kept staring at the lord.

"Fight with me, Cain," he said.

Lord Cain was still roaring his laughter, chest heaving. "Aye, I'll fight with you, lad. We two... we will shed blood together." He raised his fist and roared. "We will roast Frey's warty backside, and the south will be mine! House Cain will rise!"

His soldiers repeated the cry, raising fists and howling the name of their lord.

Rune stood still, blood dripping. Valien approached him, eyes somber, and clutched his shoulders.

"You did well, Rune," the older man said.

Rune did not turn to look at him. He only stared down at the brute's corpse.

Killing him was a mercy, Rune told himself, and his eyes stung. *Cain tortured him. Cain drove that axe into his face, then forced him to beg for treats like a dog. It was a mercy.*

And yet Rune's heart twisted, and he couldn't swallow the lump in his throat.

Lady Lana approached him too. Rune looked up at her, wondering how a woman so fair, her face pale and noble, could have been born to a monster like Cain.

"Rune," she said softly. "Stay with us tonight. Feast with us. We will tend to your wounds, then eat and drink."

Rune looked over her shoulder at Lord Cain; the man was roaring with laughter and pointing at the dead Doog.

Kaelyn's words echoed in his mind, soft and kind.

The wise work with small devils to slay the big ones.

Rune closed his eyes. She had spoken those words about Beras, and Rune clung to them now, but they could not warm the ice in his belly.

"We're leaving this place," he said and opened his eyes. He looked at Valien. "We leave now. Come, Valien. There's still an hour of daylight. We can cross a few miles before night falls." His voice sounded too dry to him, too pained. "We're going back."

Without waiting for a reply, Rune shifted into a dragon, took flight, and soared. The canyon walls blurred at his sides. When he reached the forest above, he landed among the trees, shifted back into a man, and gritted his teeth so hard they hurt. He walked through the forest, refusing to look back.

SCRAGGLES

He walked through the forest, hungry and thirsty and so weary he almost fell. His tongue lolled. His belly twisted, feeling so shrunken it could touch his back. The trees rose around him in the sunset, branches creaking and reaching out like cruel men in armor. They frightened Scraggles, but he had to keep moving. He had to find food. He had to find water. And more than anything, he had to find his master.

He had been walking for a long time now. Scraggles could barely remember the last time he lay upon a blanket, ate a true meal, or felt warm and safe. Yesterday he had caught a robin and eaten it, then retched it up later. He had not eaten since. A few miles back he had drunk from a stream, but the water had tasted foul, and his throat still blazed.

I need food, he thought. *I need real food--roast meats and stewed vegetables and anything hot and hearty.*

He thought back to the food at the Old Wheel. His master would feed him from his table, and Scraggles would feast upon roast boar, fresh bread, and cheese, and he would even drink of the tavern's ale. There had been a warm fireplace too, a rope to gnaw, and a blanket by the hearth Scraggles would rest on. There had been his master tending to him, patting him, and hugging him in the cold nights.

All that was gone now. The woman with the pale hair had snatched his master from the tavern. The dragon had swooped and its fire rained. Scraggles had barely escaped the flames. He had raced through the city, his fur smoking, seeking his master, but could not find him. He had spent moons on the boardwalk, waiting for Master to return, never losing hope. Finally he had set out into the forest, seeking him.

How far back was the town? Scraggles didn't know. How many days had he been wandering this forest? Far too many. He was so thin now. So hungry. So weak and afraid.

But I must keep going, Scraggles thought, panting as he walked over the fallen leaves. *I must find Master. I must find Rune.*

He tossed back his head and yowled. Back at the Old Wheel tavern, whenever he'd yowl, his master would come with food, with pats, with warmth and companionship. Scraggles howled again and again in the forest, as he did every day, and every time, he held his breath and expected Rune to come racing between the trees.

But he never did.

And Scraggles just had to keep walking.

Head hung low, he forced himself to move on, ignoring the pain in his paws. The sun was falling fast. If Scraggles could not find food before the darkness, the hunger would gnaw on him all night, keeping him awake. He looked around, seeking more birds, but they all stood high upon the branches. He saw a squirrel and made a halfhearted attempt to grab it, but it fled into the canopy.

Maybe I should turn back, Scraggles thought. *I could return to the town. I might find food there. I could eat dead fish on the beach or beg for scraps from passersby.*

But no. He couldn't go back. He'd come too far already. There was nothing left for him in the town. His master was no longer there. Scraggles had seen it. The pale woman had become a dragon, lifted his master, and flown off into the forest.

I will find you, Master, Scraggles thought. *I'll keep going forever, even if I die here.*

He kept walking.

The sun fell behind the trees. Long shadows stretched out, then faded into darkness. Only the stars lit the night. The wind moaned, the trees creaked, and a distant wolf howled.

Fear filled Scraggles and he mewled. Two days ago, a jackal had pounced and bitten his flank. The wound still blazed. And wolves were even larger; Scraggles had seen one howling upon a hilltop last night.

If they catch me, they will kill me, he thought and whimpered again.

He kept walking. He had to keep going. He dared not sleep, not with wolves nearby. The trees creaked in the darkness and branches snagged him. More howls rose. Scraggles walked on.

I have to rest, he thought. He was so tired. So very tired. He had to lie down. He could curl up here. He could place his head against his paws, close his eyes, and wait for death to find him. It wouldn't be long. Another day or two, and the thirst would claim him, or maybe the wolves. And his pain would end.

He blinked. He took another step. He was so weary.

I'll lie down for only a bit, he thought. *I'll close my eyes. Maybe I'll dream of Master.*

He sat upon the forest floor, the wolves howled, and Scraggles whimpered.

I miss you, Master. Do you too wander this forest? Do you too seek me?

Scraggles lay down. He placed his head on his paws and shivered in the cold. He was about to close his eyes when he glimpsed the flicker of light.

He raised his head.

He stared.

There, he saw it! Light ahead! Firelight!

Scraggles leaped to his feet. Memories of the fireplace back home filled him. He could almost feel that warmth again. A fire crackled ahead! The scent of smoke wafted, rich and intoxicating in his nostrils, overpowering. Another scent wafted beneath it; the scent of a traveler.

Master?

Scraggles ran.

He ran through the darkness. His paws banged against a root, he fell hard onto the ground, then leaped up and kept running. He followed the scent, and the light grew ahead.

He raced around an oak and saw it there.

A campfire.

A human sat there, shivering in the cold.

Master?

Scraggles froze. He stood in the shadows. He sniffed.

The human was grumbling and rubbing shivering hands before the fire. Scraggles stared, frozen in place, his tail straight like a branch. His nose twitched.

"Damn the stars and damn the Legions and damn this stupid cold!" the human said and spat.

Scraggles didn't understand those words, but the voice sounded angry.

It's not Master's voice.

Disappointment curdled in his belly like that time he'd eaten moldy cheese. Scraggles took a step forward, keeping himself hidden in the shadows, and stared more closely.

He'd have to be careful. Humans could be dangerous. Scraggles had learned that in this forest. He had come across humans here before. One had kicked him, and another had drawn his sword and scared him off. Even back home, some humans on the street would treat him cruelly, mocking him.

Some humans were friends, others were foes. Scraggles did not understand humans well, but he knew that much. He'd have to tread carefully here. If this one was a friend, there might be food and warmth here. Or there might be stones and kicks and swords.

He inched closer, crept around a tree, and stared at the traveler by the campfire.

It was a young woman. She was much smaller than his master. She was the size of a child--maybe even smaller than Scraggles--but her face seemed older, the same age as Master's face. She had short, brown hair that fell across her brow. Her face was orange in the firelight, her nose upturned, and her eyes dark.

A memory stirred in Scraggles.

He knew this one! He remembered her scent.

The memories blazed so powerfully he almost fell. In his mind, he was running along the beach again. The sand flew from beneath his paws. The salty wind filled his nostrils, rich with the scent of fish, crabs, and seawater. He ran through the waves, lapping the salty water and spitting it out, and rolling through the sand. And she was there too. This young woman with short hair would pet him, feed him scraps, and wrestle him in the sand.

She was from home!

"Good pup!" she had said on the beach, hugging him. "Good pup. You love your Aunt Erry, don't you?"

Scraggles burst into a run.

He leaped from the shadows, raced around the campfire, and stood panting before the woman.

She gasped. Her eyes widened. Scraggles froze, hesitating, not sure she would remember him. He wanted to leap onto her, but waited, a hint of fear still inside him.

Erry rubbed her eyes and blinked.

"Merciful stars!" she blurted out, squinted, and tilted her head. "I'm dreaming! Scraggles?"

It was her.

Scraggles grinned, leaped onto her, and began licking her face.

"Burn me!" she said, laughed, and fell onto the forest floor. "Scraggles, what the Abyss are you doing here? Is Rune here?"

He leaped onto her, licking her face and wrestling her and not letting her rise. She laughed, ruffled his fur, and finally pushed him off.

"Bloody stars, Scraggles, I was sure you were a wolf or outlaw or something." She looked around at the dark forest. "Cadport must be leagues from here. Are you lost? Where's Rune?"

Scraggles panted, tail wagging furiously. He didn't understand all of that. But he knew that Cadport was the name of his home. And he knew that Rune was the name of his master. She was asking about them. She wanted to find Master too, he realized.

Thinking of Master, his joy left him. Ice filled his belly, and he gave a plaintive yowl.

Erry's eyes softened. She sighed.

"You're lost too, aren't you, Scrags?" she said. She scrunched her lips, tapped her chin, and looked up at the trees. "Bollocks, old boy, but I've only been walking for three days. We must be leagues and leagues away from Cadport, *days* away." She frowned at him. "How the Abyss did you make it this far?"

He panted, leaped onto her again, and nuzzled her cheek. He wanted to tell her so much. He wanted to speak like humans, to tell her of the long days in the forest, the Old Wheel burning, and the pretty woman stealing Rune. Never before had Scraggles wished for the gift of speech so badly. He tried to talk now, giving a rumbling whine. Whenever he attempted speech back at home, Master would laugh and pat him, but Erry only sighed.

"Oh Scrags, what are you trying to tell me?" She raised her voice and cried out. "Rune! Rune, are you out here? Stars, Rune!"

The wolves answered. Their howls surrounded the camp. Erry closed her mouth, hissed, and grabbed the hilt of her sword. Scraggles tensed, his tail shot out like an arrow, and he growled.

"I think," Erry whispered, "we better be a little more quiet." She took a step closer to the campfire, keeping her hand on her sword. "Stay close to the fire, Scraggles. Wolves fear fire. But you're brave, aren't you?"

The wolf howls continued for long moments before dying off. Erry remained standing for a while longer, staring around, then finally sat down. She rummaged through her pack and pulled out bread rolls, smoked sausages, and cheese.

"It's not much," Erry said, "and it's all the food I have left." She sighed. "I was going to save half for breakfast tomorrow, but damn it, Scraggles, you look thinner than fish bones."

Scraggles salivated and his belly rumbled. The scent of the food filled his nostrils and his head swam with hunger.

"Here, you old mutt," Erry said, sighed, and gave him a bread roll. "Eat it."

Drooling more than he ever had, Scraggles scarfed it down.

They shared the rest of the food in silence. Erry had a canteen of water too, and she let Scraggles drink half. When their meal was done, they lay down by the fire. The trees creaked, the wind moaned, and they huddled close for warmth. Scraggles sneaked under her cloak, tossed a leg across her, and licked her cheek.

"God, Scrags, your breath stinks," Erry said. "Breathe the other way!" She pushed his head away, then sighed. "Oh, Scrags, what are we even doing here? We're both lost. We both have no idea where to go."

Scraggles didn't understand that, but he knew she was sad. He could hear it in her voice. He nuzzled her with his nose, trying to comfort her, and she rubbed his neck.

"We'll figure something out," she said. Her voice cracked and her eyes dampened. "I promise you. We can't go back to Cadport. There are too many soldiers there. I bet that's why you escaped." She sniffed. "And we can't go back to the Legions anymore, not after what I did; they'd bloody hang me for that. Looks like it's just you and me in the forest from now on, pup."

Scraggles whimpered and shut his eyes. Erry sighed and held him close. The fire died to embers. They slept.

LERESY

He was drinking around the campfire with his men, singing old war songs, when his guards dragged in the kicking, muddy girl.

They had been living in the woods for many days now, never staying in one place for more than a night. A thousand gruff, loud men who loved to sing and burn bright campfires, they hid about as well as a naked prostitute among priestesses. And so Leresy had been driving them southward day by day. When the clouds offered cover, they flew. When the skies were clear, they walked under the forest canopy. When darkness fell, they drank and sang the nights away. League by league, they moved south, away from the capital, away from the emperor.

He'll come after me soon, Leresy knew. *My father will not tolerate me stealing a thousand of his soldiers. He'll send an army after me. Maybe he already has.* The thought tickled him. *Let him come! I'll slay him and his men.*

And so they sang in the dark forest, raised smoke from a hundred fires, and kept their armor on and their swords polished.

"Let Frey Cadigus fly here!" Leresy cried in the night. He drank deeply from his mug of ale. "Let him come and die in our fire."

He stumbled toward his campfire where a suckling boar was roasting. Leresy laughed to see it. The poor beast had a spit stuck up its bottom, and an apple filled its mouth. Fat and juices dripped into the embers below. Leresy imagined his father and sister roasting in his camp. They too were pigs. He would shove spits up their bottoms too and cook them alive. He gave the boar a turn, allowing the fire to roast its back.

"Tonight we drink and dine!" he shouted and waved his mug. "By the moon's turn, we will reach the sea, men. We fly south to unknown lands! We fly to Terra Incognita where no dragon has ever flown. We will claim the wild lands and live like kings!"

They cheered and waved mugs.

"My father claims he slew all other races, purifying the world," Leresy continued. "But I say he lies! I say many foreign women still live--lush, nubile women of the southern wilderness." His men cheered, and Leresy raised his voice. "We will be explorers, and we will find them! They are waiting for true men of the north to bed them. We will make them ours!"

The men howled.

One of them stood up, a gaunt and tall man named Yorne. His hair was brown and shaggy, his face weathered, and his forearms tattooed with dragons.

"To Leresy!" he announced, raised his mug, and drank.

Leresy raised his own mug in salute. "We are Leresy's Lechers!" he said. "We are an army. We will rule the wild lands overseas, and if my father flies against us, we will roast his head upon our fires."

They were carving the boar, opening another cask of ale, and singing hoarsely when the guards dragged the girl into the camp.

"Let me go, you reeking, toad-warted sons of whores!" the girl was screaming, floundering in the grip of the guards. "Let me go now, maggots, or I'll gut you like fish and piss on your graves!"

Leresy blinked, rubbed his eyes, and couldn't help but laugh. The young woman was barely larger than a child, her face still fresh with youth. Her cheeks were red, and mud caked her short hair. Her wrists were tied behind her back, and Leresy's guards manhandled her forward. The girl kicked and screamed and tried to bite, but could not free herself.

"You yeasty, sheep-bedding halfwits!" she shouted, tossing her head from side to side. "Face me like men, you puny boy-loving eunuchs! I'll crush you like the worms that you are."

The guards kept dragging her forward, moving between the campfires until they stood before Leresy. The girl kept screaming. A bruise spread beneath one of her eyes, and her lip swelled.

"Lord Leresy!" one of the guards said. "We caught this one slinking outside our camp. A common thief. Probably wanted to steal food. She had a dog too, but the mutt ran off."

"You are dogs!" the girl screamed. "Your mothers were bitches and your fathers pissed on walls!" She kicked wildly, held in midair. "Give me back my sword, and I'll slice you into rat food!"

The men of his camp gathered around and laughter roared. The young woman couldn't have weighed more than a hundred pounds in armor, and even held above the ground, her head barely reached the guards' shoulders. And yet she squirmed, shouted, and kicked like an enraged bull.

"I know this one," Leresy said. He tapped his cheek, stepped closer to the girl, and scrutinized her. "I've seen her before somewhere."

She spat at him.

The glob hit Leresy's forehead and dripped down his face.

"And I know you, Leresy Cadigus," the girl said. "You tell your thugs to untie me, or by the stars, next thing that hits your face is my boot."

Leresy cleared his throat. Stiffly, he lifted the hem of his cloak and cleaned her spit off his face.

"You know, I do love a wild woman," he said, reached out to caress her cheek, and pulled his hand back when she snapped her teeth. "I bet you're a wild one in bed."

"I thought you only bed sheep," she said and raised her chin, still held in the guards' grips.

He sighed. "Your name is Erry. I remember. Periva Erry Docker, the daughter of a whore from Cadport. You served me in Castra Luna. By the Abyss, I'm pretty sure I paid good copper for your mother a few years back." He tilted his head. "How much do you charge now? I bet you bed men for bread crusts."

"I bet you bed them for gold, Leresy," she said. "Oh yes, you're a pricey one."

He stared at her top to bottom, considering. The girl was too scrawny. She stood barely taller than a child, she had no teats to speak of--at least, none that he could see under her tunic--and her hips were narrow like a boy's. Leresy liked his women rounded enough to grab on to. This one was filthy besides, all caked in mud and sweat. And yet... she was still the only woman he'd seen in days. If he closed his eyes when bedding her and thought of Nairi instead, she would serve.

He turned his attention to the guards holding her. "Let her go. This runt used to be my soldier. She will serve me here too."

The guards hesitated. "My lord?" one said. "She bit my arm back in the forest. She kicked Joran in the shin. She might be a runt, but she's wild."

"I like them wild," Leresy said. "I will tame her. Leave her arms bound, but let her stand. She's cranky because she's hungry and thirsty. We'll let her eat and drink." He looked at her. "Share our meat and ale, Erry Docker. You were my soldier. I'll look after you." He touched her cheek. "Be a good girl now."

The guards released her. Erry landed on her feet, hissed, and whipped her head from side to side. She tugged at the ropes binding her wrists but could not free herself. Panting, she stared around the camp, letting her gaze fall upon the men, the campfires, the roasting boars, and the copious amounts of ale. Her eyes narrowed.

"Bloody shite, Leresy," she said. "You look like a pack of outlaws. Burn me!"

Leresy cleared his throat. "Well, we *are* outlaws now, in a sense." He shrugged. "I got weary of life in the court. All fancy dress and pomp and fake flattery. I told my father to go shag a dog, took my men south, and here we are. Behold!" He waved his mug around. "My new domain and my new band of merry men. Meet Leresy's Lechers!"

Erry snorted. "Leresy's Lechers? Did you invent that name?" She tossed back her head and laughed. "Merciful stars, it's not very intimidating, is it? Why not... Leresy's Lepers, or... Leresy's Bastards or something? If you're outlaws, you need to sound tough and scary, not just lustful."

"Well, the first one's disgusting," Leresy said, "and the second one don't rhyme."

"Leresy's Lechers don't rhyme either," Erry retorted, chin raised. "You're thinking of alliteration, not rhyming."

He snorted. "Big words for a dock rat." He grabbed her shoulder. "Watch your tongue, little one, lest I cut it from your mou--"

He had not finished his sentence when a shadow leaped. Wild barking rose.

A black dog came running into the camp, a beast nearly as large as a wolf. The hound snarled and came racing toward Leresy.

"Scrags, no!" Erry shouted.

The guards cursed and one kicked, hitting the dog in the belly. The beast fell, mewled, and leaped back up.

"Scraggles, down!" Erry cried. She leaped toward the dog and leaned over it, whispering into its ear. It growled beneath her and stared at Leresy, seemingly unsure whether to huddle with Erry or resume the attack.

"Bloody stars!" Leresy cursed. "Men, kill that flea-bitten thing."

"No!" Erry shouted, and tears brimmed in her eyes. "Please, my lord! Don't hurt him. He's my dog. Well, he's a friend's dog. But I'm looking after him now." Wrists still tied behind her back, she huddled over the mutt. "Don't hurt him. I'll do anything, but don't hurt the dog."

Well well, Leresy thought. The little urchin who screamed, cursed, and kicked had a soft spot. That was good. The dog would help tame this one. He licked his lips. *And she said she'd do anything...*

"Men!" he said. "Do not harm this hound. Give him water. Feed him. Treat him as if he came from my royal kennels." He reached down and touched Erry's hair. "Stand up, child. Your dog will be safe. I'll protect him, and I'll protect you."

She stood up and glared at him. "Child? I'm nineteen years old, Leresy, same age as you."

Yet her voice had lost its fire, and her eyes were still damp.

"Very well, you're a big girl now," he said and gave her a mocking smile. "And I'll feed you too, Erry, and I'll treat you well-- as well as I treat my dogs. Come with me into my tent. We'll eat and drink there, and we'll be warm." He looked at the mutt. "The dog stays here."

They stepped into his tent, leaving the songs and cheer outside.

It was a small tent, no larger than the room he'd frequent in the Bad Cats brothel. He had a cot with an old blanket, a chest of clothes, and a table laden with jugs. It was enough for Leresy. His days of pomp and grandeur seemed but a distant memory; he had lost the desire for pomp when the resistors slew his wife upon the forest.

"Stars, Leresy," Erry said softly. "I've been to your chamber at Castra Luna. You had tapestries. A stained-glass window. A bed larger than any I've ever seen. You had fine cloaks with fur and embroidery." She looked around the tent and smiled crookedly. "You live like a common soldier now."

He snorted, walked to a table, and poured a mug of wine.

"What were you doing in my chambers in Castra Luna?"

She shrugged. "Rifling through your chest of undergarments, of course. Stars, Leresy, you own more corsets than I do."

"Funny," he said. "Funny girl. That chamber, Docker... that chamber was nothing but a fisherman's hut compared to the grandeur of the capital." He stared at the tent wall, lost in memory. "Have you ever seen them? The walls and towers of Nova Vita?"

She shook her head. "I've seen the boardwalk at Cadport and I've seen forts. I've never seen grandeur, my lord."

He closed his eyes. "The walls rise so tall there, Docker. Taller than you can imagine. The towers rise above them, and ten thousand banners fly. The streets are so wide twenty soldiers march abreast. And the palace! The palace scratches the sky itself, and--" He stopped himself. He clenched his jaw. "But I will build myself a new kingdom, a better kingdom, a realm of wonder in the south, far beyond my father's reach." He turned toward her. "I will take you there with me. You are mine now, Erry Docker, and I will look after you. You are safe with me. All conquerors have concubines; you will be mine."

She gave him a crooked smile. "Will you untie me first?"

He raised an eyebrow. "Why would I do that?"

She slunk forward, pressed herself against him, and looked up into his eyes, her chin against his chest.

"Because I'm asking you nicely?"

He snorted. "I prefer you tied up."

She rolled her eyes, turned her back toward him, and bent her knees. Fast as a weasel, she reached out her tied hands, grabbed his dagger from his boot, and leaped away.

"Thief!" he shouted and gasped.

She spun back toward him, dagger clutched behind her, and flashed a grin.

"It's how I survived in Cadport." She twisted her lips, then brought her hands forward. The rope that had bound her fell severed at her feet. "How would you like your dagger back? In your neck or in your chest?"

"How about," he said, "you hand it over hilt first, and you may eat our boar, drink our wine, and share my bed. Surely those pleasures eclipse the pleasure of stabbing me."

She twisted her lips. "How fatty is the boar?"

"Very."

"We shall see. Let's eat first; I'll keep the dagger in the meanwhile."

He shouted for his men, and one brought in a plate piled high with steaming roast meat. When the man left, Leresy held out one of his two chairs.

"Sit," he said to Erry, "and we'll dine."

He had never seen a woman eat so fast.

Erry was perhaps as small as a child, but she attacked the roast boar like a starving jackal. She stuffed the meat into her mouth until her cheeks bulged, gulped noisily, and drank wine directly from the jug. After every bite, she wiped her lips with the back of her hand, then reached for more.

"Have you ever heard of chewing?" Leresy asked her, nibbling his own serving.

She glared at him over her plate. "Chewing is for fine, fancy-pants princelings like you." She stuffed more meat into her mouth. "But I'm from the docks and mgfdfffgg..."

He shook his head sadly. "You're eating your own weight in food. How do you stay so small?"

She grabbed the jug of wine, held it up with both hands, and guzzled. When she slammed it down, wine dribbled down her chin.

"I'm like a snake," she said. "I eat a lot when I can find it. It usually has to last a while."

When the plate was empty--Erry had eaten most of the meal--she licked it clean. With a sigh, she leaned back, kicked off her boots, and slammed her feet onto the table.

"I don't want to see your smelly feet," Leresy said, staring at them in distaste.

She wriggled her toes and raised an eyebrow. "They're not smelly. I'm not one of your filthy men. I'm a petite, lovely young maiden."

"I wouldn't know by the way you eat," he said. "You could eat and drink my men under the table."

She closed her eyes, and an impish smile spread across her face. After a moment, she nodded and rose to her feet.

"Very well," she said. "I'm ready now."

She walked to the bed, turned toward him, and began to undress.

Leresy stared in disbelief, one eyebrow firmly raised. Erry did not undress seductively like Dawn and Dusk and the other girls at the Bad Cats. She made it seem as casual as a girl getting ready to bathe. When all her clothes were gone, she stood before him, staring at him curiously.

"Well?" she said. "Are you just going to sit there?"

Leresy stared at her.

Bloody stars, he thought. *I was right. Barely any teats on this one.*

And yet his loins stirred, and he found himself marveling at how smooth her skin was and how lithe her limbs.

"Do you always undress in strange men's tents?" he asked, still seated at the table.

"You're not a stranger, my lord," she said. "In Castra Luna, I dreamed of this. Whenever I sneaked into your chambers--and I did several times--I dreamed of this. But I was always afraid, unsure if you wanted me. You fancied Tilla then, I knew it." Her eyes hardened. "But Tilla is gone from you now. And I'm here. You said that I'm yours now, Leresy. So make me yours."

She climbed onto his bed, lay down upon her belly, and closed her eyes.

Leresy stood up, walked toward the bed, and stared down at her. *Flaming Abyss,* he thought. He had never known a woman to give herself to him so easily--at least, not one he wasn't buying. Without her muddy clothes, and despite her boyish hair and boyish frame, she seemed oddly intoxicating to him. He sucked in his breath, and he took her.

He took her roughly. He conquered her. He had never taken a woman so roughly, not in all his days of conquering them. He hurt her. He was sure he hurt her, yet she made not a sound. She had let many men hurt her, he realized. She had let many men claim her like this, lying down with her eyes closed, offering her body to get what she needed--if not money then food or protection or shelter. Leresy did not care. From this day she would be his alone.

When he was done with her, he wanted to toss her out of his tent. He hated women sleeping in his bed; he always had. He slept alone; he always did. He going to grab her, to toss her out, but he found himself holding her desperately and stroking her hair, and tears filled his eyes.

"I love you, Nairi," he whispered. "I love you."

They lay in his bed as his candles guttered. He kept stroking her hair, short hair like a boy's, and holding her so close, and his eyes stung. He had never let a woman sleep in his bed. Tonight he slept with Erry Docker in his arms.

KAELYN

She walked through Lynport, her cloak wrapped around her and fear gripping her heart.

Soldiers lined the streets, standing vigil at every corner, their helms hiding their faces. An imperial dragon patrolled the sky, clad in black armor bearing red spirals, his flames crackling in a wake. Kaelyn tightened her cloak around her, struggling to calm her trembling fingers. She felt bare without her sword and bow, as fragile as a mouse treading among cats.

I've walked here before in disguise, she told herself. She had visited Lynport--Cadport to her father, but always Lynport to her-- dressed as a priestess twice before. *I will live today too.*

She walked around a bakery where a white scarf hung at the window, a sign of mourning. This house, like many in Lynport, had lost a soldier in Castra Luna. Kaelyn swallowed an icy lump in her throat.

Today Lynport is more dangerous than ever, she knew. *Today the resistors are no heroes here, but demons. We slew the youths of this city.*

Kaelyn reached for her sword--the hundredth time today-- and found it missing. She took a deep breath, steeling herself, and kept walking.

She passed by a tannery, a chandlery, a smithy, and a dozen other workshops. They were built of wattle and daub, white clay filling the space between their timber frameworks. From the ground floors wafted the sounds and smells of their trades: the ring of hammers on anvils, the tangy scent of beeswax molded into candles, the creak of looms weaving cloth, and more. At their top floors, where the tradesmen and their families lived, shadows moved behind windows and more white scarves flew.

So many scarves, Kaelyn thought, eyes stinging. *So many youths we killed.*

As she walked down the cobbled road, she looked to her left. Alleys sloped between houses down to the boardwalk. The sea churned gray there, waves spraying foam like watery phoenixes rising. She glimpsed the cannon, the oldest one in Requiem, watching the southern horizon.

The Old Wheel used to stand nearby, Kaelyn thought. As she walked by another alley, she stared south and saw an empty patch of rubble and ash. She whispered a prayer.

Yet today she had a new errand here. She raised her head and looked northwest instead. There, upon a hill, she saw the fortress rising. Kaelyn squared her shoulders and clenched her fists.

Castellum Acta rose craggy and tall, a single tower above a wide hall. Bird droppings and moss stained its tan bricks. Arrowslits lined its walls. Battlements crowned the tower, and two dragons perched there, clad in bladed helms, watching the city. Flags of the red spiral thudded around them.

Castellum Acta, Kaelyn thought with a shudder. For five hundred years, benevolent lords had ruled here, governing a prosperous port. Today a general of the Legions, a pet of the emperor, lurked behind those bricks.

The man I must kill today, Kaelyn thought.

She trudged up a narrow, cobbled road that climbed the hill. The fortress rose above her. Boulders and brambles littered the sandy hillsides, and gulls circled above, cawing in mockery. As she climbed higher, Kaelyn rose above the city roofs. When she looked behind her, she could see Lynport's boardwalk lined with rotting shops, the docks that stretched into the water like fingers, and the sea rolling into the horizon. The scent of saltwater tickled her nostrils, and the waves whispered in her ears.

"Girl!" rose a growl. "Girl, halt!"

Kaelyn spun back toward the fort, which rose a hundred yards away upon the hilltop. Two soldiers came walking down from its gates, swords drawn. Upon the tower, the sentinel dragons glared, smoke rising from their nostrils.

When the guards reached her, Kaelyn curtsied.

"Good morning, sons of Requiem," she said. "I've come to see General Gorne, lord of this fort." She handed them a scroll sealed with a snake stamp. "A birthday gift from Lord Teus of Castellum Sil. It is General Gorne's birthday, is it not?"

The soldiers frowned, and one snatched the scroll from her hand.

"What's this then?" he demanded. "This scroll is a gift?"

Kaelyn gave him a crooked smile, pulled open her cloak, and revealed the scanty silks she wore beneath.

"No, my lord," she said. "I am. Lord Teus, a friend of your commander, already paid for my services. I shall be spending the night."

Their eyes widened, and Kaelyn sighed inwardly. Men were so easy to fool. She tugged her cloak back shut and glared at them.

"Well, take me to your lord," she said. "He would not like you delaying his gift."

Soon they entered the gates of Castellum Acta. Inside the main hall, Kaelyn held her breath and her heart pounded. The whisper of waves and the salty air faded behind; she stood among stone and shadows.

Columns supported a vaulted ceiling. Doorways led to other halls; through them, Kaelyn saw a dining room, an armory, and a barracks full of cots. Dozens of soldiers moved through the chambers, and the clank of armor echoed.

At the hall's end, a trestle table stood below a banner of the red spiral. General Gorne, Lord of Cadport, sat at the head seat.

"Commander Gorne!" cried one of the guards, slamming fist against chest. "A gift for you, Commander. Lord Teus sent her."

General Gorne leaned across the table, and his eyes narrowed. Upon his breastplate, he sported an engraving of a boar, sigil of his house. The man himself bore a striking resemblance to his emblem. He was beefy and pink-skinned, and his wide nose spread across his face like a snout. His hair was such a pale blond, it was nearly white, cut to stubble too sparse to hide his scalp.

Please don't let him recognize me, stars, Kaelyn prayed, and her fingers trembled. Gorne had visited the capital eight years ago and dined with her family. Kaelyn had been only a child, but still she caught her breath. *If he recognizes me, all is lost.*

"Teus?" the porcine lord said and rose to his feet. Despite his hoggish appearance, his eyes were shrewd. "Lord Teus is an old goat's piddle stain." He glared at Kaelyn. "Who are you, girl?"

She curtsied, allowing her cloak to open seemingly by accident, revealing the silks she wore beneath. The thin cloth showed more than it hid.

"Your birthday gift," she said. "That is all, my lord. Teus has paid for me already."

Gorne stomped around the table, frowning. He moved at a waddle, nearly as wide as he was tall. When he reached her, he placed a finger under her chin--that finger was wide as a sausage-- and lifted her face toward his. He scrutinized her. His eyes were pale blue, and his nose was bulbous and veined.

"Teus must be after my son," he said, disgust dripping from his voice. "The old bastard's daughter is coming of age. The pathetic gutter lump must want to soften me before suggesting a marriage between our houses." He snorted, shoved Kaelyn back, and roared to his hall. "As if House Gorne would stain its blood with the venom of Teus!"

The soldiers across the hall cheered at this--Kaelyn guessed they'd cheer at anything their commander announced loudly enough. She cursed inwardly, and sweat trickled down her back.

He might not have recognized me, but he'll send me away, she thought with a chill. *Stars, or he'll imprison me, or he'll toss me to his men, and our plan is doomed.*

"My... my lord?" she asked. She straightened, allowing her cloak to open another inch. "Shall I return to Lord Teus? I'm already paid for, and... if your lordship would return me, I will gladly warm Lord Teus's bed instead."

He spun toward her. His lip curled back, revealing small, sharp teeth. With a hand like a paw, he grabbed her arm.

"Oh, I'll have my gift," he said, and his eyes simmered. "Teus beds only the goats he raises on that forsaken farm he calls a fort. We'll have a taste of you, girl."

He dragged her from the hall, his men howling behind, and onto a staircase. They climbed up the tower. His fingers dug into her arm, and she stumbled behind him, struggling to climb fast enough. As the stairs spiraled up, pocked with embrasures, Kaelyn glimpsed the southern boardwalk, houses stretching east and west, and the northern forests. Looking upon those misty trees, her eyes stung and her throat tightened.

You wait for me there, Valien, she thought. *I will not fail you.*

They climbed hundreds of steps, and General Gorne was wheezing when they finally reached the tower top. He yanked open a doorway and dragged her into a chamber.

Daniel Arenson

Kaelyn felt herself pale. Her breath died.

"Stars," she whispered.

General Gorne snorted and dug his fingers deeper into her arm.

"Aye, you're a fine gift, child," he hissed. "A gift I won't be returning soon."

Kaelyn's eyes dampened.

Stars, oh stars, she thought.

A dozen women filled Gorne's dusty chamber. A bed rose in the back, but the women sat upon straw piles. They were naked and sallow, and chains bound them to the walls. They stared at Kaelyn with blackened eyes, and their swollen lips moved silently. One was pregnant, her belly swollen but her limbs scrawny and her eyes sunken.

"Filthy lot!" General Gorne said and spat. "Grown old and sickly, these ones have." He turned toward Kaelyn and licked his chops. "Aye, but you're fresh. You'll make a good addition to my collection."

The harem writhed upon the straw, and chains clattered. One woman, her nose bashed and bloody, reached out and whispered. Her voice was too soft to be heard, but Kaelyn could read her lips.

I'm sorry, the woman whispered. *I'm sorry.*

"You... collect them, my lord?" Kaelyn asked, heart thrashing against his ribs.

Gorne was already unbuckling his armor. His breastplate clanged to the floor, sending the women to cower against the walls.

"I bought them," he said. "They are scum, all of them. Nothing but seaside whores who polluted our docks. I gave them a home here. I cleaned up the boardwalk from its filth."

And you bedded them, Kaelyn thought. *And you beat them.* It took all her will not to snarl. *And now you will pay for your sins, Gorne.*

"They were like me," she whispered.

Gorne hissed and drooled. "You will be one of them, whore." He tugged off his tunic and boots. "I will break you in before I chain you among them."

As he began to undo his belt, Kaelyn doffed her cloak. She stood before him in her silks, legs and belly bared.

354

"I am yours, my lord." She climbed onto the bed, lay down, and looked up at him. "Please, my lord, be gentle with me."

He tossed off his trousers and stood naked before her, sweaty and pink. Spittle dripped down his chest.

"I will be as rough with you as I like," he said, walked toward the bed, and lowered himself atop her. "I'm going to hurt you now, and you're going to love it."

Kaelyn reached to the silks around her thigh and drew her poniard.

General Gorne's girth pressed down against her.

Her blade entered his neck.

He gasped. His eyes widened. His mouth opened and closed, struggling for words, dripping blood and saliva onto Kaelyn's chest.

She gave him a crooked smile. "I thought you liked it rough, my lord."

She twisted the blade, and he gurgled. He pawed at her, and his sausage fingers grabbed her throat.

He squeezed.

Kaelyn gasped and stars covered her vision.

She drove the blade deeper. His hand kept squeezing her throat. His blood poured down his neck, yet still he choked her. She squirmed and kicked beneath him. His body pressed against her, thrice her size and slick with sweat.

She couldn't even wheeze. Her lungs burned. She thought he'd snap her neck.

Stars damn it, die! She pulled her blade back. She thrust it again, piercing his shoulder, and more blood flowed, but he kept choking her. His eyes stared into hers, and he licked the blood on his lips.

"You..." he croaked, "will be mine..."

She felt his arousal against her. Panic flooded her and she floundered like a fish.

Oh stars, he's going to bed me here, he's going to take his prize, even as we both die.

Blackness spread across her vision, a midnight sky strewn with stars.

Her legs felt numb.

Her lungs faded into blazing embers.

Before her in the night, she saw the stars of Requiem, the stars of her fathers. The Draco constellation shone above her. She was flying toward it, a green dragon in the night. The starlit halls of her ancestors glowed above, the columns white, and Kaelyn wept for she had failed her people.

I failed you, Requiem.

She winced.

No. No, Requiem. She screamed. *Not today! Not today! Someday I will fly to you, starlit halls of spirits, but not this day. This day is for sunlight.*

With a choked cry, she thrust her poniard again.

It crashed into the general's mouth, punched through his palate, and crashed into his skull.

His fingers loosened.

Kaelyn gasped for breath.

She sucked in air, a breath she thought could swallow the chamber, the tower, and the sea outside. The blackness withdrew from her eyes like curtains lifted. Her head exploded with starlight.

She kicked, shoving the boar of a man onto the floor. She leaped over the corpse, raced to the window, and kicked it open. The sea breeze whipped her hair and stung her cheeks.

Behind her, the women whimpered. She looked over her shoulder to see them reach out to her, their chains clattering, their eyes pleading. Kaelyn sucked in her breath.

"I will return to you," she whispered... and jumped out the window.

She tumbled down from the tower, silks flapping, her bloody poniard still in her hand.

Before she could hit the ground, she shifted into a green dragon. She beat her wings, whipping the bushes and raising clouds of dust. She soared.

She rose above the tower. Upon its battlements, the two dragons shrieked. Kaelyn blasted them with fire.

They howled, blinded and burning. Before they could spray their own flames, Kaelyn swooped. She lashed her claws and swiped her tail. Blood sprayed. The tower guardians screeched, tumbled backward, and crashed to the hillside in human forms.

Kaelyn hovered above the tower, tossed back her head, and shot a pillar of flame skyward.

The fire crackled, a blazing typhoon. Kaelyn looked to the northern forest, heart thrashing.

Six thousand more flaming pillars rose from the trees. Howls shook the sky. Six thousand of her comrades--dragons of the Resistance and the canyon--rose from the forest, roared, and flew toward the city.

Below her, legionaries were streaming out of the fortress. Kaelyn blew flames, torching the Regime's banners that hung from the tower. She soared higher and cried for the city to hear.

"General Gorne is dead! Lynport is liberated! Legionaries--lay down your arms and live!" Tears budded in her eyes, and she streamed over the city streets, roaring her cry. "Requiem! May our wings forever find your sky. Lynport is free!"

The Resistance raced over the city walls, wings blasting air. The imperial dragons swarmed from their fort, leaderless, confused, howling and sputtering flame. The forces crashed above the streets and blood rained.

TILLA

She stirred in her sleep, caught in her nightmare's claws.

"No," she whispered and kicked her blankets, struggling to wake up, but the dream pulled her deeper, and the blankets wrapped around her, and Tilla walked down dark halls while eyes burned and faces floated in mockery.

"Lowborn!" they chanted. "Lowborn scum!"

Punishers lashed out. Everywhere she turned, more faces floated, laughing, spitting at her. Lightning burned her. She ran down the hall, but more of her tormenters awaited her there. They leaped from every shadow, demon creatures with masks twisted in eternal scorn.

"I am Tilla Siren!" she shouted, eyes burning. She had chosen the name of her new, noble line; it was a strong name, the name of a mythical creature said to live in Cadport's waters. She shouted it as a charm, a spell to save her from her lowborn roots, from her shameful past upon the boardwalk, from all her dirt and misery here in the purity of the academy.

The other cadets laughed around her, beautiful youths from noble houses, their blood old and pure, their highborn accents meticulous.

"Tilla Roper!" they said, laughing. "Seaside scum. Lowborn whore. Weave us a rope, Roper!"

Again their punishers lashed out.

Tilla screamed and fell. Lightning raced across her, burning her clothes, burning her skin, crackling her bones.

"I am... Cadet Tilla... Siren!" she gasped, but tears ran down her cheeks, incurring more laughter.

They kept burning her. They hunched over her like vultures over prey, and she wept. And she begged. And still they burned her.

"Lowborn worm," one boy said and spat upon her. "Go back to Cadport, peasant."

Her screams echoed through the black halls of Castra Academia.

Her eyes rolled back, and she thought she would die.

But I did not die, her thoughts whispered in the dream, and her fists clutched her blankets. She snarled, struggling to rise from slumber, but falling back in.

I survived!

No matter how badly the highborn beat her, Tilla kept training. She did not quit. When they spat into her meals, she ate sullenly around the spit. When they dumped chamber pots on her clothes, she growled and washed them herself and trained even harder. When they beat her, she fought back, and fell, and hurt, then healed and walked again.

She fought with swords.

She flew as a dragon down dark halls.

She learned to plan battles, to break spirits, to *command.*

She was Tilla Siren, a commoner thrust into a fortress full of the children of nobles, and they tortured her, and they beat her, but she fought them and every lash made her stronger.

Every night she clutched the shield Shari had given her, the shield with her sigil--a cannon overlooking the sea, a symbol of home.

I will be like a cannon, she swore every night, lying in whatever filth her fellow cadets had soiled her mattress with. *I will be strong as iron. I will slay my enemies. I will outlast sword and fire.* She growled every night as her tears burned. *I will become an officer.*

Tilla thrashed in her bed, opened her eyes, and sat up with a pant.

Cold sweat washed her, and her chest rose and fell. Her heart thrashed. She winced and raised her arms.

"Please, don't hurt me," she whispered. "Please. No more."

But no punishers burned her. Tilla opened her eyes to slits, then let out a shaky breath. She sat in bed, shuddering. The sheets were soaked with sweat.

"Just a dream," she whispered. "Just a memory."

She had survived for six moons in Castra Academia, the great school for the Legions' officers, and she had graduated first among her class.

I am a lanse now, she reminded herself. *I wear red spirals upon my shoulders. I command. I'm south in Castra Luna now, far from the academy. I no longer have to be afraid.*

She looked down at her arms. The scars of old burns still spread there. Tilla tightened her throat.

"Scars make us strong," she whispered.

She rose from her bed, shivering; the chill of autumn filled the night. Her tent was small and barren, its black walls shuddering in the wind. A hint of light shone through the tent flap; dawn was near. With stiff fingers, Tilla approached her table, lit her tin lamp, and held her hands above it, allowing the flame to warm her.

In the flickering light, she stared down at the weapon on her table. Her punisher.

Hilt untouched, its tip was cold, but when Tilla's fingers grazed the grip, the punisher crackled to life. Lightning raced across the rod's rounded head, red and creaking like shattering bones. She pulled her fingers back and the lightning vanished.

I burned her, Tilla thought, staring down at the weapon. *I burned Erry. I burned my friend.*

"Damn it, Erry," she whispered, and her throat tightened. "Why do you still have to act like a seaside urchin? What else could I have done?"

Tilla's eyes burned, and she blinked them furiously.

No, she told herself. *Show no weakness, not even when alone. Let no pain fill you. You must be strong to survive.* She squared her shoulders.

"Only the strong will survive in the Legions," she said, staring down at her punisher. "I had to be strong, Erry. Scars make us strong."

Yet now Erry was gone, a deserter from the Legions, an enemy to be hunted and killed. Now Rune too was an outlaw, calling himself Relesar Aeternum, the heir of the fallen dynasty.

How had all this happened? Only a year ago, Rune had been a humble brewer, and she had been only a ropemaker. And now... now she was an officer in the Legions. Now Rune had a new name, proclaiming himself true king. Now he fought for Valien, the man who had slain Tilla's brother.

They all turned against me, Tilla thought and clenched her fists, and a lump filled her throat. None of them understood. None of them knew the law of this land.

"Cadigus reigns, and his law is the blade, the punisher, and the iron fist," she said, repeating the words she had learned. "The weak must be purified."

She took a deep breath, closed her eyes, and let her own weakness flow away. She let all those thoughts of home drip from her mind like poisoned blood from a wound.

I will be strong.

She dressed in her steel armor, grabbed her sword and shield, and left the tent.

The camp stretched around her, kindled with the first hints of dawn. In the eastern sky above the trees, pink tendrils stretched across blue fading to black, and the stars vanished one by one. In the west, shadows still cloaked the ruins of Castra Luna, hiding the strewn bricks and fallen walls like the midnight sea at home. Around her in the camp, the first siragis--hardened, lowborn warriors--marched between tents. Shouts rang across the clearing, and soldiers emerged for morning inspection.

As Tilla walked between the tents, whatever troops she passed--be they hulking warriors or green youths fresh out of training--stood at attention, saluted, and hailed.

She was an officer now. She bore the red spirals. She was a goddess to them.

When she reached a dirt square, she shifted into a dragon and took flight. She flew across the camp, her white scales clattering, her horns gilded like those of all officers. Below her, tents spread in rows and troops bustled. Five milanxes mustered here, moved from the western mountains, five thousand troops in all.

We will find the Resistance in these forests, Tilla vowed as she flew, *and we will crush them.*

She looked across the camp to the northern trees. The white tombstones rose there. Hundreds of youths from her home lay buried under that soil. Mae lay among them.

"I will avenge you, Mae," Tilla whispered.

She returned her eyes to the camp. A ring of dragons surrounded a dirt field. In its center rose a towering tent, large as a house and topped with the banners of Cadigus. Golden embroidery formed flying dragons across its black walls. Soldiers guarded the tent entrance, clutching halberds.

Tilla flew toward the field. She landed before the guards, shifted into human form, and raised her chin. The guards saluted her, slamming fists against chests.

I might be only a junior officer, Tilla thought. *But I'm the junior officer who saved Shari's life.*

She walked past the guards, stood at the tent entrance, and shouted her salute.

"Hail the red spiral! Tilla Siren reporting."

The princess's voice came from within. "Enter."

Tilla stepped inside. Opulence filled the tent, befitting a daughter of Cadigus. A plush bed, armchairs, and giltwood divans stood upon bearskin rugs. Golden vases of wine, platters of fruits and cheeses, and a roast goose topped a table. Racks of swords, helms, and breastplates stood everywhere, a collection worthy of an armory, all belonging to the princess of the empire.

That princess stood clad in black armor, its plates filigreed with golden dragons. Her longsword hung at her left hip, her punisher at her right. Her mane of brown curls cascaded across her pauldrons. Her back was turned to Tilla; she stood before an easel, staring at a parchment the size of a door. Upon the parchment appeared a sketch of a castle, its dozen towers lofty, its walls topped with cannons.

"Castra Sol," Shari said softly, not turning to acknowledge Tilla. "Fortress of the sun. It will rise from these ruins, thrice the strength of old Castra Luna." She caressed the parchment, fingers gloved in black leather. "It will be mine to command, a glorious castle built for one purpose--to crush the Resistance."

Tilla took a step farther into the tent.

"They toppled this fort, Commander, so we will build one larger and greater. For the glory of Requiem."

And for Mae Baker, she added silently. *For hundreds of youths from my home.*

Shari turned toward her. Her face, tanned a deep gold, had aged six years in the past six moons. Shari was only twenty-nine, but weariness filled her dark eyes, and the first lines of an eternal frown had begun to frame her lips.

She's beginning to look like her father, Tilla thought. *A face as hard, cruel, and unyielding as stone.*

"Tilla, we've received reports from the south. The news is grim." Shari reached for the table, grabbed a mug of wine, but did not drink. "We've been betrayed. House Cain has joined the Resistance. Rebellion flares in the south."

Tilla sucked in her breath. "They say Lord Devin Cain is mad! They say he's not left his canyon since we crushed his last rebellion. Does he fly against us?" She clutched her sword. "We will crush him again! Let him fly to us. We will slay him and his men upon the forest. We--"

"Tilla," Shari said, her voice softer, and ghosts filled her eyes. She winced and her left arm twitched--the side where she'd lost her wing.

"Commander?" Tilla whispered, and suddenly fear flooded her.

There is worse news, she thought and her innards trembled.

"Valien and Cain have joined their forces, and they've struck in the south. They've taken Cadport. The city has fallen."

Every weapon in this tent seemed to stab Tilla with cold, biting steel that drove the breath from her lungs.

Cadport fallen. My home. My father.

She couldn't help it. She trembled. Red flooded her eyes.

Cadport. My home. My father.

Her eyes stung and her breath shook.

"We must fly there!" she finally managed to say, speaking through stiff lips. "We will crush them, Commander. I will slay this Valien myself, and Cain, and the rest of them, and--"

Shari clutched her shoulder and glared.

"Soldier!" the princess said. "Calm yourself. Do not forget your station. I command this garrison. You command a mere phalanx. Steel yourself and stand straight." Her voice softened, her grip loosened, and she sighed. "Tilla, I know this news is difficult, but please, listen to me. Sit and drink my wine. We will not leave Cadport in their hands."

But Tilla would not sit. She would not drink. The tent swam around her.

"We have to save Cadport," she whispered. Rage flared through her, and she drew her sword. "We must slay them, Commander!"

Shari bared her teeth and grabbed Tilla's wrist. Tilla was among the tallest and strongest women in this camp, yet Shari stood even taller, and she snarled down at her like a lion staring down a wolf.

"Tilla Siren," she said, "the Resistance has given us a great boon."

"They've captured my home, Commander!" she said. Her voice shook. "They will slay the people there. They--"

"They have emerged from hiding," Shari finished for her. "They muster in a city we know, a city we can attack, a city we can trap them within. We will not let Cadport remain in their hands. Five thousand troops garrison here now, and already dragons fly to bring my father the news. When he hears of Cadport, the wrath of the Legions will muster here... and descend upon the city."

Tilla breathed heavily, chest shaking. "We will lead the charge. We will kill Valien and his men."

"But we will take Relesar alive," Shari said, and her eyes blazed; she still clutched Tilla's wrist. "You will capture him, Tilla. You will capture the heir of Aeternum, and you will carry him to the capital in your claws."

Rage pounded through Tilla. Fire pumped through her veins and spun her head.

Relesar Aeternum. She means Rune.

She thought of him again, her dearest childhood friend. The boy she would wrestle. The boy she would whisper and cry with. The boy she had kissed upon the beach and vowed to see again.

The man who led the Resistance into these ruins, she thought, *who slaughtered hundreds of our townsfolk, who now brings war to our home.*

She took a shuddering breath, squared her shoulders, and stared into Shari's blazing eyes.

"I will capture him," she whispered. "He will be ours."

RUNE

He stood upon the balcony where, only moons ago, Shari had slain a girl and severed her head. He squared his jaw, took a deep breath, and gazed down upon thousands of townsfolk who filled the square below.

Rune had faced crowds many times in the past year. He had spoken to hosts of resistors in their shadowy halls. He had fought thousands of legionaries in battle. Yet standing here, facing the people of Lynport, he felt very young and nervous, and his head spun. The crowd covered the square below--tradesmen, children, farmers, and even legionaries who had stripped off their insignia after Gorne's death. Rune wore armor now, the plates bright and the pauldrons wide, and he bore the longsword of kings, yet facing this crowd, he did not feel like a warrior or royalty.

I feel like a young brewer again, he thought.

He looked aside. Valien stood at a doorway, leaning against the doorframe, arms crossed. His hair hung wild around his leathery, scruffy face. He wore his old patches of steel over hardened tan leather. Rune wanted the man to guide him, to speak for him, but Valien didn't even step onto the balcony. He only stared at Rune from the doorway, eyes inscrutable, saying nothing.

Rune turned to look at Kaelyn. She stood beside him upon the balcony, clad in her forest garb: tall deerskin boots over gray leggings, a green tunic with a golden belt, and a blue cloak. Her sword hung at her hip, her quiver hung over her shoulder, and her golden hair billowed in the breeze. She raised her hand, two fingers pressed together in the salute of the Resistance, and spoke to the crowd.

"People of Lynport!" she said. "I've asked you to gather here today. I see skilled tradesmen, the heartbeat of this town. I see farmers, the pillars of our society. I see warriors--men who abandoned the cruelty of Cadigus, tore off their red spirals, and joined the light of old Requiem. I am Kaelyn Cadigus! I am the daughter of the tyrant. I am here to tell you: That tyrant will fall! You are free."

She stood panting and her eyes glistened. She paused as though expecting cheers or applause. The people, however, only stared at her silently. A few muttered.

Rune sighed. *Kaelyn has always seen the resistors as heroes. She will learn not all see us the same.*

With a tug on her quiver's strap and a clearing of her throat, Kaelyn collected herself. She raised her chin and kept speaking.

"People of Lynport! I present to you your new king--the true king of Requiem. Here stands Relesar Aeternum, son of Ardin, King of Requiem." She knelt, eyes damp, and stared up at Rune. "May the stars bless him."

She paused again, craned her neck up, and peeked down at the crowd. She seemed to be waiting for them to kneel too, but the crowd only muttered louder. One man grumbled, shook his head, and turned to leave the square. The rest bustled restlessly.

"Kae," Rune said softly, "I don't think they care much about old dynasties here. We're far from the capital."

She rose to her feet and glared at him. "Of course they do!" she said, turned back to the crowd, and raised her voice. "Do you not remember House Aeternum, people of Lynport? Relesar is heir to an ancient dynasty, to--"

One man below groaned. "That there's only Rune Brewer!" he shouted up at her. "Bloody Abyss, the boy sold me ale about a hundred times."

"More like a million times, Tam," said the man's wife and poked his ample gut. "Boy darn well turned you into a boat."

Nervous laughter spread through the crowd. One woman, emboldened by the chortling, pointed up at Rune and cried out.

"I used to watch him as a babe, I did! Changed his swaddling clothes more than once. Boy sure knew how to soil them!"

The laughter grew, and Rune felt his face redden. Wearing armor definitely wasn't making a difference now. Desperate, he turned to look at Valien. The gruff old knight stood in the doorway, muttering and fuming, his eyes dark. Rune wanted to plead with him for help, but Valien wouldn't even meet his gaze.

The crowd's laughter grew, and more people called out their own stories of Rune--how he'd once cried when his father wouldn't let him keep a stray kitten, how he'd walked into a cart when gaping at a pretty woman whose skirts had blown in the wind, and how his singing voice once caused flowers to wilt--honest to goodness, half a dozen people saw it.

Rune only stood sighing upon the balcony, but Kaelyn shouted over the crowd.

"You speak of your king!" she cried, face red and eyes blazing. "Relesar is descended of a proud dynasty, of legendary Queen Lyana who founded this city, of the great King Benedictus who fought the griffins, and of the first King Aeternum himself who raised the marble halls. Relesar is a light upon Requiem, and--"

Rune placed a hand on her shoulder. "Kae," he said, "I don't think they're listening. Let me try."

She bit down on her words and spun toward him, fuming. Pink splotches spread across her cheeks. She seemed too enraged to even breathe. Rune looked back at the crowd below. They were still laughing, and many were leaving the square.

"People of Lynport!" Rune shouted out to them. "My friends. Listen to me please. For just a moment."

Grudgingly, they turned back toward him and watched, silent. Rune felt his head spin--so many eyes stared at him!--but forced himself to plow on.

"Look," he said to the crowd. "You're right. Don't follow me because I'm so-and-so fancy king's son. Don't follow me because I'm Relesar Aeternum, an heir from some old legend. You're right, I'm just Rune Brewer."

At his side, Kaelyn gasped and began to object, but he held up his hand, hushing her.

Rune continued speaking to the crowd. "Follow me *because* I'm Rune Brewer. Follow me *because* I'm nothing but a common son of this city. Follow me because I know what it's like living here, because I felt the scourge of Cadigus, because I--like you--saw the light of our home fade."

This got their attention. Their mirth died, and the people stared up at him, silent and listening.

Rune took a deep breath and saw Tilla's father in the crowd, a tall and wiry man with black hair. Rune pointed at him and spoke for the people to hear.

"Heri Roper, you used to sell many ropes to sailing ships. Traders from Tiranor docked here often, and your shop thrived. When the Cadigus family burned the kingdom of Tiranor, and our port rotted, you lost your livelihood." Rune turned toward another woman. "Meti Weaver, you used to sell silk to the south. You ran a shop full of seamstresses. Now you can barely sell cotton to hungry folk too poor to buy it." Rune turned to another man. "Your three sons were taken away from this very square, carted off to the Legions, and never returned."

The crowd mumbled, but this time nobody turned to leave, and no scorn filled their voices or eyes.

Rune looked upon them--his people, his townsfolk, his friends. He glanced over at Valien, and the man stared back, and now his eyes shone with approval. He gave Rune a small nod and an almost imperceptible smile. Rune turned back toward the crowd below.

"We all lost something to the Cadigus family," he said. "Some of us lost our livelihoods. Some of us lost our faith; this courthouse where I stand was once a temple to the Draco constellation, our forbidden gods. Some of us lost our loved ones. How many people did the Regime murder in this very square, beheading or whipping or breaking them upon the wheel?"

Eyes in the crowd darkened. People muttered and cursed. Anger brewed below like a sea about to erupt into a storm. But the anger was not directed at him, Rune knew. He raised his hands and spoke louder.

"Do not listen to the lies of Cadigus! They told you the Resistance is evil, that resistors hunt and kill for sport. The Resistance is not your enemy, but your ally."

Some in the crowd looked skeptical, but others were muttering their agreement, especially those old enough to remember the days before the tyrant. Voices began to rise in cheers, crying out their approval. Rune spoke louder to be heard above them.

"I am Rune Brewer!" he said. "I lived on the boardwalk. The Regime murdered my father and burned my home. I say: We are not Cadport, named after a tyrant who crushed us under his heel. We are a far older, nobler city. We are Lynport and our light will shine again." He shouted for the city to hear. "The tyrant must fall! We will fly as dragons again."

Below in the square, the crowd stared up silently. Tears filled the eyes of elders. Fire and passion filled the eyes of youths. One young woman, a farmer holding a basket of fruit, raised her head and cried out in a clear, high voice.

"Requiem! May our wings forever find your sky."

The crowd repeated the forbidden prayer, tears fell, and Rune knew: They were his.

"Blessed be the children of Requiem," he whispered, looking upon his home.

Kaelyn reached out and held his hand, her eyes swimming with tears, her lips whispering prayers.

Rune held her hand, turned his head, and looked across the roofs of Lynport. Beyond the city walls, golden forests rolled into mist.

Frey Cadigus waited there. The Legions would be mustering.

Frey will descend upon this place with all his wrath and malice, Rune thought and shivered. *Today Lynport is free. Tomorrow blood will soak these streets.*

The people sang for stars, for Aeternum, and for Requiem, but Rune only shivered and held Kaelyn's hand tight.

LERESY

"No!" he said and slapped her hand. "Damn it, girl, I told you a million times. The griffin only moves two squares."

Erry glared at him over the board of Counter Squares, a game of the capital. Her lips twisted in a snarl; she looked to Leresy like some puppy trying to seem fierce.

"This game is bloody complicated," she said. "You said the griffin can move diagonally across the--"

"That's the *dragon*," Leresy said and rolled his eyes. "By the Abyss, woman, do you think a griffin would beat a dragon?"

The pieces were arranged across the board: griffins, dragons, phoenixes, and other creatures carved of obsidian and ivory.

Chewing her lip, Erry reached for an obsidian wyvern that stood upon a white square. Leresy slapped her hand again.

"No, Erry, if you move your wyvern, my salvana will capture your mimic. See?"

Erry fumed, her face red. "No it *won't*," she said. "Do you want to know why?" She leaped to her feet and tossed the board sideways, sending pieces flying across the tent. "Because I bloody quit this stupid dumb game you just invented!"

Leresy looked at the pieces strewn across the ground. "Counter Squares was invented hundreds of years ago."

"And it was bloody dumb then too!" Erry crossed her arms and sulked. "Who the Abyss ever heard of stinkin' griffins hopping squares, and phoenixes that can't even fly, and ivory codpieces--"

"Those are salvanae, Erry, true dragons of the west."

"Well they look like codpieces to me! Sweaty, stinking ones." She snorted. "You fancy-arse nobles with your fancy-arse games. Burn me. Give me a mug of ale, a sword to swing, and a song to sing, and I'm happier than playing any game for prissy princelings."

He reached across the table and grabbed her wrist. "I'll give you something else."

She raised her chin and shot him a haughty stare. "What is that, princeling? Another la-dee-da game a little princess taught you to play?"

He rose to his feet, pulled her from her chair, and glared down at her.

"Your big mouth is going to get you into trouble one day," he said.

She smirked. "Am I in trouble now, oh lord princeling?"

He wanted to think of some clever retort, but he was too busy tearing off her clothes; they always came off so easily in his hands. She stood naked before him, smirking, no taller than his shoulders and slim as a twig, and yet she heated his blood to a boil.

He grabbed her shoulders. He pulled her to his bed. Her eyes closed, and he took her until finally the smirk left her face.

When he was done with her, again he wanted to kick her out of his bed, out of his tent, out of his camp. Stars damn it, he was Prince of Requiem, and no woman deserved sharing his bed. Yet again, as always, he only lay on his back, and she lay in his arms, her head upon his chest, and he stroked that short, brown, boyish hair of hers. She mumbled something sleepy, and he kissed her forehead, and his heart felt more confused than all the rules to all the games in the world.

What is it about you, Erry Docker? he thought, looking down at her as she slept, her cheek against his heart.

She should be nothing to him. She *was* nothing. She was only flesh, that was all. Only a body to warm his bed and feed his hunger. She meant nothing to him, nothing! She was no better than any whore from the Bad Cats back in the capital.

Leresy took her twice a day, morning and night, and sometimes a third time at noon, thrusting into her, using her to vent all his rage, all his grief, all his pain. And she never made a sound. She did not moan, or yelp, or cry. She never wept. She never demanded love or affection or money or power--any of those things all the women in Leresy's life had demanded. She simply let him use her as he would, a doll, a toy, that was all... and then slept in his arms, her head upon his chest.

And he used her. Not for his physical needs--those had lost all flavor--but to drown the pain that forever clawed his chest. To forget the capital. To forget Nairi. And so he took her again and again, and every time he did, he could forget a little more.

"Stupid, sweaty codpiece dragons," she mumbled, and he stroked her hair, and she fell silent, her sleepy breath tickling his chest.

"Stupid, sweaty, seaside urchins," he answered softly, his arms wrapped around her.

Slowly, night by night, Leresy came to realize that more than he craved her sex, he craved to hold her. More than he wanted to enter her, to grab her, to claim her body, he craved to stroke her hair, hear her mumble, and feel her breath against him.

You came to my camp muddy and scruffy and screaming like an enraged beast, he thought, holding her close. But in his arms now, she was a frail doll, delicate and pure and so fragile she seemed made of porcelain.

And slowly, he came to feel ashamed of how he'd scorned her that first day.

"Erry Docker," he whispered. "You stupid, stupid girl."

In the morning, he walked through their forest camp. Campfires crackled around him. Men lay snoring, cursing, or squabbling over their last sausages and eggs. Some men had risen early and were banging swords together, eyes grim, still soldiers even here in the forest. Many had drawn black dogs on their shields, and some had sewn black dogs on their sleeves; Erry's mutt had become something of a mascot. As Leresy ambled through the camp, surveying his men, a smile tingled the corner of his lips.

"Good morning, you bastard prince of lechers!" one man shouted out.

Leresy gave him a mock salute. "Go shag a dog, you son of a whore."

The man roared with laughter, grabbed a skin of ale, and drank deeply. The brew dribbled down his bare chest. Few men here were better dressed. Armor lay strewn across the camp, dulled and muddy. Men roamed about shirtless, barefoot, and scruffy. Most had not shaved for days.

Leresy looked down at his own raiment. A year ago, it would have disgusted him. He wore nothing but the garb of a forester: tan breeches, a rough black tunic, and a green cloak. Yet he did not miss his fine embroidery or filigreed plates of steel.

Those were trifles of the capital, he thought, grabbed a turkey leg from a wandering drunkard, and bit into the meat. He chewed lustfully. *Here we are true men of mud, steel, and sweat. The capital can burn to the ground.*

Tears stung his eyes, but Leresy furiously blinked them away and gnawed his meat with more fervor.

"Quite a camp of disciplined soldiers you've got here," Erry said, walking at his side. Her dog trailed behind her, sniffing at campfires and catching scraps the men tossed his way.

"They are hardened men," Leresy said. "True men, not bastards like my father, and not soft boys like that so-called King Relesar. They will build me a kingdom."

As they walked through the camp, many men paused from eating, drinking, or fighting and gaped at Erry. Drool thick with crumbs dribbled down some men's chins. Erry was perhaps as scrawny and short-haired as a boy, but she was the only female in camp, and these men had seen no other woman in many days.

Sooner or later, I'll have to keep her guarded and chained in my tent, Leresy thought, *or I'll have to share her with the camp.*

The meat tasted foul in his mouth, and he tossed the turkey leg aside, grabbed a jug of wine from a man, and drank to cleanse his mouth. Thinking of Erry naked and writhing beneath these muddy, scruffy men disgusted him.

Why? he wondered. He had shared his women with these men before. He had dragged many of his whores from the Bad Cats to his barracks, allowing his troops to share in the flesh.

He looked at Erry. She was still walking beside him, one hand on her dog's back, the other clasping a bread roll. She was chewing vigorously--stars, the damn girl never closed her mouth when chewing--and mumbling something about how this camp needed some good fish to cook.

They want her too, Leresy thought as the men crawled toward her. *They will try to take her from me.*

He gripped his sword's hilt. It was the simple, unadorned weapon of a common soldier. Fleeing the capital, Leresy had left his true sword behind--a priceless artifact with a filigreed blade, a platinum hilt shaped like a dragonclaw, and a scabbard glittering with more jewels than most treasure chests. That weapon probably still lay in the Bad Cats, but his new sword, grabbed from a Lecher who'd fallen to fever, could still kill.

"Bloody bollocks, Leresy!" said one man, a drunken fool with flushed cheeks, a week-old beard, and red eyes. He tottered forward, clutching a tankard. "When are you going to share your woman with us?" He waved his drink around. "I haven't tasted me a woman since I left the capital."

Stumbling forward, he reached toward Erry's backside.

With a growl, Leresy drew his sword, swung it down, and severed the man's hand.

Erry yelped and jumped. The man screamed. Across the camp, men stumbled back and cursed.

Leresy stood shaking. *Damn him! Damn the man!* His sword wavered in his hand. Blood pounded in his ears. He could barely see through his rage.

The maimed man stumbled back, clutching his stump, and tripped over a root. He crashed to the forest floor and writhed. Leresy stepped above him and raised his sword, prepared to finish the job.

"This one is mine!" he shouted. He looked around the camp at the men who watched. His eyes burned, and spittle flew from his mouth as he shouted. "You hear that, sons of dogs? Any one of you touches my woman, I'll slice *you* into a woman and give you to the camp!"

He swung his sword down.

"Leresy, no!" Erry cried and slammed into him.

His sword drove into the dirt, missing the wounded man by an inch.

Leresy slapped her.

He slapped her so hard Erry stumbled back and clutched her cheek. Her eyes widened, and her dog barked madly, and the world spun around Leresy.

Damn it, I didn't mean to--

"I'm sorry," he whispered and reached out to her. "Erry, please, I'm only trying to protect you, I..."

She glared at him, still clutching her cheek, and shook her head wordlessly. She grabbed her dog's collar and ran back to their tent.

Leresy stood, his bloody sword still in his hand. He felt everyone staring at him. Nobody said a word.

Stars damn it, he thought. *Stars damn these men and stars damn Erry.*

He lifted the fallen tankard and drank what ale remained inside. He tossed the empty vessel down.

"I'll let this one live!" he announced. "See my mercy. Any one of you other dogs lays a hand on what's mine, I'll cut that one too."

A few of the men were grumbling. A few clutched swords. Their eyes darkened and Leresy swallowed, suddenly afraid. There were a thousand of them, and each one was older and stronger.

Without my embroidery and armor, am I still a prince here, or only a man for them to slay?

He gritted his teeth, refusing to show fear. His father had to deal with a rebellion among his people; Leresy wouldn't allow the same misfortune to strike him.

"You shall have women!" he shouted, raising his sword high. "Have I not given you women before? You will have ten thousand more! We travel south to Terra Incognita, to the great unknown grasslands east of Tiranor. There are dusky women there of legendary beauty. They run topless through fields, clad in only skirts of grass, and they crave northern men to pleasure. We will rule them!"

This assuaged the men. A few began to cheer, and soon the rest joined in.

"We will be lords of our new kingdom!" Leresy shouted. "I've given you food, drink, and gold. Stay with me, and soon we will live as kings!"

They howled their approval, waving food and drink and fists, and Leresy took a shuddering breath.

Oh stars, he thought, *please let there be women in that forsaken land we seek. If we find nothing but empty grasslands, they'll have my head... and Erry's body.*

He was about to return to his tent, speak with Erry, and try to make amends when wings thudded overhead.

The foliage rustled and bent, and Leresy cursed. His heart thudded, and for a moment, he was sure the Legions had found them. Before he could flee, a lone brown dragon crashed down through the canopy, landed in front of Leresy, and shifted into human form.

Leresy glared at the man and spat. "Damn it, Yorne. I thought you were my damn father. I told you--we don't fly in daylight, not until we leave Requiem."

Yorne spat too, expelling a great glob Leresy thought could drown a rodent. The man had served in the Legions for twenty years; he'd worn six red stars upon his armbands before Leresy had ordered the Lechers remove their old insignia. The son of a lowborn fisherman, Yorne had never gone to Castra Academia, but he had served the Legions long enough, and he'd slain enough men, to fight alongside generals and send troops to die. Tattoos of dragons coiled across his ropy arms, and his shaggy hair could not fully hide a scar that snaked across his head. He was a tall man, the tallest among the Lechers, but gaunt and weathered as a strip of dry meat.

"Your father's busy dealing with bigger problems," Yorne said. He cleaned his teeth with his tongue. "Big news stirring across the empire. The Resistance has taken Cadport."

Leresy snorted. "Cadport? It's a damn backwater. I visited once and couldn't tell their fort apart from their latrines. Who cares?"

Yorne raised his eyebrows and thrust out his bottom lip. "Aye, a backwater to us, but fifty thousand folk live there. It's the largest town on the southern coast. Lots of dragons, if the Resistance has them shifting and flying against the capital."

Leresy stomped toward a campfire, grabbed a roasting sausage, and bit into it. The skin *cracked* and juices filled Leresy's mouth.

"Let them fly," he said. "Let them burn down the damn capital. I care not. Let all of Requiem burn! We are the Lechers. The unknown lands beyond the sea will be our kingdom. Let the Legions and the Resistance kill each other until none are left."

Yorne nodded, eyebrows still firmly raised, and scratched his chin. "More like the Resistance is going to be slaughtered, seems. Your sister's mustering an army in the ruins of Castra Luna. Whole brigades gather there, and more troops arrive every day. The emperor himself will arrive with the Axehand. They'll invade Cadport by winter, they say, and stamp out the Resist--"

"I care not!" Leresy said. "Damn it, Yorne, I don't give a damn about Requiem politics. We travel overseas, and--"

He bit down on his words.

He understood.

His heart leaped.

Oh bloody shite.

His sister. His father. The two people he hated most-- traveling south into battle. There would be cannons firing, dragons flying, blood and chaos and death.

It will be my chance, he thought and clenched his fists. *My sweet vengeance.*

His thoughts returned to his last night in the capital. Shari had dragged him by the hair from his fort, tossed him at his father's feet, and seen him banished. She had stolen his fortress, leaving him nothing but a wretch.

But now, sister, now you fly to war. And when you crash against the Resistance, a host of bloodthirsty barbarians, beware... beware of the shadow at your back.

Leresy licked his lips and grinned.

"Yorne," he said, "get this camp cleaned up. I want men wearing their armor. I want guards on patrol. I want some discipline here, damn it. Whip these warriors into shape!"

With that, he spun on his heel, left the men, and stomped back toward his tent.

When he stepped inside, he found Erry sitting on the cot, hugging Scraggles and muttering curses. She raised damp eyes and glared at him. The mark of his hand still shone red upon her cheek.

He approached her. She hissed and tried to rise. He shoved her down, grabbed a fistful of her hair, and forced her to look at him.

"Dearest little urchin," he said. "Poor, pathetic little wench. What do you know of pain?"

She growled. "If you strike me again, I will slay you."

He grabbed her arms and yanked her to her feet. She stood before him, glaring up at him, her hair tousled. Leresy caressed her bruised cheek.

"I promised that you will be my southern mistress," he said. "I promised you a land of wild grass, endless summer, and lazy days of sun and starry nights. To the Abyss with that." He placed a finger under her chin, kissed her forehead, and twisted his lips into a grin. "I will make you the concubine of an emperor."

VALIEN

He stood upon the breakwater, staring out into the sea, and remembered the day he met his wife.

Boulders formed the breakwater, their lower halves green with moss, their upper halves white with gull droppings. The waves slammed against the stones, turning from gray to blue and showering foam. The breakwater ended with a cairn, and there rose Lynport's lighthouse, a tower of empty windows, craggy bricks, and memories of better days.

Valien grumbled as he walked across the slick boulders--this was easier when he was younger--and placed his hand against the lighthouse. The old bricks were clammy and mossy, but he remembered years ago when this tower was new, when he had climbed its steps to view the sea and found her above.

The lighthouse doors had rotted or burned years ago. Valien stepped through the archway and climbed the stairs again, the first time he'd climbed them in twenty years. Shattered clay jugs, an abandoned glass bottle, and an old shoe littered the steps now. A feral cat hissed at him, bristled its fur, then fled. But as Valien kept climbing, he barely saw the stairway's current state. He saw himself a young man, twenty-one years old and only knighted that summer, visiting fair Lynport to protect the sea.

He reached the lighthouse top. He stepped into a round chamber where no more fire burned. Today this chamber was empty but for a discarded mattress, a cracked pipe on a windowsill, and three kittens nestled in the corner. Outside the windows, the sea stretched into the horizon, a gray sheet splotched with patches of green and blue where the water was shallow. But when Valien closed his eyes, he saw this chamber twenty years ago. A great beacon had burned here then, the fire shimmering behind glass panes, and upon the sea a dozen southern ships had sailed, bringing their treasures into Requiem.

"And you were here, Marilion," he whispered. "You shone brighter than all the beacons in the world. You guided me home."

He could almost see her again at the window, watching the sea. She had worn a white dress that day, its hem stained with salt and sand, and her feet were bare, but Valien had never seen a more beautiful woman. Her hair cascaded down her back, the color of honey, and when she turned toward him she smiled.

"Good morning, my lord," she said. "I'm sorry. I've come to watch the sea."

She was a commoner, born and raised in the south, her only jewelry a string of seashells. She was wild and beautiful, a creature of sea and sand. Standing beside her, Valien felt stiff and awkward in his armor, a relic of ancient tradition, out of place here like some dusty grandfather clock in a fairy fort.

She laughed. "Can you speak, sir knight?"

He cleared his throat. "You have nothing to apologize for. This is your town. I've only just arrived here from the capital. I serve in Castellum Acta. I--"

"You talk too much," she said and laughed again. "Listen! Do you hear it?"

Valien listened. He heard it--the waves whispering, the seagulls calling, and the forest rustling. The girl returned her eyes to the sea, inhaled deeply, and a smile touched her lips.

"I sometimes stand here silently for hours," she whispered. "The sea speaks to me."

They spent many days that summer standing in the lighthouse, walking upon the shore, or ambling between the shops along the boardwalk. During lazy days, they caught fish and cooked them on campfires, and Marilion would play her flute and he would sing softly. At nights, they would lie upon the sand, watch the stars, and hold each other. In the autumn they wed in this very lighthouse.

Valien stood in the barren chamber, twenty years older, his hair now wild and grizzled, his armor dented and dulled, and lowered his head.

I took her with me to the capital, he thought, and agony burned his throat. *She never returned.*

Valien closed his eyes and clenched his fists. The emperor's words from last winter echoed in his mind; they hadn't stopped echoing since.

"Marilion lives!" Frey had shouted, cackling and bleeding. "She lives in my dungeon, you fool!"

Valien's fists shook. His teeth grinded. Fires burst inside him.

With a howl, he opened his eyes and pounded the wall. Blood splattered his knuckles, but Valien felt no pain. He panted and growled and shook.

"You lie!" he hissed. He stormed toward the window and stared out at the sea, as if Frey hid among the waves. "You lie, dog. She died. I saw her die! I held her as she died."

Again the blood danced before his eyes--Marilion lying upon the bed, Frey's sword in her chest, her eyes glassy and still.

"I held you," Valien whispered. Tears stung his eyes and his voice shook. "I held you as your soul rose to the starlit halls. You've been waiting for me there, Marilion."

And still Frey's voice echoed, cackling madly. "She lives!"

Valien clutched the windowsill, fingers trembling.

He was lying. He was trying to break my mind, to drive me mad. He's lied so many times before.

With a shuddering breath, Valien turned from the window and left the lighthouse.

He flew over the city, a silver dragon, slower and wider than he used to be, his left horn broken off years ago. Lynport stretched below him, a crescent moon of houses and streets embracing the coast. The cliffs of Ralora rose west of the town, while forests rolled into the north. The southern sea whispered, a deep blue patched with green, lines of foam racing across it. The smell of seawater filled Valien's nostrils even up here.

He flew toward the northern walls that separated wilderness from city. They rose a hundred feet tall, overlooking oaks, maples, and pines, the trees golden and red and filling the air with their scent. A dozen dragons hovered above the walls, wings beating, holding four cannons aloft. Below upon the battlements, men waved, cried out, and guided the cannons down into place. Dozens of cannons already topped the battlements, pointing north toward the capital.

We took a hundred guns from Castra Luna, Valien thought, gliding toward the walls. *Yet ten thousand warriors will descend upon us, maybe more. These guns will not hold them back for long.*

He spotted Kaelyn standing in a turret, a small guard tower that jutted out from the wall. Valien filled his wings with air, descended, and landed outside the structure.

Around him across the wall, men scurried to bolt cannons down, and dragons hovered above, their wings whipping Valien's hair. Valien knew he should walk among them, inspect the batteries, encourage the troops, and prepare for battle. But he only stood, staring into the guard tower, and his throat constricted.

The turret was only large enough for a single archer. Kaelyn stood inside, her back to Valien. She held an arrow nocked in her bow, and she stared out an arrowslit, watching the forest. Wind whistled through the embrasure and ruffled her golden hair.

And suddenly she was not Kaelyn, and she did not stand in a turret. She was a woman years ago, standing in a lighthouse, her hair billowing in the sea breeze. Valien stood staring and his eyes stung.

"Damn you, Kaelyn," he whispered.

Damn you. Why do you have to look like her? Why do you have to fill me with those memories, with that old sweet pain? Why do I have to fight not to hold you, not to love you, not to lose you?

She turned around and saw him, and a smile split her face, showing white teeth--*her* smile.

"Valien," she said. "How are the defenses along the boardwalk?"

He entered the turret and stood beside her. While Kaelyn was slim and barely filled the place, Valien felt burly and clunky in here, a bear trapped in a box. He peered out the arrowslit at the forest; it swayed like a sea in sunset.

"The batteries of guns are being raised, and troops are manning them," he said. "A hundred will point to the sea, should the Legions invade from the south. More guns rise upon the courthouse roof and upon Castellum Acta."

Kaelyn nodded and clasped his arm. "When the Legions arrive, we will triumph."

Valien sighed, a long sigh that clanked his armor and bones. "We will slow them down. We will slay a few. But our outfliers report ten thousand legionaries already mustered in Castra Luna; they call the place Castra Sol now. More will gather there. We have only three thousand resistors and three thousand canyon warriors." He grumbled. "Lord Cain left the bulk of his forces in the canyon. The man is mad, but we will take what help he offers."

Kaelyn's eyes shone. "Our six thousand fight for justice. One man fighting for justice is worth ten who fight under the whips of a tyrant." Her voice softened, and she held his arm. "Valien, I am afraid. I see the same fear in your eyes. But know this: I fly with you today and always. I fought with you in our long years of hiding; I will fight with you now as we make our stand."

Valien stared at the rustling forest, imagining the assault--an entire brigade of dragons descending upon this city. Was he foolish to stay? Could they truly defend this city?

"We need more men," he whispered. "We need more guns. We need more time to train. Damn it, Kaelyn, we've never made a stand before. We've hidden in forests and ruins. We've attacked the Regime, then fled back into shadow. Never have we waved our banners, raised our heads, and invited the enemy to come."

Kaelyn nodded. "It's time to make this stand. Relesar has risen. The banner of Aeternum flies from our towers and walls. I feared battle in Castra Luna, and I cautioned you against it. Yet we flew out, we faced Cadigus in open battle, and we triumphed. I believe we will triumph here too." She touched his cheek, and her eyes softened. "Do not lose hope, Valien. We defeated the enemy at Luna. We will defeat them here."

Marilion lives! She lives in my dungeon, you fool!

The words echoed, and Valien saw that night again: His love in his arms, the sword in her chest, and the blood everywhere... so much blood.

He looked at Kaelyn--her young face, her nose strewn with freckles, her hazel eyes so large and earnest, eager for victory.

I cannot lose you too, Kaelyn. I cannot tell you how much I love you, how little I fear for my own life, how much I fear for yours.

He touched her cheek, his fingers so coarse and calloused against her pale skin. She smiled and embraced him, and her hair tickled his nostrils.

I love you, he thought, holding her close... not knowing if he meant a memory or the woman in his arms.

SHARI

Dawn rose golden over the forest, and Shari took her ward to see a man tortured.

They walked through the camp rather than flew. Shari wanted them to walk. She wanted Tilla to see the troops up close, see every spiral upon every breastplate, every eye burning with rage, every sword bright under the sun.

In battle, she will not command from above, a goddess overseeing her slaves, Shari thought. *She will fight among them in the blood and fire.*

And so they walked down the lines. Thousands of troops stood at their sides, three soldiers deep, forming palisades of metal. Their tents rose behind them, banners streaming. They stood at attention, fists against chests, men and women of the Legions. Every soldier wore a black helmet and breastplate; a longsword and dagger hung from every hip.

"We caught him lurking in the forests," Shari said as they marched down the dirt road between the troops. "He was spying on our camp and armed with a sword. I've broken him in, but I've left most of his flesh for you."

Tilla marched at her side, face blank and staring ahead. She wore the fine steel of an officer now, not merely a breastplate over a tunic like a common soldier, but full plate armor that covered her from toes to neck. She carried her helmet, a work of art shaped as a dragon's head, under her arm. She had taken well to command, Shari thought; she walked with the pride of nobility.

"I will break him," the young officer said, no emotion in her voice or eyes.

Shari smiled.

Good, she thought. *Good.*

Tilla was learning. Shari thought back to the first day she'd seen the woman in Cadport; it was nearly a year ago now. Back then, Tilla had been only a filthy commoner, but Shari had seen something in her even then. Unlike the other peasants, Tilla had not cowered before her. Tilla had not wept, fled, or broken even under the punishers of her commanders in Castra Luna, nor under the punishers of her fellow cadets at the academy.

Shari smiled. She knew, of course, of Nairi burning Tilla to near death. She knew, of course, of young nobles torturing Tilla for moons in the academy, burning her flesh and breaking her mind. She herself had ordered the punishment.

It made her strong, Shari thought, looking at the icy young officer. *It made her deadly. She will be a great commander yet. She will be like me.*

As they walked through the camp, heading toward the shack where they kept the prisoner, pain flared in Shari's shoulder. She winced and sucked in her breath. The injury still hurt most days. Even in human form, she felt the pain of her phantom wing. The wound had healed across her shoulder blade, leaving but a scar, yet the agony lingered.

Relesar tore a part of me away, she thought. *He crippled me. He made me weak.*

She had her prosthetic wing now, a creaking mechanism of wood, rope, and leather, and she had taught herself to fly with it, even to shift with it. Yet she would never fly as smoothly again. She would never swoop as fast. She would never kill with such deadliness.

Shari looked over at Tilla. The young woman, ten years her junior, walked clutching the hilt of her sword. Pauldrons covered her shoulders, and steel coated her limbs, yet Shari could see her body's strength. Her every movement spoke of a huntress. Her eyes stared ahead, narrowed the slightest, always scanning for danger, always shining with pride.

I am crippled, but she is strong, Shari thought. *She will grow stronger. She will be my killer, my sweet bringer of death.* Shari ground her teeth against the pain. *Relesar took my wing. I have taken his beloved from him... and I will make her kill him.*

That would be her greatest revenge.

They passed the last tents and troops, walked down a path, and reached the hut.

Small as a prison cell, its walls had been carved from the surrounding forest. The smell of blood, sweat, and urine flared. Flies bustled. Mewling sounded inside, a sound like a kicked dog.

Shari stood outside the door and looked at Tilla.

"You must make him talk," Shari said. "He will lie to you. He will deny all accusations. Yet you must remain strong, and you must hurt him. For the glory of the red spiral, we must shed blood."

Tilla stared at the hut. Her face remained still and pale, but Shari saw small signs of her fear: a twitch to her lips, a line on her brow, and a shadow in her eyes.

There is still softness in her, Shari thought. There was still weakness here to purify, even after a year of training. Shari allowed a thin smile to touch her lips. *I will crush that weakness. She will be my perfect killer.*

"I will make him talk," Tilla said.

Shari nodded, opened the hut door, and they stepped inside.

The man cowered there, if he could still be called a man. Blood and welts covered his flesh; he looked no better than a rotten corpse. He winced in the light, huddling deeper into the corner, clad in chains. Shari herself had given him these wounds. It was something Tilla had to see. Training was clinical. Battle was chaotic. Here before her bled the true face of war.

"Please," the man whispered through cracked lips, "no more, please. I'm only a quarryman, I--"

Shari drew her punisher and held it against him.

Lightning crackled across the man. He yowled and writhed on the floor, and still Shari held her punisher against him. She waited until his skin cracked and bled, then finally pulled the weapon back. The man lay twitching, smoke rising from him.

"You are a resistor," she said. "You serve Valien Eleison, the traitor. Why else would you lurk in the forests outside our camp?"

"I work in the quarry!" he said, blood in his mouth. "Please, ask the men who work there; they all know me. I cut bricks for this very fort! Please...."

Shari looked over at Tilla, studying her. The young woman stared down at the burnt man, face pale and lips tight.

This still frightens her, Shari thought. *Blood and burns still twist her innards. She will have to be hardened.* Shari nodded. *I will harden her soul like a smith hammering a blade.*

"Tilla," she said, "draw your punisher. Burn him."

Tilla hesitated for just an instant, the length of a breath, and her eyes gave the slightest blink, her lips the slightest twitch. But Shari saw it, and she vowed to eradicate that weakness.

"Yes, Commander," Tilla said and drew her punisher. Its tip crackled to life, racing with red energy.

And she burned him.

"Keep it there," Shari said. "More. Keep it burning."

Tilla obeyed. She held the punisher against the screaming man until welts rose, skin cracked, and blood spilled. As she worked, Shari stared at Tilla's eyes, watching, studying, smiling when she saw the weakness fade into grim intent.

"Enough," she said.

Tilla pulled back, leaving the wretch to writhe and mewl, half dead but still whimpering about his quarry.

"Now draw your blade," Shari instructed. "Slice his belly. Make him bleed out. We will not give him the mercy of a quick death."

Tilla hesitated again. Her hand closed around her sword's hilt, but she did not draw the blade.

"Commander," she said, "should we speak to the quarry? Maybe--"

Shari laughed. "You believe his lies? Resistors always lie. The punishment is death. He should be thankful for that. We could have kept him alive here for moons, even years. Cut him! Slice him open. He serves the Resistance, the rebels who slaughtered your friends, who captured your town. Even now, they slaughter innocents in Cadport."

Tilla's eyes burned with rage and pain. Her cheeks flushed and her lips twisted. With a hiss, she drew her blade.

"Cut him!" Shari commanded. "Make it hurt. He would do worse to you."

Tilla clenched her jaw. "For Cadport," she whispered... and lashed her blade.

The man screamed. Blood gushed from his stomach. He clutched at the wound uselessly. Tilla stared, and her fingers trembled, and her eyes flinched. She raised her blade again, prepared to strike the killing blow.

"No," Shari said. She caught Tilla's wrist, holding her sword back. "No."

Tilla looked at her. Sweat beaded on her pale brow. "Commander," she said. "I can kill him. I--"

"Let him die slowly," she said. "It's good enough for him. Come with me, lanse. We'll let him die alone."

They left the hut and returned to the sunlight. When Shari looked at Tilla, she found the woman still pale, yet her eyes were dry and her lips tightened.

"Killing is hard," Shari said. "But it gets easier. Harden your soul, and you will kill many more for the Regime." She slammed her fist against her chest. "Hail the red spiral!"

Tilla returned the salute, chin raised. "Hail the red spiral."

"Return to your phalanx. We prepare for war. Soon we will fly to Cadport, and we will face the Resistance in battle... and you will face Relesar again. And you will be ready for him."

With that, Shari shifted into a dragon and took flight, her true wing thudding, her prosthetic creaking. She rose above the camp, filled her maw with fire, and blasted a flaming jet across the sky.

She grinned as she soared higher. Of course, the man *was* only a quarryman. But Tilla didn't have to know that, and Shari had enough quarrymen to spare. What mattered was not another death, but Tilla's soul--a soul Shari would break and reshape into her greatest weapon.

When she rose high enough, Shari saw the entire camp sprawled below. Across the ruins of Castra Luna, her workers were digging ditches, raising scaffolding, and building the first walls of her new castle, the glorious Castra Sol. In the forest clearing beyond the construction, her army mustered, ten thousand strong, men and women all in steel, drilling and saluting and preparing for battle.

Shari turned her head north. The forests sprawled red as blood into distant mist. Upon the horizon, she saw dragons fly, thousands of troops joining her from their northern forts.

More will muster here, Shari thought. *We will gather in strength, a great hammer ready to fall. We will fall upon the south, and Cadport will burn.*

Shari howled, roared her fire, and grinned.

ERRY

She walked through the forest until the sounds of the camp faded behind her. Scraggles walked at her side, tail slapping branches and bushes, and gave her a plaintive look. The dog could feel the sadness inside her--Erry knew that he could--and he licked her fingers.

"Come on, Scrags," she said and gave him a pat. "We have to keep moving."

Shouts rose behind her.

"Erry!" The prince was hoarse. "Damn it, Erry, come back here."

She kept walking. She was small and sneaky and silent. She had lived for years alone upon the docks, fleeing wild dogs and those who'd steal her food or break her body. If she did not want the Lechers to find her, they would not.

"We'll find a better place," she said softly to Scraggles, keeping one hand on his back as they walked. "Leresy can go eat furry bear droppings."

Scraggles wagged his tail in approval, and they kept walking through the forest. She had to move slowly--dry leaves carpeted the forest floor, crackling beneath her boots, and there were plenty branches to snap underfoot. But she was far enough now. They would never find her, not if they uprooted every tree here.

Erry reached into her pocket and fished out her medallion. She gazed at it--a silver sunburst upon a leather thong. A prayer in foreign letters gleamed upon it. It was the language of Tiranor, which she could not read.

"Tiranor," Erry whispered, caressing the medallion. "My other home."

She had never been to that southern desert kingdom. She had never met her father, the Tiran who had bought her mother upon the docks. With this medallion, the sailor had paid for his night of pleasure, then vanished back overseas the next day. When

Erry was younger, a feral urchin upon the docks, she would often gaze at this sunburst and dream.

"The desert is a better place," she would whisper, shivering and cold and hungry enough to eat dead fish. "There are oases there full of dates and figs, and sandstone columns rise into the sky, and my father is a wealthy man. Wealthy enough to have paid for my mother with this silver medallion, not just copper coins. He is a great prince."

She would weep and dream of flying to that desert, but never did. The Legions had burned Tiranor years ago; everyone knew that. No more ships sailed to Requiem from that distant land. No more life filled the dunes. Her father was dead; the Legions had slain him.

And so Erry had remained in Requiem. But she had kept this medallion. She never wore it around her neck; if any caught her wearing a symbol of Tiranor, they would slay her. But she kept it always in her pocket. A prayer she could not read. A memory. A hope that a better world did exist out there.

"Maybe we should fly there, Scrags," she said, walking through the forest, her father's medallion in her hand. "Maybe he still lives out there, a prince of the desert, and we can find him."

Scraggles licked her hand, and Erry patted him, sniffed back her tears, and kept walking.

"Erry!" Leresy shouted behind; he sounded hundreds of yards away, his voice so dim, she could barely hear. "Erry, damn it, will you listen to me?"

She touched her cheek where he'd struck her. It still tingled and Erry sighed. Men had struck her before--many times and much harder. During those long years, orphaned on the docks, she had suffered many bruises and cuts. Men had tried to hurt her for sex, for theft, for pleasure, and Erry had always fought them, and she had always healed.

"He's just another one of them, Scraggles," she said, a lump in her throat. "Just like the drunkards on the boardwalk."

She had bedded such men before, so many she could not count. She had given her body for food, shelter, or warmth on a cold night. The other girls in town called her a whore, but the other girls had roofs over their heads and food on their tables.

"I never took no money," she whispered to her dog. "Never! No man ever paid for me. I am not my mother. I took food. I took a bed and a roof when it rained. But I never sold myself for money."

And then... then she had joined the Legions. Then she had met Tilla and Mae, two souls she loved dearly. Then she had a roof over her head, even if it was only a tent roof. Then she had food to eat, even if it was only scraps. Then she had protection, a sword to fight with, a *home*.

She sniffed and wiped her eyes. Yet Mae was dead and buried, and Tilla was dead inside, and here she was again. Feral and alone. Hungry. Lost.

And now... now, after all these men, it was Leresy, the prince of Requiem himself, who filled the same old role. Now another man wanted her body for food, for shelter, for promises of protection. And again--only days out of the Legions--she was selling herself.

"But no more, Scraggles," she whispered, and a tear trailed down her cheek. "I'm done with this life. I can't be that old Erry again. I can't let more men beat me, use me, toss me scraps to eat and worthless promises. I'd rather live alone in the wilderness with you, Scraggles, even if we starve to death."

The forest was thick. The fallen leaves rose above her feet. Bushes, wild grass, and ivy tangled around her legs, rising to her shoulders at some spots. The trees crowded around her--twisting oaks, craggy pines, and white birches with peeling bark. Red and golden leaves rustled above her, hiding the sky. Erry didn't even know in what direction she walked. She couldn't see more than several yards ahead. Yet she kept moving, just to get away from the Lechers, from Leresy, and from her past... from the old Erry she vowed she'd never become again.

"No more," she whispered. "Never again. I can't go back to the person I was."

His voice rose behind her. "Erry!"

He was in dragon form now; his voice was deeper and louder, ringing across the forest. Wings thudded in the distance. Erry kept moving.

"He can't see us down here," she whispered. "The trees are too thick."

She kept walking, and the wings kept beating above, and Leresy roared. The trees bent madly and leaves showered down; he was flying right above. Erry found herself gripping her sword but released it with a shaky breath.

He still can't see me, she thought. This forest rolled for leagues and leagues, and the canopy was thick as a ceiling. The dragon would have better luck finding a single fish in a murky ocean.

And then Scraggles began to bark.

"Hush!" she whispered, knelt, and grabbed the dog. "Scrags, quiet!"

Yet he kept barking madly at the sky, tail straight as an arrow. Erry tried to calm him--hugging, petting, and whispering to him-- but he kept barking. Even when she tried to hold his mouth shut, he tore himself free--he was stronger than her--and barked some more.

The dragon above roared.

The canopy crashed open. Claws glinted. A red dragon swooped down into the forest, fire trailing from his maw. His tail lashed, tearing down trees, and his wings raised fallen leaves into a flurry.

Erry turned and ran.

She leaped over roots, bushes, and rocks. She didn't turn to look back. A root snagged her foot, and she crashed down into fallen leaves, filling her mouth with mud and moss. She leaped up. She kept running.

"Erry, damn it!" Leresy shouted behind her. "Stop and listen to me. I'm not going to hurt you."

"You already did, you dung-sucking gutter stain!" she shouted over her shoulder.

She could not see him, but he was near, and she cursed herself for yelling and revealing her location. She kept racing. Scraggles ran at her side. A rock twisted under her foot, and she fell again. She pushed herself up, but before she could keep running, something grabbed her tunic.

She spun around, swinging her fists, and struck Leresy hard on the jaw; he was back in human form. He grunted, his lip bleeding, but kept holding her. She struggled and screamed, but he grabbed her arms. She tried to kick, but her feet found only dry leaves, showering them onto Leresy.

"Damn it, woman," he said and spat out leaves. "Will you just listen to me? Calm down and let's talk. I just--"

Scraggles bit him.

Leresy screamed.

The black mutt clung to his leg, digging his teeth deeper. Leresy kicked, trying to shake Scraggles off, and screamed again. The dog would not release him.

"Good boy!" Erry shouted. "Bite his leg off!"

Cursing, Leresy drew his sword and raised it above the dog.

Fear flooded Erry like a bucket of ice.

She screamed, leaped, and grabbed Leresy's arm, pulling his sword down. The blade sliced her thigh, she fell to her knees, and blood dripped into the leaves.

The fight froze.

Teeth deep in Leresy's leg, Scraggles stared at the blood, released the prince, and mewled. Leresy too stared at Erry's wound. His eyes widened, and he tossed his sword into the leaves like a viper.

"Oh stars," he whispered and knelt beside Erry. "I didn't mean to... Damn it, that dog of yours, he--"

She punched him again.

She punched him so hard his head snapped sideways, and he fell onto his back.

"You drunken, flea-bitten bastard!" she said. She rose to her feet, blood dripping down her thigh, and glared down at the prince. "You gelatinous piece of chamber pot goo. You--"

Lying bleeding in the leaves, he reached up, grabbed her wrist, and pulled her down.

She fell atop him, snarled, and tried to bite his face. He held her back; her teeth missed his nose by an inch.

"Erry," he said, "listen to me, damn it. I love you, all right? And I'm sorry. I'm sorry I struck you."

She spat on his face, hitting him square in the forehead.

"Go to the Abyss," she said. "I'm not one of your whores."

"I don't want you to be one," he said, blood and spit and mud mingling on his face. "I don't want a whore. Stars, Erry, I'm too poor to afford one now anyway."

She rolled her eyes. "Your sweet talk is truly winning me over."

Yet she felt her anger ebb as her blood dripped. She rolled off him and lay at his side, staring up at the canopy.

"Erry," he said, voice choked. When she looked over, she was surprised to see his eyes dampen. "Erry, I... I haven't been right since the battle. Everything is just... my mind is all..."

"Tiny?" she suggested. "Slow as a snail? Nonexistent?"

"Muddled," he said. "Too much damn drink, and too many damn memories. Since Nairi died--since everyone died there--I just keep seeing it. The blood. The corpses. The Resistance flying against us. Stars, Erry, there were so many of them, thousands of dragons and soldiers. They knew me. They knew my name. *Death to Leresy!* they shouted." Tears joined the mess of blood, saliva, and mud on his face. "So I drank too much, and I whored too much, and I hit you. I'm sorry."

She snorted weakly and her eyes stung. "And you think you can tell me you love me now? And I'll forgive you? Did you say that to Nairi or all the girls you bought?"

"Nairi?" he said. "No. I never loved Nairi. I thought I did. She was young, beautiful, and powerful, and... a typical young man, I courted her. But loved her?" He sighed. "I loved her power. But you, Erry, you have no power."

"Again, my prince, your sweet talk is falling somewhat short of my standard."

He propped himself up onto his elbows. "Erry, damn you. You're nothing but a feral little beast. You have no money. You have no noble blood, no influence, no standing at court." He stared down at her chest. "Stars damn it, you've got barely any meat on your bones. But... you joined my camp. You wanted to be with me. And I wanted you."

"To bed me every night and dawn," she said bitterly. "To use my body, and because I'm so poor, I'd let you do it--for food, for shelter, for your promises. And I did that for a while. Because you fed me, and because you protected me." She rose to her elbows too and looked at him. "But then you struck me, so deal's off, Leresy. No more."

"The deal was off a moon ago!" he said, voice rising now. "The deal was off after the first two days." He snorted. "Use you? For sex? Erry, I don't care about that. You know what you gave me? You gave me intolerable arguments over that stupid game you just can't play. And you gave me cuss words I never even knew existed; I use some of them now. And you gave me somebody to hold at night. I never held a woman before; I never held Nairi or the others. But I hold you all night, and I stroke your hair, and I kiss you, and... when I do that, it's better than all the booze and sex. It's not just forgetting the past with you. It's seeing a future."

She was about to snort again. She was about to spit at him, punch him, and run. But she only sighed.

"Stars damn you, Leresy Cadigus," she said.

He held her hand. "Erry, I'm sorry. I'm truly deeply sorry. I... I want to show you something."

He rolled up his sleeve and she gasped. She covered her mouth and her eyes stung.

"Stars, Ler," she whispered.

He sighed and nodded. "My father gave me that scar. He burned me because I couldn't learn a sword thrust fast enough. I was only six years old." He unlaced his shirt, pulled it down, and showed her a scar across his chest. "And he gave me this scar with a hot poker. I was ten and I couldn't remember the name of some ancient fort that no longer exists." He closed his shirt. "I have about a dozen more scars across me, a dozen more stories. Erry, my siblings and I... we were raised in violence, in fear, in hate. My sister Shari turned into a heartless killer; my father broke her mind. My sister Kaelyn fled. And I, well... I'm a damn broken wreck. I drink too much and I hit you, and my past can't justify that, I know. I know it's not an excuse. I don't ask for acceptance, only for forgiveness. Will you forgive me, Erry?" His voice shook and his eyes dampened. "Because I don't want you to leave me. Please. *Please* don't leave me."

Her own eyes watered and she embraced him, laid her cheek against his chest, and felt her tears wet his shirt.

"I have scars too," she whispered. "You only have a dozen? You weakling. I have more. And I'll probably have another one on my leg from your damn sword."

He held her close, nearly crushing her. "I'll never hurt you again, Erry Docker. I promise. I promise. Just stay with me, and we'll figure things out. We'll find a home somewhere, you and I. You won't have to be my concubine or my mistress. You will just be... whatever you want to be, so long as we're together."

A weight pressed down onto Erry's shoulder; Scraggles had joined the embrace. The three lay in the forest, dry leaves falling around them, and Erry sighed.

"All right, Leresy," she whispered as he stroked her hair, not knowing if she made the right choice, but feeling too weak to run. "All right."

TILLA

On a cold rainy morning in Castra Sol, the Emperor of Requiem arrived with all his contingent and asked to speak with her alone.

Tilla was drilling that morning outside her tent, sparring with her troops and imagining swinging her blade against resistors. The forest bobbed and dripped rain beyond their tents, the wet autumn leaves turned dark as blood.

When we reach Cadport, she thought, thrusting blows against one of her troops, *they will flee into houses and holes. It will be a battle of blades then.*

The soldier before her, a young flight leader with two red stars upon his armbands, cursed as he parried. Sweat dripped down his temples. Tilla kept attacking, using every thrust she'd learned at the academy. She shuffled forward with small, quick steps, sword swinging down from side to side. It was all her opponent could do to parry. Finally Tilla slammed her sword--a dulled training blade-- hard onto his pauldron.

"That's a kill!" she said.

He grunted and tossed down his own training sword.

"Commander," he said, "your sword wouldn't break through this steel. My armor is thick, and--"

"And my true blade was forged in dragonfire from northern steel," Tilla said, interrupting him. "A thrust this hard, with two hands, would cleave your armor and bone; your arm would be lying in the dust."

The young corelis--he ranked above a green periva, but below a hardened siragi--cracked his neck.

"The Resistance don't got northern steel forged in dragonfire," he argued. "Bastards fight with rusted, chipped blades."

Tilla fixed him with an icy stare. "Valien Eleison carries the sword of a knight, a blade of the old order of bellators. It would cut through your armor like parchment. Do you not dream of slaying Valien?"

The soldier stared back, then nodded and lifted his blade.

"Next man!" Tilla shouted.

Yet before another soldier could step forward to drill, roars trumpeted in the distance.

Tilla froze, sword raised.

The roars pealed across the sky, thousands of them rising from the north. The beating of wings rose like a storm. A distant voice cried out, hailing the red spiral, and countless voices answered in a chant.

"Keep training!" Tilla said. She turned to her siragi, a brawny soldier with dark eyes, her right-hand man in the phalanx. "Siragi, take command."

The man nodded and Tilla shifted. She rose from the square, white wings raising clouds of dust, her flames crackling.

She soared high above the camp. Lines of tents sprawled before her like a great city; fifty thousand now mustered here, marching and drilling. Beating her wings and rising higher, Tilla raised her head and stared into the north.

She gasped. A shiver clanked her scales like a purse of coins.

"By the Abyss," she whispered.

A great army flew ahead, as large as the army mustered below. Tilla had never seen so many dragons fly together; she could barely breathe. They flew in five great squares across the sky--five brigades, each one ten thousand dragons strong. Within each brigade, the square further divided into ten milanxes, then into ten again, forming phalanxes of a hundred.

"Fifty thousand dragons," Tilla whispered, hovering in the air, watching them fly from the north.

This was not only a force to capture a city.

This was a force to finally slaughter every last resistor.

At the head of this army, a black triangle of dragons flew like an arrowhead, and another shiver ran through Tilla.

"The emperor," she whispered, "and the Axehand Order."

They still flew a league away, but Tilla could make out Frey Cadigus, a great golden dragon, flying at their lead. Around him flew the Axehand Order, his fanatic warrior-priests. They wore black armor bristly with blades, and axeheads shone upon their stumps. They shrieked to the sky, hailing their lord, worshiping him as their god.

"Five hundred axehands fly here," Tilla whispered, "and they frighten me more than the fifty thousand legionaries behind them."

She hovered in place, watching as the northern army swallowed the forest under their shadow, roared their arrival, and descended into the camp. For the past few days, Shari had ordered troops to tear down thousands of trees north of the ruins, carving a great clearing. Now the northern host descended here in a storm of wings, an inferno of flame, and a cacophony of howls and roars and grunts. Dragons shifted into men. Legionaries took formations, tens of thousands forming lines and squares. The Axehand swept between them as ghosts, hidden within black robes and hoods. A great tent rose, its walls bedecked with spirals; the emperor strode into it.

Tilla descended, shifted into human form, and returned to her tent.

She stared into her small mirror.

A pale woman stared back, her dark eyes cold, her smooth black hair cut neatly, falling just above her chin. She knew that many called her face icy, the face of a statue. Her townsfolk had whispered this in Cadport, back when Tilla had lived as a commoner. Today her troops whispered it; she could hear them. They said her face and heart were carved of ice. They said her eyes were stone marbles, devoid of life, pity, or any feeling.

Yet they did not see her nightmares. They did not see her heart. And today... today that heart twisted with fear. That heart was not carved of ice; the ice coursed through her veins and belly.

"When I joined the Legions," she whispered to her reflection, "I vowed to banish all fear from me. Yet today I'm more afraid than ever."

She reached to the small box she kept on her table. Her fingers shook, but she took a deep breath and opened the box.

Her eyes stung.

She pulled out a seashell necklace.

"Damn it," she whispered, eyes dampening.

She caressed the seashells, listening to them chink. It was her one memento of Cadport. It was her one memory of her lowborn roots, of a ropemaker's daughter too poor to eat dinner many nights.

"It's my only memory of Rune," she whispered.

He had collected these seashells, strung them together, and given her this gift on her fourteenth birthday. Five years had passed since then, and Tilla had a sword now, fine armor, and silver in her purse, yet she kept this humble necklace.

It's the most precious thing I own, she thought.

She placed the necklace back into her box and closed her eyes.

"Oh Rune," she whispered. "Why did you do this? Why did you fall to evil? Now the Legions muster... and they will break you."

Her eyes stung. She knew what they'd do to him. Frey Cadigus would shatter Rune's bones, flay his skin, but leave him alive. The emperor would parade his trophy across the capital, letting all hear Rune scream, then finally--after days or moons or even years--he would allow Rune the mercy of death.

"Why, Rune?" Tilla whispered, clutching the box. "Why did you have to betray your kingdom? Why did you let the Resistance turn you against Requiem?" Her fingers shook. "Now I will have to hurt you, Rune. Now I will have to fight you. You could have stopped this. You forced me to do this."

Her tent flap opened behind her.

At the sound, Tilla spun around, clutching her punisher. Her troops were never to barge into her tent; she would burn anyone who did.

Her snarl died on her lips, and she released her punisher. A new gush of fear flooded her.

Two axehands stood at her tent entrance.

Their black robes draped across them, but the sleeves were short enough to reveal their deformity: axe blades strapped to their left stumps, the very blades they themselves had severed their hands with. Their hoods cast deep shadows, but Tilla caught hints of their iron masks; those masks were bolted on to the flesh, impossible to remove. Around their waists, they displayed the tools of their trade: pincers, needles, and blades for torturing their enemies.

They will use these on Rune, Tilla thought. *They'd use them on me if they knew I still cared for him.*

She slammed her fist against her chest, struggling to hide her trembling.

"Hail the red spiral!" she said.

One of the axehands spoke, his voice a hiss behind his mask, an inhuman sound.

"You are Tilla Siren. You will accompany us. His holiness, the great God of Dragons, will speak with you. Follow."

They reached out their right hands. Their fingers were scarred and wrinkled as if dipped in acid, and Tilla shuddered.

They chopped off their left hands to prove their loyalty, she thought. *What did Frey demand they do to their right hands?*

She took a deep breath, clutched her sword, and followed them outside.

They shifted into dragons. They flew over the camp; a hundred thousand troops drilled below them. As they dived toward the emperor's tent, Tilla's heart twisted, and smoke spurted from her nostrils.

Stars, he knows, she thought. *Somehow Frey knows about the seashell necklace. He knows I grew up with Rune.* Her scales clattered. *He'll have me tortured and killed.*

Yet what could she do? She could not flee; they would catch her. All she could do was fly with the axehands, speak with the emperor... and beg.

They landed outside the emperor's tent. It rose like a mansion before her, black walls thudding in the wind. A hundred axehands surrounded the tent, their black robes swaying like ghosts at midnight.

Tilla shifted back into human form, and an axehand opened the flap to Frey's tent, revealing shadows.

"Enter," the dark priest hissed, beckoning with his blade.

Tilla raised her chin, squared her shoulders, and sucked in her breath.

Strength, Tilla, she told herself. *Always be strong. Show no weakness. Weakness is death.*

She stepped into the darkness.

The tent was large and bare. Ten dragons could have stood in here, but Tilla saw only a table, two chairs, and one man.

Frey Cadigus, Emperor of Requiem, stood sharpening a dagger, rubbing stone and blade together. He stood in profile to her, staring at his blade, as if he hadn't noticed her enter. Tilla had never seen him up close before. He was a tall man, and his pauldrons flared out from wide shoulders. His armor was meticulous, the black plates lines with golden dragons, bolted together into a second skin. He wore no helm today. His face was cold and hard, the nose hooked, the brow high. Grooves framed his thin lips.

More than his blade, his armor, or his cruel mouth, his eyes frightened Tilla. When they turned to stare at her, they were cold, hard, and penetrating as swords.

Tilla saluted, slamming fist to chest.

He returned the salute, his eyes digging into her--into her mind, her heart, her oldest secrets.

"Lanse Tilla Siren," the emperor said. "Tilla of Cadport. My daughter speaks of you often." He gestured at the table. "Sit."

When Tilla stepped closer to the table and chairs, she sucked in her breath. She felt the blood leave her face.

What she'd first taken for wine jugs were actually glass jars. Inside each vessel floated a head, its mouth open in a silent scream.

Frey studied her. "Do they frighten you, child?"

Tilla tightened her lips and sat.

"No, Commander," she said and met his gaze.

A frightened child would die today, she thought. *A soldier, heart hardened, will live.*

Frey still stood. He caressed one of the jars; inside floated the head of a child, her hair long and braided, her eyes still wide with fear.

"The Aeternum Dynasty used to rule in splendor," Frey said. "They governed in halls of marble, harps, and starlight." He snorted. "They were weak. They were soft. They sang music and drank wine in their halls while our enemies mustered. They prayed to the stars as griffins, wyverns, and phoenixes slaughtered our people." He caressed a second jar; the head floating inside looked eerily like Rune. "Look at them now, lanse. Look what their weakness brought them."

Tilla stared. Bile rose in her throat. By the stars...

"The... Aeternum family," she whispered.

Rune's family.

Frey gazed at the jars as if lost in thought. "I take them with me always. I sleep by their side. I dine with them on my table. Do you know why, lanse?"

Tilla raised her chin. "To remember."

He barked a laugh. "Yes. To remember. To remember their weakness. To remember their punishment. To remember why we fight." He nodded and met her gaze. "My daughter speaks highly of you. She says you serve the red spiral well. She also says... that you knew an Aeternum."

Finally he sat too. He leaned forward in his seat and stared at her. The jars rose upon the table between them. The severed heads seemed to stare at Tilla too.

"I knew Relesar in Cadport," Tilla said, and her insides twisted. Her voice softened. "He was called Rune then."

She stared at the jars. *Rune's parents and siblings.* Tilla's throat tightened, and under the table, she twisted her fingers together. She could imagine Rune's head joining the others, staring at her with dead eyes, begging her. Tilla had to suck in her breath and grind her teeth to stop her eyes from watering.

"Tell me about him," said the emperor. "Tell me about our enemy. But do not tell me about Relesar Aeternum. I hear stories of Relesar all day from a thousand men--Relesar the brutal warrior, or Relesar the frightened pup, or Relesar the figurehead dancing to Valien's flute. I hear only stories. I hear men brag and boast, and I hear men whisper in fear." He leaned closer across the table. "Do not tell me about the heir of a fallen dynasty. Tell me about Rune. Tell me about the boy you knew."

Tilla swallowed, wanting to flee, wanting to vanish, wanting anything but this.

Stars, Rune, why did you have to join the Resistance? Why didn't you just run?

"He grew up thinking he was a mere brewer," Tilla said, and now her eyes stung. "He never spoke against the Regime. He never spoke of the lost days of Aeternum. He did not know of his heritage until the Resistance found him. He was just a commoner. He was my friend."

Those days returned to her, so powerful she could barely breathe. In her mind, she walked along the beach with him again, collecting seashells under the sun, swimming among the waves, and laughing and telling stories. And she remembered that last night. She could feel his embrace and kiss again.

"And yet," Frey said. "And yet... he rose against us. He flew against this very fortress. He slaughtered hundreds here--hundreds of youths from his own town."

Tilla nodded. "I know," she said softly. "And I hate him for it. And I fought him that day. We locked swords in the clock tower." She looked again at the jars, then raised her eyes and met the emperor's gaze. "But Commander, I believe that he did not choose this fight. I believe that Valien Eleison poisoned his mind. I believe that the Resistance kidnapped him, forced him to hate us, forced him to fight. And I believe--I *must* believe--that he can be saved. That deep inside, he still loves Requiem."

Frey raised his eyebrows. "I should think that an officer in the Legions would crave to behead our greatest enemy."

Tilla swallowed. She had to tread carefully here. A wrong word and she herself would lose her head. She glanced again at the jars. She hated Rune. She hated all that he'd done. Yet for her memories, for her seashells, and for that kiss, she had to save him. She had to.

She returned her eyes to the emperor.

"Our greatest enemy is no single man, Commander," she said. "Our enemy is an *idea*. Our enemy is *defiance*. The Resistance is small; they cannot defeat us with strength of arms. They fight not with blades, but with foolish dreams. That's why they did not attack the capital, but plastered their words across our walls." Tilla trembled, knowing she could die any second, but kept talking. "To the Resistance, that's all Rune is. Not a warrior. Certainly not a leader. He's an *idea*. He's a memory of older days."

Frey stared at Tilla, and his eyes narrowed, and his lips tightened, and she could not breathe. She was sure he would kill her. She was sure this was her last flicker of life. When Frey opened his mouth, she expected him to call the axehands to torture and slay her.

Yet only a laugh burst from his lips, a snort of amusement.

"Ha! My daughter was right." Frey's lips twisted into a mockery of a smile. "You are a wise one, Lanse Siren. But tell me--should rebellious ideas not be crushed? A figurehead rises against us. Should we not behead him?"

Tilla shook her head, breath shaky. "Commander, it's not my role to dictate policy. You are wiser than I am. Yet if you ask me my thoughts, I will say: No." She gripped her hands under the table. "You cannot slay an idea with a blade. If you kill Relesar, you give the Resistance more power. You would turn Relesar into a martyr. The people would rally around his death; the idea would live on."

Frey nodded slowly, lips pursed. "So are we to let him live, you say? Are we to let him keep fighting, keep slaying our troops, keep spreading this *idea*?"

"No," Tilla said. "We cannot do that either. Again, Commander, you are wiser than I am. Yet since you ask me, I speak to you freely." She raised her chin and stared at him, forcing herself not to look away. "Commander, we must capture Relesar, and we must force him to abandon this idea. We must stand him upon the towers and walls of Nova Vita, and we must have him hail the red spiral. The people will see that even Relesar Aeternum, heir of the old dynasty, worships your glory." She nodded. "All fire would drain from the Resistance. Valien would be left with nothing but a few haggard fighters."

Frey nodded. "You speak wisely, child. A dead martyr is far more dangerous than a living servant. People still fight for their dead. Have their hero foreswear his fight, and their courage will abandon them. And yet, what makes you think we can sway Relesar? With torture?" He raised an eyebrow. "Would you have us torture your childhood friend?"

Tilla swallowed, remembering the man in the hut, the man she had burned and cut.

"If need be," she said softly. "Yet I believe that I can sway him more easily. Tortured lips reveal their pain; a forced vow of loyalty would sway few." She leaned across the table. "I can sway him with words, Commander. With my punisher if I must, but I believe my words will work better. Please, Commander. I know Rune. I grew up with him. He loves Requiem, yet Valien has poisoned his mind. Allow me to show him your glory! Let us capture him. Let us bring him north. I will show him your light and the errors of his ways. He will become not a tortured, sniveling slave, but a true warrior to our cause." She allowed herself a small smile. "Can you imagine a greater blow to the Resistance?"

The emperor was silent.

Tilla sat still, refusing to break their stare.

Please, Tilla prayed silently to whatever gods, new or old, might be listening. *Please let him agree. Please. I cannot see Rune beheaded, despite all his sins. I must save him.*

The emperor's stare seemed to last forever. His gaze bored into her, seeking, rifling, searching for any trace of betrayal. Tilla forced herself to stare back, chin raised and jaw squared.

Finally the emperor rose to his feet.

"You are wise, Lanse Siren," he said. "And you speak truth. My daughter is right to groom you." He placed his hand on one jar; inside floated the head that looked like Rune. "We will take Relesar alive, and it will be your task to sway him. You will use words, or you will use your punisher." His lips pulled back in a snarl. "Relesar Aeternum will stand upon the tower of Tarath Imperium, gaze upon the empire, and roar his loyalty to the red spiral. And if he will not... his head will join the others."

As Tilla flew back to her tent, her insides roiled and her wings shook.

I saved your life today, Rune, she thought as she flew over the camp. *You might never know it, but today I saved you.*

Below her, a hundred thousand troops saluted and roared. War was near.

KAELYN

My father is coming to kill me.

The words echoed through Kaelyn's mind as she crawled down the tunnel. The dirt walls closed in around her, reinforced with wooden slats. Resistors crawled behind, lamps shining, boasting of how many soldiers they'd kill. Kaelyn barely heard them.

My father is coming to kill me.

The words kept rattling in her skull. Kaelyn held a tin lamp and a parchment map of these tunnels. She knew that she crawled beneath the tannery, heading toward the butcher shop. Yet in the shadows, this seemed an older, darker place. In the shadows, she was a frightened girl again, hiding under her bed as her father raged. Again she saw his hands reaching to grab her, his rod raised to strike, his eyes blazing.

"No, Father," she whispered. "Please."

She winced. The scars flared across her body, all those scars he'd given her and Leresy. She had escaped. She had left her twin behind. She had grown into a strong woman, a warrior, a leader. Yet here in the darkness, the walls closing in around her, that strength vanished. Here she was young and afraid.

My father is coming to kill me.

"Kaelyn," Rune whispered behind her. "How far is it?"

She looked over her shoulder and saw him there, covered in grime. He crawled on his belly, holding a lamp.

"We're under Market Street," she said, checking her map. "The fur shop is above us; the butcher shop is ahead. That's where the tunnel goes."

His face was young and earnest. He still did not know enough fear. He still had not seen enough of her father's cruelty.

Kaelyn kept crawling.

Again my father reaches for me, she thought. Only now he reached toward her with an army. And if he caught her this time, if she could not scurry deep enough into the shadows, he would not just beat her. He would kill her and display her mutilated corpse to the empire.

The tunnel curved up, leading to floorboards above her head. Kaelyn pushed them aside and crawled onto the floor of the butcher shop. Rubbing dust out of her eyes, she reached down and helped Rune enter too. Ten other resistors followed, clad in leather armor and bearing swords and bows.

Kaelyn looked around her and nodded, satisfied. Large slabs of meat hung from hooks, providing many places to hide. Cleavers hung upon walls, providing extra weapons. A barrel of gunpowder stood at the door, wired to blast outward should the Legions burst into the shop.

"I want to be stationed here when the fighting starts," Rune said. He looked around, smacked his lips, and nodded. "Lots of nice, fresh slabs of ham. Perfect if you get hungry during the fighting." He nodded. "Definitely the best place to be."

Kaelyn glowered and jabbed her finger at his chest.

"You," she said, "will fight from Castellum Acta with me and Valien."

Rune rubbed his chest and moaned. "Can I fight from the bakery?"

"No!"

"How about the wine shop? I can--"

"Rune!" Kaelyn grabbed his collar. "Will you *please* stop thinking about your belly for once? The Legions fly here, and you need to stay near me and Valien in the fortress. I need to look after you."

He cleared his throat. "I am, you know, your king." He puffed out his chest. "I could just command myself to stay here with the nice food."

"You're not my king yet," she said, fixing him with her best glare. "Until we win this war, you're nothing but a silly boy with a very hungry belly and a very empty skull. Now come on, we have more tunnels to inspect."

They returned to the tunnel. They kept crawling.

They crawled for hours.

During the past two moons, they had dug a network of tunnels under every main street in Lynport. As Kaelyn crawled, she examined her map.

"In these tunnels, we can scurry between every shop in town," she whispered to herself. "We can crawl from courthouse to castle, from cobbler shop to chandlery, from forest to sea."

He is coming to kill me.

She sucked in her breath; it trembled in her lungs.

"Every doorway is booby trapped with gunpowder," she whispered. "Archers stand in every window, watching every street and alley. When the Legions swarm, we will slaughter them everywhere."

Yet her heart kept thrashing, and her fingers kept trembling, and she couldn't stop that voice from echoing.

So come, she thought and tightened her lips. *Come and let us fight. Come and let it be done.*

When evening fell, she and Rune rose from the tunnels, shifted into dragons, and flew toward the fortress on the hill. Castellum Acta now displayed the banners of Aeternum, a silver, two-headed dragon upon a green field. The Regime had been cleansed from this place. Its troops had joined the Resistance or sat chained in its dungeon.

From here we will command the battle, Kaelyn thought, flying toward the tower. *Here our fate will be decided.*

Sunset gilded the tower and the whispering sea. The scent of salt filled Kaelyn's nostrils, and the northern forest murmured and swayed. She looked toward the setting sun and felt small.

If I could fly high as the sun, she thought, *this war would seem so small to me. We would all be but specks crashing together upon the land. And still the sun would turn. And still the sea would rise and fall.*

A lump filled her throat, for this sunset, these waves, and these trees--the land itself--seemed sad to her. Kaelyn had never known peace; she'd been raised in Tarath Imperium under her father's heel. Yet here in Lynport, she caught glimpses of what peace could mean. It was a whisper of waves, a song so ancient it had no words. It was the sway of trees, an eternal dance. It was orange sunset fading into starry night.

This is what Rune always meant, Kaelyn realized. He had talked of walks along the beach, of laughter with his friends, of peace, of hope. Kaelyn had never known such things, yet she saw them in the waves, and she heard them in the wind.

And I will fight for them, she thought, the scent of water and leaves in her nostrils, tears in her eyes. *And maybe someday I will know peace too.*

"Kaelyn," Rune said, flying beside her. He nudged her with his tail. "Are you all right?"

She managed a smile. "No. I'm not all right. None of this is." She blasted smoke. "But we're going to fight nonetheless."

The two dragons reached Castellum Acta and landed upon its tower. The battlements rose around them in a henge. The town stretched below along the coast, trapped between sea and forest.

Kaelyn took a deep breath, inhaling the crisp air.

Come and fight me, Father. I'm ready.

As if in answer, a roar sounded in the north.

Kaelyn whipped her head around. Her heart thudded. For an instant, she was sure the battle had come, that Frey Cadigus flew toward them with all his wrath and might. But it was only a single dragon flying across the forest. The dragon was still distant, but when Kaelyn squinted, she saw black scales crested with a white stripe.

"Lady Lana Cain," she whispered.

At her side, Rune growled. Smoke rose from his nostrils.

"She brings news," he said. "News is never good."

The striped dragon flew closer, swallowing the miles and roaring her cry. When finally Lana reached Lynport, she flew at a wobble, smoke trailing from her nostrils. With a last flap of her wings, Lana all but crashed onto the tower top. She shifted back into human form and lay panting, a woman clad in yellow and gray, a streak of white blazing through her black hair. A pin bearing the sigil of Cain, two statues guarding an archway, fastened her cloak.

"Lana!" Kaelyn said. She too shifted into human form and knelt above her friend. "Lana, are you all right?"

Lana lay wheezing. Her skin was pale, and her fingers trembled when she adjusted her eyepatch.

"The Legions," she whispered. Fear filled her one eye. "So many... so many."

Whenever Kaelyn had seen Lana, her friend had seemed a confident warrior, a smirk on her face, her hand always clutching her saber's hilt. Yet now she trembled like a woman returned from the Abyss.

"Do they fly south?" Kaelyn whispered and clutched her friend's hand. It was ice cold. "What have you seen?"

Lana reached up. She grabbed Kaelyn's shoulder, her fingers desperate, her lips white. She seemed like a drowning woman clinging on for life.

"Kaelyn," she whispered, "we must flee."

VALIEN

He stood in the grand hall of Castellum Acta, stared into the crackling fireplace, and growled.

I need a drink.

He clenched his fists. His head spun. His throat constricted; he could feel the soldier's fingers squeezing him again, that grip from years ago that had ruined his voice. Rye would cure that pain. Rye would erase that memory. Valien grumbled.

I had to hide the boy in the nearest tavern, didn't I? Now it's burned down and my throat is parched.

"Valien," she said behind him. "Valien, please."

He turned and saw her there. As always, when his eyes first fell upon her, he saw his wife again, saw Marilion staring from beyond the years, beckoning, pleading, waiting for him to save her.

"Valien," Kaelyn repeated. "What do we do?"

He tightened his lips.

It was Kaelyn, of course. It was always Kaelyn, a new light in his life, a reminder of throbbing shadows.

Marilion lives! She lives in my dungeon, you fool!

"Valien?" she asked, voice hesitant.

She sat at the table, her quiver slung across her shoulder. Rune sat at her side, clad in black wool and brown leather, the Amber Sword fastened at his belt. Lady Lana sat there too; her face was still pale, and her fingers still trembled as she brought a mug of soup to her lips.

"We flee," Valien said. "Simple as that. We cannot fight this."

Kaelyn and Rune leaped to their feet so fast their chairs crashed down. Both began to protest at once.

"But... we've dug all these tunnels!" Rune said, face red. "We've lined the walls with cannons. We've recruited three thousand townsfolk, armed them, given them positions, trained them to fight--"

Valien glared at the boy. "Three thousand townsfolk who would die when Frey arrives."

"Valien!" Kaelyn said. She marched around the table and grabbed his arm. "We've dug in here for two moons now, and... how we can just abandon this city? After all the work we've done?"

The two kept protesting. Valien ignored them. He looked past them to Lana. She still sat at the table silently, clutching her mug of broth but not drinking. She met his gaze.

"Valien, *why?*" Rune demanded.

But it was Lana who answered.

"Because I saw a hundred thousand bloodthirsty beasts," the lady of the canyon answered. "Because I saw the cruelest army that's flown since the great wars. We've mustered fighters here, yes. We have three thousand resistors. We have three thousand townsfolk who've taken arms. We have three thousand of my own men, warriors of the canyon." She shook her head and blew out her breath. "We are outnumbered. We are outnumbered more than ten to one. We expected one brigade to fly against us, maybe two. Not this." She lowered her head. "Not this."

Rune spun toward her, glaring, and pounded the table.

"One man fighting for his home is worth ten dragons!" he said. "One resistor fighting for justice is worth ten more." He drew his sword. "I bear Amerath, the Amber Sword of Aeternum. This sword stands for light, for truth, for courage. How can I bear it and run from battle?"

Valien looked at the boy, and sadness welled up inside him.

He is like me, he thought. *Rune is like me when I was his age. Brass. More brave than wise. So often, youth speak of justice and righteousness as if they alone can win wars.*

Rune had grown in the past year; Valien had seen it. The boy had come to him green, frightened, and soft. He stood in armor now. His face was gaunt, his grip strong. Ash and stubble covered his cheeks. He was a warrior now, yet he was not wise. Not yet. Not here.

"We've been running and hiding for almost twenty years," Valien said. "We are the Resistance. We are those who strike from shadow. We are those who leap and kill in darkness. We are the demon always in the corner of the legionary's eye. This is how we've always fought."

Rune snarled at him across the tabletop. "Yet now we're here. We've chosen to take this city. We've chosen to raise our banner in the sunlight. We've chosen to defend this place. I say we stay and defend it! Yes, we expected ten thousand to fly against us. A hundred thousand? Let them come. More for us to kill."

Valien roared, a sound that echoed, hoarse and torn, in the hall.

"You crave killing, boy?" He pounded the table so hard it cracked. "Have I taught you nothing? Are you but a mindless, bloodthirsty beast? You speak of death. You speak of blood. You have seen these horrors. Would you be ready to kill your friend, the girl who saved Shari, if she meets in you battle?" When Rune paled, Valien snorted. "I thought not. You speak folly."

"I speak," Rune said, eyes burning, "like you taught me."

Valien howled again. He tossed a chair aside; it smashed against a wall.

"I taught you none of this!"

Rune stood, chest heaving and eyes still blazing. He walked around the cracked table. He clutched Valien's arm and stared at him, teeth bared.

"You taught me justice, Valien," he said. "You taught me to stand tall and fight. Before I met you, I hid in shadows, a brewer, afraid." His voice shook. "You gave me courage. Do not let that courage abandon you." He swept his arm around the hall. "Look at the sea outside the arrowslits. Look at the forest. Look at the city and its people who stand tall, ready to fight, ready to die. This is my city. This is Lynport. I will not abandon it. Not if every last legionary flies against us."

Valien's eyes narrowed. "Not even if you die? Not even if we all die?"

Kaelyn had watched the exchange silently, hands on the hilts of her sword and dagger. Finally she spoke.

"We can still win this," she said. "We will do as we planned. Nothing changes. We will fight house to house, tunnel to tunnel, alley to alley. The town is stocked with gunpowder; every door, every window, every alleyway is rigged to slay them. We have maps. We can scurry, hide, and fire arrows while they burn." She nodded and gripped his arm, her eyes large and eager. "We can *win*, Valien."

And if I lose you? he thought, gazing upon her, and his chest tightened. *If I lose you like I lost her?*

She looked up at him. Large, hazel eyes. *Her* eyes.

What would you have me do, Marilion? Valien thought, fists tight at his sides, and his eyes burned. *Would you want me to run, or would you stay here and fight?*

He turned aside. He looked out the hall's southern arrowslit. A mile away, the breakwater thrust into the sea, and the lighthouse rose. The waves crashed against it, a heartbeat, an eternal whisper of the day he'd met her.

You stood barefoot in a homespun dress, and you wore seashells around your neck. And he killed you. He thrust a sword into you, and I couldn't save you. I had to save him, Marilion. I had to. I had to save the boy.

He spun back to the hall. He stared at Rune. His wife was dead, but that babe was still here. He stood before Valien now as a man, clad in armor, Aeternum's sword in his hand, ready to fight-- ready to do what Valien had saved him to do.

I saved him for Requiem, Marilion, he thought. *I saved him for this day, so we can save our kingdom. Your death will not have been in vain.*

"For Requiem," Rune whispered.

For Marilion, Valien thought.

He marched across the hall, his throat still aching. He turned toward the northern arrowslit. He pointed at the walls that guarded the forest.

"Rune, take your men and guard the northern walls. When the enemy arrives, fire all our guns into their ranks. Slay as many as you can before rushing into our tunnels."

Rune pounded the table. "Yes."

Valien turned toward Kaelyn and fixed her with a hard stare. "Kaelyn, when they fly across the city--and they will fly past the walls, even with all our cannons--you will lead our men through the tunnels. You know them best. You will emerge from every window, hole, roof, and gutter to slay them with arrows, then retreat into shadow."

She nodded, teeth bared, and drew her sword. "Yes!"

Finally Valien turned to Lady Lana.

He paused.

Iciness filled him, and he approached her slowly. She was still seated, and he knelt before her and took her hand.

"Lana, you know your task."

She nodded, face pale, and said nothing.

Valien squeezed her hand. "Lead them to safety, Lana. Tens of thousands live in this city, but they are not warriors. They are mothers, children, and elders. You must defend them. You must lead them out now--at once. Take them into your canyon. Hide them in your father's halls." He rose back to his feet. "This city will be a bloodbath."

Lana stood up too. She gave him a silent stare, then pulled him into a crushing embrace. She was a slender woman, but she gripped him with the might of a burly blacksmith.

"Be strong, warrior of Requiem," she whispered into his ear, then--surprising him--kissed his cheek. "Remember always, Lord Valien Eleison, knight of the realm--you are the light of stars."

With that she spun around. Gripping her saber, she marched toward the fortress doors, stepped outside, and shifted into a dragon. She glided across the city, roaring her call.

"People of Lynport--the time has come! We evacuate! All those who are not fighters--shift and fly. Follow me to safety!"

Valien turned from the doors, clanked up the stairs of Acta's tower, and emerged onto the battlements. He stood and watched the city. Rune and Kaelyn came to stand beside him, the wind whipping their hair.

"People of Lynport!" Lana cried, flying over the roofs. "We evacuate!"

Valien gripped a merlon, struggling to calm the tremble in his fingers. Thousands of people were emerging from their homes below. They shifted into dragons like they had drilled a dozen times; Valien himself had drilled them. They took flight.

Myriads rose into the air, a tapestry of scales of every color, shimmering and streaming across the city. Wings beat. Smoke rose in plumes.

They wobbled as they flew. Before Lynport's liberation only two moons ago, the Regime had outlawed shifting into dragons. Many elders had not flown in eighteen years. Many youngsters had never shifted at all until winning their freedom that autumn. Others had broken the laws of Cadigus, shifting at night over the sea, but most still flew as hesitantly as baby birds.

"Fly, people of Lynport!" Lana cried. "Fly with the magic of Requiem."

They flew northwest.

They flew toward the canyon, to safety underground.

Below them, the warriors--resistors, men of the canyon, and those townsfolk brave enough to raise a weapon--manned the walls.

"It is here," Valien whispered. "The great battle of our uprising. The Battle for Lynport."

He looked north. In the distance, leagues away, a shadow fell.

TILLA

They swarmed over the wilderness.

They covered the sky, a hundred thousand strong. They flew in perfect formation--ten chevrons, one after the other, ten brigades howling for blood. The beat of wings scattered the clouds and bent the forests below. Eyes blazed and scales clattered in a storm. Fire rose between fangs, shining against spiked armor. The sky burned.

War, Tilla thought, flapping her wings and staring forward with grim intent. *Blood. The great battle to end the Resistance.*

And it would be fought at her home.

She peered ahead, trying to see Cadport. She thought she glimpsed the sea, a narrow thread of blue ahead. The city was but a speck.

He's waiting there. Tilla let flames crackle in her mouth. *Rune. The man I loved. The man who turned against me. The man I must capture and convert to glory... with words or with pain.*

"You will fight well tonight, lanse," said Shari. "You will make me proud."

The blue dragon flew beside her, leading the foremost chevron of dragons. She was clad in glory. Her black armor shone with golden dragon motifs and spirals. Blades topped her helm. Her breastplate, large as a boat, shone with rubies.

"I will fight for you, Commander," Tilla answered, flying to her right, her head only several feet farther back. "We will crush them. And we will catch him."

Please, Rune, she thought as she flew. *Do not force us to hurt you. Because we will. We will.*

She looked behind her. Her phalanx, the Sea Cannons, flew there; they would lead the charge. The hundred dragons were snarling, smoke streaming from between their fangs. Tilla had been training them for two moons now, and she trusted each dragon; they were the finest warriors she knew. Behind them rolled the rest of the army. It spread into the horizon, a sea of scale, claw, and tooth.

"Does the emperor not fly with us, Commander?" Tilla asked her princess. "Nor the Axehand Order?"

Shari turned her head and stared at her, eyes shrewd, and flames sparked between her teeth.

"Emperor Frey has his own battles to fight," she said. "Do not question his wisdom. I will lead the battle today, and you will fight at my side."

Tilla nodded. She stared ahead again, squinting. The speck grew to a dot.

Cadport. Home.

As the forest rustled below, Tilla imagined the sound of waves. As dragonfire rose, she felt the warmth of the Old Wheel's hearth. As she flew to battle, she remembered flying with Rune over the sea in darkness, a dance of starlight.

Home. Her old shop. Her father. Scraggles leaping onto her. A young ropemaker with calloused, thin fingers. Weaving, dreaming, hiding.

It was her home, it was her youth, it was her family and the man she loved.

The Resistance took all that from me, Tilla thought, and flames swirled in her belly. *I will save my home. And I will save you, Rune.*

She roared a battle cry and blew fire. Behind her, a hundred thousand dragons answered her call. The might of the Legions stormed south.

KAELYN

They stood on the walls, silent.

They stared into the north.

Nine thousand men and women--resistors, warriors of the canyon, and townsfolk armed with axes and sickles. Nine thousand. Still. Watching. Awaiting the night.

The sun dipped into the west, spreading red tendrils across the sky. Clouds thickened overhead. It would be a night of no stars. A night of dragonfire.

"Whatever happens, I fly by your side," Kaelyn whispered to Valien; he stood to her right upon the wall. "Always, Valien. Always."

She reached out and held his hand, a great paw, calloused and warm and enveloping.

"Stay with me, Rune," she whispered and turned to look at him; he stood at her left. "We will roar our fire together. We will defeat them."

She grabbed his hand too and squeezed it. He stared into the northern darkness. He nodded.

"I will fly with you."

Kaelyn took a deep breath, raised her head, and stared into the shadows. She held their hands--the two men in her life, the two men she thought she'd always be torn between.

Valien--the man who'd saved her from her father, who protected her, who fought for her through blood and rain and fire. Valien--the gruff, weathered knight whose soul was torn, whose soul she had vowed to mend. She looked at him--tall, burly in his armor, his hair wild and grizzled. And she loved him. She loved him more than she'd ever loved another. Once she had thought him like a father to her, but now... now she loved him not as a daughter, but as a woman.

She looked to her left. Rune. The boy she had saved. The boy she had watched grow into a warrior. He was two decades younger than Valien, and less pain filled his eyes, and far more rage and fire. Scruff covered his cheeks now, and his body had grown hard with training. He stood clad in leather and wool, his sword upon his back. Once Kaelyn had thought him a foolish boy, then a figurehead, then a king of legend. But now, looking upon him, she did not see those things. She saw a friend. She saw a soul she loved. She saw the young man she had kissed that night, the man in whose arms she had slept.

And I love you too, Rune, she thought, looking at him. *I love you as much as I love anyone. I will fight with you to victory or death.*

She placed her hand upon a cannon and watched the northern forest. A red glow rose from the horizon like a dawn of fire. She couldn't see the Legions yet--standing upon the walls, close to the surface of the earth, the horizon only lay a dozen miles away. But she knew that glow. That was dragonfire. They flew beyond the horizon and they would soon emerge like a cruel sun.

They will be here within the hour, Kaelyn thought and sucked in her breath.

Shouts and roars rose from the east.

Alarm bells clanged.

Kaelyn's heart burst into a gallop.

The alarm. We're under attack! But how?

She shifted into a dragon. She soared and filled her maw with fire. At her sides, Valien and Rune rose as dragons too, snarling and leaking fire.

When Kaelyn looked east, she saw them there, and the breath left her lungs.

A league away from Lynport, a thousand dragons were flying along the beach, roaring and blowing fire.

"The vanguard," Kaelyn whispered, her belly twisting.

She understood at once. *Of course.* These thousand dragons, brazen legionaries, had traveled the forest as humans, hidden under the canopy, and only now emerged.

"Resistance, shift!" Kaelyn shouted, beat her wings, and rose higher. "Follow!"

She growled, narrowed her eyes, and shot eastward across the houses. The enemy hadn't reached the city yet, but they were moving fast along the shore. They flew only a moment away.

Damn my father, Kaelyn thought as she flew. *He knew we'd see his army from a distance. He knew we'd be watching the north. And his elite warriors sneaked up from the eastern trees.*

She roared and shot forward, wreathed in flame, ready for battle. She streamed over the last few houses, her fellow dragons at her sides, and dived along the shore. The horde approached.

Kaelyn was about to blow fire... when she gasped.

This is wrong.

The thousand dragons did not fly in formation, but in a confused mass. Only a handful wore armor, and even that steel was muddy and dented. They bore no red spirals.

These are not legionaries, Kaelyn realized and gasped.

The dragon at their lead, a young red beast, blasted fire and shouted out.

"Hello, sister!"

Kaelyn spat her flames onto the shore below.

"Stars damn it!" she said, turned her head around, and shouted at her warriors, hundreds of dragons who flew behind her. "Hold your dragonfire! Do not attack." She sighed. "It's my idiot of a brother."

The thousand dragons ahead halted and hovered in midair, wings whipping the sand and water below. Leresy gave her a crooked, toothy grin.

"You've got to be an idiot to fight here today," the red dragon said. "Burn me, Kae, did you know that about a million legionaries are flying your way?"

"I had an idea," she grumbled, hovering before him, her wings blasting him with air. "So... these are the famous Leresy's Lechers. I've heard of your new band of outlaws." She sniffed and wrinkled her snout. "By the stars, you lot stink."

Leresy sniffed beneath his wing and winced. "Aye, we're a salty bunch. What is the old saying? True men stink of oil, soil, and other toil. Villains smell of roses."

"What are you doing here?" Kaelyn demanded. Valien, Rune, and her other dragons hovered behind her, hissing at the beasts ahead.

Her brother twisted his scaly brow into an expression of surprise. "What do you think? I'm here to join the fun. I'm not letting you kill Father without me. I intend to roast his scaly arse myself. And looking at you lot, you could use some help."

At her side, Rune blasted flame. "I say we kill them here on the beach. Slay two villains in one day."

Leresy looked at the young black dragon. "Well well, and this must be the pup who styles himself the heir of Aeternum. Quite a temper you've got, boy. But can you back it up with fire? Fly to me; let's see."

Rune growled and made to charge, but Kaelyn darted forward, slamming him back.

"Enough!" she howled. "Leresy, we don't have an hour before Father arrives. With me--to the walls. We'll talk there. Now!" She spun toward Rune and the others. "Let him through. He won't cause trouble. If he does, I'll kill him myself."

They flew back to town.

Soon Leresy stood upon the city wall in human form, gazed north at the gathering storm, and spat.

"Burn me," he said. "Father is mad at you this time, Kae."

His Lechers stood in a courtyard below, also in human forms--a thousand sweaty, bearded men clad in motley patches of armor and leather. Their shields and sleeves bore their sigil, a black dog. Their stench wafted even to the top of the wall, where Kaelyn stood glaring at her twin.

"Leresy," she said, "this isn't one of your Counter Squares games. You don't know what you're getting into." She stared at a scar that ran down his cheek. "Is that the scar I gave you?"

He shrugged. "Father's given me worse. Now it's time to kill him. You and me. Together." He sketched a theatrical bow. "I have officially changed sides."

She grabbed and twisted his collar. "Leresy! You will die here. You don't know how to fight."

He snickered. "And you do, Kae? Look at you." He swept his arms across the walls and courtyards. "You have... what, fifteen thousand warriors here?"

She sighed. "Nine thousand," she confessed.

"Bloody shite. Well, ten thousand now with the Lechers." He pried her hands off his collar. "Sister, you need me. Let me help you."

He stared at her, his eyes earnest, and Kaelyn felt her chest deflate.

"Leresy, you are a bastard."

"That's what you need here--not righteous, noble warriors of light, but a right bastard like me and the Lechers." He winked. "We fight dirty."

She stared at the mud caking his clothes. "I'm sure you do... in more ways than one."

Rune stomped up toward them, glaring and gripping his sword.

"I've heard enough," the young heir said. "Merciful stars, Kaelyn. He's a *Cadigus*. He's a prince of the empire. We're here to kill Cadiguses, not fight alongside them."

As Rune talked, Leresy held up his hand, moving his fingers like a chattering puppet.

"In case you haven't noticed, boy," Leresy said, "you've been fighting alongside one Cadigus for a while now. Granted, she's got nicer teats than I do, but you'll find my sword just as sharp."

Rune glowered at the outcast prince. "I trust Kaelyn. She is brave and wise and loyal. I don't trust you. This is all some scheme of yours to... to take the throne for yourself! I see your ambitions, Cadigus. This is no game."

"Oh, but it is a game," Leresy said and grinned. "And you need my pieces."

"Like a pig needs more slop!"

Kaelyn watched the two argue and sighed. Though she hated to admit it, both Rune and her brother were right. She couldn't trust Leresy, and most likely, this *was* some plot of his--he would attempt to slay their father in battle and seize the throne. And yet, Leresy was right too. She did need his men.

Rune grabbed her arm and glared.

"Kaelyn!" he whispered. "You can't be considering this. We can't trust him. They say he..." His voice dropped. "They say he captures women in the capital, murders their families, and rapes them. They say he uses them for a night, then tosses their corpses into the garden."

Leresy overheard and grinned.

"Oh, they still tell those stories, do they?" he said. "Excellent! It's all rubbish, of course. Never did anything of the sort. I spread the rumors myself." He hid his mouth and whispered theatrically. "It's good for the old reputation."

Kaelyn looked at her twin--her poor, haunted, miserable brother, whose quips masked pain she could never understand. She looked at Rune who was still fuming. She looked over at Valien, who stood by a cannon, staring north and ignoring them.

She whispered to herself, "The wise work with small devils to slay the big ones."

She had spoken those words to Rune last year about Beras the Brute. They still rang true. She nodded, stepped forward, and meant to shake her brother's hand... yet she found herself embracing him.

"You poor, miserable fool," she whispered to her twin. "You know we'll both probably die here, don't you?"

He snorted a laugh. "Death's not that bad. So long as we take the old man down with us."

Tears burned in Kaelyn's eyes. The memories pounded through her: her father's hands reaching under the bed, grabbing her, pulling her out, holding her down, beating and whipping and burning her.

Please, Father! Leresy would cry. *Please. Don't hurt her. Hurt me instead. It was I who broke the toy. Please, don't hurt Kaelyn.*

She closed her eyes.

And their father had obeyed. Their father had beaten Leresy until he blacked out in a pool of blood.

All to save me... all to save his sister.

She blinked tears away and touched her twin's scarred cheek.

"Thank you, my brother," she whispered. "Welcome home."

She returned her eyes north and stared. Her brother, her companions, and all her soldiers stared with her.

In the night, the horizon burned as if the forest blazed. Distant shrieks rolled like thunder. Yet what flew toward them, just beyond the horizon, was crueler than forest fire or storm.

Death itself flew ahead.

Rain began to fall, pattering against helmets, cannons, and battlements. It soaked Kaelyn's clothes and steamed over the blazing horizon, rising as clouds.

Standing upon the wall, Kaelyn looked at her brother. She looked at Rune and Valien. She gripped her sword and sucked in her breath.

"With rain and fire," she whispered, "it begins."

RUNE

He stood upon the wall, staring north at the encroaching wave of shadow and fire.

They will be here in moments.

He swallowed and gripped his sword. He did not know if he'd live today. But if today was his death, he would die upon the walls of his home, his friends at his sides.

"That's not a bad way to die," he whispered.

I only wish I got to see you again, Tilla, he thought. *Do you fly here too? I only wish I got to hold you one last time, Scraggles. Do you run through starry meadows in the night sky?*

As if to answer his thoughts, barking rose behind him.

Rune spun around, stared down at the courtyard, and gasped.

His eyes widened.

His heart leaped.

"Scraggles?" he whispered. "You're... alive?"

The black mutt stood below, barking up at him. His tail stood out straight; he was confused, not sure if his master truly stood above.

"Scraggles!" Rune shouted.

He had a few moments. Stars damn it, he had time enough! He shifted into a dragon. He leaped off the wall, glided, shifted back into human form, and landed before his dog.

Scraggles leaped back, eyes widening. He stared, standing still, as if struggling to believe Rune truly stood before him.

"Scrags," Rune whispered, and his eyes dampened. "It's me! You remember me, right?"

He reached out to pet Scraggles, but the dog took a step back, eyes still wide, tail still straight, still unsure. His eyes seemed to say: *It looks like you, but how can this be? How can you be here?*

Rune laughed. "It's me, Scrags. I've come back."

The dog leaped.

He crashed against Rune, all one hundred furry pounds of him. His tail wagged furiously and his tongue lapped at Rune's face. Rune laughed, fell down, and the dog jumped onto him, squirming and leaping and licking him.

And then something happened that made fresh tears bud in Rune's eyes.

Scraggles began to cry.

Long, plaintive mewls rose from him, sounds of loneliness finally ended, of joy and disbelief. As he kept leaping and squirming over Rune, his cries rose across the courtyard.

Rune held the dog close.

"I'm back, my friend," he whispered, nuzzling the dog. "I'm home."

A woman's voice spoke somewhere ahead.

"Well, leaky maggot guts." A sniff sounded. "Got me all teary eyed, you two did, and I ain't cried since I stepped on a Counter Squares piece a moon ago."

Lying on the ground, his dog upon his chest, Rune looked up and his eyes widened. A scrawny young woman stood in the courtyard, barely taller than a child. She wore bits of armor over ragged wool, and mud caked her short brown hair.

"Erry?" Rune's voice rose incredulously. "Erry Docker?"

The urchin waved. "Hullo, Rune, old boy. Heard you snogged Tilla." She grinned. "Burn me, never thought you had it in you."

Rune rubbed his eyes, taking in her ragged clothes and the black dog sewn on her sleeves. "Erry! You're... one of the Lechers?"

"Of course I am! Resistance is too noble. Legions are too stiff. Both of you are mental." She shrugged. "Lechers got booze and song and you don't have to be clean. In fact, dirt is quite encouraged. I *like* that." She flashed a grin. "Rune, my dear boy, Leresy Cadigus is a right bastard, a sneaky little weasel, and a bloody pain in the arse. But he'll fight with you." She nodded. "If there's anyone he hates more than the Resistance, it's his father."

Rune rose to his feet. "Erry, I have to put Scraggles somewhere safe. We have only a few minutes. Damn!" He held the dog close. "The castle is too dangerous; there will be fighting there. There will be fighting in every damn tunnel we dug."

He looked down at the dog. Scraggles stood at his side, pressed against him, looking up with a goofy grin.

Did I find you only to lose you again, boy? Rune thought.

Erry grinned. "You resistors with your tunnels and castles. You want secret hideouts nobody can find? Ask a dock rat." She shifted into a thin, copper dragon with clattering scales. "Come on! I know a place. We have just enough time."

Rune shifted too. He was a larger dragon, his scales smooth and black, his claws long. When he flapped his wings and ascended, he lifted Scraggles in his claws.

"Hurry, Rune!" the copper dragon said, soared into the air, and winked. "We haven't got all minute."

They rose from the courtyard. They raced south over the city roofs, heading toward the boardwalk. When Rune looked over his shoulder, he could see the Legions closer now; they were rising from the horizon, a great storm cloud raining fire.

The two dragons reached the boardwalk, the place where Rune would walk so often with Tilla, the place where Erry had lived feral and orphaned.

"Here!" the copper dragon said, dived down, and landed by a crumbling windmill. Its vanes had burned years ago; an empty stone shell remained.

Rune hovered above the boardwalk, wings stirring sand and dust across the cobblestones, and placed Scraggles down. He landed and shifted back into a human.

Erry shifted too, raced into the windmill, and grinned. "Come on! Step in."

He glanced at the windmill. Rune remembered that years ago--stars, it must have been over a decade--the windmill would grind wheat into flour. An old fire had put an end to that, burning the sails, the gears inside, and the old man who had operated the place. Rune had not thought it occupied since, but when he stepped inside after Erry, he saw a tattered mattress, a few old blankets, and a colony of feral cats. The place smelled of mold and cat urine.

"Welcome!" Erry said. "Welcome to my old home. Well... one of my old homes. Well... mostly a home for my cats. Well... mostly a place my cats ate what food I found for them, then buggered off to scrounge elsewhere." She sighed and looked around the place. "It's not much, but it'll keep old Scrags safe. It kept me safe during a few storms."

Erry stood a moment, staring at the place, and to Rune's surprise, she began to weep.

"Erry," he said softly and took a step toward her.

Guilt pounded through him. He had known Erry all his life. He had often brought food to her various hideouts, played mancala with her on the beach, and once--during a heavy storm--let her sleep in his tavern. But Erry would always run off. She'd stay one night, eat one meal, then vanish for days.

I should have done more, he thought, looking at the ruin of this place. *I should have let her stay with us forever, not just once during a storm.*

"Stars, Erry," he said and tried to embrace her. "Are you--"

She growled through her tears and shoved him back. "I don't need no hugs! I don't need no pity." She knuckled her eyes dry. "I never did. I've always fought, and I've always survived here in this damn, stupid, dirty boardwalk in this gutter of a town." She looked around the old windmill, her eyes still red. "It's dirty and it's cold and it smells like piss. But it's home." She looked up at Rune. "It's *our* home. And we're going to fight for it. Right, Rune?"

He nodded and clasped her arm. "Damn right, Err."

She nodded, sniffed, and gave Scraggles an embrace. "Stay here, boy. Stay here and be safe. Try not to wet the bed."

With that, Erry and Rune left the windmill, closing the door on Scraggles. As they shifted into dragons and took flight, Rune heard his dog crying for him and scratching the door.

I don't want to leave you, boy, he thought. *I don't want to leave you again. I'll be back soon. I promise.*

The two dragons flew back north toward the wall.

Above the forest ahead, a hundred thousand dragons screamed, blew fire, and stormed toward them.

LANA

They flew on the wind, a host of chinking scales and pluming smoke, fleeing across the forests.

"Lord Eranor!" she shouted, voice rolling across the sky. "Take your dragons and guard the northern flank. Lord Ferin! Guard the south. Fly them as fast as they'll go."

The two dragons, knights of the canyon, nodded and snorted and barked orders. The warriors they commanded, dragons clad in armor bearing the sigil of Cain, flew behind them, forming a guard around the dragons they shepherded.

We must fly fast, Lana thought, looking over her shoulder as she led the flight. *Stars, we must fly fast, or all here will perish.*

The people of Lynport flew within the ring of warriors-- women, elders, and children. Their scales were soft. Many dragons had lost their fangs to old age; others had not yet grown them. The youngest of Lynport were too young to shift; their mothers flew as dragons, holding human babes in their claws.

"Forty-seven thousand townsfolk," she whispered into the wind as she flew. "Only a handful of warriors to guard them."

A shiver ran from her horns to her tail, clattering her scales. *If the Legions catch us out here, they will slaughter us all.*

Looking upon the dragons, Lana winced, the old pain flaring. Her right eye saw refugees fleeing over autumn forests, frightened but flying fast. She had lost her left eye years ago, yet forever it kept staring, showing her a mirror image of the world. With this phantom eye, she saw the refugees dying. She saw fire wash them, cracking their scales and burning their flesh. She saw their blood rain. She saw them fall dead upon stone, emaciated, pale skin draped over their bones.

Lana grimaced, the two images overlaid before her, life and death, present and past. Always two lives flickered within her. The eye she saw with. The eye she remembered with. Which vision would prove true this day?

"Follow, dragons of Requiem!" she shouted over her shoulder. "Fly as fast as you can. Safety lies ahead."

She returned her eyes to the northwest. The forests spread into the horizon. The canyon still lay too far to see. Lana filled her maw with flame. They didn't have enough time! Damn it, they should have fled Lynport earlier. She peered east, seeking the enemy, but could not see them. Yet she knew they flew there, a hundred thousand strong.

Lana cursed.

"Fly, dragons of Requiem!" she called. "We fly to safety."

Yet they could not fly faster. These were no warriors. They were elders, youngsters, the ill and wounded.

Why didn't we flee earlier? Stars, why did we wait?

The forests streamed below them.

The sea disappeared behind.

They raced over the wilderness, alone.

Weariness tugged on Lana's bones. She spat flames and forced her wings to keep beating. Yet the people trailed behind; Lana was faster and stronger. Fear twisting her gut, she forced herself to slow down.

"Eranor, keep guarding the north flank!"

She kept flying. She forced herself to breathe, to calm her racing mind. The Legions did not care to slaughter innocents, she told herself. They wanted to crush the Resistance. They wanted Valien, Kaelyn, and Rune. It was Lynport--Cadport as they called it--that they craved, not these people.

Yet still fear pounded through her. Until she shepherded these townsfolk into the Castle-in-the-Cliff, protecting them behind strong walls and the Stone Guardians, she wouldn't feel safe.

She lowered her head as she flew, gazing down at the oaks and birches. Perhaps it was still that night she feared, that horrible night worse than any.

She had been twelve, only just leaving her childhood, the winter the Cadigus family seized the throne. How her father, huddled in his canyon, had railed against them! He had pounded the table, shouted threats, and bragged that he'd slay any man who tried to claim his dominion.

"I am lord of this canyon!" Cain had shouted, voice echoing in his hall of stone. "For too long did I serve the Aeternums. Now is our chance for glory. Now is Cain's chance to rule! I will bend the knee to no Cadigus. I will be King of the South."

And even in the northern cold, in the distant capital of Nova Vita, the Cadigus family heard word of his treason. Their spies lurked everywhere, even in those days. They descended upon the canyon that winter, tens of thousands of them, an army that covered the sky.

Cain would not fly out to meet them. He hunkered in his canyon, shouting threats in the hall, inviting the Regime to enter their tomb.

And we remained in our hole, Lana remembered. For days, for moons, for a year.

Toward the end, men were drinking their piss and eating their dogs. Thousands fell ill. The Regime tossed rotted corpses into the canyon. Stars, how it stank! The fumes seeped into the Castle-in-the-Cliff and men vomited. The old and weak perished first, then the strong began to follow. Hundreds died of starvation, thirst, or disease.

How long did it last? Lana thought. *Fifteen moons? Sixteen? More?*

Finally they could bear it no more, and Lord Cain and his household flew out to meet the Regime in battle.

They fell that day.

Thousands fell dead.

Lana fought too, young but strong enough to fly, to blow her fire, to slash her claws. She faced Frey himself in duel that day. She never forgot the heat of his fire bathing her, the agony of his claws, the sting of his tail lashing her. She never forgot her three brothers falling around her, burned with the flames of Cadigus.

And she never forgot his fangs.

She never forgot the pain of his teeth digging into her face.

"You took my eye that day, Frey," Lana whispered as she flew now, years later, a grown woman yet still so afraid, still so hurt. "When I finally woke from the sleep of wounds, I wore an eyepatch, and a trail of white filled my hair." She snarled. "You fly south again. And I will fight you again. I will fight you with every breath I have in me."

Her father had bent the knee that day long ago, and Frey had taken all their forests, fields, and hills, leaving them but a crack in the earth.

"I will not slay you, Devin Cain," the emperor had said, a great golden dragon with blood on his teeth, pinning the canyon lord beneath his claws. "Death would be too kind to you. Your punishment will be to serve me forever. But not as lord of the south. You will have no more sunlight to rule. You have holed up in your canyon for over a year now, and you will remain there for the rest of your days. In shadow. In fear. If you emerge, I will crush you. I will slay you like I slew your sons. Stay in your tomb, Lord Cain, and whenever you look upon your daughter's face, the face that I ravaged, remember my wrath... and remember my mercy."

Seventeen years had passed since. Yet still the rage pounded through her father. And still the nightmares filled her. And still her phantom eye saw that death wherever she looked.

"And still we fight," she whispered. "And I will fight you, Cadigus. Forever. For the wound you gave me. For my people. For Requiem."

They streamed over the forests, heading north, heading to safety, memory, and throbbing old pain.

RUNE

The rain fell, pattering against his helm, as fires rose ahead.

He clutched his sword with one hand, his tinderbox with another. He stared ahead. He waited.

The swarm oozed across the night, a black puddle lit with countless fires like flaming stars. The host seemed a sky of some distant, demonic nightmare spilling into the waking world. Howls and grunts rang out. Flaming pillars rose and crumbled like cathedrals of gods. They flew six miles away, then five, then only four. They covered the horizon. They drowned the land.

"Be strong, Rune," Kaelyn whispered at his side. Her face was pale, her lips tight. She clutched his hand and squeezed. "Whatever happens, be strong. I'm with you."

The Legions howled ahead. Flames roared. Their cries pealed across the sky like demon howls echoing in buried chambers.

"Crush the Resistance!"

"Slay them all!"

"Break their bones and drink their blood!"

"Burn this city!"

Rune sucked in a shaky breath and tightened his lips. He could not stop his chest from shaking. The walls themselves seemed to shake beneath his feet; he didn't know whether his legs were trembling, or whether the Legions were rattling the very earth. The rain kept falling. He kept staring, wanting to flee, wanting to shift and fly away across the sea.

He forced himself to stay still. To stare ahead. To wait.

They flew three miles away. Then two.

War. Blood. The greatest battle of our time.

"You will fight well, Rune," Valien said, standing at his left side. His voice was raspy as ever, but deep and solemn. "Your wings will find the sky. Starlight will bless you." The gruff, taller man looked at him and managed a wink. "Today we fight together as brothers."

Rune did not reply. He did not trust his voice to remain steady. All across the walls of Lynport, his fellow warriors stood, thousands of men and women in leather armor, manning cannons or holding arrows nocked in bows. They were thousands of brave fighters, and they would fight well, yet Rune had never felt more fear.

"Slay them all!" rose a shriek ahead.

"We will break them upon the wheel!"

"We will flay their skin and drink their blood!"

"Grab Relesar alive--he will suffer most!"

Rune clenched his teeth, and his sword shook. They were coming to capture him, to torture him, to break his every bone and hear him scream. They were coming to kill Valien, Kaelyn, Erry, and all those he loved. They were a hundred thousand strong. He had but ten thousand with him.

We can't win this, he thought, and his eyes burned, and his breath trembled. *We will die. We will fall. We--*

He snarled.

No, he thought. *No.*

He could not let fear claim him. Not now. Valien's words from his training returned to him.

All wise men fear battle. Only brutes rush fearless into a fight. The true warrior is not he who feels no fear, but he who conquers fear.

Rune nodded.

"I will fight," he whispered through clenched teeth. "For the Resistance. For my friends. For my home." The rain streamed down his face. "For Requiem."

The Legions swarmed ahead, closer and louder. Their roars crashed against the walls. Rune could see individual dragons now. Their eyes blazed red in the firelight. Their fangs shone. Their claws reached out. Flames blasted from them, lighting the night. They rolled into the horizon. Shari Cadigus flew at their lead, clad in black armor, spraying her flames and shrieking, her head undulating in the heat waves.

"Slay them all!"

Rune lit his tinderbox.

At his sides, Kaelyn and the other archers tugged back their bowstrings.

Beside him, Valien drew his sword and held it aloft. The blade caught the firelight.

"Archers!" he shouted. "Fire!"

A rain of arrows shot forward, shards of red in the night, and slammed into the horde ahead. The dragons shrieked. Blood splashed. They kept flying.

Valien shouter louder. "Cannons--fire!"

Rune brought tinderbox to fuse.

The smell of smoke filled his nostrils.

The dragons ahead shrieked and stormed forward, only several heartbeats away from the walls.

The fuse burned.

"No fear," Rune whispered.

An explosion rocked the city walls.

Fire exploded.

The cannons thrust backward so violently they almost fell off the wall. Light flared. A hundred cannonballs blazed into the night. The smell of gunpowder flared. Through clouds of smoke, Rune saw the volley slam into the Legions. Where the cannonballs struck scales, fire screamed and blood rained. Dragons lost their magic. Human bodies tumbled, torn apart into limbs and torsos and severed heads. Already men were loading new gunpowder and cannonballs, driving ramrods into muzzles.

"Archers!" Valien howled, sword raised and voice hoarse. "Fire!"

A second volley flew. Arrows whistled and slammed into the beasts ahead. Men shoved gunpowder into muzzles, leaped back, and more fuses burned.

"Cannons, fire!"

The walls shook. The cannons jolted backward again. Flames roared and exploded across the sky, deafening. The Legions were close now, so close Rune could count their teeth. The cannonballs ripped through them. One projectile tore into a beast only a hundred yards away, shattering its head into red mist, leaving a human body to tumble.

Yet still so many swarmed. Still the thousands streamed forward, howling and raging and blowing flames.

"Archers! Fire! Keep those arrows firing!"

More arrows whistled. More blood spilled and more dragons fell dead.

"Cannons!"

A third volley of cannonfire rocked the city. The smoke rose thick and black and rich with the smell of gunpowder. A hundred cannonballs ripped into the horde ahead, tearing through armor and scales, showering blood and flame.

And then... then the Legions were upon them.

"Fall back!" Valien shouted, waving his sword. "Fall behind, into the tunnels, go!"

Rune leaped back, ears ringing, and shifted into a dragon. At his sides along the walls, thousands of resistors shifted too.

"Fall back!" Valien howled, a silver dragon with one horn. "Into the tunnels!"

Rune flapped his wings, flew backward, and beheld the wrath of Cadigus descend upon the city. The dragons covered the sky, a burial shroud of scale and flame. Their fire shot down, blasting walls and roofs. A few resistors were too slow to shift; they were still loading cannons or nocking arrows. The Legions slammed into them, and claws ripped them apart. Other resistors managed to shift but were too slow to fly back; flames blasted them, cracking their scales and melting their eyes.

"Rune!" Kaelyn shouted. The green dragon slammed into him, pushing him lower. "Fall back!"

Hovering above the roofs, he looked around wildly.

"Where's Erry! Where's--"

"Rune!" Kaelyn shouted. "Into the tunnels!"

He nodded. They turned and dived. The rooftops and streets rushed up toward them. All around, jets of flame crashed down onto Lynport like comets, burning roofs and tearing into dragons.

"There, the smithy!" Kaelyn cried. "Fly, Rune!"

They dived over the roofs. Already many homes, those built of wood and clay, were blazing. The brick smithy, however, rose strong from the smoke. Rune and Kaelyn hissed. A stream of fire crashed down before them. They scattered, skirted the flames, and kept diving.

They all but crashed onto the cobbled road outside the smithy. When Rune glanced above, he saw the Legions covering the sky of Lynport. Thousands of flaming jets slammed down. Thousands of wooden homes blazed. Resistors were blasting flame upward and scurrying into those houses built of stone. Some resistors--or maybe they were Lechers--were brazen enough to soar, howling, into the sky of legionaries. Claws and fangs tore them apart, and they tumbled as ravaged humans. Blood filled the rain.

"Rune!" Kaelyn shouted, smoke and flame around her. "Inside!"

She shifted into human form, fired one arrow into the sky, and leaped through the smithy window. Rune blasted his flames upward into the dragon storm, shifted too, and leaped. Flames crashed down where he'd stood, missing him by inches. He scurried through the window and slammed its shuttered panels shut.

Ten other resistors filled the stone house. Their clothes were singed and sweat soaked them. A few winced; welts rose across their skin. They all held swords.

"Into the tunnels, like we trained," Rune said.

He doubted they could hear him; he could barely hear himself over the ringing in his ears. Outside the windows, scales flashed and fire blazed. The walls shook. Dragons were landing outside, claws scratching cobblestones. The legionaries' battle cries thundered as loud as the cannons.

"Find Relesar!" a voice roared outside. "Slay all others."

When he peeked between the shutters, Rune saw the imperial dragons shifting into warriors clad in black armor. Helms covered their heads and their swords blazed red in the firelight. Boots thudded across the streets.

Breathing heavily, Rune turned from the window. He stomped forward, grabbed the floorboards, and pulled them loose. A tunnel delved below.

"Follow!" he said and placed a leg into the darkness.

Before he could enter, the smithy door jolted open.

Ten legionaries stood behind it, their armor reflecting the fires, their swords raised.

A rope, attached to the door, creaked.

A barrel of bolts and gunpowder fell against the soldiers.

The explosion rocked the smithy. The door shattered, raining wood. Armor tore apart. Limbs flew across the street outside, and a severed head rolled into the smithy. Blood pooled and smoke rose. The doorway had vanished. Bodies lay strewn outside. One man still lived, screaming, his arms torn off and his entrails spilling.

One leg still in the tunnel, Rune stared.

His heart seemed to stop.

The world shook and his ears rang. He could no longer hear anything but the ringing, see anything but the ravaged bodies, the man writhing, the blood, and oh stars, he was still alive, and--

"Rune!"

Kaelyn was shouting above him. He could barely hear her beyond the ringing. He looked up and saw her face splashed with blood. She was shoving his shoulders, trying to push him into the tunnel. Outside the doorway, more legionaries were racing through the streets, and more explosions rang. Through the windows, blood and debris flew everywhere. A man ran down an alley, aflame and screaming.

"Rune!" she screamed.

He nodded, tightened his lips, and plunged into the tunnel. He fell down a shaft, hit an earthen floor, and beheld a burrow driving forward. He crawled. He had forgotten his lamp somewhere above. When he glanced behind him, he saw Kaelyn and the others crawling too; a few held flickering lanterns.

The tunnels shook, raining dirt. Blood smeared Rune's face and his arm burned. As they crawled through the darkness, he could still see the bodies and hear the screams.

TILLA

Her city burned beneath her.

The flames rose everywhere. Houses, shops, trees--they all blazed. Tilla flew, eyes stinging, the smoke swirling around her. Blood spilled. Dragons burned and fell dead. Soldiers ran, swinging swords, and explosions tore through alleyways, ripping men apart. Streets cracked. Buildings tumbled. Walls fell. Any house built of wood blazed. From the brick structures--the fort, the courthouse, the silos and shops--cannons were still firing through embrasures in the walls, tearing into dragons.

My home, Tilla thought. Her heart thrashed, her eyes stung, and the terror gripped her. *Cadport. My home. It's burning.*

"Rune!" she howled, flying above the destruction. "Rune, end this! Fly to me, Rune. Stop this warfare!"

She flew in circles above the city, seeking him. The resistors scurried below, leaping from street to street, shadows in the night. They fired arrows, then vanished into doorways and windows and holes. Cannons blazed and smoke unfurled. Imperial dragons blasted the streets with fire. Their claws tore at homes and walls crumbled. Bodies littered the streets.

"Rune!" she roared, flying above, trying to find him but seeing only shadows, only dragons drenched in fire and blood, only death and destruction.

No! No. None of this should have happened! They were supposed to capture this city, not destroy it. They were supposed to capture Rune, not topple her home above him.

"Rune, surrender yourself and this will end!" she cried, flying above the streets. A cannonball flew from a silo, and she barely dodged it. Fire rose from a rooftop, blasting her tail, and arrows shot from windows, clattering against her armor. Tilla roared, dived, and bathed the buildings with fire.

"Rune, hand yourself in!" she called. "We don't have to watch our city fall."

She looked around, seeking her old home, but could not see through the smoke. She tried to look toward the beach, that place where she'd walked with Rune so many times. Dragons flew above the boardwalk and fire rose in walls.

Cadport was crumbling below her, and she could not stop it.

"Find the boy!" Shari shrieked. The blue dragon flew at her side, howling fire. "Find Relesar. Search every building until he's found! Slay all others in your path."

Below, legionaries in human form snaked through the streets, armor clanking. They yanked open doors, only for barrels of gunpowder to burst, scattering gore across the street. They tried to climb through windows, but arrows peppered them. Every instant, resistors burst from a hole, shot arrows and thrust swords, and vanished back into hiding. The larger houses held dragons; their fire erupted from chimneys and windows, blasting any legionary who approached.

"It's like fighting gophers," Shari said in disgust. Her blue wings churned the smoke and she roared. "Tear down every house until you find him!" She whipped her head around, stared at Tilla, and snarled. "Lanse! Lead your phalanx to the courthouse; they're firing cannons from within. Stop them."

Tilla had trained for this. She had spent a year training for this. Yet now she only wanted this to end, to stop this desecration of her memories. How could she fight for the force that toppled Cadport? How could she lead dragons to burn her home? Why did Rune not emerge and end this?

"Lanse!" Shari shouted. "I gave you an order. Lead your dragons! Stop those cannons."

Fire blazed inside Tilla.

You force me to do this, Rune, she thought.

Her eyes stung and she roared.

Rune had attacked Castra Luna with his Resistance, slaughtering hundreds of soldiers from Cadport. Rune now lurked here like a coward, firing cannons from shadow rather than facing her in open battle.

"Dragons!" Tilla shouted. "Follow!"

She began to fly over the burning homes, heading toward the square. Everywhere below her, buildings burned and collapsed. Still the resistors fought from hiding, emerging from holes, windows, and tunnels to fire arrows, then scurrying back into shadow.

You did this, Rune! Tilla thought with a growl. *You hide in homes, forcing us to topple them. You lurk like a coward, forcing us to destroy our city.*

She howled, racing above the streets. Her phalanx roared behind her. Beyond roofs and alleyways, they reached the city square. The courthouse, the place where Tilla had seen Pery beheaded, rose ahead from smoke.

Its portico shook. Smoke blasted and fire blazed. Cannonballs shot from between the columns toward Tilla's phalanx.

She swerved. One cannonball roared over her head, another beneath her wing. Beside her, a projectile slammed into one of her dragons. The warrior didn't even have time to roar. The cannonball tore through his magic, leaving him to tumble to the ground in human pieces.

"Burn them!" Tilla roared. "Before they reload!"

She dived lower and skimmed over the square. The cobblestones raced beneath her. She beat her wings, racing toward the columns ahead. She could see more cannons there, their muzzles lowering to face her.

She roared her fire and soared.

The flames blasted between the columns. The cannons inside jerked violently like marionettes whose strings were tugged. Fire blasted and more cannonballs flew. Tilla rose higher, screaming. One cannonball slammed against the tip of her wing, tearing off her claw, and she howled in agony. The pain blazed through her like a fingernail ripped off a hand. Her dragons blew fire around her. Cannonballs tore through two dragons at her side, scattering human limbs across the square.

"Fill this place with fire!" Tilla screamed.

She rose above the courtyard roof. Holes had been carved into the stone; she saw them too late. Arrows fired from within, and Tilla screamed. Several arrows shattered against the breastplate that protected her belly. Two more pierced her wounded wing, tearing straight through the skin. The pain nearly blinded her, but she turned and dived.

She swooped down along the columns and sprayed her fire into the courthouse shadows.

Cannons blasted from within. A hundred cannonballs flew skyward, tearing into dragons; one skimmed along her breastplate, raising sparks. Tilla snarled. Beyond the shadows and smoke behind the columns, she saw men scurry to scoop gunpowder from barrels.

Tilla growled and blew fire.

Her flaming jet spun between two columns, raced by a cannon, and slammed against the barrels.

Tilla soared.

Arrows whistled and shattered against her armor and scales. One scraped alone her tail. Tilla kept rising.

An explosion rocked the courthouse below.

Smoke burst skyward, enveloping Tilla.

Chunks of stone flew, peppering her breastplate and slamming into her wings.

She kept soaring. The dragons of her phalanx rose along with her, howling and coughing.

"Get back down there," she shouted, "and slay them all!"

She dived back into the square. She drove through the smoke, heading toward the courthouse. She beat her wings, shoving the smoke back, and revealed three shattered columns. A chunk of roof had fallen, and blood seeped from beneath. Some columns still stood, and cannons lay overturned beside them. Resistors scurried deeper into the crumbling building.

"Warriors!" Tilla howled. "Human forms--enter after me!"

She landed by the standing columns, shifted into a human, and drew her sword. Behind her, dozens of dragons followed suit.

"Slay the Resistance!" Tilla shouted. "Slay them all."

She ran between the columns into the shadows. Her men ran behind her. Arrows flew from within, and one grazed her armor. Others slammed into men behind her; some arrows punched through steel, and the men fell.

"Slay them!" Tilla shouted. She ran, sword held above her, into a shadowy hall.

They waited there, a hundred resistors. They were ashy and bloody, yet they drew their blades, shouted, and ran toward her.

"Hail the red spiral!" Tilla cried, slammed into their ranks, and swung her blade. At her sides, her fellow warriors clashed against the enemy. Swords lashed and men fell dead.

You made me do this, Rune, Tilla thought as she swung her sword, slicing into flesh, slaying men at every turn. She screamed madly, painting the hall red. *You made me kill.*

Tears burned in her eyes, but still Lanse Tilla Siren fought and killed as her city burned around her.

RUNE

He crawled from the tunnel into the silo, covered in dirt and ash. At least, once this place had been a silo. The grain had been emptied, and the chamber now served as a pillbox, a brick outpost with embrasures along the walls for firing arrows or dragonfire.

The corpses of two archers lay here, charred black.

Fire can be blown inward too, Rune thought with a grimace, stepping over the remains.

The brick walls surrounded him, sooty and still hot. Rune sucked in his breath and shifted into a dragon, all but trapping himself between the stone walls. Through the slits, Rune glimpsed legionaries running through the city streets, shouting in the night.

He thrust his jaw against an arrowslit, sucked in his breath, and sprayed the street with fire.

Screams rose.

When his flames died, he saw soldiers falling ablaze, tearing at their red-hot armor.

"A hundred or more outside!" Rune shouted over his shoulder to the hole in the floor; more resistors hid there.

"Hold them back!" Kaelyn shouted from below.

Rune peered out the arrowslit. A dozen soldiers had fallen. A dozen more were rushing forward. He blasted them with more flames, and they fell.

A dragon shrieked.

Blasts of air pounded the street, scattering dust, discarded armor, and a severed hand. Rune glimpsed blue scales in the night--a dragon swooping toward the pillbox. A boom echoed. The walls creaked and rained dust. The dragon slammed into the walls again, shrieking, and through the hole, Rune glimpsed a blue tail lashing.

"Damn it," he muttered. He blasted flames out the arrowslit, and the blue dragon shrieked. Rune glimpsed the beast stumbling back in the street, and his heart seemed to freeze.

The dragon had only one wing. The other was built of wood, rope, and leather.

"Shari Cadigus," he whispered.

Charred and howling, the blue dragon faced the silo again. Through the arrowslit, her eyes met Rune's.

He blasted more fire outward.

Shari shrieked.

"Resistor in the silo!" rose her howls. "Topple it down. Tear down the walls!"

More dragons slammed into the walls. Loose bricks fell and clattered.

"Get out of there, Rune!" Kaelyn shouted below.

He blasted more fire out the hole, scorching Shari, and shifted back into human form. The walls trembled and cracked around him. He leaped into the tunnel and plunged into darkness.

Kaelyn grabbed him, and they crawled as fast as they could. Above him, Rune heard the silo collapse. Bricks and dust tumbled into the tunnel, and he coughed, blinded.

"Keep crawling!" Kaelyn said and tugged his arm. They raced down the burrow. A dozen resistors crawled ahead of them, holding lamps.

Shari's voice echoed above, muffled beyond the debris.

"Clear the bricks and into the tunnel! The rats scurry there."

Rune crawled as fast as he could, burrowing forward on his elbows. Heat blazed behind him.

"Rune, they're coming after us!" Kaelyn shouted, crawling before him.

"Keep moving!" he shouted back.

Where's the rope? Damn it, where is it?

He heard the legionaries tug bricks, clearing a path to the tunnel. Rune hissed and kept crawling. Armor clanked behind him, and the cries of legionaries filled the tunnel.

There!

The rope dangled from the tunnel roof. Rune scurried by and tugged.

Hands reached out and grabbed his feet.

The tunnel collapsed behind him.

Bricks and soil crashed down, burying the legionaries who'd grabbed him. Dust blinded Rune, heat bathed him, and he coughed. When the debris cleared, he breathed raggedly.

"Another tunnel lost," he said hoarsely, tugging himself free from the dead man's grip.

They had been fighting for a night and day now. They had lost a dozen tunnels, a dozen homes, and a dozen pillboxes. The courthouse had fallen.

So many were dead.

Kaelyn coughed ahead of him, smeared with dust and dirt. She reached out and grabbed his hand.

"Come on, Rune," she said. "We have to keep moving. Keep crawling. We're almost at Castellum Acta."

He kept crawling, following her and the others. The sounds of battle faded behind. Judging by the other tunnels they had sabotaged, it would take the legionaries an hour to clear the rubble and crawl in pursuit.

But they always did follow.

They always emerged into the next hideout, swinging their swords and blowing their fire.

But he kept crawling.

He kept fighting.

It had been a night and day, and he had not eaten, drunk, or slept, but he kept going.

"How many still fight in the fort?" he asked, pulling himself through the darkness. It was almost winter, but the air was sweltering down here; he could barely breathe.

"Six hundred men last time I was there," Kaelyn replied. "But the damn Legions keep blasting fire at the walls. We're down to only ten barrels of gunpowder."

Rune felt his belly sink as he crawled.

"We will not last a day there," he said. "They are too many."

Still wriggling along the tunnel, Kaelyn snarled at him over her shoulder. "We will last a moon. We will keep slaying them. Their bodies litter the hillside, and we will slay ten of them for every one of us they kill."

They crawled for an hour, passing many forks in the tunnel where other resistors moved. Many were bloodied. Some were missing limbs. Some screamed as their comrades pulled them into safe burrows for healing. Rune could not guess how many had died already, but at every house and street where he had fought, he saw them there--the corpses of his brothers and sisters.

Finally they reached the tall, narrow shaft that rose upward into shadow. A wooden sign stood here, bearing the word: "Library". The actual library lay hundreds of yards west of here; all the signs in these tunnels were mislabeled, meant to confuse the Legions should they crawl here. Kaelyn, Rune, and the other resistors climbed the shaft, clinging to its wooden ladder. They opened a trapdoor and emerged into the hall of Castellum Acta, the fortress on the hill.

A hundred resistors stood here, surrounding a table heavy with maps, swords, and wooden pieces carved as dragons. Kegs of gunpowder rose at the back. A dozen archers stood along the walls, firing arrows from slits.

Valien stood at the table, clad in leather armor, glaring down at a parchment map of the tunnels. Other resistors stood around him, caked with dirt, and moved pieces around the map.

"Valien!" Kaelyn said, walking toward him. "The silo at Well Road has fallen. We destroyed the tunnel before fleeing."

Valien looked up, cursed, and slammed his fist against the table.

"Stars damn it." He lifted a piece of coal, and crossed out an outpost on the map. "Is the silo claimed or completely fallen?"

Rune marched forward too, wincing. Welts blazed across his body.

"Damn walls fell all around me."

Grumbling, Valien moved several small wooden dragons across the map. When Rune stood closer, he stared down at the parchment and cursed.

"Merciful stars, Valien," he said. "We've lost, what... a quarter of our tunnels already?"

The grizzled old knight nodded. "And losing more fast. I--"

Shrieks sounded outside the hall. The archers shouted and fired with more fervor.

"Another assault!" one archer cried over his shoulder. "Two phalanxes--and they're angry."

Valien was already shouting orders at his men. "Send two hundred dragons out--stop that assault!"

Resistors leaped onto a stairway and raced up, leaving the hall and climbing the tower. Wings thudded and more dragons shrieked. Through the arrowslits, Rune glimpsed hundreds of resistors flying as dragons--they had emerged from the tower top-- and crashing against the enemy. Blood rained.

Rune began marching toward the tower stairs; the hall doors were bricked up, but the tower still held a trapdoor for fighters.

"I'm joining them," he said, grinding his teeth.

Before he could reach the staircase, Valien grabbed his arm.

"No, Rune," he said and glared. Weariness filled his eyes, but fire too. "You do not fly out as a dragon. You fight in the tunnels. We've discussed this. They know the color of your scales; they would mob you on sight."

Rune growled. "I want to fight in the sky!" he said. "I will not watch my comrades fly out while I cower here."

Valien tightened his grip. "Cower, Rune? No. You fight the way I need you to fight--in shadow. Striking from the dark. That is your task."

He looked out the arrowslits. The imperial dragons were crashing against the resistors. Scales flew like kicked seashells. Smoke and fire stormed across the sky. As dragons died, their magic vanished. Human bodies tumbled to the hillsides.

"We won't last much longer here," Rune said. "They fight too well in the air."

Valien nodded, released him, and returned to the table. "Which is why we must keep fighting underground. Tunnel by tunnel. House by house."

Rune walked to the table too; he had to lean against it for fear of falling. He sighed and wiped sweat off his brow.

"They are too many," he said. "They've claimed too much. How much longer can we hold out, Valien?"

He no longer asked: Can we win? He knew the answer. They could not.

"As long as we can," Valien replied. "A few days. Less than a moon. We cannot hold this city forever. But we can make them pay a heavy price here. We can make them bleed."

Rune left the table. He walked toward the back of the hall. He faced the second, smaller staircase. This one plunged down into shadow, dug into the hill. It led to a tunnel, yet not one that linked to the network.

"When do we take these stairs?" he asked softly.

Armor creaking, Valien came to stand beside him. The older man placed a hand on Rune's shoulder.

"I will not yet give the order," he said. "We cannot be seen to flee so quickly, not if we've already begun this fight."

Rune looked at him. Valien's face was haggard and leathery beneath his beard. His eyes stared grimly at the shadowy stairs. A struggle raged behind those eyes, some old memory of pain. The man's calloused fists clenched at his sides.

The tunnel leads into the sea, Rune thought, looking back at it. It led into the water where he'd swim with Tilla. The water where ships had sailed. The water this town had grown along, that had brought it life... that could now save them.

He tried to imagine crawling down this tunnel on his elbows until water roared, dark and salty and stinging his wounds. He would swim--for how long? He'd have to hold his breath for as long as he could, swimming south. He'd emerge from the sea, breathe air, sink again and swim some more.

He would flee his home... and Lynport would burn behind him.

The bodies would remain behind him.

The memories, his childhood, and Tilla... they would all remain behind.

He turned away and marched back toward the table. Kaelyn and several other resistors were frowning at the map, tracing tunnels and discussing troop movements. Rune jabbed his finger against the parchment.

"We'll strike them here in the butcher shop, the eastern gates, and the old smithy." He looked up and met Kaelyn's gaze; she stared back, eyes haunted in her sooty face. "Are you ready to fight some more, Kaelyn?"

She managed a trembling smile, her teeth white against the mud and ash on her face. "Always."

They returned to the tunnels.

They fought on.

LERESY

He could not breathe.

The fear pounded through him. His pulse beat in his ears like war drums. The air was cold in the potter shop--he knew it was--yet sweat soaked his clothes. At his side, Yorne, that gaunt bastard, was peering out the window's shutters and saying something to Leresy, but he couldn't hear.

The damn blood in my ears is too loud! Leresy thought. He pawed at those ears, as if he could tear out the sound, but his fingers trembled. His breath shook.

He looked around him. Twenty other Lechers filled the brick shop. The shelves had fallen and the pottery lay smashed. Their tunnel gaped open in the floor. Leresy had a map of the network, and Yorne claimed to have memorized it already. But it was all a mess to Leresy. It was all a confusion of darkness and blood and everywhere his father's soldiers. How many tunnels had he crawled through? How many men had he seen torn apart, their blood splashing the city? He did not know.

I made a mistake, he thought, lips trembling. *I should never have come here. Yet how can I flee without seeming the coward?*

Yorne turned toward him. The gruff, tattooed man was still talking, but still Leresy couldn't make out the words.

I'm going to die here, he thought, staring at his men. *The enemy approaches. I'm going to die with this lot of stinking, drunken louts. Oh stars.*

"Ler!"

A small hand grabbed his arm. Leresy turned and saw Erry. The urchin was kneeling by the front door. She gave him a glower, peered out the keyhole, then turned back toward him. Soot filled her hair and coated her leather armor. A bandage wrapped around her arm.

"Erry," he whispered.

He tried to imagine the day she had first come to his camp, how they had eaten the boar, how he had taken her into his bed.

He tried to imagine holding her again, stroking her hair, kissing her head, and protecting her.

When I protected her, I myself always felt so safe, he thought. *I wish I could feel safe now.* His eyes stung. *I want to be back in my tent, back with Erry in my arms, not here waiting with her to die.*

"Ler, damn it!" she said and tugged his collar. "Are you listening to me?"

She had been talking, he realized. He forced himself to swallow. He forced himself to speak through tight lips.

"Yes," he said.

She glared. "Good! They'll be here soon. They're down the block now, twenty of them, moving house by house." She grinned. "Ler, you take these ones out. It's your turn. Looks like a good batch of them too." She winked. "You'll find one of them familiar, I think."

Leresy sucked in a shaky breath.

Be strong, he told himself. *Be strong. You're a Lecher. You lead the Lechers! Show Erry you're strong.*

He moved toward the door and peered through the keyhole. A small mirror was placed across the street, hidden in a water spout. In the reflection, he could see them.

"Burn me," he whispered.

Twenty legionaries were moving down the street, bedecked in black armor. They bore loaded crossbows. They were tall, strong men, an elite group of fighters, yet their commander towered above them. The brute stood seven feet tall and wide as an ox. He did not wear the polished black armor of the Legions, but patches of rusted iron cobbled together over strips of chainmail. Scars rifted his stubbly head, and dark circles hung under his beady eyes.

"Beras the Brute," Leresy whispered. Through he still hid in the pottery shop, hidden from view, he clutched the hilt of his sword.

He kept watching, sweat trickling down his spine. The legionaries were marching down the alley; it was too narrow for a dragon. They stopped at a barbershop about fifty yards away. Beras approached the door, grunted, and kicked.

The door shattered open.

At once, the legionaries leaped forward. Crossbows thrummed. Bolts shot into the house.

"Slay all inside!" Beras howled and burst into the barbershop. His men followed, drawing their swords.

Curses rose and echoed down the alley.

"Nothing but damn dummies again!" Beras shouted. "Don't touch them, men. Damn Resistance has rigged up these bastards with Tiran fire. A spark from your sword can set them off."

The brute trundled back into the alley, and his men followed.

"Damn it," Leresy whispered. "They figured out the dummies."

He himself had almost died touching one of the straw men; Kaelyn had pulled his hand back, saving his life. The Resistance had spent days sewing these decoys together. They wore armor and helms, and they carried swords, but inside their suits, they were only straw soaked with Tiran fire. The liquid was costly--a single vial of Tiran fire cost more than ten barrels of gunpowder--but it would ignite on a single spark. Any soldier within ten feet of a Tiran straw man would be torn apart.

As Leresy watched, Beras and his men kept moving down the street. They passed by the next house. A family had lived in the small, clay home before being evacuated. Since then, Leresy knew from his map, a family of Tiran dummies had taken residence.

"Load your crossbows," Beras ordered and kicked in this door too.

The men stepped forward. Crossbows fired.

An explosion rocked the street.

The house crumbled.

The clay walls shattered and the roof blazed. One man fell back, burning and screaming.

"More dummies," Beras said. He hawked, spat, and glared at the burning man. "Somebody put that bastard out. We keep moving. Bloody resistors are in one of these houses; dragons keep rising from this alley. Their tunnel is here somewhere."

Leresy gulped.

Stars, they're only a few doors away now, he thought. He clutched the hilt of his sword, but his hand was so sweaty the hilt kept sliding. *They will be here in moments.*

"How far are they?" Erry asked, kneeling beside him.

He pulled away from the keyhole. "Five doors down." The sounds of shattering wood and thrumming crossbows rose outside, and Leresy swallowed. "Four."

Erry sucked her teeth. "Ready?"

He nodded.

He looked up at the rope. It dangled over the pottery shop doorway. He traced it up to the rafters, where it vanished into a hole in the ceiling. Leresy tried to draw a deep breath, but it shuddered and only entered his lungs in spurts.

Another door shattered outside. More crossbows thrummed.

"Three," Erry whispered, replacing him at the keyhole.

Leresy could barely breathe. His throat was too tight. His pulse raged in his ears like galloping horses. He looked behind him at his twenty men, hardened Lechers with stubbly faces and dour eyes. They clutched the hilts of their swords, ready for battle.

Oh stars, the blood will spill. Oh stars, I'm going to die.

Leresy closed his eyes for just an instant, but it was enough. He could see the battle again, the massacre at Castra Luna. Behind his eyelids, he saw his soldiers fall screaming, so many youths torn apart.

You died there too, Nairi, he thought, and his eyes burned with tears. And now Erry was here, a new light in his life. Now Erry was in danger.

Another door shattered outside, and Erry peeked through the keyhole.

"Two," she whispered.

His throat was so dry. His breath panted. The room spun. He looked over at Erry, and his chest twisted. She was so young. She was so small. Beneath the mud caking her, she was only a frail doll, so delicate, so fair.

I can't lose her too. I can't...

A door shattered outside.

"One more door," she whispered, peering out the keyhole. "Wait for it..."

Leresy grabbed the rope. His hand shook, damp with sweat, but he clutched the rope tight like a drowning man. He could hear the soldiers creaking outside, only a few yards away. He could smell their sweat and leather.

I don't want to be here, he thought. *Stars, I want to be back home. I want to be back at the Bad Cats. Anywhere but here...*

"Wait for it...," Erry mouthed, not even daring to whisper.

Boots thudded.

Shadows fluttered under the pottery shop doorway.

"Now!" Erry screamed.

Leresy started. He stared.

"Now, damn it!" Erry cried, grabbed his hand, and yanked the rope down.

Shouts sounded outside. Leresy knelt, stared through the keyhole, and saw three barrels crash down from the pottery shop roof. They hit the alleyway and slammed into the soldiers.

"Back, damn it!" somebody cried and yanked Leresy backward.

The world seemed to explode.

Gunpowder blasted, so loud Leresy thought it would tear his eardrums. The pottery shop door crashed open. Leresy fell onto his backside and stared, eyes wide. Outside in the street, the barrels were gone. Flames roared. Soldiers lay dead, torn apart. A severed head burned. Blood spilled. A few men still lived; they clutched at their cracked armor as their innards leaked. They wept.

"Attack!" Yorne shouted, leaped over Leresy, and burst into the alley. The other Lechers ran behind him, swords swinging. Erry ran among them, howling for battle and waving her blade.

Leresy sat in the pottery shop, unable to rise, unable to breathe, just staring through the shattered door.

Five or six legionaries still stood. They swung their swords against the Lechers. Blades clanged. Yorne's sword cleaved a man's leg, then slammed down against his helm. Erry screamed as she duelled another legionary.

Leresy could only stare.

So much blood, he thought, chest rising and falling like a frightened hare. *So much death.*

"Leresy, damn it, come on!" Erry screamed outside. She gestured toward him, then cursed and raised her blade, parrying a blow.

He wanted to fight. Truly, he wanted to! He tried to rise. He could not. His legs had stopped obeying him. It was all he could do to even breathe.

"I..." he whispered and licked his lips. "I can't... I..."

He managed to rise to his feet. He gripped his sword's hilt, but his hand was too sweaty to draw it. He stumbled two steps forward, and blood flowed around his boots. He clenched his jaw and struggled not to gag.

Outside the smashed door, Beras came lolloping down the alley, boots crushing planks of wood and corpses. The brute snarled. Half his face was burnt away, yet still he raised his axe.

Erry stood with her back to him, dueling another man.

The axe rose higher above her.

Finally Leresy could move. His heart seemed to stop and his lungs to collapse, but he leaped forward. A torn howl left his lips. Screaming, he managed to draw his sword but not raise it. He flung himself into the alley and crashed into Beras, driving his shoulder into the beast.

"Erry!" he shouted.

Beras was so large he didn't fall back a single step, let alone fall; Leresy might as well shove a dragon. But his shove *was* enough to throw off the brute's aim. His axe swung down and missed Erry by an inch; it embedded itself into a corpse at her feet.

With a grunt, Beras turned toward Leresy.

The brute looked less like a man and more like a demon. The burnt half of his face twisted and leaked blood. Drool dripped between his teeth and down his chin. He towered, a foot taller than Leresy and twice as wide.

Leresy stumbled and raised his sword.

With a lurch, Beras tore his axe free from the corpse and swung it, knocking Leresy's blade aside. The man's hand--large and hairy as a paw--reached out and grabbed Leresy's throat.

Leresy sputtered. He tried to raise his sword, but Beras squeezed tighter, and the weapon fell from his hand. Stars spread across his vision.

"Well if it isn't the young princeling," Beras said. He grinned and licked his lips. "My my. Or is it princess? I never could tell with you. A pretty one, you are."

Leresy kicked. He scratched at the hand, but it was like scratching at stone. He couldn't breathe. He couldn't scream. He tried to look around for Erry, for Yorne, for the others, to plead for aid, but he could only see the burnt, drooling mask before him.

"I'm going to cut you slowly," Beras said. Blood dripped down his wound into his mouth. "I'm going to savor this, princess."

Stars floated and blackness spread.

Still clutching Leresy's throat with one hand, Beras drew his dagger and raised it.

"I'm going to start by slicing your pretty face," he said. "Then I'm going to--"

Beras howled.

His fingers opened.

Leresy gasped for breath, fell to his knees, and saw Erry behind the beast. She leaned against her sword, driving it deeper into Beras's unarmored leg.

With a thud that shook the alleyway, Beras fell to his knees and howled.

Erry. No. I can't lose you too, Erry, I can't.

Leresy grabbed his fallen sword, rose to his feet, and thrust the blade.

The steel crashed into Beras's neck and emerged bloody from the other side, missing Erry by an inch.

Leresy stood still, clutching the hilt, staring with wide eyes. His breath froze.

Blood spurted from Beras's mouth. His dagger clattered to the ground. He raised his hand, and for an instant Leresy thought he'd choke him again... and then he fell.

Beras the Brute, enforcer of Cadigus, the beastliest man Leresy had ever known, lay dead upon the ground.

I killed a man, Leresy thought, staring down at the corpse. *Stars, I killed a man.*

He had dreamed of this moment. For years, he had dreamed of making his first kill. In his fantasies, he'd always brag, walk into the Bad Cats with his victim's head, and be hailed a hero. Dawn and Dusk would welcome him with kisses, and later that day, his father would host a feast in his honor. Today Leresy doubled over and heaved; if he'd had any food in his belly, he'd have lost it.

Erry approached him, grumbling under her breath.

"Damn mule of a man," she said, staring down at the corpse. The bodies of the other legionaries lay around them, torn apart, bones rising from gore like shattered branches. The Lechers stood above the remains; Yorne was busy tugging his blade free from a breastplate it had cleaved.

Leresy took two great steps forward, climbed over the corpse, and pulled Erry into his embrace. He held her so tight he must have hurt her. Tears filled his eyes and he kissed her head, smearing his lips with mud.

"Thank the stars, Erry," he whispered.

Shrieks sounded above. Fire crackled.

"Dragons!" Yorne howled. "Into the tunnels!"

They ran. They raced back into the pottery shop. Outside, fire bathed the alley. They leaped into the hole in the floor.

They crawled in darkness, heading toward their next house.

They had been fighting for two nights and days, and Leresy hadn't slept and had barely eaten, but his body tingled with fire.

"I killed Beras the Brute," he whispered in darkness, knuckled his eyes, and snarled. "And I will kill you, Shari. And I will you, Father. I will kill every last one of you, I swear."

As they crawled, he could not stop his damn tears.

LANA

In the sunset, she saw the canyon ahead, and tears filled her good eye.

"Home," she whispered.

She beat her wings with more vigor. She glided over the forests, heading toward the chasm. The refugees of Lynport flew all around her, tens of thousands of dragons. When they saw the canyon, they wept in relief, blessed the stars, and blasted fire.

"Home," Lana repeated as she flew. "Safety."

She took a shuddering breath. Almost two decades ago, she had hidden from Cadigus for a year in this canyon. She had seen so many die around her from starvation, thirst, and disease. She herself had dwindled to only skin and bones and trembling fever.

"I lost my eye that year to his fang," she whispered. "I lost my three older brothers. Do I fly into another year of agony?" She looked behind her toward Lynport, but the city was too distant to see. "Fight well, Valien. Make this our shelter, not our tomb."

The dragons pulled their wings close and dived down, a great herd descending above the forest. The trees creaked below, the last of their autumn leaves tearing under the flap of wings. Lana sucked in the cold air, tightened her jaw, and dived into the canyon. Behind her, the refugees followed, a mass of scales and smoke and wings that blocked the sky.

The canyon walls rushed at her sides. Behind her, the myriads of dragons filled the canyon like a rushing river. She raced down this great stone corridor. The old pain pounded through her, and her missing eye blazed again, and her body shook with memory of fever. She flew.

The Castle-in-the-Cliff loomed ahead, its facade carved into the living rock of the canyon. Its limestone columns rose hundreds of feet tall. Its Stone Guardians, great statues with fists like carriages, flanked its doors.

"Home," she whispered. "Memory. Salvation."

The City of Cain delved deep into the cliff, a network of great halls, chambers, bridges, and corridors. Libraries lit with hundreds of lamps hid behind the stone. Staircases rose and fell, leading to kitchens, armories, nurseries, and barracks. All those Cain ruled lived here--the Vir Requis of the Canyon, the dwellers in stone.

We will barely squeeze Lynport into our halls, Lana thought. *They will sleep in our libraries, our armories, our corridors, and our pantries. They will hide under the stone.*

"They will survive," she whispered. "Fight well, Valien. Fight well, Rune. Defend your home. I will protect your people."

Her belly twisted with the old hunger, and her two eyes blazed, the one in her head, and the one that still screamed. One eye always seeing the present, the eye of a woman, a warrior, a leader. And one eye torn away, taken by Cadigus, the eye of a girl grown up too fast... always seeing old hunger and blood.

She landed outside the Castle-in-the-Cliff, her claws clattering against the canyon floor. She shifted into human form and gripped the hilt of her sword. She raised her eyes and stared at her home: the statues, the columns, and the wide stairs that led to a shadowy archway.

The dragons of Lynport landed around her and took human forms. Mothers clutched their children. Elders prayed to the stars, the forbidden gods of Requiem. They huddled close and gasped at the castle carved into the canyon's facade.

Lana climbed a dozen steps toward the palace doors, then turned to face the people. The Stone Guardians rose at her sides.

"I welcome you to the Castle-in-the-Cliff!" she called, her voice echoing across the canyon. With this welcome, the Stone Guardians would accept them. "Enter my home. Enter safety."

She turned, climbed the last steps, and walked through the archway.

The shadowy grand hall greeted her. Two lines of columns ran into the depths of the cliff. Braziers crackled between them, lighting a path toward her father's throne. Beyond the columns, darkness spread; Lana knew that it spread through many chambers and halls. Figures stood in those shadows, still and silent. Her father always boasted that his guards stood in darkness like vipers, ready to strike any who strayed from the path of light.

Lana turned around to face the gateway. The people of Lynport stood there, glancing into the darkness but daring not enter. They were humble townsfolk; most had never left Lynport before. They clutched their belongings: packs of clothes, bundles of firewood, pots and pans, and sacks of grain.

One eye of hope, one eye of pain. One eye saw frightened townsfolk. The other saw starving, haggard people at siege, dying upon the staircase as the Legions swarmed upon them.

"Enter my hall, people of Lynport!" she called. "Enter and find shelter, warmth, and food."

She beckoned to them. They hesitated, glancing around nervously, and Lana remembered that to outsiders, her home looked like a mausoleum to giants. Yet she kept calling to them, and they climbed the stairs. They entered the shadows.

Lana turned back toward the throne; it rose distant across the hall, so small she could hide it with her thumb. She walked across the mosaics, her boots clattering, and breathed deeply of the warm air. The shadows of soldiers fell between the columns, and the braziers crackled and tossed red light.

"Father!" she called out. "Father, I've returned."

When she drew closer, she frowned. Her father sat hunched over in his throne, wrapped in a great bear hide. A man stood beside him, clad in a red cloak lined with gold. A crimson hood hid his face. Lana gripped the hilt of her sword.

The colors of Cain were yellow and gray. The colors of the Resistance were silver and green. Who would wear red here, the color of Cadigus?

She kept walking forward. When she looked over her shoulder, she saw the townsfolk of Lynport follow, elders on canes, mothers holding babes, and children staring with wide eyes. Again her phantom eye saw them starving, naked, and begging for water. She blinked and returned her gaze ahead.

"Father!" she called.

She was close enough to see his face now. He looked up at her from under heavy eyebrows. His hair, red streaked with white, hung wildly around his leathery face. His shoulders stooped, and circles ringed his eyes.

"My daughter," he said, voice gravelly. "My daughter... He killed them. He killed your brothers." Devin Cain's fists trembled and his eyes watered. "He killed them all and he took your eye."

Lana paused. She sucked in her breath. She gripped her sword.

"That was almost twenty years ago," she whispered. "Father, we can save these people now. We can--"

Lord Cain rose to his feet. "No, daughter. I will not suffer another siege. I will not lose another child." He turned to the man robed in red. "Take your blood. Take it all and leave."

The man pulled back his crimson hood, turned toward Lana, and smiled thinly.

"Hello, Lady Lana," said emperor Frey. "It's a pleasure to meet you again." He grinned wildly and raised his voice to a shout. "Purification!"

From among the columns, the soldiers leaped. They were not men of Cain, robed in gray and wielding sabers. A thousand legionaries leaped into the hall, clad in black steel and bearing longswords, red spirals blazing upon their breastplates.

"Purification!" they cried.

The people of Lynport began to flee.

Shrieks echoed as Frey Cadigus shifted into a dragon, opened his maw, and blasted fire across the hall.

The flames roared. The people of Lynport fell and burned. Outside, the shrieks of more dragons rose, chanting for the red spiral and blasting their flames.

Lana screamed.

"Never again!" she cried. "Never again, Frey Cadigus! The Resistance will not fall."

She leaped from fire, shifted into a dragon, and flew toward him across the hall.

Crossbows thrummed. Bolts slammed into her. Before her, Frey--a golden dragon twice her size--laughed and blasted her with flame.

She fell. Her head tilted back. She stared upon carnage: people burning, people falling to the blade, people screaming as they died.

For the first time in almost twenty years, both her eyes saw the same world.

FREY

He flew back into Cadport with five hundred vermin in his claws.

His wrath spread behind him. His thousands of claws tightened, crushing the traitors. Their blood fell like drool. He laughed and blew fire from a forest of maws and lit the heavens that he ruled. He spread across the land, a beast with two hundred thousand wings, a hive of scale and steel and everywhere the red spiral that snaked through his mind.

"We have your pets, Relesar!" he shrieked from his golden head, letting the cry roll across the city of ruin and death.

Behind him, his lesser heads howled with laughter, this sea of might, this writhing cloud that cloaked the city, and Frey laughed and blasted flame and his claws dug into flesh.

It burned inside him, twisting, always aflame, always bleeding.

Hail the red spiral!

It coiled around his spines, pulsing with his blood, a parasite sucking on his marrow and organs and essence.

Hail the worm!

"Relesar!" his jaws cried. "Relesar, emerge from your hiding, or they will die."

He cackled, staring at the fortress that rose upon the hill. The boy still hid there, cowering. The fallen knight still lurked there, broken and trembling. His daughter still huddled behind those bricks, spreading her legs for the men he would kill.

"Relesar!" he howled.

Behind him, the many heads of the beast roared flame and chanted his cry.

"Relesar! Relesar!"

"Purification!" the golden head cried.

"Purification!" the minions answered.

Frey howled, spraying drool and flame. "Hail the red spiral!"

His heads answered the cry, and Frey cackled. He remembered a day long ago when he was just one body. He remembered a thin, pale youth, the son of a logger. He remembered walking through the forests at night, desperate for firewood, desperate to appease the father who'd beat him.

The boy hated the darkness. He boy hated the woods and the shadows that lurked there. Things crawled in the dark, insects and rodents and worms that broke under his bare feet. How they stained his feet! How the crushed, coiled things bled upon his soles, red spirals that stained him, that he could never wash off, that tainted him anew every night.

The curse of the woods. The worms left it on him. A curse he could never shake, that invaded through his feet into his bones, into his heart, into his skull, that wrapped around his spine and drove him to greatness.

It made him strong.

"Hail the red spiral!" he cried.

Now he was many. Now he was Legions. Now he no longer feared monsters, for he himself was a beast, a hive of flame and steel and worship and purity.

He flew down above the roofs of the seaside city. The ragged men all hid in their tunnels, fearing his might. The cannons had fallen silent. The boy still had not emerged.

"I will slay one of your precious vermin every minute until you face me!" Frey shouted and laughed. "I snatched them from your canyon, boy. I killed most but not all. I will kill the rest here until you emerge."

In his lead claws, the claws of the emperor, he held two of the townsfolk, a brother and sister. He clutched them so tightly they could not shift into dragons, only writhe as frail humans. He flew with them near the tower upon the hill. They no longer shot arrows. They no longer fired guns.

Frey grinned.

"You fear to slay the people I hold!" he shouted. "You fools. You should slay me on sight. Now they shall die!"

Frey tossed the brother and sister from his claws. They tumbled through the sky, bleeding and nearly dead. Before they could shift into dragons, Frey blasted them with flames.

They screamed.

They died.

They fell and crashed, burning, onto the roofs below.

Now howls rose from the tower. Now arrows whistled and cannons blasted. Frey laughed and flew backward, dodging the fire.

"Emerge and fight me, Relesar!" he shrieked. "Emerge or I will kill two more. Face me in battle, coward, or they all shall die!"

The beast laughed with a hundred thousand jaws, and its wings and scales spread into the distance. The city below lay in shadow and desolation.

Frey smiled.

"It is pure."

TILLA

He was killing them.

Oh stars, he was killing them.

Tilla wanted to howl. She wanted to weep. She wanted to blow fire against the emperor. She wanted to fly between cannonballs and arrows, to capture Rune or die upon the roofs of their city.

He was killing them. Oh stars, he was killing them all.

Flying a hundred yards away from the emperor, Tilla stared, barely able to breathe, not even able to cry. Among the five hundred prisoners, she saw her own father. The old ropemaker was bleeding, his face pale, struggling in the grip of a drooling dragon.

He will kill him. Tilla panted. *My emperor will kill my father.*

"Relesar!" the emperor cried, laughing in the sky. His great wings beat. Flame wreathed him. He grabbed two more townsfolk from the claws of his minions, gripped the bodies so tight their ribs snapped, and raised them.

"Relesar!" Frey called. "I will slay two more. Emerge and fight me, or all will die."

Tilla knew those two in Frey's claws, an old man and a woman. She had grown up with them. She had bought pottery from their shop. They had looked after her when she'd been a girl, she remembered. They had always been so kind. She could not let them die.

She whipped her head around and stared at Castellum Acta. The fort rose upon the hill. Cannons lined its battlements and windows. Archers stood firing from its arrowslits. Behind iron, steel, and stone, Rune hid.

And they were dying.

Tilla knew the price of disobedience. Soldiers were to fly in silence, to laugh only when the emperor laughed, to cheer only when he cheered. They were nothing but reflections of his glory.

Yet today Tilla had to risk her life. She had to save what she still could of Cadport, her home which lay in ruins below.

"Rune!" she called out. "Rune, please! Come out to us. He will kill them!"

More arrows flew from the fort. More cannons fired, tearing into imperial dragons who flew too close.

Yet he did not emerge.

"Hear them scream, Relesar!" Frey cried, laughed, and tightened his claws.

The two potters tore apart.

They fell to the city below, lacerated, and crashed into the rooftops.

"No..." Tilla whispered, and tears budded in her eyes.

I can't do this, she thought and panted. *I can't fly here anymore. I can't take part in this massacre. I can't let my father die.*

She looked at Frey; he was grabbing two more prisoners in his claws. She looked down at her hometown which lay in ruin, bodies and blood and debris everywhere.

"How can I fight for this?" she whispered, her voice too soft in the battle for any to hear. "How can I serve this Regime that crushes my home?"

Tilla raged.

She raged against the Regime.

She raged against the emperor.

She wanted to fly at Frey, to burn him, to slay the beast and tear out his heart.

I served you, Frey, she thought, and fire crackled in her maw. *I served the glory of the red spiral, and now you crush my home. Now you kill all those I've ever known.*

She looked at the fortress where the last resistors hid, bloodied and dying. She looked down at the city where thousands lay rotting.

She lowered her head.

There was no fighting the Cadigus family, she knew. Even with thousands of warriors, the Resistance only crashed against the might of the Legions and died. And the city died. And all its refugees died.

"You cannot fight him, Rune," Tilla whispered. "He is too great. You can only serve the red spiral. To fight him brings death to us all." She raised her voice to a howl. "Rune, please! Emerge! I will protect you, I promise."

Yet still he hid, and Tilla roared, wept, and raged.

Why would he not come to her?

Did he not care that Frey was butchering his people?

Tilla trembled, her wings roiling smoke and fire around her.

I serve Requiem, she thought. *I serve life. I serve my city.*

"And you're letting it fall, Rune. Your rebellion killed them all." Again she cried out. "Rune!"

The Legions howled and jeered around her. The emperor cackled and grabbed two more prisoners, mere children.

"Relesar, two more!" the emperor cried.

Two more bodies fell.

Two more lights went dim.

Tilla wept and roared her fire and called his name, but he would not come.

RUNE

"Let me go," he said, eyes burning, and tried to wrench himself free. His throat tightened. His legs shook. He twisted and tugged, but Valien would not release him.

"You cannot," said the older man. His teeth were bared. His eyes blazed. He clutched Rune's arms, holding him back. "Rune! Do not give him what he wants."

Yet Rune kept struggling. He kept staring through the hall's arrowslits. The scaly mass covered the sky outside. Frey Cadigus cackled, claws still stained with blood and bits of flesh. Behind the emperor, his dragons held hundreds of other townsfolk.

"They're going to die, Valien!" Rune called, struggling madly. He wanted to break free, to rush up the tower, to leap from the battlements and shift into a dragon, to fly at Frey and slay the man with all his fire and rage.

"If you fly out there, *you* will die," Valien said, refusing to release Rune; the man's grip was iron. "Rune. Look at me. Listen to me."

Rune spun away from the arrowslit. His eyes were damp and burning, but he stared at Valien. The leader of the Resistance stared back, eyes hard as his grasping fingers. Behind him, the other resistors stood gazing at Rune too. Their eyes were haunted. Their faces were somber. Even Kaelyn stared silently, her eyes large and cold like frozen dreams of winter.

"They will all die," Rune whispered.

Valien would not release him. "Rune, if you fly out, he will kill you." Valien ground his teeth. "But not at once, Rune. He will take you alive to the capital. He will torture you. He will display your mangled body to the masses and have you wail for their amusement. Years down the line, when your mind is broken like your body, then, Rune... then he will finally give you the mercy of death. If you fly out to meet Frey now, that is your fate."

Rune swallowed and trembled. Sweat drenched him. He panted, barely able to suck breath down his throat.

"I cannot simply let them die," he whispered. "Valien... stars. He has hundreds out there. Did he already kill the others?"

He did not want to weep. Yet his voice cracked, and a lump filled his throat, and he could barely see through his burning eyes.

Tilla, he thought. *Stars, do you fly there too? How can you serve him? Tilla, what do we do?*

Valien's eyes softened just the slightest. His grip loosened by just a thread.

"I don't know," he said, his voice raspier than ever. "He might have killed them all, yes. If he met the people of Lynport on their way to the canyon, he might have slain all those he didn't bring here to torture. Rune--do not let their deaths be in vain."

Rune peered back outside. Frey grabbed two more prisoners in his claws. He rose higher, disappearing from the arrowslit's range of view, but his voice still rolled across the city.

"I have two more, Relesar!" the emperor shrieked, his voice demonic, the sound of storm and lightning. "Emerge to fight me, or they too will perish."

Rune looked back at Valien and the others.

"I can't let them die," he whispered. He turned to face Kaelyn; she stared back with haunted eyes. "Kaelyn, tell him. Tell him we can't let them die."

She stepped closer, her lips trembled, and she touched Rune's arm. A tear streamed down her cheek.

"They must die," she whispered.

Behind Rune, two screams pierced the sky.

Kaelyn lowered her head and her tears fell. Rune started, gasped, and tried to turn around, but Valien still held his arms, refusing to release him.

"Come, Rune," the man said. "Into the tunnel. You do not need to hear this. It's time to leave."

Outside the tower, the emperor's voice roared across the sky.

"Two more dead, Relesar! Hundreds more remain. Emerge from your hole, coward!"

Rune shook. He let Valien guide him away from the arrowslit. They walked toward the narrow staircase that plunged into the hill. The stairs led to a tunnel, Rune knew. The tunnel led to the sea.

"Rune," Kaelyn said softly, holding his arm, "you must do this for their memory. The people of Lynport will die. But if you are captured, all hope is lost. Millions across Requiem will suffer." Her tears fell. "For those millions, you must live."

Rune let them walk him across the hall.

So here is how it ends, he thought, eyes stinging. *Lynport is fallen; all we tried to save here will die. And we will flee. And we will fight on. To dream of another battle, I must let all my memories, all my soul, all my past perish.*

Yet how could he fight again with such pain inside him?

Rune looked up at Valien, looked at this broken man with hard eyes, with old pain, with creases of endless nightmares across his face.

This is what I would become, Rune realized. A broken man. He would grow old in hiding. He would grow old in pain, the past always clutching, always pulling him deeper into darkness.

No. He could not do this.

Valien held his arm, guiding him forward, and for the first time since Rune had met him--for the first time in a year of blood, fire, and death--Valien's eyes dampened, and his voice tore with pain.

"We will not forget them, Rune," he said. "We will enter this tunnel. We will crawl through darkness to the sea. We will swim. We will flee this battle." His voice shook and his jaw twisted. "We will fight another day."

They walked toward the tunnel.

Valien looked around the hall at the resistors who gathered, several hundred in all.

"We've been fighting for seven nights and seven days," he said, looking at his men. "We've killed thousands of the enemy. We've shown that we could bleed them." He raised his hand, two fingers pressed together. "The Resistance will live on! Relesar Aeternum will reign. Today we flee into the sea. Today we lose a battle. Tomorrow we will rally, and we will grow in strength, and we will give the Regime no rest. Into the sea! Into darkness and water. Requiem! May our wings forever find your sky."

The men returned the salute. They chanted the prayer together. They began to enter the darkness.

Into the sea, Rune thought, watching them leave. *Into hiding. Into war and pain and endless memory.*

More men stepped down the staircase, one by one, their eyes hard and their faces ashy, warriors of Requiem. Rune watched them leave.

Valien released his grip on Rune and placed a hand on his shoulder.

"It's time," the gruff man said.

Kaelyn held his hand. "We will still fight together, Rune," she whispered. "I promise you. Always. I will always fly by your side."

Rune stared at the men stepping into the darkness. He could imagine them crawling underground, emerging into the sea, swimming through darkness, leaving this ruin behind, and rallying in some distant land for another battle in another town.

"They will fight on," Rune whispered. "And they will still have courage in their hearts." He looked at Valien and Kaelyn, his guiding stars, two people he had followed through fire and blood, two people he loved. "But my heart will not mend after this day. My heart is forever in Lynport. This is my home, and here I must fall." His voice tore and his eyes swam. "Goodbye."

He broke free.

Before they could grab him again, Rune ran.

"Rune!" Kaelyn shouted behind him, voice torn.

He did not turn back. He raced across the hall. He leaped onto the tower staircase.

"Rune, do not do this!" Valien roared behind. "Rune, listen to me!"

But he would not listen.

I can't, he thought, eyes burning. *I can't let them die. If torture and death await me, so be it. I cannot let the last of my townsfolk perish here.*

He ran up the tower stairs.

"Rune!" Kaelyn cried; he heard her running upstairs a few steps behind. "Rune, please!"

"Go to the sea, Kaelyn!" he said. "Go with Valien. Fight on. Fight for my memory. Go!"

He ran.

He reached the tower top.

He raced between guards, crashed through a trapdoor, and emerged onto the battlements. He shifted into a dragon.

The sky writhed, a canopy of scales and flames and claws. The Legions stormed above him in a whirlpool, wings roiling smoke and fire and drool. Rune soared toward them, a single black dragon entering the storm. The emperor himself cackled above, the epicenter of terror, a shard of gold like a cruel sun, death and blood in his claws.

"I fly to you, Frey!" Rune cried. "I fly to you. Release them. Let them live."

Below him upon the tower, Kaelyn's voice rose, torn and pleading.

"Rune!"

He looked back at her. Kaelyn stood upon the tower, still in human form, reaching up to him, pleading, tears on her cheeks. The wind from countless wings billowed her hair. Tears filled her eyes. Ash and soot coated her cheeks.

"Rune," she said, lips trembling. "Please. I love you. Please."

The Legions cackled and roared above. Claws reached down to lash Rune. Pain drove through him. The swarm engulfed him.

"Goodbye, Kaelyn," he whispered as the beasts tightened around him, a great serpent of the skies, hiding all from view.

Scales and flame rolled across him.

He saw nothing else.

Goodbye.

Flapping his wings within the storm, caught in the whirlpool of fangs and steel and fire, he looked above him, seeking the emperor, seeking the man who'd destroyed his town, his soul, his life.

Yet when he looked above, the golden dragon was gone.

A white dragon hovered there, her scales glimmering, her eyes soft with tears.

Rune breathed shakily.

"Tilla," he whispered.

Her tears fell. She glided down toward him, a moonlit angel of celestial halls, and her claws shook.

"Rune," she said. "Rune."

And he was flying with her again, side by side over the sea at night. They danced around the moon. They stood upon the beach, held each other, and shared a kiss of farewell.

"Rune," she had said to him that day, a barefooted youth with seashells around her neck. "Fly with me. One last flight."

They had flown together then, two youths entering a war too big for them, leaving their home and flying into a battle they could not win.

They flew together now too, gliding in darkness and fire.

Tilla. Pillar of my memory. Anchor of my soul.

She reached out toward him, the Legions at her back, a hundred thousand demons cackling and howling for his death.

"Tilla," he whispered again, too tired to fight, too torn to shout.

Her claws wrapped around his shoulders, and her tears fell upon him.

"It's over now," she whispered. "We're together again."

The emperor laughed in the distance, and the Legions tightened around Rune. Claws cut him. Tails lashed him. His blood spilled. His breath died.

His magic left him.

He floated among the Legions in human form, cut and bleeding, Tilla's claws wrapped around him. The last things he saw was her eyes, dark and whispering of home.

KAELYN

She stood among the ruins, staring north across the sea.

The wind caressed her hair like his fingers had that night long ago, hiding in different ruins so far away. That had been in the cold north, in Requiem, in the land they had fought and killed and bled and cried for. That had been home.

That land had fallen.

"Relesar Aeternum," she whispered into the waves that rolled below the hill, and her voice shook. "Rune."

This southern island was small, smaller than the town she had fled. Standing here upon the hilltop, she could see the shore encircling her, forming a sanctuary in the Tiran Sea. The hillsides rolled below her, thick with boulders and cedars and pines. Where hills ended, wild grass and mint bushes faded into golden sand and azure, glimmering waves.

Where Kaelyn stood, high upon the island's peak, old ruins rose. An orphaned archway stretched above her, green with creeping ivy. The wall that had once held it lay fallen; grass and weeds overgrew its bricks. An ancient stairway plunged down the hillside, most of its steps now buried under dirt and grass. Three columns stood below upon the beach, the remnants of some old port or temple. A dozen more columns lay fallen among palm trees and brambles. Gulls, cranes, and small birds she could not name flew above.

"You would have liked it here, Rune," she whispered to the trees, the wind, and the sea that spread deep blue into the horizon. "You would have stood here with me, hand in hand, and told me about the old ships that would sail here, and you would name the birds that fly."

It was an island too small for maps. An island too small for the Legions to find.

An island you will never know. Tears filled her eyes and her throat tightened. *I miss you Rune.*

"Kaelyn."

The voice rose behind her, raspy like wind over gravel. She turned to see Valien.

He wore his old furs and wool, but his armor was gone. His hair hung around his face, streaked with more white than she'd ever seen in it. His face had always seemed so hard to Kaelyn, a face like tough leather, like a craggy cliff, a face with the strength of ancient stone. His eyes had always seemed so wise, eyes that hid all the secrets in the world, eyes she would follow into the Abyss itself.

Yet now... now she saw the sadness in him. Now the sunlight fell upon that face she loved. Now those eyes gazed north across the sea, and she saw the pain of her heart reflected in them.

He misses him too. And he misses her. His Marilion.

Kaelyn stepped toward him. She took his hands--great, calloused paws twice the size of her small, white palms. He towered over her, and she looked up at him, a deer before a bear.

He lost her, but he has me. He has me always.

Valien embraced her, and she laid her head upon his scarred chest, and she felt warm, and though fear trickled through her, there was still some safety here in his arms. He stroked her hair.

"Will we ever see him again?" she whispered.

Valien held her close. He was silent for a long time.

"I don't know," he finally said, voice soft. "But we will not abandon him to torture and death. And we will not abandon Requiem." He held her cheek and looked into her eyes. "I don't know what strength I still have, Kaelyn. I don't know what battles I can still win. But so long as breath rattles through me, and so long as my sword can swing, I will fight. I will fight for our home... and for him. For Relesar Aeternum."

She shook her head. "Don't fight for a king. Fight for Rune."

They turned back toward the north. They stood under the stone archway. Ivy dangled around them and mottles of sunlight danced like fairies. The wind from the sea played with their hair and filled their nostrils, scented of water, salt, and cedar. The waves whispered below across the sand and ruins.

"Lynport too now lies in ruins upon a beach," Kaelyn whispered. "I will not forget you, Requiem. I will not forget you, Rune."

They stood for a long time, silent, watching the sea.

476

LERESY

They lay on the beach at night, watching the moon and stars. The waves whispered, the trees rustled, and the sea glistened in the moonlight, but Leresy could not see this beauty.

He saw men torn apart with gunpowder, screaming in the dirt, their severed limbs littering the street.

He saw Beras clutching his throat and raising his dagger.

He saw his father flying above, tearing bodies apart, cackling like he would years ago when beating Leresy and his twin.

He closed his eyes.

How can you forget? he thought. *How can you forget old pain? When night falls and all sound and light of the day fade, how do you stop the memories from rising?*

Food had lost its flavor. The world had lost its beauty. This was all the remained to him now. Memories. Visions of blood. A chill in his belly he could not shake.

"Ler?"

She lay beside him in the sand, her dog curled up and sleeping on her feet. Leresy turned his head and looked at her.

"Erry," he whispered, and his eyes watered.

Erry Docker.

She lay naked in the sand, her slim body caked with the stuff. He had once mocked her skinny limbs and boyish frame, her short hair that always lay tangled across her brow, and her lowborn blood. Today Leresy could not see the light of stars, nor hear the music of the waves, yet Erry was beautiful to him. She was a precious doll. She was his to protect, to cherish. She was the only thing good he had left.

No, he thought. *The only thing good I ever had.*

He placed a hand on her waist and stroked her. He leaned forward in the sand and kissed her lips.

"I'm sorry, Erry," he whispered.

He expected her to snort, to laugh, or to launch into some creative string of cusses. This was Erry Docker, after all; she was a snort and a curse wrapped in skin. Yet her eyes only softened, and she touched his cheek.

"For what?" she said.

It was he who ended up snorting, though it sounded almost like a sob.

"Do you need to ask?" he said. "Do I really need to list everything?"

This made her grin, her huge grin that showed so many teeth. She stuck her tongue out and poked him in the ribs.

"Not forgiven," she said. "Damn it, Leresy, you are a bloody piece of work, you are." She sighed. "I don't know why I lie here with you."

"Because I'm devilishly handsome?" he suggested and blinked to clear his eyes. "Because I saved your life? Because I'm your knight in shining armor?"

She sighed. She rolled onto her back and looked up at the night sky. Her dog stirred and fell back into sleep.

"You're not," she said softly, and her eyes grew somber. "You're not, Leresy. You're not heroic. You're not noble. You're not a knight." She looked at him. "You're a damn bastard, but... so am I. And we have each other. And we're learning. And we're getting a little better. That counts for something, doesn't it?"

He nodded, throat tight. He could speak no louder than a whisper, not without chancing his voice cracking.

"It counts for a lot."

She lay still for a moment, watching the stars, then propped herself up on her elbows. She placed a hand on his chest, leaned over him, and dusted sand from his hair.

"Valien and the others want to keep fighting," she said. "They counted over a thousand surviving resistors on this island. They think more might have fled into the forests of Requiem." She bit her lip. "They will go back, and they will find new allies, and they will fight on. What do we do, Ler? Do we join them?"

He touched her cheek, marveling at how her features were so soft and small; she seemed made of porcelain.

"I gave Valien the rest of the Lechers," he said. "Three hundred battle-hardened brutes. That's my gift to his Resistance. May they fight well. The bloody lot stank anyway; I couldn't stand the stench." He sighed and looked up past Erry at the stars. The

Draco constellation shone, the old gods. "But I won't join him. You're right, Erry. I'm not a hero. I'm not a knight or a warrior at all." His throat tightened. "I thought I was. When I ruled Castra Luna, I thought I was a great fighter, but... I was a boy. A foolish boy."

She nodded. "A very foolish one. I remember."

It was his turn to stick his tongue out. "You fancied me even then. I knew it." He smiled weakly. "You were bad at hiding it. So what will you do, Erry Docker of Lynport? Will you fly off with the warriors and fight and maybe die another day? Or will you stay here with me?"

She raised her eyebrows, still playing with his hair. "With you and what--sand?"

"Sand," he said. "Palm trees heavy with dates and pines heavy with nuts. Mint bushes for tea. A spring of fresh water. All the fish that we can catch." He grinned. "I'd rather like seeing you wear a skirt of leaves and clam shells on your breasts, a wild islander."

"I should think," she said and straddled him, "that you should prefer me like this--naked as the day I was born."

He chewed his lip and looked up at her, examining her body in the moonlight. "You are damn right."

He made love to her, the sand beneath them, the stars of his fathers above. So many times he had taken her to his bed, had used her, had clung to her to forget his pain. Yet now he made love to her, and now he loved her, and for a moment under the stars, Erry Docker in his arms, Leresy Cadigus could forget. He could no longer see the memories.

They will always be with me, he thought, holding Erry as she slept against his chest. *But so will Erry. So will this woman that I love. And that's not too bad.*

He closed his eyes, kissed her cheek, and slept.

RUNE

They flew in darkness for a long time.

She held him in her claws like a mother bird clutching her young. Sometimes he heard her say his name. Sometimes he felt the rain and the wind, and sometimes he could see her, a white dragon under the sky. Sometimes he thought he could hear the sea below.

He dreamed.

He had lost so much blood. The chains bound him so tightly. A sack covered his head, leaving him always in night, always in sleep and memory and nightmares. They flew. They flew in darkness. They flew for a long time.

"Rune," she said softly. "Rune, I'm here."

It was her voice. Tilla. She stood before him on the beach, and he embraced her, and they kissed. The waves raced over the sand and wet their feet, and she scurried away like always, and he laughed.

The sky cackled and creaked and clattered. Heat blasted him and he heard dragonfire storm all around. He floated through the sea at home. He floated through a sea of dragons in the sky. But she was here. His love. His Tilla.

"Rune," she whispered, her claws gentle around him. "We're almost home."

He tried to open his eyes. He saw nothing but the sack. He tried to call to her, but his throat was too parched, and he was too weak. So many wounds. So much blood lost.

They flew.

They flew in darkness for a long time.

After dreamscapes and eras of memory, trumpets sounded ahead.

"Silver trumpets will call you home," a knight had said in eras long forgotten.

And now they called. And Rune knew them. He saw only darkness, but he heard their song. They were calling him to his new home. To Nova Vita. To the capital of Requiem.

To the place where they would break him.

"Rune," she whispered. "Do not be afraid. I'll be with you."

Rain pattered him. Clouds grumbled above. And the dragons roared. Thousands of throats bellowed their rage. Dragonfire crackled and heat blasted Rune. Air from countless wings pummeled him, and the emperor howled ahead, a shriek like wind through canyons.

"We have captured the heir! Relesar Aeternum is ours!" The emperor's voice rose like steam from a kettle, a voice of demons. "Purification! The Resistance is fallen. Requiem is pure!"

And they cheered.

Rune heard them cheer below.

A million people lived in the capital, they said. Rune could not see them. He could see nothing but the sack around his head and blurs of red where firelight flared. But he heard them. He heard the million. And they howled for his death.

"Hail the red spiral!" the emperor shrieked, and they answered. The cry rolled across the Legions. It rolled across the city below. It tore through Rune and it tore through the kingdom he loved.

"Hail the red spiral! Purification!"

The rain fell, and Tilla's claws tightened around him, but her grip did not hurt.

She did not mean to hurt him.

She was protecting him.

"Rune," she whispered. "You will worship him. You will join us. And the pain will end."

The roaring swelled like an ocean below.

Wind shrieked and his ears popped as they descended.

He did not know where they landed. They left the sack over his head. They left the chains wrapped around him, binding his arms to his sides.

And they shouted.

And they shoved him.

Rough hands grabbed and tugged him. Something sharp jabbed his side. Something hard--perhaps a steel-tipped boot--drove into his spine, and he fell to his knees and cried.

"Move him forward!" rumbled a deep voice.

"Get him into the darkness!"

Tilla's voice rose too. "Leave him! He is mine. He is my catch. He is mine to break!"

Steel hissed--blades being drawn from sheaths. Swords clashed. Hands grabbed him and tugged him to his feet.

"You will have your chance, Siren," spoke another voice, and Rune recognized it; it was Princess Shari speaking. "He tore off my wing. He will be yours, but first I will have vengeance."

Boots kicked him. He fell again. Fists landed upon him. Something heavy clashed against his head, and his cheek hit the ground, and laughter rose, and voices screamed. He screamed too. He screamed louder than them all.

He fell into darkness.

He floated on the sea.

He flew under the stars with her at his side.

They stood again on the beach, and he embraced her, and she kissed him, and her fingers touched his hair.

"Rune," she whispered. "Rune, I'm here."

Her lips were soft. Her hands caressed his cheek. The waves rolled around them, the stars shone above, and the cliffs of Ralora rose behind them. He was home.

"Rune," she whispered again. "Rune, they're gone. Open your eyes. Look at me."

I can see you, he thought. *We stand on the beach again. Your face is pale like moonlight, and your black hair is waving in the wind, and you are mine. You are the woman I love.*

"Rune... Stars, Rune, can you hear me?"

He opened his eyes.

And he saw her.

Dream melted into pain.

She knelt above him, no longer the pale youth he'd known, but a woman with haunted eyes, her face smeared with ash, her cheek scarred with war. Brick walls topped with battlements rose behind her.

"Tilla?" he whispered.

He could not rise. He could barely keep his eyes open. They had broken his body. They had shed too much blood. She squeezed his hand, but he could not squeeze back.

"Rune," she whispered, and a trembling smile found her lips, and her tears fell upon his face. They stung.

She was here. This was real. She was with him again, and he wept.

"It's over now." She kissed his lips. "You saved our people. It's over. They will no longer hurt you. You only have to do what we say. You only have to join us, to hail the red spiral, to serve the emperor." Her tears ran along her lips. "And we'll be together again."

"I..."

I can't do that, Tilla, he wanted to say. *I can't. Let me die. Let me die here in your arms.*

But his throat felt too tight.

"Come, Rune, you must stand now," she said. She placed her arms around him and tugged. "We have to go. Quick, before they return."

He rose to shaky feet and leaned against her. Chains still wrapped around him, slick with blood. He wore nothing but rags beneath. Tilla stood clad in fine armor, holding him up.

"You'll be with me now, Rune," she said. "You'll be safe if you obey."

They limped across a courtyard. All around them, the brick walls rose in the night, topped with battlements. Clouds hid the stars. They stood in the courtyard, alone.

"Tilla," he whispered hoarsely. "Tilla, fly. Take me in your claws and we'll fly from here."

She helped him walk, her arms around him.

"There is no fleeing him," she said. "There is no fighting him. You must join us. That is all you can do. You must serve him like I do."

He looked ahead. A barred door stood open in a wall, leading to a cell. Inside he saw a pile of straw, a hole in the floor, and chains dangling from the ceiling. Old blood encrusted the walls.

"Tilla," he said, nearly too parched to speak, "what is this place?"

"You won't have to stay here long," she whispered, guiding him toward the cell. "Only until he thinks you're broken. Only until he hears you worship him. Rune... it doesn't have to hurt. Your pain can end."

The courtyard swam around him. He would have fallen were Tilla not holding him. He tried to break free from her, but he was too weak. He tried to shift into a dragon, but couldn't muster the magic.

"Tilla," he whispered, and his voice cracked, and his eyes stung. "Please. They're gone now. The legionaries. The dragons. The emperor. They're gone. Shift into a dragon, Tilla! Shift and hold me in your claws and fly from here."

She shook her head, and her tears fell, and she kept moving forward, pulling him with her.

"I cannot," she whispered.

"We can escape," he said, looking above. The sky cleared. He could see the stars. "I can fly myself, maybe. Let's fly from here. Let's fly home."

They reached the cell. She paused. She released him, and he stood on shaky feet before her, the world spinning.

"Rune," she whispered, and she was beautiful in the starlight, a statue of marble. "Do you remember that night on the beach? Our last night?"

He nodded, a lump in his throat. "I never forgot."

She embraced him. She touched his cheek, and she kissed him. They shared a long, deep kiss, a kiss like that last night, a kiss of goodbye. It tasted of tears and of memory.

She pulled back, and her lips shook.

"That was our home," she whispered. "But it's gone now. The city burned. There is nowhere left to fly to." She gripped his arms. "Rune... you *are* home."

She shoved him into the cell.

He fell to the floor, landing on old blood.

"Tilla!" he shouted. "Tilla!"

He rose to his feet and stumbled toward her.

She gave him a last look, her eyes large and haunted, eyes that reflected the sea, the stars, and the city that was no more.

She slammed the door shut, leaving him alone in darkness, hurt and cold and mourning the burning of his home... and the breaking of her soul.

BOOK THREE:

A MEMORY OF FIRE

KAELYN

Kaelyn was scouting the islet when fire blazed, rocks flew, and she met the crazy old man who changed her life.

Many islands dotted this sea, rising in a ridge like the spine of some sunken, ancient sea god. This islet rose leagues away from the others, barely larger than a rock. When Kaelyn first saw it from above, she was going to keep flying. Valien had sent her to find new bases for their Resistance, and this place looked too small to even host a single fighter. A carob tree crested its peak, and two palm trees swayed across its shore. The cay seemed no larger than Kaelyn's old bedroom back at the capital.

A green dragon on the wind, Kaelyn was gliding directly above the islet, heading farther south, when the explosion rocked the sea.

The sound roared in her ears, loud as cannon fire. The shock wave tossed her into a spin and cracked two scales. Before she could right herself, a cloud of dust burst from below, enveloping her. Rocks pummeled her stomach and she yelped. The skin on her belly was thick, but those rocks jabbed her like arrows.

A volcano? she wondered. No. The smell of gunpowder flared here. After fighting the Regime for three years, Kaelyn would recognize that smell anywhere.

Blinded, she beat her wings mightily, churning the dust and ash. She rose higher, grimacing. Fire blazed below and smoke twisted around her like demons. She flew, not even knowing what direction she headed, until she emerged back into blue sky.

"What in the Abyss?" she said, coughing, and looked behind her.

Dust still plumed from the islet, trailing north with the wind like a rising serpent. Kaelyn hovered in place, whipping her head from side to side. Was somebody attacking her? Did imperial ships sail here armed with cannons? Had her father found her?

That was when she heard laughter and saw the old loon.

He burst out from the smoke below, racing across the islet. He wore only a loincloth, and his long, white hair hung wild about his sooty face. He ran down the islet's slope, laughing, and danced a jig.

"Fire!" He jumped and snapped his ankles together. "Explosion! *Boom!*"

Kaelyn squinted, hovering above. The man seemed unharmed, if blackened with soot. This was no enemy. This was... who was he? Kaelyn dived a hundred yards lower, heading down to the islet.

When the old man saw her, he waved enthusiastically, his whole body swaying with the gesture, and grinned.

"Hello, pretty green bird!" he said. "Caw! *Caw!* Are you a bird or a dragon? Bantis kills dragons. Bantis booms them away. Go, dragon, go!"

Kaelyn kept diving. She circled above the islet, taking a closer look. The man was still dancing, waving his arms, and cackling. His left arm ended at the elbow, she noticed. He wore a prosthetic topped with a blade.

Kaelyn gasped.

"An exiled axehand?" she whispered. She squinted, bringing him into clearer focus.

No, she decided. The Axehand Order, a fanatical priesthood whose warriors wore axes upon their stumps, had been founded fifteen years ago. The elder below, even back then, would have been too old to join.

She filled her wings with air, descended, and landed upon the shore. The old man cawed before her, waving his arms and kicking sand as if trying to scare her off. Kaelyn released her magic, returning to human form.

"Caw!" the old man said, standing on one scrawny leg and flapping his arms like wings. "Go, dragon! Leave. No dragons allowed on Genesis Isle."

Kaelyn stared at him, head tilted. The air still smelled of gunpowder and smoke, though the dust was settling, revealing a hole upon the islet's hillside. When Kaelyn looked back at the old man, she saw that he wasn't wearing an axe upon his stump after all--it was a hammer. Several other prosthetic arms hung from his belt; one ended with a shovel, another with a knife, and a third with a hook.

"Are you hurt?" Kaelyn asked him.

The man stopped jumping and waving his arms. He hunched forward, tilted his head too, and squinted at her. He was rail-thin; Kaelyn could see his ribs pushing against his sooty skin.

"Is Bantis hurt?" he asked, voice high and quavering like a taut lute string. "No. Well, yes. Some hurts run deep. Some hurts are... inside. My heart." He slammed his prosthetic hammer-hand against his chest, then yelped. "Hurts! Heart hurts! Wait. No. That's just my hammer. Wrong hand."

He danced another jig, pulled off his hammer prosthetic, and tossed it aside. He grabbed a different prosthetic from his belt--this one shaped as a shovel--and attached it to his stump.

"Better," he said and grinned. "See? Right hand. Bantis is a digger. Bantis digs! Bantis digs for a big, big weapon. Kills dragons! Come, come, Bantis show you."

With that, he spun around, darted across the sand, and began to climb the island's hillside.

Kaelyn followed, waving aside the last plumes of dust. Despite his scrawny frame and advanced years, Bantis scuttled up the hill like a spider, scampering over boulders and bushes. Even Kaelyn, slim and young and light on her feet, struggled to keep up. Soot darkened her long yellow hair, and her bow and quiver swung across her back.

As she climbed and the dust cleared, she saw many strange items strewn across the hillside. Some she recognized: barrels of gunpowder, a cannon, and tinderboxes. Other items were foreign to her: iron spheres that looked like cannonballs but were topped with fuses; shafts of wood topped with metal pipes, possibly miniature cannons; and larger pipes--these ones made of leather and wood--with glass circles filling each end.

"Did you invent these things?" Kaelyn said, treading carefully between them, unsure if they'd explode under her feet.

The old man hopped ahead. "Invent them? Yes, yes. Bantis is the inventor. Bantis deals with booms. But now Bantis digs for greatest weapon. Here, come!" He leaped onto a boulder, turned toward her, and gestured her onward. "Come, see it, see it!"

She followed, climbing over the boulder, and beheld a cave upon the hillside. Smoke still rose from it, and the smell of gunpowder invaded her nostrils.

"Bantis made this hole," the elder said, nodded, and scuttled down into the darkness. "Bantis boomed it. Bantis digs! Come, see. Biggest weapon buried below. Kills dragons."

With that, he disappeared into the cavern. Kaelyn climbed the last few feet, coughed, and peered into the shadows.

"Be careful!" she cried down to him. "It's not safe."

His head peeked out from the pit. He grinned, revealing only three teeth. "Safe? No. No, it's not safe here. It's not safe anywhere from the cruel dragons. But Bantis will kill them. Yes. Yes, Bantis will dig. Dig!"

He raised his shovel-hand and spun back into the cavern.

With a sigh, Kaelyn followed into the darkness.

"Who are you?" she called after him. "Where are you from?"

She had never heard such an accent before. Could this man be... a foreigner? Not Vir Requis like her, but a survivor of the great wars?

Kaelyn sucked in her breath.

He has to be, she thought.

She had been only a child when Emperor Frey Cadigus, her cruel father, had begun his conquests of "purification". His Legions had swept across the known world in those years, burning all foreign lands. The griffins, the true dragons of the west, the wyverns, and all other flying beasts fell. They burned in dragonfire, her father's vengeance for ancient wars a thousand years gone-by.

And he burned men too, Kaelyn remembered. Two great kingdoms of men had bordered Requiem in those years: Osanna in the east, an ancient land of forests and plains, and Tiranor in the south, a desert realm. No magic had blessed their people. They could not become dragons like the Vir Requis, but rode horses, built great cities, and lived in peace with Requiem.

Until my father burned them all, Kaelyn thought. *Until he deemed them impure, slaughtered them, and annexed the wastelands.*

Could this frail old man be a human survivor--a true human with no dragon form?

"Bantis, where are you from?" she said in the darkness.

When she crawled deeper into the cavern, she found him at the bottom. He was staring at a wall of earth and stone, scratching his head.

"Have to dig *deeper*," he said. "Deeper! Buried here, it is. Bantis feels it. Big weapon."

He knelt and began digging with his prosthetic shovel, tossing dirt and rocks over his shoulder. Kaelyn coughed and spat out dirt.

"Stop that!" she said. "Talk to me. Do you need help?" Her voice softened. "How long have you been here?"

He looked over his shoulder and flashed his snaggletoothed grin.

"They sent me here. They banished Bantis! Poor poor Bantis. The others want to fight. They don't think Bantis can help." He snorted, spitting out dirt. "All because Bantis blew up their camp. And their ship." He tapped his cheek. "And the palm grove. And maybe their last sheep." He raised his shovel in indignation. "Sheep, palm, ships, camp... Who cares? Bantis deals with explosives. Bantis deals with weapons! Bantis will find big weapon here on Genesis Isle. Big weapon to fight the dragons."

Kaelyn's breath left her.

"The others," she whispered. "Are there others like you? Others who live on these islands?"

He was digging again.

"You talk too much." He frowned over his shoulder at her. "Bantis busy digging. Bantis dig for weapon to kill you. You burned us. You burned our lands. You will die! Let Bantis dig so he can kill you."

"I'm not your enemy," Kaelyn said. "Are you... from the south? From across the sea? Do you fight Frey Ca--"

Bantis screamed.

His face twisted. He fell and cowered and covered his head with his arms.

"Do not say his name!" the old man wailed. He shivered. "Do not say the name of the demon! He will fly here. He will burn us. He burned my brothers, he is a demon, he must die, I am scared. Please, please, don't burn me, dragons. Don't burn..."

Kaelyn gasped and knelt by the man. She touched his shoulder, but he only cowered farther into the corner.

"We fight a common enemy," she said. "Don't be afraid. I too seek to kill the tyrant."

The old man peeked between his fingers. "You... you are..." He voice dropped to a whisper. "You are Vir Requis?"

"I am Kaelyn Cadigus of Requiem. I fight for the Resistance, a band of Vir Requis who hate the tyrant and seek to dethrone him. We're your allies, my friend. Will you come with me to meet our leader? Will you help us, and will you let us help you?"

He lowered his arms. His eyes lit with fire, and anger twisted his face. His hair stuck out, white and wild.

"The tyrant burned Bantis's land," he said. "The tyrant slew Bantis's brothers. Show me your army, dragon. And then... then Bantis will help you."

TILLA

They stood atop Tarath Imperium, a princess and a soldier, and gazed upon a dark empire.

From here upon the tower, a thousand feet above the world, Tilla could see for many leagues. The city of Nova Vita spread below like a breaking wheel, the tower rising from its center, its boulevards like spokes. Between the streets stood houses and shops, countless buildings of brick, their roofs white with snow. The great Castra Draco rose to the south, a castle with four towers, the heart of the Legions. The twisting, black Castra Academia rose in the east, the school that had broken and remolded her into a commander. The arena where prisoners died, the smithies where steel rang, and the monolithic statues of Frey Cadigus--they all seemed so small from here, toys Tilla could lift and break.

But it's Rune I will break, she thought. *The empire seems small from here, but it is mighty. And Rune will serve it.*

At her side, Princess Shari Cadigus spoke.

"Has he confessed his sins?" She snarled into the wind, eyes blazing. "You've had a full moon with him, Tilla Siren. Have you broken him yet?"

A gust of snowy wind whipped Tilla's hair, pinched her cheeks, and stung her eyes. Tilla was a child of the south, of warm Cadport with its mild winters and sea breezes to scatter any snow clouds. Here in the north, in the capital, there was snow and ice and biting winds like blades. Tilla wore steel plates over wool, not enough to warm her, but she was a soldier of Requiem; she buried cold, pain, and weakness deep within her.

The emperor's daughter does not shiver in this wind, she thought. *Nor will I.*

"I need more time, Commander." Tilla clutched her sword, seeking comfort from the well-worn leather grip. "He is still shocked, hurt, and confused. He will worship our glory. I will sway him."

Shari spun toward her, teeth bared. Tilla was a tall woman, but Shari loomed above her, a beast of black steel, wild dark hair, and eyes like forge fires. Her pauldrons flared out, and her gloved hands clutched the dagger and hammer that hung upon her belt.

"Your words are useless, Siren," the princess said. "I will make him confess his sins. I will have him beg to praise us." She drew her weapons, raising hammer and blade. "I will begin by cutting off his nails, then his fingers, then his manhood. I will proceed to hammer his bones, shattering one at a time, until all are broken. I will flay his skin and pull out his bowels as he watches. I will laugh as he begs for death. And I will drag him here to this tower, stand him above the empire, and make him scream his loyalty. I will make him praise the red spiral so the entire empire hears."

Shari's eyes flashed with bloodlust. She licked her lips and her chest rose and fell.

Rune tore off her wing, Tilla remembered. *She beat him bloody the day he arrived here, but that only whet her appetite. She could never hurt him enough.*

"Commander," Tilla said and lowered her head, knowing she must speak carefully. "I know Relesar. We grew up together. Please give me more time, and I can sway him. If the empire sees a beaten, flayed, mutilated wreck hailing the red spiral, it would instill only rage in their hearts. The Resistance would gain more power. More would rise up against us." She dared to meet Shari's eyes. "But if Relesar stands here tall and unhurt, and he proudly shouts out his allegiance, the empire will see that even the heir of Aeternum worships our glory. The Resistance will lose all legitimacy. Their fire will disperse."

Shari snorted. "Yes, I've heard of your little plan, Lanse. My father told me. You begged him too for this pup's safety. He agreed with you then, I know it. The man is a fool." Shari reached out, grabbed Tilla's arm, and thrust her face so close their noses almost touched. "But I am not. I see what you're doing, Siren. You still care for the boy. You try to protect him. But you cannot protect him from me."

Tilla stared back, daring not look away; looking away would show weakness. Shari was stronger, older, and certainly higher-ranking than her, but if Tilla wanted to save Rune, she had to hold her ground.

"Care for him? Protect him? Commander, he slew my comrades in Castra Luna." Tilla allowed herself a snarl. "He cowered in my city, letting us destroy it. I survived nine moons of training to become an officer. I fought at Luna and in Cadport. I slew men for the red spiral, and I watched my own men die." She slammed her fist against her chest. "I hail the red spiral! I wear that spiral upon my shoulders. I worship our cause with every fiber of my being, and Relesar is an enemy of that cause. He will be our greatest champion. Protect him? No, Commander. I care not to protect him. I want him to fight for us--not cower for us, not bleed for us, not scream and weep--but *join* us. That will be our greatest triumph--not to torture him, but to turn him against Valien."

As she spoke these words, staring firmly into her commander's eyes, Tilla's insides shook. Did she speak truth or lie? Did she still love Rune, or did she only love the red spiral? Did she truly want him as a champion, or was Shari right--was Tilla just trying to save an old friend?

I don't know, she thought, her throat tight. *He was my childhood friend and then the man I loved. Who is he now?*

Tilla swallowed, looked inward at her fraying soul, and saw the answer. She knew why she had to convince Rune to join them.

Because I am torn between my past and my present. Because I am torn between Rune and the red spiral. Because if he joins us, I can have both, and I will no longer feel broken.

Shari stared at her, silent, still gripping her arm. She raised her dagger, bringing it between their faces. Tilla sucked in her breath but refused to flinch.

"When Relesar tore off my wing, you saved my life, Lanse," Shari said, eyes narrowed. "For that, I will grant you more time. You have until the new moon to sway him. And if you cannot..." Shari growled and tilted her blade. "This steel will make him scream so loudly the entire city will hear."

With that, Shari spun around, marched to the tower battlements, and shifted. She took flight as a dragon, one wing wide and blue, the other constructed of wood, rope, and leather. With a blast of fire, she flew into the distance.

Tilla remained upon the tower. She placed her hands against the battlements, blew out her breath, and found herself shivering. If she could not sway Rune soon, she suspected that blade would cut her too.

"Stars damn you, Rune," she whispered into the wind.

She shifted into a dragon. She flew.

The snowy wind roared around her. Tilla dived across Cadigus Square, a cobbled expanse larger than all of Cadport. Leaving the palace grounds behind, she flew over crowded streets and houses. Troops marched below and dragons shrieked above.

A mile south of the palace, she saw the Citadel, a crumbling edifice rising from snow.

Many years ago, this fortress had been called Castra Murus, the barracks of the city guardians. When Frey had established the Axehand Order, he drafted the old City Guard into his Legions, then turned the castle into a prison. The Citadel, they called it now--a place of pain, blood, and screams. No more noble warriors filled its halls. Today prisoners languished in its cellars, chained and beaten. Today blood stained the old bricks. Today she would find Rune here.

When first bringing Rune north, she had imprisoned him in a cell by the courtyard. When he would not cave, she had moved him to the dungeon. She had hoped the darkness, the echoing screams, and the smell of blood would sway him. Yet still Rune would not hail the red spiral. And so Tilla had moved him again. Now Rune languished in the cruelest cell this prison contained, a place where minds had broken, where prisoners had smashed their skulls against the wall to end the pain.

She flew above the prison courtyard and halls, heading toward the Red Tower.

Four towers rose from the Citadel, but the Red Tower was the most infamous. Its bricks were as gray and craggy as the rest of the keep; it was named after the blood that flowed within. Frey had imprisoned and tortured his greatest enemies here. Generals loyal to the old king, lords sworn to Aeternum, and resistors caught lurking in the city--all had languished here.

Tilla landed in a courtyard below the tower, shook her head to scatter her smoke, and returned to human form. The tower guards saluted her, and Tilla stepped between them and through the doorway. She climbed the spiraling staircase, heading up toward him.

She climbed many steps, and her breath was heavy when she reached the tower top. An oaken door stood here. Tilla wore the key on a chain around her neck. With a creak, she opened the door and stepped into the darkness.

The day was bright outside, the sun glittering across the snow, but shadows filled this room. Two arrowslits, vestiges of the Citadel's olden days, allowed narrow beams of light to fall into the chamber.

One beam, which lit the western wall, fell upon horror. A stretching rack stood here beside an iron maiden. Smaller torture instruments hung on pegs: hammers, thumbscrews, pliers, floggers, and a dozen other tools of mutilation. Dried blood covered the instruments; Shari had used them many times upon her prisoners.

The second beam, which lit the northern wall, fell upon Rune.

Tilla released her breath and her belly twisted.

"Rune," she whispered.

He sat against the wall, his wrists manacled behind his back. A chain ran from the manacles to a bracket, only a few feet long. Dirt and old bruises darkened his skin. Shari had beaten him the first day, but she had not tortured him yet.

I have until the new moon, Tilla thought. *Only eleven days to sway him. And then Shari will pull her tools off the wall, and when I visit Rune again, I will not recognize him.*

He looked up at her between strands of scraggly hair.

"Tilla," he said hoarsely, lips cracked.

Chains clanking, he struggled to stand up. He winced, still weak and haggard, then fell back down and sat panting.

"You used to be so strong," Tilla said. "We'd fight with wooden swords on the beach. We'd run and wrestle and swim and fly. Oh, Rune. It doesn't have to be this way."

He glared up at her, chest rising and falling, as if every breath was a struggle. Tilla stepped toward him. Armor clanking, she sat down and leaned against him.

"It doesn't have to be this way," Rune repeated, raspy. "You are right, Tilla. You are right. We could have fled this place the first day. We can still flee. You carry the key around your neck.

You just need to unchain me. There are only two guards outside. We need only break past them and fly."

Tilla laid her head against his shoulder, placed a hand on his thigh, and sighed. "You know I can't do that."

Rune wriggled away as best he could in his chains. "And you know I can't do what you ask."

She turned to look at him, narrowed her eyes, and held his shoulder. "Why? Why, Rune? I... Oh stars, look at you." Her eyes dampened. "It hurts me to see you like this. Thin. Haggard. Your body bruised. I can't see you like this, Rune, chained here. If you just hail the red spiral, if you just join Frey, we can--"

"And it hurts me to see *you* like this," he said, and his eyes flashed. "Chains? Bruises? They are nothing compared to what I see. I see a girl from Lynport, a friend, a kind woman clad in black steel, bearing the sigil of evil. I see a roper's daughter, a woman I love, serving a beast and wielding his weapons and--"

"I serve Requiem!" she said, her turn to interrupt. "Frey is a beast? Yes, Rune. Frey is evil? Perhaps. But we cannot save the world. We cannot defeat him. So we must serve him, and we must serve Requiem. Rune, please. None of this should have happened. None of it! If you hadn't joined the Resistance, Castra Luna would still stand, and our friends would still live--Mae Baker and all the others. Cadport--and yes, I still call it Cadport--would still stand." She dug her fingers into his shoulders, hurting him but not caring. "But you fought against Requiem. You killed thousands. You lured the Legions to our city, and you watched that city burn, and now everyone from our home is dead. Everyone we grew up with. Everyone we ever knew. Dead, Rune. Dead because of you."

"Not because of me!" He shouted now. "I fought for our city. I fought for our kingdom. I fought for you, Tilla. I fought to save you from him, and now... now you imprison me here, and you ask me to praise your lord? To praise the man who burned our city?"

"I ask you to live!" she said. "I ask you to... to avoid that wall." She gestured at the western wall where the torture instruments hung. "She will torture you, Rune. You do not know what she can do. She will dislocate your bones. She will cut off your manhood and force you to watch her burn it. She will flay your skin, remove your organs, and make you scream for the red spiral. She's done this to enemies before. You've been in this chamber for long days. You've studied her instruments. Why do you still refuse to join us?"

Rune closed his eyes and his face paled. He shook his head.

"You won't let them do that," he whispered. "I have to believe, Tilla. I still believe in you. You will not let them do that."

"I cannot stop them. Only you can."

He opened his eyes and looked at her.

"Tilla," he said, "do you remember our last night in Lynport? Not the battle. The night before you joined the Legions."

Her throat constricted. Her eyes dampened, and she blinked and clenched her fists.

"I remember," she whispered.

"We can find another beach," he said. "We can flee to distant lands together, to unexplored countries, or to the deserts across the sea. We can be together again. Not in this place. Not here in this cruel city. We can be like we were."

Tilla tasted a tear on her lips, and she hated herself for it, and she hated Rune for making her cry. She had not shed tears for moons in Castra Academia as her tormentors burned her, but she cried here.

"Those days are gone." She held his shoulders, knelt above him, and stared into his eyes. "They are gone, Rune. They are over. You cannot flee Frey; his arm is too long. You cannot fight him; he is too strong. But we can be together here. We can serve him together, two soldiers for his cause."

He shook his head. "Never. I will never serve him, and I will not watch you serve him."

She pulled his hair back from his brow and found herself caressing it. She leaned forward, kissed his cheek, and whispered into his ear.

"Please. Please, if you have any love for me, if our memories together mean anything to you... do as I say. Worship him. Save yourself."

She rose to leave. She walked toward the door, tears in her eyes.

His voice rose behind her. "I surrendered myself to save the last people of Lynport... but also to save you, Tilla. Also to save you."

She could not bear to turn and look at him. Her tears streamed down her cheeks. She left the chamber, closed the door behind her, and bit her lip until she tasted blood.

VALIEN

He stood upon the beach, watching the old man caw, run in circles, and plead for his life.

"Calm yourself, friend!" Valien said. "We won't harm you."

The old man wore but a loincloth and a belt strung with his prosthetic hands. His eyes bulged with fear. He tugged at his long white hair, and his chest, frail enough to reveal his ribs, rose and fell as he panted.

"You... you are Vir Requis!" he said, voice high and quavering like a bird's call. "You burn us. You burn my home! You burn Tiranor. But Bantis will fight you. Bantis invents. Bantis booms things. Big weapon. Bantis dig for it. Bantis kill you all!"

With that, he resumed running in circles. He raced toward his beached raft, an old thing of rotten wood and rope. When he saw the two resistors who stood nearby, he turned the other way and ran, nearly slamming himself against two more. He fell into the sand, leaped up, and began to wave his arms like a man trying to shoo away squirrels.

Standing at Valien's side, Kaelyn sighed.

"He was like this when I found him," she said. "He was living on a rock he called Genesis Isle. I think he was alone there for a very long time. But he spoke of other survivors. I thought my father killed all Tirans, but... Oh stars, I hope he's not the last."

Valien looked at her, and as always--no matter how many times he gazed upon her--he felt his fear melt under sadness. Kaelyn had always been pale, but the southern sun had bronzed her skin. Her hair, once dark as honey, had lightened under this sunlight into a bright gold. Instead of her forest garb, she stood barefoot in the sand, clad in a white tunic, a wild thing swept from the sea onto the shore, a mythical creature of sand and sun and secrets. But her eyes were the same--hazel, soft, and kind, the eyes that had warmed Valien through the years of war.

"He's a Tiran," he said. "I visited Tiranor years ago. I was little older than you are now, and I still served the old king." He looked across the sea and inhaled deeply, remembering the scent of the southern desert, a perfume of sand and spices. "The Tirans were a proud people, tall and golden-skinned and blue-eyed, their hair a platinum so pale it seemed almost white. They lived in oases where palm trees soared, cranes sang, and limestone palaces rose into blue skies. They spread across dunes and mountains, bringing life to the desert. I spent a year there, an ambassador of Requiem. I still miss the sweetness of Tiranor's wine, figs, and dates; her music of lutes and drums; the song of her trees and birds; and mostly her people, an old enemy of Requiem grown into a close friend." Valien returned his eyes to Kaelyn and his voice soured. "Frey Cadigus burned that land and slaughtered those people, his revenge for a war seven hundred years ago. He burned the oases. He butchered mothers and babes. He toppled temples and slew every Tiran he found. I thought they had all died. And here we have this one... a survivor."

Bantis was crouched in the sand, hopping like a frog. Hearing Valien's last sentence, he looked up and tilted his head like an inquisitive owl.

"Survivor?" he said, hopping around on his hands. "Yes, yes, Bantis survived! Others too. Army! Army like this one, yes." He gestured at the resistors who covered the beach and hills of the island.

Valien looked around him and sighed.

Army? he thought. No, this was no army. These were but ragged survivors too.

The island was small, no larger than the city of Lynport back in Requiem. Valien had named it Horsehead Island due to its shape. Perhaps it had no true name; it did not appear in the maps of Requiem. Located a three-day flight from the empire's southeastern shore, it housed the remains of his Resistance. Three thousand men and women lived here in huts, caves, or simply upon the beach. Their clothes were ragged and their weapons dulled, but their eyes still shone. Some of these resistors had been following Valien for years--they had hidden with him in the ruins of Confutatis, fought with him at Castra Luna, and crawled with him through tunnels in Lynport. Others had just recently joined his command--some were men of Cain's Canyon, outcast from Requiem after fighting Frey, and others had once followed the outlaw Leresy Cadigus. They walked across the beach, moved between the huts, and climbed the hills, haggard and long of hair and tanned of skin. An army? Valien did not know.

Maybe we're little better than old Bantis, he thought.

A voice rose behind him, twisted with contempt.

"I say we put the old bugger out of his misery."

He turned to see Leresy walking across the beach, a smirk on his face.

Valien growled. "And since when did anyone care what you say, boy?"

The young, outcast prince ignored him. Strutting as if he still wore finery rather than sandy rags, Leresy approached the old Tiran. He sniffed and wrinkled his nose.

"Stars above, the old man stinks," he said. He lifted a stick and jabbed Bantis with it. "All scrawny too, ribs showing and all. I say we put him down. He's no use to us."

Bantis seemed to find his courage. He snapped his teeth at Leresy, shoved the stick aside, and barked like an enraged dog.

"Scrawny?" the old man demanded. "No use? Bantis has many uses. Bantis is an inventor. Bantis invented hand cannons. Bantis invented glass eyes that can see far. Bantis is digging-- digging for big weapon. Genesis Isle is little, but *big* weapon is there. Weapon to slay dragons." He puffed out his chest. "Bantis smells like gunpowder; he no *stinks.*"

With a grumble, Valien trudged forward, shoved Leresy aside, and stared at the wild-haired old man.

"Bantis, you said there are others," Valien said. "Where are they? Did other Tirans survive?"

"Oh yes, oh yes!" Bantis said and resumed hopping, spinning around, and kicking sand. "Many others survived. They live on Maiden Island. Big island, it is, big like this one. But they banished poor Bantis. All because Bantis loves explosives. Poor poor Bantis. He built them hand cannons and fireballs and lots of things that go *boom*! And poor Bantis now lives alone."

Valien looked up and met Kaelyn's gaze. She nodded and he returned his eyes to the old man.

"Bantis, will you show us there? Will you lead us to the others?"

The old man's eyes widened. He tugged at his long, white hair and bounced about in circles like a monkey on a leash, slapping the sand.

"Take you there? Yes, yes. Bantis take you to the others. Bantis trusts you. Follow! Follow. We go to their island. But not as dragons, no! Shoot you they will. Kill you with my inventions." He hopped toward his raft, which lay upon the shore. "We oar our way there, yes."

He detached his shovel prosthetic, slung it from his belt, and lifted an oar from the raft. He attached the oar to his stub, grinned, and looked at Valien eagerly like a dog begging for a walk.

"Follow, follow! Bantis take you." He began to paddle the raft through the sand, seemingly unaware that it wasn't moving. "Follow!"

Valien sighed and looked at Kaelyn. She gave him a grin, her teeth bright white against her tanned face. She hefted her bow across her shoulder and gripped her sword.

"Ready for another adventure?" she asked.

Valien's heart twisted again. Her golden hair, her blue eyes, her smile that spoke of all the fire, blood, and rain they'd flown through--every time they hurt him.

"Never and always," he answered.

He gave a few orders to his men, then began pushing the raft toward the sea. Kaelyn pushed at his side. Scrawny Bantis stood upon the raft, rowing as if he himself were moving the vessel. He whooped as it splashed into the waves.

Valien and Kaelyn waded through the water, pushing the raft deeper. Waves rose and fell. Bantis kept oaring upon the raft, but the waves grew larger, splashing and shoving the raft back toward the shore.

With a grumble, Valien shifted into a dragon.

He flattened himself so his belly grazed the sea floor, and his nostrils rose above the water. He beat his tail, driving forward and pushing the raft.

"Bantis oars fast!" Bantis said upon the raft, his oar barely even skimming the water. "No waves can stop old Bantis."

Valien rolled his eyes, snorted smoke, and kept shoving the raft. The waves crashed against them. The raft rose and fell violently, almost flipping over. Still in human form, Kaelyn climbed onto the vessel and crouched low. She pulled Bantis down beside her.

"Hold on tight while you oar, friend," she said. She looked back at Valien and winked.

The waves grew larger and larger, crashing against them. The last one would have overturned the raft had Valien, swimming behind, not held tight with his claws. Past the last breaker, he shifted back into human form, climbed onto the raft, and shook water from his hair.

"Poor poor Valien," said Bantis, looking at him in concern. "Waves were too strong for you. You fell overboard. It's okay, Bantis steered us through."

Valien grunted, spat overboard, and watched Horsehead Island dwindle behind them. A single, orphaned archway rose upon its peak, green with ivy. Three columns, the vestiges of an ancient temple, still stood upon its shore; twenty other columns lay fallen around them. Resistors moved across the beach, between the trees, and upon the hilltops.

It was not a bad life. Valien could stay there, lead his men, and find a new life with Kaelyn. A life of sunlight. Of peace. Of trees and whispering waves and no more war, no more fire or blood.

He gritted his teeth. But no. They'd been living here for a moon now. The time would come for them to fly again. To fight. To bleed.

Valien lowered his head and thought of Rune.

I will not forget you, Rune. I will not leave you to a life of torture and darkness.

He had known Rune since the boy's birth. He had fought at his side, bled with him, killed with him. Rune had become more than just the hope of Requiem.

He is like my son, Valien thought. *He is like the son Marilion and I never had.*

"And I will save you," he rasped, voice too low for the others to hear.

The island grew smaller and smaller behind them, and Bantis began to sing and dance as he rowed, surefooted even upon the swaying raft.

He oared for a long time.

They traveled south until Horsehead Island dwindled to but a
green smudge upon the horizon. The sun dipped into afternoon,
casting silver light upon the sea. The water spread across all
horizons, deep green and blue. Fish leaped every few moments,
and a pod of dolphins swam in the distance.

Kaelyn leaned against Valien. "The sea seems endless," she
whispered. "There is no pain here. No people to lead. No wars to
fight. I can imagine that the whole world is like this. Blue and
quiet and... simple." She looked up at him. "I wish he were with
us. I wish he could see this water too."

Valien placed an arm around her. "They will not kill him.
He's worth more to them alive."

A tear streamed down her cheek, and she closed her eyes.
"That's what I fear. Those are the nightmares that fill me, even
here, surrounded by this peace. Because I know, Valien... I know
that death would be a kindness to him now. I can't even imagine
what--"

Valien growled. He pulled Kaelyn's face up toward his. She
opened her eyes and he glared at her.

"Do not think such thoughts," he said. "Do not, Kaelyn.
They will haunt you. They will hurt you. We don't know that Rune
is tortured. The dragon who captured him--the white one--was his
friend. She is protecting him."

Kaelyn nodded and leaned back against him. "Maybe you're
right. I pray that you are. I just wish we could be with him.
Fighting for him. Saving him and everyone else."

"So long as I breathe," Valien said, "so long as I can stand
and fly, I will fight. We hide now, but we will seek allies, and we
will regroup, and we will not abandon Rune. We will not abandon
Requiem. I swear this to you."

The sun was nearing the horizon, casting a golden path
across the water, when they saw Maiden Island.

Valien now understood how the island got its name. It rose
from the water like a woman lounging on her side, a forested hill
forming her hip. A waterfall cascaded from a smaller hill like hair
from a head.

"Welcome, welcome!" Bantis said, hopping around the raft.
"Bantis led you to Maiden Island. To hope. To his army.
Together we will fight, yes."

As they oared closer, Valien looked for signs of life but saw only seagulls and trees. The waves whispered across virgin sands. No huts, no smoke from cooking fire, no men or women to be seen.

"Bantis," Kaelyn said, "how many survivors did you say live here?"

He pirouetted upon the raft, nearly falling into the water. "Thousands! Thousands of survivors live here, yes. Bantis's friends. Bantis's son leads them, yes. Bantis lived here too. Bantis loves explosives. Bantis lives alone now."

They oared closer. Valien guessed the island stretched two miles long, maybe three. He still could see nobody. The shores were smooth. No trees had been hewn. No huts or tents rose. Valien let out his breath.

Crazy old loon, he thought. *He's been alone too long. He invented himself an army of friends.*

They let the waves carry them to shore, then walked along the sand. Cliffs rose above them, topped with palm trees. Pelicans and gulls flew overhead. Kaelyn chewed her lip as she walked, staring up at the trees, while Valien grumbled. No footprints marred the sand; Valien wondered if they were the first to ever walk here.

Yet Bantis ran ahead, eager as a dog released from a house, kicking sand and spinning in circles every few feet.

"Come, come! Follow old Bantis. He will lead you to them. Hurry, Vir Requis!"

Valien sighed. He looked at Kaelyn and saw her sigh too.

"Let's humor him," he said in a low rumble; Bantis was running too far ahead to hear. "We'll see what he wants to show us."

Kaelyn hefted her bow across her shoulder. Her cheeks were reddening in the sun, and sand clung to her clothes.

"Might be we'll find only thousands of skeletons."

"Or thousands of ghosts," Valien said.

Bantis scampered ahead, leading them toward a rocky hill. He raced up the slope, turned toward them, and gestured for them to follow. They climbed the Maiden's waist, moving between boulders, mint bushes, and rustling pines. Frogs trilled and herons flew overhead. The waterfall sang in the distance.

When they reached the hilltop and saw the southern sea, Bantis stopped walking and stretched out his arms. "Here! Here is my army. Meet them! Meet them!"

Valien looked around and saw only the trees, the frogs, and the birds. He grumbled and heaved the longest sigh of his life.

"Not skeletons," he muttered to Kaelyn, who stood by his side, chewing her lip and searching the trees. "Not ghosts either. He led us to an army of frogs."

She grinned and leaned against him. "I suppose we could unleash them in the capital. We'll teach them to swarm the emperor and give him warts."

Valien grunted, wiped sweat from his brow, and hefted his pack across his shoulders. "Come on. Let's go back."

He had taken two steps downhill when the forest leaped at him.

A hundred people or more sprang from the trees. They wore clothes of grass, leaves filled their hair, and mud smeared their faces. They bore what looked like miniature cannons mounted upon wooden shafts.

"Capture them!" spoke one, a tall man with blue eyes peering from a painted face. "Take them alive."

Valien growled, shifted into a dragon, and soared.

He shot through the trees. Kaelyn flew beside him, a green dragon, her wings bending the trees below.

A boom tore through the air.

Smoke blasted from one of the men's sticks. Fire blazed out. A projectile whizzed by Valien's head.

"I said alive!" shouted the tall man below.

Valien beat his wings, rising higher, and growled. At his side, Kaelyn sucked in her breath, and flames crackled between her teeth. She rose, then turned and assumed a swooping position, prepared to blast her fire downward.

"Kaelyn, no!" Valien shouted, flew toward her, and knocked her aside. Her flames cascaded down the hillside, missing the men. "They're refugees. They're frightened. They're--"

Metal creaked below upon the hill.

Men covered in leaves and mud raised metallic tubes and pulled levers. Grapples shot skyward, dragging chains behind them. Valien banked, but two grapples swung across him, then tugged down. Chains wrapped around him, and one grapple dug into his leg. He howled and dipped in the sky.

At his side, chains swung around Kaelyn too. She howled and drew more fire into her maw. When she blasted the flames downward, the men scattered and vanished between the trees. The fire crashed down against boulders. From the canopy, more grapples flew.

Chains encased the two dragons. They beat their wings, struggling to rise, but the chains tugged downward, and Valien glimpsed men turning winches.

Valien and Kaelyn, dragons of Requiem, crashed against the hillside. A dozen chains swung from the trees and crashed down atop them. Men cheered.

"Cursed be Requiem!" cried one man.

"For the glory of Tiranor!" cried another.

Men leaped onto their backs, and Valien howled and tried to shake them off, but the chains held him down. Arms reached across his head, fastening a muzzle over his mouth. He growled and blasted fire from his nostrils, but he couldn't free himself--not without killing the men, which he wasn't prepared to do. From the corner of his eye, he saw a dozen men muzzling Kaelyn too as she flailed.

"Death to Requiem!" they cried. "The dragons are ours!"

LERESY

He pulled her along the beach.

"Come on," he said and rolled his eyes. "Will you stop leaning down to collect seashells?"

Crouched in the sand, Erry glared up at him. Leresy held her hand, trying to tug her along. With her other hand, she lifted a large pink shell.

"This is a *conch*, you fool," she said. "This isn't an ordinary seashell. It's rare and-- Ow! Stop pulling me."

He kept walking, squeezing her hand, forcing her to trail behind. She glared and spat and kicked sand.

"It looks like a damn seashell to me," he said. "Do you want to collect shells like a little girl, or do you want to find this big weapon the crazy old man talked about?"

"Collect shells."

He paused, turned toward her, and held out his hand. "Let me see."

She shook her head.

He grabbed the conch, wrenched it from her fingers, and tossed it into the sea.

"You bloody piece of pig shite!" she shouted and tried to kick him, but he held her shoulders at arm's length, and her short legs only kicked the air.

"Call me what you like, soon I'll be pig shite with a weapon to take the throne." He spat. "You'll be thankful I let you trail behind me then. Now come along. This is where the old loon landed with his raft. Shift with me and let's find this damn Genesis Isle he came from."

She raised her hands to the heavens. "Damn it, Leresy, how are you going to find his island? Kaelyn said it's barely bigger than a rock, and there are about a million islands around here. The man was crazy! Cawing like a bird and dancing around. What weapon could he possibly have been seeking?"

"I don't know. We'll find out."

With that, he shifted into a dragon and took flight.

Damn, flying feels good, he thought.

That grizzled fool Valien had insisted nobody shift upon the island. The man was paranoid, sure that imperial dragons were scouting the sea and would see their fire. But Leresy knew his father. The old man had his prize; the boy Relesar was his.

Give the dog a bone to chew, and he'll keep himself busy, he thought.

He rose higher on the wind, inhaling the salty air. The southern sun, warm even in winter, heated his red scales. He sucked fire into his maw and blasted it skyward.

"Erry!" he cried down to her. The urchin still stood upon the beach in human form, scowling up at him, hands on her hips. "Are you coming, or are you going to stay and sulk like a baby?"

She spat and shifted too. She soared as a copper dragon, eyes narrowed and fire trickling from her nostrils. They flew east, the direction Bantis's raft had come from. The sea sprawled below them, blue and green under a clear sky, and Horsehead Island--their home since fleeing Requiem--dwindled behind.

Erry shot up to fly beside him, snorted a blast of fire, and glared. "I can't believe you're still obsessed with your damn throne. I thought you gave that up when we moved here. What about all that sweet talk? Living on an island paradise. Forgetting about the war. Making love every day, eating wild grapes, and wearing grass like beautiful savages."

"Well, that was before I heard about this big weapon."

"And now I suppose if you do find some weapon, you'll want to fly back to Requiem." She growled. "Well, I'm not going with you, Leresy Cadigus. Not for any throne or palace or gold."

He hissed. "You'd rather stay alone on this island, a dirty and miserable outcast? You'll turn into another Bantis." He shook his head. "I'm not letting that happen to me. I'm not turning into some crazy-haired, wild-eyed old man. I'll find that old bugger's weapon and slay my father once and for all."

"Leresy!" She slapped him with her tail. "There is no damn weapon. The man is crazy. His weapon is probably just an angry sea sponge he thinks he can slay monsters with."

"A sea sponge with teeth can work," Leresy said. "I'll give it to my father and tell him to wipe his arse with it."

She sighed. "Always poetry with you."

He flashed a toothy grin and flew on.

Their island dwindled behind them, a patch of gray and green shaped like a horse's head. The sea stretched on. The world became nothing but blue--the sky above, the sea below, and two dragons in the middle. As they flew, Leresy found himself antsy. Back at the island, there were many distractions--swords to sharpen, huts to build, boars to catch, trees to fell, and Erry to bed. But here, trapped between blue and blue, nothing stopped his memories from resurfacing.

An image flashed before him, and Leresy winced.

Suddenly he wasn't flying over the sea but was back in Lynport. The barrels of gunpowder rolled. Blasts tore the door open, and outside, he saw them. Men torn apart. Limbs and heads severed. Men screaming, clutching at spilling entrails and stubs. Beras the Brute swinging his axe at Erry, and so much blood, and--

No. Leresy growled and blasted flames down into the water. *No more memories. No more pain.*

His heart thrashed, and he wondered if Erry was right. Why did he need to return? Why not leave Requiem--all that fire and pain--behind?

Or course, he knew the answer.

I've left Requiem. But she did not leave me. She will not until I can return and slay those ghosts.

He looked over at Erry who flew beside him, grumbling and muttering to herself. He didn't want to leave her. He didn't want to lose her. She was the only good thing he had left, but the ghosts of his pain tainted her too. When he looked at her, he still saw Beras with his axe.

So I will slay those ghosts, he swore, flames crackling inside him. *For us.*

They flew until they saw a group of islets ahead, a dozen or more rising like a spine ridge, leafy with palms. The two dragons made their way forward, and Leresy lowered his altitude.

"I told you," Erry said, "damn too many islands here. How are you going to find the right one?"

He glided toward the first island. "Well, Bantis said he was digging, so we find the island with the big hole."

The first island he flew over seemed a poor candidate--nothing but palm trees upon a cliff. The second was barren, a mere pile of mossy rocks. He had flown over ten islands, and his wings were aching with weariness, when he saw the distant patch of green.

"There's another one there, farther off," he said. "Erry, come on."

She panted. "Can't we land on one of these? My wings hurt more than a mare in heat locked up with stallions."

"We'll rest once we find what we seek."

His own wings ached, and every breath felt like a saw in his lungs, but he forced himself onward. The sea streamed below. The distant islet lay miles away from the others, an isolated rock no larger a humble house. When he flew above, he twisted his jaw into a grin.

"Here we are. Genesis Isle."

A rocky hill rose upon the island. A hole had been blasted into the hillside, forming a cave. Rocks and dust littered the slope. Leresy glided down and landed upon the shore.

Erry landed beside him, shifted back into a human, and plopped herself down onto the sand. She lay back, closed her eyes, and let the waves wet her toes.

"Bloody stars, I'm tired. I'm going to lie here while you go searching for your toy."

He shifted back too, reached down, and grabbed her hands. "You're searching with me. We'll lie on the sand later. *Both* of us."

She gave him a sidelong look. "Oh you'd like that, wouldn't you? Bet you're after another treasure here. An island all to ourselves..." She reached down to his breeches, teased him with a caress, then slapped his face. "But since you tossed away my conch, no treasure for you today."

He sighed, grabbed her wrist, and pulled her after him. "Help me dig."

She growled and cussed but followed. They climbed the hillside between boulders and fallen trees. Items lay strewn across the slope, gray with dust. Leresy saw a wheeled cannon, a few shovels, and barrels of gunpowder.

"Hello, what are you then?" he said and leaned down by a fallen tree.

He lifted a shaft of sanded wood the length of a sword. A metal pipe was mounted upon it. A trigger, like that of a crossbow, fit his finger.

"Is this your secret weapon?" Erry said. She leaned down and lifted another one of the contraptions. "What is it? It looks like a crossbow, just without the bow."

Leresy hefted the device, sniffed at it, smelled gunpowder, and smiled.

"Very nice," he said and caressed the wood. "Very good work that Bantis did."

Erry glowered, holding her own shaft. "Leresy, are you going to tell me what this is?"

He pointed the muzzle at her. "Can't you see? It's a hand cannon."

She glowered and shoved the barrel aside. "Well, don't point that thing at me then, you dolt! Who the Abyss heard of a hand cannon? Cannons are, well... they're bloody huge."

"Not this one." Leresy pointed it skyward and pulled the trigger, but nothing happened. "Not loaded. I reckon you place miniature cannonballs into it, then go shooting down dragons."

"Leresy!" Erry stamped her feet and tossed down her own hand cannon. "The muzzles on these things are tiny. I can barely fit my finger in. How will a cannonball this small kill anyone?"

"The same way a crossbow bolt does. With a lot of speed and power." He grinned. "But this weapon here, my darling... I wager it has more power than any crossbow. Why use a string when you can use gunpowder? Let's see if we can find some rounds."

He kept climbing, moving between the rocks and fallen trees, searching for the miniature cannonballs. He wanted to try this weapon. Instead he found another strange object, one whose purpose he could not determine.

"Hello," he said, placed down his hand cannon, and lifted the new contraption. "And who are you?"

It looked like a scroll formed of tough, hardened leather bolted together. A round, wooden lid sealed each end of the tube. When he unscrewed the lids, he revealed glass circles like the bottoms of jars. Leresy had never seen anything like this.

"What is it?" Erry demanded and reached out for it. "Give it here."

He stepped back. "No touching." He brought the contraption close to his eye. "Let's see then. A cylinder of boiled leather, glass at each end. A container? Maybe the ammunition is in here."

He peeked through one glass circle, trying to see inside, and sucked in his breath. A grin spread across his face.

"Bantis, you bloody old genius," he said.

He aimed the cylinder at the sea, still holding it to his eye. Through the glass, the distant batch of islands, which should have appeared as mere specks, loomed large enough for him to count their trees. He lowered the cylinder, raised it again, and laughed.

"Give it here!" Erry demanded, leaped up, and snatched the cylinder. She stared through it and gasped. "Bloody piss pots! It's magic."

She spun in a circle, staring through the cylinder at the sea and the hill behind her.

Leresy shook his head. "Not magic. I don't think so. Bantis said he's an inventor, not a magician."

She lowered the cylinder and narrowed her eyes. "Well, how the bloody Abyss do you invent *glass* that makes things *bigger*?"

"I don't know." He shrugged. "How do you invent clocks? Or gunpowder? Or steel? Damned if I know. So long as it works. But it's not magic. Magic feels... different. You know how you feel when we shift into dragons? How it sort of... tickles, like soft light, but you can't really feel it? At least, not how you feel a feather or a blanket or heat. You sort of feel it inside you, whispering. That's how magic feels. This?" He took the cylinder from her and stared through it again. "This is clever and I don't understand it, but it feels... mechanical. It's an invention like the great clock back at Castra Luna."

Erry tapped her thigh. "So is this the big weapon? Portable cannons and a magnifying machine?" She scrunched her lips. "Good weapons for Tirans, perhaps. They need the help. But we're Vir Requis. We can turn into dragons. I'd take dragonfire any day over these hand cannons."

Leresy shook his head again. "No. Bantis said he was digging for something. Digging for a *big* weapon." He gestured at the hole that loomed above. "That's where he was digging. Let's take a look."

He shoved the cylinder under his armpit and lifted one of the discarded shovels. They continued climbing the hillside. They reached the hole--it loomed about the size of a doorway--and peered inside.

"Nothing but dust and rubble," Erry said. "Damn old man was crazy, I told you."

"Crazy enough to invent a magnifying machine and portable cannons. If he says there's a weapon here, I'm digging deeper." He climbed into the hole, thrust his shovel down, and scooped pebbles and dirt. "Now go grab another shovel and help me, damn it. I'm not digging alone."

She grumbled but she grabbed a shovel.

They dug.

They dug for a long time.

After digging through several feet of soil and rock, sweat soaked Leresy. He wiped it off his brow and stripped off his shirt.

"Feel free to do the same," he told Erry, but she only slammed the shovel against his legs.

They dug some more, and the sun began to dip into afternoon, casting golden beams into the cave. Still they dug, tossing shovel after shovel of dirt outside.

"Leresy, damn it!" Erry said. "There's nothing buried here."

"We haven't dug deep enough." He mopped his brow and dug some more.

Erry tossed her shovel down and placed her hands on her hips. Dirt covered her.

"It's an island!" she said. "A damn, stinkin' island in the middle of nowhere. Burn me, it's barely even that. More of a forsaken rock than an island. Why why *why* would there be a weapon buried here?"

He gritted his teeth and kept shoveling. "Because there has to be one."

"What do you mean?" she demanded and grabbed his arm. "Ler, what--"

He reeled toward her, teeth bared, and tossed his shovel down. It thumped against the dirt.

"I mean," he hissed, "that I'm not going to believe this is it. All right? I'm not going to believe that... that things just end like this. That my father wins. That Shari wins. That there's blood and fire and pain in Requiem, and we're just going to hide here and remember it and..." Tears budded in his eyes, and he hated himself for it. He spun away lest she saw. "There has to be some way to fight him, Erry. To kill that bastard and to kill the memories."

He stood, chest heaving and legs shaking, staring at the dirt. He felt her small hands on his shoulders.

"Ler," she said quietly. She walked around to face him, and her eyes were soft. "And if there isn't a way to fight? If this is all that's left, isn't that enough? You and me?"

He lowered his head and pulled her into an embrace. He held her tightly, crushing her against him. He smoothed her hair and closed his burning eyes.

"I thought it would be," he said, voice choked. "I wanted to forget. I wanted to just live here with you. To start a new life. Not a prince of Requiem and an orphan from Lynport, but just... just two people on an island. But I can't forget. I can't." His voice cracked. "I still see it, Erry. All of it. The dragons burning Castra Luna and killing so many, killing Nairi and the others. And the war and blood at Lynport. And my father... my father grabbing me and Kaelyn, beating us, laughing as we bled and screamed. I can't forget it. You can't know what that's like."

She held his head with both hands and growled up at him. "Can't I? I was there with you. At Castra Luna. At Lynport. I fought through the mud and fire with you. And no, your father never beat me when I was a girl. But enough men did. I grew up a dock rat, filthy and skinny and afraid. I know what pain is. And I can't forget either, and I never will. But that doesn't mean we have to go back. We don't have to go chase that world again. That life of ours... that life is over. We have a new life here."

"I don't," he said. "I don't think I ever will. Not until I go back and face him. Not until I close that door. The door is distant, all the way across the sea, but I can feel the cold wind still blowing through it. So I have to find this weapon. And I have to kill my father." He lifted the shovel again. "So please, Erry, please. Help me dig."

Night was falling, and the cave was almost pitch black, when Leresy's shovel *crunched* and red light glowed.

His heart burst into a gallop. At his side, Erry gasped. The soft red light gleamed under the soil. Leresy drove his shovel deeper, loosening the dirt. The red glow intensified.

"Burn me," he said, knelt, and began to clear away soil with his hands. "Erry, look at this."

She knelt and helped clear away the dirt. Hundreds of red shards glowed below, each one no larger than a pea.

"They look like pomegranate seeds," Erry said, lifting one in wonder. It glowed in her hand.

"Or like droplets of blood," said Leresy.

He grabbed a few and held them in his palm. They felt unnaturally cold. He raised them to his eye, scrutinizing them. Each stone seemed made of glass, and red liquid swirled within. Their surface was angular as cut gems, though each pebble had a different shape.

"What are they?" Erry asked. "Some kind of crystal?"

Leresy smiled and closed his palm around them.

"Magic," he said. "Our big weapon."

SILA

He stood upon the deck of his ship, stared at the cove that surrounded him, and clutched the railing until his knuckles turned white.

Sila didn't know why he still came here. His ship, a three-masted carrack named the *Golden Crane*, had not raised its anchor in eighteen years. Its planks had begun to rot, and barnacles covered its hull. Its hold still whispered with ghosts. Dragonfire had blackened its starboard, and though the sails were now folded, Sila knew that burnt holes still peppered them. Only the ship's figurehead, a flying crane of giltwood, still bore some former glory.

And what of myself? he wondered. Did he too bear any lingering glory, a golden figurehead for his people? Or was he but a rotting hull, as captive on Maiden Island as his ship?

Once Sila had captained this vessel through storms and battles. Once he had led refugees out of fire and into new life. Once he had been a leader, a savior, a man who made his father proud.

"And now I linger, a relic like the rest of this wreck," he said to his ship.

And now his people needed him again. Now two of their ghosts had washed ashore with the old man. Now two demons of the past, mere nightmares for so long, breathed upon Maiden Island, this sanctuary Sila had protected for so long. Now he needed to decide. And yet he only stood here upon his deck, far from his people and their tormentors--a place of solitude, of memory, of thoughts that whispered like the sea.

Cliffs rose above the surrounding shores, topped with palms. Nestled into the small of the maiden's back, the cove faced south, hidden from the northern enemy. Five other ships rose around him, each as barren as the *Golden Crane*. Often Sila thought of burning these ships. Should the dragons scout these seas from the south, the masts would reveal their sanctuary. Yet for eighteen years, Sila had hidden his people among the trees and kept his ships alive. He had watched his daughter born and raised into a woman on this island. He had watched his people, once ragged refugees, build a new life. And he had kept these ships. He had kept his vengeance burning.

"Because I have to believe," he whispered to the cove. "I have to believe that we can go back. That we can still fight the enemy. That we can still rebuild our desert home."

Tiranor, his land of dunes and oases, had burned in the fire of the red spiral. But those dunes still whispered inside him. He kept that memory as alive as his fleet.

"Father! Father, why do you do this?"

The voice came from behind him, and Sila turned to see his daughter emerge from the hull. She joined him on the deck.

"Miya!" he said and a frown twisted his face. "How long have you been here? What are you doing on the *Golden Crane?*"

Miya glared at him, fists on her hips. "And why shouldn't I stand here? I'm your only daughter, and this ship is my birthright. She's as much mine as yours."

Eighteen years old, Miya had been only a whisper in her mother's womb when Frey Cadigus had burned their kingdom. She had been born in the shallow waters of this very cove, shaded by cliffs and palms, and grown wild along the beaches and among the trees. Today she stood before him as a golden-skinned, scabby-kneed island girl with fiery blue eyes, long platinum hair, and a shark-tooth necklace. While the older folk Sila led still wore the traditional robes of the desert, Miya was a wild thing, dressed in leaves and caked in sand, a primordial child who'd never known civilization. In her left hand, she held a spear with a stone head, and across her shoulders she wore the bow she had carved herself and stringed with vine.

"This ship will be yours when I'm dead," Sila said to her. "And I plan on living as long as your grandfather."

She stomped up closer. "Father, how long do you plan to keep this up?"

He turned away from her, leaned across the railing, and stared at the cliffs that ringed the cove. Gulls and herons flew among the trees above. Somewhere between those trees the two sat chained.

Sun God bless us, he thought with a chill. *Two living Vir Requis. Two demons from the past--here, chained on my island.*

"Father, don't ignore me." Miya came to stand beside him and glared. "You cannot simply keep them chained up like that, like... beasts."

He raised his eyebrow. "I seem to have been doing a good job of it."

She groaned. "They're not here to hurt us. They could have burned us all from the air. They didn't blow fire. They let themselves be caught rather than kill us. And now you will keep them chained and--"

"Miya!" He spun toward her. "For years, I've let you nurse baby birds that fell from nests, toss back fish you pitied, and collect your baskets of caterpillars. But these are no poor animals for you to tend to. These are dragons. These are--"

"They are not dragons," she said, eyes flashing. "Not anymore. They are humans now--a man and a woman--and you chained them to a tree."

"Shapeshifters," he said and spat overboard. "Demons. You weren't there, Miya. You weren't in Tiranor when they burned us."

She looked up into his eyes. "Did they burn us--those two? Valien and Kaelyn?"

"Oh, so they have names now?"

"Yes! They do. I've talked to them, and they have names, and they have stories of their own. They are good Vir Requis, Father. They're... different from the ones you fought."

He snorted.

The ones I fought.

No, Sila had not fought the dragons eighteen years ago. His brothers had. His friends had. They had all burned. But Sila... he was either wiser or he was a coward. Sila had fled. He had loaded his ships with survivors and sailed away. And he left the others behind. He left the millions to burn.

He looked down at the hull of his ship. He could still see those fingernails clawing at the wood, still hear the people begging to be saved.

"The ships are full!" he had shouted that day. "I will return for you. I will return!"

They had wept. They had tried to swim after him. He had loaded his fleet with men, women, and children, cramming them like cargo, a weight nearly too great to bear. He brought them to these islands. And when he sailed back to Tiranor for the others... they were all gone. He found only bones and ash and lingering screams over the water.

"They are all demons," he said, voice barely more than a whisper. "And you should not have talked to them, daughter. I forbid you to speak with them again."

It was her turn to snort. "I speak to whoever I like. Remember what you used to call me when I was a child?"

"You are still a child."

She shook her head. "I am eighteen."

He nodded. "A child."

She growled and stamped her feet. "What did you always call me?"

He groaned and felt his pain melt. "An insufferable, pigheaded, scrawny-legged pest?"

"Father!" She gave a sound like an enraged hippo. "No! You know what you called me. Princess of the Islands. That was your name for me. I was born here, the daughter of our leader. Not born in Tiranor like the rest, but born wild and free, an islander. A princess." She swept her arm through the air, gesturing at the cove. "This is my kingdom, and I go where I like, and I speak to whom I please. So I spoke to your prisoners. And they told me stories. And they want to speak to you too. Will you listen to them?"

He sighed.

He had led merchant fleets through storms. He had battled pirates and kraken. He had led thousands of refugees from inferno into safety. His arms were thick and tattooed with serpents, his shoulders were wide, and his stare, he knew, caused even the strongest sailors to mutter and look away. Yet Miya, it seemed, never saw him as a hero. To her, he was not the burly captain with the withering stare, only her lumbering, old-fashioned father.

Perhaps no man is a hero to his eighteen-year-old daughter, he thought and grumbled.

"I will speak with them once, Miya," he said. "I will let them tell their story. And if I am not satisfied... they will suffer my justice."

Miya sucked in her breath and narrowed her eyes. She began to object, but he hushed her with a glare. Sila had not condemned a man to death in ten years, not since one sailor had slain another after losing a game of dice. He had turned Maiden Island into a land of order, of harsh discipline, and of harsh justice.

If more of those beasts follow, he thought, *all this will end. The new life I built for my people will burn too.* He closed his eyes and saw the dying again, thousands in the water, screaming for him, thrashing like flies in blood, scratching at his hull as he sailed away. *If Requiem flies against us again, Maiden Island too will burn.*

They took a rowboat to the beach, then walked the hidden paths up the maiden's waist. Mint bushes rose around them, bustling with mice. Cedars grew like dark columns. Carob, olive, and pear trees rustled, heavy with fruit. Vines crawled over boulders and the branches of oaks. Frogs and crickets trilled in the grass, herons and jays flew overhead, and turtles sunbathed upon rocks.

I gave Miya a good home here, he thought, looking at her walking beside him, her face tanned deep gold, her blue eyes bright. *I will not let this place burn too.*

A mile from the cove, they reached the maiden's neck, a declivity between the hills of her head and shoulder. The waterfall crashed down ahead, the maiden's hair, and between the trees, their village sprawled.

Sila wasn't sure when he'd stopped calling this place a "camp" and started calling it a "village." They had landed here eighteen years ago as refugees, shivering and afraid and famished. Today were they still refugees or simply islanders?

Four thousand souls lived upon Maiden Island, survivors of the slaughter and those born upon the island. Their huts spread between the trees. Some elders still bore the white, woolen tunics of Tiranor, sturdy garments that had lasted the years. Most now wore clothes of *maidenspun*, a fabric they wove from local leaves and wild cotton. Some, especially the children, simply wore clothes of grass, leaves, and fur.

Looking at the children who ran around, near naked and laughing and wild, Sila sighed.

"We came from a land of golden obelisks, temples that kissed the sky, libraries with a million books, and statues of such beauty that grown men wept to behold them. We fled a beautiful, wise civilization that had ruled the desert for thousands of years." He shook his head ruefully. "And eighteen years later, we're running around half-naked in the mud."

His daughter, her own legs muddy up to the knees, flashed him a grin. "And we thank you for it."

Walking across a grassy plateau dotted with gopher holes, he saw a squad of arquebusers drilling a volley. They stood in five lines, ten men in each, holding their guns to their chests. Across the plateau rose a dragon effigy, life-sized and built of wood, grass, and wicker. Sila paused from walking and placed a hand on his daughter's shoulder.

"Watch," he told her.

The first five men stepped forward, standing in profile to Sila. They raised their arquebuses, masterworks of oak and iron, and pointed the muzzles toward the wicker effigy. They pulled the triggers, and booms *crashed* over the island, so loud that even Miya, who had seen these drills before, jumped and winced. Smoke blasted. The smell of gunpowder flared. Rounds crashed into the wicker dragon, tearing holes through it.

"Good," Sila said. He raised his voice to a shout. "Next line--faster!"

The five shooters, their arquebuses still smoking, marched behind the formation and formed a new line. There they began to reload their guns. As they worked, the next line of men stepped forward. They pulled their triggers. Five more arquebuses fired, roaring across the island, loud as cannons. More holes tore through the wicker dragon.

Sila nodded in approval. For a long time, he had insisted his men drill with empty guns. Iron and gunpowder were rare upon these islands. But yesterday two dragons had flown here, speaking of three thousand more.

"Today we drill with live fire," he said softly.

After each line of gunmen fired, they stepped behind the formation to reload. It was a slow, tedious process. Damn too slow. Sila watched, grumbling.

First the men pulled gunpowder from pouches and refilled their barrels. New rounds--balls of iron the size of marbles--followed, pushed down with ramrods. Some rounds were the wrong size; they had to be wrapped in leaves to snugly fit. Once the barrels were loaded, the men filled the guns' flashpans with more gunpowder. These small, iron receptacles stuck out from the guns like ears; when ignited, they would deliver a spark into the barrel, lighting the main charge. Once barrel and flashpan were ready, the men strung fuses through their matchlocks like tailors stringing thread through a needle. When finally ready to fire, they'd light their fuses, pulling the triggers to bring matchlocks to flashpans.

"It's still too damn slow to reload," Sila said and spat. The whole process took a full minute, even for the fastest fingers.

By the time the first five arquebusers had reloaded, their comrades had all fired their guns. This formation--ten lines of gunners, the front line firing while the others reloaded--meant Sila could maintain gunfire throughout a battle without pause. But it also meant that, at any given moment, most of his men were reloading rather than fighting.

"Grandpapa will find a way to make the guns faster," Miya said.

Sila grumbled. "Your grandfather is a dangerous man. He nearly blew himself up--and half this island--with his inventions."

"And he invented these guns you now use!" she said. "And he invented the scope, which you're always looking through. And he invented the canals to bring water from the spring to our camp. And--"

"Yes, yes, I know all about his inventions," Sila said. "Half the time they work. Half the time they nearly sink the island. We should send him back to his rock."

Miya stamped her feet. "No! You cannot send him back. He's your father. When you're that old, would you like me to banish you to deserted rock?"

"I don't blast huts apart when trying to invent an ice-making machine."

He sighed. He didn't know how he--a burly, laconic captain--
had been born to a scrawny, wild-eyed inventor like Bantis.
Sometimes Sila wondered if the man had simply swapped his true
babe with another, too consumed with a new invention to notice.

"Keep drilling!" he called out to his men. "I want you to
double your speed. When the dragons fly here, it will save your
life."

They nodded and Sila kept walking, crossing the grassy
plateau toward a hill thick with mint bushes, brambles, and trees.
These men drilled to slay dragons, but today Sila had two dragons
he needed very much alive.

When he reached the hill, he turned to Miya.

"Stay here," he said. "I'll speak to them alone."

Her eyes flashed and she raised her fists. "I will go with--"

"You will do as I say," Sila said. He sighed and softened his
voice. "Miya, you are young and fiery and proud. You grew up in
peace, in sunlight, wild among the trees and upon the beach. I gave
you a good life here. Or at least, I tried to."

She lowered her head, then looked up again, stood on tiptoes,
and kissed his cheek. "You did."

"I gave you a life most of our people never knew. They
burned, Miya. I watched them burn. I watched the Vir Requis
burn them and laugh. I saw flesh peeling from bones, and I saw
the proud palaces and temples of Tiranor fall. I saw women and
children swimming after my ships, begging for room I did not have.
I will speak to these shapeshifters now. I will ask them why they
did this to us. I won't hurt them, but I will demand answers. Stay
here, Miya. Stay in this valley in sunlight, grass and trees and water
around you. I will step back into the fire."

Tears gleamed in her eyes, and she nodded. He left her there
and turned toward the hill.

He began to climb. A natural path led up the hillside, carved
by eighteen years of footsteps. Alongside the pebbly trail, mint
bushes, olive trees, and brambles bustled with birds and mice. Ant
hives and groundhog holes rose from wild grass. Boulders of chalk
and granite speckled the hillside like white clouds upon a green sky.

A twisting carob tree crowned the hill, the tallest tree upon
Maiden Island. Its branches spread out like a crown, thick with
dark leaves. Its roots rose from a carpet of fallen fruit. Wooden

strands wove together into its bole, forming a grandfatherly face, complete with two burrows for eyes. Sila often thought of the tree as the island's grandfather, an ancient sentinel watching over him. Sila was not a religious man--back in Tiranor, he had spent little time worshiping the Sun God, the lord of the desert--yet he often thought this tree holy.

You've watched over us for eighteen years, Old Carob, he thought, climbing the trail toward the tree. *Today you watch our greatest enemy.*

Climbing the hill, he could see the island spread all around. The hills rolled down, thick with brush, to golden shores. The sea spread into every horizon, azure under the clear sky.

Maiden Island, he thought and clenched his jaw. *A new haven. I will not let it burn too.*

He took the last few steps toward the hilltop, approached Old Carob, and stared at the two prisoners tied to the trunk.

"Vir Requis," he said, hand on the pommel on his saber.

They stood in human forms now. The ropes binding them to the tree would keep them humans. It had taken a hundred men to cudgel the dragons, knocking their magic out of them. Bruised and bound, the two hardly looked threatening now, but Sila had seen their dragon forms: one dragon large and silver, missing a horn, the other slim and green.

Demons.

The silver dragon now stood as a man, his dark hair streaked with white, his leathery face thick with stubble. He stood tall and wide; his shoulders bulged under his tattered tunic. Sila was among the tallest, strongest men on this island, and this man seemed his match. He seemed on the wrong side of forty--about the same age as Sila--but his eyes seemed older, haunted with ghosts. Those eyes glared now, steaming with rage, but Sila had stared into the eyes of enough enemies to recognize old pain.

Two men of an age, Sila thought. *Two warriors with dark eyes. What secrets do your eyes keep?*

He turned to look at the second Vir Requis. This one was as different from the man as fire from ice. She was a young woman, perhaps twenty years old. Her hair cascaded in waves the color of dark honey, and her hazel eyes blazed with fury. She hadn't the skin for the southern sun, and her nose and cheeks had begun to peel, and her lips were dry and cracked, but she still exuded a northern beauty. Her sharp features and golden mane gave her feline look, a tied lioness who couldn't wait to rip out his throat.

"Two Vir Requis sweep onto our shore," Sila said, flexing his fingers around his hilt. "Two dragons are captured. What should we do with them?" He turned back toward the beefy, haggard man. "You. You have the bearings of a soldier. How did you find us?"

The man's eyes simmered like smelters. When he spoke, his voice was raspy like a man being strangled, a mere death gasp.

"I thought all Tirans were dead. How did *you* get here?"

Sila raised his eyebrows and thrust out his bottom lip. "Asking questions, are we? My friend, where I come from, the man with the sword asks the questions. The man beaten and tied answers. So tell me. We have hidden here for years. How did you find us, and how many will follow you?"

The man spat, nearly hitting Sila's boot. "You hide here from Frey Cadigus. So do we."

Sila blew out his breath and shook his head. "Of course you would claim that. Yet how can I believe you? You perhaps convinced my daughter, but she is young and naive. I've seen too many of your kind. I know your evil, weredragon."

For the first time, the young woman spoke up, straining against her ropes.

"You will not call him that word!" she said and bared her teeth. "You will not use that... slur. He is *Vir Requis*. He is the son of a noble, proud race fallen into darkness, and he fights to restore its light. You speak to Lord Valien Eleison, leader of the Resistance. For twenty years, he's been fighting Frey Cadigus, the man you fled. Show him respect."

Sila turned back toward her. "So quick to change flags, are we? I know you lie. I know you scout these islands for Frey Cadigus, your lord. Are Frey's soldiers so cowardly that a few bruises and a rope make them turncoats?"

She fixed him with a steady, haunted stare. "Yes, I am a turncoat. I turned against Frey Cadigus. But not because of your bruises or your ropes. I rebelled against him three years ago, and I've been fighting him since. I hid from him in mud and ruin. I flew through fire and rain to charge against his lines. I crawled through darkness, and I killed, and I watched my comrades die. And I still fight him. Until my last breath." Her eyes bored into him. "Frey destroyed Tiranor and he destroyed Requiem too. He burned your land; he cloaked ours in darkness. I hate him more than fire hates the rain."

For a moment Sila could say nothing, only stare into the woman's eyes. He had commanded merchant ships through storms. He had commanded ships in battle. He had led men from fire into light. He could read eyes like other men read books, and he could spot a lie like a hound spotting a hare. There was no deception in this woman's eyes. She either spoke truth, or Vir Requis could tell lies like the greatest actors.

He turned back toward the haggard man, this Valien Eleison. "How many do you lead? My father spoke of seeing hundreds of you upon your island. Why are you there? Do you plan an attack against us?"

"We plan an attack against Requiem," Valien growled, and again Sila was taken aback by the sound. The man's voice was little more than a hiss like leather dragged over stone. "We lost a battle upon Requiem's southern coast. We fled to these isles to regroup. We will fight again. You are not our enemy, Tiran. We share an enemy. I lead three thousand fighters, all sworn to slay the emperor. Free me... and join us."

Sila barked a laugh. "Even if I did believe you were a rebel Vir Requis, now you truly speak madness. We are no army here, Valien Eleison. We fled war. We built a new life here. We are people of peace now."

"Is that why I hear gunfire?" Valien grumbled. "Is that why your men carry hand cannons and grapples? Those are tools for slaying dragons."

"Aye." Sila nodded. "For slaying dragons who would attack our shores."

"And yet you did not slay me and Kaelyn. You hear me speak and doubt seeps through you. Deep inside, you believe me, Sila of Tiranor. Because I am like you, and you see it."

It was Sila's turn to growl. His fist clenched around his hilt, and he drew a foot of steel.

"We are nothing alike, weredragon," he said, and his voice shook. "I know your kind. I saw thousands of you swoop and burn my home. I saw--"

"You saw the soldiers of Frey Cadigus," Valien interrupted. "You saw dragons in armor, their helms displaying the red spiral. You saw men march in black steel, the sigil of Frey upon their breasts. You did not see me. You did not see the Resistance. And yes, Sila of Tiranor, we are alike. We both lead men. We both carry the scars of war; I see them in your eyes." His mouth twisted into a mockery of a grin. "And we both hate Frey Cadigus. The question is, Sila... will you hate him in hiding, or will you fight with me?"

Sila found that his fist trembled. Sweat trickled down his back. *Damn it. Damn it!*

He took a step closer, muscles tense and heart pounding. He stood only a foot apart from Valien and stared into his eyes, seeking deceit and finding none.

"Frey cannot be defeated," he said. "All of Tiranor fought him. Three million of my people perished in his flame. You lead a few thousand warriors. Among my people, only two thousand are strong enough to fight. We cannot defeat him."

Valien's twisted grin--a wolf's grin--only widened.

"A few thousand dragons... bearing two thousand gunmen on their backs. The world has never seen such an army. We cannot fight him? Oh... I think we can."

Sila stared at him a moment longer, silent and still.

Then he drew his sword, thrust it forward, and sliced Valien's ropes.

"Come with me to my camp," he said.

As they walked down the hillside, Sila's throat tightened and he could not stop his heart from thrashing. When he looked toward the sea, he saw the waters turn red again, and he saw the refugees begging and scratching at his hull.

I fled war, he thought, fists clenched. *Curse the Sun God. Now it returns to me not with fire, but with a whisper and a hope.*

When they reached his daughter, and she stared at him with earnest eyes, Sila decided that he believed Valien's story... and that frightened him more than a hundred enemy dragons.

LERESY

He spent all night in the hole, digging with his shovel, collecting soil thick with gems, and sifting with a canteen he'd punched full of holes. Erry had given up only an hour after sundown, then gone to sleep upon the beach, but Leresy would not sleep. This was too important.

"Here is my salvation," he whispered as dawn crept through the cave entrance. "Here is my father's death."

He had fashioned his shirt into a sack. Inside glowed thousands of red crystal shards. Each one was no larger than his smallest fingernail, and inside them glowed swirling red liquid like lava.

He straightened, and his back creaked after so many hours hunched over. He lifted the sack of shards, tossed it across his shoulder, and climbed outside the hole into daylight.

Genesis Isle sloped down around him, littered with the barrels, tools, and weapons Bantis had built. Below upon the sand, Erry lay sleeping, her cheek on her hands.

"Wake you, you lazy dog's bottom!" Leresy called out and began walking downhill. "I damn well broke my back while you were dreaming of unicorns."

She sat up, moaned, and rubbed her eyes. "Bloody bollocks, Ler. I wasn't dreaming of no damn unicorns. I was dreaming that you actually had some muscles on you." She stared at his bare torso and grinned. "A good night of shoveling didn't help that dream come true."

He stomped down to the beach, kicked sand onto her, and placed down the shards as she cursed.

"I dug them all up," he said. "What do you reckon they are?"

She spat out sand. "Ladybug shite."

"Be serious." He growled and lifted a shard; it was the size of an apple seed. "These aren't natural gems. They're polished. It looks like... like pieces from a smashed stained-glass window, but there's some liquid inside. They almost look like drops of blood."

He blew out his breath. "Bantis said they're a great weapon. How do you kill with them?"

Erry chewed her lip. "Well, we can tell Frey they're candies and maybe he'll choke. Or we can call him over, then spill the shards onto the floor, so he trips and breaks his neck. Or wait--I know! We can wait until he's very frail and old, and then pelt him to death with them--death by a thousand tiny jabs." She nodded thoughtfully, lower lip thrust out. "Quite a weapon. Definitely more powerful than dragonfire."

Leresy waited and sighed. "Are you done?"

"Or maybe we can--"

"You're done!" he said. "Be quiet. Burn me, I preferred you sleeping. Let's take these shards and find Bantis. He'll know what to make of this."

He cracked his neck and summoned his magic, preparing to shift.

He cleared his throat.

He twisted his toes.

"Or maybe we can make him a necklace so pretty, he'll abandon his wars and become a bar singer named Freyina," Erry said brightly, ignoring him.

Leresy grumbled.

What the Abyss is wrong?

He strained again, tugging at his magic, but no wings sprouted from his back. No scales grew across his body. He remained standing in the sand, a human.

I'm just tired, he thought. He had been digging all night, and was just too weary to fly.

"Or maybe we can--"

"Shut up, Erry!" he said. "I'm trying to focus here."

He gritted his teeth, closed his eyes, and searched deep inside him for the old magic of Requiem, the magic that flowed from the old gods, that let his people become dragons. He felt the flickers inside him, mere whispers. He tried to grab them, but it was like trying to catch the memory of a fading dream; it slipped from his consciousness like smoke between fingers.

He opened his eyes, kicked sand, and shouted.

"Stars damn it! What the Abyss?" He looked at Erry. "I can't do it. It won't work."

She snickered, reached over, and patted his privates. "So it's finally happened."

He grabbed his wrist, tugged her hand away, and snarled. "Don't you worry about that. *That* is fine. I can't... oh bloody stars, I can't shift into a dragon."

She frowned and tilted her head. "What are you on about?"

"You heard me." He spat into the sand. "I can't shift."

"Why not?"

"I don't know. Maybe it's the damn shards."

He looked at the sack of them. They were glowing behind the cloth. And Leresy understood. He clutched his head, leaned over, and laughed.

"Oh maggoty dog vomit," he said, borrowing one of Erry's cusses, and laughed again. He looked up at Erry and grinned. "Erry! He's a genius. Bloody stars, the man is a genius."

"What are you talking about?" she demanded again, glaring. "Stop laughing like an idiot. If you can't fly home, I'm flying without you."

She raised her chin and stretched out.

Nothing happened.

She growled, strained, and hopped about.

She remained a human.

"Having trouble?" Leresy asked.

She roared and glared at him, barely five feet tall but looking fierce as a demon.

"What did you do, you gutter stain?" she said. "Damn you, you sheep-shagger, what the Abyss did you do?"

He grinned. "I didn't do anything." He gestured at the sack of glowing shards. "They did. The red shards. Don't you see?" He whooped, joy brimming in him. "They cancel out magic! They're like... like anecdote to poison. Like light to shadow. Like song to silence."

"Like booze to your brain," she said. "Pretty much wipes it out."

"Pretty much," he admitted. "By the stars, Err! The old man got it. Bantis figured it out." He gave a little Bantis-style jig himself. "No wonder the bugger was dancing about. He knew the way to kill my father all along. Imagine it! The Legions flying toward you, hundreds of thousands of dragons roaring for blood.

You wave these shards around, and they fall from the sky as humans. If any survive the fall, you blast them to death with hand cannons." He punched the air. "This is what I'm talking about. This is how you take Nova Vita."

Erry rolled her eyes. "Yes, yes, that's all fine and dandy, except for one little problem. Nova Vita is far in the north across the sea. And we're, well... stuck on this damn rock!" She shoved him. "How the Abyss do we get back now? We can't fly, you idiot, and Bantis has the raft."

Leresy tapped his cheek. "We were able to fly here, back when the shards were underground." He stared at his makeshift sack of cotton. "See how they glow through the cloth? We need a thicker barrier against whatever magic they're spitting out. It's the light that does it, I reckon."

He looked around the beach, considering. If he had a wooden chest, cast iron pots, or even a sack made of thicker cloth than his old tunic, perhaps he could contain the shards' magic and fly. Would he have to rebury them after all that work?

"How about this?" Erry said. She scampered across the beach, lifted one of the magnifying cylinders, and waved it about. "The ladybug shite can go in here."

"Will you please stop calling them that?" Leresy said.

He grabbed the cylinder from her. It was made of hard, boiled leather like the armor his recruits used to wear. It could work, he had to confess. He popped off the lid, revealing the glass lens, and drew his dagger.

"Don't scratch it," Erry said.

"Be quiet. I'm working."

With a few twists and pokes of his dagger, he pried the lens off the cylinder. He revealed a hollow receptacle about a foot deep. He filled it with red shards, popped the lens back in, and screwed the lid back on. Erry, meanwhile, scurried around the beach and returned with three more magnifying cylinders in her arms. She dumped them at his feet, and Leresy filled those too. It took four cylinders to seal all the red shards.

"Now try to shift," Leresy said, holding the cylinders. "The shards are sealed. No more light. Go on, fly!"

Erry gave a few stretches, touched her toes, and shook her legs. With a clearing of her throat, she shifted.

Wings burst out from her back. Copper scales rose across her. She took flight, her beating wings tossing sand onto Leresy.

"Moldy troll toes, it works!" she said and flew over the water, heading back west. "Now come on, fly after me. We're getting out here."

Leresy unscrewed the lid off a cylinder and pointed it at her. Red light shone out the lens.

Erry's magic vanished.

She tumbled in human form and crashed into the water.

"Leresy, you dung-sucking puddle of codpiece-juice!" She floundered in the water. "I'm going to shove these shards down your throat!"

She swam back to shore, stepped onto the beach, and marched toward him. With a glower that could wilt flowers, she grabbed the cylinders from him and shoved him back.

"Give me those, you piss-drinking maggot worm breath."

"What does that even mean?"

"It means you're a damn child."

He shrugged. "I had to test them. And they work beautifully. Thank you for your dedication to our cause."

She kicked his shin, and when he cursed and leaped with pain, she sealed the open cylinder. She held all four cylinders to her chest and shifted back into a dragon, taking the vessels into her larger form. She beat her wings and flew again.

Leresy summoned his magic. It crackled through him, as familiar as a warm, old cloak. He rose as a dragon, blasted fire against the sand below, and flew after Erry.

As they dived across the sea, heading back to Horsehead Island, Leresy imagined the Legions flying toward him, a storm of scale and fire covering the sky.

And he imagined them falling.

"I'm coming home, Father," he said into the wind.

As he flew onward, a grin stretched across his face, wide enough to hurt his cheeks. He had to keep grinning. He had to keep drowning that fear under rage, or he would see the blood again, the fire and death and guns blazing.

"I will face you again, Requiem," he swore. "And this time I will not run. This time I will win."

He flew. He kept grinning--forced himself to keep grinning--even as his tears fell and his belly twisted.

RUNE

He sat in his cell, chained and bruised, and stared at the wall that awaited him.

He had stared at these instruments for so many days, they had become like people to him, staring back at him, waiting, thirsty for his blood. The thumbscrew hung from the wall, its two bolts like eyes watching him, its vise like a mouth waiting to bite his fingers.

I will crush your fingers and toes! it cried to him, staring, waiting. *Your bones will snap between my jaws.*

Rune turned his eyes toward the stretching rack. Knots in the wood reminded him of a face, sagging and cruel.

I will tear your bones from your sockets, Rune, the face hissed at him. *Come lie with me.*

The pliers laughed from the wall, tiny iron crocodiles hungry for his fingernails. The rusted hooks sang for his entrails. The floggers screamed for his flesh.

We await you, Rune! The instruments sang and danced upon the wall. *We will make you sing with us. We will dance with blood.*

Chained to the wall, Rune only smiled at them.

"I won't fear you," he said. "You're my friends. I can't fear friends."

That confused them. They fell silent. Good. Good. If they had faces, friendly faces that were funny, he would not fear them. He would only laugh at their taunts.

Friends.

Tilla had been his friend once. Once. Years ago. Eras ago. In a different world, one that had burned. A world of sand and water and dreams now buried under ash.

"Are you still my friend?" he whispered into the shadows as the sun fell outside.

He did not know. Tilla served the red spiral now. She served those who hurt him. Tilla tried to protect him, but... she wasn't always here. She wasn't here when the guards kicked him, when they spat in his food, when they spilled his water across the floor, leaving him to lick moisture from dust and encrusted blood. But she had been there when Lynport burned. She had flown above, watched their city fall, and fought for *him*.

"For the demon," Rune whispered through cracked lips.

For the golden beast. For the creature with many heads. For Frey Cadigus.

Rune could see it again in the darkness. His home burning. The golden dragon above, his minions behind him, a hundred thousand strong. Kaelyn cried for him from the tower, and everywhere below the corpses lay, all those he'd grown up with, all those he'd loved, burnt and torn apart. So many screams. So much fire. Evil itself, a blanket of scale and smoke and fang, swirling above in a storm.

And her.

"And you."

The white dragon. A single beam of light breaking through the storm, warm and kind, caressing him, taking him under her wing. His dearest friend. His love. His Tilla.

"I have to save you from him," he whispered, his throat dry, his lips cracked and bleeding. "Even if they break me. Even if all those tools on the wall hurt me. I have to save you from him."

He tried to imagine it--Tilla leading him outside the tower, holding his frail body in her claws, and flying south. Flying away from the capital. Flying to the sea, across the waters, and into distant lands where Frey could not find them. They would find another home. Another beach to walk along, sand to caress their feet, water to wash away their pain. He would hold her in the night, kiss her lips again, and they would be as they were.

"And you will be good again," he spoke into the darkness, voice choked. "You will be Tilla Roper again, not Lanse Tilla Siren, not this creature they molded you into. And I will just be Rune. Not Relesar Aeternum, not any king. Just Rune and Tilla on the beach. That's all I want."

For a year, fighting in the Resistance, Rune had prayed to see her again. And now he saw Tilla here every night. She came to him in her armor, a machine of the enemy, and she spoke to him. Sat with him in the dark. Held him in her arms, and whispered to him, and kissed his cheek, and begged him to join her.

"But I will not let this happen to us. I cannot forget who you were."

The sun fell outside, casting orange light through the arrowslits. On cue, keys rattled in the lock. The door creaked open. And there she stood.

"Hello, Tilla," he said, sitting in the corner, his arms and legs chained.

Her sword hung from one hip, her punisher from the other. She had never used the instrument on him, but when the moon fell to darkness, when her time to sway him ended, would she burn his flesh?

As always, she sat by his side. As always, she wore her armor, the fine black plates of an officer. She stared at the wall with him, saying nothing.

"A fine pair we make," he said. "Me wearing my prisoner rags, you wearing your steel. Me with my face all dirty and thin, you with your face so pale, your eyes sad."

"It doesn't have to be this way," she whispered, her voice choked. She looked at him. "You can wear armor too, not rags. You can fight with us. For Requiem."

He looked away from her, leaned back as far as he could in his chains, and smiled softly. "Do you remember the mancala board I carved that winter, the one with the seashell pieces? It was such a cold winter, too cold for the south. Rain and thunder and wind every day. We sat in the Old Wheel most nights by the fire. You'd wrap a blanket around your shoulders. And we'd play mancala and drink ale, and Scraggles would lie at your feet. Do you remember? We--"

"Stop it," she said.

He let his smile widen and closed his eyes. "And the apple pies my father would bake! Stars, the whole place would smell of apples, and--"

"Stop it!" she said, more vehemently this time, and grabbed his arm. "Rune, those days are gone. The Old Wheel burned. You know this." Her fingers tightened and she stared at him. "Our home is gone. Everything we've ever known is gone."

He looked into her dark eyes and shook his head. "You're still here."

"I am not the woman I was."

"You are Tilla Rop--"

"I am Lanse Tilla Siren!" she said and bared her teeth. "I serve the red spiral. I follow Frey Cadigus. And so will you, Rune. So will you." She rose to her feet. "I placed you in the dungeon so you could hear the prisoners scream, see their blood, and languish in the dark. And still you did not worship him. So I placed you here, in this tower, so you could stare at the instruments of torture and imagine their pain. And still you do not join me."

"And still you, Tilla, do not join me," he said. He struggled to his feet, the chains so heavy, and stood before her. "You can end this. You have the key. You can flee with me."

She stared at him coldly, face blank as always, but something filled her eyes this time, something cold and afraid. She touched his cheek and whispered.

"So I will take you to a third place. And in this place, Rune... you will join us. I promise you. This place will break you."

She reached behind him and unchained him from the wall. She left his wrists manacled, but for the first time in days, no shackles bound him to the wall.

She held his shoulder and guided him toward the door. He walked with small steps. For nearly a moon now, he'd languished in irons. His chain had been long enough to let him stand and lie down, but not to walk. Walking now, every step ached, shooting pain from his toes, up his legs, and down his spine to the tailbone. He winced and almost fell, but Tilla held his arm, a gentle jailor, helping him onward.

The climb downstairs seemed an eternity. Rune did not count the steps, but there were hundreds, maybe a thousand. Each one shot more pain through him, and his head spun. He was too weak, too hungry, too hurt. The guards had kicked him too strongly. When they finally reached the bottom, Rune panted and swayed.

They stepped through the doorway, past the two guards with the mocking eyes, and into a snowy courtyard. The walls of the Citadel rose all around them. More guards stood upon the battlements, faces hidden behind helms. From within those walls, screams rose, a chorus of a thousand prisoners mad and beaten and dying. Rune had spent his first week here with them, and just hearing their screams, he could imagine their anguished faces.

"We fly from here," Tilla said. "I'll carry you."

"Unchain me and I'll fly with you."

He had tried to shift many times in his chains, only to find he could not. Whenever he'd summon his magic, the ancient starlight of Requiem, his body would start to grow, and wings would start to sprout from his back... and then the chains would slam him back into human form, leaving him panting and dizzy. Rune could shift with clothes, with weapons, even with armor; those were parts of him like his skin. The chains were foreign objects; they shackled his human form, and they shackled his dragon magic.

Tilla shook her head. "I cannot unchain you. Not yet. Not until you join us. I'll carry you."

She stepped away from him, leaving deep prints in the snow, and shifted. Her scales were white as the snow, but her eyes were black, two pools of night against a starry field. When she flapped her wings, she scattered snow across the courtyard, revealing its cobblestones. Smoke plumed from her nostrils, and fire glowed between her teeth, a single patch of color in a white and black world. Rune stood before her, chained and shivering, and she reached out her claws. She lifted him, an owl lifting a mouse, and flew.

Wind whistled. Snow swirled around them. The Citadel dwindled below. Rune watched it shrink until it looked like a toy, just a pile of blocks white with snow. The city streets snaked around it, bustling with people, thousands of men and women and children all going about their lives. Thousands of souls who cared not for his war. Thousands of souls who knew him as an outlaw, a killer, a beast to be tortured.

They flew over the streets, the city arena, and a dozen towering statues of Frey. They flew toward a fortress with black towers, a place Rune had only seen once in darkness.

"Castra Draco," he whispered. "Bastion of the Legions."

The Legions had many forts across the empire. Some trained recruits. Most housed garrisons of troops. Some, like the Citadel, housed prisoners, and one--Castra Academia--trained nobles for leadership. Draco was the heart of them all. If the Legions were an empire of their own, this would be its imperial palace. From this place did the generals command.

Will she take me there for torture? Rune thought, watching the fortress grow nearer. *Will she place me in another dungeon and in more chains, and will the whips of her comrades tear my skin?*

Yet when they almost reached the castle, Tilla banked and descended toward a street lined with tall, narrow houses. Rune remembered this street. Last year, he had rummaged here with Kaelyn through a barrel for posters. His heart twisted at the memory.

"Kaelyn," he whispered, and his eyes stung.

Last year, running and hiding with Kaelyn through the wilderness, Rune had often found comfort in thinking about Tilla-- remembering her dark eyes, her smooth black hair, her soft lips, and his childhood spent with her upon the boardwalk. Hiding with Kaelyn, a wild rebel with flashing eyes, Rune had sought his comfort with the ghost of an old love.

Today, clutched in that same old love's claws, Rune thought of Kaelyn.

For so long, Kaelyn, I wanted to escape you, he thought. *I wanted to go back home, back to Tilla, to never see you and Valien and war again. But now I miss you.*

He missed her eyes rolling at him. He missed her finger jabbing his chest. He missed the sound of her groaning at his jokes. And he missed her smile. He missed her courage, her light that shone in the dark, and her love of life and home.

He wondered if she even still lived. Last time he'd seen the young woman, she had stood upon the tower of Castellum Acta, dragon wings billowing her golden hair, and she had cried his name. Had she fled with Valien through the tunnel? Did she live now in exile, and was she thinking of him too?

Wings puffed out, Tilla descended into a side street in the shadow of Castra Draco. Narrow, three-story houses lined the street, their tiled roofs white with snow, their gray bricks frosted. She placed Rune down outside one house, shifted back into human form, and stood beside him.

Rune stood on shaky feet, shivering in the snow. He wanted to hug himself, but manacles still bound his wrists behind his back. Orange light glowed from windows, and oil lamps flickered along the street, but Rune saw no other people. Tilla walked toward the house, unlocked the door, and led him inside.

"Welcome," she said, "to my home."

A cozy room greeted them. An armchair stood by a fireplace. Leather-bound books stood upon shelves. Plates of bread, cheese, ham, and fruits stood upon a wooden table. Tilla stepped toward the fireplace and soon flames crackled, filling the room with warmth and light.

"You are a legionary," Rune said, looking around the chamber. "I thought you would live in a fortress, surrounded by blades and shields."

Tilla locked the door behind her, then began unbuckling her armor and hanging the pieces on pegs.

"The common soldiers do. I'm an officer. I'm the officer who saved Shari's life." She gave a rare, crooked smile. "Some comforts are allowed for me here in the capital. The house is mine. When I asked to be stationed in Nova Vita, the Cadigus family bought it for me, a place of my own outside my barracks."

Rune wondered who had lived here before Tilla, and if Cadigus had truly "bought" the place, or if he'd made the previous occupant conveniently vanish.

"Why did you bring me here?" he asked, hearing the bitterness in his voice. "To gloat? To show off your comfort while I languish in a cell?"

Her eyes flashed with rage, then softened, and she sighed. She unbuckled her last plate of armor and stood before him in a woolen tunic. Suddenly she looked so much like the old Tilla--Tilla Roper from Lynport--that Rune could almost smell the sea.

"Not to gloat," she said. She began to load a plate with bread slices, slabs of ham, cheese, and grapes. "To share this with you. Come, sit with me and eat."

The armchair was wide enough for two. Tilla sat in one corner, the plate on her lap, and patted the space beside her.

"Will you unchain me before our meal?" he asked, standing before her.

"You know I can't. Not yet. Sit by the fire with me. Eat and drink with me. Please."

He wanted to refuse. He wanted to barge against the door, break it open, and run into the street. Yet he doubted he was strong enough. He was barely strong enough to stand. He was too famished, too thirsty, too tired. He sat by her in the armchair, his wrists still bound behind him, and let the flames warm him. It was a tight squeeze. Pressed against him, Tilla's body warmed him as much as the fire.

"It's a bit hard to eat with my wrists chained," he said.

She held a grape up for him. "Pretend I'm not your jailor, but your beautiful serving girl, feeding you grapes in luxury."

"Is that a joke, Tilla? You can joke at a time like this?"

"Eat."

He could not refuse it. He needed this food. He took the grape into his mouth, chewed, and swallowed. The juices flowed down his throat, sweet and healing. He had never known food to taste this good.

They ate, the fireplace warming them. Tilla held out pieces of cheese, ham, and bread for him, and he ate those too. He drank wine from her mug.

"It feels almost like the old days," she said. "Sitting by the fire at the Old Wheel."

He swallowed another grape and looked at her. She stared at the fire, her face golden in the light, as if lost in memory.

"I thought you didn't like to remember," he said.

She looked at him, her eyes soft. "I always remember, Rune. Always. I never forget. We can have a life again. Together. Here in this home." She held his knee and leaned closer, bringing her face but an inch from his. "I spoke to the emperor about it already. He will let you live here with me." A tear trailed down to her lips. "You and me together again. Always."

He looked away from her at the crackling fire. "And at what cost? I would have to serve him."

"You would. You would join the Legions. You would train. The training is difficult, but you will survive it, and I will be there, watching over you. You will fight for Cadigus, a soldier like me. You will raise his banners and bear his sigil. You will hail him in the days like I do. But at night, Rune... at night you can come back here to me."

Suddenly the food tasted stale.

"I cannot serve him," he said. "How can you serve him, Tilla? How can you wear that armor? Bear the red spiral? Worship the man who killed my father, who burned our home, who crushes Requiem under his heel?"

"Because I want to live!" She grabbed his cheeks and forced his face back toward her. Her eyes flashed and her lips peeled back. "Because I'm a survivor. Damn it, you don't have to love him. Do you think I do? Do you think anyone does? Do you think I love the man who burned our home? You don't have to love him, Rune. You only have to fear him."

"Is that what you do? Fear him? Are you a warrior or a coward?"

"A survivor," she said. "I joined the Legions and I served him. I did what I had to do to live. And I'm trying to save your life too. Call it cowardice if you will. I'd rather be a live legionary than a dead resistor."

Rune thought of Kaelyn again, the woman who hid in burrows, crawled through the mud, and fought through fire and rain. He thought of Valien, his guiding star, the man who lived in ruins but sang for light. They were brave. They were noble. Did they even still live?

"I don't want to die," he said, Tilla's hand still holding his knee. "But I have to believe they're still alive somewhere. Kaelyn. Valien. The others. I have to believe there is still hope for them. For Requiem. And for you, Tilla."

She blinked tears from her eyes. She rose to her feet.

"Come with me, Rune. I want to show you something."

She helped him to his feet and headed toward a staircase. They climbed upstairs into a bedchamber. A clock stood upon a bureau. An iron spiral hung upon the wall over a bed. Outside the window, beyond a few snowy trees, loomed the towers of Castra Draco.

"What did you want to show me here?" Rune said, lips twisting bitterly. "The spiral that hangs over your bed? The fortress that shadows you even here?"

She shook her head. "No. I wanted to show you this."

She stepped toward her bed and lifted something off her pillow. When she turned back toward him, a shaky smile trembled on her face, and her eyes were moist.

A string of seashells lay in her palm.

Rune blinked and felt his own eyes dampen. The memories pounded through him. Once more he was walking along the beach under the cliffs. The waves glistened in the sun and splashed over his bare feet. A boy of fourteen, he collected seashells into a pouch, choosing only the nicest ones. He strung them along a string for her. He gave her this gift for her birthday, and she laughed and tousled his hair.

"You kept it," he whispered.

She placed it around her neck and touched his cheek. "It means more to me than all the spirals and forts in the world. It means more to me than my sword, than my shield, than my empire. It's our childhood. It's our memory. It's our love."

She kissed him. Her lips were full and soft, and her tongue sought his, and her fingers smoothed his cheeks. It tasted like salt-- the salt of her tears and the sea. Rune closed his eyes and he hated her, and he hated what she fought for, and he loved her.

"I want you to come into my bed," she said. "And I want to make love to you. Because I love you, Rune Brewer. I always have, and I can't bear to lose you."

She took him into his bed. It was soft and warm and so was she. She removed their clothes, held him close, and kissed him again. Their bodies moved under the blankets, a dance more intoxicating than wine, than all their flights over the sea. He had never lain with a woman before, but this felt right. This was home.

When it was done, they lay together in bed. He lay on his back, and she leaned up on her elbows, kissed his lips, and played with his hair.

"I want us to stay here forever," she said. "Stay with me here."

He looked at her pale face, her smooth black hair, her dark eyes that spoke of so many years and lost memories. He wanted to stay here with her. He wanted to choose her kisses, not the whips and the rack.

He looked up at the iron spiral that hung above them. He looked out the window at the fortress towers. And he thought of Kaelyn--his comrade, his friend, the woman he had fought with. He thought of her still fighting in the mud.

"Flee with me," he said to Tilla. "Flee south with me, and we'll fight him together. But I cannot join him. I cannot serve him. Not for you. Not for anything. Flee with me south and fight with us... or return me to my cell."

Her tears splashed against his chest. She took him downstairs. She flew with him. And she returned him to his cell.

ERRY

She wandered along Maiden Island, tears in her eyes.

"Tirans," she whispered. "My father's people."

She reached into her pocket, found her father's medallion, and clutched it so hard it hurt.

All her twenty years, Erry had lived among Vir Requis, her mother's people, an ancient race with the magic to become dragons. She had lived with them in Lynport upon the docks. She had served with them in the Legions. And finally, she had spent moons with ragged Vir Requis refugees upon Horsehead Island. Erry had inherited Requiem's magic from her mother, and she too could become a dragon, unlike her father's people. Yet she had always felt the outcast. A half-breed. The scrawny bastard of a whore and a foreign sailor.

But here... here on this southern island shaped like a sleeping woman... here the dormant half of her, her southern desert blood, blazed with waking fire.

"They're real, Scraggles," she whispered to her dog. "Stars, they survived. They live. My people."

Thousands wandered the camp around her. Erry had imagined Tirans to be short and scrawny like her; she had always blamed her father's blood for her diminutive frame. And yet they were a tall people, maybe even taller than Vir Requis. Their hair shone a platinum so pale it was almost white. Their eyes were blue as sapphires, their skin golden. Rune had once shown her a painting of Tirans he kept hidden, and in that painting, they wore golden armor and rode horses between palisades of columns. Yet here around her, they lived as wild islanders, clad in leaves and homespun; only a few of the elders still wore old, embroidered cotton of the desert.

Erry wiped tears from her eyes.

"Damn it, Scraggles," she whispered, then knelt and hugged her dog. "We... we could have been here with them. All those years I spent on the docks. All that damn year in the Legions. All those cold, lonely, painful nights in Requiem... and they were here. In sunlight. Happy. Alive. I could have been here with them."

Scraggles licked the tears from her cheeks.

Erry kept moving through the camp. Elders sat upon logs, singing old songs about Tiranor: her golden dunes, her lush oases of fig and palm trees, her fallen temples of sandstone and platinum, and her wisdom lost. Children scampered about, laughing, the sun shining upon their pale hair. Young couples walked hand in hand, whispering and smiling secret smiles. They were refugees. Their land had fallen. And yet still they seemed to Erry happier than she herself had ever felt.

"Do you think they'd let me live with them?" she asked Scraggles. She bit her lip and her eyes still stung. "Or would I be an outcast here too?"

She was half Tiran, that was true, but she looked Vir Requis. Her hair and eyes were brown, not platinum and blue. She was scrawny and short, not tall and noble. She spoke with the rough accent of Requiem's southern coast--odd enough among northerners like Leresy, Kaelyn, and Valien--not the flowing lilt of the desert.

"But I have this," she whispered. "I have my father's medallion."

She pulled it from her pocket and slung it around her neck. She had never dared wear her father's memento in Requiem, not in that empire that had burned the desert and hunted its people. Yet here she could wear it freely, and she clutched the silver. The medallion was shaped like a sunburst, symbol of Tiranor, and it had often comforted Erry during the long, cold nights. Her father, a Tiran sailor, had paid for her mother with this medallion, hiring her for a night of pleasure before sailing back south. Some would see it as shameful--the cost of a whore--but to Erry, the medallion had always brought hope. It had always been a symbol of another world, a better place.

And now I've found that place, she thought, looking around the camp of sunlight, greenery, and noble folk of her blood.

A young woman was climbing a fig tree ahead. She was reaching for the fruit, but the figs hung just beyond her grasp. When she saw Erry, the youth waved and cried out.

"Can you help me?"

Erry stepped closer, hesitant. A life upon the docks had taught her to fear strangers; those who asked for help often wanted more than she could give.

"What do you want?" she said, approaching the fig tree. Could this girl somehow see her Tiran blood, and would she mock her for it, call her a half-breed and bastard?

"I need a push," the girl said. "Please?"

She clung to the tree trunk, several feet above the ground, straining to reach a branch heavy with fruit. Yet far as she stretched, the branch remained an inch out of reach.

Erry realized her belly was rumbling. If she helped, perhaps the girl would share the prize. She wove her fingers together, forming a little shelf with her hands, and pushed up the girl's foot. The young Tiran snagged some fruit, smiled, and hopped down to the ground.

"Thanks," she said and grinned. Her teeth were very white in her golden face. Her long hair was almost as white, a smooth flag that swayed in the breeze. Her eyes seemed like sapphires to Erry, blue and bright.

"Now give me half of those fruits," Erry said.

The girl laughed. "You deserve them, fair enough. Come, eat with me." She reached out her hand. "My name is Miya."

Erry stared at the oustretched hand, not moving. So many times upon the docks, people had offered her food, but they had always wanted something in return. So many times, Erry had accepted an outreached hand, only to have that hand beat her later. So many men had offered food and shelter for her body. Leresy too had offered a smile and meal, only for him to later use and strike her.

How can I trust anyone? Erry wondered.

As the girl's smile faded, Erry lowered her head.

I can't be the old Erry here, she thought, *afraid and angry and hiding. These are Tirans. Their blood pumps through me. Miya is only a youth, not a man who lusts for me. I'll have to be different here, or I'll forever be the dock rat.*

She reached out, grabbed Miya's hand, and shook it.

"My name is Erry. Let's eat."

They sat upon a flat boulder under the shade of a pine. Wildflowers and fallen needles spread around them. The hillside sloped down at their feet, leafy with mint bushes, mulberry trees, and swaying wild oats. Far below, a golden shore faded into the sea. For a moment, the two young women sat silently, watching the waves and eating the figs.

"Is it true?" Miya finally asked, breaking the silence. "Your leader, the man Valien... he says he can defeat Frey." She looked over at Erry, her eyes wide. "Do you believe him?"

Erry shrugged and took another bite. She chewed for a moment, considering.

"I don't know. Sometimes I think he's mad."

"And yet you fight with him."

Erry allowed herself to laugh, but her eyes stung. "Frey burned my home. And so I fight. I have nowhere else to go. Can we win? I don't know. But fighting is better than just lying down and dying."

As she spoke those words, Erry didn't know which home she meant: Lynport... or the desert kingdom she had never seen.

Miya bit into a second fig. "He burned my home too. I've never seen Tiranor. I was born here on this island. But my father... he speaks of home often." She gazed across the sea as if she could see that distant, fallen kingdom. "He said that most of Tiranor was just desert--dunes, mountains, and endless plains of sand. But a great river flowed through it, the Pallan, a giver of life. Oases grew alongside its banks, lush with fruit trees, shade, and a thousand kinds of birds. Limestone towers rose among them, capped with platinum. Great cities sprawled between the trees, centers of learning, their libraries and universities as large as palaces." Miya's eyes gleamed. "I wish I could have seen Tiranor. But she is fallen now. We are all that remains."

Erry stared across the sea, trying to imagine it.

"It sounds a lot nicer than Requiem," she said. "I wish I could have seen it too." She reached under her collar, pulled out her silver amulet, and showed it to Miya. "Can you read the letters here? I've never known what it says."

Miya's eyes widened. "This... this is Tiran silver! This is the sunburst of our god. How did you get this?"

Erry glared. "I didn't steal it, if that's what you mean."

"I didn't mean..." Pain filled Miya's eyes. "I'm sorry. Let me see."

The young Tiran girl held the amulet, leaned closer, and examined it.

"Well, can you read it?" Erry said. She herself had never learned to read; she didn't even know whether Tiranor and Requiem used the same letters.

Miya nodded and closed her eyes, saying nothing.

"Well, what does it say, damn it?" Erry scowled. "Won't you tell me?"

Maybe she had been wrong to trust this girl. Would Miya accuse her of being a thief? All her life upon the docks, fellow girls would accuse Erry of being a prostitute, a burglar, and a bastard. Men would beat Erry; girls would taunt her, their words more painful than blows. Was Miya just one of them, a pretty young thing who thought it fun to mock the orphan?

"Well, forget it then, damn you!" Erry said. She yanked the amulet back, rose to her feet, and was about to stomp away... and froze.

Tears were flowing down Miya's cheeks.

Erry stared. "Bloody stars, what...?" She sat back down. "Miya, why are you crying?"

The young Tiran sniffed and smiled tremulously.

"The words on your amulet... My father used to speak them. I haven't heard them in many years. Your amulet bears our Old Words, the prayer of Tiranor. *We Will Never Fall.*" She blinked tears from her eyes. "For thousands of years, our people spoke those words in the desert."

Erry felt all her rage flow away, and her own eyes stung. She clutched the amulet to her chest.

"We will never fall," she repeated in a whisper. "I like that."

Miya sighed and lowered her head. "And yet we did fall. Perhaps that prayer is meaningless now."

Erry shook her head mightily. "We did *not* fall. Look around you." She swept her arm around, gesturing at the camp. "I see thousands of survivors. I see a new life for our people. This amulet is right. We *will* never fall."

The young woman looked up and tilted her head. "Our... people? Erry, aren't you--"

Before she could complete her question, a shout rose from among the trees.

"Erry Docker! Damn you, you filthy urchin. Docker, where are you?"

Erry sighed. It was Leresy.

"Oh, bloody bollocks," she said and watched the outcast prince emerge from the trees.

Leresy stomped forward, hands on his hips, his chin raised with the same old vanity of royalty. A few dried leaves topped his golden hair instead of a crown, and he wore only tattered rags rather than finery, but he still strutted around as if he owned the world.

And as if he owns me, Erry thought.

He pointed at her. "There you are. Stars damn it, woman, didn't you hear me? Come with me. The council is about to begin, and I need you there."

She glared and spat at his feet. "Go find a rotting turtle carcass to shag, Leresy. I'm eating figs. I don't need no fancy-arse council for princelings."

He groaned and rolled his eyes. "Burn me. I need you to demonstrate the damn shards. Remember? Valien will be there, and so will my sister. The leader of this rabble will be there too, some oaf named Sila."

It was Miya's turn to glare. The young woman hopped onto her feet, crossed her arms, and growled.

"Sila is a great captain," she said. "He is my father. You will show him respect."

Leresy guffawed. He looked at Miya as if noticing her for the first time. His eyes trailed up and down, taking in her golden skin, pale hair, and slim body clad in leaves.

"Well, burn me," he said. "Another damn urchin. As if one weren't enough."

Erry grabbed a pine cone and tossed it at him. "She's got more bollocks than you do, Leresy. Brains too I reckon, but so does this pine cone. And I'm not some trained monkey. You want to demonstrate the shards? Use them on yourself, preferably while flying over a campfire."

He groaned, walked forward, and grabbed her arm. "Just come on. Bloody Abyss. Eating figs! We've got more important things to do. Planning how to kill my father, say." He began pulling her down the hillside, then called back up toward Miya. "You! Little girl. You come with us too. You'll want to see this."

Miya fumed, her arms crossed and her eyes blazing. She looked ready to claw Leresy to death. But it seemed curiosity overcame her anger. Grumbling under her breath, she followed.

They made their way downhill, heading toward the southern shore. Back at Horsehead Island, where the Resistance had been camping, Erry would fly from hilltop to beach. Since arriving here at Maiden Island that morning, she had been walking everywhere.

"These people watched dragons burn down their kingdom," Valien had told her. "We don't wish to stir those memories. Do not take dragon form around Tirans."

And so they walked, though Erry's soles ached, and rocks and thistles covered the hillside. Birds and mice rustled in the bushes, wild oats swayed taller than Erry's knees, and a falcon chased starlings overhead. The stems of old walls rose from the grass, only a foot tall and smoothed to lumps. Grass, vines, and cyclamens all but covered them.

"Somebody once lived here," Erry said.

Miya nodded, walking at her side, the wind in her hair. "My father said the Ancients lived on these islands. They were a wise people who vanished thousands of years ago. Father said they were great explorers who sailed around the world, navigating by the stars."

Walking ahead of the two, Leresy snorted. "Lot of good it did them. Nothing left of the buggers but a few old bricks."

He kicked an old wall, stubbed his toe, and wailed. Erry and Miya nearly fell over laughing.

After an hour of walking, they had crossed the island's waist and beheld a cove. Erry's eyes widened and she gasped.

"Stars above," she said. "Would you look at that."

Leresy frowned. "What the Abyss are those things?"

Erry grinned, remembering the paintings Rune had kept hidden under his floorboards. "They're ships. Tirans use them to navigate the seas."

Leresy guffawed. "Those things? Primitive. I'd take flying any day."

Erry glared at him. "Is it hard work being such a horse's arse, or does it come naturally to you? Tirans can't fly, and I think their ships are beautiful."

She stood a moment, admiring them. Six ships floated in the cove, their sails folded upon their masts. From bow to stern, they looked longer than the greatest dragon from snout to tail's tip. Cannons lined their decks, and their figureheads were shaped as birds. Their hulls sported sunbursts, the paint faded to dull ocher, and beneath them appeared words Erry could now read.

"We will never fall," she whispered.

Miya nodded. "See the largest ship, the one with the crane figurehead? That's the *Golden Crane*, our flagship. My father is captain. Our council will be held there."

They walked downhill, heading to the cove. A small oared boat waited at a dock, and they climbed in. As they rowed, Erry stared up at the *Golden Crane*, clutched her medallion, and felt peace flow across her. Leresy be damned, this ship was beautiful. It was not merely a vessel, she thought, but a symbol of a better time. It was Tiranor in her golden age, navigating the seas, a proud desert kingdom of spice, song, and secrets. It was Lynport before the Regime, a thriving port town, welcoming such ships to its docks.

Long ago, these ships would sail into Lynport, Erry thought. They had brought southern silk, spice, and gems. The boardwalk had been alive then, not a ruin of rotten wood and urchins rifling through trash, but a hub of trade. Rune's father would sell his ale to these sailors, and Tilla's father would sell his ropes, and Mae's father would sell bread.

And my mother sold her body, Erry thought. *I come from these ships. They brought me too into Requiem.*

When they climbed onto the deck, she saw Valien and Kaelyn already there. They had shed their charred, torn leather and wool-- the clothes they had fled Lynport with--and wore tunics of *maidenspun,* a fabric the Tirans wove from wild cotton. They still bore their swords of Requiem. A heavy, two-handed sword hung across Valien's back, an ancestral weapon of House Eleison. Kaelyn wore Lemuria upon her hip, her thin sword of dragonforged steel. They were ancient blades, weapons of honor and history and tradition.

Yet honor, history, and tradition are passing from the world, Erry thought. She looked at a rack of hand cannons that lay against the bulwark--*arquebuses,* she had heard the Tirans call them. *Our blades will rust; gunpowder will rise, a demon of greater malice.*

"Welcome to the *Golden Crane.* Welcome to my council."

Erry turned toward the voice. She saw a man emerging from the ship's hold. He was tall and wide--as large as Valien--and almost as gruff. His face was wide, leathery, and golden, his nose flat and his jaw heavy. Stubbly platinum hair covered his scalp, cut so short he was almost bald. Grooves lined his face; Erry couldn't tell if they were wrinkles or scars. He wore maidenspun, a wide belt, and baggy pants--simple garb, yet he moved with the aura of command.

Miya approached the man, kissed his cheek, and introduced him.

"This is my father, Captain Sila. Father, this is Leresy Cadigus, the outcast prince of Requiem, son of Emperor Frey. His companion is Erry Docker, once a soldier in the Legions. Both now fight for Valien."

"*With* Valien," Leresy corrected, raised his chin, and cleared his throat. "I serve no man."

Erry jabbed him with her elbow, glowered, and hissed from the corner of her mouth. "Quiet, Leresy. Nobody cares about your stupid pride."

Under the noon sun, pelicans flying overhead and the ship gently rocking, the council began.

Valien spoke the most, straining to hiss the words through his ruined throat, but never slowing his speech. He spoke of battles they'd fought: the Battle of Castra Luna, where Erry had flown in the Black Rose Phalanx, fighting against the Resistance; and the Battle for Lynport, where Erry had fought on the other side. And he spoke of older battles too, battles that had raged in the north years ago, back when Erry had still lived upon the docks. And he spoke of future battles: of his plans to storm the capital of Nova Vita, to surround Frey in his palace, and to slay the man.

Sila spoke too, gruff captain of the *Golden Crane,* and Erry learned that he not only ruled this ship, but all the island. He spoke of leading a merchant fleet years ago, of fighting the Legions when they had invaded his homeland, and of fleeing burning Tiranor with all those he could load onto his ship.

"We've trained for battle," Sila said. "My father invented the arquebus, and we've forged two thousand of the guns here on this island, melting down everything from swords to belt buckles for the metal. I've drilled an army of men and women. We know how to fight." He grumbled. "Yet we've only trained to fight off dragons should they attack our island. We've never dreamed of invading Requiem, let alone her capital. How would we? We are only a few. The Legions are half a million strong, they say."

Valien nodded. "We are few and they are many. Yet now we have new weapons. Now we have hope. Leresy!" He turned toward the former prince. "Show him the scope."

The young man nodded, rummaged through his pack, and produced one of the leather magnifying cylinders; Erry had learned the Tirans called them *scopes*. It rattled, still full of the glowing crystal shards they had found.

"Erry, go on, fly around a bit," Leresy said.

She placed her hands on her hips. "I'm not doing it again. Just tell them how it works."

"Bloody griffin vomit, Erry, they need to see it." Leresy scowled. "Just fly around, for stars' sake. It won't kill you."

Erry gave the loudest, longest groan of her life. Eyes rolling, she jumped off the ship, shifted into a dragon, and flew.

The beating of her wings blasted the hull, rocking the ship. She flew in circles, scales clattering, and blew fire upward--just to impress them a little more. She rose higher, roared to the sky, and swooped toward the ship, claws outstretched, feigning an attack.

Upon the deck, Leresy--still in human form--pointed the scope at her, then unscrewed the wooden lid.

The gems inside glowed. Their light blasted out from the lens, drenching Erry.

Like a tugged tablecloth, her magic vanished.

Erry returned to human form, fell through the air, and crashed into the water.

She sputtered, cursed, and swam back to the ship. When she stood back upon the deck, she shook herself wildly like a dog, spraying water onto the others.

"That," Leresy said, "is how we fight the Legions. I've got four scopes full of these shards. We fly to Requiem. My father's dragons will drop from the sky like dead flies." He nodded. "I've called my weapons Leresy Scopes. They will win me the throne."

The others began to growl and roll their eyes. Before they could object too much, however, a high voice rose above them.

"Big weapon! Big weapon is no Leresy Scope. Genesis Shards they are, yes. Bantis knows them!"

Erry looked up and raised her eyebrows. Crazy old Bantis, still clad in only a loincloth, perched upon a mast. His white hair billowed in the breeze and he laughed. Fast as a monkey, he scurried down the mast, landed upon the deck, and danced a jig.

"Grandpapa!" Miya said. "Have you been up there all along?"

The old man grinned. "You cannot hold councils without Old Bantis, no. Foolish boy, give me that." He reached toward Leresy, grabbed the scope full of shards, and began tugging, struggling to free it from the younger man's grip. "Mine. Mine!"

Leresy growled and held the scope firmly.

"Leresy, let him have it!" Erry said and kicked his shin.

The prince yelped, his grip loosened, and Bantis scurried back with his prize.

"These are Genesis Shards," the old man repeated. "Yes, that is their name. Bantis has been seeking them for many years, yes. They have languished underground for a thousand years. Dragons buried them! They did not want them found, no." He cackled. "Yet now Bantis has big weapon. Kills dragons!"

Leresy rubbed his shin. "Bloody Abyss. Why are they called Genesis Shards?"

Bantis hopped around on one leg, cawed like a bird, then smiled mischievously. "Created all life, they did. Ten thousand years ago, the gods created Animating Stones, *big* gems--big like chicken eggs!--that raised dust, earth, and water into men and beasts. Created us Tirans too, they did." He laughed, head tossed back. "Powerful magic, yes. Powerful enough to raise matter into life. Powerful enough to cancel out all other magic around them. Even the magic to become dragons." He winked. "The old Vir Requis found the gems a thousand years ago. They feared them. They broke them into tiny shards. They can no longer create life, no, not broken like this." He laughed and gave a quick dance. "But they can still cancel dragon magic. So they buried the shards. Buried them deep in a distant island. But Old Bantis found them! Old Bantis will take them to Requiem. And dragons will fall from the sky!"

Bantis himself fell onto his back, arms and legs splayed out, imitating a fallen dragon. He lay upon the deck, grinning.

Leresy began to pout and object, shouting that *he* had found the shards, and that they *were* called Leresy Shards. Kaelyn, Erry, and even Miya began to shout him down--and soon to kick him. Sila howled at everyone to be silent, and Bantis kept laughing. The council collapsed into chaos, and soon everyone was yelling above the others.

Only Valien stood silent, staring across the water, lost in thought. After a long moment, he nodded and spoke, but his voice drowned under the shouting.

"All of you, be quiet!" Erry howled, hopping up and down. "Valien is talking. Let him be heard!"

When finally everyone was silent, Valien stared at them one by one, then spoke again.

"We've fled here to these islands, two camps of refugees. On Horsehead Island, three thousand Vir Requis dream of reclaiming their homeland. Here upon Maiden Island, four thousand Tirans have found a new life, refugees from their fallen kingdom, and they too dream. They dream of returning to the desert, unafraid, of rebuilding their homeland without the threat of Cadigus looming. For long years, both our camps hid and fought separately, but we shared the same vision. We sang the same song. We dreamed of going home."

As they listened to the speech, Erry saw that Kaelyn and Miya had tears in their eyes. Kaelyn dreamed of returning to Nova Vita, the capital Erry herself had never seen. Miya dreamed of returning to Tiranor, land of her fathers, the desert kingdom her people still yearned for.

Yet what home do I dream of? Erry wondered. *I never had a home, unless the docks at Lynport were a home. If we truly win this war, what awaits me if not more pain?*

Valien continued speaking, voice scratchy but clear, the voice of wind over sand. "For many years, this was but a dream, a whisper of a hope. But today we found new hope--a hope that blazes bright as a pillar of fire. We no longer need hide. Together, with our magic and your machines, we can defeat the Cadigus regime. We can both reclaim our homes." He lifted a scope in one hand, an arquebus in the other. "I will lead my people into Requiem. We will fly as dragons, roaring and blowing fire. Upon our backs, we will bear you, noble people of Tiranor, and you will wield your weapons. You will point the Genesis Scopes at the Legions; they will fall from the sky. We will fly for days, felling the armies that storm toward us, until we reach the capital. We will storm the palace as men, firing our guns. The Axehand Order defends the palace, and they fight with blades; we will shoot them from a distance. We will find Relesar Aeternum, true King of Requiem, and free him from captivity. We will find Frey Cadigus, the usurper, and slay him." The grizzled man's eyes gleamed. "The war will end. Fear will fade. We will return home."

The council dispersed one by one. Leresy shifted and left first, flying off with a puff of smoke, still muttering about how *he* had found the shards. Kaelyn followed him, a slim green dragon, calling him a woolhead for all the island to hear. Miya left in her boat, while Bantis opted for leaping off the hull, crashing into the water, and swimming to shore. Valien departed with a grumble, a silver dragon with clattering scales and one horn.

Erry remained standing on the deck, watching the others leave. She placed her hand upon a cannon, remembering the battles she had fought, the friends she had seen die, and the men she'd killed. She lowered her head.

A voice spoke behind her.

"Will you not fly with your friends, Erry of Requiem?"

She turned to see Captain Sila. His golden, weathered face still seemed rough to her, a patch of leather left out in the sun, but she saw softness in his eyes.

"They're not my friends," she said. "I'm just here because..."

Because what? she wondered. Because the docks had burned? Because Tilla had turned into a killer, little better than Shari Cadigus? Because Leresy fed and sheltered her, or because she felt she had to heal him?

Sila nodded. "I understand. You are here for the same reason I am."

"And what is that?" she demanded.

He smiled wryly. "Because there's nowhere better to be."

"Valien thinks there is. And he wants to fly out and fight for it. Will you fight with him, Captain Sila? Will you leave your haven for a chance to win this war?"

He cleared his throat, came to stand beside her, and placed his hands upon the railing. They both stared at the beach.

"My people mistrust dragons," he said at length. "Some were born here upon the island, but most remember the war. They remember thousands of dragons burning their homes, killing their families, and toppling their kingdom. They might not distinguish between the Resistance and the Legions; both are beasts to them. Yet I will do my part to sway them. I believe we should fight with Valien. I believe he is an honorable man."

Erry swallowed. "Maybe I... maybe I can help sway them. Your people, that is. The Tirans here." Her throat felt so tight, and her eyes dampened. When she looked back up at Sila, her vision was blurred. "I can tell them that not all Vir Requis are bad."

He smiled. "What makes you think they'd believe you and not me?"

Now her tears did fall. She had never told anyone here of her heritage--not Valien, not Kaelyn, and certainly not Leresy. Yet now she blurted out the words, voice choked.

"I'm half Tiran." She trembled. "I'm... I'm a bastard orphan. My mother was a Vir Requis from Lynport, a town in southern Requiem. My father was a sailor from Tiranor, though I never met him. I can shift into a dragon like a Vir Requis; I got that from my mother. But... I'm Tiran too." She rubbed her eyes. "I'm one of you, or at least half of me is. I can tell the people. I can tell them that Vir Requis and Tirans can work together. I'm living proof."

Sila laughed softly, and Erry sucked in her breath, sure that he was mocking her, but his smile was kind.

"There's no shame in mixed blood," he said. "Do not cry, Erry. Did you know? After the great Griffin War, a massacre a thousand years ago that left only seven Vir Requis alive, Requiem's survivors mingled with the people of Osanna and Tiranor. Most Vir Requis today carry some mixed blood."

Erry blinked at him, tears still falling. "Really?"

He nodded. "Many years ago, there was a great queen in Requiem, Luna the Traveler of House Aeternum. She visited

Tiranor and appears in our lore. They say she wed a Tiran prince, and that her children inherited the magic of Requiem and became princes of your realm. Perhaps all Vir Requis have some Tiran blood deep inside them. Be proud of it, child. You are a noble daughter of starlight and of sand."

She nodded, blinking her tears away. That didn't sound too bad. A thought struck her, and she reached under her shirt, slung her medallion off her neck, and held it out.

"This is my only memento from my father," she said. "He was a Tiran sailor. He gave this to my mother in Lynport twenty years ago. Sila, you commanded a merchant fleet. Maybe you recognize this medallion?" Her voice shook. "Maybe you knew my father?"

His eyes narrowed and he took the medallion from her palm. He examined it, turning it over and over, and exhaled slowly. Old dreams seemed to dance in his eyes.

"I know this medallion," he said.

Erry trembled like the last leaf on a tree. "Do you know who gave it to my mother?"

He nodded, placed the medallion back in her palm, and closed his hands around hers. He smiled again, a soft, secret smile full of pain and memory.

"Of course I do. I did."

TILLA

"The moon is new," said Shari. "The time for his torture has come."

They stood in the Citadel's courtyard, torchlight illuminating the falling snow. The walls rose all around them, lined with cells. From behind a hundred oaken doors, prisoners howled, wept, screamed, and begged. Below Tilla's feet, she could feel the cobblestones trembling; down in the dungeon, racks turned, whips lashed, and flesh tore. The very stones of this place shook with pain.

Now that pain would tear through the man she loved.

Tilla looked up at the Red Tower. It rose into the night, wreathed in snow, a bone rising from a grave. In that tower he waited, chained, foolish, still hoping he could sway her to his cause. In that tower he would now scream.

"I will begin with my punisher," Shari said. "I will burn every inch of him. His skin will crack and fall." She sucked in her breath. "Every day I will introduce a new instrument. Tonight the punisher. Tomorrow the rack. The third day the hammers. I wonder how many days he will last."

Tilla returned her eyes to her princess. It was the first time she had seen her commander without armor. Shari had not dressed for battle today; she had dressed for torture. She wore tall boots over black leggings, a leather apron, and thick gloves. Her mane of dark curls cascaded down her shoulders, and her eyes shone with bloodlust. Her punisher crackled in her hand, red energy racing across its tip.

Today she does not look like a warrior, Tilla thought and shivered. *Today she looks like a butcher.*

"Commander," Tilla said, "I need more time. I am beginning to sway him. I--"

"You've had long enough," Shari said and caressed the dagger that hung on her hip. "Are you softening to his cause, Lanse? Whose side are you on--ours or his?"

Tilla's heart pounded. Her voice was weak. "Commander, a flayed, beaten, broken man cannot fight for us. He cannot break the spirit of the Resistance, only embolden them. If I can sway him with words, and he joins us willingly, the Resistance--"

Shari snarled, reached out, and grabbed Tilla's throat.

"The Resistance is scattered!" she said and squeezed. "They fled into the sea with their tails between their legs. Most likely they all drowned." Shari growled like a feral dog. "I grow tired of your excuses, Lanse."

Tilla gasped for breath. The fingers were crushing her. She thought Shari would snap her neck. Stars, the woman was strong. How could anyone be so strong? She grasped at Shari's hand, trying to pry her fingers off, but could not. She was seeing stars and her legs were wobbling when Shari finally released her.

Tilla clutched at her throat, wheezing, and stared up with burning eyes.

I saved your life! she wanted to say. *Rune almost killed you, and I saved you from him!*

Yet she could not speak those words, even if she had breath for them. To speak them was death. Shari was too enraged now.

I am her groom, Tilla thought, sucking in air. *And I saved her life. And I fought at her side in battle. Yet if I cross the line, she will still kill me. And she will enjoy it.*

"Commander," she managed to say, voice raspy. "Let me do it. If I cannot sway you, let *me* hurt him."

Shari laughed, the laugh of a madwoman. "A moment ago, you were pleading for him."

Tilla took a deep breath, unable to conceal its shakiness. "I thought I could sway him with words. But if we must use pain, we must hurt him fully. We must break him." She allowed herself a small, crooked smile. "What would hurt him more than his dearest friend torturing him?"

Please let her agree, Tilla prayed silently. *Please, old and new gods, let her agree.*

If she could torture Rune herself, she could perhaps hurt him less than Shari would. She could make him scream, but not cause permanent damage. If Shari tortured him, she would drive all her malice into her work; she would break his mind. Tilla could still save him... save him by burning him herself.

Shari reached over and touched Tilla's punisher, which hung at her hip. Her gloved fingers caressed its leather grip.

"You will torture him," she said and sucked in her breath. "Yes. That will hurt him, and it will harden you. We begin. Now. We enter the tower."

They crossed the courtyard, a chorus of screams rising from the cells alongside. They entered the Red Tower, climbed its stairs, and emerged into his cell.

Oh, Rune, Tilla thought, and her eyes stung.

He stood bound, arms chained to the ceiling. He met her gaze and did not break it. He knew what was coming. He had been waiting. He was ready.

"Begin," Shari said.

Tilla wanted to flee. Yet if she fled, Shari would give him a worse fate. She wanted to plead with Shari again, but if she did, she too would suffer this pain.

I'm sorry, Rune, she thought.

She drew her punisher.

She did as she was trained.

At first he withstood it. Then his screams joined the rest of them.

"You don't have to do this!" he cried, voice torn, as her punisher burned his flesh. "Tilla, you don't have to--"

But his voice drowned in his agony.

And she kept working.

It seemed an hour, maybe more, before Shari nodded and placed a hand on Tilla's shoulder.

"Good, Lanse," she said. "Good." She admired the welts that rose across him. "You did well for tonight. Tomorrow you will continue. You've made me proud."

Tilla stood shaking. Sweat and tears burned in her eyes. She looked at her commander.

"Will you not ask him to join us?" she whispered. "Will you not ask him to hail the red spiral?"

"In time," Shari said and smiled. "When he's suffered enough. Not this night. Not until my vengeance is sated. Your work here only begins."

With that, Shari turned and left the chamber. Tilla remained in the tower. A moment later, she heard a roar and, through an arrowslit, saw a blue dragon fly into the distance.

"Tilla..." Rune spoke in a choked whisper.

Now she could not curb her tears. They stung her eyes and streamed down her face, and she took two great steps toward him. She wanted to embrace him but froze; embracing him would only double the pain in his wounds. Instead she stood trembling and touched his cheek, the only part of him not scarred.

"I will heal you," she whispered. She rummaged through her pack for bandages. "I will bring you laceleaf milk for the pain. I--"

"I don't want you to heal me," he said, hanging from his chains. "Will you heal me only to hurt me again? Tilla... flee with me."

She shook her head, tears streaming down her cheeks.

"I cannot," she whispered. "He would hunt us. He would kill us. I have to make you serve him. I have to save you."

His eyes softened, and alongside the pain, she saw pity in them. Despite what she had done, he pitied her.

"And I must save you," he whispered. "I must save you from what you've become, what they turned you into. My body is burned. But worse is the pain of seeing your soul broken."

Tilla closed her eyes and trembled. She remembered Nairi burning her a year ago; that pain had only lasted for several minutes, and it had left Tilla in an infirmary for days. Now she had burned Rune for an hour, maybe longer, and still he only thought about her. Still he cared for her soul more than his pain.

She opened her eyes and kissed him, a kiss deeper than any they had yet shared, and she loved him more than any love she had felt.

"You are noble," she said through her tears, "and you are brave, and you love me. But you are wrong. My soul was never broken. I do what I must to survive. Please, Rune. Tomorrow when Shari returns, hail the red spiral. Worship Frey Cadigus. And this pain will end."

"It would only begin," he replied.

She looked at his manacles. She had the keys on her belt. How easy it would be to unlock him, to fly with him again! They could fly like in the old days, find some distant beach, heal together, kiss in the sand, and--

No, she told herself and tightened her lips. Those were the dreams of youth. She had to follow this path--for Requiem, for herself, and for his life.

She left him in the tower.

She returned to her home.

She sat upon her bed, pulled out her string of seashells, and held them all night.

ERRY

She sat on the islet, eyes burning, and stared out across the sea.

"Pissy pig-shagging maggots," she said, eyes burning, and clenched her fists--small fists no larger than a child's. "Damn bloody gutter shite." She snarled and shouted to the waters. "Damn you, you latrine-licking dog's son, and damn all of you beef-witted cockroaches, you... damn..."

Her throat tightened. Her eyes watered. She pulled her knees to her chest, lowered her head, and let her body shake.

"My father," she whispered. "He is my father. Damn him. Oh stars, damn them all."

She looked at the sea. The waves shimmered through her tears. It was easy to remember like this. It was easy to pretend that she still sat at home, on the beaches of Lynport.

Her belly rumbled with the old hunger, and she remembered rifling through trash for scraps, eating live fish when she could catch them, dead ones that washed ashore when she couldn't. She remembered all those men who had taken her in the sand, all those times she had spread her legs for a meal, a roof in a storm, or a broken promise. And most of all, she remembered the demon inside her, the icy tendrils that clutched her belly and heart and mind, pulling her into shadows of loneliness and gloom worse than any blow. So many times she had lain in the sand, stared up at the stars, and prayed to die. So many times she had walked into the sea, sunk under the water, and tried to drown but never found the courage to swallow the water.

"I spent eighteen years on the docks," she whispered. "I lived with cats and I became a feral beast, and I fought and I hurt. And you weren't there. You left me to that nightmare."

She still clutched his medallion in her palm. She looked at it, her face twisted, and she emitted something halfway between growl and sob. She had thought this amulet a symbol of hope, of home, of a better world. Yet now it disgusted her.

She whispered through tight lips, "You abandoned me."

She rose to her feet. She tossed the amulet into the sea.

The sun began to set, and Erry stood watching it, frozen as a statue, just standing, just staring, alone. So many nights she had stood like this, watching the waters, dreaming of what lay beyond. But now she knew.

"They were there. My father. My sister. Living in peace. They left me."

Darkness fell and the stars emerged. It was her seventh night alone on this islet. The others had been searching for her; she had seen the dragons flying overhead, calling her name. She had hidden among the trees until they passed.

"They can all leave," she said. "They can all fly to their war, and I will stay here, and they can all go die. Especially him. Especially Sila." She clenched her fists. "I hope he dies first."

She howled at the moon, fingers raised like claws.

But no. She could not let him die like this. Not yet.

She shifted into a dragon, rose into the air, and roared fire across the sea.

"You will answer to me first."

She howled in the darkness. She beat her wings. She flew through the night.

The sea spread below her. The sky spread above. Erry flew between black and black, her fire lighting the way. Her blaze reflected against the water, and her roars pealed. The night was clear but she was a storm.

"I've been hiding and running all my life," she spoke into the wind. "But now I will learn the truth. Now I will learn why I suffered."

She flew for hours before she saw Horsehead Island ahead, a dark patch upon the inky sea. They would be mustering for war now. Tomorrow they intended to fly out, to invade Requiem, to kill and to die. That was their war; Erry fought her own, a battle that had been raging inside her since her birth upon the boardwalk.

She crashed down onto the beach in a cloud of smoke and flame. Valien had forbidden them to light fires, worried the Legions were patrolling the seas, but Erry didn't care. She howled and sprayed her flames, lighting the island.

"Sila!" she cried upon the beach. "Come see me. I'm here. Come face me!"

She tossed her head, scattering fire, not caring that others saw. She beat her wings, raising the sand into a storm. They stood upon the beach, Vir Requis and Tirans, gaping at her.

Let them gawk, she thought, eyes burning. *Let them see the orphan, the dock rat, the creature. He made me this thing.*

Through the smoke and flying sand, he emerged, walking grimly and staring ahead. Captain Sila of Tiranor. Her father.

"Erry," he said.

She growled and snapped her teeth at him, still in dragon form. He stood before her, wide-shouldered, leathery-faced, gruff and strong and weathered, but still only a man. She was a dragon. She was fire and claw and fang, and she could kill him. She could make him hurt like she hurt.

But her eyes only dampened again.

She lowered her head, blasting the sand with smoke, and growled and clawed the beach.

"Why?" she said, spitting the words out with spurts of fire. "Why did you do this?"

He stood before her, not cowering back even as her smoke and fire flickered. Sparks from her flame burned upon his tunic, but still he stood firmly, staring at her steadily. His eyes were still hard, his face inscrutable.

"Will you face me as a woman?" he said.

She growled. "Will you face me as a man? I don't see a man. I see only a coward. I see only a whoring sailor. I see a dog who... who abandoned my mother." Her tears streamed now, steaming in her fire. "A dog who abandoned me."

He met her gaze steadily. "Return to human form, Erry, and we will talk."

She howled. She wanted to blast him with fire. She wanted to dig her claws into his flesh. But he only kept staring, eyes hard, lips tight, silent. He stared her down. With a yowl, she blasted a pillar of fire skyward, and she released her magic. She returned to human form and stood in the sand, panting. Her flames rained around her as sparks.

"Speak to me!" she said. "Tell me why you did it. You abandoned me!"

"Is that what your mother told you?" he asked.

She could barely see through her tears. "She never told me anything! She died when I was only five. You didn't even know, did you? You didn't care. Frey killed her, and you only lived here on the island. You never cared about her. You only fled here, a coward."

People were gathering around them, but Erry didn't care. She panted and rubbed her eyes and stared at this man she hated.

"Erry, where is the medallion I gave her? The medallion you carried all these years?"

"I threw it into the sea. It's a piece of garbage. Meaningless. It's a trifle you paid for a whore." She snorted through her tears. "I hope you enjoyed bedding her that night. I hope it was your best damn time. I hope your silver bought you an hour of joy. It bought me a lifetime of pain."

He remained calm and cold. If any pain filled him, his eyes did not betray it. He had a captain's eyes, eyes for staring down mutinous sailors and enemy ships, for staring down death and life.

"You have lived for years upon the docks. You have served in the Legions. You have seen the underbelly of the world. Have you ever, Erry, in all those years, seen a man hire a whore with a silver medallion?"

She gritted her teeth. "You probably spent your last few coins on booze."

He shook his head. "I never did drink booze, not then and not now. No, Erry. I did not hire your mother for a night of cheap passion. I loved her. I courted her. I wanted her to marry me, to return with me to Tiranor. When she refused, I gave her my amulet, a parting gift. I never knew she was with child. You must believe that. Had I known, I would have returned for you."

"I don't believe you!" Her body trembled, and she could barely breathe. "If this were true, my mother would have told me."

"Would she have? Would she have told a toddler of these things even adults struggle to grasp? Yes, Erry, I loved her. She was a flower blooming in the sand. I found her living in boardwalk squalor, and I wanted to save her, to show her a better life. I would have brought her to the desert and built a palace for her. But she would not leave her home. Her heart was in Requiem, land of her fathers, not my desert. She stayed--with my medallion, with my heart... and with my daughter."

Erry shook her head, staring at her feet. "I am not your daughter. By blood? Maybe. I don't care." She looked up at him, and her voice cracked. "Do you have any idea how I suffered? I was an orphan. I slept on the docks. I always wanted to know who you are, but now... now I hate you."

Finally something changed in his eyes. Finally some of that hardness shattered, and for a moment, his soul shone through, and it was hurt. It was as hurt as hers.

He took a step toward her. "Erry," he said softly. "Erry, I am sorry. I am so sorry."

Her tears fell. "I hate you."

"I know." Now his voice too cracked with pain. "You are my daughter. And you suffered. And I hate myself for this too. Erry, my child. I cannot change the past. I cannot make you forgive me. I cannot undo any of this or make any of it right."

She sobbed. "So what can you do?"

"Be with you now," he answered, reaching out to her. "I cannot heal you, and I cannot make you forget those years, but I can be with you now and always. You are my daughter. Let me learn how to love you. Let me learn how to be your father."

A shadow appeared behind him. A platinum-haired girl stepped around the captain. Slim, golden-skinned Miya walked across the sand, and her eyes shone with tears. She reached out to Erry.

"I have a sister," the girl whispered. "I have an older sister."

Erry wept. She looked away. She wanted to fly. She wanted to flee this, to return to her island, to roar her fire, to drown in the sea, or to be a wild beast, but not face this. Not feel her heart shatter. Not feel love fill her; love hurt too much. She had known too much pain to feel love now. It frightened her more than all the dragons and horrors in the world.

Yet she could not move, and when Miya embraced her, she could not resist. She wept against her sister's shoulder. Miya was only eighteen, two years younger than Erry, but taller and stronger. Erry had grown up with a tight belly, and she was so small, a runt of a thing, but her sister held her nonetheless, and she felt warm.

"I have a sister," Miya whispered and cried. "Erry, you are my sister. I see it in your eyes."

574

Erry looked up. Sila stood there, a foot away, looking upon them, still gruff, still the captain. But then his throat bobbed, and he sucked in air, and he took a great step forward and joined their embrace. Erry wanted to scratch and kick him, to break free and burn him, but she found herself holding him tight. She pressed her cheek against his chest and wept.

I have a sister, she thought. *I have a father.*

She spoke through her sob, voice shaking. "I'm so scared."

They held her close, keeping the night at bay, strong and warm and enveloping her.

"I know," Sila said. "But we'll be here with you. We'll help you face it. We'll help you heal. You'll never more be alone."

Held in their arms, Erry raised her head. She looked at the sky. The Draco constellation shone there, stars of Requiem.

"And... you don't care that I'm half Vir Requis? That half my blood is that of your enemy?"

Sila laughed and squeezed her tight. "The only thing I care about," he said, "is that you curse more than most sailors in my fleet."

She closed her eyes. "You're talking bloody pig shite," she whispered.

She stood in the sand, letting them hold her, and she thought of home. Mae had died, Tilla had betrayed her, and Leresy could go lick codpieces. Erry sniffed and rubbed her eyes.

I have a family.

VALIEN

They flew above Horsehead Island in the sunset, one dragon scarred and silver and brawny, the other green and slim and fast. They glided silently. They surveyed their army that mustered below.

"Three thousand Vir Requis," Valien said, voice nearly lost in the wind. "Two thousand Tirans strong enough to fight, each armed with an arquebus. A handful... against the might of half a million legionaries."

Here was his new Resistance, a patchwork. Only a seed of his original fighters remained. The rest Valien had woven in from other forces. A few hundred had served as Leresy's Lechers. A thousand had been men of Cain's Canyon. Now two thousand Tirans joined his cause, foreign warriors who could not shift into dragons. A patchwork, that was all. A few thousand souls who hated Frey enough to join here upon these beaches.

It wasn't enough.

Flying at his side, Kaelyn grinned, showing all her teeth. "Since when did we care about being outnumbered?"

Valien snorted a puff of smoke. "Since we lost most of our men in Lynport."

Since I lost my wife, he thought. *Since I fled the capital with Rune in my arms and Marilion's blood in my nightmares.* Yet he did not speak those words. He would not speak of Marilion to Kaelyn, this new woman in his life.

She lives! She lives in my dungeon, you fool!

Emperor Frey's words still echoed. They filled his mind now as they did every waking moment. Valien had seen his wife die. He had held her lifeless body. Her blood had coated his hands.

She lives!

He knew the emperor was lying. He knew that Frey only wanted to hurt him. Yet still Valien dreamed--even as he flew here above the island. Still her eyes haunted him, and still he saw her in the lighthouse, smiling at him, waiting for him always.

When I fly to free Rune, will I find you in that dungeon too? Have you been waiting for twenty years, Marilion?

He growled. *No. Frey lied.* Valien blasted fire. *All he does is lie.*

Kaelyn flew around him in a circle, nudged him with her tail, and smiled. "Come, Valien, let us land and sleep. Night falls. Tomorrow our battle begins."

Below upon the island, men and women sheathed swords, slung arquebuses over their shoulders, and retreated into huts and tents. Even flying high above, Valien could sense their fear; their every movement spoke of it. These people had seen war and death, and tomorrow they would fly back into the fire. Valien growled, forcing his own fear down his throat. *The battle-hardened always fear war more than the green soldier.*

The two dragons spiraled down and landed upon the shore. When they shifted back into humans, Valien looked at Kaelyn, and his heart twisted. The sun dipped into the sea behind her, painting her orange and gold. The wind blew her hair and dress, and she seemed so sad to him, a sea nymph lost upon the shore.

"Kaelyn," he began, voice low, but could say no more.

I couldn't bear to lose you too, he wanted to say.

Stay on this island in safety, he wanted to say.

I love you more than Requiem and all that's in it, he wanted to say.

Yet he could say none of those things. And so he only stood in the sand, looking at her, at the sunset in her hair, at her soft eyes, at her tanned and feline face. And Valien realized that for the first time in three years, when he looked upon Kaelyn, he did not see the woman she looked like. He no longer saw Marilion.

"I see you, Kaelyn," he whispered.

Here upon the beach, on this last night before the fire, she was not a ghost, but a living flame.

She embraced him and whispered into his ear, "I'm afraid."

He cupped her pale cheek in his hand. "I know."

She clutched his hands and squeezed them. "I'm afraid for Rune. And for our people. But mostly I fear this night, this darkness, this silence before the storm." She smiled shakily. "The last night before battle always seems so long, doesn't it?"

He nodded. "I never know if I want these nights to end quickly or last forever."

"To last forever," she said and touched his cheek. "I wish tomorrow would never come. Valien, will you share my hut tonight? Hold me on this long, dark night, for tomorrow the fire will burn."

They walked to her island home, a shelter woven of branches and leaves. Valien had spent his nights sleeping alone upon the island's peak, perched upon the hilltop in dragon form, always half awake and ready to fly should the Legions find their haven. Yet tonight he entered her hut, a little nook with a bed of grass, womb-like and warm.

He stood at the entrance. Kaelyn sat down upon the grass, pulled her knees to her chest, and looked up at him. Suddenly she laughed shyly and lowered her eyes.

"I'm sorry!" she said. "It's not very roomy, but... it's warmer and cozier than the hilltop you sleep on."

She looked down at her knees and her cheeks flushed.

Feeling awkward and cumbersome, far too clunky and rough, Valien cleared his throat. He sat beside her, leaned back, and allowed himself a smile.

"Very warm and cozy," he said. He lay down and placed his hands behind his head.

She lay on her side, facing him, her hair brushing his shoulder, her body an inch away from his. She looked at him silently, and Valien was struck by how young she seemed. She was only twenty. He was more than twice her age--and probably twice her weight. Lying beside her, he felt too old, too grizzled and ragged, a disheveled bear sharing a den with a graceful young lioness.

"Valien," she whispered as darkness fell, "can we win this?"

"We will win."

"Do you think... do you think Rune is still alive?" Her voice trembled.

Valien closed his eyes. He hadn't stopped thinking of Rune since arriving on this island. Yet tonight, Kaelyn's soft breath against him, he did not want to remember Rune or Marilion or Requiem. He wanted this one, last night in shadowy warmth. He wanted no more ghosts, only this woman beside him.

"I don't know," he said. "All I know is that we must fly. We must keep fighting. We must fly to victory or death. We are Requiem. Our wings forever seek our sky."

She nodded. "For so long I hid in darkness. For so many years, my father beat me, burned me, broke my body, and I hid under my bed, and in the dungeons of our tower, and in the shadows of my own mind." She held his hand tight. "You taught me to fly, Valien. And I will keep flying with you. Always."

He wiped a tear from her cheek. She gazed at him with damp, huge eyes, and her lips shook. She placed a hand on his cheek, leaned forward, and kissed his forehead. He smoothed her hair, and she kissed his lips.

She had never kissed him before. Her lips were small but full, pink and very soft, and they shot warmth through him, warmth better than all the rye he would drink in his years of darkness. She was too young for him, her hair too soft in his calloused fingers, her eyes too fair for the pain he carried. Yet he held her close, her body lithe and warm under his hands, and he kissed her, and she smiled. He had never known eyes so large and bright, even here in the shadows.

She climbed atop him. She began to unlace his shirt, her fingers shy and hesitant at first, then gaining speed, and soon she tugged at the cloth with the hunger of a starving man for food. His hands moved over her body--large, rough hands that could encircle her waist. He pulled the tunic off her, and she sat atop him, naked in the last glimmers of sunset. Her body was slim, her breasts small and pale, and he kissed her neck, and she buried her hands in his hair.

He wanted to stop this. She was too pure, too young and virginal, too full of life for an old, scarred wreck. But he could not stop. He needed this; he needed her now more than he'd ever needed his rye or vengeance or starlight. They moved faster, naked in the darkness, and the last light faded. He rolled atop her, and she gasped and moaned and clutched his shoulders. He held her hands, and she shuddered and arched beneath him, legs wrapped around his back. He moved above her. In the darkness he felt like a dragon flying through a storm, fleeing a burning city, roaring in pain as the terrors of the world chased him.

I couldn't save you, Marilion.

He clutched the babe in his claws and flew, rising and falling on the wind, seeking shelter in the night. Still he flew through that storm. Still that darkness wrapped around him.

Fire blazed through him, and Kaelyn gasped below him, and her fingernails almost tore his skin. She bit his shoulder to stifle her cry, and they lay still.

He rolled onto his back, and she nestled against him, her head on his chest, her body soft and small in his arms. She mumbled and smiled and slept, her breath playing against his neck like waves over the sand. He held her close and the pain dug through him.

Valien had bedded women during his long years of exile. He had found comfort with outcasts, wanderers, and urchins, women who came and left his life during the long years on the road. During his darkest hours, when the rye would not dull his pain, he had found comfort in brothels, and those memories still throbbed inside him like old scars. But he had not loved a woman until Kaelyn. He had not slept with one in his arms since Marilion.

He kissed her head, and his throat constricted, and he was afraid.

Love weakens us, he thought. *I cannot lose you, Kaelyn. Tomorrow we fly to war. Tomorrow I will be afraid for Requiem... bust mostly for you. Mostly for you.*

Only a beam of moonlight lit their bed. Kaelyn mumbled something in her sleep, nestled closer, and smiled softly. Valien lay awake for a long time, holding her close.

The dawn rose gray and rainy. As fighters took formation on the beaches, they frowned skyward, cursed, and muttered of signs. For many days they had lived here in sunlight and warmth; on the eve of battle, the sky gods raged. Wind whipped the palms, the waves crashed like watery demons, and the sand blew.

The land itself rages today, Valien thought. He stood on the beach, staring north into the roiling waters. *Today the wrath of man and sky will descend upon you, Cadigus.*

His fighters stood around him, standing still in their formations, staring north with hard eyes. The wind whipped their hair, and the rain stung their faces, yet they did not flinch. Five thousand fighters marshaled here. Vir Requis and Tirans stood together; today they were one army.

Valien looked at them one by one. He wanted to see warriors. He wanted to see howling, bloodthirsty fighters chanting for victory. He wanted to see a hammer ready to crush the Legions.

Instead he saw friends.

He saw families.

He saw Kaelyn, the woman he loved, her hair a banner of gold under the clouds.

We are not warriors, he thought. *We are husbands, wives, brothers, sisters. We are outcasts and we are dreamers. We are a single light shining through the storm.*

He shifted. He stood upon the sand as a dragon, roared so the island could hear, and blasted fire upward, a pillar to lead his people.

"Arise!" he howled, his voice still strangled but loud enough to peal across the beach. "Arise, dragons of Requiem! Arise, warriors of Tiranor! Today our hiding ends. Today we fly--to war, to glory, to victory!"

Around him, his fellow dragons shifted too. Three thousand scaly beasts roared, blew fire, and lit the storm.

Glory? he wondered. *Victory?* What did those have to do with war? War was not glorious. War never ended with victory. They flew to men screaming in the mud, limbs torn off, bones shattered. They flew to more grieving widows. To more pain. To more death and nightmares that would forever haunt them.

Yet Valien was a leader. He was heir to great rulers who had led Requiem in battle. Roaring upon the beach, he thought of those who had come before him: the legendary King Benedictus who had fought the griffins, the noble King Elethor who had defeated the phoenixes, and the wise Queen Lyana who had slain demons and raised Requiem from ruin.

I am no noble, brave leader like they were, Valien thought, the rain peppering his scales. *I am too hurt, too haunted, too afraid.*

Yet the people needed that leader now. They needed a king, a hero, a leader of legend. And so he roared for glory, for victory, for freedom. And so he gave them the courage he himself lacked.

The Tirans, men and women without the ancient magic, mounted the dragons. Each fighter wielded an arquebus, a saber, and a spear. Miya climbed onto Kaelyn's back, grabbed the horn of her makeshift saddle, and raised her chin. Her father, the gruff Sila, climbed onto Valien's saddle.

"So," said the merchant captain, "I've gone from leading a fleet of ships to a flight of dragons."

Valien grumbled beneath him. "You could steer your ships, captain. This dragon flies where he will." He gritted his teeth. "Hold on tight. You might have sailed through storms, but you've never flown through one."

With that, he kicked off the sand, beat his wings, and soared.

Around him, the dragons of Requiem rose, roaring fire through the rain. The wind whipped them, but their wings beat powerfully, driving them forward. They soared through the storm. The waves crashed below. Fire, wind, and water churned like a primordial world before creation.

They left the island behind. They left the children, the elders, and the infirm. They flew through the storm, five thousand souls, a drop against the ocean of the Legions. The sea rolled beneath them. A haze of darkness lay ahead.

Valien looked at Kaelyn, who flew at his side. Their eyes met through the rain. Her scales glimmered with raindrops, and her eyes were sad yet hopeful and knowing. He thought of last night, and the memory warmed him.

I fight for the memory of Requiem. I fight for a legacy of light. But I also fight for you.

The storm clouds broke ahead, and a single ray of light fell into the sea, a glowing column of gold. Valien flew toward it. It would guide him home.

TILLA

Rune hung on the chains before her, welts covering his body, his eyes swollen and his lips bleeding. He moaned, head lowered. If not for the chains that held up his arms, running from his wrists to the ceiling, he'd have collapsed.

"Tilla," he whispered through cracked lips. "Please."

She had not wanted it to come to this. Why wouldn't he just speak the words? Why wouldn't he join her, worship the red spiral with her?

"Oh, Rune," she whispered, punisher in hand. "Why do you do this? You can make it end. Just say the words..."

He looked up at her, blinking, his face pale and splashed with blood. And yet he managed to fix her with a stare, a deep gaze like the one he would give her at home. In his eyes she saw Cadport again--their youth in the sand and sun and their home burning. His lips were silent; his eyes did the speaking. And he was speaking to her of home... and of the woman she used to be.

"Hurt him some more!"

Shari stood at her side, wearing her butcher's apron, her voice thick with bloodlust, her eyes alight. She seemed like a woman in rapture. Her teeth were bared in a wolf's snarl. Her chest rose and fell as she panted. Rune's blood stained her clothes.

"Drive your punisher against him!" the princess commanded, hissing through her teeth. "Make him scream. Make him worship the Regime."

And Tilla obeyed.

And he screamed.

But he did not obey.

"Just speak the words, Rune," Tilla whispered. She touched his cheek. "Just hail the red spiral. And you will join me. And this will end."

He raised his head, spat out blood, and stared at her.

Silent.

Tilla turned toward her commander. "He will not join us. I've hurt him more than anyone's hurt another. This is hopeless."

She prayed that Shari would listen. She prayed that Shari would abandon this quest of pain.

Just... just let Rune be our prisoner! she wanted to cry out. *Let him stay in this cell, but make his pain end.*

Yet Shari only smiled and licked her lips. "His pain is only beginning," she said. "The punisher is but a caress compared to what I still plan. It's time, Tilla. It's time to make him truly suffer. Draw your dagger."

Tilla's eyes burned, but she tightened her lips, refusing to show emotion. Her insides trembled.

She didn't want to do this. She didn't want to hurt him. She wanted this to end--to flee this tower, this blood, this pain. Yet if she ran, Shari would never stop hurting Rune. If she ran, they would hunt her down, and she would hang here too.

"Rune," she whispered. She held his cheeks, moved her face close, and pleaded with him. "Please, Rune. Do as I say."

Hands grabbed her shoulders. Shari tugged her back.

"Lanse!" she said. "Do you disobey me? Draw your dagger. Do it now!"

The princess growled, face red and wild, the face of a demon. If Shari lunged at her, sank her teeth into her flesh, and feasted like a wolf, Tilla would not be surprised.

"I'm sorry, Rune," she whispered. "I must do this."

She coiled her trembling fingers around her dagger's hilt. Her breath shook as she drew the blade. The dagger felt so heavy in her palm. It caught the torchlight and gleamed red as if already bloodied.

"Now..." Shari tapped her fingers against her hip. "This boy tore off my wing. He crippled me. He made me only half a dragon. I think... it's time to repay him in kind. What do you think, Lanse?"

Tilla swallowed.

Please don't make me do this, she prayed. *Please, stars, please, old gods or new.* Her heart raced. Sweat drenched her. Her chest tightened and she thought she would collapse.

"I... Commander, what do you plan?"

Shari laughed, approached Rune, and stroked the manacles binding his left arm.

"We don't need him chained by two arms. I do believe he can hang from one just as well." She licked her lips. "A hand for a wing; seems fitting, does it not?"

Tilla felt the blood leave her face. "I can't," she whispered.

"You will!" Shari said. "Do the deed. Now. Cut him. He took my wing; you will take his hand."

Rune began to pant. He looked up, bleeding and beaten, and his chest shook, and finally fear seemed to fill him.

"Tilla," he said and pulled his chains. "Tilla, please. Don't. You can end this. You can--"

"Cut him!" Shari screamed. Her voice echoed in the chamber. "Cut him, and we will force him to eat his own hand, and he will scream, and he will worship us. Hurt him!"

Tilla stood trembling. She wept. Her dagger wavered.

"Please, I cannot... I can't do this..."

"You must cut him! You were his love. You were his friend. You must do this deed." Shari laughed maniacally. "Watch, boy. Watch! The woman you loved, the woman you wanted to bed--she will cripple you. Lanse Tilla, cut him! Cut him or you will join him in chains."

Tilla shook. No. No! She couldn't do this. What could she do? She took a step closer to Rune. He tugged mightily on the chains, struggling, shouting at her.

"Please, Rune," she whispered, tears on her lips. "Please..."

She raised the dagger. He trembled. She positioned the blade, ready to cut through the joints of his bones.

"Do it!" Shari screamed.

"Rune, please," Tilla whispered.

He stared at her.

The room seemed to freeze.

All sound died, and even the torches seemed to fall silent.

He lowered his head, and his chest shook, and he nodded.

"I hail the red spiral," he whispered.

Tilla let out a sob, trembled, and gasped for breath. She pulled her dagger back. It was over. Thank the stars, it was over. She could be together with Rune now--like they used to be. They could leave this place. They could worship Frey together. It was over.

"Speak it louder, Rune," she said, smiled tremulously, and touched his cheek. "Worship the red spiral with all the strength in you."

He shook, his teeth ground together, and he let out a howl, a howl louder than any of his screams of pain.

"I hail the red spiral!"

He swung on his chains, heaving and shaking.

He raised his eyes and looked at her... and she expected to see relief in them. She expected to see resignation or pain but also relief... relief that the game was over. That he had lost and the agony would end.

But instead... instead she saw horror.

It was not only horror for himself. She could see that. His eyes were haunted for her.

She saw her reflection in them--a young woman, her face so pale, her heart withered. She looked upon herself as she was. She looked upon herself in his memory. She saw both her lives, past and present. A ropemaker's daughter and a torturer.

And she understood.

He's given up on me, she thought. *That is the horror in his eyes. He thought that by taking my pain, he could save me. And now he realized I'm lost to him forever.*

She knew then that even now, even if Shari freed him, even if he lived with her in her home, she was lost to him. They would never be together as they were.

The Tilla he loved died. I killed her.

Shari nodded.

"Good...," the princess said, savoring the word. "Good, very good. He's finally broken. Sooner than I'd have liked, but I'm pleased."

Tilla lowered her head, trembling, not knowing if she was relieved or terrified. "I'll take him to my chamber," she said softly. "I'll find him armor. Tomorrow he can join the Legions and serve the emperor."

Shari raised her eyebrow. "Oh... my dear lanse. I believe you've misunderstood. He's not yet paid his price. Raise your dagger! I will still have you sever his hand."

Tilla gasped. She could barely see, and she heard Rune gasp too. She raised her head, eyes wide, and stared at Shari.

"But... Commander! He's broken. He hailed the spiral. He--"

"He is not broken," Shari said, smiling thinly. "He's still in one piece, isn't he? My dear child, you are young and innocent. Relesar is lying. He hailed the red spiral only to save his hand. His words reek of dishonestly." Shari snickered. "But I see through his lies. You will break him. Fully. You will sever his hand. And then you will shatter his bones. And then you will cut off his manhood and burn it. You will have him crawl in the dust, no longer a man, no longer human, but a creature, a sniveling maggot that you created with your blade and hammer. But you'll leave his tongue so that he can still scream and worship the spiral. It will be all he can do. And then... then he will be fully broken. Then I will be avenged. Then, Lanse Tilla Siren, you'll have proven yourself worthy." Her voice rose to a shout. "Now obey me and bring me his hand!"

Tilla stared at her princess, barely able to breathe.

She's mad, she realized. *She's gone mad entirely.* Tilla's eyes burned. *How... how can I do this? How can I worship her? Even Frey did not want this! Even Frey sees reason, not just mad vengeance.*

"Your father--" she began.

"My father isn't here! I am your commander. It is I you must obey. Obey me! His hand!"

"Tilla!" Rune cried, voice choked. "Tilla, please, don't listen to her--"

"Cut him!"

Tilla shook. What could she do? Stars, what could she do? For so long, she had blamed Rune for this. For so long, she had thought that if Rune only worshiped the spiral, this would end. But it wasn't ending. The pain would only grow, and her soul would only darken, and Rune would only wither into a beast.

"This is not the way, Commander," she whispered. "The red spiral is about the glory of Requiem. If Rune can join us, he--"

"He will join us as a freak, as a creature for a cage! Cut him! Maim him!" Shari screamed, saliva spraying from her mouth. Sweat soaked her hair. She seemed not a human, not a dragon, but a demon. "Cut him now, or I will cut him, and I will cut you, and I will sew your twisted bodies together, forming you into conjoined, diseased twins for my court. Cut him! Cut him or you will suffer!"

Tilla turned back toward Rune.

She shook so madly she could barely grip her dagger.

She took a step toward him.

Rune stared at her, eyes wide and damp, and shook his head. His lips trembled.

"Tilla, no," he whispered, voice cracking. "Please. Tilla..."

She took a shuddering breath.

She placed her dagger against his wrist, and he closed his eyes and whispered prayers.

She saw it again--the sea at home. She wove ropes with her father. She sat in the Old Wheel, drinking ale with Rune, petting his dog, feeling warm and safe. She walked along the beach, barefoot, and he gave her a seashell necklace, and she kissed him. And he bled. And her home burned. And so much blood covered her hands.

I'm scared too, he had said to her that day two years ago, standing with her on the beach in the night, the night before the Legions had drafted her. *But it will be fine. I promise you, Tilla. Everything will be fine.*

"You promised," she whispered, tears on her lips, and she kissed him again, a last kiss like their first one, a kiss that tasted of her tears and his blood.

She nodded.

"I have to do this," she whispered... and spun around.

She thrust her dagger with a scream.

The blade crashed into Shari's chest, driving between her ribs and into her heart.

Shari's eyes widened. She stared, mouth wide, and for a moment the chamber froze. Nobody breathed.

"When we first met," Tilla whispered, "you told me that you'd keep an eye on me. You should have kept closer watch."

Snarling, Tilla twisted her blade.

Blood spread across Shari's tunic. She stared, silent, and her lips peeled back, and her eyes blazed, and her hands rose... and she crashed to her knees.

Tilla yanked her blade back. Shari Cadigus, heir to Requiem, crashed facedown onto the floor. Her blood pooled.

Tilla spun back toward Rune. He hung from his chains, frail and beaten, struggling for every breath. Tilla's fingers shook so madly she could barely grab her keys.

"We have to flee," she whispered. She touched his cheek and tears stung her eyes. "It's over now, Rune, but we must flee. Fast. We must run."

Her heart pounded. Stars, if they were caught...

She unlocked his manacles, freeing his arms from the chains. For so long, only the chains had held him standing, not his own feet. Now he wavered and nearly fell. She grabbed him. She held him up. He leaned against her, legs rubbery; she supported all his weight.

"I'll have to tie your wrists," she said. "There are guards downstairs. They'll think I'm moving you to another cell."

He nodded weakly. She took a rope from a table. She tied his wrists, making sure the knot was weak.

"Now let's go," she whispered. "Step by step. I'm with you."

She slung his arms across her shoulders. She began to walk. One step. Another. Holding him up. He moaned and his feet all but dragged across the floor. He was too hurt, too famished, near death perhaps.

"We have to keep moving," she said.

He limped along, his weight against her, and she heard the smile in his voice.

"I knew you were still there, Tilla. I knew it."

They reached the chamber door. Tilla yanked it open, revealing the staircase that spiraled down the tower. She took the first step, holding Rune tight. He wavered and Tilla nearly fell. She grabbed the wall for support.

"I know you're hurt, but we'll have to do this quickly," Tilla said.

With every step, her heart raced faster, and sweat trickled down her spine. She tried to calm herself. Shari had died silently; no guards would know Tilla had slain her. She just had to keep descending, step by step. She just had to pass the guards outside; they had seen her move Rune through the Citadel before, and they would let her pass.

And then... what then?

She kept climbing down, Rune's arms around her.

And then they would have to leave the city. To flee into the wilderness. They would be hunted. Frey would never rest from hunting them--the heir of Aeternum and the woman who slew his daughter.

"We'll find some faraway place," she said, and her voice shook. "Like you wanted, Rune. We'll fly as far as we can. We'll keep flying--to the very end of the world. We will not let them catch us."

She knew what the wilderness held. Soldiers. Forts. Perhaps starvation and thirst. It was likely they would fly to their deaths. Yet they would die together, holding each other, Tilla Roper and Rune Brewer. It would not be a bad way to die. It would be infinitely better than the death Frey would give them.

After what seemed like hours, they reached the bottom of the tower.

Tilla froze and steeled herself. She forced a deep breath. Behind those doors, two guards awaited, armored and armed with halberds.

They will know, she thought. *They will see Shari's blood on my hands. They will know and raise the alarm, and a thousand more soldiers will swoop upon me.*

"Be strong, Rune," she whispered. "You'll have to walk now on your own. I'll pretend to manhandle you. Act like my prisoner; there are guards outside."

He nodded.

With another deep breath, she opened the door.

They stepped out into the courtyard.

The two guards stood there, covered in black steel. They slammed their gauntlets against their chests.

"Hail the red spiral!"

Tilla shoved Rune forward. He stumbled and all but fell, but she grabbed his arms and manhandled him forward. She glared at the guards as she passed by.

"Stand straight, men!" she barked. "You're slouching again. Commander Shari will descend soon, and if she sees you hunched over, she will flay your hides."

They straightened like blades, chins raised.

"Yes, Commander!" they said.

Tilla inspected them, eyes narrowed. Despite the horror pounding through her, she still outranked these men. She nodded and kept walking, shoving Rune before her. He limped and stumbled, his blood dripping.

"Move, worm!" she shouted at him.

The courtyard seemed miles long. Walls and towers rose around her; screams rose with them. She kept walking, shoving Rune forward. Step by step. Past more cells. Past more towers. Past more guards who marched, armor clanking, whips in hands.

"Move!" she screamed at Rune as five guards marched by. "Move, maggot, or I swear, I will break every segment in your spine. Move, scum!"

She kept shoving him, and the guards marched by.

Oh stars, they will find Shari soon. They will shout. They will descend upon us.

She walked. Step by step. Drop by drop of blood.

It seemed hours before she reached the Citadel's gates. More guards stood here, their black helms spiked, their hands clutching swords.

"I'm taking this one to Tarath Imperium," she told them and forced herself to snicker. "The emperor wants to see his blood. I will return him tonight."

She sucked in her breath. The guards stared at her silently. Tilla nearly fainted and her heart pounded. Surely they sensed the ruse. Surely they would capture her, capture Rune again, torture them both, and--

"Yes, Lanse," the chief guard finally said. He drew a scroll from his belt--it held the names of all prisoners who came and went--and made a marking. "Hail the red spiral!"

She shakily returned the salute.

The guards opened the gates... and Tilla and Rune stepped out into the city streets.

Snow fell around them. The houses rose alongside. The city seemed strangely beautiful to her--the snowy roofs, the trees glimmering with icicles, the small sun behind the clouds... On any other day, she would marvel at this beauty.

She turned toward Rune. He stood looking at the snow too. He stood on his own now, frail and burnt, but he inhaled deeply. He smiled and tugged his bindings, freeing his bloodied wrists.

"I'll carry you in my claws now," Tilla said. "But once we're outside the city, we'll fly together. Side by side. Like we used to."

She shifted into a dragon. She beat her wings, scattering snow off the cobblestones, and rose several feet into the air. She reached down and scooped Rune up into her claws.

She flew.

The city spread beneath them, countless houses and streets, statues and forts, ponds and parks, a million souls who knew none of her pain. Tarath Imperium, palace of the emperor, rose in its center, a thousand feet tall, the heart of the empire. Once Tilla had dreamed of serving in that palace. Once she had stood below it, shouting for the spiral, worshiping the tower's might.

Today she flew away.

She flew south.

She flew across Nova Vita, over the city walls, and above a frosted forest.

She flew into the wilderness, Rune in her grip, and her heart shook and she could barely breathe.

VALIEN

Sunset gilded the land when he beheld the shores of Requiem.

He had been flying all day. His ruined throat wheezed, his lungs burned, and his wings shot agony through him with every stroke. The scars on his body blazed as if freshly cut. He was too old, too wounded, too haunted for these long flights and so many battles, and yet he flew on.

His army flew around him, a thousand dragons. Each beast bore several riders, a mix of Tiran arquebusers and Vir Requis in human forms. They had been flying for three days over the sea. Every few hours, they swapped--one Vir Requis rider would leap from the saddle, shift into a dragon, and take the load, allowing the exhausted flier to resume human form and ride. They slept in the saddle. They kept flying northwest. Three days and three nights of water.

And finally the shores of Requiem emerged.

The coast stretched ahead, a mere hint upon the horizon. All around Valien, dragons chanted for home. They sang the old songs of the forest. They cried for starlight and birch leaves and marble columns. They sang for Requiem, but Valien only lowered his head.

No. This was not Requiem ahead. This was not Aeternum's kingdom. They flew now toward the shore of another realm, a fallen land once named Osanna, an ancient kingdom Frey had burned. Valien had spent years hiding in these ruins with the Resistance. He had seen thousands of Osanna's burnt skeletons littering the ash. Frey had annexed his conquest years ago, and today his banners flew here too, but no--this was not home, no more than the ruins of Tiranor were.

"We will free Osanna too," Valien said as he flew over the water. "We will liberate this fallen land for the memory of her people." He raised his voice to a howl. "Children of Requiem! Every Vir Requis--take dragon form. Every Tiran--load your guns. Scope bearers--ready your beams."

As the coast drew nearer, his army formed ranks.

All Vir Requis in human form leaped from saddles, shifted into dragons, and howled. Jets of fire lit the twilight. Soon three thousand dragons roared, flying in four units. Upon their backs rode Tiran arquebusers. They streamed over the water, chanting for victory. Valien roared with them, hoarse but pealing his cry across the sea.

"Death to Cadigus! Dragons--fan out!"

Their four formations spread side to side. Ahead of each flew a scope bearer--a Tiran rider clutching a cylinder full of Genesis Shards.

Valien led one group, and upon his back rode Sila; the gruff captain held one of the scopes. Kaelyn and Erry each led another group, scope bearers upon their backs. Leresy held the fourth scope in his own claws; the prince had refused to let anyone ride him.

Only four scopes, Valien thought with a grumble. Even with a hundred, fear would have filled him today. They had tried dividing the shards into smaller batches, but found the magic too weak, and so with four scopes they flew, and fear filled his belly.

He looked across his army. Three thousand dragons. Two thousand riders. Four scopes. It wasn't enough. Even with the Genesis Shards and the arquebuses, superior weapons, it wasn't enough. Not against half a million legionaries, howling for blood and firing cannons.

We must fly to Nova Vita without rest, he thought and snarled. *We must engage no enemies along the way. We must storm the palace and slay Frey, fast and deadly as an arrow shot from shadow.*

He roared. The coast loomed only ten miles away. There would be a small patrol; the Legions patrolled every mile of this beach.

"Slay every legionary you see!" Valien called out. "Let none flee to bear news."

They streamed toward the shore. The sun sank below the horizon. The sea vanished into shadows.

From ahead upon the shore, thousands of flaming pillars blazed skyward.

Roars pounded across the sky.

"Hail the red spiral! Hail Frey Cadigus!"

Valien felt as if a hammer slammed against him.

By the Abyss...

The horizon blazed. Fire streamed like a storm of comets, like an erupting volcano, like the Abyss risen into the world. Shadows broke apart from the distant shore, rising like demonic crows from a rotten tree. Ten thousand dragons ascended from fire, shadow, and smoke, shrieked to the sky, and streamed across the sea.

He knew, Valien thought, for a moment unable to breathe, barely able to flap his wings. *Frey knew we were coming.*

Around him, his fellow dragons cursed and roared. They glanced around. They blasted flame in a confused array.

"Damn it, Valien, you said these coasts weren't guarded!" Leresy shouted somewhere in the distance.

Valien growled and snapped his teeth. He beat his wings mightily, rising higher in the night. The sea streamed below him. The beasts raced ahead.

"Dragons of Requiem!" he howled. "Show the enemy no mercy. Fly! Meet them head-on. For Requiem!"

Upon their backs, the Tirans blew their war horns. The cries trumpeted across the sea. The dragons of the Resistance answered the call, roaring their own battle cries, wordless howls of rage. Ahead, the Legions streamed across the miles--five miles away, then four, then three--bellowing and hailing the spiral.

"Scope bearers!" Valien shouted. "Ready your weapons!"

The armies streamed closer. Three thousand dragons of the Resistance. Ten thousand legionaries, a cloud of flame and shadow.

"Hold!" Valien howled.

They flew, howling. Three miles. Two.

"Ready your scopes! *Hold!*"

The Legions howled and laughed ahead. Their flames crackled, lighting the sea below. The dragons of the Resistance growled and snarled. Not a gun or flaming jet fired.

"Hold!"

Two miles.

One.

"Slay them all!" roared the Legions.

"Break their spines!"

"Feast upon their flesh!"

"Hail the red spiral!"

Valien gritted his teeth, sucked in his breath, and reared in the air.

"Scope bearers--fire!"

At his side, Kaelyn's rider unscrewed a scope first. The red light blazed out in the night, a beam piercing the shadows, an explosion as bright and furious as dragonfire. A heartbeat later, beams blasted out from Erry and Leresy, humming and slamming forward. Upon Valien's own back, Sila howled and his beam shone, nearly blinding Valien, stretching over his head to crash into the imperial dragons ahead.

The Genesis Beams hit the Legions with the fury of ten thousand cannonballs.

Where the red light struck, dragons vanished. Men and women tumbled, screaming, to crash into the sea below.

Valien howled. "Resistance--dragonfire!"

He blasted his flames. They rained onto the falling legionaries, burning them as they fell. The troops tumbled, blazing comets, to slam into the water. Around Valien, thousands of dragons roared their fire.

The legionaries screamed. They fell. They died. The beams ripped through them like great, glowing blades. Hundreds tumbled into the water.

"Slay them all!" Valien roared. "Show them no mercy. Leave none alive!"

The two armies crashed together.

Valien barreled through a swarm. Legionaries flew everywhere, a dark horde, their armor bladed, their fire raging.

"Sila, cut them down!" Valien said.

Upon his back, the captain spun his beam, clearing a path. All around, the legionaries fell. Any who flew near met the beam, lost his magic, and crashed down in human form.

"Break their lines!" Leresy shouted somewhere in the distance, laughing.

The battle descended into chaos. Legionaries flew at all sides, mingling with resistors. Beams shot every which way. Fire blazed. Arquebuses fired. The air exploded into a storm of gunpowder, flame, and light.

"Scope bearers, fan out!" Valien roared. "Leresy! Erry! Fly to the east. Kaelyn, take the south. Surround our forces!"

He cursed, trying to find them. Their formations were falling apart. A phalanx of legionaries flew toward him, roaring fire. The flames blasted Valien's belly and he yowled.

"Sila!"

The captain's beam fell upon the enemy. They fell. Valien bathed their tumbling human bodies with fire.

"Scope bearers, surround our forces! Hold the enemy back."

He whipped his head from side to side, seeking them. He howled curses. They had drilled for this. On order, the four scope bearers were to surround their army, forming four pillars of defense, cutting down the enemy while allowing their comrades to blow fire from within the shield. Yet now they flew in disarray.

"Leresy, damn it, take the east!" Valien roared.

The red dragon was crashing into the enemy above, laughing madly, clutching a scope in his claws. He spun it around every which way. Behind him, legionaries--still in dragon form--were crashing into resistors, tearing them down.

"Leresy, damn you!" Valien roared.

The red dragon blazed his beam upward. When humans tumbled down, he caught them in his jaws, bit their bodies apart, and spat out the pieces.

"Valien!" the young prince shouted, laughing, blood on his teeth. "We will slay him. We will slay my father!"

Valien blasted fire. "Leresy, behind you--"

Ten imperial dragons swooped from above. Their claws reached out. They crashed into the prince.

Leresy yowled, a high-pitched sound, and reared. His beam shot out wildly, whipping from side to side. A legionary bit into the prince's back. Leresy's claws opened, and the scope tumbled from his grasp.

"Damn it, Leresy!" Valien said. He shot forward and reached out, trying to grab the scope.

The cylinder spun wildly as it fell, shining light every which way. The beam blazed against Valien.

Like a sword pulled from his back, his magic vanished.

Valien tumbled through the sky, a human. Above him, Sila tumbled too, torn free from the saddle, his beam still shining.

The water raced up toward them.

Valien roared, swearing to slay the boy.

An instant before he could slam into the sea, he emerged from the beam's light. He sucked in his magic. He shifted back into dragon form.

His claws grazed the water. He beat his wings and soared. He grabbed Sila before the captain could crash into the sea.

"Back into the saddle!" he said.

He rose higher, looking around him. The battle had become a brawl. Rather than protect their comrades, the scope bearers flew aimlessly. For every legionary they cut down, ten swooped from behind. Arquebuses fired, cracking and shattering the air. Dragonfire blazed.

"This is no battle," Valien growled. "It's a bar fight."

He soared higher. Sila blazed his beam upward. They tore through the hosts, legionaries falling around them.

"Kaelyn!" he said, spotting the green dragon ahead. "Take the east. Go! Erry--go west. Shine that beam. Leresy, damn you, find your scope!"

The red dragon still flew, blood seeping down his shoulders, his scope gone from his claws. Kaelyn and Erry roared and darted out, blazing their beams, holding the enemy back. Thousands of legionaries still flew, mingling together with the resistors.

Valien cursed. "Sila, what can you do?"

Upon his back, the captain shouted, "Damn armies are too mingled! I can barely shine the light upon a legionary without hitting a resistor too. This is a damn mess."

"Do what you can. We have to separate the forces."

The battle continued for hours. Dragonfire, Genesis Beams, and gunfire lit the night. Men and women fell all around, some still alive and blazing, others charred corpses. Legionaries flew everywhere. The beams mowed down some; others crashed into the Resistance, blowing fire and lashing claws. Smoke and blood rained into the sea below.

Dawn rose before the Resistance made its way onto the empire's shore.

The sunlight rose upon a world coated in blood and ash.

Valien filled his wings with air, grunted with the pain of a dozen cuts, and landed upon the beach. His fellow resistors landed around him, wheezing and puffing smoke. Their scales were cracked and charred. Cuts and burns covered them. Their blood dripped. Upon their backs, many Tirans clutched wounds and welts. Some dragons bore only corpses upon their saddles.

All around them, the bodies of legionaries swept onto the shore. Every wave brought a new pile of their bloated, lacerated corpses. Death covered the beaches, thicker than the seashells, a blanket of flesh.

Sila dismounted and Valien took human form.

"Teramil, bring me reports!" Valien barked at one of his lieutenants, a tall and dour man with cold eyes. "Count the living. Aranor!" He turned toward another commander, a former priest turned resistor. "Organize the survivors into new phalanxes. Make sure every man is armed. We fly within an hour. They know we're here."

He moved along the beach, giving orders. With every wave, new corpses floated toward him. Blood painted the sand. Most of the dead were legionaries, clad in black armor; many were resistors, wearing only leather and wool, their flesh burnt black, their mouths open in silent anguish.

Some soldiers washed ashore still writhing and screaming. Some had lost limbs; they clutched at their bleeding stumps. Others screamed with burns, their skin peeling, their flesh twisting. Some bore gaping wounds, exposing or losing organs, crying for home. They had brought only a hundred healers--not enough, Valien knew. Not enough. With every step he took, another wounded man or woman fell silent, joining the dead.

So many more dead, Valien thought, walking among them, gritting his teeth. *We should have stayed on the islands. Stars damn it, this shouldn't have happened. Frey knew. He waited for us.* Valien's throat tightened. *And now more blood stains my hands.*

Yet as he walked among the dead and dying, his thoughts centered on only one soul.

"Kaelyn," he whispered.

He walked through the sand, seeking her. He saw her in every charred body. His fists shook. He wanted to shout out for her, but could not; the leader of the Resistance could show no emotions for one woman. He kept moving, quickening his step, his boots slogging through the blood.

I can't lose you too, Kaelyn. His breath shook behind his clenched teeth. *Where are you?*

"Valien!"

Her voice rang across the beach. He turned and saw her there, and his eyes dampened.

"Thank the stars," he whispered.

He took three great strides toward her. She ran and crashed into his arms, and he held her. Blood smeared her.

"Kaelyn, you're hurt," he said, her golden hair a tangle beneath his chin.

She shook her head. "The blood isn't mine. Not most of it. I'm scratched and a little burned, but I'm fine." She looked up at him, her eyes large and afraid. "He knew we were coming. How did he know?"

Still holding her in his arms, Valien looked over the beach. For a mile or more around him, the corpses lay. Crows and crabs were already swarming for the feast.

"He always knew we were on the island," he said, throat tight and voice a mere hiss. "I should have known islands that size, even so far away, would not go unnoticed. He patrolled from the air or from the sea, but he knew, and he waited for us."

When his lieutenants returned with the news, Valien felt his stomach sink. His head spun. He gritted his teeth and could only stand in the blood, fists clenched. He had flown here with five thousand souls; four thousand remained.

This was always a fool's quest, he thought, head lowered.

Kaelyn clutched his arm. Her hair flew in the wind, stained red. A cut ran down her cheek, but her eyes still blazed.

"We fly on," she said. "We tore through the Legions upon the beach. We will tear through them at the capital."

Valien growled and shook his head. "We've lost too many. Even with full force, we were unsure. We lost a thousand warriors before even landing on the beaches."

"And yet we did land," Kaelyn said and bared her teeth. "Valien Eleison, do not give up hope now. Keep fighting or I will smack you." She dug her fingers into his arms, her head no taller than his shoulders, her eyes shining like the red beams of ancient stones. "We fight on. You and me. As we always have. We fly to the capital and we win this."

Valien looked around. His fighters surrounded him and he gazed into their eyes, each one in turn. Sila and Miya stared back steadily; their faces were ashy and bloody, but their backs were straight. Erry stood with her chin raised, snarling, her eyes lusting for the fight. Thousands of fighters spread beyond them--cut, burnt, and weary, but their eyes all shone the same. They shone for battle. For victory.

They are brave and strong, Valien thought, *yet I am afraid. They need me to lead them, but do I only lead them to more death?*

"Move. Move it!" An arrogant, high-pitched voice rose among the crowd. Leresy came trudging forward, elbowing men and women out of his path. "Where's Valien, damn it?" When the prince emerged from the crowd and saw them, he glared. "Are you having a council without me?"

Kaelyn rolled her eyes. "Brother, do be quiet."

Her twin snorted. "Me, be quiet? My scopes won this battle for us." He raised his chin. "*I* dug up the Genesis Shards. *I* built the scopes. Thanks to me, we're in Requiem now. What are you planning next? I demand to know."

Valien growled. His rage fumed inside him like dragonfire. For many days, he had ignored this pup, letting Kaelyn and the others scold him into silence. Today, these dead around him, this blood on his boots and hands, he could not curb his fury. He marched through the sand.

When he reached Leresy, the prince smirked at him. Valien could not stop himself. He growled and backhanded the boy, putting all his rage into the blow.

Leresy yowled like a kicked dog. He cowered, raising his arms to protect his face, and scampered back. Valien would not let him flee. He grabbed the boy, twisted his collar, and glared down at him.

"You foolish child," he said, clutching the prince. "You lost a scope. You were too proud to bear a rider, and you let your scope tumble into the sea. Did you find it?"

Leresy tried to shove him off, but could not, so he only raised his chin and glared. His lips shook, and his cheek reddened where Valien had struck him.

"How the Abyss can I find it?" His voice cracked, but he swallowed and glared, struggling to reclaim some pride. "The damn thing sank. It fell by you. Why didn't you grab it?"

Valien howled and shook the prince. "Its light tore away my magic. I could have died because of your foolishness, boy. I let you carry a scope, and you proved yourself useless."

Leresy clenched his fists and glared, but his knees trembled and sweat drenched him.

"Unhand me!" he demanded. "I am Prince Leresy Cadigus. I am the son of the emperor. I order you to--"

"You are a fool," Valien said and spat.

He shoved the prince away. Leresy tumbled into the sand, hissed, and glared. Valien turned and marched away. He shouted out for his army to hear.

"Warriors of the Resistance! We will not linger here. We fly! Carry the wounded with you. We fly on."

They took flight, four thousand souls, one of their scopes lost, leaving their dead to the sea. They would need to set camp soon. They would need to rest, to eat and drink, to sleep, to nurse their wounds before the fight ahead. But not here. Not upon this beach of death.

They flew through the night, a small light in the endless darkness. As Valien flew at their lead, he could not swallow the pain that filled his throat.

RUNE

They had flown for barely a league when the city erupted behind them.

Rune had never found flying harder. He had not taken dragon form in many days, not since surrendering himself. His wings felt as creaky as the old chains. His scales clanked and slammed together, sending jolts of pain through him. When he twisted his head and looked at his body, he did not see the slim, strong black dragon he had been, but a wretched beast, haggard, his ribs pushing against cracked scales.

He looked at Tilla. She flew at his side, a white dragon clad in black armor, the red spirals still blazing upon her steel. She looked behind her and cursed.

"They found her," she said. "They found Shari and they'll scour the sky until they find us."

As Rune flew, he again glanced over his shoulder at the city. Alarm bells clanged. Pillars of fire shot skyward, thick as a forest. Dragons began to rise, tens of thousands of them, like flies rising from a disturbed carcass. Their shrieks rolled across the land. The Legions began spreading out from the city in every direction, a puddle oozing across the forest.

"Oh stars damn it!" Tilla said and panted. "They'll find us. They'll bring us back. Oh stars."

Rune shook his head. He wheezed and barely forced the words from his lips.

"They won't find us," he said. "I've hidden from the Legions for two years. Follow me."

He spotted the place ahead. Two piney hillsides dipped down, creating a fold between them. The trees were thick and white with snow, but Rune knew that a stream ran beneath them, hidden from the air. He began descending, the wind rushing against him. Fire crackled and shrieks rose behind.

"What are you doing?" Tilla said. "We have to fly far. We have to fly south. They're chasing!"

"Trust me," he said. He slapped her with his tail, gesturing her on. "Follow. I know a hiding place. Don't blow fire. Glide dark and silent as a ghost."

He glanced behind him. The Legions were swarming closer. Firelight glinted against armor. Tens of thousands of dragons were flying out, shrieking, blowing fire and lighting the night. Rune was a fast flier, but he was too weak now, too slow and hurt. They would have to hide.

He dived down, silent in the night. Tilla dived beside him. They crashed through the forest canopy, stretched out their claws, and landed on the forest floor. Rune allowed only a glint of fire to fill his maw. The orange light fell upon a frozen stream, boulders, and snow. Hillsides flanked them, thick with birches and pines, forming two walls.

"We're too close to the city," Tilla said. The white dragon glanced up nervously. Their pursuers shrieked above; they would fly overhead in moments. "They'll uproot every tree here."

Rune grunted and wheezed. "Uprooting trees takes a while. And they won't burn the forest. They want us alive or dead. Burning us gives them only ash. Follow me. We're close. It's somewhere around here."

"What is?" she said. "Rune, we must head south. We must get as far from the capital as possible. I can carry you if you can't fly. But we--"

"We cannot flee," he said. "They're too many and too fast. Tilla, trust me. I've spent two years fighting with the Resistance. I know how to hide. We walk in human forms from here; walking as dragons disturbs the trees."

He shifted back into a human. His head spun and he nearly fell. Tilla had burned him with her punisher; every inch of his skin ached. But she didn't know of his deeper wounds, those kicks and punches the guards had given him at nights while she slept. He could barely walk. Every step blazed. Yet he forced himself to move, one step after another.

Tilla walked at his side. Perhaps sensing his weariness, she held his hand.

"Are you all right?" she whispered.

He could barely see her; she was but a shadow in the night. He squeezed her hand.

"Keep walking. Let's be silent. We're almost there."

His throat burned. More than he worried about the dragons hearing him, he worried about his voice cracking. They walked atop the stream, the ice coarse with fallen pine needles. The dark trees creaked, a wolf howled, and the dragons screamed above.

"Find them!"

The cry rang out. Wings beat. Wind howled and trees bent.

"Find the heir! He's in these trees. Find him!"

Rune cursed and began to move faster, limping. Wings thudded above. Claws tore at trees. Firelight blazed overhead.

"Rune..." Tilla said. She clutched the hilt of her sword. "I won't let them take us alive. I..." She shook. "It doesn't have to hurt. One thrust into the heart. I--"

He growled and grabbed her wrist. "What are you talking about? Stars! Come, quickly. We're close."

They ran along the stream. Ice creaked and the fire blazed above. A thousand shrieks rose.

"Find the prisoner!"

A dragon swooped ahead. A lashing tail shattered a pine. Branches snapped and icicles fell. To their left, claws uprooted an oak. Dirt and snow rained.

Tilla froze, whispered a prayer, and lifted her sword.

Rune grabbed her and tugged. "Here!"

As trees snapped behind them, they scurried up a hillside. Brambles tore at their legs. Rune knew this place. Boulders should rise in a henge nearby, their surfaces carved with ancient runes. He ran among the trees, seeking them.

"Come on, where are you?" he whispered, and fear pounded through him. Had he flown to the wrong riverbed? Had he already passed the boulders?

"Uproot every tree!"

Fire cracked. Branches tore. Red light blazed against scales, and Rune cursed and ran at a stoop.

There!

In the firelight, he saw the boulders. He ran, ignoring his pain, pulling Tilla behind him. He raced around the henge and behind an oak. He knelt, fished through snow and fallen leaves, and cursed again.

"Where are you...?"

A tree ahead crashed down. Claws glinted. Rune's hand closed around the rope.

With a tug, he opened the trapdoor, revealing an earthen tunnel. He leaped in and pulled Tilla with him. He tugged the rope again, and the trapdoor closed above.

They slid down in the darkness, mud and moss smearing against them, and landed in a cold chamber. They lay silent for a long moment. Rune barely dared breathe. He couldn't see in the darkness, but he felt Tilla grab his hand.

"Did they see us?" she whispered.

He squeezed her hand. Her body pressed against him.

"No," he whispered back. "But wait. Listen."

They lay in the burrow. Above them, he heard the shrieks of the dragons, claws lashing at wood and soil, and wings beating. The Legions howled. Fire crackled. With every heartbeat, Rune squeezed Tilla's hand tighter, praying the dragons didn't find the trapdoor.

After what seemed an eternity, the shrieks grew distant. The dragons flew on.

Rune let out a shaky breath.

"We're safe for now," he said. He leaned his head back against the soil. Every part of him throbbed with pain. Every last shred of his skin burned. His bones themselves felt ready to shatter, his muscles to tear. He could do nothing but breathe.

In the dark, Tilla reached her arms around him. She held him and kissed his lips, and her tears splashed his face.

"I'm so sorry," she whispered, voice trembling. "I'm so sorry that we hurt you. I love you."

He held her for a moment, too pained to move or speak. Finally he raised his head.

"Let's crawl deeper in. There's food and supplies here."

They wriggled through the darkness. Rune felt around, arms outstretched, tracing the walls. He soon felt the wooden chest, opened it, and rummaged. It took long moments to find what he sought: a tinderbox and an oil lamp.

He rubbed flint against steel. When the lamp flickered to life, it illuminated a chamber the size of his old prison cell. Shelves lined the walls, laden with jars of preserves, dried meats, jugs of wine, and wheels of cheese. Swords and crossbows hung upon another wall. In a second chest lay blankets, bandages, cloaks, and leather boots.

"What is this place?" Tilla asked. She stood hugging herself and shivering in the cold.

"A gopher hole," Rune said. "The Resistance uses them. Hundreds exist across Requiem. They're safe places for us to hide and recover from injuries." He smiled wanly. "I suppose I no longer have to worry about sharing our secrets with you."

He took a step toward a shelf of food, but his legs swayed. His knees buckled, and he found himself on the ground.

"Rune!"

Tilla knelt above him. She placed her hands on his cheeks, her eyes soft with concern. He looked up at her. Her face was so pale, her eyes so large, her hair so smooth.

"There you are," he whispered. "My Tilla. Tilla Roper."

The coldness, the cruelty, the red spiral--they were gone from her eyes. In them he saw his old friend, his *best* friend, the woman he loved. The woman he had saved. In her eyes, he saw the waves and sand of their home.

"I'm going to heal you," she said. "I'm going to nurse you back to health. When you're strong enough, we'll find a place for us. A safe place to live."

Rune's eyes fluttered. He tried to hold her, but he had reached the end of his strength. She bustled around the room, fetching supplies. She bandaged his wounds. She laid fur blankets atop him. She held a mug of cider to his lips, and she fed him preserves and cheese and wafers.

"What else can I do?" she asked. "Tell me. Would you like more food? More drink? Another blanket?"

He laughed softly. "You've gone from soldier to a fussy old aunt. I want to sleep. Sleep beside me, Till. Remember how we used to sleep on the beach at home, wrapped in a blanket, watching the stars?"

Eyes damp, she nodded. "Of course."

She removed her boots, tunic, and leggings, remaining in her underclothes. Gently she crawled under the blanket and huddled close to him, embracing him.

"Does it hurt when I hold you?" she whispered, her lips touching his ear.

He shook his head. "Never."

She held him tighter, her body warm. "Good. I don't want to ever let you go." She blinked away tears. "You should never forgive me, Rune. I don't deserve your forgiveness. But know that I'm sorry. Know that I love you. I'll never let you go, and I'll never let you forget that." She kissed his lips. "Goodnight, Rune Brewer of Lynport."

"Goodnight, Tilla Roper."

The lamplight guttered away. They slept in each other's arms.

LERESY

As the high command convened, moving pieces across maps and discussing battle plans, Leresy crossed his arms, stood in the shadows, and fumed.

How dare he slap me? he thought, grinding his teeth. *How dare he? I am prince of Requiem!*

Fists clenched, Leresy stared at this Valien Eleison, this ragged, outcast knight--no better than a common outlaw--who styled himself the leader of the Resistance. The vagabond stood at the table, moving his finger across a parchment map. His hair was long, scraggly, and streaked with white. Salt-and-pepper stubble covered his cheeks, while the rest of his face looked like beaten leather. Even his dress was coarse; the man wore leathers, furs, and wools, the raiment of a beggar.

And my sister follows him? Leresy scoffed.

"At dawn, we fly northwest," Valien said, tracing his finger along plains and forests. "We head straight to the capital. We cannot win a slow war; we are too few. We must seize Nova Vita before the Legions learn to fight our Genesis Shards. Speed is our ally."

His lieutenants stood at his sides: Kaelyn with her ever-present bow and quiver, that southern creature Sila, and a dozen resistors with gaunt cheeks and somber eyes. The rest of their forces camped below the hill, a few thousand men and women nursing wounds, eating and drinking, and polishing swords.

They are a rabble, Leresy thought, disgust rising in his throat. *They are nothing but outlaws. They only won a battle because I found the Genesis Shards.* He looked back at Valien and hissed under his breath. *And Valien takes credit for this victory.*

"Let us fly out at once," said Kaelyn, chin raised. "We've lingered here long enough."

Valien shook his head. Leresy was surprised the decrepit thing didn't shed dust with every movement.

"We'll fly at dawn," the outlaw said. "We've been flying with no rest for days now, and too many are wounded. Our fighters need one night upon solid ground, not in the saddle. They need a night to nurse their wounds, to eat, to ready their weapons and their souls. At dawn we fly. We will fly for seven days and nights, and we will fall upon the capital." He pointed at the map. "And we take the throne."

Leresy hissed again from the shadows. They had invited him to their council, but he would not speak here. He would not dignify this mob rabble with his wisdom.

You want the crown for that pup, Rune, he thought, glaring at the man. *You want to pull his strings even as he sits upon the Ivory Throne. I know your mind, Valien Eleison, traitor of Requiem.*

Leresy couldn't help it. He had vowed to remain silent, but words fled his lips.

"I demand another Genesis Scope," he said, taking a step closer to the table.

All eyes turned to stare at him. Some glared with open disdain while Kaelyn sighed and gazed with pity. No emotion, however, filled Valien's eyes; his stare was cold and dead.

"You lost your scope, Leresy Cadigus," the outlaw said. "You insisted on clutching your scope in your claws, for you were too proud to bear a rider. You will have no new scope. Kaelyn, Erry, and I will bear the remaining three."

Leresy bared his teeth and hissed. "It's I who found the Genesis Shards. They are my weapons! It's my ingenuity that won us the battle upon the coast. I will have a new scope!"

Valien himself bore one scope upon his belt. Leresy marched up toward the man, prepared to wrestle the scope free, but froze a few paces away. His heart raced and sweat trickled down his back. Leresy was a strong warrior--he had proven himself in battle--yet Valien was still taller and wider.

"Hand me your scope!" Leresy barked. When Valien said nothing, Leresy spun toward his sister. "Kaelyn--you bear a scope too. The one I gave you. Return it to me! Or give me half the shards within so I can build a new one."

His sister shook her head. "Stars damn it, Ler, you're drunk. There aren't enough shards to go around, and you know it. Go to bed. Sleep it off."

Leresy cackled. "Oh, I'm very sober. I see things very clearly." He pointed a shaky finger at them. "You want the throne for yourselves! You want to use my weapon--mine!--to seize my prize."

"Leresy!" Kaelyn shouted, her voice ringing across the hill. She stomped forward, eyes blazing, and grabbed his arm. She leaned close, sniffed, and wrinkled her nose. "Damn it, you reek of booze." She looked back at the council. "I'll take him to his bed."

When she began dragging him downhill, Leresy struggled, but she was damn strong for her size. He couldn't pry her fingers off his arm, so he only stumbled after her.

"I had only a few sips," he said, tugging his arm but failing to free himself. "Kaelyn, damn it! Release me. Give me my scope back. You want the throne too! You want all the glory, and you don't care about anything I do." Tears of rage stung his eyes. "I found the weapon. I should lead this rabble, not you and that outlaw. Did you bed him, Kaelyn?" He spat. "The camp says you did. Are you a princess or a whore?"

She gave his arm a twist. Her eyes blazed. "Leresy, damn you!" They reached his tent, which stood in a valley by an oak. "Sleep it off. I'll forget what you said here, but promise me--sleep it off, and no more booze tonight."

With that, she shoved him into his tent. He stumbled backward, his heels hit a chair, and he fell down hard. The tent flap closed, and he could hear Kaelyn march away, returning to her council.

Leresy wanted to run after her. He wanted to shout, to fly as a dragon, to torch the council and burn them all. How dared they steal his weapons? How dared they send him to bed--as if he were some temperamental child, not a prince? He grabbed a bottle of rye from his pack, uncorked it with his teeth, and drank deeply.

"I am prince of Requiem!" he said, speaking to his bottle. "I'm the one who found the Genesis Shards. And now they plot to take my throne. Valien wants what is mine!"

His head spun and the spirits burned down his throat. He barely felt the hand touch his shoulder. He spun around, spilling half his drink, and saw Erry there.

The little urchin was staring up at him, her eyes solemn, that ridiculous short hair of hers falling across her brow. Leresy had forgotten he'd let her stay in his tent, warming his bed at night.

"Ler," she said softly and tried to take the bottle from him. "You've had enough."

He scoffed. "I can hold my liquor. I'm larger than a shrimp like you. I'm a man! I'm a prince. And Valien..." He hissed and took another swig. "He's a pig who plots to steal what is mine."

The solemnity left Erry's eyes; they flashed with rage. She pulled the bottle from his grip and tossed it aside.

"You fool!" she said, teeth bared, no taller than his shoulders but snarling like some wild beast. "Valien doesn't want the throne. He's fighting to restore the throne to Rune. You know that. You're drunk, Leresy. Go to bed."

He stared at the fallen bottle; its precious liquids had seeped into the earth. He spoke through a tight jaw.

"Oh, but Rune is only a puppet. Valien is the one pulling the strings. Even should he place Rune upon the throne, Valien would still be the master, controlling the boy-king's every move." He looked back at her, shaking with rage. "It's not right, Erry. The man is a cunning devil, a slimy worm. Why should I follow at his heel like a dog? I cannot bear him!"

Something cold and afraid filled Erry's eyes. She froze for just an instant, a deer staring at a hunter. Then the moment was gone. She tightened her lips, stepped toward him, and pressed her body against his.

"Forget about them for tonight, my prince," she whispered and reached down to his pants. "Come to bed. I'll help you forget them."

He shook his head, but let her stroke him. "I will not forget their insolence. I'm their prince. I do not forget. I do not forgive."

She reached into his breeches, her fingers deft. "Let them play their games, then, my lord. The important thing is that they'll kill Frey. That's why you're here, isn't it? To help kill Frey?"

He snorted, wanting to push her away, but letting her do her work; it was why he kept her.

"Killing Frey is no longer enough for me," he said. "I now have a second enemy. Valien must die."

Erry's fingers froze. She inhaled sharply. She pulled away and stared silently.

"You are a fool," she whispered. With one fluid movement, she pulled her tunic over her head. She stood naked before him. "Come to bed, Ler, and forget this foolishness."

He stared at her naked flesh and licked his lips. He stepped forward, grabbed her arms, and shoved her onto the bed. He mounted her at once, making her gasp.

"I can't kill him in the open," he said as he moved atop her. "No... the men would see me as a murderer, a usurper. I could kill him in the capital... yes, in the chaos of battle, I could kill him."

Erry closed her eyes and placed her hands in his hair. "Be silent, my prince. Be silent and take me harder."

He took her harder, but he would not be silent. "No, if I kill him in the capital, it would be too late. The capital must see me as a savior, *leading* the Resistance to slay the tyrant, a hero liberating his homeland." He hissed down at Erry. "Valien will have to die soon, and I will take over this ragtag army of his."

Erry moaned, moved her body beneath him, and placed a finger against his mouth.

"Please," she said, eyes closed. "Please stop talking. Harder."

He snarled, fists clenched, moving faster atop her. "I'll have to slay him in the shadows. No one must know it was me. And then, Erry... then I can take over his Resistance, use my Genesis Shards to claim the throne, and be hailed a hero." He grinned, breathing heavily. "Valien will be dead, I will be a beloved emperor, and you will be my concubine."

He closed his eyes and gritted his teeth, then lay atop her, drained and weary. She held him close, silent, her eyes still afraid.

TILLA

She lay in his arms, the burrow cold and his embrace warm, and she had never felt so lost, and she had never felt so much in just the right place.

"I never want to leave," she whispered, nestled against him under the blankets.

Lying on his back, he laughed. "So we'll spend the rest of our lives here, in a gopher hole a league outside the capital?"

She shrugged. "It works for gophers. Why not for us?"

They had been here, in this underground hideaway, for three days now. They had been the worst three days of Tilla's life: three days of nursing Rune's wounds, shivering in the cold, and mostly worrying. She worried about the Legions finding them. She worried about her father and whether he'd survived the slaughter at Lynport. She worried about where they'd go next, whether they'd spend their lives in hiding or seek distant lands. Yet they were also the best three days of Tilla's life: three days of holding Rune close, kissing his lips, making love to him in the dark, and whispering of memories.

"Last I checked, we were Vir Requis," Rune said, "meant to fly as dragons, not huddle underground as gophers."

Tilla propped herself up on her elbows, leaned over him, and kissed his lips. "But I like huddling here. It's safe and it's warm and it's better than any of that damn world above us, a world of fire and blood and cruelty. Here there are none of those things. Here I'm happy."

She kissed him again and he touched her hair.

"I have to check your wounds," she whispered and began to unlace his shirt.

"Again?" he asked.

She nodded, pulled off his shirt, and began to work at his trousers. "You were very wounded. I have to make sure you're all right."

He raised an eyebrow. "So why are you removing your clothes too?"

"I have a little scratch. Can you check it for me?"

He nodded. "Show me. Where--"

She did not let him finish his sentence. She kissed him again, a deep kiss, their hands clutching. She needed this. She had needed it for so long--during her cold days in the Legions, during those bloodred nights of seeing him chained, perhaps for years upon the beaches. She had him now. She had him here underground, hers alone, her Rune. All her world had burned above. All her dreams, her hopes, her life itself had collapsed, and yet she had him. He was all she had left. She would not let him go. And so she made love to him again; she had lost count of how many times she'd loved him here underground. Countless times was not enough.

She lay in his arms for a long while. She looked around the burrow, seeing shelves of food and drink, enough to last for moons. A soft laugh fled her lips.

"I was an officer in the greatest military the world has known," she said. "I lived in a large home all my own. I commanded men in battle. I was groomed by the princess of Requiem herself. But I'm happier here. I would be happy staying in this burrow forever with you."

"And yet we can't stay forever," Rune said, one hand against the small of her back, the other on her thigh. "My wounds are healing. We'll have to move soon."

Tilla closed her eyes. She had known this day would come, though she feared it.

"Let's run far away, as far as we can," she said. "We'll travel across Requiem, through the ruins of Osanna, and to the eastern sea. We'll fly from there. We'll head south to Terra Incognita, the unexplored country." She squeezed Rune tight. "We'll find a new life there, far from the Regime, far from everything we've ever known. Just you and me."

She tried to imagine that southern land of myth. The empire of Requiem stretched across forests, seas, mountains, and deserts. Yet there were lands beyond the empire too, lands no dragon had ever flown to. What lay beyond the edges of maps? Would they find lush forests full of fruit and game? Would they find foreign civilizations or strange animals? Were there forests there or deserts, mountains or plains? Would they find a new life, Tilla and Rune in unknown landscapes of adventure? She nodded, tightened her lips, and drew comfort from the warmth of his body.

Yet he remained silent, and when Tilla looked at him, his face was somber.

"Rune?" she said and touched his cheek. "What's wrong?"

He sighed, staring at the ceiling of wooden slats. "Can we really abandon home?"

Tilla leaned her head against his shoulder. She spoke softly. "Our home burned. Lynport is gone."

I burned it, she wanted to add, but her throat tightened, and she could say no more. The memories and guilt clutched her. She saw herself a dragon again, flying over Lynport, burning its roofs, shattering its columns, slaying its defenders. Her eyes stung.

"I don't just mean Lynport," Rune said. "All of Requiem is our home. This is the land of our forebears. The land my father governed. Can we truly abandon it, flee to distant lands and forget all who suffer here?"

She gripped his shoulders. "I will not have you imprisoned again. I will not lose you again, Rune Brewer. Do you understand?" She squeezed his shoulders painfully. "You might be thinking you can find the Resistance, that you can fight on, but I won't let you. I won't. I..."

Her eyes dampened, her throat constricted, and she could only lie against him and hold him close.

"I must find them," he said, embracing her. "Valien and Kaelyn still live. Hundreds of resistors still live, and they will fight on. *I* must fight on." He smoothed her hair. "I won't ask you to join me. If you want to flee, you can--" He bit down on his words and scrunched his lips. "Oh, bloody Abyss. I *will* ask you to join me. I *am* asking you. Find the Resistance with me. Fight with us."

She squeezed him so tight he grunted. Her rage exploded inside her like dragonfire, and she almost shouted. Her heart thrashed and she forced herself to take slow breaths between her clenched teeth.

He wants me to fight for Valien! she thought, reeling. He truly thought she'd fight for the man who had murdered her brother? She dug her fingernails into him. He wanted her to fight with

Kaelyn, that... that little harlot he lusted for? Tilla ground her teeth, her tears drying under her anger. She had heard tales of Kaelyn Cadigus's beauty. Rune's eyes had always wandered to beauties in Lynport; he would have noticed Kaelyn too. *Did he bed her too, kiss her like he kisses me?*

Rune grunted and Tilla forced herself to loosen her grip on him. She would not sway him with anger. She knew Rune; whenever confronted with anger, he became stubborn like a mule. She'd have to sway him with calm words, not shouts.

"You can't keep fighting," she said. "Damn it, Rune, look at you. You're still wounded. You're still too thin. I've had enough of fighting." Her eyes watered and her chest shook. "I slew too many. I want to run away from all this. Maybe that is weakness, but I don't care. This whole empire is rotten. I want to run. I never want to kill again. There is enough blood on my hands."

He nodded and whispered, "That is why you must stay."

"To kill more? For more blood and death?"

He shook his head. "For redemption."

She rolled away from him. "I redeemed myself when I slew Shari Cadigus. I redeemed myself when I saved you, the heir of Aeternum."

He placed a hand on her waist. "Yet in Terra Incognita, would I be an heir? You saved Relesar Aeternum. That is who I am; I cannot run from it. Not while Frey still lives and still subjugates our people."

"The Resistance is smashed," Tilla said. "It burned in the fires of Lynport. It is gone."

Rune shook his head. "Not so long as I live. Not so long as Valien and Kaelyn live." He touched her cheek, turning her head back toward him. "Tilla, you saved me from the Red Tower. And now I must do what I can to save my friends. I must keep fighting."

Finally Tilla could not hold back the pain. She let the words slip from her mouth; they tasted like poison. "Fighting with the man who killed my brother."

Rune became quiet. For a few breaths, he said nothing. When he spoke, his voice was low and careful.

"Valien slew many, it's true. Did he himself kill your brother? Maybe. So many died in battle on both sides. War makes victims of us all."

She snorted, trying to feign some strength as her tears fell. "Is that some poetic way of saying I should forget Valien's sins?"

"He himself does not forget his sins. I've seen Valien drink, brood, and howl in the night, lamenting those he killed and those he let die. He bears much blood on his hands. So do we. Our hands will never be cleansed; perhaps there is no true redemption for us, killers in war. I don't believe there is running from this. I don't believe that even distant, unknown lands could purify our souls, could wipe the memories and grief away. So I will stay. I will keep fighting. You cannot run from a demon, only charge him head-on and slay him. Our demon is Frey Cadigus. I will not rest until he's dead. Tilla, fight him with me."

She sat up and regarded him. She ran her fingers along his face, tracing the old familiar features, and she wondered if she even still knew him. Was this truly still Rune her friend? Or was he now fully Relesar, a stranger? He needed to fight, but she needed different things. She needed him far from war. She needed him away from Valien, who led him into blood, and she needed vengeance for her brother. She knew what she must do, and it chilled her.

I must kill Valien.

She nodded. "All right, Rune. I'll help you find the Resistance. We'll find them together."

And then I will slay him, the man who took my brother from me, the man who's taking you away too.

Rune didn't seem to suspect her deeper motives. He pulled her into an embrace.

"Thank you. I promise you--once you meet them, you'll see the Resistance in a different light. We'll fight this together, you and me."

She rose to her feet, leaving the warmth of the blankets. The cold air raised goose bumps across her naked skin, and she grabbed her clothes and began to dress.

No, Rune, she thought. *I will not fight with you. We will be together, yes... but not like this.* She tugged up her leggings and slipped her tunic over her head. *I will kill anyone who comes between us. When your friends are dead, I will be avenged.*

She buckled her sword to her waist, but she left her armor behind; it would slow her down in the wilderness, and her days of donning imperial steel were over. They left the gopher hole, carrying what supplies they could, and emerged into the forest.

Dawn fell between the branches and the snow glittered. Icicles hung from birches, oaks, and pines. No dragons flew above, and the scents of the forest filled the air. It was a beautiful morning, but darkness filled Tilla. She walked silently, staring ahead, not speaking to Rune and not squeezing his hand when he held hers.

She gripped the hilt of her sword and took a deep breath.

I will do as I promised, Rune, she thought. *I will help you find your friends... and then I will drive this sword into them.*

VALIEN

"The boy is a burden." He sneered, facing the tent wall. "He's been a burden since he joined us."

He heard Kaelyn sigh behind him.

"He is an oaf," she said. "He is a whiny brat. Yet he fought with us at Lynport. He slew legionaries. And he did find the Genesis Shards."

Valien spun toward her, enraged, but his snarl died on his lips. He found it impossible to rage against Kaelyn. She stood before him, looking up with those large eyes, and his anger melted. He too sighed, a creaky sound.

"You have sad kitten eyes," he said. "You always get what you want with those eyes, don't you?"

"I don't want any of this," she said. "I don't want Leresy here, but... what can we do? I can't just banish him now. He's my twin. And he means well."

Valien snorted. "He still hopes to seize the throne for himself."

"Leresy doesn't know what he wants. He only knows that he hates our father. He has no cunning, no wit, only hatred. He's foolish and rash, but I know him. I can control him."

Valien grumbled. "One more mistake or outburst from him, and I banish him. Simple as that, sad kitten eyes or not."

She touched his cheek. "Do not weary your mind with him. We have greater things to worry about."

"And I worry about them all. Tomorrow we will fly again, and we will not rest for days, not until we reach the capital. It all ends now. This is our last battle, for victory or for death. Perhaps worrying about Leresy is easier than thinking about the battle ahead."

"Think of neither tonight," Kaelyn said. "My brother is in his tent, Erry is soothing him, and the fight continues tomorrow. Tonight let *me* soothe *you*."

She unclasped her cloak and let it fall. With a single movement, she pulled her tunic over her head. She stood nude before him, her body slim and pale, and gave him that look of hers, her kitten eyes. She pressed herself against him, stood on tiptoes, and kissed his lips.

"Think only of me tonight," she whispered. "Let me love you. This is what you need. This is what *I* need."

She tried to kiss him again, but he turned his head away. She held him, but he took a step back.

"I can no longer do this," he said. "The last time was a mistake."

He saw the hurt in her eyes; this time it was real hurt, deep and cutting.

"Why?" she whispered.

"Because we are warriors. Because we cannot love. Love weakens us."

She laughed mirthlessly. "Must warriors feel only bloodlust? That is my father speaking, not you."

He looked away from her. He stared at his cot, remembering a night long ago when he had found her, Marilion, in his old bed in the capital.

"For years I refused to love you, Kaelyn," he said in a rasp. "Do not make me love you now."

She came to stand beside him. She held his arm.

"Is it because of her?" Her voice was soft; there was no jealousy there, only compassion and understanding.

He turned back toward her. He held her hands in his, two white flowers in his calloused paws.

"The gods, fate, or chance have been cruel," he said. "You look like her. For years, I refused to love you, for you were as a ghost. But now I don't see you as an echo. Kaelyn, you have flown by my side through fire, blood, and rain. You have been my torch in these cold, dark years. I love you, Kaelyn Cadigus, for the woman you are. And that is one emotion we cannot feel. If one of us should fall, the other must keep fighting, heart whole, fire bright. I cannot bear the fear of losing another love."

Tears filled her eyes. "And I love you, Valien Eleison. I came to you as a muddy, bruised youth, a frightened girl fleeing her father's rod. For a long time, you were as a father to me, wiser and nobler than my true father ever was. But I now love you not as a daughter, but as a woman. And I cannot quell that feeling. I will not. And I will not believe it weakens me. Tomorrow we might fall, so let us love today all the brighter." She began to undo the lacing on his tunic. "Save your troubles for tomorrow. Tonight you are mine."

He closed his eyes. He let her undress him, and their naked bodies pressed together, hers slim and soft, his scarred and rough. The candles flickered around them and he loved her. And he forgot about all else.

LERESY

He slunk through the camp, clad in cloak and hood, the clouds hiding the moon above. The booze still coursed through his blood, but he walked silently, the yellow grass muffling his boots. Inside the shadows of his hood, he grinned, licked his lips, and hissed.

"Backhand me, will you?" he whispered, still feeling the sting on his cheek; it had left an ugly bruise. "You do not strike the prince of Requiem and live, old man."

His hiss rose into a chuckle. He reached into his cloak and gripped his dagger. The cold hilt felt heavenly. Thrusting this blade into Valien would feel better than thrusting into a woman.

"You all abandoned me," he whispered, slinking between the shadowy tents. "You all stole my Genesis Shards. Now you will pay. Now you will bow down to me, and I will be your emperor."

His chuckle rose into a laugh, and Leresy bit down, cursing. No. He could not laugh now. He would save his laughter for later. For now he must move silently as a shadow. No one must know it was him who struck this night. He wanted to be remembered as a savior, not a murderer.

The camp slept around him, thousands of soldiers exhausted from the long flight and battle, many of them wounded. They lay as lumps in the night, wrapped in blankets, sleeping upon bare grass. As Leresy moved among them, they breathed and snored in a chorus. A few guards patrolled the perimeter of the camp, but they were gazing outward and upward, scanning for the Legions. Here among the sleeping troops, cloaked in darkness, Leresy walked alone, no eyes upon him.

Fools! he thought, adjusting the scarf that hid his face. *They should be watching the enemy within, not shadows beyond.*

A hill rose ahead, a slumbering giant in the night. Tents stood atop it like warts. Leresy growled. The high command slept upon that hilltop, Valien leading the Vir Requis and that glorified fisherman Sila leading the Tirans. Both men were filthy, common outlaws. Leresy sneered. He would have lunged uphill now and slain them, but guards surrounded the hill, a ring of sentinels armed with swords and shields. Leresy could not attack those tents now, not unless he shifted into a dragon. As a dragon, he was a great warrior, a champion, a beast of red scales and flame who had slain many... but tonight he was a shadow. Tonight he would strike as a viper.

"If I cannot sneak past your guards, I will draw you to me," he whispered.

He kept creeping among the sleeping men and women, common soldiers who lay upon grass, no tents above them. He only had to find a suitable one, a frightened one, one who would scream. Yes, she would have to be a screamer.

As he passed soldier by soldier, Leresy frowned. Most were men. Among the women, most were ugly freaks, their faces scarred with war, their lips chafed and their hair in disarray. Truly, this was a rabble of filthy commoners.

Finally, by a clump of maple trees, he found a match. He grin widened and his mouth watered.

The girl slept below him, her face upon her palms. Even in the darkness, her beauty shone.

"Miya," Leresy whispered.

Erry's half sister.

He had been eying the girl for a while, a wild thing with golden skin, bright blue eyes, and platinum hair. She was young and blooming into womanhood, a forbidden fruit, and Leresy was famished. He had known no woman but Erry for too long.

Foolish girl, he thought, standing above her. *You should have stayed with your father upon the hill, safe behind guards, not here among the commoners.* He licked his lips. *Tonight you are mine, Miya. You sister is mine and you will be too. And then... then my dagger will strike.*

He glanced around him. The other resistors all slept. Leresy sucked in his breath and knelt above Miya.

"Hello, my sweetness," he whispered, kissed her cheek, and caressed her hair.

She mumbled in her sleep. Leresy reached down to undo her clothes.

"Hush and sleep," he whispered and kissed her.

Her eyes opened. She gasped and he clutched her throat, constricting her, and smiled. She sputtered, staring with wide eyes, and kicked.

"Are you ready to scream?" he said. She kicked madly. She punched him, but he only hissed and ignored the pain. He kept tearing at her clothes.

"Now scream, little one," Leresy said, grinned, and released her throat.

She sucked in breath... and she screamed.

He stepped back from her. She leaped up. All around, soldiers rose from their slumber, drew swords, and came running forward.

"Father!" Miya cried, tears in her eyes, and began racing uphill. She clutched the tatters of her clothes to her body. "Father, help!"

As the camp erupted into chaos, Leresy crept behind the maple trees, disappearing into shadow.

Resistors ran through the night. A dragon took flight and blazed fire overhead, lighting the camp. Miya was still running uphill, crying for her father. Atop the hill, Sila emerged from his tent, ran downhill toward her, and embraced her. Men burst out from the other tents too, the officers of their force.

Leresy grinned in the shadows.

The camp had fallen into chaos.

"What is the meaning of this?" rose a raspy voice. Valien emerged from his tent and marched downhill, scowling and drawing his sword. He wore but a tunic, no armor. "Miya, what happened?"

Men were gathering around the haggard old knight. Miya wept and began blubbering about a masked man attacking her. Resistors began sweeping through the camp, holding torches.

In the madness, Leresy crept uphill, moving through the crowd.

"A man... a masked man," Miya said, tears on her cheeks. "He choked me. He tore my clothes. Father..."

Sila held his daughter in his wide, tattooed arms, and his eyes burned. Kaelyn stood nearby, whispering soothing words to the girl, while dozens of others gathered around.

Leresy crept closer, step by step, the people crowding around him.

Valien stepped toward Miya, his lips tight. Unlike the others, the gruff outcast had no embraces or soothing words. He was gritting his teeth, and his eyes burned with rage rather than pain.

"Miya," he rasped in his gravelly hiss of a voice. "Can you describe him? Do you know who did this?"

Leresy crept around the group, placing himself behind Valien, and inched closer. He reached into his cloak and clutched his dagger.

Miya shook her head. "I... I don't know, I... he wore black, and..."

Leresy stepped around a few resistors. Valien stood only two feet away.

Sweat soaked Leresy's back.

Do it now! a voice screamed inside him. *Now, while they're all distracted! Stab him! Kill him!*

Sweat covered his palm. Inside his cloak, he almost dropped the dagger. People were still shouting and moving about. Chaos covered the hill like a kicked ant hive. It was the time to strike, yet Leresy could barely breathe. The sweat now soaked his tunic, and his pulse thudded in his ears.

"We must find him," Valien said. "Sila, take Miya into your tent. I'll search the camp."

Stab him! Kill him before it's too late!

Leresy shook and his throat constricted.

Valien took a step away.

I can't do it, Leresy thought and tears filled his eyes.

He closed his eyes, and he saw his father again. He saw Frey beating him. He saw the emperor spitting upon him, casting him from his court, banishing him into the wilderness, turning him from a prince into this wretch.

Leresy had to kill the emperor. He had to. He had to seize Frey's throne for his own. And only one man stood between him and the crown.

Valien took another step away.

With a hiss, Leresy leaped forward. His dagger gleamed. He slammed the weapon against Valien's back.

His blade slashed through the man's tunic... and clanged.

Pain shot up Leresy's arm.

He yowled, dropping the dagger like a man dropping a viper.

So fast Leresy could not react, Valien spun around and grabbed him. Leresy yelped and Valien twisted his arm behind his back.

"You..." Leresy sputtered, clutched in the man's grip. "You... you should be dead! What kind of man wears armor under his tunic?"

Valien growled and tightened his grip. Leresy struggled, but the man was too large, too strong; Leresy would have better luck breaking iron shackles.

"Unhand me!" he screamed, tears budding in his eyes. "Leave me alone, savage!"

Resistors were gathering around, shouting. Some eyes widened with shock; others blazed with hatred. All the faces swam around Leresy. He could barely see them. He thought he saw Kaelyn there, her eyes sad. Sila was shouting something. Miya was gasping and pointing at him. A thousand others swirled around him like some mad puppet show.

"I did nothing!" Leresy screamed. "Let me go."

Valien gripped him only tighter; Leresy thought the man would break his bones.

"I think," Valien rasped, "we have found our villain. Is this the man, Miya?"

She nodded tearfully, and Leresy screamed louder.

"She's lying! I never touched her. Let me go!"

Valien began manhandling him forward. "Make way."

Leresy screamed and howled, but the men pushed and dragged him. A path cleared through the crowd. He kicked and pressed his feet into the dirt, but too many hands now gripped him, moving him forward. When Leresy saw the fallen log ahead, he began to weep.

"Please," he said, mucus and tears running down his face. "Please, don't... don't kill me. I didn't do anything."

Valien growled. "You assaulted a woman, and you stabbed me in the back, Leresy Cadigus. If I hadn't been warned of your treachery, you'd have killed me. Now be silent, place your neck upon this log, and I will make your death painless. Struggle and I will make it hurt."

Leresy howled to the sky. He kicked wildly. He could barely see through his tears.

"Treachery!" he cried. "Who warned him? Who? I've been betrayed!"

He panted, shaking and trembling... and he knew.

He had told only one soul.

Oh stars, no...

Icy water seemed to flow through him, drowning his fear and rage, replacing it with something colder and deeper--the ghostly stab of betrayal.

"Erry..."

He looked through the crowd, seeking her. Not Erry. No... she couldn't have betrayed him. She... she was his woman. She was his love. Not Erry...

"Erry," he said, weeping. "Erry, where are you?"

He raised his head, still clutched in the grip of so many men, and saw her ahead.

His tears fell.

She stood among the crowd. Men almost hid her from view, but he could see her face. She gazed at him, her expression hesitant, almost shy. Her eyes were soft, the eyes of an abandoned child. Suddenly she seemed so young to him. She *was* only a child, only a little doll.

"I vowed to protect you, Erry," he whispered. "You were my woman. You told him?"

She looked at him and her eyes dampened, but she said nothing. And he knew the answer.

She betrayed me. Erry Docker, the love of my life, the only woman I've ever loved... betrayed me.

They shoved him toward the log. Hands gripped his neck, pushing it down. Steel hissed against leather. Cheek pressed against the wood, Leresy raised his eyes, and he saw Valien drawing his sword. The sword was massive, a hunk of steel wide enough to behead an ox.

Leresy did not want to gaze upon this. No. He did not want to see this bear of a man and his steel; that would not be his last vision.

He turned his eyes back toward Erry.

He looked at her--at her soft face, her small features, her short hair he would always mock. She was beautiful. He would die gazing upon her.

"I love you, Erry Docker," he said, waiting for the steel to fall.

The camp fell silent all around.

Leresy held his breath, waiting to die.

A single, high voice broke the silence.

"Wait."

Leresy twisted his head and saw her there, golden through the veil of his tears.

His twin.

The second half of his soul.

"Kaelyn," he whispered.

She held up her hand, a sign of redemption, of mercy, pointing upward to the heavens and stars of his forebears.

"Wait," she said. "Valien, wait. Don't kill him. He is my brother."

"Sister," Leresy whispered. "Kaelyn... he hurt you... I'm sorry. Please. He hurt you so much. He would beat you. I have to kill Father... I have to..."

His twin looked upon him, eyes soft and full of pity. She stared at him, but she spoke to Valien.

"He is miserable, he is sad, he is drunk and pathetic and a wretch. But he is my brother. Please, Valien, spare his life."

Valien growled, a deep sound like a wolf disturbed in its den. He held his sword high above Leresy's neck.

"He assaulted Miya," he said, eyes staring down, cold with fury. "He stabbed me in the back. And you would spare his life?"

Kaelyn nodded and now tears streamed down her cheeks. "He deserves death, it's true. I've tried to kill him myself in our years of battle; I gave him that scar on his cheek. But now I look down upon him and I pity him. And I see myself. His soul is bound to mine. Our father would beat us; he would beat us until we bled, wept, and blacked out. He nearly beat us to death. I fled from my father, but Leresy was not as strong. My father broke his soul. All my brother does--all his sins--are driven by his madness."

Valien refused to lower his sword. "Life is hard in this land. Many children suffer under the scourge of Frey Cadigus. Past suffering does not excuse present cruelty. Leresy is no longer a child but a man--a man capable of his own choices, a man responsible for his actions."

He raised his sword higher.

Leresy whimpered.

"He saved my life!" Kaelyn blurted out. "Please, Valien. He saved me. When we were children... one night... oh stars." She trembled. "One night Father beat me so badly, all because I picked fruit from a garden tree. He meant to kill me. He *would* have killed me. Leresy begged. Leresy pleaded with our father. 'Beat me instead!' he said. 'Kaelyn did nothing, beat me! I picked the fruit!'" Kaelyn lowered her head. "And he beat Leresy so badly he broke his arm. My brother saved my life that night. Let me save him now. Let me repay that debt. Please, Valien, I cannot watch him die. Banish him from our camp, but let him live. I love him."

Leresy lay still, face pressed to the log, watching his sister, and the pain of that night returned to him. He remembered his father's fists striking him, his punisher burning him, his boots bruising him. But as bad as that pain had been, it was better than seeing Kaelyn hurt. He had saved her that night; it was the best thing he'd ever done.

"I love you too, my sister," he whispered. "I'm sorry for what I became. I'm sorry for the man that I am. I'm sorry I could never be strong like you. I know what I am... and I'm sorry. I love you."

The silence seemed to stretch forever.

Valien stood, sword held above.

Nobody spoke. Even the wind seemed to die.

Finally, with a grunt, Valien swung and slammed his blade down. It banged against the log an inch from Leresy's face, scattering chips of wood.

Leresy gasped and flinched, for a second not sure if he was alive or dead.

"Get up," Valien said in disgust.

He grabbed Leresy's collar and yanked him to his feet. Leresy stood on shaking legs. His pants clung to him, and he realized that under his cloak, he had wet himself.

"Thank you," he whispered.

Valien shoved him away from the log.

"Leresy Cadigus," he rasped, "I will spare your life tonight, but if our paths cross again, I will slay you. Do not doubt that. Leave this camp. Leave into whatever exile you choose. Fly from here now and thank the stars for my mercy."

Leresy wobbled. The world still spun around him, and he fell to his knees. The resistors all wavered, a sea of faces, and Leresy hissed at them.

"Stand back!" he screamed. "Do not touch me!"

He leaped up and shifted.

He beat his wings. He soared as a red dragon, a legendary beast, a monster none could hurt. He blew fire, lighting the sky.

"You will regret this!" he howled. "I am your prince. I will be your emperor. The throne will be mine, and I will hang you all!"

He soared uphill. The tents rose ahead. Cackling, Leresy stretched out his claws, grabbed Valien's tent, and tossed it aside, exposing the bed and table within.

"You will all kneel before me, and I will break you!" he shouted.

Laughing madly, he reached down his claws.

"Leresy, no!" Kaelyn shouted.

He ignored her. His eyes damp with laughter, he could barely see. He grabbed Valien's Genesis Scope from the table. He soared.

"Stop him!" rose a voice behind. "Bring him back! Kill him if you must."

Leresy beat his wings and flew, racing over the hill, a field, and trees. A jet of fire blasted above him, searing the tips of his horns. He looked over his shoulder to see dragons chasing, a hundred or more. Fire blazed his way.

"Requiem will be mine, fools!" he cried. He tore the lid off the scope and pointed it at them.

Red light bathed the world.

The dragons lost their magic and tumbled.

Laughter in his throat, tears in his eyes, and fire in his heart, Leresy turned and flew. He raced into the night, blowing flames, leaving his love, his sister, and his hope behind. He wept and laughed as he flew.

"You banished me," he said into the darkness, "but I will not forget you, Requiem. I will win my throne. You will all see and you will all be sorry, but I will not forgive you. I will be Emperor Leresy Cadigus and you will worship me."

Over a dark forest, miles from the camp, he crashed down onto a bed of pine needles. He shifted back into human form. He lay down, pulled his knees to his chest, and shivered until the dawn.

VALIEN

They crossed the border of Old Requiem at dawn.

Sunbeams broke between the clouds, shining golden over frosty forests and fields. The southern islands had been warm, but here in the north winter covered the land. A distant ruined castle caught the sun and blazed, a beacon of molten bronze. A frozen stream snaked across the land, glimmering silver in the light. Hills rose from mist, earthen children waking from slumber.

For days now, they had been flying over the ruins of Osanna, a fallen kingdom Frey had burned and annexed into his empire. Yet now... now they flew over the ancestral home of the Vir Requis, an ancient land of memory and starlight. Flying at the head of his army, Valien whispered the Old Words, the prayer of his people.

"As the leaves fall upon our marble tiles, as the breeze rustles the birches beyond our columns, as the sun gilds the mountains above our halls--know, young child of the woods, you are home, you are home. Requiem! May our wings forever find your sky."

At his side, Kaelyn spoke the prayer with him. He turned to look at her. The green dragon bore four riders on her back: a Tiran scope bearer and three Vir Requis in human forms, resting from flight. All four slept, wrapped in their cloaks. Gliding on the wind, Kaelyn met his gaze, and her eyes shone.

"We're home," she said.

Valien looked to the east. The sun was rising, but they would not see the capital this day. Even flying without rest, Nova Vita still lay days away.

"If Frey knows of our scopes, he will send no more dragons our way," he said. "He will hole up in the capital, ready his cannons, and sharpen his swords. He will fight house to house, chamber to chamber, not in the sky. We should have a clear flight to the city, but once there..."

He let his voice trail off. The thought had been rattling through his mind for days now. The boy Leresy had lost one scope in the sea, then stole another. Valien looked over his shoulder at his army, and his heart sank deeper. Four thousand fighters, that was all. Four thousand against the might of the Legions.

"We're down to two scopes," he finally said. "We are outnumbered more than a hundred to one. We are home, Kaelyn, yet my heart is heavy. We might be flying to our deaths."

She nodded. "I am willing to die for Requiem."

"Yet I want to live to see you live." He spat flames. "Kaelyn, we can still turn back. We can return to our islands. We can find another life together, you and me, away from all this."

The idea had been taking root inside him. With every disaster--the lost scopes, the fallen men upon the beaches, the betrayal in their camp--the temptation had grown stronger. He could flee. He could find new life with the woman he loved--with Kaelyn, the light of his heart. He needn't fly here to war, to blood, to death.

"We can," Kaelyn said. "We can find a small island, and we can grow old together, and we will never know war again. But we would not know peace, Valien. Forever we'd be haunted. Rune would languish in his prison. Requiem would moan under the scourge." She shook her head, scattering smoke. "I don't want to die. I want to live too. I want to win."

"Can we still win?" he asked. "We were to fly here with four scopes, one on each side of our army. We shouldn't have lost so much so soon."

She snarled and her eyes blazed. "We lost men, it's true. And we lost scopes. But we smashed an army on the beaches, and we will smash the capital. This is the greatest flight of our lives. Poets will sing of us."

He twisted his jaw. "Aye, but will they be our poets, or those of the emperor?"

Such was youth, he thought. *Rune is like this too; he is like her. They are young. They fly with conviction. Justice lights their hearts. But I am old and I've seen that justice often fails, that the righteous often die while evil lingers.*

And yet he flew on, for he knew Kaelyn was right. He would find no peace upon a distant island. He was a soldier. He had been a soldier for most of his life. All he could do was fight on.

Even if the battle is hopeless, I will fight it, he thought. *Better to die fighting than to flee and wither in pain.*

They flew on, the valleys and hills rolling below.

They flew over sprawling Lanburg Fields where snow glimmered, the place where long ago the griffin armies had slain all but seven Vir Requis, the last of their race. They flew over the rolling farmlands of Oldnale, the great wheat basket of Requiem for thousands of years. They flew until they saw King's Forest ahead, its birches coated in ice, where the Vir Requis had first risen, where their magic had first shone.

They flew across Old Requiem, land of their ancestors, until at sundown the first roars of the enemy sounded.

They looked ahead and saw them upon the wind.

A host flew their way, and Valien hissed and felt his belly knot.

"Resistors!" he called and blasted fire skyward. "Spear formation! Cut through them."

His dragons roared behind him. Roused by the alarm, those Vir Requis who slept in human forms leaped off their saddles, shifted into dragons, and blew their flames. Tirans leaped from dragon to dragon in midair, spreading themselves out across the hosts.

Ahead, flying from the west, the Legions covered the sky. Ten thousand or more flew toward them, clad in armor, chanting their battle cries. The banners of Cadigus flew upon them, black streams emblazoned with red spirals. They were a storm, a demon of the air, a great beast of metal and fire and scale. They howled for death.

Valien growled.

If Frey sent this host our way, he thought, *he knows we're coming. He knows of our triumph on the coast. He knows of the scopes. And he knows we'll fell his dragons from the sky.* Valien bared his teeth and hissed. *He sends myriads to die under the Genesis Light... just to slow us down.*

"Kaelyn!" he shouted. "Take the right flank."

She nodded and banked north. Miya rode upon the green dragon's back, her hair streaming, a scope ready in her hands.

"Sila, ready your scope!" Valien said to the rider on his own back. "And hold tight."

He banked south, and their army flew forward, a great snake in the sky, driving toward the enemy. Valien and Kaelyn flew ahead of the force like two horns.

The Legions swarmed toward them.

Dragonfire blazed.

Red light beamed.

Screams filled the air.

The Genesis Light tore through the sky, two beams thrusting forward. By the hundreds, dragons lost their magic. Human legionaries fell from the sky, screaming.

"Kaelyn, keep your beam on those falling!" Valien roared. "I'll keep sending them down."

She nodded and dipped in the sky. Legionaries tumbled down, and Kaelyn followed, shining her light upon them, not letting them shift back into dragons. They crashed against the hills.

"Sila, sweep the beam across them!" Valien said.

They flew, swinging their beam from side to side, tearing into the dragons, scattering humans like a broom scattering a swarm of vermin. The legionaries tumbled.

"Burn them!" Valien howled.

Behind him, his fellow resistors roared. Jets of fire blasted, burning the falling legionaries. Arquebuses blasted and iron rounds tore into dragons and falling men alike. Some legionaries managed to dart around the beams, reach the Resistance, and blaze their fire, but they too fell; the arquebuses punched through scales like arrows through flesh.

Valien roared. "Slay them all!"

Only four thousand souls, the Resistance tore through the Legions like a wolf tearing through a herd of deer.

Resistors were chanting for victory, and even Valien's heart was rising, when he heard the howls behind him.

"Slay the Resistance!"

"Hail the red spiral!"

"Hail Cadigus!"

The roars shook the sky. Fire crackled in a typhoon. Heat blazed.

Valien turned his head... and felt his heart sink down to his tail.

A second army flew from the south, twenty thousand strong--two brigades chanting for death and spreading out wide, a claw ready to engulf them. For several heartbeats, Valien could not move.

"Slay every last resistor and drink their blood!" the Legions cried. "Hail the red spiral!"

The western host, cut down to half their size, roared with renewed rage. The eastern host stormed. From the north and south, more forces appeared, chanting and blasting fire.

We are trapped, Valien thought. *We are encircled. We will die.*

He growled.

Then let us die well.

"Resistance!" he said. "Do not lose heart! I, Valien Eleison, fight with you. Howl for Requiem! Blow your dragonfire! Fire your guns! We will overcome."

They gathered around him, a small host of survivors trapped in a storm, and they roared for their home, and they blasted their fire.

"Valien!" Kaelyn said. She flew up toward him, eyes damp but burning with rage, and upon her back Miya was aiming her cone from side to side. "Let us fly around our men in rings."

He nodded. "Fly clockwise! I'll fly the other way."

She nodded.

They flew.

Darkness swarmed from every side.

They fought like a sun engulfed by night. The Resistance roared their dragonfire and shot their guns. Their beams blasted out, felling legionaries, but they could not cover the entire sky, not with only two scopes. Always they left a flank exposed, and the legionaries swooped against it, blasting fire and lashing claws. Valien flew from flank to flank, cutting the Legions down, but only exposed more resistors behind him.

Blood rained.

Corpses littered the hill below.

The sun sank and still they fought. Fire lit the night.

When dawn rose, it illuminated a world red with blood and black with soot.

Lashed with claws, his scales cracked with dragonfire, Valien descended toward the hills. He grunted and puffed smoke, his blood leaked, and every flap of wings blazed. He landed upon a hilltop and wheezed. The bodies of legionaries spread around him, tens of thousands. The survivors of the Resistance landed too, lacerated and burnt, coughing smoke and all but collapsing.

Valien resumed human form and walked among the dead, clutching his wounds. Kaelyn strode toward him, her cheeks ashy, her clothes torn and bloody.

He marched toward her and she crashed into his arms. Blood smeared her hair. Crows cawed, picking at the fallen.

"We won," she whispered, holding him tight.

He nodded, looking around at the dead, the screaming wounded, and the gore covering the grass.

"We lost half our people," he said. "But yes, Kaelyn, we won. We won."

She wept against him, and he held her in his arms as ash fell from the sky.

The capital still lay leagues away. They were down to two thousand fighters, and horror clutched Valien's heart so tightly it could barely beat.

RUNE

They crouched between the trees as the sky burned.

The Legions swarmed overhead, a storm of howls, blasting fire, and swirling smoke. The trees bent as if cowering from the host. The scents of fire and oiled steel filled the air, overpowering the smells of the forest. When Rune peered between the branches, he couldn't see the sky, only scales, armor, and smoke. Ten thousand dragons or more flew above, shrieking and chanting.

"Death to the Resistance! Hail the red spiral."

Rune scrunched his lips and crouched lower. Tilla knelt at his side. Both wore garments woven of pine branches, lichen, and twigs. Even kneeling beside her, Rune could barely see Tilla; to the world, she looked like a snowy evergreen.

"They're flying to battle," he whispered. "The Resistance must be near. They're still fighting."

Hope sprang inside him, but fear too. This meant Valien, Kaelyn, and the others were still alive. It meant there was still light shining in the darkness. It also meant war was flaring again... that everyone Rune still cared for could burn.

"How far do you reckon the Resistance is?" Tilla said.

"I don't know," Rune said, "but the Legions are flying east, so we'll follow. We'll follow until we find them."

They knelt until the last formations passed overhead, leaving a sky of smoke and raining ash. With the shrieks distant, Rune and Tilla rose to their feet, two leafy figures like storybook monsters invented to frighten children away from the woods. They shivered, brushed snow off themselves, and kept walking.

The snow was deep and progress was slow. The trees rustled, their icicles gleaming. Rune could not stop shivering, and soon he began to cough. Taken from the gopher hole, his clothes were woven of thick wool, and his cloak was wrapped tight around him, but still his teeth chattered.

"I wish we could fly," he said. "I'm never cold as a dragon. We should fly tonight."

Tilla shook her head forcefully. "No flying! Not until there's a cloudy night. We would be seen in the moonlight. You know only legionaries are allowed to fly as dragons. And you know those legionaries are looking for us."

Rune grumbled. "At this point, I'd welcome a fight against the legionaries. This snow is nastier than every dragon who serves Frey."

Tilla's eyes flashed, and she seemed ready to snap at him, but she bit her lip, stared ahead, and walked silently. Her body was stiff, her shoulders squared.

Rune looked at her and sighed.

What's wrong, Tilla? he wanted to ask but dared not. For the past couple days, it seemed whenever he asked her anything, she had only an angry retort. Her eyes were always flashing, her mouth was always frowning, and fire always seemed to simmer inside her. A root snagged her boots, and Tilla swayed and cursed. When Rune reached out to hold her hand, she glared and pulled herself away. She kept walking silently, not looking at him.

Bloody stars, Rune thought, looking at her, but she ignored him. *What happened to you?*

For three days--for three wondrous, magical days in the burrow--Tilla had kissed him, whispered of her love, and... Rune's blood heated to remember what else they would do, their naked bodies moving together under the blankets, their lips locked together, their...

He forced the thought away. As lovely as those days had been, they seemed over. Since he'd insisted on seeking the Resistance, Tilla had been cold as a statue.

"Tilla," he said, making one more attempt to soothe her, "I was thinking that after this war is over, we can return to Lynport. Maybe we can rebuild the Old Wheel. I--"

She spoke harshly, not bothering to look his way. "Don't talk to me of Lynport. Please. Just walk silently, all right?"

Rune sighed again; he had lost count of how many times he'd sighed since leaving the burrow.

"I know you're angry," he said, voice softer. "I know you wanted to flee Requiem, not seek the Resistance, not march right back into war. But I promise you, I--"

"Rune!" She snapped her head toward him. Her eyes narrowed and her cheeks flushed. "I told you. I don't want to talk. I agreed to find the Resistance with you. So we will find them. But that doesn't mean I feel like talking to you, all right?"

Rune lost his breath. He had never seen Tilla so angry. He had argued with Tilla before--he had spent his childhood bickering with her about a mancala move, wrestling her on the beach, or just arguing about minutiae like the name of a star. But this was worse. Tilla had changed in the Legions, grown both colder and more fiery. She seemed like a growling wolf now, not even human.

He nodded.

"All right, we'll walk silently for a while."

"Not just for a while. For the rest of the way."

They kept walking. He spoke no more, but his mind raced.

Was Tilla simply mad because he'd insisted on rejoining the Resistance? Or could something darker be stirring in her mind? He glanced at her as they trudged through snow. She stared ahead, face pale, eyes hard, her mouth a thin line. Her hand clutched the hilt of her sword, ready to draw and fight. She moved like a warrior, a slinking beast ready to pounce.

Rune swallowed. Tilla had trained for a year in the Legions. She had fought for them in battle. She had killed for them. Could she still be loyal to the red spiral?

Stars, he thought. *Did she free me so I could lead her to the Resistance? So she could draw her sword and slay Valien, the man who killed her brother?*

Rune felt dizzy. His throat dried out. Tilla wore pine needles and twigs now, no longer armor, but her every movement still spoke of a huntress, a warrior, a woman ready to kill. Rune felt faint. Was he leading an enemy into his camp?

No, he told himself. *No!* It was impossible. Tilla had saved him. Tilla had slain Shari. Tilla had made love to him in the burrow. This was no ruse. She was simply... simply mad that he refused to flee with her. That was all.

And yet Rune decided to keep a close eye on her, and he couldn't eliminate the chill in his belly.

They walked in silence, following the trail of fire that blazed across the sky.

In the afternoon the forest thinned out, and they found themselves walking in open sunlight. The snow was deeper here, and Rune began to worry about their tracks being seen from the sky. Maples and ash trees grew upon scattered hills, and frozen streams crossed the land. Rune stuck his hands under his armpits, but he couldn't stop shaking, and his cough ripped at his throat.

As the sun dipped behind them and dusk painted the sky, clouds moved in from the east. Another mile and the clouds thickened above, hiding the sky. Fresh snow began to fall. Finally, after hours of silence, Tilla spoke.

"We will fly."

Without waiting for a reply or even glancing his way, she shifted. She rose as a white dragon, soared straight up, and vanished into the clouds. With a breath of relief, Rune shifted too and followed.

Stars, this feels good, he thought. He had not shifted in so long. Fire filled his belly and throat. The magic warmed him, flowing through his veins like wine. For the first time this winter, he felt warm.

For a moment he flew blinded, seeking Tilla but seeing only snow and clouds. He pounded his wings, trying to clear the clouds, but they were too thick.

"Tilla?" he called.

He flew on, grumbling, wondering if she'd flown off and if he'd ever see her again. Perhaps she had decided to abandon him, to find her own life away from his war. His belly sank.

"Tilla!" he called again.

A grumble rose in the darkness. Her head thrust out from clouds, and her wings blasted him with air.

"Hush!" she said. "The Legions fly here too. I spotted a battalion flying east about a mile away. We're heading the right way. Now fly quietly!"

Her words were harsh and biting as ever, but Rune breathed in relief. Angry or not, at least she was still with him.

They kept flying, the clouds streaming around them, the snow flurrying. Rune kept close to Tilla, but he could barely see her; he only caught glimpses of her white scales between the wisps. Every few moments, the two dragons rose higher, emerging above the clouds, then sinking again, like whales rising for a breath.

During these breaches, Rune could see the Legions ahead beyond the storm. The armored dragons flew east, their fire bright, their howls a distant thunder.

They fly to Valien... and to Kaelyn.

At the thought of Kaelyn, his heart gave a twist, and his eyes stung. He missed her. He missed Valien too, and he missed Erry, and he missed all the others... but he mostly missed her. With Tilla's words still stinging, Rune yearned for Kaelyn's kind eyes, soft touch, and smiling lips. He thought back to that night in the ruined, hilltop temple, the night they had kissed.

I always thought Tilla was the love of my life, but now I miss you, Kaelyn. Now I wish I were back there in those ruins, holding you.

He looked at Tilla, who flew beside him, her scales glimmering, and guilt choked his throat, and he had never felt more confused.

A roar sounded ahead, and fire pierced the clouds.

Rune started. At first he thought it was Tilla roaring fire, but she looked just as bewildered. Rune sucked in his breath and stared ahead. Tilla's eyes narrowed and she bared her fangs.

The roar sounded again, five hundred yards away or closer, and more fire blazed, painting the clouds red.

Rune snarled. The main battalion was still distant; this was probably a lost soldier or a small patrol. Rune dipped lower in the clouds, gestured at Tilla, and she followed his lead. They sank fifty yards, staying within the cloud cover.

"Keep flying," he mouthed and pointed his claws ahead. "We'll fly under them."

She nodded, moved closer to him, and they shot forward through the clouds, silent and straight.

The roars continued above and fire cascaded down.

"They betrayed me!" roared a dragon; perhaps there was only one. "They stabbed me in the back. But I will make them kneel."

Rune frowned as he flew. He knew that voice from somewhere.

"How dare they banish me?" The dragon flew directly above now. "I'm their prince. I'm their savior! I--" The voice halted, then spoke louder. "Who flies below? I see your wake through the clouds. Is it you, sister? Have you come to kneel?"

Rune cursed and kept gliding forward. He gestured with his claws for Tilla to follow. He cursed under his breath. They'd been spotted, but perhaps they could still lose this dragon in the clouds. Tilla glided beside him, silent.

A jet of fire crashed down, missing Rune by a foot. Wings beat, scattering clouds, and air whistled. The dragon above was swooping.

"You cannot escape me!" cried the beast. "I see your wake. Come and die, dragons! I will kill you. I will kill you all."

Rune growled and filled his maw with fire.

"Stars damn it, there's only one," he said to Tilla, not caring if the beast above heard. "Let's kill the bastard."

Tilla gave a battle cry, and flames crackled to life between her teeth. She and Rune reared, soared, and blasted flame upward.

The fires roared, scattering the clouds. From the smoke and flame and mist, a red dragon came barreling down, bellowing and clawing the air.

Rune's heart skipped a beat and his anger flared.

"Leresy Cadigus," he said.

The young prince, twin to Kaelyn, looked haggard and nearly mad. The gilt on his horns, a sign of nobility, was peeling. Grime clung to his scales. But worse were his eyes; they were a madman's eyes. Something inside them had broken like snapped springs inside a doll. The red dragon cackled and leered.

"Hello, dragons!" he said. "You will kneel too. But first you will fall, yes. Fall!"

He raised his claws, holding up a cylinder of leather and glass.

Rune wasn't sure what the contraption was, and he had no time to contemplate it. He soared with Tilla, and they blasted fire again, shooting the jets up at the prince.

Red light shot down.

At first Rune thought it a stream of fire. Then he realized—red light was streaming from the cylinder like a sunbeam. Rune roared, tried to fly higher, and gasped.

An unseen claw tugged at his magic.

He growled, trying to cling to it, but the magic was jerked away like sleep vanishing under shaking hands.

Among the clouds, he resumed human form.

He tumbled.

At his side, he saw Tilla falling too. They pierced the clouds. They fell through open sky. The black fields below spun, racing up toward them. The red light still bathed them.

"I can't fly!" he shouted.

Even as she plummeted, Tilla managed to glare. "I noticed!"

He grimaced and tried to summon his magic again. Its tendrils coiled inside him, but whenever he reached for them, they slipped from his mind. It felt like trying to remember a fading dream.   Leresy still flew as a dragon. He cackled and dived, aiming the cylinder down. The red light still bathed Rune and Tilla.

"It's that damn light of his!" Rune shouted. "It's canceling out our magic."

Tilla shouted in frustration. "Yes, Rune, I can see that! Thank you, Sir Obvious."

The ground grew closer. Rune winced. He had only seconds to live.

"Damn it, Leresy!" he shouted up. "We're not your enemies. It's Rune and Tilla. You know us! Take that light off!"

But the red dragon seemed fully mad. He laughed, head tossed back, and blasted fire across the sky. His chest rose and fell, and smoke sputtered from him. He seemed like some cracked, leaky cauldron about to shatter.

"Rune and Tilla, Rune and Tilla!" he chanted. "I know you. Yes, I know you! Rune the silly boy my father wants. Tilla the tall woman with the nice, pale skin to kiss, yes." He howled with laughter. "I craved you both once, one to kill and one to bed, but which was which?"

The air howled around them. The ground loomed so close, they could count the boulders and trees. They had only a breath or two left.

"Leresy, stars damn you!" Tilla screamed. "Stop shining the light!"

"Take it off, Leresy!" Rune shouted, panic thudding through him. "We're not your enemies! We're your friends!"

The wind roared.

The ground reached toward them.

Rune winced and knew: *This is it.*

He reached out and held Tilla's hand.

He held his breath.

Leresy laughed and soared, and the red light vanished.

Treetops skimmed Rune's boots.

Roaring, he shifted into a dragon.

His wings bent the trees below. He blasted fire and sucked in air and his eyes watered.

I'm alive, stars, I'm alive.

Tilla soared at his side, howling.

Still laughing, Leresy made a lazy arc in the air, turning back toward them.

"Tilla, fly down and land!" Rune shouted.

They swooped.

They crashed between the treetops.

Several feet above the forest floor, the red light bathed them again. They lost their magic and thumped into the snow in human forms.

Rune moaned. The fall wasn't high enough to break his bones, but he would bruise. He raised his head, coughed, and struggled to rise. Tilla moaned at his side and pushed herself up onto her elbows.

Before they could stand, the red dragon crashed down through the trees. His claws thrust out. One dragon foot slammed against Rune, shoving him down. Snow filled his mouth and he moaned. The second foot slammed against Tilla and pinned her down.

"So, Rune and Tilla, Rune and Tilla," said the dragon. "Or should I say... Relesar Aeternum and the famous Lanse Tilla Siren?" He cackled and spat fire. "Oh yes, I've heard of your ascension, girl." He thrust down his head, reached out a tongue the size of a human arm, and licked Tilla's head. "Oh my, but you taste delightful. You taste like honey and moonlight. I've wanted to taste you for a long while."

She spat and her face twisted in disgust. "Go lick gutter shite, Leresy. Get off me."

She struggled and kicked but couldn't free herself. Rune squirmed too. The cylinder's light no longer shone upon him, but Leresy's foot pressed down too mightily. Whenever he grasped his magic and tried to shift, the weight squeezed it away like juice from a fruit, leaving Rune in human form.

"What do you want?" he demanded, twisting his head to stare up at the dragon.

Leresy laughed. "What do I want? Oh, silly child of the woods. What do I want?" He lowered his scaly head, and his smoke fluttered across the forest floor. "I want to kill all my enemies. I want to bed every woman in the world. I want power and money and booze. I want to forget the blood, the screams, the fire. What do I want, lost children?" His voice strained, shoving out each word through a clenched jaw. "I want the *throne*."

The claws dug into the soil beneath Rune, then tightened, coiling around his torso like a steel cage. Rune grimaced, his arms pinned to his sides, and glared up at Leresy.

"Go take your damn throne then," he said. "Go fight your madman of a father. Or if you want to face me, face me like a man, or let me shift and face you as a dragon. Or are you a coward?"

Leresy laughed and lifted Rune from the ground. In his other foot, he held Tilla, squeezing and pinning her arms to her sides. The red dragon bucked and tossed his head, blasting smoke across the forest.

"A coward?" he said. "Am I a coward? I slew Beras the Brute. I found the Genesis Shards. I will kill my father. I will kill my sister Shari. I will--"

"Your damn sister is already dead," Tilla spat out, squirming in the claws. "I killed her myself. Stabbed my blade right into her chest."

Leresy froze.

He panted, not moving, holding Rune and Tilla still in his claws. His eyes widened.

"My sister... Shari... dead?"

Rune nodded. "I saw her die. Tilla is speaking truth. You've been away from the capital for too long."

For a moment Leresy stood frozen. Fire crackled in his maw. Then, with a howl, he reared. He tossed back his head and blasted fire, igniting the treetops. He laughed. His tail lashed, slamming into trees. Flaming branches fell and sparks showered. The grass kindled.

"Shari is dead!" Leresy howled and laughed, sounding like a demonic child overcome with joy. "Dead, dead, dead! Shari is dead!"

He bounced around with glee, tail knocking down trees, still clutching Rune and Tilla. Smoke filled the forest. Trees blazed. Rune coughed, blinded. Before the flames could burn him, Leresy leaped up and soared, rising into the night sky, still clutching his prizes.

"Dead, dead! Shari is dead! Happy night, happy night, Shari is dead!"

Rune coughed and squirmed, trying to free an arm, trying to shift, but the claws clutched him so tightly he could barely breathe.

"Stars damn you, Leresy, I thought we were fighting together. You helped us in Lynport. Now free me!"

Leresy laughed and began flying back west, back toward the capital. The clouds streamed by, the forest below burned, and the wind roared.

"Shari is dead!" he cried into the night. "I am heir. I am heir to Requiem!"

Tilla kicked wildly.

"Leresy, you bloody fool," she shouted into the wind. "Your father banished you. He will kill you if you return. You're no heir, damn you."

But the red dragon kept flying, clutching them, and roared fire over their heads. He beat his wings, flying faster, streaming over the forests.

"Banished me?" He laughed. "Yes, yes, that he did. But now I return. Now I bear his greatest prizes--Relesar, the lost whelp of a miserable dynasty, and Tilla Siren, the traitor who murdered his daughter. Frey Cadigus will name me heir now. I will be his golden child." Leresy howled and his fire bathed the sky. "It is Leresy's turn to rise. Requiem is mine."

Rune and Tilla cursed and shouted and squirmed. The red dragon tightened his claws, grinned, and flew through the night.

KAELYN

A thousand dragons, their scales chipped and charred. A thousand riders on their backs, bandaged and burnt and bearing their guns. A ragtag force of refugees and rebels. A whisper in the night. A single flicker in a storm. They flew through the night and beheld the capital of Requiem ahead, rising from the dark forest like a crown of fire.

"Nova Vita," Kaelyn whispered, flying ahead of her people.

The capital had many names. Jewel of Requiem. Gloriae's City. Light of Aeternum. Yet to Kaelyn it was more than that. It was her home, her haunting pain, and her glittering prize. It was all that mattered in the world.

"Nova Vita." Her voice shook in the wind. "City of our ancestors. City of my pain and hope. Today I liberate you, Nova Vita, or I die upon your walls."

The city still lay miles away. From here it seemed no larger than a ring she could slip onto her finger. Fires blazed upon its walls, countless torches to light the night. More fire crackled within the ring--dragons flying over the roofs in patrol, blasting their flames. All around the capital, the land slept in darkness, a black sea.

Kaelyn took deep breaths, narrowed her eyes, and flew faster. The others flew at her sides: Valien, her guiding light; Erry Docker, a coppery dragon with flames in her nostrils; and two thousand more of her comrades, the dearest souls she knew.

"And you wait for me there, Rune," she whispered. "I will find you and I will free you. Be strong, my friend."

At her side, Valien raised his head, and his eyes shone in the night. He gazed upon his city and began to sing. His voice was a low rumble, a thunder rolling in a distant storm. Kaelyn knew the song. He sang Old Requiem Woods, an ancient tune, a song the Vir Requis would sing before they had a kingdom, before marble columns stood, before books were written and myths were told. It was a song of days before gunpowder, before walls of stone, before bloodshed and swords and a land that was torn, a song of the Vir Requis living in this forest below, wild children of the woods.

Kaelyn joined her voice to his. He sang in a rumble, but her voice was soft and pure as summer wine. Behind her, the others joined. A thousand dragons raised their voice in song.

"Old Requiem Woods, where do thy harpists play, in Old Requiem Woods, where do thy dragons fly..."

They flew closer. The city blazed ahead, a disk of light in the darkness, the beacon of her heart. With every mile they crossed, more details emerged, and Kaelyn could soon see dark towers and battlements. The streets stretched out, lit with palisades of lamps, shaped like a wagon wheel. In the wheel's center, like an axle, rose the black tower of Tarath Imperium, a thousand feet tall.

A rumble sounded ahead, a distant chant.

The Resistance flew onward, singing their song.

Ahead, the walls of Nova Vita blazed with torchlight. Specks upon the walls grew larger, revealing themselves to be dragons, tens of thousands of them. Smoke plumed from their nostrils, and flames blasted from their maws. A thousand cannons rose between them, small as matches from here but growing larger with every flap of wings. The rumble upon the walls grew louder, becoming a battle cry, a howl for blood.

"Hail the red spiral!" rose thousands of distant voices. "For the glory of Cadigus! Purification!"

Kaelyn snarled. Her heart twisted. Fear pounded through her. But she flew on and she kept singing. She raised her voice, letting her song ring out. All around, the other dragons sang with her. Their voices rose in hope, in light, in memory.

The Legions howled ahead upon the walls.

"Slay the Resistance!"

"We will break them upon the wheel!"

"We will drink their blood!"

"Leave none alive!"

Kaelyn shivered as she flew. Her heart pounded in her throat. Ice seemed to wrap around her spine. Myriads roared for her death ahead--hundreds of thousands. Half a million troops or more waited here, each bred and broken into a machine of perfect hatred, a killer who longed for her blood. Half a million demons... flaming and screaming for her death.

She flew among two thousand.

The miles blurred below. The walls grew ahead. The Legions screamed and blasted flames. The Resistance sang their old song, voices clear and deep, a psalm of old.

In darkness and firelight, with song and with prayer, after two decades of fighting in shadows, the Resistance flew toward the ancient walls of Nova Vita, capital of Requiem.

"Old Requiem Woods, where do thy harpists play, in Old Requiem Woods, where do thy dragons--"

A thousand fuses burned. Upon the walls, a thousand cannons blasted.

Fire ripped across the sky. Smoke blasted upward. Cannonballs blazed through the night, streaked like comets, and slammed into the Resistance.

Blood sprayed. Iron tore through dragons. In death they lost their magic; they scattered in a shower of blood and human limbs.

Their song rose louder.

Kaelyn sang out the old words. Her comrades sang with her. They flew on. Their flames lit the night. They sang and they flew and though fear filled her, Kaelyn felt the light of Requiem guide her onward and glow within her.

"Cannons!" rose howls from officers ahead. "Fire!"

The Resistance sang as they flew.

Matches burned. Explosions rocked the walls, blasting smoke and flame.

A thousand more cannonballs flew through the night.

The rounds ripped into the Resistance. Hundreds of dragons howled, lost their magic, and fell dead as ravaged men and women.

Kaelyn kept singing, staring ahead.

The others flew around her.

The walls loomed closer.

Cannons fired. Smoke and blood filled the sky.

They flew over the last fields, and Kaelyn tossed back her head and blasted a jet of flame.

"Arquebuses!" she cried.

At her side, Valien roared. "Tirans, fire your guns!"

The dragons of the Resistance swooped toward the city walls.

The cannons blasted and smoke blinded them.

Hundreds of arquebuses blasted. With an explosion of smoke and flame, with a thousand *cracks* of gunpowder blasting, the iron rounds pummeled the city battlements.

Legionaries fell.

Iron rounds tore through armor, more powerful than any sword or arrow, cutting into steel like knives into butter. Blood sprayed in a mist. Men and women tumbled from the walls.

"Dragonfire!" Kaelyn shouted. She dived toward the battlements and rained her flames.

Around her, a thousand dragons of the Resistance swooped and blew fire. The walls rose in flame. Barrels of gunpowder burst, and smoke and fire covered the sky. Stone cracked. Kaelyn roared and beat her wings, churning ash and smoke. Below, she beheld a wall crumbling. Bricks rained and cannons tumbled, disappearing into clouds of dust.

"Fly, Resistance!" she shouted through the inferno. "Fly to Tarath Imperium. Crush the tower!"

She could no longer see the city, only a storm of gray and red. Cannonballs flew through dust and smoke and ash. Dragons screamed around her, lost their magic, and collapsed into bits of flesh. Kaelyn screamed and kept flying.

"Forward, Resistance!" Valien howled somewhere ahead. "Fire your guns. Blow your fire!"

Kaelyn couldn't see. She could barely hear beyond the ringing in her ears. A cannonball blasted ahead of her, missing her by inches. A second round flew behind her; it banged against her tail, knocking off a spike, and she screamed. Yet she flew on. Through the dust and smoke, she could still hear the Resistance singing their song.

"To the tower!" she cried. "Fly on, Resistance. For Requiem!"

They flew over the walls. Through the smoke, Kaelyn glimpsed the city roofs and streets. Nova Vita sprawled below her, a labyrinth of shadows and firelight.

Shrieks tore through the sky ahead.

Flames blasted toward her.

Through the thinning smoke, she saw them swarm: countless dragons of the Legions, beasts clad in steel, death in their eyes, fire in their jaws.

"Miya, are you still there?" Kaelyn shouted above her shoulder.

Upon her back, the young woman shouted back. "I'm here!"

"Fire your beam!"

Kaelyn snarled and flew toward the Legions ahead, a mass of scales and metal and smoke. They covered the sky.

"Miya!" she screamed.

The Legions howled and charged toward her, their fire blasted, and Kaelyn winced.

Red light blazed above her head and slammed into the horde. They lost their magic.

They fell as men and women, clad in armor and bearing swords, and crashed onto the roofs and streets below.

Ahead, she saw a second red beam pierce the smoke and fire. Valien flew there, her lord, the man she loved. The silver dragon flew through fire and blood, roaring his cry. The Legions fell before him and his fire rained.

For Requiem, Kaelyn thought. *For Rune. And for Valien Eleison, the greatest man I know.*

Their guns blasted. Their beams blazed. Their fire lit the night. The Legions surrounded them, darting between the beams to burn them down. Cannonballs flew from every tower, crashing into their ranks, felling them from the sky.

The Resistance flew over the city, and they died. They died by the hundreds. Their corpses covered the roofs and walls below.

And yet the survivors flew. And they sang. They fought on, and even as their ranks crumbled, and their comrades fell dead around them, they shot forward. They plowed through the Legions, an arrow driving through a giant's flesh.

Tears in her eyes, her scales cut and burnt, Kaelyn saw it ahead, rising from smoke and fire.

Tarath Imperium soared in the night, the tower of Requiem, the pillar of Cadigus, the heart of the empire.

My childhood home.

Smoke and light filled the night. The city burned and crumbled, and thousands fell dead all around. It was the greatest battle of her life, the last battle she would fight. It was the end of the war.

With song and blood and blazing light, the remains of the Resistance, only a few hundred strong, dived over the last streets toward the dark tower.

LERESY

Leresy flew high above the city, watching it burn.

The capital blazed and crumbled, a painting in red and black. A chunk of eastern wall had fallen, and scattered fires burned around it. Cannons and arquebuses rang out, dragonfire blazed, and smoke filled the sky. Corpses lay upon roofs and towers, and blood painted the streets. The Legions covered the sky, hundreds of thousands of dragons roaring. The Resistance drove through them, shining their two remaining Genesis Scopes, cutting down thousands of dragons, sending men crashing against roofs, walls, and cobblestones.

Leresy had fought in battles before. He had defended Castra Luna. He had fought in the great Battle of Lynport. He had slain legionaries upon the beaches. Yet he had never seen such death, thousands falling from the sky, a rain of corpses. For every resistor killed, the beams sent a hundred imperial dragons falling, yet the Legions kept swarming.

"Fly at them!" their officers shouted, voices ringing across the sky. "Fly and slay them, fly around their light, fly and die for the red spiral."

As Leresy flew above, watching the carnage, a chill gripped his heart. His father was willing to send thousands to die in the Genesis Beams, all to slay only a handful of rebels. Was the death of a resistor so worthy, the life of a legionary so expendable?

"Leresy, damn you!" Tilla shouted, clutched in his left claws, still in human form.

"You're going to die here with us, Leresy!" shouted Rune, also in human form, clutched in his right claws. "The Resistance is slaying your father's troops, and they will slay you too."

Leresy snorted fire. He tightened his claws, almost snapping his prisoners' ribs; they grunted and fell silent. He shook his head wildly, clearing it of morbid thoughts. He could not contemplate morality now. He had to deliver his gifts, claim his inheritance, and save his city.

"Oh, but you are wrong, little ones," he said. "The Resistance will fail. I will save this city in its hour of need. I will deliver you to my father." He tossed his scaly neck, allowing his Genesis Scope to swing on its rope like an amulet on a chain. "Then, with my scope, I will cut down your feeble Resistance and save my empire."

He grinned. With Shari dead and his newfound glory, everything was finally falling into place.

You will finally see my worth, Father. You will finally name me your heir.

Below him, the Resistance had crossed the city center. They were attacking the palace of Tarath Imperium, the great axle of the wheel. Cannons were blazing from its walls, ripping into resistors. Imperial dragons were leaping from its tower, only to crash into the Genesis Beams and tumble a thousand feet to the ground. Dragonfire bathed the tower, smoke unfurled, and the walls shook.

Leresy laughed. "Now, Father... now as you huddle in the darkness, waiting to die, it is I--Leresy, the son you outcast and shamed--who will save you."

He cackled, almost tempted to let the Resistance swarm the palace and kill the bastard. But no. Valien would only seize the throne for himself, one despot replacing another. Leresy did not crave to see this rabble rule his empire.

"So I will save you, Father, though you disgust me," he said. "In return, I will watch you age and wither until the throne is mine."

He blasted fire, narrowed his eyes, and dived.

Smoke raced around him. Flames exploded like fireworks. A stray cannonball whistled by his side. Still he swooped, snarling, his captives clutched in his claws. Rune and Tilla screamed--human bodies were so frail, the skulls so small, squeezing under a fast descent. Yet Leresy would not slow his flight, and he sprayed fire, crashing down like a comet.

A Genesis Beam blazed his way, red and humming.

Leresy banked sharply, skirted around the beam, and kept diving. The beam shone upon a battalion of imperial dragons to his north, scattering a rain of armored men.

The steeple of Tarath Imperium reached up from a sea of smoke and fire. Black spikes crowned the tower like the claws of a giant. In the inferno of war, the tower seemed like the charred hand of a corpse. Cannons fired from its battlements, and a hundred men in black robes stood upon its roof, warriors of the Axehand Order, awaiting the resistors.

Valien and his mob swarmed from the east. The Legions surrounded the tower and covered the city. Here above the tower's crest, Leresy flew alone. Laughing, he dived toward the outreached claw of battlements. Several feet above the tower roof, he stretched his wings wide. They caught the smoky air, billowing like sails, slowing his descent. He reared in the air and shot a blazing inferno skyward.

"I am Leresy Cadigus!" he howled, beating his wings, a beast of wrath and glory. "I bear Relesar Aeternum and his whore in my claws. Open the tower doors, axehands!"

Shrieks sounded behind him.

Leresy spun to see a dozen resistors shooting toward him, rabid dragons bearing riders. Guns blazed from their saddles. Their fire crackled. An iron round slammed into Leresy's shoulder, digging through scales into flesh, and he howled.

He landed upon the tower, pinning Rune and Tilla down under his feet. He twisted his neck, grabbed his Genesis Scope between his teeth, and popped off the lid with his tongue. More guns fired, and another round slammed into his flesh. Grimacing, holding the scope in his mouth, Leresy aimed the beam.

Red light blasted forward, lighting the resistors.

A dozen dragons, only feet away and howling for his death, lost their magic.

They resumed human forms--wild, long-haired men and women clad in leather and rags. They tumbled. Most crashed down beyond the tower and into the night. Three, the closest to Leresy, crashed against the tower roof. The Axehand Order swept forward, black robes swaying, and swung the blades strapped to their stumps. Resistors screamed and died.

Leresy panted and mewled. Two iron rounds dug into his flesh. Each was small, only the size of a marble, but crackled with agony.

He limped across the tower roof. With every step, he pressed his captives down against the floor, all but crushing them. He had to beat his wings to keep moving. The battlements towered around him, fifty feet tall, their obsidian reflecting the firelight. Across the roof, axehands chanted prayers, blades swung, and dragons roared. Fire crackled and cannons blasted, their booms deafening. Leresy's ears rang. His blood dripped. Yet he gritted his teeth and kept moving, his claws wrapped around his prisoners.

The tower trapdoor lay ahead. Fifty axehands surrounded it, blades raised. The firelight pierced their hoods, painting their iron masks a demonic red.

"Let me through," Leresy demanded, limping forward, slamming Rune and Tilla down with each step. "I've caught the escaped heir. Let me pass!"

As the battle raged beyond the battlements, the axehands stood in the firelight and smoke, hissing. One spoke, his voice ghostly, a sound like steam fleeing a kettle.

"You are Leresy the Outcast. Our lord, the God of Dragons, has banished you. Leave this place, or we will feast upon your organs for the glory of the red spiral."

Leresy hissed and blasted smoke their way. "The city is burning. I have the heir of Aeternum in my claws. I have the traitor Tilla Siren, the killer of Shari Cadigus. I have a Genesis Scope, the only weapon that can stop the Resistance now." He spat flames at their feet. "Let me pass or watch this tower fall."

The axehands stared, silent. Jets of dragonfire crisscrossed overhead. Arquebus rounds blazed; one slammed into an axehand, knocking the man down. Dragons screamed and flew above and corpses showered down. The tower shook. But Leresy only stared at the axehands, smoke rising from his nostrils, his claws gripping his prizes.

Finally, after what seemed an eternity, the axehands parted, clearing the way to the trapdoor.

Leresy barked a laugh and stepped between them, still in dragon form.

"Now grab these prisoners!" he said. "Chain them up. Drag them behind me, and we will present them to the emperor."

He tossed Rune and Tilla down, then shone his scope upon them. They were bloodied, bruised, and weak; he wondered if he'd snapped their bones. The wretches tried to escape. They could not shift under the light, but they crawled across the tower, coughing and struggling to rise.

Pathetic, Leresy thought. And yet... he found his blood heating. The boy Rune was a maggot, but Tilla... even as she crawled and gasped for breath, her skin bloody and ashy, Tilla was more intoxicating than wine. Her clothes were tattered, revealing her shapely flesh. Her eyes blazed with fury, shining like two black gems. Leresy watched her struggle and licked his lips.

I've craved you since I first saw you at Luna, he thought, and his drool dripped between his teeth. *I will bed you yet. You will be my prisoner and my concubine.*

The two struggled to their feet, pitiful lovers. Before they could take a step, the axehands swarmed around them. The robed warrior-priests grabbed them, shoved them down, and pulled chains from their cloaks. The two traitors screamed and kicked and punched. Rune managed to knock an axehand down. But they were too weak, and the axehands were too many. Within moments, the prisoners were chained, and the axehands were dragging them into the tower.

"Wait!" Leresy said. "I will lead the way. Drag the prisoners behind me."

He shifted into human form. His wounds blazed with new agony, and blood soaked his clothes, but he ignored the pain; soon all his pain would end. As the sky burned and bled, he stepped toward the prisoners. Rune and Tilla stood before him, struggling in their chains, screaming for his blood.

"My sweetness," Leresy said, approaching Tilla. Her wrists were bound, and four axehands held her still.

Leresy caressed her cheek, then pulled his hand back as she tried to bite. She spat at him but missed his face, and her spit landed at his feet. Iron rounds and fire crashed all around them, and dragons fought overhead. Blood pattered down. Chipped scales clattered around them like hail.

"I will kill you, Leresy Cadigus, you gutter worm," Tilla said, her cheeks red with fury.

He licked his lips. "Good. You're still feisty. I like that. I want you to struggle tonight as I make you mine." He snapped his fingers. "Axehands! Follow."

Grinning, he stepped through the trapdoor and into the tower.

He walked down a coiling staircase. Torches lined the walls, and the axehands walked behind him, dragging the kicking prisoners. Guards stood every few steps, armed with halberds and swords and shields, clad in black steel.

Soon they will serve me, Leresy thought. *Soon these soldiers will hail Leresy as their god.*

He laughed as he descended the steps. Finally, after all this blood and fire and pain, glory was his. Finally Shari was dead. Finally *finally* after all the agony, he--Leresy Cadigus--had emerged triumphant.

"Tonight you will see, Father," he said to the shadows as he descended. "You will see that Shari was weak, that she died like a dog. You will see that Kaelyn is a mere worm. You will see that I, your outcast son, am the strong one, the glorious one, the heir to your crown." Tears burned in his eyes, but Leresy forced himself to grin. "And you, Erry... you betrayed me. You will watch me rise to glory, and I will hunt you down, and I will force you to kneel. And I will force you to kneel too, Tilla. I will force this whole damn world to kneel and worship my glory."

He reached a corridor and marched across its black tiles. Guards stood alongside, swords drawn, waiting for battle. Within moments, Leresy knew, the Resistance could swarm down these halls like poison through the arteries of a giant. By then it would be too late for them; Leresy would have claimed his domain.

"Leresy, fight us like a man!" Tilla screamed behind, but hands muffled her cry.

Leresy's grin widened and he kept marching. When he reached a tall, bronze door, he paused and inhaled deeply.

Father's door.

The tower of Tarath Imperium rose from a sprawling palace, a complex of halls and courtyards. The throne room, far below this place, loomed so large a hundred dragons could fly within it. Intricate mosaics covered its floors, gold shone upon its columns, and paintings of dragons bedecked its ceiling. The Ivory Throne rose there, resplendent... and usually empty.

Lowborn Frey Cadigus was a soldier at heart, disdainful of pomp. Once or twice a year, he entertained guests in his throne room, putting on a show of majesty. The rest of the time, he lurked here in this tower, in the austere chamber of a soldier, a place where he could butcher his animals, torture his prisoners, and--so many times--beat his children.

Standing before this door, Leresy's knees shook, and he clenched his fists. He closed his eyes.

No, Father! cried a small voice within him. *Don't hit her. You're killing her, Father! It's I who stole the fruit. Beat me instead.*

He had stood shaking outside this door so often as a child. Beyond this door, he had screamed, bled, and hurt so much. The throne room was a place of glory, but here... here beyond this door lurked blackness, pain, and terror.

He sucked in breath.

I must not fear the shadows today, he told himself. *I suffered here as a child. But now, as a man, my glory will blaze within this darkness.*

He opened his eyes, grabbed the doorknob, and pushed the door open.

Shadows greeted him. He entered the wolf's lair.

The place looked less like the chamber of an emperor and more like a butcher shop. The bricks were rough and gray. Meat hooks hung from the ceiling, holding animal carcasses. One poor lamb was still kicking as it bled out. Some slabs of meat, those in the shadowy back, looked oddly human, skinned and red. The stench of blood and offal filled the place. Leresy swallowed, feeling ready to gag.

Emperor Frey Cadigus stood before a table laden with cleavers. Despite the battle raging outside, he hadn't donned his armor, perhaps too proud to admit any danger. Instead, he wore his bloodstained butcher's apron. In recent years, Frey spent less time governing and more time with his passion, cutting and dissecting beasts and men. The meat was never eaten. Frey Cadigus never ate meat; he only craved to cut it.

"Father!" Leresy said, marching toward him over the bloodstained floor. "I've returned."

Frey stared at him across his table. His eyes were cold chips of obsidian.

"My son," he said, lips curling in disgust. "Have I not banished you? You return now as battle rages?"

"I return now to win your battle!" he said and tossed the Genesis Scope forward. It thumped against the table. "Have you wondered how the Resistance has been felling your dragons from the sky? They're using these weapons. Here is yours--a gift worthy of an emperor. And I bring further gifts, my lord." Leresy snapped his fingers and raised his voice. "Axehand! Bring forth my prisoners."

The robed priests entered the chamber, dragging the bound Rune and Tilla. Leresy pointed at the floor, and the axehands shoved the prisoners down. Smirking, Leresy placed a boot against Tilla's neck, shoving her face against the tiles. He drew his sword and held the blade against Rune's neck, keeping the boy too pinned down.

"Behold!" Leresy said. "I've brought you imperial gifts: Lanse Tilla Siren, the traitor who slew your daughter, and Relesar, the heir of Aeternum. It is I, your son, who captured them. They are yours, Father. Accept my gifts. All I ask is that you return me to your good graces. Name me your heir, and these prizes are yours."

His heart thumped and his chest rose and fell. He had rehearsed this speech all day. His fingers trembled, and he took a shaky breath, expecting his father to beam, to embrace him, to shower him with love and approval.

But Frey only stared silently, no emotion on his face.

Leresy hissed. His breath rose to a pant. He pushed down with his foot, pressing Tilla's face hard against the tiles. The axehands knelt around him, holding the prisoners still. Frey only stared, eyes cold, saying nothing.

"Well, Father?" Leresy demanded, able to wait no longer. "Here is your key to victory! Here is your vengeance, the prize you have sought for years. I brought you victory, I brought you Shari's killer, and I brought you Relesar. I brought you all that you've ever desired. Will you not speak?"

Frey reached across the table. Leresy thought he'd grab the Genesis Scope, but instead, his hand clutched a meat cleaver. Finally he spoke.

"Is that so, Leresy?" he said, his voice dripping the same old disgust. "Did you bring me all I've ever desired? What of my desire for a worthy son, a noble heir of my own blood?"

Leresy pounded his chest. "I am here, Father! I've proven myself worthy. Reward me!"

Frey lifted the meat cleaver and turned the blade, letting the torchlight glimmer against it. "Is that all you seek, Leresy? Rewards? A treat for a begging dog? You have spoken here of yourself, of your own vainglory, of the gifts you demand. Not once have you mentioned the glory of Requiem, the honor and strength of our empire. Even now, as the Resistance smashes against our walls, as blood and fire purifies our empire... even now, you only care for your own power."

Leresy realized his error and his eyes watered. He screamed hoarsely, already knowing it was too late.

"I care for you, Father!" His voice sounded too young to him, no longer the voice of a hero, but the voice of frightened child. "I brought these for you, for--"

"For me?" Frey snorted. "I am a soldier. I fight for the eternal glory of Requiem. It is Requiem I serve, not my own hubris. It seems you've learned nothing from me. Still, after all the times I've disciplined you, you care only for yourself." He turned to stare at the axehands. "Men! Take the girl to the Red Tower. Chain her but do not torture her; that will be my pleasure. Take the boy down into my bedchambers. Chain him there; should Valien reach my halls, I would have him gaze upon the boy."

The axehands bowed and hissed.

"Yes, God of Dragons, Lord of Spiral."

They retreated from the chamber, robes swaying, clutching the screaming and kicking prisoners.

Leresy stood alone before his father.

"Well, Father?" he demanded, tears in his eyes. "Will you say no more?"

Frey fixed him with a glare. "What would you have me say?"

Leresy snorted a laugh, but it sounded more like as a sob. "Thank you, son! You saved the empire! You made me proud!" Tears ran down Leresy's cheeks and his lips shook. "I love you, son. Welcome back to my court." He hated himself, but he couldn't stop his tears, and he couldn't stop his knees from shaking. "Any of those thing would do splendidly, Father. But you have no emotion in that rotten, shriveled-up organ you call a heart. Even now, as I won you the war, as I brought you all your desires, you only stare at me like... like I'm some worm. Like I'm nothing but a common soldier." He screamed, tears falling. "I am your son!"

Frey stared at him silently for a long moment.

"Are you quite finished?" he finally said. "Yes. Yes, you are my son. As shameful as that is to admit, it's true. I do not know why the gods have cursed me so. I had two strong children; one now lies dead, and the other flies against me. Alas, it is my son--my *son*, who should be my greatest warrior--who snivels here before me, weeping like a child. But yes, Leresy. Yes, you are my son. And yes, you brought me gifts that I desired. For that, you shall be rewarded."

Leresy gasped. Hope sprang inside him, and he rubbed his eyes.

"I... I will receive your grace?" he whispered.

Frey lifted a whetting stone and began sharpening his cleaver. "When the battle is over, and we've crushed the Resistance, I will welcome you back into this city. I'll give you a small house to live in, somewhere... far in the shadows, out of my way. Perhaps in the slums around that brothel of yours. You would like that. And you shall be allowed to live out the rest of your days there, in the darkness, drunk and surrounded by your whores."

Leresy took a step forward and raised his fists. "I demand more! I demand to live in this palace. I demand to be named your heir, Father!"

Again Frey snorted. "My heir? I would sooner bed a peasant girl and name her whelp my heir than you." He fixed Leresy with a stare like stabbing daggers. "You will never be my heir. You will never be more than a miserable drunk. Now leave this palace. It is forbidden to you."

Leresy stood speechless.

His hands dropped to his sides.

His mouth worked silently.

Frey walked around him, heading toward the door. "And now I have a battle to win. I have a Resistance to crush. When I return with the head of this Valien, I expect to see you gone."

Leresy fell to his knees. He reached out, grabbed his father's leg, and clung.

"Father, please!" he said hoarsely. "I am your son!"

Frey grunted, kicked himself free, and shoved Leresy down.

"And so you keep reminding me," the emperor said. "It's a disgraceful truth I wish I could forget. If you have any honor, boy, fly out now against the Resistance and die in their fire. That is the greatest gift you could give me."

With that, Emperor Frey exited his chambers, leaving Leresy in darkness, tears, and old clutching pain. He lay on the floor, punched the tiles, and screamed.

VALIEN

He ran up the stairs, scales clattering, and slammed into the palace doors. They creaked and stood strong. Valien cursed, stepped down a few steps, and ran again. He was a burly dragon, yet when he slammed into the palace doors again, he groaned and thought his bones would crack.

"Valien, we can't hold them back much longer!" Sila shouted, standing upon the staircase. Ash, sweat, and lacerations covered the Tiran captain. He fired an arquebus, smoke blasted, and he spat.

The staircase led from the Square of Cadigus, a cobbled expanse larger than most towns, to the palace gates. The remains of the Resistance covered the steps, swords and guns in hand. Looking upon them, Valien felt his heart sink.

How many were left? Four hundred? Five? No more than that. Horror pounded through him. They had flown here with thousands... now only a handful remained.

These surviving resistors were firing arquebuses. The smoke hung thicker than storm clouds. Only Kaelyn and Erry held no guns; they were shining Genesis Scopes in every direction, holding back the swarms.

The Legions covered the city streets, the square below, and the sky above. Hundreds of thousands swarmed, a tightening noose, a puddle of scales and flames. Wherever the beams shone, imperial dragons fell from the sky. Wherever men charged in armor, swinging swords, arquebuses cut them down. Thousands fell. Their corpses covered the square in a demonic carpet of flesh. Yet for every legionary who died, more emerged. Cannons fired from within their ranks. Dragonfire blasted. Arrows flew. Every moment another resistor screamed and fell.

Valien slammed into the palace gates again. At his sides, two other dragons, gruff warriors of the Resistance, charged with him. Yet the doors were too thick, their oak iron-banded; even three dragons could not break them.

"Valien!" Kaelyn cried below, shining her Genesis Scope at a swooping battalion of dragons, sending them falling. "Valien, hurry!"

He looked upon his forces and could barely breathe. They were trapped here; the enemy surrounded them, miles deep, a colony of ants surrounding a piece of fruit. More resistors fell, torn apart by cannons and claws. Soon they were down to four hundred men, then only three. Valien could feel those old hands clutching his throat again.

We will all die.

He tossed back his head and roared, blowing fire.

Then we will die fighting.

He beat his wings and soared. He shouted commands at the two dragons who fought by his side.

"With me! Fly high."

They ascended along the palace walls, leaving the doors below. The palace bricks blurred. Arrows fired from slits, clattering against them, and one sank into Valien's shoulder. He grunted but kept flying.

A thousand imperial dragons howled above. Their claws reached out. Their maws opened, swaying in heat waves, smelters spilling fire.

"Kaelyn," Valien shouted, "your beam!"

He kept soaring, his warriors at his sides. The imperial dragons shot down. Fire blasted, and Valien winced and rose through the flame. One of his dragons screamed in the fire, lost his magic, and fell burning.

"Kaelyn!"

The Legions cackled above, their claws extended, their fangs bared, a shimmering cloud of steel and scale, and Valien kept soaring, flying into his death. Fire blazed, and his second warrior howled and fell.

Valien winced, seconds from slamming into the enemy.

Red light blazed.

The Genesis Beam slammed against the horde.

The imperial dragons lost their magic. Dozens tumbled down, screaming troops in steel.

Just below the beam, Valien growled and kept soaring. Upon the stairs below, Kaelyn kept raising the beam, clearing a path through the sky.

Through fire and smoke, Valien saw his target--the battlements of the palace hall. They overlooked the square, lined with cannons. Beyond them, Tarath Imperium rose from flames, but Valien did not care for that tower now. He shot toward the hall's crenellations.

Cannons blasted his way and Valien banked, dodging the missiles, and rose higher. He blew his flames.

Gunners screamed and fell ablaze. Some rolled upon the walls, clutching at their heated armor. Others tumbled off the battlements, living comets, burning and screaming before crashing onto the stairs below. Barrels of gunpowder exploded. The walls shook. Fires blasted out.

Valien shot toward a cannon that stood between two merlons. Its gunners were busy reloading; one man was pressing a ramrod down the barrel, while another was already lighting the fuse. When they saw Valien charge toward them, a howling silver dragon, they leaped back and drew their swords.

With a roar, Valien clawed them apart. They fell lacerated from the walls. Tail lashing, knocking back charging men, Valien grabbed the cannon.

He roared. The barrel was still searing hot; it burned his feet. He grunted and beat his wings, struggling to rise. The cannon must have weighed more than he did. He grimaced and lifted the gun into the air. With two great flaps of his wings, he cleared the battlements and began his descent.

Dragons howled and charged around him. Kaelyn was blazing her beam, carving him a path through the horde. Arrows flew. Two slammed into Valien's chest, and he roared and nearly dropped the cannon. He plummeted down, nearly at a free fall. The stairs rushed up toward him. Hardly three hundred resistors remained fighting; the rest lay dead upon the steps. Groaning, the searing barrel clutched in his claws, Valien stretched his wings wide. He slowed his fall and dropped the cannon onto the stairs, its muzzle pointing at the door. It came free from his grip with bits of seared flesh, cracking the stone steps.

"Clear the way!" he howled.

Between him and the door above, arquebusers moved aside, firing their weapons at the encroaching Legions. Bleeding and burnt, nearly too weary for fire, Valien managed a puff of flame, igniting the cannon's fuse.

He winced and stumbled aside.

The cannon fired.

Smoke blasted out, covering the stairs. The cannon flew backward, tumbling down the staircase, crashing into charging legionaries. Its projectile slammed into the palace gates.

With flame and a shower of splinters, the doors crashed open.

Valien bellowed and raced up the stairs.

"Charge!" he shouted, his voice a mere rasp, but loud enough to carry across the battle. "Resistance, into the palace. Death to Cadigus!"

The remains of his forces howled, three hundred scarred and burnt souls. They charged. They swung swords and screamed for blood.

"Death to Cadigus!"

Shouting, Valien ran through the smoke. Still in dragon form, he crashed through the shattered doors and into the palace hall.

Ahead in the shadows, palisades of columns held a grand, vaulted ceiling painted with scenes of flying dragons. A mosaic of aerial battles covered the floor, depicting wyverns and phoenixes. Far ahead rose the Ivory Throne, but tonight it stood barren.

Between Valien and the throne, hissing and glaring, stood a hundred dragons. Each wore an iron mask like a muzzle; the metal was bolted on to the flesh. Each was missing his front paw; instead, their legs ended with raised axe heads.

"Hail the red spiral!" the deformed beasts cried. "Hail Frey, God of Dragons!"

Valien blasted his dragonfire.

His flames filled the hall.

The axehands shrieked and charged.

With a roar, a green dragon shot into the hall, flew over Valien's head, and blazed a beam of red light.

The Genesis Beam fell upon the deformed dragons. They shrieked and ran afoot, men clad in black robes, swinging their axes.

Valien roared his flames. Behind him, dozens of resistors swarmed into the hall, running between and around his legs. Their arquebuses fired. The rounds tore into the axehands; the dark priests fell, writhed, and burned.

"Find the emperor!" Valien shouted, running into the hall. He whipped his head from side to side, blowing fire. Between the columns, dozens of guards were charging his way, swinging swords and firing arrows. His flames washed them. His gunners cut them down.

"Where's Frey?" Kaelyn shouted at his side, still in dragon form, her beam clutched in her claws.

He growled and stared at the throne. It was so close, only a hundred yards away, rising from fire. He could run over and seize it. But no; without Rune here, and without Frey's body, it was an empty prize.

"Kaelyn, climb the tower," he said. "Take half our forces with you. Seek Frey there."

She nodded. "What of you?"

Arrows and iron rounds blazed around them. Legionaries fell dead at their feet.

"I'll search the ground complex," Valien said. He swung his tail and sent a legionary flying.

As the fires roared and the blood spilled, she met his gaze, and for an instant they stood still, staring at each other. Her eyes glimmered, those hazel eyes that had guided him for years, the beacons of his soul, his starlight in the dark. He loved her, and he saw the love in her eyes, and he knew her thoughts. They were the same thoughts he himself was thinking.

I might never see you again.

He wanted to hold her, to speak of his love, to share a last embrace. But the battle raged. Soldiers fell dead all around. One arrow flew between them, and another snapped against his scales.

"Valien," she whispered.

"Go!" he said. "Climb the tower and find him."

She nodded, shifted into human form, and ran between the columns. She shouted orders, and men ran behind her, firing guns and clearing a path through the Legions.

Valien grunted, spun around, and flamed three charging men. He shifted into human form too, drew his sword, and bared his teeth. About a hundred resistors stood around him.

"Sila!" he shouted to the sailor. "Take your men and search the dungeons. Everyone else, follow me. We'll find the bastard."

Snarling, he raced between the columns, leading fifty warriors. He swung his sword, and gunners fired around him. They moved into a corridor, cutting men down, splashing the walls with blood. They fought for every step.

As he killed, Valien could not stop seeing her eyes in his mind, and the terror ignited his blood. He might die this day. He might find Rune dead in the dungeons. He might never seize the throne. But most of all he feared for Kaelyn. He roared, swung his sword, and carved a path of corpses.

KAELYN

She ran upstairs, swinging her sword and cutting men down.

Fifty resistors ran behind her. Two ran at her sides; the stairway was just wide enough for three to climb abreast. Legionaries shouted above, running down toward them, swinging longswords.

"Fire!" Kaelyn shouted.

The resistors at her sides pulled their triggers. Their arquebuses blasted; they were so loud her ears rang. Four legionaries crashed down above, pierced with the rounds. Two more raced her way, and Kaelyn swung Lemuria. Her sword crashed through one's armor, severing his arm. She parried the second man's blow, swung down, and cleaved his helm. Their bodies crumbled, and Kaelyn ran across them, climbing higher.

"Men, swap!" she cried.

The men at her sides, their guns smoking, retreated down the staircase to reload. Two more fighters, their guns loaded and ready, replaced them.

"Hail the red spiral!" cried legionaries above, swarming downstairs.

"Fire!" Kaelyn said again, and two more guns blasted. Two more men retreated to reload, and two more, their guns ready, replaced them. Kaelyn screamed and thrust her sword. She trampled corpses and climbed on.

She climbed for hours, it seemed, corkscrewing up the tower. Her men kept firing and retreating, moving in a constant cycle. Their guns cut down the legionaries, blasting through armor, killing two--sometimes three--men deep. All those legionaries who escaped the gunfire met Kaelyn's blade.

A hundred cuts covered her. A gash on her thigh bled--the same place Shari had wounded her almost two years ago, the night she had flown to Lynport, seeking Rune. She howled, driving onward, climbing floor by floor. Her limbs shook and her ears rang, but she fought on.

I will always fight on, she thought. *Until my last drop of blood. Until the last beat of my heart.*

"Father!" she shouted as she climbed. "Father, come face me! Are you a coward?"

But she heard only his Legions, the endless chants, the bloodthirsty cries of those he'd molded into killers. And she killed them. She slew them with steel and iron, and their blood covered her, stinging her lips, coppery and sweet.

You made me a killer too, Kaelyn thought, swinging her sword. *You made me a greater killer than any in your Legions. I can forgive you for killing my people. But I can never forgive you for making me kill yours.*

"Father!" she shouted. "Face me! It's me, Kaelyn. Do you hear?"

Arrows whistled down from above. The men at her sides screamed and fell, and their guns clattered down. Kaelyn ducked. An arrow flew over her head, slicing her hair. She grabbed a fallen arquebus, screamed, and fired. The gun blasted, blinding her with smoke, nearly knocking her down the steps. When the smoke dispersed, she saw two fallen legionaries above, but more stood behind them, ready to charge.

She rose to her feet. She swung her sword and cut a man down. She fought on.

When shouts rose behind her, she cursed. The Legions were charging up the stairs from below too, trapping her and her men. She fought onward, killing with every step. An arrow slammed into her left arm, and she cried out in pain. She kept climbing.

"Father, come and face me!"

She ascended another few steps. Men fell before and behind her. The stairs were slick with blood.

"Father!"

A cackle rose above, muffled behind the walls. "Kaelyn, my sweet traitor! Have you fought all this way to scream under my punisher?"

She sucked in air. It was his voice, the voice she had heard a thousand times in her nightmares.

My father.

She kept climbing. Her left arm hung uselessly, pierced with an arrow. Her leg bled. Her head spun. Yet still she killed. Cut, burnt, and pierced with arrows, her men fought around her. Ten more steps, and Kaelyn saw a red door. The cackling rose beyond it.

The sight of this door pierced her with more pain than her wounds.

"No," she whispered. "Oh stars, no, not here."

Frey Cadigus kept many chambers in this palace. His throne room, a hall of glory, lay far below. Still farther above, near the tower's crest, festered his butcher room, the place where he slaughtered both beasts and men. Yet here, Kaelyn thought, here behind this door lay the true heart of his madness.

"His trophy room," she whispered. "The center of his pride and insanity."

"Kaelyn!" he shouted, voice echoing beyond the door. "Kaelyn, my sweetest betrayer. Do you remember this place? Come inside, Kaelyn, and scream for me."

Guns fired over her shoulders. Legionaries clattered down. Kaelyn could no longer see the men battling around her. She could only stare at that door. She could only see the old nightmares.

"This is the room you are most proud of," she whispered. She grabbed the arrow in her arm, grimaced, and pulled it out with a gush of blood. "This is the room where I kill you."

She kicked the door open, barged inside, and swung her sword.

A crowd of axehands ran her way.

Kaelyn clutched her sword with both hands and ran toward them.

Behind her, her fellow resistors charged into the room. Guns blazed. Smoke filled the chamber; Kaelyn couldn't see farther than her blade's tip. She spun in circles, cutting limbs, kicking men down. All around the guns fired, steel sparked, axes flashed, and blood sprayed. The iron masks of the axehands leered at her. A blade sliced across her side.

"Father!" she shouted. "Face me alone! Call back your thugs and face me, coward."

The clanging of steel and crashing of guns rang out. Every heartbeat, more bodies thudded to the floor. Blood sluiced around her boots. When the screaming died and the dust settled, Kaelyn found herself standing alone. Corpses surrounded her, resistors and axehands alike.

All lay dead.

Kaelyn stood panting, Lemuria still clutched with both hands.

I stand alone.

She took a step farther into the chamber, sword trembling in her hands.

"Father?" she whispered.

Her head spun. She walked hesitantly, stepping over corpses. She saw nobody living. Could Frey have died among his axehands? Heart thudding, she stepped deeper. Her knees shook. Her breath shook in her lungs. Blood dripped from her wounds, but she moved on, whipping her head from side to side, seeking him. The eyes of the dead stared up at her. The stench of death flared so powerfully Kaelyn almost gagged.

Deeper into the chamber, candles glowed and she saw his trophies.

A chill ran through her.

Thousands of years ago, the first King Aeternum had raised a marble column in the forest. King's Column had stood since; ancient magic protected it. Frey had smashed the rest of the old palace, but King's Column remained, and all his cannons and dragons could not topple it. Instead, Frey had built Tarath Imperium around the pillar, a black tumor growing around a single white bone. That ancient marble rose inside Frey's tower, the stairway coiling around it like a snake coiling around a rod.

In this chamber, surrounded by black walls, Kaelyn saw the capital of Aeternum's ancient monument.

The column rose only three hundred feet tall; most of Tarath Imperium still towered above. This room was Frey's museum for Aeternum's fallen glory. The column's capital stood forlorn, pale and glimmering, carved in the shape of rearing dragons. If Frey could not smash it, he would display it like a master displaying a chained slave.

All around the marble artifact, he displayed the rest of his trophies. The severed heads of the Aeternum family floated here in jars, each standing upon an obsidian pedestal. Their faces stared at Kaelyn, still torn in anguish. Their swords lay shattered upon the floor.

A glass tank, six feet tall, stood here too. Kaelyn had never seen this trophy before. Liquid filled the container, and a woman floated there, her body naked and cut with red spiral scars. She had wavy hair the color of honey, feline features, hazel eyes, and a pale face strewn with freckles.

The woman looked exactly like Kaelyn.

"Marilion," she whispered.

A voice spoke in the shadows.

"Marilion Brewer of Cadport, that was her name. Wife to Valien. Sister of that drunkard who raised Relesar in his tavern. Such a beauty. Such a waste." Frey emerged from the shadows, placed a hand upon the glass, and admired the floating corpse. "I told Valien that she still lives in my dungeon. The fool must have believed me. He took the bait and came here. I lured him out of his hiding and into my lair." He turned toward Kaelyn. "And now he will die, my daughter. Now you will die too. You both will float here with her."

Kaelyn screamed and charged.

Frey stepped back, and Lemuria slammed against the tank, scratching the glass. The woman inside swayed and seemed to stare at Kaelyn, eyes still wide in pain, mouth open in a silent scream.

Kaelyn raced around the tank, all her weakness gone, all her pain drowning under rage. She swung Lemuria and met her father's blade.

He had drawn his sword, a monstrous hunk of black steel named Fellwair, a weapon as long as Kaelyn's entire body. She had seen him sever his enemies' heads with this steel, seen him hack into flesh and lick the blood. It was the blade he had killed the Aeternum family with, the blade that had slaughtered the last soul of Osanna, that had killed Marilion.

Now this terror swung toward her, and Kaelyn screamed as she parried.

"You've returned to me, my daughter," Frey said, and a cold smile twisted his face. "Do you remember this chamber? Do you remember how I chained you here, how I forced you to stare at the heads, how I beat you until you wept?" He snarled and swung his sword. "I will hurt you here again, my daughter, more than ever. I will hurt you here for years before I let you die."

She screamed and thrust Lemuria.

"You will never more hurt me." She could barely see him; she had lost too much blood, was too hurt, too weak, but she fought on. "You die tonight, Father. No, you are no father to me. You are nothing but a beast."

He laughed, a mirthless and cold sound.

"Is that so, daughter?" he asked. "Already you weaken. I see the blood soaking your clothes, draining from your flesh, leaving you weak and pale. You cannot best me in swordplay. Nor can your pitiful Resistance hurt me." He blocked another blow and sighed. "Oh, my dear, foolish daughter. Do you not see? I have planned all of this."

She screamed and swung her blade. It sparked against his own.

"Silence, liar! For years I suffered under your heel. For years I fought you. Tonight you die."

He parried languidly. He did not even bother attacking.

"Do you not see, my wayward child? I knew of your island all along. I let you linger there. I placed the lure and watched you come. I drew you into my trap... and now you are here. Your warriors lie dead outside. Your friend Valien seeks me in the twisting halls; his men too are dying." He shook his head in mock sadness. "Oh, my poor child. You and Valien have done exactly what I wanted. Soon you and he will scream here together. The boy Relesar will scream too. Who will scream the loudest, I wonder?"

She trembled as she fought. Her eyes stung.

"You lie!" she screamed. She slammed her sword against his breastplate, but could not pierce it. "All you do is lie."

"And yet you shiver. And yet you weep. Your Resistance is fallen; you know this. All your hope is faded like the starlight of old gods." His face hardened. "My eldest daughter proved herself weak. My son proved himself a fool. And you, Kaelyn... you are the worst among them. You are a traitor." He snarled and his eyes blazed. "Now is your time to suffer."

Finally he thrust his blade.

Fellwair, black and wide and over five feet long, swung through the air. The blade caught the firelight and burned red. Kaelyn raised her sword, her slim and short Lemuria, and the blades clashed. Sparks rose in a fountain. She wanted to thrust again, to chip at his armor, to crack the steel and slay him. But she was too slow. She had lost too much blood. It was all she could do to parry.

Frey fought with bared teeth, eyes narrowed, his face demonic. He swung his sword again and again, slamming it into Lemuria, showering sparks. With every blow, pain shot up Kaelyn's arm. She thought her shoulder would dislocate.

She panted. Sweat and blood drenched her. Fellwair swung down. With a scream, Kaelyn raised her sword and parried.

The blow knocked her to her knees.

She knelt before her father, panting, bleeding, praying. He raised his sword again.

No, she thought, *no, I can't die now. I must live. For Requiem. For Valien. For Rune and my brother and everyone else.* She took a shuddering breath.

"I am Kaelyn Cadigus," she whispered. She struggled to rise, legs shaking. "But I foreswear your name. Know this, Father. When you are dead, I will marry Valien Eleison. Your grandsons will carry his name." She stared into his eyes and raised her bloodied blade. "But they will not know of you. They will not know you are my father. Your legacy will die."

With a howl, she drove forward, exposing her left side, ready to suffer his sword for a chance to pierce his neck.

But he did not take the bait.

He could have stabbed her left arm, severing it. He could have attacked and maimed her, allowing her right arm to slay him. But he only stepped back defensively. His blade swung sideways, biting Kaelyn's fingers.

Her blood spurted.

She screamed. Her sword flew from her hand; so did two of her fingers.

She howled. She tried to grab the dagger in her boot, but her left arm was numb from the arrow. Her right hand gushed blood. And Kaelyn knew she had lost this battle.

The chamber spinning around her, she tried to retreat. She took a few steps back, her heels banged against a corpse, and she fell. She landed upon bodies. Before she could scramble up, he was upon her.

Frey's hands reached out. His one hand clutched her throat and squeezed. The other pulled her hair. He leered down, his face twisted into something between a grin and a snarl, something monstrous and insane.

Please, Father, I'm sorry I ate the fruit! Please, don't hit me.

Again she huddled under her bed, a screaming child, as his hands reached into the darkness, clutched her, pulled her into this very chamber to beat her.

"Please, Father," she whispered.

His grip on her throat tightened. Her eyes rolled back. Darkness fell into nightmare and endless screams echoed.

Daniel Arenson

VALIEN

He stumbled down the corridor, bleeding and alone. With a final gasp, the last of his warriors--a young woman with flaming red hair--fell dead.

So weak he could barely see, Valien leaped forward. He swung his sword, shattering the head of her killer. The axehand, his blade dripping, crashed down.

Valien stood in place, panting. His chest rose and fell, and his breath wheezed. He looked around and saw nothing but dead. They filled the hallway, axehands and resistors alike. Their blood pooled and splashed the walls.

And so the Resistance ends, he thought. If Kaelyn and her men fell too, he was the last. The last resistor. The last hope of Requiem. And his light too was flickering. Valien wanted to fall, to lie down, to join his comrades. He would close his eyes, let his blood flow, and his soul would rise to the starlit halls of his ancestors.

He fell to his knees, head spinning, blood flowing down his arms. His sword clanged to the floor.

The dead woman stared up at him, and her face did not seem pained or frightened, but soft, welcoming, her eyes large and green. She was at peace. She sang among the white columns of their forebears, a land of eternal glory.

On his knees among the corpses, Valien looked up. The ceiling was black and bloody, but Valien imagined that he could see beyond it. The old palace of Requiem rose among the stars, celestial and shimmering.

"The true palace still shines above," Valien whispered, gazing up at the ceiling. "A reflection in the stars. You wait for me there, Marilion. You wait for me there, all those who fell."

He took a shuddering breath and reached up, almost feeling that warmth, almost seeing that glow.

A scream shattered the illusion.

Valien lowered his gaze and stared down the hall.

The scream sounded again--high, pained, and pleading.

Valien inhaled sharply.

"Kaelyn," he whispered.

With a raspy breath that burned his throat, he pushed himself to his feet. He lifted his sword and took a step forward. Grunting, he trudged on.

He wanted to shout her name but forced himself to remain silent; he would not reveal his location. He stepped over corpses, moving silently, barely daring to breathe. His hair dangled over his face, slick with blood.

The scream sounded again, then died off. Valien hissed and clutched his sword. The call had come from nearby, only a chamber or two away. He kept moving down the corridor. Torches crackled on the walls and blood trickled between the floor tiles. No more guards filled this place; he saw only bodies.

I'm coming for you, Kaelyn, he thought. His chest shook and he plowed on. He could no longer hear the scream. Had Frey killed her? Would he find her dead, Frey's sword thrust into her belly, like he'd found Marilion all those years ago?

A whimper rose down the hall.

Kaelyn. It was her; he was sure of it.

Breath shuddering, Valien trudged onward. He held his sword in bloodstained hands. As he walked down the hall, he realized that he knew this place. He had walked here before. Twenty years ago, white tiles had covered the floor, and instead of an eastern wall, a portico of marble columns had revealed forested hills. Today the hall was black and narrow but... this was the same place. Valien could feel it.

Sweat beaded on his brow and his fingers shook. A few more steps and he saw a door--a door he knew would be there.

He stepped forward. Hand slick with blood and trembling with weakness, he pulled the door open. He stared into the chamber.

His breath left him and his eyes watered. He felt like ash melting in the rain, all his hardness fading into shimmering memory.

In the past twenty years, this palace had spread and rotted like a canker, but his chambers had remained untouched. His old tapestries still hung from the walls, depicting scenes of sunset over forests and mountains. The same vases and mugs still stood upon his table; even the dried roses were still there. His bed stood by the wall, topped with the quilts Marilion had woven--the bed where he would love her, where he'd sleep holding her, where he'd found her dead.

"He kept it the same," Valien whispered. "Why?"

A voice answered him. "Because I knew you would return."

Valien growled, stepped into the chamber, and turned to his right.

His world seemed to burn and his heart froze.

"Let them go," he rasped and raised his sword. His heart unlocked and burst into a gallop. His fist shook around his hilt. "Let them go, Frey."

The emperor smiled thinly. "Welcome to my bedchamber, Valien Eleison. Welcome to your old home."

Frey Cadigus stood clad in his imperial armor, a suit of black plates that covered him from toe to neck. His pauldrons flared out, and motifs of golden dragons coiled across his breastplate. His sword hung across his back. He held an arquebus, the gun bloody. The fuse was crackling like a pipe, the flashpan full of powder.

Before the emperor, in sight of his muzzle, Rune and Kaelyn sat tied to chairs.

Valien struggled for breath. He took a step closer, reaching out to them, but Frey pulled the trigger back a hair's width. The gun creaked. Valien froze.

"Rune," he whispered. "Kaelyn."

They were wounded; they looked within a few breaths of death. Burns and welts rose across Rune's flesh, peeking from the tatters of his clothes, and he was thin, thinner than he'd ever been. His cheeks were ashen, his eyes sunken. He met Valien's gaze. His mouth was gagged, but in his eyes, Valien saw relief mingling with fear.

Heart wrenching, Valien turned to look at Kaelyn. Blood seeped between the ropes that bound her to the chair. More blood dripped down a wound in her arm; it looked like the hole of an arrow. A gash ran across her thigh, and two fingers were missing from her right hand; the stumps bled. She too was gagged. She too looked at him, her eyes wide and fearful but loving.

"It's all right," Valien whispered to them. "I'm going to get you out of here. This ends now."

Frey grinned, gun in hands. "Yes... you can save one of them." He licked his lips, turned his eyes away from his prisoners, and looked at Valien. Mockery filled his eyes. "I have only one round for this crude contraption I stole off one of your warriors. I can slay only one of your little friends."

Valien took another step forward, but Frey *tsk*ed and hefted his gun. Valien froze.

"Frey, enough of this," he rasped. "Put the gun down and draw your sword. Face me like a man, not a coward."

"Oh, but I will face you," said Frey. "We will duel with swords, the duel we should have had years ago, the duel you fled from. But first... first, my old friend, I will slay one of these two wretches. And I will let you choose." His licked his lips. "Choose, old friend."

Valien snarled and raised his sword. "Enough of these games. I've not come here to play, but to fight you. Place down your gun. Do not toy with me."

Frey only laughed, a sickly sound, and sucked in air between his teeth. "Will you have me choose then? Perhaps the boy?" He turned the muzzle toward Rune. "Ah... the young heir of Aeternum. The babe you saved all those years ago. The whelp you fought this war for, the hope of Requiem, the backside you hope will warm my throne." The emperor chuckled, a sound like blood bubbling from a wound. "Should I slay him with my single round?"

When Valien hissed and took another step forward, Frey shook his head and turned his muzzle toward Kaelyn.

"Or perhaps," Frey said, "I will slay my daughter. The fair, beautiful Kaelyn. The woman who betrayed me. The woman you love." He raised his eyebrows. "She has spread her legs for you, I know it. She is a whore and yet you love her. Perhaps I should fire my gun at her?"

Valien stood frozen, shaking with rage and fear, daring not take another step. "Fire your gun, and before you can draw your sword, you will die."

Frey nodded. "Perhaps. But I think I should have enough time to draw my sword, to duel you, perhaps to slay you too. Who would win a fight between us? I do not know. I know only one thing." He stared at Valien, all amusement gone from his eyes. "One of these two will die. Rune or Kaelyn. The heir or the lover. Twenty years ago, you chose Rune over the woman you loved. You saved him and let your wife die. She died in this very chamber, in this very bed where I now sleep every night. Choose again, Valien Eleison. Choose now or I will choose for you."

Valien wheezed for breath. He looked back at them. Both Rune and Kaelyn struggled in their bonds. They stared at him, eyes pleading, and he saw the words in their gazes. They each wanted him to choose the other.

"Choose!" Frey demanded. "The fuse burns low; you have only a few heartbeats left. Choose, Valien! The boy who can heal Requiem or the woman who can heal your heart. Choose!"

The fuse flickered. Frey raised his gun and bared his teeth, ready to fire.

Valien grimaced, his eyes burned, and his breath froze.

I cannot choose, he thought. *I cannot!*

Again that night returned to him, that night twenty years ago. Frey's men had swept through the halls, killing all in their path. Marilion had waited in this chamber, Rune in a nursery across the palace.

I chose Rune then, he thought. *I chose hope for Requiem.*

He looked at Rune now, a grown man, a man he could crown tonight. He looked at Kaelyn, the woman he'd flown with for so long, the woman he loved, the woman who filled his heart with so much light.

When Marilion died, he thought, *I broke. I fell into darkness, into drink, into madness.* He looked into Kaelyn's hazel eyes. *You saved me, Kaelyn. You saved me from the wreck that I was. You gave me strength to fight. You gave me something to fight for. I cannot lose you too.*

"Choose!" Frey shouted. "Choose now, Valien!"

Valien lowered his head.

All sounds faded.

He closed his eyes.

"Spare Kaelyn," he whispered.

For a moment the silence continued. Then Frey began to laugh--a dry, crackling sound like twigs breaking. His laughter grew until he was cackling.

He pointed his gun at Rune.

Tied in the chair, the young man looked up and gave Valien a last look. Rune nodded and Valien's eyes dampened. In his eyes, Rune was saying: *I understand. I accept. Goodbye.*

A scream rose outside.

A shadow darkened the window.

Frey pulled the trigger.

The arquebus blasted smoke.

A red dragon crashed through the window, roared, and shifted into human form.

"I will kill you, Father!" screamed Leresy, leaping through the air, a dagger in hand. "Die, bastard!"

The iron round slammed into Leresy's chest, spraying red mist.

Still screaming, the prince slammed against Frey and drove his dagger into the man's neck.

Father and son crashed down, screaming and struggling. Leresy howled, pulled his dagger back, and thrust it down again and again, stabbing madly and screaming. Frey gasped, blood spurting from his neck and cheeks.

"Die, you bastard!" Leresy cried. His tears poured and blood covered his arms. "Die! Die... I..."

The prince coughed blood, fell over the corpse of his father, and trembled.

Valien raced toward the shattered window. Rune and Kaelyn still sat tied to their chairs, glass shards in their hair. Valien cut through the ropes, freeing them.

They rose on shaky limbs, and Valien pulled them into an embrace, a crushing grip, and his eyes watered, and he held them and gasped and wept.

"It's over," he whispered, chest shaking, and held them close. "It's over. You're safe. You're safe."

He kissed their bloodied cheeks and tasted their tears.

KAELYN

Countless thoughts rattled in her head, vying for dominance.

We won the war.

I'm wounded and bleeding.

My father is dead.

Rune is alive.

My fingers are gone.

She trembled in Valien's embrace, and each thought howled inside her, each alone enough to overwhelm her. Yet as the voices rattled, one emerged above the rest, bringing tears to her eyes.

My brother is hurt.

She disentangled herself from Valien, limped forward, and fell to her knees above Leresy.

"Oh, Ler," she whispered.

He had fallen off their father. He lay on his back, smiling wanly. A hole gaped open in his chest. He placed a hand against the wound and coughed weakly, blood on his lips.

"Look at us, sister," he said. He coughed again but did not lose his soft smile.

She wept. She knelt over him, touched his cheek, and placed her second hand above his.

"I'm going to take care of you," she whispered. "You're going to be all right."

He laughed--a weak, choked sound. "I've got a hole in my chest a rodent could crawl through. But I killed him, Kae. I killed him for us." His smile turned into a sob. "He can't hurt you anymore. Never again."

She nodded. Her voice was so soft she could barely hear herself. "He can't hurt anyone anymore." She looked over her shoulder at Valien and Rune who stood watching. "Get bandages! Get medicine! We have to heal him, we--"

Leresy gripped her hand. "It's too late for me, sister. Look at me again. I want to die seeing your face."

She turned her eyes back toward him. "You can't die. I won't let you."

With a shaky hand, his fingers bloody, he reached up and touched her cheek. He whispered so softly she had to lean down to hear.

"Sister... make this a good kingdom. Whoever takes this throne... make sure they do a good job."

She nodded. She could no longer even whisper, only mouth the words. "I will."

"Find Erry." Leresy blinked his damp eyes. "Look after her. Give her gold and a house to live in. Make sure she has a good life. Tell her... tell her that I forgive her. No. Don't tell her that. Tell her that she was right and that I'm sorry. Tell her that I love and that I'm so sorry."

She pulled him into an embrace. "You will tell her."

He shook his head. "Goodbye, my sister, my twin, my Kaelyn." He smiled and suddenly all pain left his face; he seemed at peace, as if already floating toward the starlit halls. "And make this a good life for you, Kae. May your wings always find our sky."

He went limp in her arms.

She held him against her for a long time, whispering to him, praying as his soul rose.

TILLA

She stood atop the tower of Tarath Imperium, gazed upon the city, and closed her hand around the hilt of her sword.

It was too quiet.

Frey Cadigus was dead, but the sun rose as always. Below in the streets, people emerged to their daily routines. Merchants hawked food in distant markets. Shops opened their doors. Hammers rang on anvils, smoke rose from smelters, and saws ground in sawmills. People moved along the streets, busy selling, buying, working, and living.

Tilla shook her head. This... this was wrong. She had expected... what? The Legions still attacking, sworn to slay the Resistance even with their emperor dead? A hundred claimants to the throne, bastards or madmen or distant relatives of Cadigus? She did not know. But when hearing of Frey's death, she had expected... not anvils ringing but cannonballs blasting, not smoke pumping from chimneys but the blaze of dragonfire.

Yet here she was. Frey lay dead and the city bustled with life.

"But I cannot forget," she whispered from the tower, eyes stinging. "I cannot just go on with my life."

She raised her chin and closed her eyes. Rune had won his war. He had slain the tyrant. But Tilla still had her war to fight. She still had her vengeance to claim.

She opened her eyes and nodded. She would do what she must.

With a deep breath, she leaped off the tower.

She tumbled down, shifted into a dragon, and caught the wind. She glided toward the Square of Cadigus below--or whatever its name might be now--and landed outside the palace gates. They still stood smashed, guarded by a handful of surviving resistors. Tilla walked between them--they knew her as Relesar's ward, the woman they had unchained from the Citadel--and entered the palace hall.

She walked between the columns, boots thudding against the mosaic, and drew her sword. Ahead rose the throne.

They stood around it, the survivors of the Resistance, no more than fifty men and women, most still wearing their tattered, bloody clothes. They were bandaged, weary, and covered in grime, and they ruled the world.

As Tilla stepped closer, her eyes stung and her breath shook.

"Which one of you is him?" she called out, voice hoarse. "Who among you is Valien Eleison, leader of the Resistance?"

She did not even need to ask. As she stepped closer, she knew who it was. Only one here stood with the aura of command. He was a tall man, broad-shouldered but haggard. His shaggy hair framed a weathered face and eyes full of scars--not the scars of knives, but the deeper wounds of the soul. Tilla almost lost her step. She had expected to see a demon, a barbaric warrior leering and drinking the blood of his enemies. Yet this man seemed weary beyond reckoning, an aging, outcast knight who longed to lower his blade. He seemed almost pathetic, a man who hated battle yet whose honor forced him to fight on.

Tilla sucked in her breath, raised her head, and banished all sympathy from her heart.

He might seem weary, even kind, but he killed my brother. She stepped toward him, sword raised. *He would not have seemed so harmless that day years ago.*

"Are you Valien?" she said.

His warriors--perhaps they were no longer *resistors*, for their Resistance had triumphed--drew blades and stepped toward her. Valien raised his hand, holding them back. They froze.

"I am Valien," he said. His voice was but a rasp, the sound of a strangled man. "Will you give me the courtesy of your name?"

She took another step toward him, sword raised. She considered giving him her new surname, the noble one Shari had bestowed upon her, but decided against it. She was no longer Tilla Siren; that woman had died with Shari.

"I am Tilla Roper," she said through a tight jaw. "Does that name mean anything to you?"

She saw that it did. Understanding filled his eyes. At his side, a young archer with long, golden hair breathed deeply, and her eyes softened.

Valien's rasp dissolved into a whisper. "Rune told me about you."

Her sword wavered in her hand. "Then draw your blade! Draw it and fight me, if you wish to die like a man, or I will kill you like a dog." She spat at him, narrowly missing his boot. "Draw your steel. Fight me and I will kill you like you killed my brother."

Her eyes burned and her chest heaved. She waited for him to rage, to draw his blade, to howl and lunge at her. But he only stood still, and no bloodlust filled his eyes, only sadness.

"I won't fight you, Tilla," he said. "I have fought for too long. I have swung my sword too many times. The war is over. Let no more blood spill."

She stepped closer, sword pointed at Valien, close enough that if she just leaned forward, her blade would cut him.

"Do you confess then that you killed him?" She wanted her words to sound strong, to speak with the authority of an officer, but today her voice cracked. "Do you confess your murder? Confess now before you die."

He looked into his eyes. There was no hardness to his stare, no malice, no fear, no hate... only weariness.

"I confess," he said, and Tilla snarled and prepared to thrust her blade, but he continued speaking. "I confess to killing many. I killed dozens with my own hands, Tilla Roper of Lynport, maybe hundreds. I sent tens of thousands to die; their blood stains my hands too. If you kill me now, you would be justified in doing so, perhaps. Thousands across Requiem grieve for brothers, sons, daughters, fathers... people I killed. Their deaths still haunt me. I will grieve for every soul I had to extinguish. Did I kill your brother too? Perhaps. You might find me heartless to say this, but the truth is, I don't know. I killed too many; I don't know their names. But know this: If your brother fell to my sword, his death too weighs upon my soul."

Her tears fell and her sword wavered in her grip. "Do you think contrition can save you now? Do you think some convoluted apology, if that's what this was, can save your life?"

He smiled thinly. "I don't know. But I know that I won't fight you; as I've said, I've fought too much already. And I know that Rune loves you. And I know that you saved his life. If you are a person he loves, I don't think you will slay me here."

Tilla's nostrils flared, her tears fell, and she panted.

You are wrong, coward, she thought, barely able to see, and readied her sword to strike.

"Wait!" rose a voice.

Tilla froze, her sword an inch from Valien's neck. She turned to see the young, golden-haired archer reaching out toward her. Tilla noticed that the woman was missing two fingers on her right hand; the stubs were bandaged.

"Wait," the young woman repeated. She heaved a sigh. "Valien did not kill your brother."

"How do you know?" Tilla demanded, teeth bared.

"Because I killed him." The archer lowered her head. "I am Kaelyn Cadigus, daughter of Frey, fighter of the Resistance." She looked back up at Tilla, and her eyes were damp. "I don't know the names of all my kills either, but I know some. I know the first one. I'm sorry, Tilla. I'm so sorry."

Tilla could barely stay standing. She hated herself for it, but her tears kept falling. She howled, the howl of a wounded animal, and spun her sword toward Kaelyn.

"Why?" she said. "Why did you kill him? He was only a ropemaker. Oh, stars. He was good."

Kaelyn nodded. "I know. Many who are good fight for evil men. He fought for Frey, same as you did, same as almost every youth in Requiem did. He flew against me. He fought well. We fought as dragons over the eastern skies. He was the first man I killed." She closed her eyes. "I was only sixteen, only a child, but... even a young dragon's fire burns bright. I still see him dying in my dreams."

Tilla closed her eyes too.

And I still see my first kill, she thought. She saw him now too, the quarryman in the hut. *I burned him. I sliced open his belly and let him bleed out. And every night, I still hear his screams.*

Tilla heard a clang and realized she had dropped her sword.

"I wasn't meant to be this person," she whispered. "I wasn't meant to hold a sword, to fight, to kill, to torture." She opened her eyes and looked at Kaelyn through her tears, not knowing why she spoke these words to this stranger, but unable to stop. "I'm just a ropemaker, but he made me a soldier. He made me kill so many. And I obeyed him. I murdered for him. I killed hundreds. And I

691

still hear their screams." She took a step toward Kaelyn. "How do you forget? How do you wash the blood from your hands?"

Kaelyn smiled, a sad smile like a single ray of light breaking through clouds. "I don't think you can forget. I think you just keep living, and you try to do good. You try to build with your hands that once swung a sword or fired a gun. You try to bring life to a world you burned."

A voice spoke behind them from across the hall, and footfalls echoed.

"And now is the time to bring life. Now is the time for laying down swords, the time to lift sickle and loom and hammer. It's time to rebuild this world."

Tilla turned around and saw him there across the hall, walking toward her.

Rune.

His dark hair fell across his brow. His scars were fading. He wore a new doublet and cloak, and his eyes were somber.

My Rune, she thought. *The boy I grew up with. My best friend. My lover. My future king... a man I no longer know. A man named Relesar. A stranger.*

"And will you rebuild this realm as king?" she asked, and a new sadness filled her. He had his throne. He had an empire to rule. And she... what did she have?

He reached her. He took her hands and squeezed them, his grip warm, and his eyes stared into hers.

"We will rebuild it together," he said.

She scoffed and her eyes still stung. "You would have me be your queen? Do you think that's what I want?" She shook her head. "You are mistaken. I don't belong in this place. I don't belong up here in this capital anymore. And nor do you, Rune Brewer." She shook her head, cursing her damn eyes that would not stay dry. "You're just a damn brewer's boy."

He smiled and nodded. "That's all I want to be. Queen? Tilla Roper, if you were queen of Requiem, the realm would just suffer under another tyrant." He winked.

She growled and tried to pull her hands free, but he held them tight. "Why do you mock me? Will you marry Kaelyn then?" Her jealousy flared, and she hated herself for that too.

He shook his head. "I will marry you."

She growled. "Damn you, Rune! I told you. I'm not going to be your damn queen."

"Oh stars, Tilla! You are dense." He rolled his eyes. "I don't want you to be my queen, I told you that. And I don't want this throne." He squeezed her hands. "I want us to go back home-- together. I want you to rebuild Lynport with me."

A stunned silence fell... and then the throne room erupted.

Everyone began shouting at once.

Kaelyn grabbed Rune's collar and shook him, yelling that he was the heir, that he had to sit upon this throne. Valien was emitting that rasp of his, insisting that they had fought this war for Rune, to return Requiem to his line, to restore the ancient dynasty of Aeternum. Other resistors all crowded around, some red with rage, others pale and shaking their heads.

"Friends, please!" Rune said, tugging himself free from their grasp. "Listen to me."

Kaelyn was snarling, her eyes flashing, and she twisted his collar tighter. "You listen to me, you stupid boy. We fought this war for you. Your forebears have sat upon this throne for four thousand years--since the days of the first king. How can you just... just walk away from it?" She released his collar and covered her eyes.

Again everyone started shouting, tugging at his clothes, gesturing at the throne, and filling the hall with echoes.

Only Tilla stood silently throughout the ruckus. She looked at Rune through the crowd that came between them. He met her eyes.

There he is, she thought and breathed deeply. *There is Rune Brewer. There is the boy I grew up with. There is the man I love.*

As the others tugged at his arms, his collar, and his shoulders, Tilla stepped forward, reached out, and held his hand. She smiled tremulously, and she was with him again on the beach. They no longer stood here in this throne room, this place that was foreign to them, this place of gold and marble and ghosts. In her mind and in his eyes, they were already back home.

She nodded.

"Yes," she whispered. She turned to Valien, who was still railing about ancient dynasties, and touched his arm.

He turned toward her, face red. "The boy is a fool!" he said, teeth grinding. "Tilla, will you talk sense into him?"

She sighed. "For the first time since I've known him, he is making perfect sense. Look around you, Valien Eleison. We don't belong here. I'm not a soldier. Rune isn't a king." Seeing him open his mouth to protest, she held up her hand. "Oh, I know all about his lineage. You've spoken of it enough. But those are old lines. Look at that throne, Valien. Is that the throne his father ruled? The Oak Throne of Requiem? No. Frey burned that ancestral seat. I see only an ivory mockery that Frey sat upon. Dynasties change. Requiem is reborn, and she is ready for a new line." She looked back at Rune and she smiled. For the first time in years, she smiled a warm smile, the sort of smile that filled one's entire body, that tickled like spring dawn after winter. "Let him return south with me. You needed him to rally hearts and win this war. You don't need his silly little backside to polish some seat." She returned her eyes to Valien and winked. "That backside of his now belongs to me."

Valien gaped at her, eyes wide, mouth open, and then something happened that caught Tilla by surprise.

Valien, the gruff and grizzled leader of the Resistance, laughed.

It was a creaky laugh, sort of like a tree thawing after a long frost. Tilla guessed that like her smile, his laugh was reemerging after long years of slumber. It started awkwardly, scraping and crackling, then became a deep, joyous sound. And Tilla laughed too.

She pulled Rune into an embrace. She held him close and would not release him, and she kissed his cheek, and she kept laughing. When finally she could laugh no more, she touched his hair and whispered softly.

"Can we do this, Rune? Can we rebuild our home?" She lowered her gaze. "Not much is left."

He held her in his arms. "*We* are left. And we are together. We can rebuild the whole damn world."

She pinched his cheek and mussed his hair. For the first time in many years, she had laughed this day. For the first time in many years, she was happy.

ERRY

She stood in the crowd, watching Valien and Kaelyn's wedding. Or was this their coronation? Erry couldn't tell and she fidgeted, hopping on her tiptoes and twisting her fingers behind her back.

"Damn ceremonies," she muttered under her breath. "Who in the Abyss gets married *and* crowned on the same day? Too much pomp and too much damn--"

"Shh!" Miya said, standing at her side. Her younger, taller sister glared down at her. "Valien is being crowned now, so hush."

Erry grumbled, frowned at the girl, and grudgingly bit down on her words.

She stood among a crowd of... stars, it must have been a hundred people. They covered the palace walls all around her-- resistors, city elders, and whatever other dignitaries Valien had deemed important enough to stand here with him. And below the walls--maggoty toe juice! Erry's head spun to see it. A great square spread below; Erry thought it larger than all of Lynport. Hundreds of thousands crowded down there, maybe a million. All of Nova Vita had come to see the coronation, it seemed, filling the square.

Upon these walls where Erry stood, no more banners of Cadigus hung, nor did they fly from the tower that rose above. Tarath Imperium had been rededicated. New banners hung here now. They were deep green, and the silver stars of Requiem appeared upon them, shaped like a dragon--the Draco constellation, the forbidden gods now worshiped again.

Miya elbowed her and whispered from the corner of her mouth. "Erry! You're not watching the coronation. This is a historical event. Stop gawping at the clouds and look at Valien."

Erry growled. "You're a pushy little sister. Remember that you're younger than me, and I can beat you up."

The young Tiran's eyes flashed. "You might be older, but I'm taller. Now hush and *watch*."

With another grumble, Erry looked up toward Valien. He stood upon the walls perhaps a hundred yards away, looking down at the crowds. Erry had always seen him wearing only furs and leathers, but now he wore his old knight's armor, the steel plates polished to a bright silver. Birch leaves were engraved on his breastplate, and he bore a new sword, abandoning his old hunk of steel for a kingly blade. For the first time since Erry had known him, his beard was trimmed, his hair brushed and neat, and his eyes bright.

By the stars, he's actually handsome, Erry thought and felt her blood heat. *Who knew?*

She turned to look at Kaelyn, who stood at Valien's side. The young princess had always been beautiful, even when covered with grime. But now, dressed in an azure gown, her hair braided and strewn with flowers, Kaelyn looked fairer than ever, so much that Erry's blood heated further. With her short hair and scrawny limbs, Erry wasn't sure if she felt jealous of or awed by Kaelyn's beauty.

Valien is a lucky bastard, she thought.

The coronation began.

Rune stepped forth, clad in green and silver, and he too looked more clean and handsome than Erry had ever seen him. The last Aeternum approached the newlyweds, bearing two crowns. When he reached Valien and Kaelyn, they knelt before him.

He spoke some words; they flitted into Erry's ears and out again. She did not understand court-speak. Rune recited some fancy talk about abdi-something the throne, passing on the torch, and naming Valien Eleison the new king. He placed the crown upon the man's head, then turned to Kaelyn and crowned her too, and then spoke some more. He prayed to the Draco Stars and blessed them.

Erry rolled her eyes and rocked on her heels. Rune had just memorized the words yesterday. He was no priest or ruler; he was just the boy from the boardwalk, the boy she would play mancala with, the boy who brought her food sometimes. And she was just a dock rat, and Tilla was just a ropemaker. They were just southern beach children. They didn't belong here. They didn't need any of this pomp and ceremony.

She sighed.

But maybe we're no longer those things, she thought and lowered her head. *Maybe we did change. Maybe we did grow. Maybe... maybe Rune is wise now, and Tilla is a warrior, and I... what am I?*

She looked at Miya who stood at her side. The young
woman's eyes gleamed as she watched the coronation. Erry looked
past Miya at the tall, golden-skinned man who stood farther back, a
captain of the southern seas.

No, I'm no longer a dock rat, she thought. *I'm a sister. And I'm a
daughter.*

Her eyes stung and her chest constricted. The urge to flee
welled inside her. She had to escape this place, to run, to get away,
to stop those damn tears from burning.

She tightened her lips, clenched her fists, and began to shove
back through the crowd. Miya gasped at her and people muttered,
but Erry didn't care. She had to get out. She couldn't... couldn't
bear this anymore, couldn't bear these feelings that stung her, that
felt so warm in her chest.

Let them have their celebrations, she thought, worming her way
between the people. Trumpets began to play and singers to sing,
but Erry ignored them. She had never needed anyone. She had
always been a lone wolf--on the docks and here in this city.

She found a staircase and descended toward a small
courtyard, moving away from the music, the crowds, the flowers,
and all those things that still stung, that still frightened a child
grown up in shadows. She walked upon cobblestones, walls and
towers at her sides, finally able to breathe, to calm her heart. She
had always felt most calm in solitude, and though she had often felt
unfortunate as a child, she found herself missing the beach, the
sound of waves, and the company of her animals. Perhaps that was
the only life she truly knew how to live.

She walked along paths and porticoes. Finally she found a
small garden between brick walls. Several oak trees grew here,
surrounding a statue of Frey Cadigus. Thousands of his statues
filled the city; many had been toppled already, but some still stood,
tucked away in small gardens or courtyards, still watching the city
and awaiting their felling.

Erry was about to sit under a tree when she noticed a figure
standing ahead, watching the statue.

Tilla.

Erry froze, not sure how to proceed. Tilla had once been her
dearest friend, but last time she had seen the woman, Tilla had
worn the armor of a legionary, and she had burned Erry with her

punisher; Erry still carried a faded scar from the attack. Today Tilla wore no armor and bore no weapon. She stood in a white tunic, a string of seashells around her neck. A breeze rustled the trees and billowed Tilla's black, chin-length hair.

She's staring at the tyrant, Erry thought. *Does she still worship him? She has removed her armor, but is her heart still dark?*

She had begun to tiptoe away when Tilla spoke, not turning toward her.

"It's a funny thing, isn't it?"

Erry paused in mid-step, turned back, and saw Tilla still staring at the statue.

"I've heard folk call Frey a god or a monster," Erry said, "but funny is a new one."

Tilla nodded, face blank. "I think most saw him as both, a monstrous god to worship not from love but from fear. That's why I served him."

When Tilla turned toward her, Erry took a step back.

No, her face isn't blank, she thought. *There is deep pain there, a horror she hides under her cold mask.*

"Well, he's dead now," Erry said, still hesitant, not sure that she wanted to be here, and the old scar on her chest burned. "So to the Abyss with his rotten carcass, and may they dump this statue in a cesspool."

She turned to leave, but Tilla called out.

"Erry, wait."

With a huff, Erry spun around and glared. "What?" Rage flared within her. "What do you want with me? You have your statue here. Go make love to it, or worship it, or spit on it. I don't care. I'm looking for a quiet place of my own."

When she turned to leave again, Tilla raced toward her, held her shoulders, and wouldn't let go.

"Erry, please. Just... wait a moment."

"Don't touch me!" Erry said and shoved her off.

Tilla took a step back and nodded. "Erry, I'm sorry, all right?"

She snorted a laugh. "Easy to be sorry now with your lord dead."

"You served in the Legions too. We both served him." Tilla lowered her head. "That doesn't mean he's my lord."

"Oh, we both served him, did we?" Erry's voice rose, torn with anger. "I never killed for him. I never collaborated with his daughter. I never..." Her eyes burned with tears, and Erry hated herself for it. "I never betrayed a friend."

"And I did," Tilla said. "I did all those things. I know it. And I'm sorry. I was... how would you say it? A horse's arse."

Erry snorted. "You were a particularly big, smelly horse's arse."

Tilla nodded. "Fair enough."

"With fleas."

"All right."

"And with an infected, maggoty red spiral brand right on it. And with some ticks and--"

"All right, Erry, I get it."

Erry sighed, knuckled her stinging eyes, and looked at her feet. She spoke in a low whisper. "You're my best friend, Tilla. You're my *only* friend. You and Wobble Lips." Now her own damn lips wobbled. "I never had any other friends." She looked up through damp eyes. "I love you, you stinky horse's bottom."

Tilla smiled, laughed, and pulled her into an embrace. "Love you too, you little shrimp."

Erry held her friend and felt warm and safe. She closed her eyes, leaned her cheek against Tilla, and thought this better than all the crowds, weddings, and coronations in the world.

Leresy would hold me too, she thought. A hundred men before him would hold her like this, but they hadn't loved her. They had all wanted her sex, or they had wanted her to heal their souls. But this felt right. This felt good.

"I'm moving back to Lynport," Tilla said. "Rune is going too. A few hundred townsfolk survived, and we're going to rebuild. Rune and I will rebuild the Old Wheel and run it together." She held Erry at arm's length. "Come with us. Brew ale with us or serve tables or cook meals... just be with us. We'll run the place together, us three."

To live with Tilla and Rune? To have a roof over her head, regular meals, a home of her own? Warmth filled Erry, spreading through her like sunrise over a rolling landscape. And yet she shook her head.

"Nah, it's called the Old Wheel, not the Third Wheel. It's not a place for me. Go and make it a great place, Tilla. You and Rune. I know that you will. But me... it's not a place for me."

Tilla's eyes softened. "So where will you go? Do you have a place? Are you sure you don't want to stay with us?"

A hesitant smile tingled Erry's lips, soon turning into a grin. "I have a place now. I have a home. I have a family."

The spring sun warmed the land, leaves budded on the trees, and new light shone across Requiem. Masons bustled in cities and villages, building new temples to the stars. Statues of Frey fell. Knives scratched red spirals off armor, swords, and shields. A new dawn rose for Requiem, and King Valien ruled with light, justice, and wisdom.

"I helped save Requiem," Erry whispered, flying over the forests and mountains of the kingdom, the sun bright above. "But not for me. It will never be a warm, safe place for me."

She had suffered here too much. Her body and soul bore too many scars. The beaches, the forests, the city walls... they all carried too many memories, too much pain.

How do you cleanse your memories of blood? she thought as she flew on the wind, the forests rolling below her, the capital vanishing far behind. *How do you find light when so much darkness still fills you?*

Erry didn't know. For so many years, she had run from pain. She had run to her docks, into forests, or into men's arms. Today too she was fleeing.

Yet now... now she had a good place to fly to. Now she had somebody to fly with.

"Hey, Erry!" Miya cried from her back, seated in a saddle. "Can't you fly any faster?"

Erry growled over her shoulder. Her little sister's hair flapped in the wind, and her cheeks were pink, yet still she pointed forward, demanding more speed. Their father sat upon the saddle too, smiling, his hard face showing rare peace.

"Do you want to fly instead, Miya?" Erry said.

"Not fair. I'm a Tiran. You know Tirans can't fly. Tirans *sail.*"

"So be quiet and let the half-dragon do her work."

Tirans sail. And Erry too had Tiran blood. She too would sail. She inhaled, already smelling the salty air.

They flew across Requiem for days. They left the birch forests behind, and they flew over the great plains of Osanna. They traveled over hills, woods, and mountains. At nights, they slept in taverns or simply under the stars. They flew until they saw the eastern sea, the blue border of the empire.

In a clear dawn, they descended toward the port of Altus Mare, an ancient city. Once a place of docks and shipyards, a great hub of merchants, the city had fallen in the wars, its original inhabitants slain. Today a small fishing village rose upon the ruins, home to several hundred Vir Requis, a tanned people clothed in canvas, their faces weathered with the sea winds.

Erry walked onto the docks, stared out into the sea, and tapped her chin.

"Now what do we do?" she asked her father and sister. "The islands with our ships are a three-day flight away. I can't fly for three days straight, not without a place to rest at night."

Her father stared into the sea, inhaled deeply, and smiled.

"We fly back the way we flew here," he said. "You take turns. Every few hours, you return to human form and sleep upon another dragon. We just need to find that other dragon."

And so they spent the night in Altus Mare, and in the morning, they paid a young fisherman three silver coins to fly with them. At first Erry didn't want him riding her. His grin was too wide, his eyes too green, his curly hair too wild. She had fallen for too many pretty boys to let another into her life.

"Not this one," she said, pointing at him upon the docks. "He's too young."

The boy flashed a grin. "I'm twenty years old. I can't be much older than you." He winked. "And I bet I can fly faster."

"You keep pretending that," Erry said. She turned back toward her father. "This one is trouble. You should never have paid him silver. I would never agree to him, had he not already pocketed the coins." She grumbled. "I fly first. And I fly fast, so hold on to your saddle."

She shifted into dragon form. They climbed onto her back. And she flew.

The sea rolled below them, blue patched with green, and he would not stop taunting her, that rude boy with the green eyes. When finally it was his turn to fly, and she rode upon his back with

Sila and Miya, she wanted to taunt him too. But she was too tired. So she only leaned back in the saddle, closed her eyes, and slept.

They flew for three days and nights, and finally they saw Maiden Island ahead, a woman rising from the sea, her hair formed of a waterfall, her hip and waist crowned with trees. In the cove between her curves, it waited--the *Golden Crane*, its masts tall, its hull emblazoned with golden sunbursts. When Erry saw it, her eyes dampened.

My new home.

"You're wobbling again," said the boy on her back. He jabbed her with his heel. "You wobble too much when you fly."

She glared over her shoulder at him. He was smiling his same mocking smile.

"Be quiet or I'll wobble so much you'll fall off."

Upon the *Golden Crane*, dear old Bantis--he had stayed to watch over the ship--danced a jig and waved and whooped.

My crazy grandfather, Erry thought and laughed.

She flew down and landed on the deck. When her riders dismounted, she returned to human form, placed her hands upon the railing, and inhaled the sea air. In her mind, she could already imagine the sails wide, the ship cutting through the water. She could fly faster than a ship could sail, and yet... flying was lonely. This ship was not merely a vessel; it was family and it was home.

Her father smiled and held her hand. Her sister and grandfather embraced her. They stood together on the deck and Erry smiled too. This was right.

"Well," said the green-eyed boy and stretched. "I suppose now it's back to the village with me. Back to fishing and lying around on the beach." He sighed theatrically. "I reckon you don't need me here, so if you could just take me a few miles back, I'll fly the rest of the way."

Erry groaned, jabbed his chest with her finger, and glared at him. "If you want a job here, pretty boy, just spit it out. Don't play your little games."

He grinned and mussed her hair. When she shoved his hand back, he only grinned wider.

"So you want me to stay! You'd love me to. I can see it in your eyes, little one."

They left Maiden Island, the wind in their sails, only five souls heading into the open sea. He was right, of course. She had wanted him to stay, that rude boy with the taunting smile and green eyes. And their first night on the waters, when her family slept, Erry was tempted again. It would be so easy! She could sneak into his hammock, doff her clothes, and let him bed her. She would look into his eyes, press her body against his, and she would feel warm, feel a respite from the chill that always filled her.

But no. Not this time. She let him sleep, climbed onto the deck, and watched the moonlight glimmer on the sea. This time she would be a different Erry. She had to be different now, not the same old dock rat, not even with this very rude, very pretty sailor. She could wait a little longer with this one.

The *Golden Crane* sailed on into the night. The wind filled her hair, the good scent of water and salt filled her nostrils, and Erry smiled softly. In the darkness, she thought of Mae Baker, and she thought of Leresy, and she thought of all those she had lost. She remembered the pain of her childhood and the wars of her youth, and she knew those memories would always fill her, that her scars would always burn. Yet standing here upon the deck, she could smile, for Erry knew that while darkness stretched behind her, light shone ahead. And that was all right. That was enough for her.

A gleam upon the sea caught her eye. She leaned over the railing and frowned. Something was floating in the water, small and bright in the moonlight.

Erry leaped and shifted into a dragon. She dived down to the water, gripped the sparkling item in her claws, and flew back onto the deck. When she shifted back into human form, she found a silver amulet in her palm, shaped like a sun.

It was her father's amulet, the amulet that had been hers for so long, that had brought her here. She slung it around her neck and stood for a long time, watching the sea.

RUNE

They walked along the beach, watching sunset gild the waves. The cliffs of Ralora rose behind them, and the sand caressed their bare feet. Seashells glimmered in the light, countless jewels hiding and emerging with every wave. The wind from the sea blew their hair, scented of home.

"Do you know why I love the sea?" Tilla said, voice soft.

Rune looked at her. She was staring into the water, her high cheeks, normally so pale, golden in the light. A smile touched her lips, but a sadness filled her eyes, a good sadness like memories that were too special, too important, for joy alone.

"Because it's always different," Rune answered.

She looked at him. "Yes. Have I told you before?"

He smiled. "Only a hundred and one times."

She looked back at the waves. "This evening the sunlight breaks through the thin clouds, rays fall upon the water, and a path of gold trails into the horizon. Yesterday birds sang here, and the water glimmered with white mottles. Sometimes the water is blue and sometimes it's green. Sometimes the sky is a single, uniform azure, and sometimes it's a patchwork of a hundred colors." She reached out and held his hand, still watching the waves. "And sometimes, standing here, we are young and scared. And sometimes we are older and scarred. And sometimes... sometimes we're just two people in the sand, a story of pain and triumph, and we too are a patchwork like the sky, a dappled painting of hurt and joy. And some days, like today, when the wind is warm and the waves whisper, when the light falls on seashells and sand, and when the sky fades into purple and indigo... I don't know who I am. But I'm happy with that. And I'm happy here with you."

Rune placed a hand around her waist, and she leaned against him. This was the same place, here under these cliffs, where they would wrestle and laugh as children. This was the place where they'd stand before the wars, watching the merchant ships rise from the horizon. This was the place where they had said goodbye two

years ago, the first place they had kissed. He smoothed her hair
now, and he kissed her again. Two years ago, it had been a kiss of
farewell, a kiss that tasted of her tears. This one was better; it was a
kiss of hope, of a future, of many more ahead.

They walked along the sand, hand in hand, heading back
toward the town. Lynport rose ahead, nestled between forest and
sea. Much of the city still lay fallen, but new buildings now rose
here like saplings rising from the ash of an old forest fire. A few
hundred survivors were finding a new life. A flame kindled in the
lighthouse, the first time it had shone in twenty years. A distant
figure stood fishing on the docks--Tilla's father, one of the few
survivors of the slaughter. Rising farther back, Rune could see the
tiled roof of the rebuilt Old Wheel. A warm meal, a welcoming
dog, and a soft bed awaited them there.

He began to walk toward the town when Tilla gasped. She
squeezed his hand and held him fast.

"Look!" she said.

He turned back toward the sea and squinted.

A small white square rose from the horizon, caught the sun,
and blazed gold. It grew taller, blooming from the water, revealing
masts and a hull. Five more ships appeared behind it, sails wide.

"They're returning to Lynport," Rune whispered. "Like they
did years ago."

Tilla nodded and smiled, and a distant scent of spice wafted
on the wind. Rune held her hand in the sunset, and they stood
together on the sand, watching the ships sail in.

THE END

NOVELS BY DANIEL ARENSON

Standalones:
Firefly Island (2007)
The Gods of Dream (2010)
Flaming Dove (2010)

Misfit Heroes:
Eye of the Wizard (2011)
Wand of the Witch (2012)

Song of Dragons:
Blood of Requiem (2011)
Tears of Requiem (2011)
Light of Requiem (2011)

Dragonlore:
A Dawn of Dragonfire (2012)
A Day of Dragon Blood (2012)
A Night of Dragon Wings (2013)

The Dragon War:
A Legacy of Light (2012)
A Birthright of Blood (2012)
A Memory of Fire (2013)

KEEP IN TOUCH

www.DanielArenson.com
Daniel@DanielArenson.com
Facebook.com/DanielArenson
Twitter.com/DanielArenson